THE 10TH WESTERN
NOVEL MEGAPACK®

THE 10TH WESTERN NOVEL MEGAPACK®

Harold Bell Wright,
B.M. Bower
Jackson Gregory
Bessie Marchant

WILDSIDE PRESS

* * * *

The Mine with the Iron Door, by Harold Bell Wright, was originally published in 1923. *Meadowlark Basin*, by B.M. Bower, was originally published in 1925. *Timber-Wolf*, by Jackson Gregory, was originally published in 1923. *Athabasca Bill*, by Bessie Marchant, was originally published in 1906.

Contents

Contents

INTRODUCTION,
by John Betancourt

I know I'm in the minority, of readers, but I love Westerns—my grandmother was a huge Western fan, and growing up, she would pick out some of her favorite books for me to read. It started with her paying me a dollar for each one I read (I had to give a book report on it. Can you tell she was a teacher?), and by the end, I was asking for more for free, just to read them.

In retrospect, I believe she curated them with a focus more toward action and adventure than anything else: I got loads of Zane Gray, B.M. Bower, and other pulp authors…and series characters like Walt Slade…which may help explain my love for pulp fiction!

Here is the tenth volume in our popular Western Novel MEGAPACK® series, which features more of the same. In this volume:

The Mine with the Iron Door, by Harold Bell Wright
Meadowlark Basin, by B.M. Bower
Timber-Wolf, by Jackson Gregory
Athabasca Bill, by Bessie Marchant

I hope you enjoy reading it as much as I enjoyed putting it together!

THE MINE WITH THE IRON DOOR,
by Harold Bell Wright

CHAPTER I
THE CANYON OF GOLD

FROM every street and corner in Tucson we see the mountains. From our places of business, from our railway depots and hotels, from our University campus and halls, and from the windows and porches of our homes we look up to the mighty hills.

But of all the peaks and ranges that keep their sentinel posts around this old pueblo there are none so bold in the outlines of their granite heights and rugged canyons, so exquisitely beautiful in their soft colors of red and blue and purple, or so luring in the call of their remote and hidden fastnesses, as the Santa Catalinas.

Every morning they are there—looking down upon our little city in the desert with a brooding, Godlike tolerance—remote yet very near. All day long they watch with world-old patience our fretful activities, our puny strivings and our foolish pretenses. And when evening is come and the dusk of our desert basin deepens, their castle crags and turret peaks signal, with the red fire of the sunset, "good-night" to us who dwell in the gloom below. Even in the darkness we see their shadowy might against the sky, and feel the still and solemn mystery of their enduring strength under the desert stars.

This is a story of some people who lived in the Catalinas.

If you would find more exactly the scenes of this romance you must take the new Bankhead Highway that, in its course from Tucson to Florence and Phœnix, runs for miles in the shadow of these mountains. From the old Mexican quarter of the city—picturesque still with the colorful life of the West that is vanishing—you go straight north on Main Street, where the dust of your passing is the dust of the crumbled adobe buildings and fortifications of the ancient pueblo that had its beginning somewhere in the forgotten centuries. Leaving the outskirts of the town your way leads over rolling lands of greasewood and cacti, down the long grade past the cemetery, past the Government hospital in the valley, to the bridge that spans the Rillito. From the little river you climb quickly up to the desert slopes that form the western base of the main range and that lie under their wide skies unmarked by human hands since the beginning of deserts and mountains. Beyond the famous Steam Pump Ranch, some sixteen miles from Tucson, the road to Oracle branches off from the Bankhead Highway and climbs higher and higher until from a wide mesa you can see the place of my story—the mighty Cañada del Oro—the Canyon of Gold.

But if you know the way you may turn aside from the main road before you come to this new Oracle branch and take instead the old road that winds closer to the mountains and for several miles follows the bed of the lower canyon. It was along this ancient trail that the eventful and romantic life of this southern Arizona country, through its many ages, moved.

This way, centuries ago, came the Spaniards—lured by tales of a strange people who used silver and gold as we use tin and iron, and who set turquoise in the gates of their houses. This way came the Franciscan Fathers to find in the Cañada del Oro gold for their mission at San Xavier. This way, from the San Pedro and the Aravaipa, came savage Apache to raid the peaceful farming Papagos and later to war against the pale-face settlers in the valley of the Santa Cruz. Prehistoric races, explorers, Indians, priests, pioneers, prospectors, cattlemen, soldiers and adventurers of every sort from every land—all, all have come this way—along this old road through the Canyon of Gold.

And because there was water here, and because there was gold here, this wild and adventurous life, through the passing centuries, made this place a camping ground and a battle field—a place of labor and crime, of victory and defeat; of splendid heroism, noble sacrifice, and dreadful fear. Set amid the grandeur and the beauty of these vast deserts, lonely skies and wild and rugged mountains, the Cañada del Oro has been, most of all, as indeed it is today, a place of dreams that never came true; of hopes that were never fulfilled; of labor that was vain.

Of all the stirring tales of this picturesque region of the Santa Catalinas, of all the romantic legends and traditions that have come down to us from its shadowy past, none is more filled with the essence of human life and love and hopes and dreams than is the tale of the Mine with the Iron Door.

But this is not a story of those old Spaniards and padres and Indians and pioneers. It is a story of today.

The old, old tale of the Mine with the Iron Door is as true for us as it ever was for those who lived and loved so many years ago. We too, in these days, have our dreams that must remain always, merely dreams and nothing more. We too, in these modern times, are called upon to bury in the secret places of our modern hearts hopes that are dead. In every life there are the ashes of fires that have burned out or, by some cold fate, have been extinguished. For every living one of us, I believe, there is a Cañada del Oro—a Canyon of Gold—there is a lost mine that will never be found—there are iron doors that may never be opened.

And yet—those who look for it still find "color" in the Cañada del Oro. Romance and adventure still live in the Canyon of Gold. The treasures of life are not all hidden in a lost mine behind an iron door.

As the old prospector, Thad Grove, said to his pardner one time when their last pinch of dust was gone and their most promising lead had pinched out: "After all, it's a dead immortal cinch that if we *had* a-happened to strike it rich like we was hopin', we couldn't never bin as rich as we was hopin' to be. There jest naterally *ain't* that much gold, nohow."

"Sure," returned Bob Hill, the other old-timer, "and ain't you never took notice how much richer a feller with one poor, little, old nugget in his pan is than the hombre what only thinks he's got a bonanza somewheres on the insides of a mountain? An' look at this, will you: If everybody was to certain sure *find* the mine he's huntin' there'd be so blame *much* gold in the world that it'd take a hundred-mule train to pack enough to buy a mess of frijoles. It's a good thing, *I* say, that somebody, er something has fixed it somehow so's *all* our fool dreams *can't* come true."

"Speakin' of love," said Thad on another occasion, when the two were discussing the happiness that had so strangely come to them with their part-nership daughter, "love ain't no big deposit that a feller is allus hopin' to find but mostly never does. Love is jest a medium high-grade ore that you got to dig for."

"Yep," agreed Bob, "an' when you've got your ore you've sure got to run it through the mill an' treat it scientific if you expect to recover much of the values."

The affairs of the old Pardners and their daughter Marta were matters of great and never-failing interest to the loungers who gathered in front of the general store and post-office in Oracle.

Bill Janson, known as the Lizard, invariably opened and led the discussions. The Janson family, it should be said, had drifted into the Cañada del Oro from Arkansas. They were, in the picturesque vernacular of the cattlemen, "nesters." The Lizard, an only son, was one of those rat-faced, shifty-eyed, loose-mouthed, male creatures who know everything about everybody and spend the major part of their days telling it.

It was on one of those social occasions when the Lizard was entertaining a group of idlers on the platform in front of the store that I first heard of the two old prospectors and their partnership girl.

CHAPTER II
AT THE ORACLE STORE

"YES, sir," said the Lizard, "I'm a-tellin' ye that them thar Pardners an' their gal—Marta her name is—are th' beatenest outfit ye er ary other man ever seed. Ain't nobody kin figger 'em out, nohow. They've been here nigh about five year, too. Me an' paw an' maw, we been here eight year ourselves—comin' this fall. Yes, sir, they're sure a queer actin' lot."

The Lizard had so evidently made his introductory remarks for my benefit that some sort of acknowledgment was unquestionably due.

"What are they, miners?"

"Uh-huh, they're a-workin' a claim—makin' enough t' live on, I reckon—leastways they're a-livin'. But that ain't hit—hit's that thar gal of theirn." He shook his head and heaved a troubled sigh. "Law, law!"

And no one could have failed to mark the eager viciousness of the Lizard's expression as the loose-mouthed creature ruminated on the delectable gossip he was about to offer.

"Ye see hit's like this: Them two old-timers had this here gal with 'em when they first come into th' canyon down yonder. She was a kid—'long 'bout fourteen, then. An' there ain't nobody kin tell fer sure who she is, ner whar she come from. They say as how old Bob an' Thad found her when they was a-prospectin' onct down on th' border somewhares—tuck her away from some Mexican outfit er other. Mebby hit's so an' mebby hit ain't. But everybody 'lows as how she ain't come from no good sort nohow, 'cause if she had why wouldn't the Pardners tell hit? An' take an' look at this dad-beatin' father arrangement—take their names fer instance: one is Bob Hill, t'other is Thad Grove, an' what's the gal's name but Marta Hillgrove—Hill-Grove—d'ye ketch hit? An' one week old Bob he'll be her pappy, an' th' next week old Thad he's her paw, an' the gal she jist naterally 'lows they both her daddies. My Gawd! Hit's enough t' drive a decent man plumb loony a-tryin' t' figger hit out."

The Lizard's friends laughed.

"Oh, ye kin laugh, but I'm a-tellin' ye thar's somethin' wrong somewhars an' I ain't th' only one what says so neither. Won't nobody over here in Oracle have nothin' t' do with her. Will they?" He turned to the loungers for confirmation.

"She's a plumb beauty, too, an' a mighty cute little piece—reg'lar spitfire, if ye git her started—an' smart—say, she bosses them pore old Pardners till they're scared mighty nigh t' death of her—an' proud—huh—she's too all-fired proud to suit some of us."

The crowd grinned.

"The Lizard, he sure ought to know," said one.

Bob grinned cheerfully.

"Mebby I ain't so much of a Christian neither," he agreed, "but if I'd a-been that old Pharaoh what built them pyramids—"

The girl interrupted:

"Now, there you go again. That's the second time. What in the world started you to talking about Egypt and pyramids and Pharaoh and mummies and things like that?"

"Oh, I jest happened to take a peek into one of them books that Saint Jimmy got us to buy for you, that's all," returned the old-timer, with a sly wink at the smiling girl. "An' anyway, it seems like I ought to know somethin' about mummies by this time, after livin' as long as I have with that there." He pointed a long, gnarled finger at his pardner. "Egypt or Arizona, livin' or dead, it's all the same, I reckon. A mummy's a mummy wherever you find it."

Thad rubbed his bald head with deliberate care.

"Daughter, does Mother Burton's brand of Christianity say anything about what a man should do to his enemies?"

"Indeed it does," returned the girl. "It says we must love our enemies and forgive them."

"All right—all right—an' what does it say about lovin' an' forgivin' your friends, heh?"

"Why—nothing, I guess."

"Course it don't," cried the old prospector in shrill triumph.

"Course it don't. An' do you know why? I'll tell you why. It's because it's so doggone easy to forgive an enemy compared to what it is to forgive a friend, that's why. The Good Book knows 'tain't necessary to say nothin' about friends, 'cause it's jest as nateral and virtuous to hate a friend as 'tis to love an enemy—that's what I'm a-meanin'."

Marta was not in the least disturbed over this exchange of courtesies by her two fathers. Rising from the table, she laughingly remarked that if they were not *too* busy they might saddle her horse, as she must go to Oracle for supplies. Whereupon the Pardners went to the barn, leaving their girl free to clear away the breakfast things, wash the dishes, and finish her morning housework.

It was an unwritten law of the partnership that the particular father of the week should stand obligated to the parental responsibilities of the position. It was by no means the least of his duties that he must endure the criticisms of the other upon the way he was "bringing up" his daughter. It seems scarcely necessary to add that criticism was never wanting and that it was never without directness and point. To compensate for this burden of responsibility, the parent was permitted to say "my gal" while the critic, by the rules of the game, must invariably say "that gal of yourn."

While Thad the father was currying his daughter's horse, Nugget—a bright little pinto—Bob squatted comfortably on his heels, his back against the wall of the barn.

"Pardner," he said, as one who speaks after mature deliberation, "I ain't meanin' to mix none in your family affairs, but as a friend I'm a-feelin' constrained to remark that you ain't doin' right by that gal of yourn nohow."

Marta's father was making a careful examination of the pinto's off forefoot and seemed not to hear.

Bob continued:

"Anybody can see that she comes mighty nigh bein' grown up. First thing *you* know somebody'll make her understand all to once that she's a woman, and then—"

Thad dropped the pinto's foot and glared at his pardner over the horse's back.

"Then *what*?"

"Then she'll be wantin' to know things. An'—it might be too late to tell her."

"You mean that I ought to tell my gal what we know about her?" demanded Marta's father. "Is that what you're tryin' to say?"

"You guessed it, Pardner," returned the critical one cheerfully. "It's time that your gal knowed about herself. Bein' her daddy, it's up to you to tell her."

The other exploded:

"Which is exactly what I tried all last week to tell *you*, when you was her daddy, you blamed old numskull, an' you wouldn't near listen to me. A healthy father you are. When it's *your* daughter that ought to be told, you can't even whisper, but when she's mine you can yell your fool head off tellin' me what *I* ought to do. Besides, you said yourself that we don't actually know enough to tell her anything."

"But that was last week, you see," returned Bob calmly. "You was doin' the talkin' then—now *I'm* tellin' you."

When Thad, without replying, fell to rubbing Nugget's glossy hide with such energy that the little horse squirmed like a schoolboy undergoing maternal inspection, Bob continued:

"Marta is bound to know, when she stops to think about it, that she jest can't have two fathers. It's plumb unnateral, even for two such daddies as she's got. So far she ain't give it much thought. She's sort of growed up with the idea an' accepted things as young folks do—up to a certain time, that is. My point is, that from now on her time is liable to come any day. Right now, if she thinks of it at all she jest smiles an' plays the game with us, but that's 'cause she's mostly kid yet. You wait till the woman in her is woke up—right there she'll quit playin' an' somethin' is due to happen. You ain't doin' right by your daughter, Thad, not to tell her—you sure ain't."

Thad Grove faced his old pardner miserably. "I know you're right, Bob. Marta ought to be told what we know about her. I can see that it'll look mighty bad to her some day if she ain't. But, hang darn it, it's jest like you said last week—we don't know enough for me to tell her anything. If I was to tell her what little we do know, it would look a heap sight worse to her than it possibly can with her not bein' told anything, like she is now. The way I figger, if the gal don't know nothin', she's got a chance to ride over it; but if she knows the little that we know she'll be plumb ruined."

"I don't reckon it's near so bad as that, Pardner," said the other soothingly. "I'm here to tell you that there ain't nothin' could ruin that gal of yourn."

At this, the fire of old Thad's soul flared up anew.

"Is that so?" he returned in a voice of withering scorn. "*Is* that so? Well, I'm a tellin' *you* that you can ruin *anybody*."

"Saint Jimmy, for instance?" retorted Bob with sarcasm.

"Yes, Saint Jimmy. You can't tell what sort of a scoundrel Saint Jimmy would a-been if he hadn't happened to a-turned sick. There's many a man in the pen, right now, jest on account of havin' too much good health."

"I reckon you're speakin' gospel for once," agreed Bob reluctantly. Then, as if he had not forgotten his critical privileges, he added: "But there's something else you ought to tell your gal—something that the best authorities all agree ought to be told every gal by somebody—an' bein' as you're her father, an' she ain't never had no real ma, why—it would look like it was up to you."

"What's that?" demanded Thad suspiciously.

"That's what they call love," returned the other gently. "Growin' up like Marta has, with jest us two old, dried-up, desert rats, she don't know no more about love an' its consequences than—than—nothin'."

Marta's father dropped his brush and kicked it viciously across the stable. Nugget danced with excitement.

"Love! Holy Cats! What fool notion'll take you next? You don't need to worry none. Some feller will happen along some day an' tell her more about love in a minute than you've ever knowed in all your life."

"That's jest it," returned the other. "Some feller is bound to tell her, jest like you say. He'll slip up on her quiet like, when she ain't suspicionin' nothin', an' break it to her sudden 'fore she knows where she's at. That's how them consequences happen. An' that's why she ought to know beforehand, so's she can be watchin' out."

Thad was rubbing his bald head seeking, apparently, for an answer sufficiently crushing, when a clear call came from the house.

"Daddy—Oh, Daddy, I am ready."

With frantic haste, the Pardners, working together as if they had never had a difference, saddled and bridled the pinto. Together they led the little horse to the house.

When the girl was in the saddle, she looked down into their upturned faces with such an expression of girlish affection and womanly thoughtfulness that the two old men grinned with sheepish delight and pride.

"You will find your dinner all ready for you," she said, while Nugget tossed his head, impatient to be off. "It is on the table, covered with a cloth. I'll be home in time for supper. *Adios.*" She lifted the bridle rein and the pinto loped away.

The Pardners stood watching while she opened and closed the gate, cowboy fashion, without dismounting. With a wave of her hand she rode on up the canyon while the two old men followed her with their eyes until she passed from sight around a turn in the canyon wall.

Thad spoke slowly:

"You're plumb right, Bob. The gal has mighty nigh growed into a woman, ain't she? It don't seem more'n a month or two neither, does it?"

"It sure don't," returned the other softly. "An' ain't she a wonder, Thad—ain't she jest a nateral-born wonder?"

"She's all of that," agreed Thad, "an' then some. It plumb scares me though, when I think of her findin' out about herself an' her all educated up by Saint Jimmy an' his mother like she is. Holy Cats, Bob! What'll we do?"

"She's bound to know some day," said Bob.

"She's bound to, sure," echoed Thad with a groan. "But my God a'mighty ain't either of us got nerve to tell her *now*. If she hadn't been goin' to school to Saint Jimmy these last five years—I mean if she was like she would a-been with jest me an' you to bring her up, it might not a-mattered. But now—now it's goin' to be plain hell for her when she finds out."

Bob murmured softly:

"Won't even let us work on Sundays 'cause it ain't the right way for Christians like us to do. We'd ought to a-told long ago, that's what we ought to a-done."

"Sure, we ought to told her," cried Thad, "jest like we'd ought to done a lot of things we ain't. But mournin' over what ought to been done ain't payin' us nothin'. What're we *goin'* to do, that's what we got to figger out. The gal's got to be told."

"Yes," returned Bob. "An' she's got to be told 'fore some sneakin' varmint beats us to it an' tells her for true what me an' you are only suspicionin'. How'll you ever do it?"

"How'll *I* ever do it?" shrilled Thad. "Holy Cats! I can't—How'll you ever do it yourself?"

Bob answered helplessly:

"I can't neither—an' by smoke, I won't."

"She's got to be told," insisted Thad.

"She sure has," said Bob.

CHAPTER IV
SAINT JIMMY

DOCTOR JIMMY BURTON and his mother spent their first year in Arizona at Tucson and Oracle. But when they were satisfied that Jimmy could live if he gave up his too strenuous professional work and remained in the South-west, and that if he did not follow that course he would as surely die, they built the little white house on the mountain side at Juniper Springs, above the Cañada del Oro. As Jimmy explained, "it was quite necessary, under the circumstances, that they live where they could see out."

It was during that first summer in Oracle that the neighbors began to speak of his tender care of his mother, for, even in those days when he was too ill to do more than think, his thoughts were all for her. And so lovingly did he try to shield her from the pain of his suffering, so cheerfully did he ac-custom her to the thought of the utter hopelessness of his professional future, and so courageously, for her sake, did he accept the pitifully small portion that life offered him, that the people marveled at the spirit of the man. It was a question, they sometimes said, with a touch of sincere reverence in their voices, if Doctor Burton needed his mother as much as the doctor's mother needed him. But Jimmy and his mother knew that the truth of the matter was they needed each other.

And so in their mutual need both mother and son found compensation for their dreams that now could never come true. In place of the professional honors that were predicted with such confidence for her boy, and toward which she had looked with such pride, the mother saw her son honored by the love of the unpretentious country folk. From plans that had failed and hopes that were buried, Jimmy himself turned to the grandeur of the mountains and the beauty of tree and bush and flower—to the limitless spaces of the desert and the peace of the quiet stars. The life of the great eastern city, with its hunger for fame, its struggle for riches, its endless tumult and its restless longings, faded farther and farther away. The simple, more primitive, more peaceful life of God's great unimproved world became every day more sat-isfying.

To the roaming cowboys and miners and their kind, and to the people of the little mountain village, that tiny white house on the hill was known. And many a man, when things were going wrong, came to spend an hour with this friend whose understanding was so clear and whose counsel was so true. Many a girl or woman in need of comfort, strength or courage came to sit a while with Mrs. Burton. And sometimes a tired rider of the range would hear in the twilight dusk the clear, sweet song of Jimmy's flute and, hearing, would smile and lift his wide-brimmed hat; or perhaps a lonely prospector, camped for the night in some gulch or wash would hear, and, hearing, would think again of things that in his search for gold he had forgotten. And this is how Doctor James Burton became Saint Jimmy and Saint Jimmy's mother became Mother Burton to them all.

It was natural that the good doctor should become Marta Hillgrove's teacher, and that Mrs. Burton should mother the girl who, until her fathers brought her to the Cañada del Oro, had never known a woman's guiding love. Indeed, it was Saint Jimmy and his mother and all that their friendship meant to Marta that had kept the Pardners in that neighborhood. Never before since the beginning of their partnership had those wanderers stayed so long in one place. For four—nearly five—years Marta had been studying under Saint Jimmy; a fair equivalent of the usual college course. With this textbook education she had received from Mother Burton the kind of training that such a woman would have given a daughter of her own. And yet these most excellent teachers knew no more of their pupil's history than did those thoughtless ones who so freely discussed the girl and looked at her askance for what they thought her parentage might be.

It should be said, too, that this schooling which Marta had received from Saint Jimmy and his mother was wholly a matter of love. As Doctor Burton explained to the Pardners, when they insisted that he should be paid "same as a reg'lar teacher," the work was really a blessing to him in that his pupil contributed more to his life than he could possibly give to hers; while Mother Burton warned the anxious fathers, gently but firmly, that if they ever said another word about pay they would ruin everything.

But as the years passed and she watched the amazing development of the girl's mind, and saw the unfolding of her richly endowed womanhood, wise Mother Burton came to wonder sometimes if Saint Jimmy's teaching was not more a matter of love than even he perhaps realized.

On that spring morning when Marta rode to Oracle and her fathers discussed the problem that so troubled them, Saint Jimmy sat in the yard before the cottage door. On every side he saw the Mariposa tulips lifting their lovely orange cups, and sweet pea blossoms swinging like pink and white fairies above a lilac carpet of wild verbena and purple fragrant hyptis, while against the rocks that were stained with splashes of gray and orange and red and yellow lichens stood the purple pentstemon. The mountain sides below were wondrous with the scarlet glory of the ocotillo and the indescribable beauty of the chollas and opuntias with their crowns and diadems of red and salmon and orange and pink. The slopes and benches of the lower levels were bright with great fields of golden brittle-bush; and beyond these, on the wide spaces of the mesa, he could see the yuccas (our Lord's candles) in countless thousands, raising their stately shafts with eight-foot clusters of creamy-white bloom.

Mrs. Burton, leaving her housework for a moment, came to stand in the doorway. When they had spoken of the beautiful sight that never failed to move them—calling each other's attention to different favorite views—Saint Jimmy said:

"Mother, doesn't it all make you sort of hungry for something—something that can't be told in words?" he laughed in boyish embarrassment.

His mother smiled.

"Marta will be coming from Oracle with the mail, I suppose—this is Saturday, you know."

"Yes, I know," said Jimmy softly, and wondered if his mother guessed what it really was that he hungered for and could not talk about even to her.

Mrs. Burton was turning back into the house when they heard someone coming up the trail from the canyon. A moment later the Pardners appeared. Saint Jimmy and his mother knew at once that the old prospectors had come on business of greater moment than to make a mere neighborly call.

When they had exchanged the customary greetings and Marta's fathers had assured their friends that the girl was well, Thad and Bob sat looking at each other in troubled silence.

"Wal," said Bob, at last, "why don't you go ahead? She's your gal this week. Bein' her daddy makes it your play, don't it?"

Thad, rubbing his bald head desperately, made several ineffectual attempts to speak. At last, with a recklessness born of this inner struggle, he addressed Mrs. Burton:

"You see, ma'am, me an' my pardner here has been takin' notice lately how my gal Marta is due, first thing we know, to be a growed-up woman."

"She is, indeed!" replied Jimmy's mother with an encouraging smile.

"Yes, ma'am, that's what me an' Bob here took notice. An' we've been figgerin' up that mebby it was time she knowed what we know about her. You an' your son knows the same as everybody does, I reckon, that we ain't Marta's real honest-to-God daddies."

"Yes," said Mrs. Burton, "but we have never, in any way, mentioned the matter to Marta."

"No, ma'am," said Thad, "an' we ain't neither."

"An' that's jest what's the matter now," put in Bob. "The gal ain't never been told nothin'."

Mrs. Burton looked at her son.

"I am sure that you men are right," said Saint Jimmy. "I have been wanting to talk with you about it. You ought to tell Marta everything you know of her and her people—how she came to you—everything."

The Pardners consulted each other silently. Then Thad turned to Marta's teacher; the old prospector's faded blue eyes were fixed on the younger man's face with a steady, searching gaze that permitted no evasion, even if Saint Jimmy had been disposed to parry the question.

"Is there, to your thinkin', any perticler reason why my gal ought to be told at this perticler time?"

Saint Jimmy smiled reassuringly.

"No particular reason, so far as I know," he said. "Of course you realize that there has always been more or less talk. Sooner or later the girl is bound to hear it. She should be fortified with the truth."

Again Bob and Thad looked at each other helplessly.

"An' if the truth ain't jest what you might call fortifyin'—what then?" said Thad at last.

"Yes," echoed Bob. "What then? What if my pardner an' me can't say that all the gossips is talkin' ain't so?"

Saint Jimmy did not answer. Mother Burton looked away. Old Thad rubbed his bald head in mournful meditation.

"Doctor Burton," said Bob slowly, as one feeling his way amid conversational dangers, "Thad an' me ain't to say blind, if we be gittin' old. We can still tell 'color' when we run across it." He consulted his pardner with a look and Thad nodded his head in approval. Bob continued: "We're almighty proud of what you been doin' for our gal," he caught himself quickly. "Excuse me, Pardner—for your gal, I mean."

Thad raised his hand—a gesture which signified that, in the stress of the situation, he waived the fine point of their usual courtesy, and for this crucial occasion acknowledged their joint fatherhood.

Old Bob swallowed, with difficulty, something that seemed to obstruct his usual freedom of speech.

"An' I reckon you understand, sir, that we ain't noways lackin' in appreciation an' gratitude to you an' your ma for helpin' Marta to grow up into the young woman she is. My pardner an' me, we sure done what we could, an' we'd been glad to a-done more if it had a-been possible, but it wasn't, not for us, an' we're sensible to what it all means to our gal. If she wasn't trained up an' all educated like you an' your ma has made her, it wouldn't much matter what her own folks was or how she first come to us."

"I understand," said Saint Jimmy gently, "and I know that the girl could not love you men more if you were, in fact, her own fathers. I know, too, that nothing could make her love you less. But I am convinced that she should know all that you know about her."

"We would a-told her the story long ago," said Thad, "if only we'd a-knowed a little more than we do, or mebby, if we hadn't knowed as much, or if what little we do know didn't look so almighty bad."

"It will look a heap worse to her now than it ever did to us," said Bob.

"It sure will," agreed Thad, "an' so, you see, we've been waitin' an' puttin' it off, hopin' that we would mebby, somehow, find out something that, as it is, is lackin'." He appealed to Mrs. Burton: "You can see how it is, can't you, ma'am?"

"I understand," said the good woman, gently, "but I agree with my son. Whatever it is, the story will make no difference in Marta's love for you, just as it has made no difference in your love for her."

"Yes," said Thad, "but how about the difference it might make to—" he paused and looked at his pardner helplessly. "Ahem—to—I mean—"

Bob spoke quickly:

"To you an' Saint Jimmy, ma'am. What difference will it make to you folks?"

Thad drew a deep breath of relief and rubbed his bald head with satisfaction.

Mother Burton met them bravely with:

"Nothing that you have to tell can change our feeling for Marta. I could not love her more if she were my own daughter."

The two old men looked at Saint Jimmy eagerly.

"You dead sure that nothin' would make you change toward our gal?" demanded Bob.

"You plumb certain, be you, sir?" said old Thad.

Saint Jimmy smiled reassuringly.

"As certain as I am of death," he answered.

With an air of excited relief Thad faced his pardner.

"That bein' the case I move, Pardner, that we tell Doctor Burton here what we know, an' he can tell our gal or not as he sees fit, and when he sees fit."

"Jest what I was about to offer myself," returned Bob. "You go ahead."

CHAPTER V
THE PROSPECTOR'S STORY

"IT was about sixteen year ago," Thad began at last.

"Seventeen, the middle of next month," said Bob.

Thad continued:

"Me an' my pardner here was comin' in to Tucson from the Santa Rosa Mountains, which is down close to the Mexican line. We'd been out for about three months an' was needin' supplies. 'Long late in the afternoon of the second day from where we'd been workin', we stopped at a little ranch house about three mile this side of the line for water. We knowed the old Mexican man an' woman what lived there all right—'most everybody did—everybody like us old desert rats, that is—an' didn't nobody know any good of 'em either."

"Some claim that the old woman was Sonora Jack's mother," said Bob. "Sonora Jack, you know, is half Mex, and a mighty bad citizen, too. He's somewheres across the line right now, hidin' out for a killin' he an' his crowd made in a holdup' bout the same time that we're tellin' you of."

Thad took up the story.

"Well, sir, we'd filled our water bags an' was standin' talkin' with the old woman who'd come to watch us—the man, he was away it appeared—when all at once a little boy come trottin' 'round the corner of the cabin from behind somewheres."

"About three or four, he was," said Bob.

"About that," agreed Thad. "An' when he seen us he jest stopped short, kind of scared like, an' stood there cryin'.

"Well, sir, me an' Bob tumbled in a holy minute that he didn't belong there. We knowed them old Mexicans didn't have no kid that wasn't growed up long ago. An' this little chap didn't look like a Mexican youngster nohow. The old woman acted kind of rattled at us lookin' at the kid so sharp, an' started in tellin' us that the muchachito was one of her grandsons. That sounded fair enough at first, but when she turned an' yelled at the kid in Mex, givin' him the devil for not stayin' behind the house like she'd told him to, we seed that somethin' was wrong. He didn't savvy Mex no more than we do Chinee.

"While the poor little cuss was standin' there scared stiff an' cryin'—not knowin' what the old woman wanted, Bob here went down on one knee an' held out his hands invitin' like. 'Come here, sonny,' says he to the kid in English, 'come on over here an' let's have a look at you.'

"Well, sir, that youngster gave a funny little laugh, right out through his tears, an' come runnin'.

"The old woman didn't know what to do; but I was keepin' one eye on her so she didn't dare try to start anything much.

"Bob, he asked the youngster, 'What's your name, sonny?' an' the little feller answered back, bright as a dollar: 'My name's Marta.'

"'Marta?' says Bob, lookin' up at me puzzled like. 'That's a funny name for a boy.'

"'I ain't no boy,' said the kid, quick as a flash, 'I'm a girl, I am.'"

"An' by smoke! she was," ejaculated Bob.

"Yes," continued Thad, "an' when the old woman seen that the little gal was talkin' to us—the old woman she didn't savvy a word of anything but Mex, but she could tell what was goin' on—when she see it, she jest naterally grabbed the youngster an' yanked her into the house an' shut the door.

"Me an' Bob made camp not far away that night, an' after supper, an' it had got good an' dark, we was settin' by the fire talkin' things over, when all at once we heard the sound of a wagon an' a child screamin'—sort of choked like. You can believe we wasn't long gettin' to where the sound come from. Them Mexicans was lightin' out with that little gal for across the border.

"By that time, me and my pardner was so plumb sure that there was somethin' wrong that we didn't waste no more strength in foolishness. We jest proceeded to give that hombre the third degree till he ups an' confesses that the baby was left with them by some white folks who was on a huntin' trip, an' that they was only keepin' the youngster till her daddy an' mammy come back for her.

"You can guess how quick me an' Bob was to believe any such yarn as that; so we figured the safest thing to do was to take the baby ourselves into Tucson; which we done.

"Well, sir, by the time we struck town the little gal had made such a hit with us both that we couldn't near think of givin' her up."

"Darndest affectionate kid that ever was," put in Bob. "Started right off first thing lovin' us two old rapscallions like we'd always belonged to her, an' callin' us both 'daddy.'"

"We sure done our best to find her real folks, though," said Thad. "We stayed in Tucson for more'n a month. But the authorities nor nobody couldn't get no hint nowhere about any kid bein' lost, nor stole, nor nothin'. Things was movin' pretty fast in this country them days, an' the sheriff always had his hands full; so it wasn't long till everybody got busy with some fresh excitement, an' me an' Bob was left with the baby on our hands. There didn't appear to be nothin' else we could do, so we jest decided that Providence, or good luck, or somethin', had fixed it so's us two old mavericks was blessed with a offspring whether we was regularly entitled to one or not. Then pretty soon we moved on over into the Graham Mountains, an' jest naterally took her along.

"We both was lovin' her so by now that we was about to fight to see which one was to be her daddy, when we compromised by agreein' to take turn an' turn about—week by week. An' that's how we come to give her both our names—Hillgrove. Her first name is Martha, we suppose; but Marta was the best she could ever tell us. An' that's about all there is of it up to the time we fetched her here an' you started in teachin' her."

"You see, ma'am," said Bob, "this here is the way me an' Thad has got it figgered: The baby must have been left with them Mexicans where we found her, 'cause she ain't Mexican nor any part Mexican herself. Wal, what kind of white folks do you reckon would go away an' leave a little gal like that, with such an outfit? They couldn't a-left her accidental like, 'cause if they had they'd a-come back for her, an' then they'd been huntin' us. With all the fuss we made about it in Tucson, somebody would a-knowed somethin' about her sure, if her people hadn't wanted to get shet of her on account of them bein' the sort they was. An' there ain't been no time since then that me an' Thad has been hard to find. Don't you see, her folks couldn't a-been decent even if her father an' mother was—was—I mean, even if she was borned all regular an' right—which don't look no way likely. Any way you take it, they must a-been a bad sort to throw away a baby like her."

"You can bet they was," added Thad mournfully, "for it's a dead immortal cinch that them old Mexicans couldn't a-come by her no other way; 'cause they never went anywhere an' if they had stole her it sure would a-raised enough interest in the country for somebody to a-heard about it. No, sir, take it any way you like, it jest naterally looks bad. An'," the old prospector finished with an air of relief, "that's all me an' my pardner knows about it."

Saint Jimmy did not speak. He was evidently deeply moved by the strange story. Mrs. Burton was drying her eyes. The Pardners waited, with no little anxiety.

At last Bob asked timidly:

"Be you still thinkin', sir, as how our gal ought to be told?"

Reluctantly, Saint Jimmy answered:

"I am afraid that Marta must know."

He looked at his mother.

"I am sure she must know," said Mrs. Burton with quiet decision. "And you, my son, are the one to tell her. It will come to her easier from you, her teacher, than from anyone else."

"Yes, ma'am," cried Thad eagerly. "That's the way me an' Bob figgered it."

"Will you do it, sir?" asked Bob.

"Yes," said Saint Jimmy, "I will tell her."

The Pardners sighed with relief.

"That sure lets us out of a mighty bad hole," said Thad. "It'll be a heap easier on our gal, too."

"It sure will," echoed Bob. "Ain't nobody can tell what kind of a God-awful mess us old fools would a-made of it. We're almighty grateful to you, sir, for helpin' us out."

"We are that," came from Thad with pathetic earnestness.

Bob said hurriedly:

"An' now that it's all settled, Pardner, I move that me an' you pulls out of here before our gal happens along. I wouldn't be ketched by her right now for all the money we're goin' to have when we strike that big vein we're tunnelin' for."

"Which ain't so much as it might be at that," retorted Thad.

"You can't never tell," returned Bob with his usual cheery optimism, "gold is where you find it."

When Bob and Thad were gone, Saint Jimmy and his mother, discussing the matter, were forced to agree with the Pardners. It certainly did look bad. In fact it looked so bad that Saint Jimmy was not at all happy under the burden of the responsibility which the old prospectors had shifted from their own shoulders to his. He foresaw that it would not be easy to tell this young woman whom he had educated, and whose fine, sensitive pride he knew so well, this story that he had just heard from her two foster fathers.

When Marta stopped at the Burtons' on her way home from Oracle, later in the day, neither Saint Jimmy nor his mother mentioned the Pardners' visit, and there seemed to be no opportunity for the girl's teacher to tell her the story he was so sure she should know. Some other time, he told himself, it would be easier, perhaps.

While the Pardners' daughter was riding home from the Burtons' that afternoon, and the Pardners were at work in their little mine, Natachee the Indian stood on a point of rock, high on the mountain side—so high that he could look beyond the Canyon of Gold and afar off, over the brown desert that, from the foothills of the Catalinas, stretches away, weary mile after weary mile, until, in the shadowy blue distance, it is lost in the sky.

To those of us who are accustomed to the present-day Indian in his white man's garb, doing the white man's work on the white man's roads and ranches, Natachee would have aroused peculiar, not to say amusing, interest. From the single feather in the headband which bound his long, raven-black hair to his beaded moccasins, he was dressed in the picturesque costume of his savage fathers. Save for a broad hunting knife, he was armed only with the primitive bow and arrows. He was in the best years of his manhood and his face and bearing would have graced the hero of a Fenimore Cooper Indian tale.

But however much he seemed out of step with the times, that lone figure, standing sentinel-like on the rocky point, fitted his wild surroundings. So, indeed, might one of his ancestors have stood to watch the strange new human life when it first began to move along those trails that, until then, had known only the sandaled and moccasined feet of prehistoric peoples.

An hour passed. The Indian held his place as motionless as the rock against which he leaned, while his somber gaze ranged over those mighty reaches of desert and mountain and sky. High over Rice Peak a golden eagle wheeled on guard before the nest of his royal mate. But Natachee seemed not to see. From a dead oak on Samaniego Ridge a red-tailed hawk screamed his shrill challenge. The Indian apparently did not hear. A company of buzzards circled above a dark object in the wash below the Wheeler Ranch corrals. Natachee gave no heed. A ground squirrel leaped to a near-by rock to sit bolt upright with bright eyes fixed upon the red man, the while he sounded a chirping note of inquiry. But the Indian's gaze remained steadfastly fixed on that distant landscape where he could see a cloud of dust that was raised by a swiftly moving automobile on the Oracle road. On the Bankhead Highway there were two similar clouds. In the purple haze beyond the point of the Tortollita Mountains, a streamer of smoke marked the position of a Southern Pacific Overland train that was approaching Tucson from the western coast.

The face of the red watchman on the mountain side was set stern and grim. In his somber eyes there was a gleam of savage meaning.

The sun was just touching the tops of the Tucson hills when the Indian started and leaned forward with suddenly quickened interest.

No ordinary power of human vision would have noticed that black speck in the vast stretch of country, much less could the ordinary observer have said exactly what it was that had attracted the Indian's attention. But Natachee saw that the tiny dot, moving so slowly on the old road into the Cañada del Oro, was a man. His interest was excited to an unusual degree because the man was walking, unaccompanied even by a pack burro.

And now the evening wind from the desert, fragrant with the smell of greasewood, mesquite and cat-claw, swept along the mountain side. The Tucson hills were massed dark blue with their outlines sharply cut against the colors of the sunset. Natachee, watching, saw that lone figure on the trail below enter the Canyon of Gold and lose itself in the gathering dusk.

As the shadows thickened, the night prowlers on padded feet crept from their dark retreats into the gloom. Owls and bats on silent wings swept by. Old ghosts of the dead past stirred again on the old desert and mountain ways. In the deeper dusk that now filled the canyon, voices awoke—strange, murmuring, whispering, phantom voices that seemed to come from an innumerable company of dreary, hopeless souls. The light went out of the western sky. Details of plant and rock and bush were lost. Weird and wild, like a mysterious spirit brooding over the scene, the dark figure of the Indian on the rocky point above the Canyon of Gold was silhouetted against the starlit sky.

In the little white house on the mountain side, Saint Jimmy was thinking of the strange story that the Pardners had told.

In their home beside the canyon creek, the old prospectors and their partnership daughter were sleeping, with no dreams of the strange leading of the tangled threads of lives to the Canyon of Gold.

Far away to the south, in old Mexico, two men sat in a cantina. Between them, on a table, with glasses and a bottle of mescal, lay a crudely drawn map. As they talked together in low tones, they referred often to the rude sketch which bore in poorly written words "La mina con la puerta de fierro en la Cañada del Oro"—The mine with the door of iron in the Canyon of the Gold.

CHAPTER VI
NIGHT

THE man who was following the old road up the Canyon of Gold had made his way a mile or more from the point where he was last seen by the Indian, when the deepening twilight warned him of the nearness of the night. It was evident, from the pedestrian's irresolute movements and from his manner of nervous doubt in selecting a spot for his camp, that not only was he a stranger in the Cañada del Oro, but as well that he was unaccustomed to such surroundings.

He was a young man of about twenty-two or twenty-three years—tall, but rather slender, with a face habitually clean shaven but covered, just now, with a stubby beard of several days' growth. His skin, where it was exposed, was sunburned rather than tanned that deep color so marked in the out-of-doors men of the West. On the whole, he gave the impression, somehow, of one but recently recovered from a serious illness; and yet he did not appear overfatigued, though the pack which he carried was not light and he had evidently been many hours on the road. In spite of his rude dress and unkempt appearance due to his mode of traveling there was, in his bearing, the unmistakable air of a man of business. But he was that type of business man that knows something more than the daily grind of money-making machines. His world, apparently, was not wholly a world of factories and banks and institutions of commerce.

Forced, at last, by the approaching darkness, to decide upon some place to spend the night, the traveler selected a spot beside the canyon creek, a hundred yards from the road. But even after he had lowered his heavy pack to the ground, he stood for some minutes looking anxiously about, as if still uncertain as to the wisdom of his selection.

Nor was the man's manner wholly that of inexperience. Suddenly, without thought of his evening meal, or any preparation for his comfort until the morning, he climbed again up the steep bank to the road, where he gazed back along the way he had come and studied the mountain sides with eyes of dread. The man was in an agony of fear. Not until it was too dark to distinguish objects at any distance did he return to the place where he had left his pack and set about the necessary work of preparing his supper and making his bed.

Hurriedly, as best he could in the failing light, he gathered a supply of wood and, after several awkward failures, succeeded in kindling a fire. From his pack he took a small frying pan, a coffeepot, a tin cup, and a meager supply of food. With these, and with water from the creek, he made shift to prepare an unaccustomed meal. Several times he paused, to stand gazing into the fire as if lost in thought. Again and again he turned his head quickly to listen. Often with a shuddering start he whirled to search the darkness beyond the flickering shadows, as if in fear of what the light of his fire might bring upon him. When he had eaten his poorly prepared supper, he spread his blankets and lay down.

There was something pitiful in the trivial and puny details of this lone stranger's camp in the wild Cañada del Oro. There was something sinister in the night life that crept and crawled in the darkness about him. There was something pathetic in the man's lying down to sleep, unprotected, amid such surroundings.

The mountains are very friendly to those who know them; to those who know them not, they are grim and dreadful—when the day is gone. Night skies are kind to those who love the stars; to others they are heavy with brooding fears. The timid life of the wild places is good company for those who know each voice and sound; to others every movement is a menace, every call a voice of danger—when the sun is down.

Cowering in his blankets the man listened for a while to the strange and fearful things that stirred in the near-by bushes, on the rocky ledges, and on the mountain sides above. He heard the canyon voices whispering, murmuring, moaning. The night deepened. The boisterous song of the creek became a sullen growl. The mountain walls seemed to close in. The stars above the peaks and ridges were lonely and far away. The camp fire, so tiny in the gloom, burned low.

The sleeping man groaned and stirred uneasily as if in pain, and a fox that had crept too close slipped away in startled flight. The man cried out in his sleep, and a coyote that was following the scent of the camp up the wind turned aside to slink into the thicket of mesquite. The man awoke and springing to his feet stood as if at bay, and a buck that was feeding not far away lifted his antlered head to listen with wary alertness. From somewhere on the heights came the cry of a mountain lion, and at the sound the night was suddenly as still as death. The man shuddered and quickly threw more wood on the dying fire. Again he lay down to cower in his blankets—to sleep restlessly—and to dream his troubled dreams.

In the first faint light of the morning, a dark form might have been seen moving stealthily down the mountain above the stranger's camp. The buck, with a snort of fear, leaped away, crashing through the brush. The prowling coyote fled down the canyon. On every side the wild creatures of the night slunk into the dense covers of manzanita and buckthorn and cat-claw.

Silently, as the gray shadows through which he crept, Natachee the Indian drew near the place where the white man lay. From behind a near-by bush the Indian observed every detail of the camp. When the form wrapped in the blanket did not stir, the Indian stole from his sheltering screen and with soft-footed, noiseless movements, inspected the stranger's outfit. He even bent over the sleeping man to see his face. The man moved—tossing an arm and muttering. Swift as a fox the Indian slipped away; silent as a ghost he disappeared among the bushes.

The gray of the morning sky changed to saffron and rose and flaming red. The shadowy trees and bushes assumed definite shapes. The detail of the rocks emerged from the gloom. The man awoke.

He had just finished breakfast when he heard the sound of horse's hoofs on the road. With a startled cry he leaped to his feet. The Lizard was riding toward him.

Like a hunted creature the man drew back, half crouching, as if to escape. But it was too late. Pale and trembling he stood waiting as the horseman drew up beside the road, on the bank above the creek, and sat looking down upon him and his camp.

CHAPTER VII
THE STRANGER'S QUEST

THE Lizard's preliminary inspection of the stranger and his camp might or might not have been prompted by a habit of caution. When it was finished he called a loose-mouthed "Howdy" and, without waiting for a response to his greeting, spurred his mount, slipping and sliding with rolling stones and a cloud of dust, down to the edge of the creek.

Dismounting and throwing the bridle rein over his horse's head, he slouched forward—a vapid grin on his sallow, weasel-like face.

"I seed yer smoke an' 'lowed as how I'd drop along an' take a look at who's here; bein' as I war aimin' t' ride t' Oracle sometime t'-day anyhow. Not as I've got anythin' perticler t' go thar fer nuther, 'cept t' jist set in front of th' store a spell an' gas with th' fellers. Thar's allus a bunch hangin' 'round of a Sunday."

He looked curiously at the stranger's outfit and, ignoring the fact that the camper had not spoken, seated himself with the air of one taking his welcome for granted.

The stranger smiled. The fear that had so shaken him a few moments before was gone, and there was relief in his voice as he bade his visitor a quite unnecessary welcome.

"Ye'r a-footin' hit, be ye?" the Lizard continued with garrulous ease. "Wal, that's one way of goin'; but I'll take a good hoss fer mine. A feller'll jist naterally wear out quick ernough no matter how keerful he'd be. Never 'lowed I had ary call t' take an' plumb *walk* myse'f t' death on purpose. Them's good blankets you've got thar. Need 'em, too, these nights, if 'tis spring. That thar coffeepot ain't no 'count, though—not fer me, that is—wouldn't hold half what I'd take three times a day, reg'lar." He laughed loudly as if a good joke were hidden somewhere in his remarks if only the other were clever enough to find it.

"You live in this neighborhood, do you?" the stranger asked.

"What, me? Oh shore. My name's Bill Janson—live down th' canyon a piece, jist below whar th' road comes in. Paw an' maw an' me live thar t'gether. We drifted in from Arkansaw eight year ago come this fall. What's yer name? Whar ye from? What're you a-doin' here?"

The stranger hesitated before he answered slowly:

"My name is—Edwards—Hugh Edwards. I came here from Tucson. I want to prospect—look for gold, you know. I heard there were some—ah—placers, I think you call them, in this canyon."

The Lizard grinned, a wide-mouthed grin of superior knowledge. "Hit's plumb easy t' see y' know all about prospectin'. Y'r some edicated, I jedge. Ben t' school an' them thar college places a right smart lot, ain't y' now?"

The other replied with some sharpness:

"I suppose it is not impossible for one to learn how to dig for gold, even if one has learned to read and write, is it?"

The Lizard responded heartily, but with tolerant superiority:

"Larn—shore—ain't nothin' t' pannin' gold 'cept a lot of hard work an' mighty pore pay. Anybody'll larn ye. Take the Pardners up yonder—old Bob Hill an' Thad Grove—they'd—" he checked himself suddenly and slapped a lean thigh. "By Glory! I'll bet a pretty you've done come t' find that thar old lost Mine with th' Iron Door, heh? Ain't ye now?" He leered at the stranger with shifty, close-set eyes, his long head with its narrow sloping brow cocked sidewise with what was meant to be a very knowing, "I-have-you-now-sir" sort of air.

The man who had given his name as Hugh Edwards laughed.

"Really I can't say that I would object to finding any old mine if it was a good one, would you?"

The Lizard shook his head solemnly and with a voice and manner that was nicely calculated to invite confidence, replied:

"Thar's been a lot of people, one time an' another, a-huntin' this Mine with th' Iron Door. Thar was one bunch that come clean from Spain; an' they had a map an' everythin'. You ain't got no map ner writin' of any sort, now, have you?"

"No," returned the stranger. "But I suppose it is true that there is gold to be found here?"

The Lizard was plainly disappointed but evidently deemed it unwise to press his inquiry.

"Oh, shore, thar's gold here—some—fer them what likes t' work fer hit. They've allus been a-diggin' in this here canyon an' in these here mountains, as ye kin see by their old prospect holes everywhar. But nobody ain't never made no big strikes yet. Thar's one feller a-livin' in these hills what don't dig no gold though; an' they do say, too, as how he knows more 'bout th' ol' lost mine than ary other man a-livin'. Some says he even knows whar hits at." The Lizard shook his head solemnly. "You shore want t' watch out fer *him*, too. He's plumb bad—that's what I'm a-tellin' you."

"Yes?" said Hugh Edwards, encouragingly.

"Uh-huh, he ain't no white man neither. He's Injun—calls hisse'f Natachee, whatever that is. He's one of these here school Injuns gone wild agin—lives all 'lone way in the upper part of th' canyon somewhar, whar hits so blamed rough a goat couldn't get 'round; an' togs hisse'f up with th' sort of things them old-time Injuns used to wear—won't even use a gun, jist packs a bow an' arrers. I ain't got no use fer an Injun nohow. This here's a white man's country, I say, an' this here Natachee he's the worst I ever did see. He'd plunk one of them thar arrers of hisn inter you, er slit yer throat any old time if he dast. I can't say fer shore whether he knows about this Mine with th' Iron Door er not, but hit's certain shore you got t' watch him. Hit's all right fer that thar Saint Jimmy an' them old Pardners t' be friends with him if they like hit, but I know what I know."

Hugh Edwards did not overlook this opportunity to learn something of the people who lived in the Canyon of Gold; and the Lizard was more than willing to tell all he knew, perhaps even to add something for good measure. When at last the Lizard arose reluctantly, the stranger had heard every current version of the history and relationship of the two old prospectors and their partnership daughter, with copious comments on their characters, sidelights on their personal affairs, their intercourse with their neighbors, their business, and every possible theory explaining them.

"Not that thar's anybody what really knows anythin',"—the Lizard was careful to make this clear—"'cept of course that old story 'bout them a-findin' th' gal somewhars when she warn't much more'n a baby; which, as I say, ain't no way nateral enough fer anybody t' believe—'cause babies like her ain't jist found—picked up anywhar, as you may say, without no paw ner maw ner nothin'. An' if thar warn't somethin' wrong about hit, what would them two old devils be so close-mouthed fer? Why, sir, one time when I asked 'em about hit—jist sort of interested an' neighborly like—they ris up like they was a-fixin' t' climb all over me. Yes, they did—ye kin see yerself hit ain't all straight, whatever 'tis. Even a feller like you can't help puttin' two an' two together if he's got any sense a-tall.

"Wal," he concluded regretfully, "I shore got t' be gittin' on t' Oracle er hit won't be no use fer me t' go, nohow." He moved slowly toward his horse. "Better come along," he added. "This here trail t' Oracle goes right past the Pardners' place, an' Saint Jimmy's an' George Wheeler's. Best come along an' see th' country an' git acquainted."

"Thanks," said Edwards, "but really I can't go today. I want to get settled somewhere before I take much time for purely social matters, you see."

"Huh," grunted the Lizard, "gettin' settled ain't nothin'; hit's all day till t'morrer ain't hit?" Then, as if suddenly inspired with the possibilities of having a friend at the very source of so much interesting, if speculative, information, the Lizard added: "I'll tell ye what ye do, you come along with me as fer as th' Pardners' place. They'll he'p ye t' get located. They're all right that a-way, an' there ain't nothin' them two old-timers don't know about th' prospectin' game. An' right up th' canyon, not more'n a half a quarter from them, is an old cabin you could take. Hit war built by some prospector long time ago. George Wheeler, he told me. Seems th' feller lived thar fer two er three year an' then went away an' didn't never come back. You might have t' fix th' shack up a bit, but that wouldn't be no work; an' thar's allus some gold t' be found up an' down th' creek. Th' Pardners they'll larn ye how, an' mebby *you* kin larn somethin' 'bout them an' that thar gal of theirn."

"Thank you," returned Edwards, "but I really can't go now. I am not packed yet, you see."

But the Lizard was not to be deprived of the advantage of his opportunity. "Aw, shucks—what's th' matter with ye? Grab yer stuff an' come along. Ye can't be stand-offish with me."

Because there seemed to be no way of refusing the invitation, the stranger hastily threw his things together and, with his pack on his back, set out up the canyon in company with the Lizard.

On the steep side of the mountain above, Natachee, creeping like a dark shadow among the rocks and bushes, followed the two men.

Saint Jimmy, that Sunday morning, was sitting with a book by the window. But Mother Burton, looking through the door from their tiny kitchen where she was busy with her household work, could see that her son was not reading. Jimmy's book was open, but his eyes were fixed upon the far distant horizon where the desert, with its dreamy maze of colors, becomes a faint blue shadow against the sky. And Jimmy's mother knew that his thoughts were as far from the printed page as that shadowy sky-line was distant from the window where he sat.

Often she had seen him in those moods—sitting so still that the spirit seemed to have gone out from its temporary dwelling place to visit for a little those places which lie so far beyond the horizon of all fleshly vision and earthly hopes and aspirations. Of what was he thinking, she wondered, if indeed it could be said at such times that he was thinking at all. What was he seeing, with that far-away look in his eyes, as of one whose vision had been trained in the schools of suffering, of disappointments, and failures, and disillusions, to a more than physical strength. Was he communing with someone over there in that world beyond the sky-line of material things? Was he merely dreaming of what might have been? Or was he living in what might be? Wise Mother Burton, to know that there were certain rooms in her son's being that even her mother love could not unlock. Wise Mother Burton, to understand, to know, when to speak and when to be still.

Saint Jimmy was aroused at last by the clatter of iron-shod hoofs on the canyon trail. An instant later, Nugget, running with glorious strength and ease, dashed into view, and Marta's joyous self came between the man at the window and the distant sky-line. Another moment and the girl stood in the open doorway.

CHAPTER VIII
THE NEW NEIGHBOR

WITH a merry greeting to Saint Jimmy, Marta ran straight to the welcoming arms of Mother Burton.

"Goodness me, child," the older woman exclaimed when she had kissed her and held her close for a moment as such mothers do, "you look as if—as if you were going to jump right out of your skin; I do declare!"

And Saint Jimmy, watching them, silently agreed with his mother, thinking that he had never seen the girl quite so animated. Her vivid, flamelike beauty seemed to fill the house with joyous warmth and light, while her laughter, in quick response to Mrs. Burton's words, rang with such happy abandon, and thrilled with such tingling excitement, that her teacher knew something unusual must have happened.

"What is it?" cried Mother Burton, shaking the girl playfully, and laughing with her. "What is the matter with you? What are you so excited about? Have Thad and Bob struck it rich at last?"

Marta shook her head.

"No, but it is something almost as good. We have a new neighbor."

Mother Burton looked from Marta to her son inquiringly, as if mildly puzzled to know why the mere arrival of a newcomer in the neighborhood, unusual as it was, should cause such manifestations.

Saint Jimmy, smiling, asked:

"What is his name? Where is he from? And what is he like?"

The girl's face was glowing with color and her eyes were bright as she answered:

"His name is Hugh Edwards. He came here from Tucson. I didn't quite understand where he lived before he went to Tucson." She paused and the ghost of a troubled frown fell across her brow. "But it was somewhere," she finished brightly.

"Quite likely you are right," said Jimmy, grave as a judge on the bench.

"Yes," she continued, "and he has come here to stay. He is awfully poor—poorer than any of us. Why, he hasn't even a burro to pack his outfit—had to pack it himself on his back, and he has been sick too, but he doesn't look a bit sick now." She laughed a little laugh of charming confusion. "He looks as if—as if—oh, as if he could do just anything—you know what I mean."

"You make it very clear," murmured Saint Jimmy.

Mother Burton made a curious little noise in her throat.

Marta looked from one to the other suspiciously. Then a bit defiantly she said:

"I don't care, he does. And he is different from anybody that ever came to the Cañada del Oro before—for that matter, he is different from anybody that I have ever seen anywhere."

"Dear me," murmured Mother Burton, "how interesting! But how is he different, dear?"

The girl answered honestly:

"I can't exactly tell what it is. For one thing, it is easy to see that he is educated. But of course Jimmy is too, so it can't be *that*. I am sure, too, that he has lived in a big city somewhere and has known lots of nice people, but so has Jimmy. I don't know what it is."

"I judge he is not, then, one of our typical old prospectors," said Saint Jimmy.

Again the girl's joyous, unaffected laughter bubbled forth.

"Old! He is no older than you are; I suspect not quite so old, and he has the nicest eyes, almost as nice as you, Jimmy—only, only different, some-how—nice in another way, I mean. And he knows absolutely nothing about prospecting. He is so green it is funny. But he's going to live in the old Dalton cabin right next door to us and we're going to teach him."

"Fine," said Saint Jimmy with proper enthusiasm, and managed some-how to hide the queer, sinking pain that made itself felt suddenly down deep inside of him. Saint Jimmy was skilled by long practice in hiding pain.

"Dear me!" exclaimed Mother Burton. "This is interesting. But I must finish my morning work," she added, moving toward the kitchen.

"I'll help," volunteered Marta quickly, and started after the older woman.

But Mother Burton answered:

"No, no, I was almost finished when you came." Then catching the girl in her arms impulsively, and looking toward her son whose face was turned again to the far-off horizon, she added in a hurried whisper: "Get him out of doors, dear, he has been sitting like that all this blessed morning—make him go for a walk."

Marta led her teacher straight to their favorite spot on the mountain side, some distance from the house. Here, in the shade of a gnarled and twisted cedar that for a century or more had looked down upon the varied life that moved through the Canyon of Gold below, they had spent many an hour over the girl's studies. Against the bole of the tree they had contrived a rude shelf and pegs for hats and wraps. Mrs. Burton had contributed an old kitchen table and two chairs that neither rain nor sun could injure, and there was a large, flat-topped rock that served as bookcase and desk, or for a variety of other purposes, as it might happen.

On this occasion, Marta converted the rock into a couch by throwing her-self full length upon it with the unconscious freedom of a schoolboy. Saint

Jimmy seated himself in a chair and, in defiance of all schoolmaster propriety, elevated his feet to the table top.

They talked a while, as neighbors will, of the small affairs of the country side. But Doctor Burton could see that Marta's thoughts were not of the things they were saying; and so, presently, from her rocky couch, the girl spoke again of the stranger who had come to be her nearest neighbor. She described him now in fuller detail—his eyes, his voice, his smile. She contrasted him with the Pardners, the Lizard, and with other men whom she had seen. She imagined fanciful stories for his past and invented for him various wonderful futures. And always she came back to the curious assertion that he was like her teacher, only different.

And Saint Jimmy, as he listened, asked an occasional encouraging question and studied her as in his old professional days he might have studied a patient. Never before had he seen the girl in such a mood. It was as if something deep-buried in her inner self was striving to break its way through to the surface of her being, as a deep-buried seed, when its time comes, forces its way through the dark earth to the light and sun.

Then for some time the girl was silent. With her head pillowed on one arm, and her eyes half closed, she lay as if she had drifted with the currents of her wandering thoughts into the quietude of dreams—dreams that were as intangible, yet as real, as the blue haze and purple shadows through which she saw the distant desert and mountains.

And Saint Jimmy, too, was still; while his face was turned away toward the far-off horizon, as if he saw there things which he might not talk about.

On the pine-clad heights of Mount Lemmon there were a few scattered patches of snow that had not yet yielded to the spring; but the air was soft and fragrant with the perfumes of warm earth and growing plants and opening blossoms. There was the low hum of the bees that were mining in the fragrant cat-claw bushes for the gold they stored in their wild treasure-houses in the cliffs. Not far away a gambrel partridge gallantly assured his plump gray mate, who sat on the nest in the shelter of a tall mescal plant, that there was no danger. A Sonora pigeon, from the top of a lone sahuaro, called his soft, deep-throated mating call. And a vermilion flycatcher sprang into the air from his perch near-by and climbed higher and higher into the blue and then, after holding himself aloft for a moment, puffed out his red feathers, and, twittering in a mad love ecstasy, came drifting back like a brilliant-colored thistle bloom, or an oversized and fiery-tinted dandelion tuft.

Marta's teacher had not forgotten that the Pardners had trusted him to tell their girl the things that they—Saint Jimmy and his mother—were agreed she should know. And Saint Jimmy meant to tell her. But somehow this did not seem to be the time. He stole a look at the girl lying on the rocks. No, this was not the time. He could not tell her just now. He would wait. Some other time, perhaps, it would be easier.

"Jimmy," said the girl at last, and her words came slowly as if she spoke out of the haze of her dreams, "when you went to school—I don't mean when you were just a little boy, but when you were almost a man—was it a big school?"

Saint Jimmy did not answer at once, then, without taking his eyes from what ever it was that he was looking at in the distance, he said:

"Why, yes, it was a fairly large school."

"And were there both men and women students?"

"Yes, there were a good many women in the University, and a few in the medical school, where I finally finished."

"I expect you had lots of friends, didn't you, Jimmy? I should think you would—men and women friends both. And I suppose there were all kinds of good times—parties and dances and picnics."

Doctor Burton turned suddenly to look at her. "What in the world are you driving at now?"

"Please, Jimmy," she said wistfully, "I want to know."

And something made him look away again.

"I suppose I had my share of friends," he answered. "And there was a reasonable amount of fun, as there always is at school, you know. But we—most of us—worked hard, too."

"Yes," she returned quickly, "and you dreamed and planned the great things you would do in the world when your school days should be over, and, in spite of all your friends and the good times, you could hardly wait to begin—yes, I am sure that is the way it would be."

Saint Jimmy did not speak.

"And when your school days were finished, and you were actually a doctor in a big city, you still had lots of men and women friends, and you found a little time, now and then, for parties and—and dinners and such things, didn't you, Jimmy?"

Saint Jimmy smiled, a patient, shadowy smile as he answered:

"My practice at first certainly left me plenty of time for other things."

The girl did not notice the smile, because she was not looking at her companion.

"You lived in a nice house, too, with books and pictures and—and carpets on the floors. Do you know, I think I have wanted more than anything else in the world to live in a house with carpets on the floors. That is, I mean, I have wanted it ever since I knew there were such things. Do you know, Jimmy, I never saw a house with carpets until that first day I came to see you and Mother Burton?"

She laughed a little.

"That was a long, long time ago, wasn't it? And I couldn't much more than read then. Gee! how scared I was of you and Mother Burton."

"You have made wonderful progress in your studies and in every way," said Jimmy, proudly.

"Yes," she returned. "The carpets did it—the carpets and you and Mother Burton. I don't see how you ever managed to teach me, though. I guess you just learned by doctoring so many sick people. It must be a wonderful, satisfying work—helping people, I mean, like a doctor, or a teacher, or any work like that. It's not like just finding gold in the ground. Even though you do have to work so hard to get the gold, it's not like—like working for *people*—or *with* people. Getting gold out of the ground seems to take you away from people. You don't seem to be doing anything for anybody—but only just for yourself. Prospectors and workers like that 'most always live alone, I have noticed. I don't think many of them are very happy either. I have seen quite a lot of prospectors in my time, you know, Jimmy. In fact, except for you, prospectors and that sort are the only kind of men I have ever known—until now."

Saint Jimmy was watching her closely.

"Yes," he said softly, as if he did not wish to disturb her mood.

"I suspect it was pretty hard, wasn't it, Jimmy, when you got sick yourself and had to give up your work and all your plans and leave your nice home and all your friends and everything and come away out here to get well, and then to find that you never could go back but must stay here always—poor Jimmy! It must have been mighty hard."

"It wasn't exactly easy," he said slowly, "not at first. I fought a good deal until I learned better. After that it was not so hard—only at times, perhaps. Even now, I rebel occasionally, but not for long."

Which was as near a complaint as anyone had ever heard from Doctor Jimmy Burton.

"Jimmy," said Marta earnestly, "I think that you are the most wonderful man that ever was—that ever could be."

Saint Jimmy shrugged his shoulders, and waved a protesting hand.

"But you are," she insisted, "and you know how I love you, don't you? Not merely because you have helped me as you have, but because you are *you*. You *do* know, don't you, Jimmy?"

There was an odd note in Jimmy's voice now—it might have been gladness—it might have been protest—or perhaps it was both—with a hint of pain.

"Marta! I—"

He stopped as if he found himself suddenly unable to finish whatever it was that he had started to say. It may be that this was one of the times when Saint Jimmy was not wholly reconciled to the part that life had assigned to him.

Apparently Marta did not notice her teacher's manner. Her thoughts must have been centered elsewhere because she said, quite as if she had been considering it all the time:

"I feel sure that Mr. Edwards has been hurt some way, just as you have, Jimmy. I mean that he has been to school, and had a world of nice friends and good times, and then started his real work and all that, and, now for some reason, has had to give up his work and home and friends and everything, and come out here. He didn't tell us much, but you could sort of feel that he was that kind of a man. You *can* feel those things about men, can't you, Jimmy?"

Jimmy nodded:

"I suppose so."

"I don't know why he didn't tell us more about himself—about before he came to Tucson, I mean. Perhaps he will some day; but he acts as if he didn't like to think about it now. You know what I mean, don't you?"

"Yes, I know."

"It is rather important that one have a past, isn't it, Jimmy?" She smiled as she added: "Rather important that one have the right kind of a past, I mean."

"To my mind it is quite important," answered Jimmy soberly. And suddenly he remembered again the story that the Pardners had told.

She nodded thoughtfully.

"You have talked to me a lot about heredity and breeding and good blood and early environment and those things. I suspect it is your being a doctor that makes you consider them as you do. And Mother Burton, she has told me a lot, too, about your ancestors, away back. And so I can see that it is your past and the things you have to remember that make you the kind of a man you are. If you didn't have the father and mother that you had, and the fathers and mothers that they had, and if you hadn't had the schools and the friends and the home with carpets and the work of helping people that you have had, why, you wouldn't be you at all, would you, Jimmy?"

Saint Jimmy moved uneasily. He wished now, in the light of the Pardners' story and their conclusion as to the birth and parentage of this girl, that he had not included some subjects in his pupil's course of study.

Marta continued as if, scarcely conscious of her companion's presence, she were thinking aloud.

"And so if—if anyone else *did* have the same kind of things to remember that you have, he would be the same kind of a man that you are—not exactly, of course. He might not be a doctor, or might not be sick, but on the whole—well—you see what I mean, don't you, Jimmy?"

Saint Jimmy was quite sure that he saw her meaning. In fact, Doctor Burton was fast being convinced that he realized, more clearly than Marta herself, the real meaning of her unusual mood. Her next words confirmed his fast-growing suspicion that, however scientifically right he had been in his teaching, he had not been altogether kind in stressing certain truths.

"It's funny that I never really thought of it before," she said, "but I don't seem to have any past at all. All I can remember is just moving around with my two fathers, who, of course, are not my fathers at all—at least not both of them. And, if it were not for you and Mother Burton, we wouldn't have stayed here any longer than we did the other places. I think I must have been born while my real father and mother were moving somewhere. I never cared much about it before, Jimmy, but somehow I wish—now—that I—that I knew who I am. I wish—I wish—I had things to remember—such as you and Mr. Edwards have—schools and friends and good times and a home with carpets—I mean."

There was a suspicious brightness in the frank eyes and her lips were trembling a little; a state of affairs very unusual to the Pardners' daughter.

Saint Jimmy realized that it was going to be even harder than he had foreseen to make known to this girl the things he had promised to tell her. Certainly he could not tell her just now.

His voice was gentle as he finally said:

"I wouldn't worry about all that, if I were you, dear. You see, it doesn't really matter so much whether you know or not—your people must have been the best kind of people because you are what you are, and after all, it is what you are right now that counts. It is your own dear self, and not what you might have been that matters, don't you see? Why, you have a better education already than most girls of your age. As for the rest—the friends and all that—those will come in time, I am sure."

She smiled her gratitude bravely, then:

"Jimmy, may I ask you something more—something real personal?"

"As personal as you like," he answered gravely.

"Well, among all your friends at school, and among all the people you met and knew afterwards, was there ever—was there ever one who was more than all the others—one girl or woman, I mean?"

Jimmy considered, then deliberately:

"You mean, in my school days and before I was forced to give up my work?"

She nodded.

"No," said Jimmy readily. "Once or twice I thought there might be, but I soon found out that I was mistaken—of course I am glad now that I found it out."

"But didn't you, in all of your plans and dreams for your life and work—didn't you ever include someone, didn't you ever plan for a—for—well, for"—she finished triumphantly—"for two little boys like the Wheelers have?"

"I looked forward in a general way to a home and children, as I think every man does," he answered.

She caught him up eagerly:

"You really think that every man includes such things in his plans?"

"At least," he replied, "I fail to see how any normal, right-thinking man can ignore such things in his life plans."

"I wonder if that could be it?" said Marta.

"You wonder what?"

"If Mr. Edwards came to the Cañada del Oro because his plans included someone who refused to be included."

"Good Lord!" ejaculated Saint Jimmy under his breath.

"No," she continued, "I don't believe that is it. He doesn't act as though that was the reason."

Suddenly her mood changed. She seemed to awaken to some hitherto unrealized possibilities of her life, and to grasp with startled fierceness a defiant truth.

"Jimmy," she cried, "just because I have no past is no reason why I should not have a future, is it?"

Before he could find an answer she went on, and her words came rushing, tumbling, hurrying out, as if the floodgate of her emotions were suddenly lifted and the passionate spirit of her released.

"I can see now that I have always been like our canyon creek in summer, just playing along any old way, taking things as they are, without even caring whether I stopped or not, but now—now I feel like the creek is today, with its springtime life, boiling and roaring and leaping—I won't—I won't be like the creek though—that for all its strength and fuss and fury just fades away at last into nothing, out there in the desert. I want to keep on going and going and going—I don't know where. I don't care where, just on, and on, and on!"

She sprang to her feet and stood before him in all the radiant, vigorous beauty of her young womanhood, and with reckless abandon challenged:

"Jimmy, let's run away. Let's go away off somewhere beyond the farthest line yonder that you are always looking at; and then let's keep on going, just you and I. Wouldn't it be fun if we were to be married? Why shouldn't we? You're not too old—I'm not too young. We could live in a little house somewhere—a house with carpets, Jimmy—and books and pictures, and you could make music, and I would take care of you—Oh, such good care of you, Jimmy. I'd cook all the things you like and ought to eat, and wash for you, and mend your things, and you could go on teaching me, and scolding me when I forgot to use the right words, and—and—wouldn't it be fun, Jimmy? Of course after a while Mother Burton would come too—and perhaps there would be a place somewhere near for my daddies to prospect—Oh, Jimmy, Jimmy, let's go!"

Doctor Burton laughed, and it was well for the girl that she was still too much of a child to know how often grim tragedy wears a mask of mirth.

When the stranger had told the Pardners and their daughter his simple story—how he had been ill and could find no work in Tucson, and so had come to the Cañada del Oro with the hope of finding enough gold to live by, and Marta had ridden away to spend the Sunday with Saint Jimmy and Mother Burton, Thad said doubtfully:

"I don't see as there's much we can do. We can't learn nobody to find gold whar it ain't, an' if we knowed whar it was we certain sure would stake out some claims for ourselves, wouldn't we? I don't take no stock in there bein' anythin' more than a color mebby, round that old Dalton cabin yonder."

"Gold is where you find it," remarked Bob cheerfully. "You can't never tell when or where you're going to strike it rich."

"That's all right," retorted Thad. "But it stands to reason that if the feller what built that cabin hadn't of worked out his claim, he'd be there workin' on it yet, wouldn't he? He quit and vamoosed because he'd worked it out, I'm tellin' you."

Bob returned with energy:

"And I'm maintainin' that no claim or mine or nothin' else was ever worked out. Folks jest quit workin' on 'em, that's all. There's many and many a mine been abandoned when three hours more—or one more shot, mebby, would a-opened up a bonanza. This young man may go right up there in the creek and stick in his pick a foot from where the other feller took out his last shovel of dirt an' turn up a reg'lar glory-hole. Don't you let him give you the dumps, Mr. Edwards, he's the worst old pessimist you ever see. There's enough gold in this neighborhood to buy all the bacon an' beans you'll need, long as you live, if you're willin' to scratch around for it; an' you've got jest as good a chance as there is to strike a real mine an' make your everlastin' fortune, too."

"If you want my honest opinion, Mr. Edwards," said Thad solemnly, as if his pardner had not spoken, "you'll be a fool to spend any time here."

The younger man smiled:

"But you see, Mr. Grove, I am rather forced to do something right now. As I told you, I'm not in a position to spend much time tramping about the country looking for what might be a better place. All my capital—all my worldly possessions, in fact—are in that pack there. After all, you know the old saying," he finished laughingly, "'It takes a fool for luck.'"

"That ain't so," growled Thad, "'cause if it was, my pardner there would be as rich as Rockefeller and Morgan an' the rest of them billionaires all rolled into one."

Bob grinned at Edwards reassuringly. Then he said to Thad:

"Now that you've got that off your mind, suppose we jest turn in an' do what we can for the boy here."

"This here's Sunday, ain't it?" returned Thad, doubtfully. "Didn't my gal tell us yesterday that we couldn't—"

"Your gal," interrupted Bob, fiercely. "Your gal—huh. I'm here to tell you that you'd best keep within your rights, Thad Grove, even if me an' you be pardners. She's my gal this week beginnin' at sun-up this mornin', an' you know it; an' besides, there's good scripture for us helpin' Mr. Edwards here to get located, even if 'tis Sunday."

"Scripture!" said Thad scornfully. "What scripture?"

"It's that there part where the Lord is linin' 'em up about what they did an' what they didn't do," explained Bob. "Says He to one bunch, 'When I was dead broke an' hungry an' thirsty an' all but petered out, you ornary skunks wouldn't turn a hand to give me a lift, an' so you don't need to figger that you're goin' to git in on the ground floor with me now that I've struck pay dirt'—or words to that effect. An' then to the other bunch He says: 'You're all right, Pardners; come on in an' make your pile along with me, 'cause I ain't forgot how when I was a stranger you took me in. You grubstaked me when I was down and out, an' for that, all I've got now is yourn'—leastways, that's the general meanin' of it."

Whereupon Thad conceded that while it would be wrong actually to work on the day of rest, it might be safe for them to show the stranger around and sort of talk things over.

And all that day, while the two old prospectors were conducting him to the cabin that, for the following months, was to be his home, while they were showing him about the neighborhood and advising him in a general way about his work, and as they sat at the dinner which Marta had left prepared for them, Hugh Edwards felt that he was being weighed, measured, analyzed. Nor did he in any way attempt to avoid or shirk the ordeal. Fairly and squarely, with neither hesitation nor evasion, he met those keen old eyes that for so many years had searched for the precious metal that is hidden in the sands and rocks and gravel of desert wastes, and lonely canyons, and those mountain places that are far remote from the haunts of less hardy and courageous men.

They did not ask many questions about his past, for it is not the way of such men to pry into another's past. By their code a man's personal history is his own most private affair, to be given or withheld as he himself elects. But what a man is, *that* is a matter of concern to everyone who is called by circumstance to associate with him. They were not particularly interested in what this man who had given his name as Hugh Edwards *had* been. They were mightily interested in discerning what sort of a man Hugh Edwards, at that moment, was.

"Well, Pardner," said Bob, later in the afternoon when Edwards, with sincere expression of his gratitude, had left them to go to the cabin which by common consent they now called his, "what do you make of him?"

Old Thad, rubbing his bald head, answered in—for him—an unusual vein:

"He's a right likable chap, ain't he, Bob? If I'd ever had a boy of my own—that is, supposin', first, I'd ever had a wife—I think I'd like him to be jest about what I sense this lad is." Then, as if alarmed at this betrayal of what might be considered sentiment, the old prospector suddenly stiffened, and added in his usual manner: "You can't tell what he is—some sort of a sneakin' coyote, like as not, a-tryin' to pass hisself off as a harmless little cottontail. I'm for layin' low an' watchin' his smoke mighty careful."

"He'll assay purty high-grade ore, I'm a-thinkin'," said Bob.

"Time enough to invest when said assay has been made," retorted Thad. "It looks funny to me that a man of his eddication would be a-comin' up here in this old canyon to waste his time tryin' to do somethin' that he don't know no more about than a baby. Hard work, too; an' anybody can see he ain't never done much of that."

"He's been sick," returned Bob.

Thad grunted:

"Huh! If he was, it was a long time ago. Did you notice the weight of that pack—He's a totin' it like it warn't nothin' at all."

"He looks kind of pale when his hat is off," said Bob.

To which Thad returned:

"He's mighty perticler about where he was an' what he was doin' for a livin' before he blew into Tucson."

"As for that," returned Bob, "there's been some things happen since me an' you was first pardners that we ain't jest exactly a-wavin' in the wind—an' look at us now."

Thad's dry retort was inevitable:

"Yes, jest look at us!"

Bob chuckled.

"*You* ain't so mighty much to look at, I admit."

"Well," said Thad, "as long as my gal thinks I'm all right, you—"

"My gal—*my* gal," snapped Bob. "Why have you allus got to be a-tryin' to do me out of my rights. You know well as I do this is my week."

"Excuse me, Pard," the other apologized in all seriousness. "And that leads me to remark that your gal didn't appear altogether indifferent an' uninterested in this young prospectin' neighbor of ours. You took notice, too, I reckon."

"I ain't blind, be I?" answered Bob. "An' why wouldn't she take notice? My gal ain't no wizened-up old mummy like me an' you. Why wouldn't she take notice of a fine, up-standin' clean-eyed, straight-limbed, fair-spoken youngster like him, heh? It's nateral enough—an' right enough too, I reckon."

Old Thad, with sudden rage, shook his long finger at his pardner and, in a voice that was high pitched and trembling with emotion, cried:

"Nateral enough, you poor old, thick-headed, ossified, wreck of manhood, you. Nateral enough! Holy Cats! It's *too* nateral, that's what I'm a meanin', it's *too* nateral—whether it's all right or all wrong—it's too almighty nateral—that's what it is."

Later, when Marta had returned to her home in the Canyon of Gold—when the sun was down and the shadow of the approaching night was deepening over desert and mesa and mountain—a cowboy on his way to the home ranch stopped to listen as the music of Saint Jimmy's flute came soft and clear through the quiet of the evening, from that spot beneath the old cedar tree, high on the mountain side. A wandering Mexican, camped near Juniper Spring below, heard and crossed himself. Natachee the Indian who was following a faint trail toward the wild upper canyon heard and smiled. Jimmy's mother heard, and her eyes filled with tears.

CHAPTER IX
"GOLD IS WHERE YOU FIND IT"

THE Canyon of Gold was still in the shadow of the mountains the next morning when the Pardners went to give their new neighbor his first lesson in the work that was to occupy him for months to come.

Hugh Edwards greeted them without a trace of the hesitating fear that he had shown during the first moments of their meeting, the day before. His eyes now met theirs fairly, with no hint of questioning dread. It was as if the restful peace and strengthening quiet of that retreat which was hidden so far from the overcrowded highways of life had begun already to effect, in the troubled spirit of this stranger, a magic healing.

"Well," said Thad gruffly, "we're here—where's your pick an' shovel an' pan?"

When the younger man had produced those implements which were so new and strange to him, Bob asked kindly if he had had a good night's sleep, if he found the cabin comfortable, and if he had fortified himself for the day's work with a proper breakfast.

Hugh Edwards laughed, and, with his face lifted to the mountain heights that towered above them, squared his shoulders and drew a long deep breath.

"I haven't had such a sleep since I can remember. As for breakfast, well, if I eat like this every day, I will exhaust my supplies before I even learn to know gold when I see it. I feel as if I could move that hill over there into the canyon."

Bob chuckled.

"You'll find you've got to move a lot of it, son, before you make enough at this gold-huntin' game to buy your grub."

"That's the trouble with prospectin' in this here Cañada del Oro country," said Thad. "The harder you work the more you eat, and the more you eat the harder you got to work. Come on, let's get a-goin'."

For several hours the old Pardners labored with their pupil beside the creek, then, with hearty assurance of further help from time to time as he made progress, they left him and went to their own little mine, some five hundred yards down the canyon.

The afternoon was nearly gone when Edwards, who was kneeling over the gravel and sand in his pan at the edge of the stream, looked up.

On a bowlder, not more than five steps from the amateur prospector, sat an Indian.

With an exclamation, the white man sprang to his feet.

The Indian did not move. Dressed as he was in the wild fashion of his fathers and with his primitive bow and arrows, he seemed more like some sculptured bit of the past than a creature of living flesh.

Hugh Edwards, standing as one ready to run at the crack of the starter's pistol, swiftly surveyed the immediate vicinity. His face was white and he was trembling with fear.

With grave interest the red man silently observed the perturbed stranger. Then, as Edwards again turned his frightened eyes toward him, the Indian raised his hand in the old-time peace sign and in a deep, musical voice spoke the one word of the old-time greeting:

"How."

Edwards broke into a short, nervous laugh.

"How-do-you-do—By George! but you gave me a start."

Some small animal—a pack rat or a ground squirrel—made a rustling sound in the bushes on the bank above, and with a low cry the frightened man wheeled, and again started as if to escape.

The Indian, watching, saw the meaning in every move the stranger made, and read every expression of his face.

With an effort Edwards controlled himself.

"Are you alone?" he asked. "I mean"—he caught himself up quickly—"that is—have you no horse?"

"I am always alone," the Indian answered calmly. Then, as if to put the other more at ease, he continued in excellent English: "Night before last, when the sun went down, I was up there on Samaniego Ridge," he pointed with singular grace. "There on that rock near the dead sahuaro, and I saw you as you came up the old road into the canyon."

Hugh Edwards again betrayed himself by the eagerness of his next question:

"Did you see anyone else?"

"There was no one on your trail," returned the Indian.

At this the stranger seemed to realize suddenly that he was permitting his fears to reveal too much, and, as one will, he sought to amend his error with a half-laughing excuse.

"Really, you know, I didn't suppose there was anyone following me." He indicated his work with a gesture. "I am not exactly used to this sort of life, you see, and—well—I confess the loneliness, the strangeness of my surroundings, and all, have rather got on my nerves—quite natural, I suppose."

The Indian bowed assent.

As if determined to correct any impression he might have made by his unguarded manner, Edwards abruptly dropped the subject, and with an air of enthusiastic delight spoke of his surroundings, finishing with the courteous question:

"You live in this neighborhood, do you?"

There was a quick gleam of savage light in the dark eyes that were fixed with bold pride upon the questioning white man, and the Indian answered more in the manner of his people:

"In the years that are past my fathers came to these mountains to hunt and to make war like men. They come now with the squaws to gather acorns, when the white man gives them permission. I live here, yes, as a homeless dog lives in one of your cities. My name is Natachee."

The deep, musical voice of the red man revealed such bitter feeling that Hugh Edwards was moved to pity. And then, as he stood there in the silence that had fallen upon them, a strange thing happened. It was as if the spirit of the Indian had somehow touched the inner self of the stranger and had quickened in him a kindred savage lusting for revenge upon some enemy who had brought upon him, too, humiliation and shame and suffering beyond expression. The white man's hands were clenched, his breast heaved with labored breathing, his face was black with passion, his eyes were dreadful with the scowling light of anger and hate.

A faint smile came like a swift shadow over the face of the watching Indian; then he spoke with deliberate meaning:

"And why have you come to the Cañada del Oro? Why should a man like you wish to live here, in the Canyon of Gold?"

Hugh Edwards gained control of himself with an effort.

"I came to look for gold; as you see," he said at last.

Again that faint smile like a quick shadow touched the face of the red man.

And this time the other saw it. Looking straight into the eyes of the Indian, he said coldly:

"And you, what do you do for a living?"

Natachee, returning look for look, answered simply:

"I live as my fathers lived."

"I have heard about you, I think," said Edwards.

The Indian's deep voice was charged with scorn.

"Yes, the Lizard called at your camp—you would hear about everyone from the Lizard."

"He told me that you were educated."

Natachee answered sadly:

"It is true, I attended the white man's school. What I learned there made me return to the desert and the mountains to live as my fathers lived; and to die as my people must die."

When the white man, seemingly, could find no words with which to reply, the Indian spoke again.

"If it is gold that brought you here to the Cañada del Oro, why do you not search for the Lost Mine with the Iron Door?"

Hugh Edwards, remembering what the Lizard had said, smiled.

"And is there, really, such a mine?"

"There is a story of such a mine."

"Do many people come to look for it?"

Natachee answered gravely and with that dignity so characteristic of a red man, while his words, though spoken in English, were the words of an Indian:

"Too many people come. As the ocean calls the water of the rivers, and the rivers call the creeks and springs; so this story of a treasure hidden in a mine that is lost has called many people to the Canyon of Gold. For many years they have been coming—for many years they will continue to come. The white people say they do not believe there ever was such a mine and they laugh about it. They look for it just the same. Even the Pardners, who dig for gold in their own little hole down there, laugh, but I know that they, too, believe even as they laugh. That is always the white man's way—always he is searching for the thing which he says does not exist, and at which he laughs."

"But what about you?" asked Hugh Edwards. "Do you believe in this lost mine?"

The Indian's face was a bronze mask as he answered:

"Of what importance is an Indian's belief to a white man? When the winds heed the dead leaves they toss and scatter, when the fire heeds the dry grass in its path, then will a white man heed the words of an Indian."

"Oh, I wouldn't say it was as bad as that," returned Edwards easily, and as he spoke he went to bend over his pan again. "Mine or no mine," he continued, as he examined the sand and gravel he had been washing, "I think I have some real gold here."

When there was no answer he said:

"You must know gold when you see it. Will you look at this and tell me what you think?"

Still there was no answer.

With the gold pan in his hand, the white man turned to face his visitor. The Indian had disappeared.

In amazement, Hugh Edwards stood staring at the spot where the Indian had been sitting but a moment before. Then, while his eyes searched the vicinity for some movement in the brush, he listened for a sound. Not a leaf or twig or blossom stirred—not a sound betrayed the way the red man had gone.

With an odd feeling that the whole incident of the Indian's visit was as unreal as a dream, the man had again turned his attention to the contents of his gold pan when a gay voice came from the top of the bank.

"Well, neighbor, have you struck it rich?"

Looking up, he saw Marta.

"I have struck something all right, or rather something struck me," he laughed, as she joined him beside the creek. Then he told her about the Indian.

"Yes," she said, "that was Natachee. He always comes and goes like that. Everybody says he is harmless. He and Saint Jimmy are quite good friends; but he gives me the creeps." She shrugged her shoulders. "Ugh! I always feel as if he were wishing that he could scalp every one of us."

"To tell the truth," returned Edwards, "I feel a little that way myself."

That evening as Hugh Edwards sat with the Pardners and their girl on the porch, he asked the old prospectors about the Mine with the Iron Door.

They laughed, as Natachee had said, but Edwards caught an odd note of wistfulness in their merriment. Thad answered his question, with a brave pretense of scorn:

"There's lost mines all over Arizona, son. Better stick to your pick and shovel if you want to eat reg'lar. You won't pan out so mighty much, mebby, but what you do get will be real."

"But this here Mine with the Iron Door is different some ways from all them others," said Bob.

And again Edwards caught that wistful note in the old-timer's voice.

"You mean that you believe there is such a mine?" he said.

"Holy Cats—No!" growled Thad. "We don't believe in nothin' till we got it where we can cash it in."

Bob was thoughtfully refilling his pipe. "They say it was made by the old padres, away back, a hundred years before any of us prospectors ever hit this country. I know one thing that you can see for yourself, easy—there's the ruins of a mighty old settlement or camp or somethin' on the side of the mountain up above the Steam Pump Ranch. They say it was there that the Papagos, what worked the mine for the priests, lived. The Papagos and the padres always was friendly, you know. The padres have got a big mission, San Xavier, down in the Papago country, right now—built somethin' like three hundred years ago, it was. I ain't never been able myself to jest figger their idea in fixin' up the mine with that iron door. Mebby it was on account of them only workin' it by spells, like when they was needin' somethin' extra for their mission or for their church back home in Spain, where they all come from, and so wanted to shut it up when they was gone away. Then one time, the story goes, along come one of these here earthquakes, and tumbled a whole blamed mountain down on top of the works. The old priests and their Papago miners figgered it out that the landslide was an act of God—Him bein' displeased with the way they was runnin' things er somethin', an' so they was scared ever even to try to dig her up again. An' so you see, after all these years, the trees and brush growed over the mountain again and the old mine got to be plumb lost for certain sure."

"An' so far as we're consarned," added the other pardner emphatically, "it's goin' to stay lost. This ain't no country for a big mine nohow. Mineralized all right, but look at the way she's all shot to pieces; busted forty ways for Sunday—ain't nothin' reg'lar nowhere, unless you was to go down a thousand or two feet, mebby, and that ain't no prospect for a poor man, I'm a-tellin' you. Find a little placer dirt, yes, and you might strike a good pocket once in a lifetime or so, but that ain't to say real minin'. Take my advice, son, and don't let this lost mine get to workin' on you or you'll go hungry."

"That's all true enough, Pardner," said Bob, "but you know how 'tis, you can't never tell—Gold is where you find it."

CHAPTER X
SUMMER

THE weeks of the spring passed. The gleaming snow fields vanished from the dark pine heights of Mount Lemmon. The creek, which ran through the Canyon of Gold with such boisterous strength that day when the stranger came and Marta talked with Saint Jimmy under the old cedar on the mountain side, crept lazily now, with scarce a murmur, pausing often to rest in the shady quiet of an overhanging rock or to sleep, half hidden, among the roots of a giant sycamore.

The Sonora pigeon, his mission accomplished, had long since ceased to give his mating call. The nest in the mesquite thicket had been filled and was empty again. The partridge was leading her half-grown covey far from the mescal plant where they were born. The vermilion flycatcher was too busy, with his exacting parental duties, even to think of indulging in those fantastic exhibitions which ultimately had placed the burdens of fatherhood upon his shoulders.

There was not a day of those passing months that the Pardners and their girl did not in some way come in touch with their neighbor. Sometimes Edwards would go to counsel with the two old prospectors as they worked in their little mine. Again, they would go over to his place to advise him, with their years of experience, in his small operations. Often he would spend the evening with them on the porch in neighborly fashion, or they would go to smoke with him before the door of his tiny cabin. Occasionally, it was no more than a shout of greeting across the three hundred or more yards that separated the two places; but always the contact that had been established that day when the Lizard brought the stranger to the Pardners' door was maintained.

Hugh Edwards might have gone from the place where he labored to the Pardners' mine, along the creek under the high bank, without passing their house at all, but he never did. That is, he never both went and returned by the creek route. Either going or coming, he would always climb out of the deep cut made by the stream to the level of the main floor of the canyon where the house stood—except, of course, when Marta had gone to the store at Oracle or to see Saint Jimmy and Mother Burton.

The girl was always included, too, in those evenings on the porch or before his cabin door. Always, on her way to the store, she stopped to see if she could bring anything for him. And often, with the freedom of the rude environment she had known since she could remember, and with the frank innocence of her boyish nature, Marta would run over to give him a lesson in the arts of the kitchen; or, perhaps, to contribute something of her own cooking—a pie or cake or pudding—that would be quite beyond the range of his poor culinary skill. It was indeed all very natural—perhaps, as Thad had said that first day, it was too darned natural.

To the Pardners, Hugh Edwards was an object of continued speculative interest, a subject of endless and somewhat violent arguments; and, it must be added, a never-failing source of amusement and delight. The genuineness and depth of this friendship for their young neighbor was evidenced at last by their telling him the story of their partnership daughter as they had told it to Saint Jimmy and Mother Burton. It was not long after this mark of their confidence that the old prospectors were led into a characteristic discussion of their observations.

Hugh had gone to them at their mine with a bit of quartz which he had picked up in the bed of the creek. The consultation was over and the two old prospectors were sitting in the shade of the tunnel opening watching the younger man as he climbed up the steep bank toward the house. Old Bob was grinning.

"He sure thought he had found somethin' good this time, didn't he? The boy's all right, don't never show a sign of bein' sore when his rich rocks turn out to be jest nothin' but rock—jest keeps right on tryin'. Don't seem to care a cuss how many blanks he draws."

Thad chuckled:

"If hard work will get him anything, he's sure due to strike it rich. Hits it up from crack of day till plumb dark an' acts like he hated even to think of sleepin' or eatin'."

"It's funny, too," said Bob, "'cause you remember at first he didn't 'pear to take no interest a-tall. Jest poked along in a come-day, go-day, God-send-Sunday sort of a gait, as if all he wanted was to git his powder back with what frijoles, bacon, and coffee he had to have. He's sure come alive, though. I wonder—"

Thad was rubbing his bald head with a slow, speculative movement.

"Had you took notice how he allus goes up to the house when he brings them pieces of fool rock to us? My gal, she says to me the other evenin'—"

"Your gal! Your gal!" Marta's father shouted. "This here's my week, and you know it blamed well, you old love pirate, you. Can't you never be satisfied with your share? Have you got to be allus tryin' to euchre me out of my rights?"

"I apologize, Pardner, I forgot, I apologize plenty," said Thad hurriedly. "As I was meanin' to say, that gal of yourn, she says to me, 'Daddy'—last Saturday it was, so she had a right to call me daddy—'Daddy,' says she, 'Hugh has changed a lot since he come to us, ain't he?'"

"Well," returned Bob, "what if my daughter did make such a remark, it—"

"She was my daughter then," interrupted Thad sternly.

"She's mine right now," retorted Bob with equal force. "What if she did say it? I maintain it only goes to show what a smart, observin' gal she's growed up to be."

Thad grunted disgustedly.

"It's almighty plain that she didn't inherit none of her observin' powers from you."

Bob glared at him.

"Wal, what are you seein' that I ain't?" he demanded. "Somethin' that's wrong, I'll bet—By smoke! Thad, if you was to happen to get into Heaven by any hook or crook so ever, you'd set yourself first off to suspicionin' them there angels of high gradin' the gold they say the streets up there is paved with."

The other returned with withering contempt:

"You've said it! But don't it signify nothin' to you when your gal—when any gal takes notice of how a feller is lookin' different from what he did when she first met up with him? Ain't it got no meanin' for you when she says, 'Since he come to us'? *Come to us—to us*—can't you see nothin'? If I was as dumb as you be, I'd set off a stick of powder under myself to see if I couldn't get some sort of, what I heard Doctor Jimmy once call, a re-action."

Bob laughed.

"I figger on gettin' all the reactions I need from you, without wastin' any powder. Hugh did come to us, didn't he? Even if that measly Lizard did fetch him far as the gate."

"Oh, sure," grumbled the other with fine sarcasm. "Hugh, he didn't come to this here Cañada del Oro—not a-tall—he jest come to *us*."

Bob continued as if the other had not spoken:

"As far as his not bein' the same as when he come, well, he ain't—anybody can see that. 'Tain't only that he's started in to workin', all at once, like he jest naterally *had* to get rich. He's different in a lot of ways. Take his looks, for instance—he used to be kind of white like—you remember, and now he's tanned as black as any of us old desert rats. He's sturdier and heavier like, every way. Hard work agrees with him, 'pears like."

"'Tain't only that," said Thad.

"Sure—his hair ain't so short no more."

"There's more than hair an' bein' tanned," said Thad.

"Yep, there is," agreed Bob. "Do you mind how, when he first come, he acted sort of scared like—right at the very first, I mean."

"That's it," returned Thad, "his eyes was like he was expectin' one or t'other, or both of us, to throw down a gun on him. An' yet I sensed somehow, after the first minute, that it wasn't us he was afraid of. He sure walks up to a man now, though, like he could jump down his throat if he had to."

"I'll bet my pile he would, too, if he was called," chuckled Bob. "And have you noticed how easy he laughs, an' the way he sings and whistles over there when he's fussin' 'round his shack of a mornin' or evenin'?"

"He sure seems contented enough," said Thad, "an' that's another thing I've noticed, too," he added slowly. "The boy ain't been out of the canyon since he come."

"Ain't no reason for him to go," said Bob. "We take out what little gold he pans with ourn, don't we? An' it's easy for Marta to buy his supplies for him while she's buyin' for us. There ain't nobody at Oracle that he'd be wantin' to see."

"Mebby that's it," said Thad.

"Mebby what's it?" demanded Bob.

"That there ain't nobody at Oracle that he wants to see—or that he don't want to see him—whichever way you like to say it."

"There you go again," said Bob. "Can't talk more'n a minute on any subject without hintin' that somethin' is wrong. The boy is all right, I tell you."

"Well, Holy Cats! who said he wasn't?" cried Thad. "I wouldn't hold it against him much if he never went to Oracle or nowhere else; jest stuck in this here canyon till he died, hidin' out in the brush somewhere every time anybody strange showed up nearer than George Wheeler's. You an' me has both suffered from the same sort of sickness more'n once, or I'm a-losin' my memory. You're allus makin' out that I'm thinkin' evil when I'm only jest tryin' to look at things as they actually are. If I'd intimated that the boy was a hoss-thief or a claim-jumper or somethin' like that, you'd have reason to climb on to me, but I'm likin' him an' believin' in him as much as ever you or anybody else ever dared to."

Bob grinned.

"It's funny how we're all agreed on that, ain't it? He is sure a likable cuss. I was a-warnin' him the other day about handlin' his powder. 'You don't want to forgit, son,' says I, 'that there's enough in one of them sticks to blow you so high that you'd think you was one of them heavenly bodies up yonder.' He laughed an' says, says he, 'That bein' the case, it would be mighty comfortin' to know there was no one to dock me for the time I was up in the air, wouldn't it?'"

"Huh!" grunted Thad, "that's an old one."

"Sure it's an old one," retorted Bob, "but nobody can't say it ain't a good one; and I'm here to maintain that you can tell a heap more about a man by the jokes he laughs at than you can by the religions he claims to believe in."

"Yes," retorted Thad grimly, "I've allus took notice, too, that them that's all the time seein' evil in whatever anybody does is dead immortal certain to be havin' a lot of their own doin's that need to be kept in the dark. As for this game of lookin' for some sort of insinuations in everything a body says, it's like a lookin' glass—what you see is mostly yourself. That's what I'm meanin'."

"Hugh is a good boy all right," said Bob.

"He's all of that and then some," said Thad.

The truth of the matter is, Hugh Edwards had found, in the Cañada del Oro, something more than the gold for which he worked so laboriously through the long days, and which he had come to hoard with such miserly care. In the Canyon of Gold, he had found more than rugged health; more than a sanctuary from whatever it was that had driven him from the world to which he belonged into the lonely seclusion of that wild country. Into his loneliness had come a sweet companionship that had grown every day more dear. In this new joy and gladness, bitterness and pain had ceased to darken his hours with hatred and with useless and vengeful longings. Crushed and beaten, humiliated and shamed, his every hour an hour of dread, he had found inspiration and spirit to plan his life anew. Out of his hopelessness, a glorious new hope had come. He had learned again to dream; and he had gained strength to labor for his dreams.

But he had not told Marta what it was that he had found. He could not tell her yet. Before he could tell her, he must have gold. And he must have, not merely an amount that would satisfy the bare necessities of life—he must have much more than that. He was not so foolish as to feel that he must be in a position to offer this girl the extravagant luxuries of life. But his need was born of a dire necessity—a necessity as vital as the need of food. Without gold, the realization of his dream was an impossibility. His only hope of happiness was in the possibility of his success in finding a quantity of the yellow metal for which, through the centuries, so many men had labored, as he was laboring now, in the Canyon del Oro. He could not explain to Marta—he could only dream and hope and work, as those others before him had dreamed and hoped and worked in the Canyon of Gold. And so, with a strength that was like the strength of Saint Jimmy, this man was resolutely hiding the love that had re-created him. Marta must not know—not now.

But Marta knew—knew and yet did not know. The girl, whose womanhood had developed in the peculiarly sexless environment that had been hers since she could remember, had formed no habit of self-analysis. She was wholly inexperienced in those innocent but emotionally instructive friendships which girls and young women normally have with boys and men of their own age. Except for her fathers and Saint Jimmy, she had had no contact with men. In her childlike ignorance she asked of herself no questions. She gave no more thought to the meaning of her interest in Hugh Edwards than a wild bird gives to its mating instinct. But as their friendship grew and ripened, this girl of the desert and mountains knew that she was happy as she had never been happy before. She felt a kinship with the wild life about her that thrilled her with its poignant mystery. The flowers had never before bloomed in such passionate profusion. The birds had never voiced such melodies. The very winds were freighted with perfumes that filled her with strange delight. The days, indeed, flew by on wings of sunshine—the nights were haunted with shadowy promises as vague and intangible as they were sweet.

Natachee, as the weeks passed, seemed to develop a strange interest in the man who was so obviously from a world that is far indeed from the haunts of the lonely red man. Frequently the Indian called at the little cabin to spend an hour or more. Always he appeared suddenly, at the most unexpected moments, as if he were a spirit materialized that instant from an invisible world, and always he disappeared in the same startling fashion.

Sometimes, when he was with Edwards and the Pardners, he would discuss matters of general interest with the speech and manner of any well-bred college man. Save for his savage costume, his dusky countenance, and a certain touch of poetic feeling in his choice of words and figures of speech, there would be nothing, on these occasions, to mark him as different, in any way, from his white companions. But on other occasions, when Natachee and Edwards were alone, the red man would, for the moment, cast aside every mark of his training in the schools, and, with the voice, words, and gestures peculiar to his race, express thoughts and emotions that were purely Indian. Much of the time, however, he would sit silently watching the white man at his work. Often he would come and go without a word. He would sometimes appear, too, when Marta and Edwards were together, and on these occasions, save for a courteous greeting, he was rarely more than a silent observer.

The Lizard had at first endeavored to cultivate the stranger's friendship, but, receiving no encouragement, had soon limited his attentions to a sullen "Howdy" when he passed on his way to or from Oracle.

But Saint Jimmy had not yet met the man who was living next door to Marta. Often the girl begged her teacher to go with her to call on the new neighbor. Mother Burton frequently scolded him, gently, for his discourtesy to the stranger. And Saint Jimmy promised many times that he would call, but he invariably postponed the date of his visit. He would set out on his social mission in all good faith, but invariably, when he came within sight of the cabin so near to Marta's home, he would stop and, instead of going on, would spend the hours alone on the mountain side looking out over the desert. Had Saint Jimmy been other than the gentle spirit he was, he might have said that he heard quite enough about Hugh Edwards from Marta without going to visit him.

Many times, too, Saint Jimmy thought to tell Marta the story her fathers had intrusted to him, but for some reason he always found it as difficult to talk to his pupil about the mystery of her early childhood as he found it hard to call on this man in whom she was so interested.

Often he said to his mother that he would delay no longer—that he would tell the girl the next time she came to see them; but each time he put it off. The girl was always so radiantly happy, so overflowing with the joy of life. Perhaps, Saint Jimmy told himself, perhaps, it might never be necessary for her to know.

The dry season of the summer passed—the summer rains came; and again the desert, the foothills and mountain sides were bright with blossoms. It was during this "Little Spring," as the Indians call this second blossoming time of the year, that Saint Jimmy finally called on Hugh Edwards.

And—it was the Lizard who brought it about.

CHAPTER XI
THE LIZARD

THE Lizard was on his way to Oracle that day when he turned aside from the more direct trail to take the path that led past the little white house on the mountain side. Approaching the Burton home, he pulled his horse down to a walk, and, as he rode slowly up the winding way, his shifty eyes searched the vicinity on every side. It was not long before he saw Doctor Burton, who was seated, with his back comfortably against a rock in the shade of a Juniper tree, reading.

As the Lizard left the trail and rode toward him, Saint Jimmy glanced up from his book. With a look of mild interest, he watched as the horse with its rider climbed the steep side of the mountain.

When he had come quite near, the Lizard stopped, and slouching down in the saddle looked at the man seated on the ground with a wide grin, while the horse with a long breath of relief dropped his head and settled himself sleepily, as if understanding from long experience that his master would have no further use for him for some time to come.

"How do you do?" said Jimmy, smiling.

"'Bout as usual," returned the horseman. "I'm eatin' reg'lar. 'Lowed hit war time I rode by to see how you was a makin' hit these days. I see ye're still alive," he laughed, in his loose-mouthed way.

"I am doing very well," returned Saint Jimmy, wondering what the real object of the fellow's call might be.

"Yer maw's well too, I reckon?"

"Yes, thank you."

"Been over t' Oracle lately?"

"I was there yesterday."

"Uh-huh! I was up t' the store myself day before. Hear anythin' new, did ye?"

"Nothing startling," smiled Saint Jimmy. "Your father and mother are well, are they?"

"'Bout as usual. Ain't seed George Wheeler lately, have ye—er any of his folks?"

"George was at our house a few days ago," returned Jimmy. "Stopped in a few minutes on his way home from the upper ranch."

"Uh-huh!—George say anything, did he?"

"No. Nothing in particular."

The Lizard shifted his slouching weight in the saddle. "I met up with one of George's punchers t'other day. Bud Gordon, hit war. He says as how th' lions is a-gettin' 'bout all of George's mule colts up 'round his place above."

"So George was telling us. It's too bad. You ranchers will be planning another hunt soon, I suppose."

The Lizard shook his head solemnly, then leered at Saint Jimmy with an evil grin.

"Thar's varmints in this here neighborhood what needs a-huntin' a mighty sight more'n lions an' coyotes an' sich."

Jimmy waited.

"You say you ain't heerd nothin'?" demanded the Lizard.

"About what?"

"'Bout that there new prospector, what's located in th' old cabin down thar by th' Pardners' place."

"No," said Doctor Burton slowly. "I have heard nothing about Mr. Edwards—nothing wrong, I mean."

"Wal, if ye ain't, hit's 'cause ye ain't been 'round much, er 'cause ye ain't listened very close. Mebby, though, folks would be kind o' slow-like sayin' anythin' t' you—seein's how you'd likely be more interested 'n anybody else."

Saint Jimmy was not smiling now.

"I think you are mistaken about my interest," he said curtly. "I have no desire to listen to you or to anyone else on the subject."

"Oh, ye ain't, heh?" the man on the horse returned with a sneer. "I 'lowed as how ye'd be mighty quick t' listen, seein' 's how this new feller's cut you out with th' gal, like he has."

When Saint Jimmy did not speak, the Lizard continued with virtuous indignation:

"Things was bad enough as they was, but now since this new feller's come, she's a-carryin' on past all reason. You kin find 'em t'gether at his shack er down in th' creek whar he's a-pretendin' t' work, er out in the brush somewhar 'most any time. An' when she ain't over t' his place er out with him somewhar, he's dead certain t' be at her house. I seed them t'gether when I passed on my way up here. She's too good t' speak to me, what's been neighbor t' her ever since she come into this country, but she kin take up with this stranger quick enough."

Doctor Burton was on his feet.

"That's enough," he said sharply. "You might as well go on your way now. You have evidently said what you came to say."

"Oh, I don't know," returned the Lizard with insolent superiority. "There ain't no use in yer tryin' t' be so high an' mighty with me. She's throwd me down fer you often enough. Now that yer gettin' th' same thing, ye ought t' be a grain more friendly, 'pears t' me. As fer this other feller, he'll sure get what's a-comin' t' him, an' so will she."

Jimmy caught his breath.

"What do you mean?"

"I mean that folks 're a-talkin', an' that they'll likely do more than talk this time. We've allus had our doubts about th' gal—who wouldn't have—her bein' raised by them two old mavericks like she war an' bein' named fer both an' both claimin' t' be her daddy—an' nobody knowin' a foreign thing 'bout who her real paw an' maw was, er even whether she ever had any. But folks has put up with her an' you 'cause you was supposed to' be a-teachin' her an' cause yer Saint Jimmy." He laughed. "Saint Jimmy—mighty pretty, heh? But this new feller that's got her now—Edwards, he calls hisself—he ain't pretendin' nothin'. Him an' her, they—"

Doctor Burton started forward, his eyes were blazing and his voice rang:

"Shut up—if you open your foul mouth again, I'll drag you from that horse and choke the dirty life out of you."

The Lizard, amazed at the usually gentle-mannered Saint Jimmy, straightened himself in the saddle and caught up the reins.

"Get out!" continued the man on the ground. "Go find some filthy-minded scandalmonger like yourself to listen to your vile rot. I've had enough."

The Lizard snarled down at him:

"If you warn't a poor lunger, I'd—"

But as Saint Jimmy reached for him, he touched his horse with the spur, and the animal leaped away.

Twenty minutes later, Doctor Burton was on his way to the cabin in the canyon.

Marta was at home, sitting on the porch with her sewing, when her teacher rode down into the Canyon of Gold. She saw him as he turned aside toward the neighboring cabin, and was on the ground in time to introduce the two men.

CHAPTER XII
GHOSTS

MARTA could not have explained, even to herself, why she was so anxious to see Saint Jimmy and Hugh Edwards together. Certainly she made no effort to find an explanation.

Through the years that he had been her teacher, Saint Jimmy had come to personify, as it were, her spiritual or intellectual ideal.

Any why not, since it was Saint Jimmy who had helped her form her spiritual and intellectual ideals? Their daily association, their friendship, their love—for she did love Saint Jimmy—had all been grounded and developed in an atmosphere of books and study that was purely Platonic. In her teacher she had come to see embodied the essential truths which he had taught. She had never for a moment thought of Doctor Burton and herself as a man and a woman. He was simply Saint Jimmy. She was his grateful pupil who loved him dearly because he was Saint Jimmy.

But from the very first moment of their meeting Marta was conscious that the appeal of Hugh Edwards' personality was an appeal that to her was new and strange—she was conscious that he had made an impression upon her such as no man had ever before made. For that matter, she had never before met such a man. As she had said so many times, he made her think of Saint Jimmy and yet he was different. And because the experience was so foreign to anything that she had ever known, she did not understand.

Because Hugh Edwards made her think so often of Saint Jimmy, and because he was so different from Saint Jimmy, she was anxious to see the two men together. Nor could the girl understand her teacher's persistent failure to call on their new neighbor. It was not at all like Saint Jimmy. Nothing, perhaps, revealed quite so fully Marta's lack of experience in such things as her failure to understand why Saint Jimmy was so slow in making the acquaintance of Hugh Edwards.

And now at last her wish to see these two men together was gratified. The girl's radiant face revealed her excitement. Her voice was jubilant, her laughter rang out with delicious abandon. She was tingling with animation and lively interest. Her two friends could no more resist the impulse to laugh with her than one could refrain from smiling at the glee of a winsome child.

As they shook hands she watched them, looking from one to the other with an expression of such eager, anxious inquiry on her glowing countenance that the men were just a little embarrassed.

"I really should have come to see you long ago," said Saint Jimmy. "The right sort of neighbors are not so plentiful in the Cañada del Oro that we can afford to neglect them. I have heard so much about you, though, that I feel as if you were really an old-timer whom I have known for years."

He looked smilingly at Marta.

Hugh Edwards did not appear at all displeased at the suggestion that the girl had been talking about him.

"And I," he returned with an equally significant glance at Marta, "have heard so much about Doctor Burton that if there was ever a time when I didn't know him I have forgotten it."

Marta was delighted. She could not mistake the fact that the two men, as it sometimes happens, liked each other instantly. They seemed to know and understand each other instinctively. The truth is that the men themselves were just a little relieved to find this to be the fact.

Doctor Burton saw in Marta's neighbor a man of more than ordinary personality. That one of such character and education should choose to live as Edwards was living, amid surroundings so foreign to the environment in which he had so evidently been born and reared, and should be content to occupy himself with such menial labor, was to Saint Jimmy a puzzling thing. But Saint Jimmy was too broad in his sympathies—too big in his understanding of life to be suspicious of everything that puzzled him. It would, indeed, have been difficult for any healthy-minded, clean-thinking person to be suspicious of Hugh Edwards.

And Hugh Edwards recognized instantly in Marta's teacher that quality which led all men, except such poor characterless creatures as the Lizard, to speak in his presence with instinctive gentleness and deference.

When they were seated in the shade of the cabin and the two men, who were to her so like and yet so unlike, were exchanging the usual small talk with which all friendships, however close and enduring, commonly begin, Marta watched and listened.

She was right, she thought proudly; they were alike, and yet they were different. What was it? Too frank to dissemble, too untrained in such things to deceive, too natural and innocent to hide her interest, she compared, contrasted, analyzed. But while she was seeking an answer to the thing that puzzled her, there was in her mind and heart not the faintest shadow of a suggestion that she was choosing.

There was no occasion for choice. Indeed, she was not in reality thinking—she was feeling.

And the men, while more apt in hiding their emotions, were scarcely less conscious of the situation.

Suddenly Doctor Burton saw the girl's face change. She was looking past them as they sat facing her, toward the corner of the cabin. Her expression of eager animation vanished and in its stead came a look of almost fear. In the same instant, Jimmy was conscious that Edwards, too, had noticed the girl's change of countenance, and that a quick shadow of dread and apprehension had fallen upon him. The two men turned quickly.

Natachee was standing at the corner of the cabin.

For a long moment no one spoke. Then with a suggestion of a smile, as if for some reason he was pleased with the situation, the Indian raised his hand and uttered his customary word of greeting:

"How."

They returned his salutation and he came forward to accept the chair offered by Edwards. And though his dress, as usual, was that of a primitive savage, his manner, at the moment, was in no way different from the bearing of any white man with a background of educational and social advantages. As he seated himself, he smiled again, as if finding these three people together gave him a peculiar satisfaction.

Doctor Burton spoke with the easy familiarity of an old friend:

"Natachee, why on earth can't you act more like a human being and less like a disembodied spirit? You always come and go as silently as a ghost."

"I am as God made me," the Indian returned lightly, then he added with mocking deference to the three white people: "Except for a few improvements added by your civilization. It is odd, is it not," he continued, "how the noble red man of your so highly civilized writers and painters and uplifters of various sorts becomes so often an ignoble vagabond once you have subjected him to those same civilizing influences?"

"Certainly no one would accuse you of having acquired too much civilization," retorted Jimmy.

"I hope not, I am sure," returned the Indian quietly. Then turning to the others, he said graciously, "You will pardon us for this little exchange of compliments. We are not really being rude to each other, just friendly, that is all. With me, Saint Jimmy always drops his mask of saintliness and becomes a savage, and I cease being a savage and become, if not a saint, at least an imitator of the white man's virtues. It is the privilege of our friendship."

"You are an old fraud," declared Saint Jimmy.

"You flatter me," returned Natachee. "My white teachers would be proud of the honor you confer. They tried so hard, you know, to educate me."

Edwards was amazed. He had never before heard Natachee talk in this bantering vein. With him the Indian had always spoken gravely. He had seldom smiled and had never laughed. The white man felt, too, that underlying the playfulness of the Indian's words and the seeming pleasant humor of his mood, there was a savage interest—a cruel certainty in the final outcome of some game in which he was taking a grim part. He seemed to be playing as a cat plays with the victim of its brutal and superior cunning.

While Edwards was thinking these things and watching the red man with an odd feeling of dread which made him recall Marta's saying that the Indian always gave her the creeps, Natachee addressed the girl with grave courtesy:

"It is really time that your teacher called upon your good neighbor, isn't it? I was beginning to fear that our Saint was harboring some hidden grievance that provoked him to forget the social obligations of his exalted position."

Marta made no reply save a nervous laugh of embarrassment.

Doctor Burton flushed and said hurriedly:

"I was just asking Mr. Edwards, Natachee, when you materialized so unexpectedly, how he liked living in the Cañada del Oro."

"And I was about to reply," said Edwards with enthusiasm, "that it is the most beautiful, the most wonderfully satisfying place, I have ever known."

The Indian smiled, and his dark eyes glanced from Marta to Saint Jimmy, as he said:

"Our canyon is being very good to Mr. Edwards, I think. It is giving him health, gold enough for the necessities of life, and that peace which passeth all understanding, with the possibility of acquiring great wealth. It delights him with the beauty and the grandeur of nature. It bestows upon him the blessings of a charming and delightful companionship. And last, but not least, it affords him a sanctuary from his enemies—if he has any. What more could any man ask of any place?"

Hugh Edwards moved uneasily.

The expression of Marta's face was that of a wondering, half-frightened child.

Saint Jimmy looked at the Indian intently, as if he, too, had caught the feeling of a hidden, sinister meaning beneath the red man's courteous manner and half-jesting words.

"Natachee," he said slowly, "I have often wondered—just what does the Cañada del Oro mean to you?"

At the Doctor's simple question or, perhaps, at the tone of his voice, the countenance of the Indian suddenly became as cold and impassive as a face of iron. Sitting there before them, clothed in the wild dress of his savage ancestors, with his dark features framed in the jet-black hair with that single drooping feather, he seemed, all at once, to have thrown off every vestige of his contact with the schools of civilization. When he had been speaking in the manner of a white man, there had been something pathetic in his appearance. Only his native dignity had saved him from being ridiculous. But now he was the living spirit of the untamed deserts and mountains that on every side shut in the Canyon of Gold. His dark eyes, filled with the brooding memories of a vanishing race, turned slowly from face to face.

The three white people waited, with a strange feeling of uneasiness, for him to speak.

"You say that I, Natachee, come and go as a ghost. Well, perhaps I am a ghost. Why not? It would not be held beyond the belief of some of your philosophers that the spirit of one who once, long ago, dwelt amid these scenes, should return again in this body that you call me, Natachee the Indian. The Cañada del Oro is peopled with ghosts. Those who, in the years that are gone, lived here in the Canyon of Gold were as the blossoms on the mountain sides in spring. In the summer months when there was no rain, the blossoms disappeared. Then the rains came—the 'Little Spring' is here—and look, the flowers are everywhere.

"In this Canyon from the desert below to the pines above, there are holes by the thousands where men have dug for gold. Climb the mountains and go among the cliffs and crags and there are more and more of these holes that were made by those who sought the yellow wealth. Walk the ridges and make your way into the hidden ravines and gorges—everywhere you will find them—these holes that men have dug in their search for treasure. And every hole—every stroke of a pick—every shovel of dirt—every pan of gravel—was a dream that did not come true; a hope that was not fulfilled.

"The Canyon of Gold is haunted by the ghosts of these disappointed ones. They are the shadows that move upon the mountain sides when the sun is down and the timid stars creep forth in the lonely sky. They are the lights that come and go in the canyon depths when the frightened moon tries to hide in the pines of Mount Lemmon. They are the voices that we hear in the nighttime, whispering, murmuring, moaning. Weary spirits that cannot rest, troubled souls that find no peace—the disappointed ones.

"And you who dare to dream and hope and labor here in the Canyon of Gold today as those thousands who dared to dream and hope and labor here before you—what are you but living ghosts among these restless spirits of the dead? What are you today but shadows among the shades of yesterday?

"You, Doctor Burton, are only a memory of dreams that did not come true. You, Mr. Edwards, are but the ghost of the man you once planned to be. You, Miss Hillgrove, are but the living embodiment of hopes that were never fulfilled.

"As the shadow of an eagle passes, you came and you shall go. As the trail of the eagle in the air so shall your dreams, your hopes and your labor, be.

"I, Natachee, know these things. But because I am an Indian, I dream no dreams—I have no hopes." He arose and for a moment stood silent before them. Then he said: "Natachee the Indian lives among the ghosts in the Canyon of Gold."

Before they could speak, he was gone; as silently as he had come he disappeared around the corner of the cabin.

The two men and the girl sat as if under a spell and in the heart of each there was a strange sadness and a shadow of fear.

As Doctor Burton made his way homeward, he wished more than ever that he had told Marta the things that the Pardners had related to him.

Ever since that day when she had first talked to him of the stranger, Saint Jimmy had watched carefully the girl's growing interest in her new neighbor. And, while Marta herself had been wholly unconscious of the true meaning of those emotions which so disturbed her, her teacher had understood that the womanhood of his child pupil was beginning to assert itself. He was too wise not to know also that the time was approaching when Marta herself would understand.

Through all her girlhood she had been no more conscious of herself than were the wild creatures that she knew so much better than she knew her own humankind. She had lived and accepted life without a thought of the part that, as a woman, she would some day be called upon to play in it. Because of this freedom from self, she had not been deeply concerned about the beginnings of her life. But with the arousing of those instincts that were to her so strange would come inevitably a tremendous quickening of her interest in herself. This new and vital interest in herself would as surely force her to inquire with determined and fearful persistency into her past. Who was she? Who were her parents? Under what circumstances was she born?

Doctor Burton knew the fine pride and the sensitive nature of his pupil too well not to realize that, when the time did come for the girl to ask these questions, her happiness might well depend upon the answers.

The Lizard's loose-mouthed gossip had brought him suddenly face to face with a situation which was to his mind filled with real danger to Marta's future. His meeting with Hugh Edwards, his quick observation of the comradeship that had developed between Marta and her neighbor, the uneasy forebodings aroused by the Indian's words, all combined now to make him resolve that, at any cost to himself, he no longer would put off telling the girl what she ought to know. If Hugh Edwards were not the type of man he was, or if Marta were not the kind of girl she was, it would not, perhaps, make so much difference. Tomorrow Marta was going to Oracle. She would stop at the little white house on the mountain side on her way home. Saint Jimmy promised himself that he would surely tell her then.

CHAPTER XIII
THE AWAKENING

MARTA began that day with such buoyant happiness that even her fathers, accustomed as they were to her habitually joyous nature, commented on it.

The air was tingling with the fresh and vigorous sweetness of the early morning. From the kitchen door, as she prepared breakfast, she saw the mountain tops, golden in the first waves of the sunshine flood that a few hours later would fill the sky from rim to rim and cover the earth from horizon to horizon with its dazzling beauty. From some shelf on the canyon wall, a canyon wren loosed a flood of joyous silvery music, gracing his song with runs and flourishes, rich and vibrant, as if the very spirit of the hour was in his melody, and while the canyon echoed and reëchoed to the wondrous, ringing music of the tiny minstrel and the girl, with happy eyes and smiling lips, listened, she saw a thin column of smoke rise from that neighboring cabin and knew that her neighbor, too, was beginning his day.

Like the puff of air that stirred the yellow blossom of the whispering bells beside the creek, the thought came: Was he enjoying with her the beauty and the sweetness of the morning? Was he sharing her happiness in the new day? Then, as she watched, Hugh appeared in the cabin doorway with a bucket in his hand. He was going for water to make his coffee. She saw him pause and look toward her, and her face was radiant with gladness as her voice rang out in merry greeting.

All that forenoon she went about her household work with a singing heart. When the midday meal was over, her fathers saddled Nugget and, as soon as she had washed the dishes, she set out for Oracle to purchase some needed supplies.

When the girl stopped at his cabin, as she always did, to ask if she could bring anything for him from the store, Edwards thought she had never looked so radiantly beautiful. Glowing with the color of her superb health and rich vitality—animated and eager with the fervor of her joyous spirit—she was so alluring that the man was sorely tempted to say to her those things that he had sternly forbidden himself even to think. Lest his eyes betray the feeling he had sentenced himself to suppress, he made pretext of giving some small attention to her horse's bridle, so that from the saddle she could not see his face.

As she rode on up the trail, he stood there watching her. When she had passed from sight around a sharp angle of the canyon wall, he went slowly to the place where through the long days he labored in his search for the grains of yellow metal that had come to mean so much more to him than mere daily bread.

Where the trail to the little white house on the hill branches off from the main road to Oracle, Marta checked her horse. She wanted to go to Saint Jimmy and Mother Burton. She wanted them to know and share her happiness. She wanted to tell them how grateful she was for their love—for all that they had done to save her from the ignorant, undisciplined and dangerously impulsive creature she would have been but for their patient teaching. In the fullness of her heart she told herself that without Saint Jimmy and his mother she could never have known the joy and gladness that had come to her. Without conscious reasoning, she realized that it was their teaching, their love, their understanding of her needs, that had fitted her for that time of her awakening to the glad call of those deeper emotions that now moved her young womanhood. But above Mount Lemmon and back of Rice Peak, huge cumulus clouds were rolling up, and the girl knew that she must continue on the more direct way if she would finish her errand at the store and return before the storm that might come later in the day. On her way back, she could stop at the Burtons, for then, if the storm came, it would not so much matter.

Through narrow, rocky ravines and tree-shaded draws and sandy washes, up the steep sides of mountain spurs and along the ridges, Nugget carried her, out of the Canyon of Gold to the higher levels. And everywhere about her as she rode, the mountain sides were bright with the blossoms of the "Little Spring." Sego lilies and sulphur flowers, wild buckwheat, thistle poppies and bee plant, and, most exquisitely beautiful of all, perhaps, the violet-tinted blue larkspur—*Espuela del caballero*—Cavalier's spur—the early Spaniards called it.

In George Wheeler's pasture, not far from the corrals with the windmill and the water tank, she met the sturdy, red-cheeked Wheeler boys and Turquoise, one of the ranch dogs, playing Indian. From their ambush behind a granite rock, they shot at her with their make-believe guns, and charged with such savage fury and fierce war whoops that Nugget danced in quick excitement. While she was laughing with them and they were courteously opening the big gate for her, their father shouted a genial greeting from the barn, and Mrs. Wheeler from the front porch called a cheery invitation for her to stop awhile. But she answered that it looked as if it were going to rain, and that she must be home in time for supper, and rode on her way to the little mountain village.

In the wide space in front of the store, a group of saddle horses stood with heads down and hanging bridle reins, waiting with sleepy patience for their riders who were lounging on the high platform that, with steps at either end, was built across the front of the building. As she drew near, Marta recognized the Lizard. Then, as they watched her approaching, she saw the Lizard say something to his companions, and the company of idlers broke into loud laughter. The girl's face flushed with the uncomfortable feeling that she was the victim of the fellow's uncouth wit. Two of the men arose and stood a little apart from the Lizard and his fellow loungers.

When the girl stopped her horse, a sudden hush fell over the group, and as she dismounted she was conscious that every eye was fixed upon her. With burning cheeks and every nerve in her body smarting with indignant embarrassment, the girl went quickly up the steps and into the store. As she passed them, the two cowboys who stood apart lifted their hats.

The girl was just inside the open doorway when the Lizard spoke again, and again his companions roared with unclean mirth at the vulgar jest—and this time Marta heard. She stopped as if someone had struck her. Stunned with the shock, she stood hesitating, trembling, not knowing what to do. For the first time in her life the girl was frightened and ashamed.

Two women of the village who were buying groceries regarded her coldly for a moment, then, turning their backs, whispered together. Timidly the girl went to the farther end of the room where, to hide her emotions until she could gain control of herself, she pretended an interest in the contents of a show case.

Before the laughter of the Lizard's crowd had ceased, one of the cowboys who had raised his hat walked up to them. With an expression of unspeakable disgust and contempt upon his bronzed face, the rider looked the Lizard up and down. Those who had laughed sat motionless and silent. Slowly the man from Arkansas got to his feet.

The cowboy spoke in a low voice, as if not wishing his words to be heard in the store.

"That'll be about all from you—you stinkin' son of a polecat. Never mind yer gun," he added sharply as the Lizard's hand crept toward the leg of his chaps. "Thar ain't goin' to be no trouble—not here and now. I'm jest tellin' you this time that such remarks are out of order a heap, here in Arizona. They may be customary back where you come from, but they won't make you popular in this country—except, mebby, with varmints of your own sort."

He included the Lizard's friends in his look of cool readiness.

Not a man moved. The cowboy carefully rolled a cigarette. Calmly he lighted a match, and with the first deep inhalation of smoke, flipped the burnt bit of wood at the Lizard. To the others he said:

"I notice you hombres are thinkin' it over. You'd best keep right on thinkin'. As for you—"

He again looked the man from Arkansas up and down with slow, contemptuous eyes. Then, without another word, he deliberately turned his back upon the Lizard and his friends and walked leisurely to his horse.

As the cowboy and his companion rode away another chorus of laughter came from the group of idlers and this time their merriment was caused, not by anything the Lizard said, but was directed at the Lizard himself.

"Better not let Steve Brodie catch you again," advised one.

"He'll sure climb your frame if he does," said another.

"Steve's a-ridin' fer the Three C now, ain't he?" asked another, seemingly anxious to change the subject.

"Uh-huh—Good man, Steve," came from another.

With an oath, the Lizard slouched away to his horse and, mounting, rode off in the direction of his home.

In the store, Marta struggled desperately to regain at least a semblance of composure.

The two women, when they had made their purchases, were in no haste to go, and, under the pretext of taking advantage of their meeting for a friendly chat, furtively watched the Pardners' girl.

Marta, pretending to examine some dress goods displayed on a table behind the stove, tried to hide herself. When the kindly clerk came to wait on her she started and blushed. Trembling and confused, she could not remember what it was that she had come to buy.

The clerk looked at her curiously. The women whispered again and tittered.

At last, in desperation, the girl stammered that she did not want anything—that she must go—that she would come in again before she started home. With downcast eyes and burning cheeks, she fled.

As she passed the men on the platform and walked swiftly to her horse she kept her eyes on the ground. She was so weak that she could scarcely raise herself to the saddle.

But the men were not watching her now. With their faces turned away they were, with one accord, interested in something that held their gaze in another direction.

Perplexed and troubled, Marta made her way slowly back toward the canyon. When Nugget, thinking quite likely of his supper, or perhaps observing the dark storm clouds that now hid the mountain tops, would have broken into a swifter pace, she pulled him down to a walk. Annoyed at the unusual restraint, the little horse fretted, tossed his head, and tugged at the bit. But she would not let him go. The girl wanted to think. She felt that she *must* think.

What was the meaning of that incident at the store? Why did those men laugh in just that way when they first saw her? Why had they watched her like that when she dismounted? Why had they looked at her so as she passed them? Why did those women refuse to speak to her?—they knew her. And what had they whispered after turning their backs upon her? She had never before been conscious of anything like this. All her life she had met rough men. She had not been unaccustomed to rude jests. She had been, in the presence of men, like a young boy—unconscious of her sex. The only close association with men she had ever known was with Saint Jimmy and her fathers—until Edwards came. It could not be that these people were any different today than on other days when she had gone to the store. It must be that she herself was different.

"Yes," she told herself at last, "she *was* different."

Just as she had found a deeper happiness than she had ever before known, she had found a new consciousness—a new capacity for feeling—that had made her blush when the men looked at her—that had made her ashamed when she had heard the Lizard's jest.

And then her mind went back to consider things which she had always accepted as a matter of course, without question or particular thought—as she had accepted her two fathers.

Why had she never been invited to the parties and dances at Oracle? Why was it that, except for Mother Burton and good Mrs. Wheeler, she had no women friends? Only men had attempted to be friendly with her, and they had approached her only when she met them by chance, alone. She knew them all—they all knew her. Suddenly she remembered how Saint Jimmy had warned her once—long before Hugh Edwards had come to the Cañada del Oro:

"You must be always very careful in your friendships, dear. Before you permit an acquaintance with any man to develop into anything like intimacy, you must know about his past. And by past, I mean parentage—family—ancestors, as well as his own personal record. For let me tell you that no one can escape these things. We are all what the past has made us."

The inevitable question came in a flash. What was her own past—her parentage—her family? The conclusion came as quickly. She understood now why the old prospectors had never talked to her of her own parents, nor told her how she happened to be their partnership daughter. She understood now the significance of her name, Hillgrove—her two fathers had given her their names because she had no name of her own. Nothing else could so clearly explain the attitude of the people which had been so forcefully impressed upon her by her new consciousness.

Just as the young woman reached this point in her reasoning, her horse stopped of his own volition. The girl had been so engrossed with her thoughts that she had not seen the Lizard ride from behind a thick screen of low cedars beside the trail and check his horse directly across the path. She was not at all frightened when she looked up and saw him waiting there, barring her way. Indeed, she regarded the fellow with a new interest. It was as if one factor in her sad problem had suddenly presented itself in a very definite and tangible form.

"Well," she said at last, "what do *you* want?"

The Lizard's wide-mouthed, leering grin was not in the least reassuring.

"I knowed ye'd be a-comin' along directly," he said, "an' 'lowed we'd ride t'gether."

"But what if I do not care to ride with you?" she returned curiously.

"Oh, that ain't a-botherin' me none. I ain't noways thin-skinned," he returned, reining his horse aside from the trail to make room for her. "Come along—ye might as well be sociable like. I know I can't make much of a-showin' in eddication an' fine school talk like you been used to, but I'm jist as good as that lunger Saint Jimmy, er that there fancy neighbor of yourn any day."

Something in the fellow's face, or some quality in his tone, brought the blood to Marta's cheeks.

"Thank you," she said curtly, "but I prefer to ride alone."

She lifted the bridle rein and Nugget started forward.

But the Lizard again pulled his mount across the trail and the man's rat-like face was twisted now, with sudden rage.

"Oh, you do, do you? Wall, let me tell you I've stood all I'm a-goin' t' stand on your account today."

"Why, what do you mean?" she demanded, amazed.

"Never you mind what I mean, my lady. You jist listen to what I got t' say. You've been a-playin' th' high an' mighty with me long enough. D' ye think I don't know what you are? D' ye think I don't know all about your carryin' on. My Gawd a'mighty, hit's a disgrace t' any decent neighborhood. A pretty one you are t' be a-puttin' on airs with me. Why, you poor little fool, everybody knows what you are. Who's yer father? Who's yer mother? Decent people has got decent folks, an' you—you ain't got none. You ain't even got a name of yer own—Hillgrove—two fathers. Yer jist low-down trash an' nobody that's decent won't have nothin' t' do with you. You prefer t' ride alone, do you? All right, my fine lady, you needn't worry none, you're goin' t' ride alone all right. I wouldn't be seen within a mile of you."

With the last brutal word, he whirled his horse about and set off down the trail as fast as the animal could run.

The girl, with her head bowed low over the saddlehorn, sat very still. Her trembling fingers nervously twisted a lock of Nugget's mane. Here was confirmation, indeed, of all the doubts and fears to which she had been led by her own painful thoughts. Here was the answer to all her questions. Here at last was the explanation of those emotions which were to her so new and strange.

CHAPTER XIV

THE STORM

THE old Pardners, when their day's work was finished, climbed slowly down from the mouth of the tunnel to the creek and, crossing the little stream, climbed as slowly up to the level above. As his head and shoulders came above the top of the steep bank, Thad, who was in the lead, stopped.

"What's the matter?" called Bob, who was close behind in the narrow path with his head on a level with his pardner's feet. "Gittin' so old you can't make the grade without takin' a rest, be you?"

"Whar's the little pinto hoss?" demanded Thad in an injured tone, as if the absence of Nugget was a personal grievance.

Bob climbed to his pardner's side.

"Looks like Marta ain't back yet."

"She ought to be," said Thad with an anxious eye on the threatening clouds that now hung dark and heavy over the upper canyon.

"Stopped at Saint Jimmy's, I reckon," returned Bob, who was also studying the angry sky. "Goin' to storm some, ain't it?"

"The gal sure can't miss seein' that," returned the other, "an' she ought to know that when we do get a storm this time of the year, it's always a buster. I wish she was home."

"Mebby she's over to Edwards'," said Bob hopefully.

They went on toward the house until they gained an unobstructed view of the neighboring cabin and premises.

"Her hoss ain't there neither," said Thad, and again he looked up at the dark, rolling clouds.

"Oh, she'll be comin' along in a minute or two," offered Bob soothingly, but his voice betrayed the anxiety his words were meant to hide.

Marta was no novice in the mountains, and the old Pardners knew that it was not like their girl to ignore the near approach of a storm that would in a few moments change the murmuring canyon creek into a wild, roaring flood that no living horse could ford or swim. The trail, on its course from her home to the Burtons, and to Oracle, crossed and recrossed the creek many times, and should the storm break in the upper canyon at the right moment, it would easily be possible for the girl to be trapped at some point between the canyon walls and the bends of the stream, and forced to spend at least the night there. More than this, there was a place where the trail followed for some distance up the narrow, sandy bed of the creek itself, between sheer cliffs. The Pardners and Marta had more than once seen a rolling, plunging, raging wall of water come thundering down the canyon from a storm above, with a mad force that no power on earth could check or face, and with a swiftness that no horse could outrun.

A few scattered drops of rain came pattering down. The Pardners without another word hurried over to Edwards' cabin.

The younger man, who was coming up the path from his work, greeted them with a cheery, "Hello, neighbors—looks like we're going to have a shower." Then as he came closer and saw their faces, his own countenance changed and the old look of fear came into his eyes. "Why, what's the matter—what has happened?" He glanced quickly around, as if half expecting to see someone else near-by.

"Marta ain't come home," said Thad.

And in the same instant Bob asked:

"Did she say anythin' to you about bein' specially late gettin' back today?"

Edwards drew a long breath of relief.

"No, she said nothing to me about her plans. But really, there is no cause for worry, is there? She always stops at the Burtons' with the mail on her way back, you know. Perhaps she stayed longer than she realized. Come on in out of the wet," he added, as the pattering drops of rain grew more plentiful. "She will be along presently, I am sure."

With a glance at the fast-approaching storm, Thad said quickly:

"You don't understand, son, we ain't worried about the gal gettin' wet." And then in a few words he explained the grave possibilities of the situation. "If she stops at Saint Jimmy's, it'll be all right, but if she's a-tryin' to make it home and gets caught in the canyon—"

A gust of wind and a swirling dash of rain punctuated his words.

Old Bob started for the canyon trail. The others followed at his heels. When they reached the narrow road a short distance away they halted for a second.

"There's fresh hoss tracks," said Bob. "Somebody's been ridin' this way. 'Tain't the pinto, though."

"It's the Lizard probably," said Edwards. "I saw him pass on his way up the canyon this forenoon."

Half running, they hurried on. Before they reached the first turn in the canyon, a fierce downpour drenched them to the skin. The falling flood of water, driven by the blast that swept down from the mountain heights and swirled around the cliffs and angles of the canyon walls, hissed and roared with fury.

"There goes any chance of strikin' her trail," shouted Thad grimly.

The three men bent their heads and broke into a run.

At the beginning of that stretch of the trail which follows the bed of the creek, Bob stopped abruptly.

"Look here," he said to the others, "we've got to use some sense an' go at this thing right. If we all of us go ahead like this, we'll all be caught on t'other side of the creek when the rise gets here. If she ain't already in the canyon, she might be at Saint Jimmy's, and she might not. There's a chance that the gal got started home from the store late an' was afraid to try comin' this way, and so left Oracle by the Tucson highway, figurin' to cut across the hills somewheres to the old canyon road an' try crossin' the creek lower down, like we do sometimes. It'll be plumb dark pretty quick an' if she ain't at Saint Jimmy's, there ought to two of us cover both trails—the one by Burtons' an' the one that goes direct, an' there ought to one of us stay on this side of the creek in case she has made it the other way 'round. You won't be much good nohow, son," he continued to Edwards, "if it comes to huntin' the hills out, 'cause you don't know the country like we do. Suppose you go back down to the lower crossin' where the old road comes into the canyon, you know—the way you come. If she don't show up there in another hour or two, you'll know she didn't go that way. There ain't another thing that you can do till daylight."

"You men know best," said Edwards and turned to go.

Thad caught the younger man by the arm.

"Wait." For a second he paused, then spoke slowly: "It might not be a bad idea while you're down that way to drop in on the Lizard."

"Come on," cried Bob. "We sure got to run for it if we beat the rise into this cut."

The Pardners disappeared in the gray, swirling downpour. Edwards, with a new fear in his heart, ran with all his strength down the canyon. But it was not alone the thought of the coming flood that made his heart sink with sickening dread—it was the memory of the Lizard's face that day when the fellow had first told him of Marta.

By the time he reached the cabin, Hugh heard the roaring thunder of the flood. For an instant he paused. Had the two old prospectors gained the higher ground beyond the stretch of trail in the creek bottom in time? He turned as if to go back, then came the thought he could not now retrace his steps beyond the first crossing. Whether the Pardners were safe or were caught by the flood, it was too late now for human aid to reach them.

Again he hurried on down the canyon. When he came to the place where he had made his camp that first night in the Canyon of Gold, it was almost dark, but over the spot where he had built his fire and spread his blanket bed he could see a leaping, racing torrent that filled the channel of the creek from bank to bank.

For nearly three hours he waited where the old road crossed the stream. Convinced at last that Marta had not come that way, he went on down the canyon, to the adobe house where the Lizard lived with his parents.

It was late now but there was a light in the window. The dogs filled the night with their clamor as he approached and he stopped at the dilapidated gate to shout:

"Hello—Hello!"

The door opened and a long lane of light cut through the darkness. The Lizard's voice followed the light:

"Hello yourself—what do you want—who be you?"

"I'm Edwards from up the canyon—call off your dogs, will you?"

From the gate, he could see the fellow in the doorway turn to consult with someone inside. Then the Lizard called to the dogs and shouted:

"Come on in, neighbor. Little late fer you t' be out, ain't it?" he added as Edwards approached, then: "Who you got with you?"

"There is no one with me," returned Edwards as he paused in the light before the door.

"Come in—yer welcome—come right in an' set by the fire. Yer some wet, I reckon." As the Lizard spoke, he drew aside from the doorway and as Edwards entered he saw the man place a rifle, which he had held, against the wall.

An old woman sat beside the open fire smoking a cob pipe. The Lizard's father stood with his back to the wall at the far end of the room. They greeted the visitor with a brief, "Howdy." The Lizard offered a broken-backed chair.

"Thank you," said Edwards, "but I can't stop to sit down. I came to ask if you have seen Miss Hillgrove this afternoon."

The Lizard and his father looked at each other. The old mother answered:

"What's the matter, come up missin', has she?"

Edwards told them in a few words.

The old woman spat in the fire and laughed.

"She's most likely out in the brush somewheres with some no-account feller like herself. Sarves her right if she gits caught by the creek. Sich triflin' hussies ought ter git drowned, I say—allus a-tryin' t' coax decent folks inter meanness. Best not waste yer time a-huntin' sich as her, young man."

Edwards spoke sharply to the Lizard, who was grinning with satisfaction.

"Did you see Miss Hillgrove this afternoon, anywhere on the trail between here and Oracle?"

The father answered in a voice shrill with vicious anger.

"Wal, an' what ef he did—who be you to be a-comin' here at this time o' the night wantin' t' know ef my boy has or hain't seed nobody?"

Hugh Edwards forced himself to speak calmly.

"I am asking a civil question which your son should be glad to answer." He again faced the Lizard. "Did you see her?"

An insolent, wide-mouthed grin was the Lizard's only reply.

The old woman by the fire looked over her shoulder.

"Tell him, boy, tell him," she croaked. "You ain't got no call to be skeered o' sich as him."

"Shucks, maw," said the son. "I ain't skeered o' nothin'. I'm jist a-havin' a little fun, that's all."

He addressed Edwards:

"You bet yer life I seed her 'bout a mile this side o' Wheeler's pasture it was. We shore had a nice little visit too. You an' that thar Saint Jimmy needn't t' think you're th' only ones."

Before Edwards could speak, the old woman cried again:

"Tell him, son—why don't ye tell him what ye said?"

The Lizard grinned.

"I shore told her enough. I'd been a-aimin' t' lay her out first chanct I got. When I got through with her, you can bet she knowed more 'bout herself than she'd ever knowed before. She shore knows now what she is an' what folks is a-thinkin' 'bout her an' her carryin' on with that there lunger an' you." His voice rose and his rat eyes glistened with triumph. "She wouldn't ride with me—Oh, no!—'prefer t' ride alone,' says she. An' I says, says I—when I'd finished a-tellin' her what she was an' how she didn't have no folks, ner name, ner nothin'—'You needn't t' worry none, there wouldn't no decent man be seen within a mile of you.' An' then I left her settin' thar like she'd been whipped."

Hugh Edwards moved a step nearer. It seemed impossible to him that any man could do a thing so vile.

"Are you in earnest?" he asked. "Did you really say such things to Miss Hillgrove?"

"I shore did," returned the Lizard proudly. "I believe in lettin' sech people know whar they stand. She's been a-playin' th' high an' mighty with me long enough."

Then Edwards struck. With every ounce of his strength behind it, the blow landed fair on the point of the Lizard's chin. The loose mouth was open at the instant, the slack jaw received the impact with no resistance. The effect was terrific. The fellow's head snapped back as if his neck were broken—he fell limp and senseless halfway across the room.

The old woman screeched to her man:

"Git him, Jole, git him!"

The Lizard's father started forward and Edwards saw a knife.

A quick leap and Hugh caught up the rifle that the Lizard had placed against the wall. Covering the man with the knife, the visitor said coolly to the woman:

"Not tonight, madam. I'm sorry to disappoint you, but he isn't going to get anyone just now."

He backed to the door and opened it with his face toward them and his weapon ready.

"I will leave this gun at the gate," he said. "If you are as wise as I think you are, you will not leave this room until you are sure that I am gone."

He pulled the door shut as he backed across the threshold.

As Hugh Edwards made his way back up the canyon he reflected on what the Lizard had said. One thing was certain, Marta had not started home by the highway. But where was she now? At Saint Jimmy's? Edwards doubted that the girl would go to her friends after such an experience. Nor did he believe that she would come directly home. He knew too well the sensitive pride that was under all the frank boyishness of her nature. No one was better fitted than he to appreciate the possible effects of the Lizard's cruelty.

Hugh Edwards knew the dreadful power of humiliation and shame. He knew the burning, withering torture of unexpected and unjust public exposure and of undeserved popular condemnation. He knew the horror and despair of innocence subjected to the unspeakable cruelty of those evil-minded gossips whose one hope is that the venomous news they spread may be true, so that they will not be deprived of their vicious pleasure. Better than anyone, Hugh Edwards knew why Marta had not come home after meeting the Lizard.

Like a hunted creature, wounded and spent, this man had come, as so many had come before him, to the Cañada del Oro. He had come to the Canyon of Gold to forget and to be forgotten—and he had found Marta. In the frankness and fearlessness of her innocence, the girl had not known how to keep her love from him. And seeing her love, hungering for that love as a starving man hungers for food, as a soul in torment hungers for peace, he had resolutely forbidden himself to speak the words that would make her his.

When he had first come to the canyon, he had hoped only to find gold enough to secure the bare necessities of life. And when out of their daily companionship his love had come with such distracting power, he had been the more miserable. But when he had heard from the Pardners their story of how they found the girl, he had seen that there was no reason save his own ill-starred past why, if he could win freedom from that past, he might not claim her. That freedom—the freedom from the thing that had driven him to hide in the Cañada del Oro—the freedom to tell her his love, could only be had in the gold for which he toiled in the sand and gravel and rocks beside the canyon creek.

As men, through all the years, have sought gold for love, so he had worked in that place of broken hopes and vanished dreams. Every day when she was with him he had sternly forced himself to wait. Every night he had dreamed, in his lonely cabin, of the time when he should be free. Every morning he had gone to his work at sunrise, buoyed with the hope that before dark his pick and shovel would uncover a rich pocket of the yellow metal. Every evening at sunset, as he climbed up the steep path from the place of his labor, he had whispered to himself, "Tomorrow." And now it had all come to this. With the knowledge of what the Lizard had done, and the full realization of all that might so easily result, the man's control of himself was broken. He was beside himself with anxiety. If Marta was not safe with her friends in the little white house on the mountain side, where was she? Had the Pardners found her? Was she wandering half insane with shame and despair through the storm and darkness? Had she been caught in that plunging flood that was roaring with such wild fury down the canyon? Was her beautiful body, that had been so vivid, so radiant with life, at that moment being crushed and torn by the grinding bowlders and jagged walls of rocks? Perhaps the Pardners, too, had been met by that rushing wall of water before they could escape from the trap into which he had seen them disappear. As these thoughts crowded upon him, the man broke into a run. There must be something—something that he could do. The sense of his utter uselessness was maddening.

At the gate to Marta's home he stopped, and in the agony of his fears he shouted her name. Again and again he called, until the loneliness of the dark house and the sullen grinding, crashing roar of the creek drove him on. At the first crossing above his own cabin, the stream barred his way. Again he cried with all his might, "Marta! Marta! Thad! Bob!" But the sound of his voice was lost, beaten down, overwhelmed by the wild tumult of the plunging torrent. At last, weary and spent with his efforts, and realizing dully the foolishness of such a useless waste of his strength, he returned to Marta's home.

He did not stop at his own cabin. Something seemed to lead him on to that house to which he had drifted months before, as a broken and battered ship drifts into a safe harbor from the storm that has left it nearly a wreck. Since the first hour of his coming, that home had been his refuge. Every morning from his own cabin door he had looked for the chimney smoke as a wretched castaway watches for a signal of hope and cheer. Every night in his loneliness he had looked for the lights as one lost in the desert looks at a guiding star. He could not bear the thought now of those dark windows and empty rooms.

As the Pardners were climbing out of the creek bed where the trail leaves the canyon for the higher levels they heard the thundering roar of the coming flood.

"Thank God, we know that won't git her anyhow," gasped old Thad. "That there run jest about winded me."

Bob, panting heavily, managed a sickly grin.

"Like as not we'll find her safe an' dry eatin' supper at Saint Jimmy's, an' ready to laugh at us for a pair of old fools gettin' ourselves so worked up over nothin'."

"Here's hopin'," returned the other. "But it's bound to be a bad night for the boy back there. Pity there won't be no way to get word to him till mornin'."

They could not go very fast, and it was pitch dark before they reached the little white house. But at the sight of the lighted windows they hurried as best they could, stumbling over the loose rocks and slipping in the mud up the narrow, zigzag trail.

In less than ten minutes from the time Saint Jimmy opened the door in answer to their knock they were again starting out into the night. And this time they separated. Thad returned to the point where the path that leads by the Burton place branches off from the main trail to make his way from there on, while Bob continued on the path from the white house which joins again the main trail at Wheeler's pasture gate.

Another hour, and the storm was past. Through the ragged clouds, the stars peered timidly. But every ravine and draw and wash was a channel for a roaring freshet.

A little way from Wheeler's corral, in the pasture, Thad met his pardner coming back. He was riding and leading another horse saddled.

"She didn't start home on the highway," said Bob.

"They seen her at Wheeler's, did they?"

"Yes, George saw her himself when she was goin', an' when she come back. George, he's saddled up an' gone on into Oracle to pass the word. He'll be out with a bunch of riders at sun-up."

Thad climbed stiffly into the saddle and for some minutes the two old prospectors sat on their horses without speaking, while over their heads the windtorn clouds swept past as if hurrying to some meeting place beyond the distant hills.

"There ain't a God almighty thing that we can do till th' mornin'," said Bob at last.

Slowly and in silence they rode back to the little white house on the mountain side, there to wait with Saint Jimmy and Mother Burton for the coming of the day.

The two old prospectors, who had spent the greater part of their lives amid scenes of hardship and danger and whose years had been years of disappointment and failure in their vain search for treasure of gold, had given themselves without reserve to the child that chance had so strangely placed in their keeping. Lacking the home love and the fatherhood that spurs the millions of toiling men to their tasks, and glorifies the burden of their labors, Bob and Thad had spent themselves in their love for their partnership daughter. But, because these men had been schooled in silence by the deserts and the mountains, they made no outward show of their anxiety and fear. They did not cry out in wild protest and vain regrets and idle conjectures. They did not walk the floor or wring their hands. They sat motionless in stolid silence—waiting.

Mother Burton, in the seclusion of her own room, found relief for her overwrought nerves in quiet tears and carried the burden of her anxious, aching mother-heart to the God of motherhood.

Saint Jimmy paced the floor with slow, measured steps, pausing now and then to look from the window into the night or to stand in the open doorway with his face lifted to the wind-swept sky, listening—listening for a voice in the darkness.

In Marta's home beside the roaring creek—alone amid the dear intimate things of her daily life—the man who had been made to live again in her love waited—waited for the eternity of the night to lift from the Canyon of Gold.

CHAPTER XV
MARTA'S FLIGHT

THE victim of the Lizard's unspeakable brutality was as one dazed by an unexpected blow. Coming, as the fellow's vicious attack did, so close upon her own uneasy thoughts, it seemed to answer all her troubled questions and she accepted every cruel word as the truth.

Nugget, wondering, perhaps, why his rider remained so motionless when the other horse and rider had gone on, essayed an inquiring step or two forward. When his mistress gave no heed to his movement, he tossed his head and pulled at the slack bridle rein invitingly. "What's the matter?" he seemed to say. "Come on—why don't we go?" But still she gave no sign of life. Slowly, as if still wondering and a bit doubtful, the little horse moved on down the familiar way toward home. At the pasture gate, the pinto, without a sign from his rider, placed himself so that she could reach the latch. Mechanically she opened the gate and the knowing animal helped her close it from the other side.

But when Nugget would have taken the trail which goes past that white house on the mountain side by which they always went home from Oracle, Marta reined him back with a sudden start. She could not go that way now. She remembered with a wave of hot shame how she had proposed to Saint Jimmy that they be married and run away somewhere—and how she had pictured their home. She understood now why he had laughed in that queer, strained way. It would have seemed funny to any man like Doctor Burton, with such a family name and birth and breeding, that a girl like her—born as she was without a name, with no right to be born at all, even—would dare to suggest such a thing.

Saint Jimmy and Mother Burton had been good to her—yes, they would be good to anyone like that. They had pitied her and had wanted to help her. But of course Saint Jimmy had laughed when she asked him to marry her. She would love those dear friends always, but at the thought of ever meeting them again she shook with terror. She felt that she would die with shame.

As she rode on, the girl gave no heed to the heavy storm clouds that were massing above the upper canyon. At any other time she would have seen and would have pushed her horse to his utmost speed in a race with the coming flood. But now she was too occupied to think of the approaching danger. In fact, her thoughts of Saint Jimmy and Mother Burton were only momentary. When her horse had turned into the direct trail to the canyon, she was fighting to keep herself from thinking of the man who lived in the cabin so close to her home. She was telling herself over and over that she must not think of him. And yet she did, and her thoughts burned like coals of fire.

Marta knew now with terrifying certainty that she loved Hugh Edwards—not, indeed, with the love that she gave Saint Jimmy and, which, until Edwards came, was the only kind of love she knew, but with that other love—the love that a woman gives to the one man she chooses above all others to be her man for all time to come, in the lives of her children—their children. Her happiness that morning had been born of the certainty that the man she had chosen wanted her. He had never spoken a word of love to her but she knew. In a thousand ways he had told her. His very efforts to keep from speaking had made her more sure in her happiness.

She had not understood. She had not even realized why she had wanted him to speak. She had only felt instinctively that she belonged to him, and that he wanted her, but that for some reason he hesitated. But now the Lizard had explained it all. She knew now that her love for Edwards was an evil love. She knew that her instinctive answer to him was a wicked thing. She knew that the emotions stirred by him were vile. She understood at last why he had not spoken the words she hungered to hear. He would never speak. He was like Saint Jimmy. The mother of Hugh Edwards' sons must not be a nameless nobody—a creature of shameful birth and evil desires—a woman upon whom decent women turn their backs and at whom men like the Lizard laughed in scorn.

The girl was almost in sight of Hugh's cabin when, with sudden energy, she sat erect and again checked her horse. Around that next turn in the canyon wall he would be waiting. She could not go on. A barrier, invisible but mightier than any mountain wall, had fallen across her way. She was separated—shut out. She was unclean. She must not go near the one she loved.

Wheeling her horse, the girl rode away up the canyon, straight toward the storm that was gathering in the mountains above. She did not know where she was going. She did not care. What did it matter where she went? She would go anywhere but there where he was waiting.

Blindly she rode into that stretch of the trail that lies in the channel of the creek between the sheer walls. But when, at the end of the hall-like passage, her horse would have followed the trail out of the canyon, she pulled him back. The pinto fretted and tried to turn once more toward home, but she forced him to leave the trail and go on up the creek.

For some time the little horse labored through the sand and gravel or picked his way, as a mountain horse will, around bowlders and over the rocks. So that when those first few drops of rain came pattering down, the girl was already a considerable distance up the canyon. Again Nugget protested, and again she forced him on.

She had reached a point beyond where the canyon turns back toward the south when the storm broke and the rain came swirling down the mountain in torrents. The fierce downpour, driven by the heavy gusts of wind, forced her to bend low in the saddle. On every side the dense gray curtain enveloped her. Her horse broke in open rebellion. Nugget knew, if his rider had forgotten, the grave danger of their position in the creek bed, and he proceeded to take such action as would at least insure their immediate safety.

There were a few preliminary bounds, then a scrambling rush with flying gravel and rolling rocks and tearing brush, with plunging leaps and straining heavy lifts, during which the girl rider could do little more than cling to the saddle. When her horse finally consented again to the control of the bit, and stood trembling, with heaving flanks, on the steep side of the mountain, Marta had lost all sense of direction. In the terrific downpour, she could not see a hundred yards. Wrapped in the gray folds of that wind-blown curtain, every detail of the landscape save the near-by bushes was obscured beyond recognition. No familiar peak or sky-line could be seen.

Suddenly Nugget threw up his head—his ears pointed inquiringly. The girl, too, looked and listened. Then above the hiss of the rain on the rocks and bushes, and the roar of the wind along the mountain slope, she heard the thunder of the coming flood. Nearer and louder came the sound until presently that rolling crest of the flood, freighted with crushing, grinding bowlders, swept past and the gray depths of the canyon below her horse's feet were filled with the wild uproar.

Marta knew that to go back the way she had come was impossible. She realized dully that Nugget had saved both her life and his. It did not much matter, but she was glad that the little horse was not down there in the bed of the creek. They might as well go on somewhere, she thought; perhaps Nugget could find some place where he at least would be more comfortable.

Giving her horse the signal to start, she dropped the bridle rein on his neck, thus permitting him to choose his own course. With sure-footed care, the little horse picked his way along the mountain side, always climbing a little higher until finally they reached what the girl knew must be the top of a ridge or spur of the main range. Following this ridge, which led always upward but at an easy grade, the pinto moved with greater freedom. They came at last to a low gap through which Nugget went without a sign of hesitation, and again he was making his way along the steep side of the mountain.

It was nearly dark when the girl became aware that her horse was following a faint trail. She did not know when they had come into this trail. It was so faintly marked that it could scarcely be distinguished, if at all. But Nugget seemed perfectly content and confident, and because there was no reason for doing otherwise, and because she did not care, she let the horse go the way he had chosen.

The night came swiftly down. The gray curtain deepened to black. The girl did not even try to guess where she was except that she knew she must be somewhere on one of the mountain slopes that form the upper part of Cañada del Oro—the wildest and most remote section of the Santa Catalina range.

She was exhausted with the stress of her emotions and numb with her rain-soaked clothing in the cool air of the altitude to which they had climbed. As the light failed and the black wall of the night closed in about her, she swayed, half fainting, in her saddle. Nugget stopped and the girl slipped to the ground, clinging to the saddle for support. Peering into the gloom she could barely distinguish the mass of a mountain cedar a little farther on.

Wearily she stumbled and crept forward until she could crawl beneath the low sodden branches.

The girl felt herself sinking into a thick darkness that was not the darkness of the night.

CHAPTER XVI
NATACHEE

AS consciousness returned to Marta, her first sensation was that of physical comfort. She thought that she was in her own bed at home, awakening from a dream. Slowly she opened her eyes. Instead of her own familiar room she saw the rough, unhewn rafters, the log walls, and the rude furnishings of an apartment that was strange.

Wonderingly, without moving, she looked at the unfamiliar details—at the fireplace of uncut rocks with a generous fire blazing on the hearth—the lighted lamp on the table—the rough board cupboard in the far corner—the cooking utensils hanging beside the fireplace—and at the skins of mountain lion and lynx and fox and wolf and bear that hung upon the walls. It all seemed real enough, and yet she felt that it must be a part of her dream. She would awaken presently she thought—how curious—how real it was.

She put a hand and arm out from under the covers and touched, not the familiar blankets of her own bed, but a fur robe. The effect was as if she had come in contact with an electric wire. In the same instant she saw the sleeve of her jacket, and realized that she was not in her own bed at all, but was lying fully dressed on a rude couch—that her clothing was still wet from a storm that was not a dream storm, and that everything else was as real.

But where was she? Who had brought her to this strange place? Fully awake now, the girl made a more careful survey of the room, and this time saw hanging on a peg in the log wall near the fireplace a bow with a sheaf of arrows, and on the floor beneath a pair of moccasins.

"Natachee!"

With a shudder, as if from a sudden chill, Marta threw back the fur robe and sat up. She was not frightened. It is doubtful if Marta had ever in her life known real fear. But there was something about the Indian that always, as she had expressed it, "gave her the creeps."

Swiftly her mind reviewed the hours that had passed since she left her home to go to Oracle. Her good-bye to Edwards, her happiness as she rode over the familiar trail, her meeting with the Wheeler children and their parents, the incident at the store, her troubled thoughts as she started homeward, and then, the crushing shame—the horror of the things that the Lizard had made known to her. Of her actual movements after the Lizard left her, she remembered almost nothing clearly. That part of her experience remained to her still as a dream. But that one dominant necessity which had driven her into the storm and the night; *that* stood clear in all its naked and hideous reality. She could not, with the burning certainty of her shame, she could not see Saint Jimmy nor Hugh Edwards again.

Rising, she went to the fireplace and stood before the blaze to dry her still damp clothing. She was calmer now. The wild uncontrolled storm of her emotions had passed. With her physical exhaustion had come a sort of relief from her emotional strain. She could think now. As she stood looking down into the fire she told herself, with a degree of calmness, that she *must* think. She must plan—she must decide—what should she do?

She was standing there, with her eyes fixed on the blazing logs in the fireplace, when she became aware that she was not alone. As clearly as if she had seen it, she felt a presence in the room. She turned to look over her shoulder. Natachee stood just inside the closed door of the cabin. He had entered, opening and closing the heavy door without a sound.

As she whirled to face him, the Indian bowed with grave courtesy.

"I beg your pardon, Miss Hillgrove, I did not mean to startle you but I thought you might be sleeping."

There was nothing either in the Indian's face or in his manner to alarm her. Save for his savage dress he might have been any well-bred college or university man. Nor did the girl in the least fear him. She only felt that curious creepy feeling that she always experienced in his presence.

As if to put her more at ease, Natachee went to bring a rustic chair from the other end of the room, saying in a matter-of-fact tone:

"I have been out taking care of your little horse. He will be comfortable for the night, I think." He placed the chair before the fire and drew back. "Won't you be seated? You can dry your boots so much better."

Marta sat down and, holding her wet feet to the blaze, looked again into the ruddy flames. The Indian, standing at the other side of the room, waited, motionless as a graven image, for her to speak.

"Thank you," she said at last.

At her words, or rather at her air of utter hopelessness, a flash of cruel satisfaction gleamed for an instant in the somber eyes of the red man.

But Marta did not see.

"It is nothing," said the Indian and his deep voice gave no hint of the fire that had, for the instant, blazed in his dark impassive countenance. "It is a pleasure to be of any service." And then with a smile which again the girl did not see, he added, "I was caught in the storm myself."

Without raising her eyes Marta said wearily, as if it did not in the least matter:

"It was you who found me and brought me here?"

"I was on my way home from the canyon below when I chanced to catch a glimpse of you and your horse against the sky. Naturally I was curious to know who it was that rode in these unfrequented mountains through such a storm and at such an hour. I managed to follow you and so found your horse. Then I found you and brought you here."

When the girl was silent he continued:

"My poor little hut is not much, I know, but it is a shelter at least, and I assure you you are as welcome as if it were the home of your dreams."

At this the girl threw up her head with a start. Staring at him with wide questioning eyes she said wonderingly:

"The home of my dreams? What do you know of my dreams?"

Natachee bowed his head.

"I beg your pardon. My choice of words was unfortunate but unintentional, I assure you. And yet," he finished with quiet dignity, "it would be difficult for anyone to imagine a woman like you being without a dream home."

With a shudder the girl turned back to the fire.

Again that gleam of savage pleasure flashed in the eyes of the Indian.

"But I am forgetting," he said, "you have had nothing to eat since noon and it is now past midnight. This is a poor sort of hospitality indeed."

As he spoke he went to the cupboard and began putting dishes and food on the table.

The girl watched him curiously—his every movement was so sure, so complete and positive. There was no show of haste and yet every motion was as quick as the movements of a deer. He gave the impression of tremendous strength and energy, yet his touch was as light as the hand of a child, and his step as noiseless as the step of that great cat, the cougar. Indeed, as he went to and fro between the table, the cupboard and the fireplace, Marta thought of a mountain lion.

"And how do you know that I have had nothing to eat since noon?" she asked presently.

Without looking up from the venison steak he was preparing, he answered:

"You went to Oracle early in the afternoon—you did not stop at the Wheeler ranch on your way back—you did not go to Saint Jimmy's—you did not go to Hugh Edwards'—you did not go home."

The girl's cheeks flushed as she persisted:

"But how do you know? Have you some supernatural gift that enables you to see what people are doing no matter where you are?"

Natachee laughed.

"My gifts are only the gifts of an Indian, Miss Hillgrove; I see with the eyes of a red man, that is all."

The girl looked again into the fire.

"I wish you did have the gift of second sight," she said, speaking half to herself.

The Indian flashed a look at her that would have startled her had she seen it.

"Why?"

"Because," she answered slowly, "because then perhaps you could tell me something that I want very much to know."

The Indian, who was behind her, smiled.

"Dinner is served," he said.

"Really I—I don't think I can eat a thing," she faltered, looking up at him.

"I know," he returned gravely, "but perhaps if you try—" He placed a chair for her and stood expectantly.

And Marta felt herself compelled to obey his unspoken will. Perhaps because of the strange effect of the Indian's personality upon her, or perhaps because she sought relief from the pain of thoughts which she could not express, the girl encouraged the red man to talk of his life in the mountains. And Natachee, as if courteously willing to serve her purpose, followed her conversational leadings with no mention of her own life in the Cañada del Oro or of her friends. Over their simple meal, of which Marta managed to partake because she felt she must, he told her of his hunting experiences and drew from his seemingly inexhaustible store of desert and mountain lore many strange and interesting things. Nor was there, in anything that he said or in his way of speaking, the slightest hint of his Indian nature.

As they left the table, and Marta resumed her seat before the fire, she said:

"But I do not understand how a man educated as you are can be satisfied to live like—" She hesitated.

"Like an Indian?" he finished for her.

"Well, yes."

There was a long moment of silence before he replied with a marked change in his voice:

"I live like an Indian because I am an Indian. Because if I would I could not be anything else."

As he spoke he came to the other side of the fireplace and seated himself on the floor and the act had for the girl the odd effect of a deliberate renunciation of the civilization which she, in her chair, seemed for the moment to personify. It was as if in answering her question he had cast off the habit of his white man's schooling; had thrown aside mask and cloak and placed before her his true self. As he sat there, in the picturesque garb of his savage fathers, with the ruddy light of the fire playing on his bronze, impassive countenance and glinting in the somber depths of his steady eyes, the young white woman looking down upon him could detect no trace of the white man's training.

"And yet," she said, "this cabin—this room—does not look like any Indian's home that I ever saw."

He answered with the native imagery of a red man:

"The cougar that has been taught to jump through a hoop at the crack of his trainer's whip is still a cougar. The eagle in a white man's cage never acquires the spirit of a dove."

"But I should think that with your education you would live among your people and teach them."

Gazing steadfastly into the fire he answered grimly:

"And what would you have me teach my people?"

"Why, teach them what you have learned—teach them how to live."

The Indian looked at her, and the girl saw something in his countenance that made her feel, all at once, very weak and helpless. She was embarrassed as if caught in some petty meanness. In her confusion she began to stammer an apology but the red man raised his hand.

"You, a white woman, shall hear an Indian. I, Natachee, will speak.

"It would be easier to number the drops of water that fell in the storm tonight than to tell the years of these mountains that look down upon the Cañada del Oro and the desert beyond. They have seen the ages pass as the cloud shadows that race across their foothills when the spring winds blow. Before the beginnings of what you white people call history they had watched many races of men rise to the fullness of their strength and pride, and fall as the flowers of the thistle poppies fall in the desert dust. In the time appointed the Indians came.

"From the peaks of these mountains Natachee the Indian can see far. From the place where the sun rises in the east, to the mountains behind which he goes down in the west, and from the farthest range that lies like a soft blue shadow in the north, to that line in the south where the desert and the sky become one, this land was the homeland of my Indian fathers. Since the God of all life placed us here it has been our home. What has the Indian today?

"Was there a place where the tall pines grew and the winter snows lingered long into the dry season to feed the streams where the wild creatures drink—'I want those trees, they are mine,' said the white man. And he cut them down and sold them for gold, and the naked mountains held no snows to feed the creeks; and the meadows that God made became barren wastes— lifeless. Was there a spring of water—'It is mine,' cried the white man, and he built a fence around it and made a law to punish any thirsty creature that might dare to drink without paying him. In this homeland of my fathers the wild life was as the grass on the mesas. The Indian took what he needed. It was here for all. The white man saw the antelopes in the foothills, the deer on the mountain slopes, the bear in the canyon, the sheep among the peaks, and he shouted: 'They are mine—all mine.' And every man in his white madness, for fear some brother would destroy one more wild thing than he himself could count among his spoils, killed and killed and killed; and only the buzzards profited by the slaughter. But I, Natachee, an Indian, here in this homeland of my fathers, because I dared to kill the deer from which we had our meat this evening, am a violator of the white man's laws, and subject to the white man's punishment.

"You tell me that I should teach my people how to live? By that you mean that I should teach them the ways of the white people? Is it the duty of one who has been robbed of all that was his to accept the thief as his schoolmaster and spiritual guide? Would you say that one who had been tricked and cheated out of his birthright must adopt the principles and customs of the trickster? Could you expect one who had been humiliated and shamed and broken to set up the author of his degradation as his ideal and pattern?

"The schools of the white people taught me nothing that would cause the white people to permit me ever to make a place for myself among them as their equal. No education can ever, in the eyes of the white man, make a white man of an Indian. All kinds of animals are educated for the circus ring, and the show bench, and the vaudeville stage. If they prove clever enough you applaud them. You reward them for amusing you. You educate the Indian. If he be clever enough you give him a place in your social circus so long as he amuses you. But do you permit him to become one of you in your homes, your professions, your law-making, your business—no—he is no more one of you than the performing bear is one of you. Do you think that I, Natachee, do not know these things? Do you think my people do not know that, when one of their boys is put in the white man's schools, he grows up to be something that is neither a white man nor an Indian? It is because they do know, that they look upon me, Natachee, as an outcast of the tribe. Would the outcast, without place or people in the world, teach others the things that made him an outcast?

"The only thing that an Indian can teach an Indian is to die. In the day of their strength and pride my fathers in these mountains saw the smoke from the first camp fire made by a white man in the Cañada del Oro. It was a signal smoke—but no Indian then could read its meaning. We know now that it meant the time had come when the Indians, too, must go into the shadows, even as the many races that had passed before them. But my people shall not be unavenged—as the red man is going, the white man too shall go.

"The strength of the Indian was the red strength of the mountains and deserts and forests and streams. The Indian is dying because the white man stole his red strength and turned it into a white man's strength, which is yellow gold. But the white man's yellow strength is his weakness. In the golden flower of his greatness are the seeds of his decay. For gold, your people destroy the forests—tear down the mountains—dry up or poison the streams—lay waste the grass lands and bring death to all life. For gold they would rob, degrade, enslave and kill every race that is not of white blood. For gold they rob, degrade, enslave and kill their own white brothers. Even the natural mating love of their men and women they have made into a thing to buy and sell for gold. In this lust for gold their children are begotten, and born to live for gold, and of gold to perish. The very diseases that rot the white man's bones, wither his flesh, dim his eyes and turn his blood to water are diseases which he buys with his gold. And the only heaven that his religious teachers can conceive for his celestial happiness is a place where he may forever wear a crown of gold, make music upon a harp of gold, and walk upon streets of gold. It was this gold, which is both the white man's strength and his weakness, that brought your race like a pestilence upon my people. By this same gold for which the Indian peoples have been destroyed shall the Indians be revenged; for by this gold shall the destroyers themselves, in their turn, be destroyed.

"There is nothing left for the Indian but to die. I, Natachee, have spoken."

At his closing words Marta Hillgrove caught her breath sharply.

"Nothing left but to die? And you—have you never dreamed of—" She could not speak her thought.

Again that quick light of savage pleasure flashed across the dark face of the red man.

"An Indian has no right to dream of love," he answered, "for love to an Indian means children. Why should an Indian wish to have children?"

When the girl hid her face in her hands, he continued with cruel purpose:

"Is it so hard for Marta Hillgrove to understand that there might be circumstances under which it would become a duty to deny one's self the happiness of loving? If it is there are two men who could, I am sure, make it clear to her."

For some time the Indian sat watching the white woman as one of his ancestors might have watched an enemy undergoing the agony of torture. Then rising he said:

"Come, it is time that you were taking your rest. You have nearly reached the limit of your endurance. You will sleep there on the couch. I shall be within call. In the morning I will take you home."

He threw more wood upon the fire and turned to leave the room.

"You are very kind," said the girl, "but I cannot go home."

Natachee faced her and she saw the savage triumph that for the moment burned through the mask of stolid indifference which he habitually wore.

"Kind?" he said with cruel insolence. "Kind! And why should I, Natachee, an Indian, be kind to you, a white woman? Make no mistake, Miss Hillgrove, if I do not tonight treat you as my fathers treated the women of their enemies, it is not because I am kind. It is only because it will afford me a more enduring and keener pleasure to return you to your friends down there in the Canyon of Gold."

The girl, cowering in her chair, heard no sound when the Indian left the room.

When morning came and Natachee again appeared he was his usual stolid, courteous self. But Marta knew now what fires of bitter hatred smoldered beneath the red man's calm exterior. He made no reference to her statement that she could not go home, nor did the girl dare to repeat what she had said. She felt that she was powerless to do other than resign herself to the will of the Indian who seemed to find a cruel satisfaction in returning her to Saint Jimmy and Hugh Edwards.

When they had eaten breakfast, Natachee brought her horse.

The canyon creek below was still a roaring torrent, impossible to cross, but the red man led her by ways known only to himself around the head of the canyon and so at last to Saint Jimmy and Mother Burton.

For the next two or three weeks Marta avoided Hugh Edwards. She saw him frequently at a distance, and when he came to spend an evening hour on the porch, but she did not go to his cabin alone and always managed that her fathers were present when she talked with him in her own home. Edwards accepted the situation understandingly, and said no word, but worked harder than ever. Neither did she spend much time with Saint Jimmy, though she went nearly every day to see Mother Burton. The girl was very gentle with the two old prospectors and with tender thoughtfulness sought to make them feel that she was their partnership girl exactly as she had been ever since she could remember. But she would not go to Oracle, so either Bob or Thad was forced to go to the store whenever it was necessary for someone to bring supplies.

Doctor Burton blamed himself bitterly for the whole affair, but the Pardners insisted that the fault was theirs.

"You can see yourself, sir," said Bob, "that if we'd raised the gal up knowin' all the time what she had to know some day, it couldn't never a-struck her like this."

And Thad added:

"The God almighty truth is that me an' my pardner was jest too darned anxious to shirk what was plain enough our duty, and so shifted the responsibility on to you. It was a mean, low-down trick an' no way fair to you, an' you jest got to see it that way. We know how you feel about not tellin' her 'cause we're feelin' that way a heap ourselves, but it ain't addin' none to our comfort to have you tryin' to shoulder the blame what belongs to us."

The two old men were so miserable that Saint Jimmy's sympathy for them lessened somewhat his own suffering, and the three agreed that the only thing they could do was, as Bob said, "to blame everybody in general and nobody in perticler and make it up to the girl the best they could."

Then came that eventful day when Sheriff Jim Burks and two of his deputies rode into the Cañada del Oro.

CHAPTER XVII
THE SHERIFF'S VISIT

THE Pardners were coming from their mine to the house for the midday meal when the officers stopped at the gate.

"Howdy, Jim?" called Bob with the cheerful grin he kept for his friends. "Which one of us are you wantin' now?"

The sheriff laughed as he shook hands with the two old prospectors.

"If you'll give our horses a feed, I'll let you both off this time."

"How about yourselves?" asked Thad. "Would you fight if we was to try to force you to eat a bite?"

"I'll say we would not," returned one of the deputies, swinging from his saddle.

"I'm that holler that I'd ring if anybody was to kick me," drawled the other.

"I'll have to hear what the boss says before I commit myself," said the sheriff. "How about it, Marta?" he called to the girl who stood in the door-way. "Are you backing the offer of these two daddies of yours?"

"You know I am, Mr. Burks," she returned heartily. "You are always welcome here. I'll be ready for you in a few minutes."

While they waited Marta's call to dinner, the men exchanged news of general interest and talked together as old friends will. And Marta, in the kitchen, could hear through the open window every word as clearly as if she had been sitting with them.

Presently the sheriff made known his mission in the Canyon of Gold. "You haven't got any strangers in the neighborhood, have you?" he asked casually.

"Nope," said Bob.

"Nary a stranger," echoed Thad.

"That is," amended Bob, "not that we have seen or heard of. This here Cañada del Oro is a pretty big piece of country, Jim, an' mighty rough, as you know, an' Thad an' me we stick kinda close to our diggin'."

"Natachee been 'round lately?"

"Oh, he drops in once in a while, same as always," returned Bob. "He was here yesterday."

"Natachee would sure know if there was anyone around," mused the officer. "There is nothing stirring in these mountains that Indian don't see. I'm looking for a convict who escaped from the Florence penitentiary," he continued. "The last trace we had of him he was headed this way. He came into Tucson and managed to get a sort of an outfit together and struck out for somewhere in this general direction."

At the officer's words old Thad rubbed his bald head meditatively. Bob bent over to pick up a bit of rock which he proceeded to examine with minute care. The girl in the kitchen caught at the table for support and, faint and trembling, with white face and horror-stricken eyes, stared through the open door toward that neighboring cabin.

Then she heard Thad say:

"We sure ain't seen nothin' like a convict in these parts, Jim. When did he make his break?"

"Two weeks ago," answered the sheriff.

The color returned to the girl's face and her trembling limbs became steady. But as she turned again toward the stove where the meal for her guests was cooking, she glanced through the open window and stood as if turned to stone.

Natachee was moving with noiseless step toward the group of men outside.

Then she heard Bob's laugh.

"Talkin' about the devil, sheriff, suppose you take a look behind you."

While the officers and the Pardners were exchanging greetings with the Indian, Marta, going to the door, summoned the hungry men. They trooped into the house and Natachee, declining the invitation to join them at the table on the plea that he had eaten an early dinner, seated himself just inside the open doorway to continue his part in the general conversation.

When the sheriff had explained his mission to the Indian, Natachee, with his eyes fixed on Marta's face, confirmed the Pardners' opinion that no stranger had recently come into the Canyon of Gold.

"That's good enough for me," said the sheriff. And then to his men: "We'll swing over into the Tortollita country this afternoon. No use wasting any more time here."

"We can just about make it over to Dale's ranch by dark," returned one of the deputies.

"We ain't due to strike no such meal as this at Dale's," said the other officer mournfully, "Dale's batchin'."

And with one accord they all smilingly expressed their appreciation of Marta's cooking and acknowledged their gratitude for her hospitality, while the girl happily assured them again of the welcome that always awaited them in her home.

For some time following this the hard-riding officers were too busy demonstrating their approval of the dinner to engage in conversation. Natachee waited.

At last the Indian spoke casually:

"You do not always succeed in finding these escaped convicts, do you, sheriff? This is a big stretch of country to cover and it's not so very far to the Mexican line. I should think a man would have a fairly good chance."

"They have more than a fair chance," returned the sheriff. "But still we get most of them. A man must have food and water, you know. If our man knows this sort of country, we can nearly always figure out about what he will do."

He put down his knife and fork and sat back in his chair with the genial air of one who is at peace with the world.

"It's mostly the strangers that drift in from other parts that we never get," added one of the deputies. "You can't tell what they'll do, nohow. Generally they lose themselves and never show up."

Rolling a cigarette the sheriff, in a reminiscent mood, continued:

"That's right. There was one that got away from San Quentin over in California about six months ago, and we lost him clean. They traced him as far as Phœnix and notified me to be on the lookout, because it was reasonably sure that he was heading south, but that's the last anybody ever heard of him. He may show up yet—if he's not dead. We always try to keep them in mind, you know."

The Indian, watching Marta, saw the terror that came into her eyes at the sheriff's words. Quietly she drew away from the group and slipped into the adjoining room where she stood just inside the half-open door listening.

The eyes of the Pardners were fixed upon the officer with intense interest.

Natachee smiled.

"What did this man look like?"

The sheriff answered:

"The description sent to me says he is a man of about twenty-two or three, tall, rather slender, gray eyes, brown hair, clean shaven, good-looking, well educated, well appearing, likable sort of a chap. Haven't seen him, have you, Natachee?"

"I might run across him somewhere, some day," returned the Indian.

There was a sound in the adjoining room and the sheriff, who was sitting with his back toward the door, turned his head inquiringly.

Old Bob spoke quickly:

"What was he in for, Jim?"

And Thad asked in the same breath:

"A killin', was it?"

The officer gave his attention again to his hosts.

From where he sat the Indian, through the open kitchen door, saw Marta running toward the neighboring cabin.

The sheriff was answering the old prospectors:

"He was sent up for wrecking a big investment company in Los Angeles. You remember—the papers were full of the affair at the time."

Hugh Edwards did not know that his neighbors were entertaining visitors. He was at work in the creek bed when the sheriff arrived and when he went up to his cabin for his noontime lunch the Pardners and their guests were on the far side of the house, so that he could not see them. He had returned to his work and was energetically wielding his pick when he heard Marta's hurried step on the bank above. The girl came running and sliding down the steep path.

At sight of Marta's face, Edwards dropped his pick and ran to her.

"Marta dear, what is the matter? What has happened?"

In his alarm for her he forgot himself for the moment, and would have taken her in his arms, but her first hurried words brought him back with a shock.

"The sheriff—" she cried in a voice that trembled with fear and excitement.

Hugh Edwards stood as if stunned by a sudden blow, staring at her dully, unable to speak.

"Don't you understand?" she said sharply. "The sheriff is here—why don't you speak? Why don't you say something?" She caught him by the arm and shook him. "The sheriff is here, I tell you. He is looking for a man who escaped from prison."

Hugh Edwards drew a long shuddering breath and the girl saw him, in obedience to his first impulse, turn and start as if to run. Then, as suddenly he checked himself, and stood looking about in fearful indecision, not knowing which way to go. Another moment and he had regained control of himself.

Facing her with a steadiness which revealed the real strength of his character he said coolly:

"This is interesting, I'll admit, but don't you think perhaps you are a little overexcited?" he smiled reassuringly. "Suppose you tell me more."

Calmed by his strength the girl answered:

"Sheriff Burks and two of his men are searching for a convict who escaped from the Florence penitentiary two weeks ago. They stopped at our house to inquire if we had seen any strangers in the canyon recently, and we asked them to stay for dinner of course. Natachee happened in as he always does when anyone from outside comes to the canyon—and—and—while they were all eating and talking I slipped out the front door and ran over here to tell you."

Edwards laughed.

"A convict escaped from Florence two weeks ago. Well, he certainly is not in the Cañada del Oro or Natachee would know."

The girl looked at him pleadingly.

"I—I—am afraid Natachee does know." She shuddered. "He—it would be just like him to bring the sheriff and his men here. Please—please—won't you go? For my sake, won't you?"

At this Edwards looked at her searchingly.

"Go where?" he said at last. "What do you think the Indian knows? Why should I go anywhere?"

"You—you do not understand," the girl faltered. "You must hide somewhere, quick—Please, Hugh, they may come any minute."

Again Edwards looked about as if, while prompted to yield to her entreaty, he was still undecided as to the best course to pursue.

"But surely you know that I did not escape from Florence two weeks ago," he said slowly.

"I know—I know," she cried, "but there was another."

"Another?"

"Yes—a man who escaped from San Quentin six months ago. They followed him as far as Phœnix. He was coming this way. He was twenty-two or twenty-three years old—tall—slender—gray eyes—brown hair—well educated—Oh, Hugh—Hugh—don't stand there looking at me like that! You must do something—you must go—quick—somewhere—anywhere where these men won't see you."

With a low cry of horror and despair the man leaped away, running like a startled deer up the creek. But before he had gone a hundred feet he stopped as suddenly as he had started and faced back toward the girl, holding out his arms in an unmistakable gesture of love and longing.

But Marta did not see. She had dropped to the ground, where she crouched with her face buried in her hands.

Still holding out his arms the man went slowly toward her. Then again he stopped, to stand for a moment irresolute, as one fighting with all the strength of his will against himself. And then once more he faced the other way, and stooping low, with head down, ran as if in fear for his life.

When Marta had recovered a little of her self-control she realized that she must not be seen near Edwards' cabin by the officers, who by this time must have finished their dinner. Hurriedly she stole away down the creek, thinking that if she was seen coming up the path that led from the Pardners' mine to the house no one would question as to where she had been.

When she had gained the top of the bank she saw her fathers just outside the kitchen door deep in a heated argument. There was no one else in sight. Catching her breath sharply, the girl hurried on until she could gain an unobstructed view of the neighboring cabin. There was no one there. With a sob of relief she almost ran the remaining distance to the Pardners, who were by now watching her expectantly, as if wondering what she would do or say.

"Where are they? Have they gone?" she cried as she came up to them.

The two men looked at each other questioningly.

"Go ahead, you old fool, she's your gal, ain't she?" said Bob. "What's the use in your standin' there lookin' at me like that, I ain't done nothin'."

"Holy Cats!" ejaculated Thad. "Can't a man even look at you without you goin' mad? I ain't a-worryin' none about what you've done or about what anybody's done, if it comes to that. It's what you're likely to do that's got me layin' awake nights."

He turned to the girl and in a very different tone said:

"Sure they're gone. Jim figgered that if the man they wanted was in the Cañada del Oro, Natachee would a-seen him and so, as long as the Indian hadn't seen nobody strange in these parts, they've pulled out for the Tortollitas. Jim said to tell you good-bye an' that they'd sure enjoyed your cookin'."

To the utter amazement of the two old prospectors their partnership girl burst into a joyous ringing laugh, and throwing her arms around each leathery wrinkled old neck in turn she kissed them and ran into the house.

Bob looked at Thad—Thad looked at Bob—together they looked toward the kitchen door through which their girl had disappeared.

"Holy Cats!" murmured Thad softly, as he rubbed his bald head. "Now what in seven states of blessedness do you make of that?"

"She must know," said Bob. "She must a-heard what Jim said—she ain't a plumb fool if she is your gal." He shook his head. "I give it up. Listen to that, will you?"

Marta, busy with her after-dinner kitchen work, was singing.

"One thing is certain sure," said Thad softly, "whatever trouble the boy may have got himself into, it's a dead immortal cinch that he ain't in no way different now from what he was before Jim Burks happened to eat dinner with us, an' that blamed Indian began askin' fool questions about what ain't none of his business."

"That's fair enough," returned Bob. "We didn't never take to Hugh for what some judge, that we never saw or heard tell of, said he was or wasn't. We threw in with him for what he is. An' if we're such a pair of boneheads as to be livin' with him like we have all this time without findin' out more about what he really is than any judge that ever sat on a bench—well—we ought to be sentenced ourselves, that's what I'm sayin'."

Thad rubbed his bald head.

"At that," he said mournfully, "it wouldn't be the first time by several, that we'd ought to a-been sentenced, would it? If young Edwards was to go to pryin' into our records—huh—I'll bet he wouldn't feel proud of his neighbors no matter what he's done hisself."

Old Bob grinned cheerfully.

"You've said it, Pardner, by smoke!—if he was to know, the youngster would be hittin' it out of this Cañada del Oro so fast you wouldn't see Mount Lemmon for dust. Come to think of it, it's generally a healthy proposition not to know too much about your neighbors—the ones that you like, I mean. What is it the good book says: 'Where ignorance is bliss a man's a darned fool to poke around tryin' to find out things?' As for my gal, it's plain to be seen that she's plumb tickled at the way it's all turnin' out an'—"

"*Your* gal!" shrilled Thad. "Your gal!—there you go again. Holy Cats! Have you got to be allus tryin' to gouge me out of my rights? Can't you never give me a fair break?"

"Excuse me, Pardner, I forgot. As I was about to say, in my opinion you'd better let that gal of yourn work her own way out of this. It's easy to see that she's in too deep for us, an' considerin' everything—considerin' everything, I say—it might not turn out so bad after all."

To which Thad replied:

"However it looks an' however it turns out, my gal knows a heap more about it than us two old sand rats ever could. We're bankin' on the boy, an' we're trustin' the gal, an' we're mindin' our own business, you bet!"

To which Bob responded fervently:

"You bet!"

CHAPTER XVIII
AN INDIAN'S ADVICE

LESS than a mile up the canyon creek Hugh Edwards stopped. It was useless, he told himself, to go farther. He would wait there until night, when, under cover of the darkness, he could return to his cabin and secure food and the small store of gold he had accumulated. Seating himself on a rock in the shade of a sycamore, where he could watch and listen for anyone attempting to follow his tracks, he gave himself up to troubled thoughts.

True, the sheriff had not come for him this time, but the officers might, while in the neighborhood, learn of his presence in the Canyon of Gold and return to investigate. Suppose, for instance, they should meet and talk with the Lizard. His supply of gold would not take him far, but he must go as far as he could; as for his dream and Marta—what a fool he had been to think that he could ever find gold enough to—

A hand touched his shoulder. With a cry he leaped to his feet, and like a wild animal caught in a trap whirled to fight.

Natachee made the peace sign. The Indian was smiling as he had smiled that night when Marta was in his cabin.

The white man's nerves were on edge. He glared at the Indian angrily.

"What do you mean sneaking up on a man like that?" he demanded. "You'll get yourself killed for that trick some day."

Natachee laughed, and there was a touch of scorn in his voice as he returned:

"Not by you, Hugh Edwards."

"And why not by me?" demanded the other, goaded by the Indian's tone and by the slight emphasis which the red man placed on his name.

"Because," said Natachee coolly, "you are not the killing kind, and because if you should, in a moment of wild madness, attempt such a thing, I—" He paused, then with an abrupt change in his tone and manner, said: "I am sorry that I startled you. It was unpardonably rude, I'll admit, and you have every reason for being angry. I did not stop to think."

"It is nothing," returned Edwards. "I was a fool to fly up over such a thing. I—I'm a bit upset just now, that's all. Forget it."

He resumed his seat on the rock. The Indian seated himself on the ground near-by.

Edwards was thinking: Marta had said that Natachee had come to the house while the officers were there. How much of the sheriff's talk had the Indian heard? How much had he guessed? What was he doing here?

Almost as if to answer the white man's thoughts the Indian said casually:

"I happened in at the Pardners' place a while ago and found Sheriff Burks and two deputies there. I am going to Tucson tomorrow and dropped in to see if I could do any errand for them or for Miss Hillgrove. Then I called at your place to offer a like service but you were not at home. I happened to see you sitting on the rock here as I came up the canyon."

The Indian did not explain how, before the officers were out of sight, he had made his way with the noiseless speed of a fox to a point where from behind rocks and bushes he had witnessed the close of the interview between Marta and Edwards; and how, after the girl had returned to her home, he had trailed the white man. Neither did he explain that he had had no thought of going to Tucson when, from the mountain side, he saw Sheriff Burks and his men ride up to the Pardners' place.

"Thank you," said Edwards, "there is nothing you can do for me in Tucson."

Natachee waited several moments before he spoke again, and the uncomfortable thought flashed into Edwards' mind that the Indian seemed particularly pleased that he, the white man, had nothing to say. Edwards, in an agony of suspense, wondering, fearing, perplexed, baffled, dared not speak.

At last the Indian said softly:

"The sheriff and his men have gone away. They are satisfied that the man they are looking for is not here. I assured them that there was no stranger in the Cañada del Oro."

"They are gone?" said Edwards doubtfully, as if he feared the Indian were playing him some cruel trick.

"For this time," Natachee said gravely.

"You—you—think they will come again?"

The Indian looked away and answered with odd deliberation:

"Who can say? There is always that possibility. Any day—any hour they may come. But if, in spite of what I told Sheriff Burks, the man wanted by him is in the Cañada del Oro, my advice to that man would be that he stay right where he is."

Hugh Edwards hesitated. He felt that the Indian was playing some kind of a game—a game which the red man seemed rather to enjoy but which left the white man very much in the dark.

"You don't think then that he—that the man could get away, out of this part of the country, I mean?" he said at last.

"The sheriff and his deputies will be watching every place but the Cañada del Oro," returned the Indian. "Because they are just now satisfied that their man is not here, this is the one safe place for him. And if they should by any chance return—"

"What," cried Edwards eagerly, "what if the officers *should* return?"

Still without looking at his companion Natachee answered:

"There are places in the Cañada del Oro where a man, if he knew these mountains as I know them, could hide from all the sheriffs in Arizona."

Haltingly, but with trembling eagerness, Hugh Edwards asked the inevitable question.

"And would you, Natachee, help such a man under such circumstances?"

"I might."

At this noncommittal answer Hugh Edwards moved uneasily.

"Do you know," he said at last, "I have fancied sometimes that you, being an Indian, hated all white people bitterly."

Natachee made no reply.

Edwards continued, as one feeling his way over dangerous ground:

"And yet you seem to enjoy the company of Saint Jimmy."

The Indian rose to his feet and stood looking down upon the white man and something in his face—a shadow of a cruel smile, a gleam of savage light in his dark eyes—something—made Edwards rise and draw back a step.

"I do enjoy the company of Doctor Burton," said the red man. "He is suffering. He is dying slowly. He is in torment. I am Natachee the Indian, why should I not enjoy the company of any white man who is like your Saint Jimmy or who can be made to suffer in any way?" For a moment he paused, then in a voice that made his words almost a command, he added: "I will return from Tucson in three days. In the meantime if it should be necessary for you to go into the upper part of this canyon, find my hut if you can and make yourself at home. You will be very welcome. If you should not find my place—if you should get yourself lost, for instance, have no fear, I will find you. But if I were you I would not leave my cabin and my friends down yonder unless it were absolutely necessary."

Without waiting for a reply the Indian turned, and climbing the steep bank of the creek with amazing ease and quickness, disappeared.

Hugh Edwards went slowly back to his cabin.

Marta, who was watching, saw him coming and ran joyously to meet him.

CHAPTER XIX
ON EQUAL TERMS

AS Marta ran to meet him, Hugh Edwards could not but see that she was elated and happy. Not since that morning before the storm had she been in such a joyous mood. The depression, that since her meeting with the Lizard had been so marked, was gone. She was again her own frank, radiant self. But Edwards did not respond to the girl's happiness. When she would have spoken of the sheriff and the escaped convict he coldly prevented her. Concealing every hint of emotion under a mask of formal politeness, he repelled every advance and received her loving overtures of sympathy and loyal comradeship in silence.

In those months when his friendship for Marta had ripened into love it had not been easy for Hugh Edwards to deny himself the happiness which the girl in her love had so innocently offered. With all the strength of his will he had fought to do the thing that he knew to be right. A thousand times he had told himself that to speak the words that would make her share the black shame of the fate that hung over him would be the part of a selfish coward. He must protect her from himself. When he had won gold enough to insure his freedom from the life of a convict, then he would tell her everything. With gold enough he could escape to a foreign land and Marta, when she knew his story, would go with him. But until he could assure himself that complete and final safety from the prison that threatened was within his reach, both for his own sake and for hers, he would not speak of his love.

And now suddenly the girl had learned a part of the truth. And it had only made her love for him more evident. At the same time the incident that had revealed to her his real purpose in coming to the Cañada del Oro had shown him that his fancied security in the Canyon of Gold was fancy indeed. Any day, any hour, any moment, the officers might come for him. The Lizard, the Indian, a chance unguarded word of the Pardners, any one of a hundred things might happen to put the men of the law upon his track. He must not— he must not—say the word that would bring upon the girl he loved the shame and misery that so surely awaited him if the sheriff should find him. More than ever now he was determined to save Marta from himself. But it was not easy. It had been hard before Marta knew what Sheriff Burks' visit had revealed to her—it was harder now. If only he could find the gold.

But nothing could dampen the girl's spirit. She was as sure of Hugh Edwards' love as if he had spoken. When she had believed that her own nameless and questionable birth was the reason for his refusal to declare his love, she had been miserable. But now that his own disgrace had been revealed she felt that the shame of her unknown parentage need be no longer a barrier between them. She did not know what it was that had made the man she loved a fugitive from the law. She did not care. She was glad—glad—because now her dream of happiness with him was possible. She saw now that the thing which had kept him from telling his love was not her lack of an honorable name but the dishonor of his own. He had been shielding her from himself. His silence had not been to save himself from the shame that she might bring to him, but rather to save her from the shame that was already his and which an avowal of his love would have led her to share.

And so she tried in every way to win through the guard he had set against her and to restore the dear comradeship which had been broken—first by the Lizard, and now through the visit of Sheriff Burks. With every wile of her womanhood—with every art of her sex—with all the frankness of her unspoiled nature—she offered herself. Secure in the confidence of his love, she tempted him to break the silence which he had with such fortitude imposed upon himself. And while her loving, generous heart was wrung with pity for his suffering, she gloried in the strength that enabled him to endure against her, and rejoiced in the knowledge that his self-imposed torture was for love of her.

When she tried to make him talk to her of his past, he was silent. When she told him of her own history, he answered, bitterly, that she was fortunate in having no parents to disgrace, no name to dishonor. When she asserted her belief in him no matter what he was in the eyes of the law, he smiled grimly and remarked that, while he appreciated and was grateful for her confidence, her opinion could in no way alter the hard facts of the case. And every day, from the first light of the morning until it was so dark that he could no longer see, he toiled with desperate strength for the gold that would enable him to escape and, by insuring his freedom, make it possible for him to ask Marta to share his future.

He no longer saw the beauty and the grandeur of the mountains. The flowers no longer bloomed for him. He did not hear the birds that filled the Canyon of Gold with music. He did not now glory in the vigorous freshness of the morning. He no longer knew the peace of the restful nights. His every thought was of gold, gold, gold, because gold to him meant Marta. As so many men in the Canyon of Gold had whispered in the night, after a day of heavy fruitless toil: "Tomorrow, perhaps," this man in the night whispered to himself: "Tomorrow, perhaps."

Then came that night when Hugh Edwards was startled out of his dream of the golden possibilities of tomorrow by a sound at his cabin door.

Springing to his feet he stood trembling with fear and dread—had the officers come?

Again came the sound of someone knocking lightly on the door.

With white lips he whispered to himself:

"It's only Thad or Bob or Marta, it's not late yet."

But he knew that it was late. He had seen the light in Marta's window go out two hours ago.

Again the knocking sounded.

In desperation he threw open the door.

It was Natachee.

CHAPTER XX
THE ONLY CHANCE

SILENTLY the white man drew back.

The Indian stepped into the cabin and softly closed the door.

Edwards waited for his visitor to speak, while the red man gazed at him with a hint of that fleeting, shadowy smile of cruel pleasure and satisfaction.

"I returned from Tucson this afternoon," he said at last. "I came back to my place another way, over the mountains from the south. When the sun was gone I came down here to you."

Edwards did not know what to say. He realized that Natachee's visit, at that hour of the night, was more than a mere social call. He felt that for some reason he, the white man, had suddenly become of more than mere passing interest to the Indian. Recalling the Indian's manner at the time of their last meeting, he waited anxiously for what was to come. He managed to murmur a few commonplace words of welcome.

Natachee said gravely:

"I have something to tell you—something which I think will be of interest."

Edwards nervously offered a chair.

When they were seated, the Indian said:

"Perhaps I should tell you that I went to Tucson in your interest." He smiled as he added: "In your interest—and for *my* pleasure."

"I can't see how my interests have anything to do with your pleasure," returned the white man, stung by the touch of mockery in the Indian's tone.

"No? I suppose you can't. But you will understand presently," said the other, as if he enjoyed the situation and would prolong the pleasure it afforded him to witness the white man's uneasy fears.

"Suppose you explain yourself and be done with it," said Edwards shortly.

"You white men are all so impatient," murmured Natachee with taunting deliberation. "Really, you should learn a lesson of patience from the Indians. An Indian has need to be patient. He must wait and watch, long and untiringly, for his few opportunities, and then when his opportunity at last comes he must not fail through ill-advised haste to make the most of it. The white man squanders his pleasures as he squanders his wealth. With reckless, headlong, swinish eagerness to drink his fill at one gulp; he spills his cup of happiness before he has really tasted it. The Indian takes his pleasures with careful deliberation, as he compels his enemies to bear the pain of the torture, and so he enjoys in its fullness, to the last drop, whatever drink his gods are pleased to set before him."

"For God's sake say what you have come to say and be done with it!" cried Edwards.

The Indian laughed.

"Many a white man, in the old days, has begged an Indian to end it all quickly and have done with it. But," he added with triumphant insolence, "the rabbit that is caught by the fox does not dictate to his captor. I, Natachee the Indian, in my own way will tell you, Donald Payne, what I have come to say."

As the Indian spoke that name, the man, known as Hugh Edwards, sprang to his feet with a cry.

Natachee watched the effect of his words with cruel satisfaction.

When the Indian's victim had gained some control of his tortured nerves and had dropped weakly into his chair again, the red man said with savage irony:

"I regret, in a way, that Miss Hillgrove is not here to listen to my story."

The white man, with his head bowed in his hands, winced.

"It would add much to my pleasure if I could watch her enjoying it with you."

Hugh Edwards groaned as one in torment.

"But all that in good time," continued the Indian. "I must explain now how it came about that the rabbit, Donald Payne, is under the paw of the Indian fox.

"When Sheriff Burks described the criminal who escaped from the California penitentiary I saw a possible opportunity that promised me, Natachee, no little pleasure and satisfaction—an opportunity for which I have been waiting. Miss Hillgrove's agitation, her going to you, and your own action, confirmed my opinion as to where the convict who had so far escaped the officers was to be found. But I realized that it might be well to learn more. Thinking it unwise to appear too interested before the sheriff, I went to Tucson—first making sure that you would be here when I returned. In the white man's city, clothed properly in the white man's costume, with careful white man's manners, I was permitted to search the files of the white man's newspapers, and, thanks to my white education, to read the shameful account of this escaped convict's crime.

"I learned how Donald Payne, a promising young business man and a graduate of the California University, had held an important position of trust in a certain investment company. This company had been specifically planned and organized to attract the savings of small investors. Its appeal was to the better class of workmen, who out of their meager earnings were ambitious to put by something for the better education of their children— widows, with a little life insurance money upon the income of which they must exist—school-teachers, who must save against that dread day when they could no longer work—stenographers, clerks, and that class of poor whose education and tastes were above their earnings, and in whose hearts hope was kept alive by the promise of safe and honest returns from their hard-saved pennies. Every dollar in that institution of trust represented honest human effort and worthy ambition and heroic selfsacrifice.

"Oh, it was a white man's enterprise, born of a white man's devilish cunning, and carried out with a white man's remorseless cruelty to its damnable end. When the people's confidence had been won, and they had been persuaded to place enough of their savings in the hands of these spoilers to make it worth while, the company failed. The investors lost everything. The promoters—the principals of the company—gained everything. But Donald Payne, the brilliant young financial genius whose manipulation brought about the wreck, went to San Quentin prison.

"He had served eighteen months of his sentence when he escaped. His mother, a widow, brokenhearted over the shame and dishonor, scorned and ostracized by her neighbors and friends, humiliated by the cruel publicity, died in less than a month after her son was pronounced guilty. Donald Payne is without doubt the most hated, the most despised name in this decade."

The man who, during the Indian's deliberate recital, had sat cowering in his chair, raised his haggard face. His eyes were dull with anguish, his lips were drawn and white; but in spite of his ghastly appearance there was a strange air of dignity in his manner as he said hoarsely:

"And is that all you know?"

The Indian waited a little as if to give the greatest possible significance to his answer, then:

"No, not quite all. I know that this escaped convict, Donald Payne, has learned to love a woman. And I know that this woman loves this man, who is hiding from the officers who would send him back to prison."

"Yes," said the white man, hoarsely, "that is true. If it is any satisfaction to you, I confess my love for Marta Hillgrove. I have every reason to believe in her love for me, and—I—dare not—for her sake—tell her of my love."

He rose to his feet and stood before the Indian with a dignity and strength that won a gleam of admiration from the dark eyes of his tormentor, and in a voice ringing with passionate earnestness cried:

"But, listen, you damned red savage. You do not yet know all the truth. Donald Payne was never guilty of the crime for which he was sentenced. I was an innocent tool in the hands of the real criminal. It was a part of his plan from the first that someone should be offered, a sacrifice, to satisfy the public. He schemed far ahead to prove someone guilty and thus secure himself. I was chosen for that end. I was promoted to a position of trust with my sacrifice in view. It was all planned, arranged, and carried out. The man who robbed the people and for whose crime I was sent to prison is today living in Los Angeles in safety and luxury with the wealth he acquired through the company which he promoted and wrecked.

"The people who hate me, because they believe me guilty, do not know. The papers that branded me with shame and heralded my disgrace to every corner of the world do not know. The jury that convicted me did not know. The judge did not know. My mother did not know. The penitentiary does not know. The officers who would drag me back to it all do not know. *But I know—I know—I know!*"

He stood madly, superbly defiant, uplifted for the moment by the strength of his own asserted innocence. Then suddenly, as a beef animal falls under the blow of the butcher's killing maul, he dropped into his chair, where he writhed in an agony greater than any physical suffering could have wrought.

The deep voice of the watching Indian broke the silence.

"Good! It is even better than I could have believed. In my wildest dreams I never hoped to see a white man suffer such unmerited torture. In time, perhaps, you will even come to a degree of sympathy for an Indian, and to understand, a little, his feeling toward the white race."

When Hugh Edwards was able to speak again he said with dreary hopelessness:

"They will come for me in the morning, I suppose?"

"They? Who?"

"The officers—have you not told them?"

Natachee laughed.

"I tell the officers what I know about you? I give you up for them to take you back to the penitentiary? No—no—you do not seem to have grasped the purpose of my efforts in your behalf. I shall keep you for myself. I have too much pleasure in you to permit anyone to take you away from me. You shall go with me, and together we, the two outcasts, we who are outcasts because of nothing that we have done, but only because someone wished by our misfortune and suffering to gain riches, we shall enjoy life together as we can."

The note of exaltation that was in his voice, or some hint of a sinister purpose in his manner, aroused the white man.

"You mean that you are going to help me to escape?"

"From your white man's laws, yes. From me, no—not yet—not until I am through with you."

"Explain yourself," demanded the other. "What is it that you propose? I don't understand."

"It is this," returned the Indian. "You cannot stay here because any day—tomorrow even—the sheriff may come for you. You cannot go from this Canyon of Gold because you would surely be caught, unless you could leave this country, and that you cannot do because you have no money. You shall come with me. With me you will be safe from the law. No one will know where you are. No one shall ever find you. I, Natachee, know these mountains as no white man can ever know them. I will hide you."

There was something in the Indian's face that made Hugh Edwards gaze at him in wondering silence.

The Indian continued:

"I will show you where you can dig more gold than ever you would find here. Who knows, perhaps you may even find the Mine with the Iron Door. With gold enough you could make your way to safety. You could even take the woman you love with you. And so you shall work and dream and dream—and I, Natachee—I will help you to dream. If your dream never comes true, if your labor is all in vain, if you never find the Mine with the Iron Door, or if, while you are toiling for the gold you need, the woman you love should become the wife of your friend Saint Jimmy, why, that will not be my fault. I will help you to dream. It will be for you to find the gold that will make your dream come true—*if you can*."

The Indian spoke those last three words with fiendish deliberation and sinister meaning that was unmistakable.

Hugh Edwards understood.

"You are a devil."

"No, I am Natachee the Indian—you are a white man."

"You would save me from prison so that you might feast your damned revengeful spirit on my suffering."

"It is a help for you to understand exactly my purpose," returned the Indian.

"What if I refused to go with you?"

"You will not refuse."

"Why?"

"If you go with me you take your only possible chance for the future. You might, you know, find the gold. If you do not go, I shall send you back to prison."

"I will go."

"Good, but—you must understand. You will leave here with me tonight. There will be no message—no hint to tell anyone why you have gone, or where, or that you will ever come again. As long as you are with me you will be as one dead to all who have ever known you."

"But Marta—Miss Hillgrove—" cried the other.

Drawing himself up with the air of a conqueror, the Indian answered coldly:

"I, Natachee, have spoken."

When morning came, Marta saw no smoke rising from the chimney of Hugh Edwards' cabin. At first she told herself, with a laugh, that Hugh was sleeping later than usual, and went happily about her own early morning work. But as the hours passed and there was no sign of life about the neighboring cabin, she became uneasy. By the time breakfast was over and the Pardners had gone to their work, the girl was fully convinced that all was not right and went to investigate.

Knocking at the cabin door, she called:

"Hugh—Oh, Hugh!"

There was no answer.

She went hurriedly to the top of the bank above the place where he worked.

He was not there.

Running back to the cabin she knocked again.

"Hugh—Oh, Hugh! What is the matter?"

There was no sound.

Pushing open the door she stood on the threshold. The room was empty.

The truth forced itself upon the girl with overwhelming weight. Hugh Edwards was gone. He had not merely left his cabin for an hour or a day. He had not stepped out somewhere to return again presently. He was *gone*. Sometime during the night he had packed his things and had disappeared with no parting word—no good-by—no promise—leaving no message. He had vanished.

The girl was stunned. She argued with herself dully that she must be mistaken—that it could not be so. Hugh, her Hugh, would never do such a cruel, cruel thing.

From the open doorway she looked out at the familiar scene, at the canyon walls, the mountain ridges and peaks, her home—nothing was changed. She turned again to the empty, silent room. Hugh was gone.

But there must be something—some word to tell her—to explain.

Carefully, with slow, leaden movements, she searched every corner of the bare room. She looked in the cupboard, under the bunk, in every crevice of the walls. She even searched with a stick among the dead ashes in the fireplace. There was nothing.

She did not cry out. The hurt was too deep. She sat on the threshold of the empty cabin and tried to make it all seem real.

It was two hours later when Saint Jimmy found her sitting there.

CHAPTER XXI
THE WAY OF A RED MAN

THE weeks of the "Little Spring" passed. The blossoms vanished from mountain and foothill and mesa and desert. The air grew crisp with the tang of frost. On the higher elevations the cold winds moaned through the junipers and cedars—wailed among the peaks and shrieked about the cliffs and crags. Again on Mount Lemmon the snow gleamed, white and cold, among the somber pines.

In the wild remote region of the upper Cañada del Oro the man, known to his friends in the Canyon of Gold as Hugh Edwards, lived with his captor, Natachee the Indian.

The white man was not a prisoner of force—rather was he a captive of circumstance. But captive and prisoner he was, none the less. He was held by the red man's threat to reveal his real name and identity as the convict who had escaped from San Quentin, together with that hope so cunningly offered by the Indian—the hope of finding the gold that would bring him freedom and the woman he loved.

Every day the white man toiled with pick and shovel in a hidden gulch where the Indian had shown to him a little gold in the sand and gravel. Every night before the fire in the Indian's hut he brooded over his memories, dreamed dreams of freedom and love, or sat despondent with the meager returns of his day's labor. And always the Indian held out to him the possibilities of tomorrow. Tomorrow he might, at one stroke of his pick, open a golden vein of such magnitude that the realization of all his dreams would be assured—tomorrow—tomorrow.

His small hoard of gold increased so slowly that, unless he should strike a rich pocket, it would be years before he could accumulate enough to win his freedom and his happiness. But gold was his only hope. And every day he found enough to justify the belief that all he needed was near to his hand if only he could find it. He was held by that chain of tomorrows.

In the meantime, what of Marta? Would her love endure? With no explanation of his sudden disappearance—with no word of love from him—no promise of his return—no message to bid her hope—would she wait for him? Was her faith in him strong enough to stand under such a cruel test?

Many times during the first weeks of his strange captivity he begged the Indian for permission to send some word to the woman he loved. But the red man invariably answered, "No," with the cold warning that if he made any attempt to communicate with anyone, he should be returned to prison. When the white man realized that his importunities only served to give the Indian a cruel pleasure, he ceased to plead.

Then one evening just at dusk the red man said:

"Come, my friend, this will not do at all. You are not nearly so entertaining as you were. You need inspiration—come with me."

He led the way to a point on the mountain ridge not far above the hut. The colors of the sunset were still bright in the western sky and behind them the higher peaks and crags were glowing in the light, but far below in the Canyon of Gold and over the desert beyond, the deepening dusk lay like a shadowy sea.

"Look!" said the Indian, pointing into the gloomy depths. "Do you see it—down there directly under that lone bright star? Almost as if it were a reflection of the star, only not so cold?"

"Do you mean that light?"

"Yes, you have good eyes for a white man," answered the Indian. "I am glad. I feared you might not be able to see it."

He paused and the other, watching the tiny red point in the darkness so far below, waited.

"That light is in the home of your friends, the Pardners and their daughter."

The Indian's victim muttered an exclamation.

"In fact," continued Natachee slowly as if to make every word effective, "it shines through the window of Miss Hillgrove's room."

The white man stood with his eyes fixed on that distant light, as one under a spell, then suddenly he whirled about, cursing his tormentor for bringing him there.

The Indian smiled, as in the old days one of his savage ancestors might have smiled in triumph, at a cry of pain successfully wrung from a victim of the torture. Then he said with stern but melancholy dignity:

"I, Natachee, often come here to sit on this spot from which one may look so far over the homeland of my Indian fathers. But for Natachee there is no light in the window of love. Where you, a white man, see the light, the red man sees only darkness. For Natachee the Indian there is no soft fire of a woman's love and home and happy children. Where the fires of the Indian's home life and love once burned, there are now only cold ashes and blackened embers. I shall often see you up here watching your star that is so near. But for me, Natachee, there is no star. The dark clouds of the white man's lust for gold have hidden all the stars in the red man's sky."

In spite of his own suffering, Hugh Edwards was moved to pity.

On another occasion the Indian told his victim of Marta's visit to his hut that night of the storm. He called attention to the fact that the very chair in which Hugh was sitting was the chair in which she had sat before the fire. The couch upon which Hugh slept was the couch upon which she had slept. Hugh's place at the table had been her place.

Invariably, when he saw that the white man was nearing the limit of his endurance, the Indian would hold before him the promise of the future—the love and happiness that would be his when he should find the gold—the gold that he would perhaps strike—tomorrow.

At times the Indian would be gone for two or three days. Always he left with no word or hint that he was going. The white man would awaken in the morning to find himself alone in the hut, or perhaps the Indian would disappear at a moment when Hugh's back was turned, or again Edwards, upon returning from his work in the evening, would find that Natachee had left the place sometime during his absence. Invariably, when the red man reappeared, he came in the same unexpected and unannounced manner. The white man never knew when to look for him, nor where. Often the captive would look up from his work to find the Indian only a few feet away, watching him.

At times, when Natachee returned from an absence of a day or more, he would tell his victim of Marta—how he had seen and talked with her—how she looked—what she was doing—painting such true and vivid pictures of the girl that the captive's heart would ache with longing. Then the Indian, watching with devilish cunning the effect of his words, would assure his victim that the girl loved him but that she believed he had left her because he did not care for her, and that the grief of her disappointment and loneliness was seriously affecting her health.

"What a pity," the Indian would say mockingly, "that you cannot find the gold!" And then he would picture the happiness that would come to this man and woman—how they would go together to a place of peace and security—how, in the fullness of their love and in the joys of their companionship, the pain and suffering would all be forgotten. "If," he always added, "you could only find the gold."

Again the red man, with fiendish skill, would tell how he had seen Saint Jimmy and Marta together. He would talk of Saint Jimmy's love for her—of his tender devotion and care, and of the girl's affection for her teacher. He would relate how they spent hours together—how, in her grief, Marta had sought the comforting companionship of her gentle friend.

"I fear," Natachee would say, "that if you do not find the gold soon it will be too late. What a tragedy it would be for you, for Doctor Burton, and for the girl, if, when you are able to go to her, you should find her the wife of your friend. But tomorrow, perhaps, you will find the gold."

Every evening at sunset, when he thought that the Indian was away somewhere in the mountains, Hugh Edwards would climb to that place on the ridge from which he could see that tiny point of red light so far below in the dark depth of the Canyon of Gold. And not infrequently, when the light had at last gone out, he would return to the hut to learn that the red man had been watching him.

When, under the torment of the Indian's cruel art, the victim would rebel, Natachee talked of the prison—of the future of shame and horror that awaited the returned convict if he should again fall into the clutches of the law. Reminded thus that his only chance was in finding gold the man would return to his labor with exhausting energy.

And Hugh Edwards, with his lack of experience in such things, never once dreamed that all the gold he dug in that hidden gulch was put there by the crafty Indian. Night after night when the white man was sleeping, Natachee stole from the hut to the place where his victim toiled, and there "salted" the sand and gravel with a small quantity of the precious metal.

In her home in the Canyon of Gold, Marta waited, as so many women have waited while their men toiled for the yellow treasure that meant happiness. She could not understand. But neither could she doubt Hugh Edwards' love. She only knew that some day he would come again. With Saint Jimmy and Mother Burton to help her, she would be patient.

More than ever, in those days of her waiting, the Pardner's girl depended for strength and courage and guidance upon her two friends in the little white house on the mountain side. More than ever, they were dear to her.

The Pardners too had faith that their neighbor would return.

"An' when he comes," said old Bob, "you can bet your pile he's comin' with bells on. We don't know what it is that has took him away so suddenlike, but whatever it is, it ain't nothin' that we'll be ashamed of when we know."

And Thad, with characteristic fervor, added:

"Well, Holy Cats, there ain't no law, leastwise in this here Cañada del Oro, that says a man has got to advertise every time he makes a move. You're tootin'—the boy'll come back, an' he'll come with head up an' steppin' high—that's what I'm meanin'."

It was on one of these occasions, when the Indian was taunting his victim with the assurance that more gold than he needed was within his reach if only he knew where to look, that the white man turned on his tormentor with a contemptuous laugh.

"Do you think that I am fool enough to believe that you actually know of any such rich deposit near here?"

The words seemed to have a marked effect upon the Indian. Hugh saw, with a thrill of satisfaction and not a little wonder, that he had by chance broken through the red man's armor of stoical composure.

Natachee threw up his head and held himself stiffly erect with the pride of a savage conqueror, while his eyes were gleaming with intense mental excitement, and his voice rang with challenging force, as he said:

"You think that I, Natachee, am lying when I say that I know where there is gold beyond even a white man's dream of wealth?"

"I know you are lying," returned Hugh coldly. "Your talk of great wealth so near when I am finding so little is pure fiction. Because you know that I would almost give my soul to find a reasonably rich pocket, even, you have invented the story of this marvelously rich deposit, to torture me. If I believed it were true, I might, under the circumstances, feel worked up over it, but as it is you may as well save your breath. You are not worrying me in the least."

"Good!" said Natachee, "the night is very dark. If the white man is not a coward he will come with me."

"Go with you?" exclaimed the other. "Where?"

"You shall never know *where*," replied the Indian. "But you shall see that I, Natachee, do not lie."

From a peg in the wall he took a short rope and from the cupboard drawer a cloth and two candles. One of the candles he offered to Hugh with an insolent smile.

"If you are not afraid of the ghosts that, in the night and the darkness, haunt the Canyon of Gold."

The amazed white man, snatching the candle, motioned impatiently for the Indian to proceed.

CHAPTER XXII
THE LOST MINE

FROM the door of the hut the Indian led the way into the darkness.

There was no friendly moon. The sky was overcast with lowering clouds that shut out the light of the stars. From the thick blackness of the canyon far below, the sullen murmur of the creek came up like the growl of angry voices from the depth of some black pit. The mountains seemed to breathe like gigantic monsters in a weird, dream world. The very air was heavy with the mystery of the night.

They had not gone a hundred yards before the white man lost all sense of direction. As they made their way down the steep side of the mountain he could scarcely distinguish the form of the Indian who was within reach of his hand.

Presently Natachee stopped, and, lighting the candle he carried, said:

"See, there is your pick and shovel. Are you satisfied that this is the place where you work?"

"Certainly, I can see that," returned the other wonderingly.

"Good!" returned the Indian. "Now we will go only a little way from this place."

He extinguished the candlelight, and the inky darkness enveloped them like a blanket.

"But," he added, "I must first make sure of your never again going as we shall go. I will blindfold you and you will follow me by holding fast to this rope. Are you willing?"

There was a taunting sneer in his tone that would have goaded the white man into any reckless adventure.

"As you like," he said shortly.

When the cloth was bound securely about Hugh's eyes, the Indian caught him by the arms and whirled him about until he was completely bewildered. Then he felt one end of the rope thrust into his hand.

"Come," said the Indian, and gave a slight pull on the rope.

It was impossible for the white man to form any idea as to their course. At times they climbed upward, then again they descended as rapidly. At other times they made their way along some steep slope. Now and then the Indian bade him go on hands and knees, or warned him to move with care and to hold fast to the shrubs and bushes. At last Hugh Edwards knew that they were entering a cavern by an opening barely large enough for them to crawl through. He could not even guess the dimensions of this underground chamber, but he imagined that it was a passage or tunnel, for as they went on he touched a wall on his right and the Indian cautioned him to keep his head down.

For some distance they walked in this fashion, then Natachee stopped, and the white man heard him strike a match. A moment later his blindfold was removed.

"Your candle," said Natachee sharply, and lighted it from the one he himself held.

The white man gazed curiously about him.

"Look!" cried the Indian. "Look and say if I, Natachee, lied when I told you of the gold that is so near the place where you work—if only you knew where to find it."

Natachee the Indian had not lied. Thousands upon thousands of dollars in golden value lay within the circle of the candlelight.

Hugh Edwards stood amazed. He could not know the full extent of the vein, but a fortune of staggering proportions was within sight. The farther end of the chamber was an irregular mass of rocks and earth that had quite evidently fallen and slid from above; but the remaining walls and ceiling were as obviously cut by human hands.

The white man looked at his companion inquiringly.

"An old mine?"

The Indian, with an air of triumph, answered:

"The Mine with the Iron Door."

As one half dreaming feels for something real and tangible, Hugh Edwards said hesitatingly:

"But why, knowing this, have you not made use of it—why do you leave such wealth buried here?"

"You forget that I am an Indian," the red man answered. "If I, Natachee, were to tell the secret of the Mine with the Iron Door, would the white men permit me to retain this treasure or to use it for my people? When has your race ever permitted an Indian to have anything that a white man wanted for himself? Suppose it were possible for me to take this treasure without revealing the secret of the mine—of what use would its gold be to me? Could I, an Indian, use such wealth without bringing upon myself and my people, envy, hatred and persecution from those who say that this is a white man's country?

"And suppose I could use this gold? What would an Indian do with gold? The things that the white man buys with gold mean nothing to an Indian. We do not want the white man's things. We do not want your factories and railroads and ships and banks and churches. We do not want your music, your art, your libraries and schools. An Indian does not want any of the things that this yellow stuff means to the white man.

"Could I, with this gold, restore to my people the homeland of their fathers? Could I destroy your cities, your government, your laws and all the institutions of your civilization that you have built up in this, the land that you have taken by force and treachery from my people? Could I, Natachee, with this gold bring back the forests you have cut down, the streams you have dried up or poisoned, the lands you have made desolate? Could I bring back the antelope, the deer and all the life that the white man has destroyed?"

Stooping, he caught up a piece of the quartz that was heavy with the gold it carried. Holding it in the light of the candle, he said:

"Before the white man came, this, to the Indians, was only a pretty stone, of no more value than any other bright-colored pebble. If the red man used it at all it was as an ornament of trivial significance—of no real worth. But to the white man, this is everything. It is honor and renown—it is achievement and success—it is the beginning and the end of life—it is sacrifice and hardship—it is luxury and want—it is bloody war with its murdered millions—it is government—it is law—it is religion—it is love. And it was this—this bit of worthless yellow dirt—that brought the first white man to the Indians. For gold, the white adventurers braved the dangers of an unknown ocean and forced their way into an unknown land. For gold, they have robbed and killed the people whose homeland they invaded, until today we are as dead grass and withered leaves in the pathway of the fire of the white man's greed. We are as a handful of desert dust in the whirlwind of your civilization."

He threw the piece of quartz aside with a gesture of loathing, and stood for a moment with his head lowered in sorrow.

And once again Hugh Edwards, in spite of the cruel torture to which the Indian had subjected him, felt a thrill of pity for his tormentor.

But before the white man could find words to express his emotions, Natachee suddenly lifted his head, and with the cruel light of savage exultation blazing in his eyes, went a step toward his startled companion.

"Do you understand now why I have brought you here? Do you understand my purpose in permitting you to see, with your own eyes, the gold of the Mine with the Iron Door?

"Your only hope of freedom, from the hell to which you have been condemned through a white man's trickery and by your white man's laws, is in gold. Only through the possession of gold can you hope to win the woman you love and who loves you.

"You say you would give your soul for the gold which means so much to you. Good! I believe you. I am glad. Here is the gold—look at it—handle it—dream of all that it would bring you. Here is freedom from your hell— here is love—here is happiness—here is the woman you love. It is all here, within reach of your hand, and you shall never touch one grain of it. If you had a hundred souls to offer in exchange, you should not touch one grain of it. Because you are a white man, and because I am an Indian.

"I, Natachee, have spoken."

The meaning of the Indian's words burned in the white man's brain. Slowly he looked about that treasure chamber as if summing up in his mind all that it might mean to him. His nerves and muscles were tense with agony. Beads of sweat glistened on his forehead. His face was twisted in a grimace of pain. And in the agony of his torture a dreadful purpose came.

The watching Indian saw, and his sinewy hand loosed the knife in his belt, as his deep voice broke the silence of the old mine.

"No, you will not try that. You are unarmed. I would kill you before you could strike a blow. There is no hope for you there. Your one chance is to dig for the gold you need. You might strike it rich, you know. Who can say—to-morrow—another stroke of your pick. The hope that brought the first white man to the Cañada del Oro is your only hope. As so many of your race have labored in the Canyon of Gold you shall labor—you shall find your gold—if you can."

The white man bowed his head.

Natachee went to him with the cloth to bind his eyes.

Quietly Hugh Edwards submitted to the bandage. The Indian extinguished the light of the candle and thrust the end of the rope into his victim's unresisting hand.

"The white man is wise to take the one chance that is his," said the Indian. "Come. Tomorrow, perhaps, you will find gold."

Through the remaining weeks of the winter Hugh Edwards toiled with all his strength for the grains of yellow metal that the Indian secretly permitted him to find. Day and night the knowledge of the Mine with the Iron Door tortured him. Many times he was tempted to abandon all hope, and, by surrendering himself to the officers of the law, escape at least the torment of his strange situation. But always he was held by the one chance—tomorrow he might find the gold that meant freedom and Marta and love.

And at last, one day in spring, when the mountain slopes again were bright with blossoms—when the gold of the buckbean shone in the glades, and whispering bells were nodding in the shadows of the canyon walls—when the glory of the ocotillo, the flaming sword, was on the foothills, and "our Lord's candles" again fit the mesas with their torches of white, Hugh Edwards looked up from his work in the gulch to see a stranger.

CHAPTER XXIII
SONORA JACK

WHEN he saw that he was discovered, the man who was watching Hugh Edwards came leisurely forward. At the same instant Hugh thought that he glimpsed another figure farther away on the mountain side.

The stranger explained his presence in the neighborhood by saying that he was hunting and had wandered farther from his camp than he had intended. For nearly an hour he and Edwards visited in the manner of men who meet by chance in the lonely open places. Then with a careless *adios* he went on his way down the canyon.

When Hugh, at the close of his day's work, went up to the cabin, Natachee was not at home. But when the white man had finished his supper the Indian appeared, coming in his usual silent, unexpected way. As he set about preparing his own supper, Natachee said:

"You had visitors today."

Hugh was too accustomed to the red man's uncanny way of knowing things to be in the least surprised at his companion's remark.

He answered indifferently:

"I had a visitor."

"There were two in the neighborhood," returned Natachee. "I saw their tracks just before dark."

Hugh told how only one man had talked with him but that he thought he had caught a glimpse of another.

"That was the Lizard," said Natachee. "I would know his tracks anywhere. I have seen them often. His right foot turns in in a peculiar way and his boot heels are always worn on the inside."

Hugh Edwards caught his breath.

"Do you think they were—"

"After you?" Natachee finished for him. "I can't say yet. It might be. What was the man who talked with you like?"

Hugh described the stranger.

"Medium height, rather heavy, black hair, eyes very dark, a Mexican, or at least part Mexican, I would say."

"Did he ask many questions about you?"

"No more than anyone would naturally ask."

"Did he show any curiosity about me?"

"No, you were not mentioned. He said he was hunting but he seemed to be rather interested, too, in prospecting and mining, and asked a lot of questions about the country up here as if he had a general idea of the lay of the land but was not exactly sure."

Natachee said no more until he had finished his supper. Then, going to a corner of the cabin at the head of his bed, he pulled up a loose board in the floor, and from the hiding place took a revolver with its holster and belt of cartridges.

Offering the weapon to the astounded white man, he said with a meaning smile:

"I brought this for you from Tucson last fall. But, considering everything, I thought that it might be just as well for you not to have it unless some occasion should arise. I am going to leave you for a little while. Until I return you must keep this gun within reach of your hand every minute—day and night."

Hugh took the weapon awkwardly.

"Do you know how to use it?" asked Natachee sharply.

The other laughed.

"Oh, yes. I know how, but I couldn't hit a flock of barns."

"You must carry it just the same," returned the Indian. "But don't do any practicing. Keep your eyes open for anyone who may be prowling around and don't let them see you if you can avoid it. This stranger may be a hunter or a prospector—he may be an officer—he may be something else. I shall know before I see you again."

Taking his bow and quiver of arrows, the Indian went out into the night.

For two days and nights Hugh Edwards was alone. Then Natachee returned.

When the Indian had eaten, with the appetite of a man who has been long hours without food, he said:

"The man who talked with you is called Sonora Jack. He is a half-breed Mexican; his real name is John Richards.

"For several years this Sonora Jack, with a band of Mexicans and white outlaws, operated in this section of the Southwest. They rustled cattle, robbed trains, looted banks and stores, and held up everybody they chanced to run across. With their headquarters somewhere south of the line, it was not so easy for the United States authorities to capture them, but after a particularly cold-blooded murder of a poor old couple who were traveling by wagon through the country, the officers and the people were so aroused that Sonora Jack, with a large reward on his head, moved on to other less dangerous hunting grounds. It is generally believed that he went south somewhere in Mexico."

"But are you sure that it was this same Sonora Jack that called on me?"

The Indian smiled.

"As sure as I am that you are Donald Payne."

Hugh Edwards flushed as he returned coldly:

"Please don't forget that Donald Payne is dead."

"That depends," retorted Natachee dryly.

The white man did not overlook the Indian's meaning. For a time he did not speak, then he asked:

"But what has brought this outlaw here to the Cañada del Oro?"

Natachee's face was grave as he answered:

"The Mine with the Iron Door."

Hugh Edwards uttered an exclamation.

"You mean that he has come to look for the lost mine?"

For several minutes the Indian did not reply, but sat as if lost in thought, then he said, as one reaching a grave decision:

"Listen—I will tell you exactly what I have learned. It is of very great importance to us both.

"This Sonora Jack, with a Mexican who I am quite sure is a member of his old band, first appeared in the Cañada del Oro several days ago. They came in by the Oracle trail and called on Doctor Burton and his mother, telling them that they were prospectors. I have talked to the Burtons and they do not dream of the real characters or mission of the two strangers who camped at Juniper Spring.

"Apparently Sonora Jack and his companion met the Lizard, for they moved down the canyon and are now living with the Lizard and his people. The Lizard seems to be helping them with his supposed knowledge of the country. Sonora Jack has a map, crudely drawn, and evidently very old. Under the drawing in one corner is written:

"'La mina con la puerta de fierro en la Cañada del Oro'—The mine with the door of iron in the Canyon of the Gold."

Again Hugh Edwards uttered an exclamation of astonishment.

"But how in the world do you know all this?" he demanded.

The Indian explained.

"In the Lizard's house the table is close under one of the windows. While Sonora Jack and his Mexican and the Lizard were looking at the map and trying to determine the exact location of a certain gulch that was many years ago filled by a landslide, I also looked."

"But those dogs," cried the white man, "they were ready to eat me one night when I happened to call there."

"You are not an Indian," Natachee returned calmly. "Bows and arrows make no sound. The Lizard will be short of dogs until he has an opportunity to steal some new curs."

"Fine!" said Hugh.

Natachee continued:

"I not only saw their map, but, as it happens, there is a little place under the sill of that particular window where the adobe wall has crumbled away from the wood, and so I could hear what was said as clearly as if I had been sitting at the table with them.

"The Lizard told them all about the Indian who is commonly supposed to know the secret of the lost mine. Some of the things he said I rather think you would agree with. He also told them a good deal about you. He knows you only by the name of Hugh Edwards, but I must say that some of the things he reported were not what you might call complimentary."

"I imagine not," returned Hugh.

Again Natachee, for some time, seemed to be weighing some matter of greater moment than the things he had related; while the white man, seeing the Indian so absorbed in his own thoughts, waited in silence.

"There was something else that Sonora Jack and his companion talked about," said Natachee, at last, "something that I cannot understand."

Then looking straight into the white man's eyes he asked slowly:

"Will you tell me all that you know about Miss Hillgrove and her two fathers?"

Hugh Edwards drew back and his face darkened. The Indian saw the effect of his words and raised his hand to check the white man's angry reply.

"I understand your thought," he said calmly. "But I assure you I am not amusing myself at your expense. It is for your interest as well as for mine that I ask."

Believing that the Indian was speaking sincerely, even though for some reason of his own, and prompted by his alarm at this mention of Marta, Hugh asked:

"Am I to understand that Miss Hillgrove was discussed by this outlaw and his companions?"

"Yes," said Natachee. "The Lizard told Sonora Jack all that he knew and perhaps more. I am asking you so that we may know how much of the Lizard's story is true."

In a few words Hugh related how the Pardners had found Marta when the girl was little more than a baby.

When he had finished the Indian said:

"I knew the story in a general way and the Lizard told it substantially as you have. But here is the amazing thing—Sonora Jack knows more about these two old prospectors and their partnership daughter than even you know."

Hugh Edwards was speechless with astonishment.

The Indian continued:

"When the Lizard first mentioned Miss Hillgrove's name, it was in connection with you, and Sonora Jack only laughed and made a coarse jest. But when the Lizard went on to tell of her relationship to Bob and Thad, the outlaw was so excited that he almost shouted. He asked question after question—her age—how long she and the Pardners had been in the Cañada del Oro—where they came from—everything—and as the Lizard answered, the outlaw would translate to his Mexican companion, who was as excited as Sonora Jack himself. And when the Lizard had told him all he could, the two talked together in Mexican a long time. I cannot repeat all that was said but Sonora Jack cried many times: 'It is the same girl, Jose, the very same—Jesu Cristo! what luck—what marvelous luck!'

"One thing is certain—this outlaw in some way expects to make a fortune through the old Pardners and their girl. I do not know how. But Sonora Jack said to the Mexican that whether they found the lost mine or not, their coming to the Cañada del Oro was certain now to make them both rich."

"Is it possible," asked Hugh, "that Thad and Bob were one time in any way mixed up with this Sonora Jack?"

"I thought of that," returned Natachee, "and the next day I watched to see if the outlaws went to the Pardners. They did—they spent nearly two hours talking with Miss Hillgrove and her fathers. Then they went with Thad and Bob down to their mine, leaving the girl at the house. They were with the Pardners over an hour."

Hugh Edwards was greatly disturbed by what Natachee had learned. His first fear, that the stranger who had talked with him was an officer, was as nothing compared with his fear now for Marta. All night he pondered over the situation with scarce an hour of sleep. When morning came he told the Indian that he was going back to his old cabin to be near the girl—prison or no prison.

"But can't you see what a foolish move that would be?" asked Natachee. "The Pardners know who you are. If they have been, in the past, connected with Sonora Jack, which is very possible, they will turn you over to the sheriff in short order to protect both the outlaw and themselves. If that should happen either through them or through anyone else, you certainly would be in no position to help Miss Hillgrove. You do not even know yet that Miss Hillgrove is in danger. Sonora Jack will do nothing until he has satisfied himself about the lost mine, which brought him into this country at the risk of his life. You can depend on that. While he is searching for the mine I may be able to learn more of his interest in the Pardners and their girl. Be patient or you will spoil everything."

And Hugh, because he felt that Natachee for the time being was his ally, listened to his advice. The white man did not deceive himself as to the real reason for the Indian's interest in the situation. Nor did the red man make any pretenses. But even at that, Hugh felt that he would be better able ultimately to protect Marta, if for the present he fell in with the red man's plan to learn the exact nature of Sonora Jack's interest in the girl.

All that forenoon Natachee did not leave his cabin. But after their noonday meal he followed Hugh down into the gulch where, for a long time, he sat on a rock watching the white man at his work. Then he went back to the hut on the mountain side above.

When Edwards, a little before sunset, climbed the steep way from the place of his labor up to the cabin, the Indian was gone.

No second glance was needed to tell the white man that the cabin had been the scene of a terrific struggle.

CHAPTER XXIV
THE WAY OF A WHITE MAN

WITH a cry of dismay Hugh ran to the place where he kept hidden his hoard of gold. His pitifully small earnings were untouched. Natachee's bow and quiver of arrows, without which the Indian never left the cabin, were in their usual place. His hunting knife, which was always in his belt, was lying on the floor. It was not difficult for Hugh to guess what had happened.

Sonora Jack, unable with the help of his map to find the Mine with the Iron Door, and believing that Natachee knew the location of the treasure had sought the Indian to force him to reveal the secret. While Natachee was in the gulch with Edwards, Sonora Jack and his companions had entered the cabin, and waiting there had taken the Indian by surprise when he returned. The ground in front of the cabin was trampled by horses, and the tracks of their iron shoes were clear, leading away down the mountain toward the lower canyon. There was no doubt in Hugh's mind but that the outlaws had taken Natachee away with them. Without hesitation he set out to follow the tracks as fast as he could in the failing light. He was wholly without experience in such matters, but the ground was soft from the winter rains and the three horses left a trail that was easy enough to follow.

When it became too dark to see, he was a mile or two from the cabin, well down on the steep slope of what he thought must be a spur of Samaniego Ridge. He had set out to follow the outlaws upon the impulse of the moment. In his excitement, he had not paused to think. But now, when he could no longer see the tracks, he was forced to stop and consider the situation with more deliberation.

Hugh Edwards realized that he was in every way but poorly equipped to meet such an emergency. What, he asked himself, could he do if he should succeed in finding the outlaws with their captive? If it had been a question of meeting Sonora Jack alone and bare-handed, he would have no reason to hesitate. Certainly he would not fear to face such an issue. Hugh Edwards was far from being either a weakling or a coward. But Sonora Jack was not alone. There were two others with him and they were undoubtedly well armed, while their desperate characters were clearly evidenced by their successful attack on Natachee. Hugh smiled grimly and touched the weapon at his side as he recalled how he had said to Natachee:

"I could not hit a flock of barns."

After all, why should he concern himself with Natachee's affairs? The red man had never professed anything even approaching friendship for him. For weeks the Indian had held him a prisoner and with all the cruelty and cunning of his savage fathers had tortured him. Why not abandon him now to his fate? Why not return to the hut, take what gold he had accumulated and make his way out of the country? But as quickly as these thoughts raced through his mind, Hugh Edwards dismissed them—Marta.

If Natachee had not told him of Sonora Jack's interest in the old prospectors and their partnership daughter it might, perhaps, have been possible for him to desert the Indian now. But in spite of his hatred for his tormentor, and in spite of the bitter, revengeful purpose which he knew inspired the red man's interest in his affairs and in the woman he loved, Hugh needed Natachee's help. Perhaps even now, at that very moment, the Indian was finding, through Sonora Jack, a key to the mystery of Marta Hillgrove's birth and parentage. At any cost he, Hugh Edwards, must find the outlaws and their captive.

But how? He could not go to Thad and Bob for help. Natachee had made the possible connection between the old prospectors and Sonora Jack too clear. Even if he could have found his way in the night to Marta's home, he would not dare appeal to them. Saint Jimmy—George Wheeler and his cowboys? It would be worse than useless for one of Hugh's inexperience to attempt to find his way such a distance through such a wild country in the darkness of the night. He realized hopelessly that he did not even know which way to start.

He decided at last that the only course possible for him was to wait with what patience he could for the morning, and then to continue following the tracks of the horses. He had barely reached this decision and settled down in the poor shelter of a manzanita bush to pass the long cold hours of discomfort and anxiety, when he saw, at some distance down the mountain from where he sat, a strange glow of light.

It was not a camp fire. It was too soft—too diffused. It was not like the light of that window which he had watched so many lonely hours. It was not so steady and it was nearer—much nearer. He could see the trees and bushes that fringed the top of a cliff. Why—that was it—the light was from below—there was a fire at the foot of that cliff. He could not see the fire itself because—why, of course—the cliff that was lighted from below was the other side of a narrow gorge. He was too far away, and the walls were too steep for him to see the bottom.

As quickly as possible, but with every care to make his movements noiseless, Hugh Edwards stole toward the light. In a few minutes, that seemed hours to him, he was close to the rim of the gorge. Lying flat on the ground, he crawled with even greater caution to the edge of the precipice, where through the fringe of grass and bushes he looked down.

The place was, as he had reasoned, a deep, narrow canyon with sheer walls of rock. The cliffs on the side where he lay were fully fifty feet from base to rim, and for about a hundred years they formed a half circle, giving a width to the little canyon at that point of about the same distance. At one end of this natural amphitheater, where a creek came tumbling down over granite ledges and bowlders, a man with his arms outstretched could almost touch both walls of the hall-like passage. The lower end was wider, with no rocks to obstruct the entrance. Except for the creek which ran close to the foot of the cliff opposite the semicircular side where Hugh lay, the floor was smooth and level with a number of mesquite trees and several giant cottonwoods. It was in the more open center of this arena that Hugh Edwards saw a thing that made him catch his breath with a shuddering gasp, while his heart pounded and his hand went to the gun on his hip.

On a large, altar-shaped rock that had been dislodged from the walls above by some force of nature, Natachee lay bound. The Indian was on his back with his arms and legs drawn down and tied securely to the rock, so that, save for his head, he was held immovable, but with no rope across his body.

Sonora Jack stood beside the rock giving directions to his companions, the Lizard and a Mexican, who were looking after the fire. Nearer the entrance to the amphitheater were three saddle horses. On the opposite side of the open space about the rock, and beyond the fire, the men had placed their rifles against the trunk of a cottonwood. The eyes of the man on the rim of the canyon wall had barely noted these details when Sonora Jack turned from his companions by the fire to Natachee.

"Well," he said, and every word carried distinctly to the man above, "how about it, Indio, you got something to say, yet?"

Natachee did not speak.

"You not want to tell, heh? All right, you're some bravo Indio, but you goin' to beg me to let you talk 'fore I get through with you. I got nothin' 'gainst you, but you know where that Mine with the Iron Door is an' sure as fire is hot you're goin' to lead me to it. I don't come all the way up here from Mexico City just for nothin'. You show me the old mine, an' you can put in the rest of your years growin' old nice an' easy. If you don't—" He paused significantly, then called to his two helpers: "Put plenty mesquite on that fire, boys, we want plenty good red coals. This Indio here needs a little warmin' up, I think." Bending over his victim he said again: "Well, how 'bout it, you goin' to come through?"

Save for the glittering light in the dark eyes of the red man, the outlaw might have been talking to a stone image.

Enraged by the silent strength of that opposing will, Sonora Jack went closer to the Indian's side.

"Mebby you no sabe what I'm goin' to do to you. Mebby you think I got you here on this rock just for a bluff. Not much, I ain't. If you don't come across an' show me that mine, I'm goin' to put 'bout a hatful of them red coals right here." With his open hand he slapped Natachee's naked chest. "You do what I say or I burn the red heart out of you, an' I ain't hurryin' the job neither. You ain't the first mule-head hombre I've made loosen up."

Hugh Edwards drew back from the edge of the cliff. For a single instant he was sick with horror. Then the blood of his race surged through his veins with tingling strength. In that moment it meant nothing to him that the man bound to the rock down there was an Indian. It made no difference that the red man, with cunning cruelty, had for weeks ingeniously tortured him to gratify a savage thirst for revenge against all white people. He did not, at the moment, even remember Marta and his need of Natachee's help. It mattered nothing that there were three of those fiends down there and that he was alone. He was conscious of but one thing: a thing that was born of his white man's soul. That deed of unspeakable brutality must not—should not—be accomplished.

Swiftly he made his way along the rim of the canyon toward the upper end of the semicircle. He felt as if he were acting in a dream, or as if some spirit over which he had no control dominated him. But even as he moved, a plan flashed before him, and he saw clearly every detail of the only part he could play with the slightest hope of success. The narrow passage through which the creek entered the amphitheater was hidden from the men by the deep shadows of the trees. Their rifles were on that side of the fire.

A short distance above the scene of the impending tragedy he found a place where he could descend, half sliding, half falling, to the creek, while the noise of the stream covered any sound from that direction. A moment more and he had let himself down over the rocks and bowlders, around which the waters roared, and stood behind the trunk of one of the giant cottonwoods, not a hundred feet from the outlaw and his companions. With sheer strength of will he restrained his impulse to rush forward and throw himself upon those fiends in human form as they bent over their fire.

He must wait. He must watch for the exact moment.

It was not long.

Sonora Jack, from the Indian's side, called to his companions:

"Ya chito tray la lumbre—bring the fire."

To Natachee, the outlaw said:

"One more time I ask you, Indio, are you goin' to take me to the mine?"

There was no answer.

The Lizard and the Mexican raked a quantity of live coals from the fire on to a flat rock.

Behind the tree, Hugh Edwards crouched in readiness.

The two men who were kneeling at the fire rose and started toward the Indian. Sonora Jack faced toward his victim. It was the moment for which the man behind the tree was waiting.

With all his strength, Hugh Edwards ran for the tree against which the three rifles were standing. He reached his goal at the same instant that the men with the coals of fire arrived at the rock.

With a shout, Hugh began emptying his revolver in the general direction of the outlaws.

The Lizard, with a scream of terror, ran for the horses. The Mexican and Sonora Jack, under the combined shock of that fusillade of shots from the direction of their rifles, with those accompanying yells and the Lizard's screaming flight, leaped for the safety of their mounts. The horses in their fright added to the confusion.

Dropping his revolver and snatching two of the rifles, Hugh ran forward to the Indian. By the time Sonora Jack and his companions had succeeded in mounting their struggling horses, he had cut the ropes that bound Natachee, and the Indian and the white man, from the shelter of the rock, were firing into the shadowy group of plunging animals and cursing men.

As the outlaws disappeared in the darkness beyond the entrance to the amphitheater, Natachee caught his rescuer by the arm:

"Quick, we must get out of this light before Sonora Jack gets hold of himself."

Swiftly he led the way up the creek.

An hour later, in the Indian's cabin, Natachee stood before his white companion. With an expression which Hugh Edwards had never before seen on that dark countenance, the red man spoke in the manner of his people.

"Before the winter snows came, a white rabbit was caught by an Indian fox. The snows are gone and the rabbit has become a mountain lion. Why has the lion saved his enemy, the fox, from Sonora Jack's fire?"

"Why," stammered Hugh, "I—I—really, you know, I couldn't do anything else. I saw the light, then I saw what those devils were going to do, and—well—I simply couldn't stand for it."

"I, Natachee the Indian, have no claim on you, a white man. I have been your enemy. I am an enemy to all of your blood. I have tortured you in every way I knew. I would have continued to torture you."

"That has nothing to do with it," retorted Hugh coldly. "I didn't do what I did because I thought you were my friend."

The Indian smiled with grave dignity.

"The live oak never drops its leaves like the cottonwood. The pine never blossoms like the palo verde. A coyote in the skin of a bear would still act like a coyote. A deer never forgets that it is not a wolf. You, Hugh Edwards, saved me, your enemy, from the coals of fire, because you could not forget your nature—because you could not forget that you are a white man. I, Natachee, will not forget that I am an Indian."

With these words he bowed his head and, turning, went to take his bow and quiver of arrows from beside the fireplace.

Standing in the doorway, he spoke again:

"I must go. Sonora Jack will not come here again tonight. If he should, I will be near. Sleep in peace. When I return I will have something to tell you."

All that following day, Hugh Edwards watched for another visit from Sonora Jack and his companions, and waited with no little anxiety for Natachee's return.

But the outlaws did not come again. It was a little after noon the second day when the Indian finally appeared. He was driving four burros equipped with packsaddles.

When Hugh expressed surprise at sight of the pack animals, Natachee offered no explanation. In stolid silence the Indian prepared his dinner. He ate as if he had not touched food for many hours. When he had finished he said simply:

"I must sleep. In two hours I will awaken. Then we will talk. Do not go away from the cabin, please. Watch! If you see anything moving on the mountain side, call me."

He threw himself on his couch and almost instantly was sound asleep.

Hugh Edwards, sitting just outside the cabin door, waited.

A gentle wind breathed through the trees of juniper and live oak and cedar and sighed among the cliffs and crags; and from below, faint and far away, came the murmur of the distant creek. He saw the sunlight, warm on the green of the cottonwoods and willows in the Canyon of Gold. He watched the cloud shadows drifting across the mountain slopes and ridges and, looking up to the high peaks, saw the somber pines against the blue of the sky.

A rock wren from a bowlder near by observed him with friendly eye and bobbed a cheerful greeting, and a painted redstart swung on a cat-claw bush. From somewhere on the side of the gulch where he worked came the exquisitely finished song of a grosbeak. The towering cliffs behind the cabin echoed the hoarse croaking call of a raven and now and then there was a flash of black and white and a bulletlike whiz, as a company of white-throated swifts shot past.

But no human thing moved within the range of his vision.

As he watched, he pondered the meaning of the Indian's manner. The red man had often remained silent for days at a time. But now, under the peculiar circumstances, Hugh felt that there was an unusual significance in Natachee's native reticence. What had the Indian been doing? Where had he been? What had he learned? What was the meaning of those four burros?

The deep voice of the Indian broke in upon his thoughts. Natachee was standing in the doorway.

CHAPTER XXV
THE WAYS OF GOD

THE Indian spoke with that strange dignity of mingled pride and pathos that so often moved the white man to pity:

"Hugh Edwards, the mountain streams that are born up there among those peaks are obedient to the will of Him from whose hand the snows fall. From their cradles among the roots of the pines, they start for the sea that lies many days beyond that faint blue line yonder, where the earth and the sky become one. Nor is there any doubt but that the waters, in the end, reach the appointed place for which they set out. But how or when, no mortal can say, for the creeks are forced to change their plans. The clearly marked trail upon which they first set out comes to an end. The waters that run with such noisy strength down the mountain's slopes sink into the desert, and are lost forever to human eyes.

"It is so with the plans of men. The will of Him who sets the unknown ways by which these mountain waters shall reach the sea determines also the unknown ways that men shall go through this life, even to that place where the spirit's journey ends. The trail, which at first is so clearly marked, sinks from sight and is lost in a desert of things which no mortal can know.

"I, Natachee, in following the trail of my destiny, have come to such a place. The course which lay before me as plain as the bed of a mountain stream is changed. I can no longer go the way I had planned. I am an Indian. You have said many times that I am a devil—good. Under certain circumstances every man is a devil. Change the circumstances and the devil becomes something else. Listen carefully now and hear with your heart what I, Natachee, shall say.

"Sonora Jack and his Mexican have left the home of the Lizard, but the Lizard has gone with them. The three are camped in the foothills a few miles from the home of the Pardners and their girl. They are hiding there because they do not know how many there were in the party that rescued me. It was well that you made so much noise. But Sonora Jack will not hide long. When he is sure that he is not being followed by a posse, he will move. But he will not again attempt to find the Mine with the Iron Door. He fears to stay longer in the Canyon of Gold lest he be prevented from carrying out some other plan. I could not learn what that other plan is. I know only that it concerns Marta Hillgrove and the Pardners. Whatever Sonora Jack plans, it is not good. We must go at once that we may protect your woman."

Hugh Edwards spoke as one who finds it hard to believe what he has heard:

"You say that *we* must go—that we must protect Marta? Do you mean that you will help me to save her from whatever threatens through this Sonora Jack?"

Natachee bowed his head for a moment, then met the white man's eyes proudly.

"Did I not say that the trail which I, Natachee, was following had suddenly changed as the course of a mountain stream is lost in the desert sands? When Sonora Jack and his companions caught me and tied me with their ropes to that rock, I was as helpless as a dove in the coils of a snake. Do you think that I, Natachee, would have weakened under their torture fire? Sonora Jack would have burned the heart out of the Indian's breast but he never would have heard from the Indian's lips the secret of the Mine with the Iron Door. It is not a new thing for an Indian to be tortured for gold. I, Natachee, would have died as so many of my fathers have died, without a word. But you, a white man, obedient to your strange white man's nature, offered your own life to save the life of Natachee the Indian, who had for months been torturing you. The trail of hatred and revenge that lay so clear before the red man is lost in the strange desert of the white man's ways. I, Natachee, cannot understand, but who am I to disobey? The life you saved belongs to you, Hugh Edwards. I, Natachee, am yours until I pay the debt. Can the heart of the white man understand?"

The Indian, with an earnestness that left no doubt of his sincerity, offered his hand. And Hugh Edwards, though he did not yet realize the full significance of the Indian's words, gladly accepted the proffered friendship, saying as he grasped the Indian's hand:

"I am more than glad you feel that way about it, Natachee, but really, old man, I'm afraid you overrate what I did. I can't believe yet that those fellows would have dared to go the limit with you. They might have burned you pretty bad, I'll grant, but—"

At the touch of the white man's hand and the hearty comradeship of his words, Natachee dropped his Indian manner and became the Natachee of the white man's schools. Smiling, he said:

"It is evident, my friend, that you do not know Sonora Jack and his methods. I hope for your sake that if you are ever introduced to him you will kill him before he can identify you as the man who blocked his way, as he thinks, to the treasure which brought him from Mexico at such a risk.

"But no more of this," he added. "We have work to do. I went to see Doctor Burton and told him everything—everything except of our visit to the mine. Together we made a plan and he bade me assure you of Marta's love and tell you how glad he was for you. Then I called on the Pardners as the Doctor and I had agreed was best. They knew no more of Sonora Jack than everyone who lives in this part of Arizona knows. I explained to the old prospectors and their girl why you had disappeared and how you had been hiding with me this winter. I told them of your innocence of the crime for which you are under sentence—of your love for Marta—of your efforts to find the gold that would enable you to leave the country and take her with you. I leave you to imagine the girl's happiness. She would have come to you with me but I would not permit it. I promised her that instead tomorrow you should go to her."

Hugh Edwards, in a fever of longing and anxiety, paced to and fro.

"But why tomorrow?" he cried. "Why not now—this moment? Who can say what may happen while we wait?"

Natachee answered:

"We have work to do first. Listen—you are not safe for a day, once you show yourself again. The Lizard has talked too much as I told you he would. Your disappearance set everybody to wondering, then to questioning and guessing. You can only save yourself and Marta by leaving the country before the sheriff learns that you are here and before Sonora Jack can carry out his plan, whatever it is. Doctor Burton will have everything arranged. Tomorrow you will go."

"But—but"—stammered Hugh—"I have no money. There is not gold enough to buy even my own way out of the country, much less to take Marta with me."

The Indian laughed.

"I told them you had struck the rich pocket that you have been working so hard to find. Bob and Thad loaned me those burros there to bring down the gold. The Pardners will cash your gold as if they had found it in their own little mine. Doctor Burton and I planned it all. He will advance money for your immediate needs until your own gold is in the bank."

"But I tell you I have no gold."

"You forget," returned the Indian calmly, "the Mine with the Iron Door."

When it was dark, Natachee said:

"Come, we must not lose an hour."

Taking one of the burros with a number of ore sacks which he had brought from the Pardners, the Indian led the way down into the gulch where he put Hugh's pick on the packsaddle. Then tying the cloth over the white man's eyes and placing one end of the rope in his hand, he went on; Hugh, in turn, leading the burro. When they arrived near the entrance to the mine, they left the pack animal and went into the tunnel.

Removing the cloth from his companion's eyes, Natachee said:

"You shall remain here to dig the gold. I will carry it out to the burro and take it to the cabin. I trust you not to leave this spot until I am ready to take you back as we came."

Hugh laughed.

"You may trust me. I'll promise not to put my head out even. I'll be too busy to waste any time investigating."

"Good!" said the Indian and the two men fell to work.

All night long, Hugh Edwards toiled with his pick, while Natachee sorted the ore, selecting only the richest pieces of quartz for the sacks. As fast as the sacks were filled, he carried them from the mine and packed them on the burro. When they had a load, the Indian led the pack animal away, to return later for another. It was a full two hours before daybreak when Natachee announced that they had taken out all that the four burros could carry. With this last load he led Hugh out of the mine and back to the cabin. Then, while the white man prepared breakfast, the Indian went once more to the mine to destroy every evidence of their visit and to obliterate every sign of the tracks they had made going and returning. When he again appeared at the cabin, the gray light of the coming day shone above the crest of the mountains. With the four burros loaded with the precious ore, the two men set out for the Pardners' home in the lower canyon.

They had reached a point on Samaniego Ridge above the house when Natachee, who was leading the way, stopped suddenly with a low exclamation.

"What is the matter?" cried Hugh.

The Indian motioned for the white man to come to his side. Silently he pointed down at the little house on the floor of the canyon below.

"Well, what is it—what is the matter—what do you see?" said Hugh, gazing at the familiar scene.

"There is no one there," returned the Indian in a low voice, "no one about the house—the door is closed—no one at the mine—no horse in the corral—no smoke from the chimney. And see," he pointed to three buzzards that were circling about the yard in the rear of the house. While they looked, another huge bird joined the group, and then another.

With a cry, Hugh Edwards started forward, but Natachee caught him by the arm.

"Wait, you do not know who may be watching for you to come—wait."

Quickly the Indian led the burros into a little hollow that was fringed with thick bushes, where he tied them securely. Then showing Hugh where to lie in a clump of manzanita so that he could watch the vicinity of the house below, the red man disappeared in the brush.

For what seemed hours to him, Hugh Edwards waited with his eyes fixed on the scene below. There was no movement—no sign of life about the little house. The Indian had disappeared as if the earth had swallowed him. The company of buzzards increased until there were eight or ten now wheeling above the silent dwelling.

The watching man had almost reached the limit of his patience, when to his amazement the front door of the house was thrown open and Natachee stepped out.

The Indian signaled his companion to come, and Hugh plunged with reckless haste down the steep side of the ridge.

The old prospector, Thad Grove, was lying on his bed unconscious from a blow that had cut a deep gash on the side of his head. Natachee had found him on the floor in front of the door to Marta's room. At the end of the living room, opposite the door to the girl's chamber, Sonora Jack's Mexican companion was lying on the floor severely wounded. Though unable to move, the man was conscious and his eyes followed the Indian with the look of a crippled animal at bay.

The body of the other Pardner was lying in a queer twisted heap in the yard, halfway between the kitchen door and the barn.

Marta was gone.

CHAPTER XXVI
THE TRAGEDY

AT first, when his mind was able to grasp the terrible facts of the tragedy, Hugh Edwards nearly lost control of himself. But Natachee steadied him. The Indian assured him with such confidence that Marta was in no immediate danger that he took heart again.

"The girl is worth too much money to Sonora Jack for him to harm her," continued Natachee. "He has carried her away, yes, but remember we know that he expects somehow to make a fortune through her. You may depend upon it he will take every care to keep her safe."

"But how can you know?" said Hugh, wondering at the certainty of the red man's words.

The Indian answered quickly:

"Because the outlaw, even in his haste, was careful to take the girl's things with her." He led his companion into the girl's room. "Look—this closet is nearly empty. The drawers of this dresser are all pulled out and there is almost nothing left in them. Her toilet articles even are not here. There are no blankets left on this bed. I tell you there is much for you to hope for yet, my friend, if you can make yourself as cool and self-controlled as I know you are brave."

When they had returned to the room where the old prospector lay, the Indian, after bending over the unconscious man for a moment, turned again to Hugh; slowly he said:

"There is no night so dark but there is a little light for those whose eyes are good. Always one can see the mountain peaks against the sky. The Mexican there will not talk, and I have not yet looked about outside the house, but some things are very clear. This happened last night, because there are still a few coals among the ashes in the kitchen stove and the clock was wound as usual. Sonora Jack will go to Mexico—he does not dare remain in the United States where there is a reward out for him. At the best possible time, it will take him two days to reach the line. He will not travel with his woman prisoner by daylight. That he expects to lay up during the day is shown by his taking every particle of food he could find in the house. It is not likely that he got started before midnight. With the girl's clothing, the bedding, the provisions, and his own things, he must have taken a pack animal. Good! I, Natachee, will follow a trail like that as fast as a horse can run."

Hugh Edwards put his hand on the Indian's arm.

"We can get horses and men at Wheeler's," he said quickly. "It ought not to take an hour to raise a posse. We can telephone the sheriff from the ranch. Come on."

He started toward the door but the calm voice of the Indian checked him.

"You forget. This is no time for you to meet the sheriff. No one but Doctor Burton and his mother must know of this, until you are safe out of the country."

"I am a fool, Natachee, I forgot. Tell me what to do."

For a moment the Indian again bent over the unconscious man on the bed, then he said:

"We cannot leave Thad like this. He must have a doctor. I am going to bring the Burtons. While I am away, you must not leave the old man's side.

He might regain consciousness for a moment and you must be ready to hear anything that he can tell you. And keep your eye on that Mexican snake out there in the other room. He is the kind that may try something desperate to keep Thad from ever speaking again, for the old prospector is the only one who can tell us exactly what happened here last night. Do you understand?"

"I do," returned Hugh. "You can trust me."

A moment later the Indian was running up the canyon trail toward the little white house on the mountain side.

Two hours later Natachee returned with Saint Jimmy and Mother Burton, who were riding and carrying on their horses a supply of food.

While Doctor Burton with his mother and Hugh were doing all that could be done for Thad and for the wounded Mexican, Natachee, with the swiftness and certainty of a well-bred hunting dog, examined every foot of the ground in the vicinity of the house, the barn and the corral.

When the Indian was satisfied that he could learn nothing more, he climbed swiftly up the steep side of the canyon to the spot where he and Hugh had left the four burros with their heavy loads of gold. Edwards was just coming from the house when Natachee, leading the burros, arrived at the gate. Together the two men took the animals with their precious burdens down into the creek bottom and across to the Pardners' little mine, where they hurriedly buried the sacks of gold in the dump at the mouth of the tunnel.

And then—not far from the house, between two wide-spreading mesquite trees, where a pair of cardinals had their nest and mocking birds loved to swing and sing in the moonlight, where anemone and sweet peas and evening primroses never failed to bloom, the white man and the Indian dug a grave.

There was no time to secure a coffin. They dared not make any public announcement now, nor wait for any formal ceremony. With tender hands they wrapped the old-timer in his blankets and gently laid him in his resting place. And who shall say that Mother Burton's simple prayer was not as potent before that One who judges not by pomp and ceremony, as any ritual ordained by church or creed? And who shall say that the old prospector himself would not have wished it to be done just that way? As Saint Jimmy said gently:

"After all, it is not the first time that Bob has slept on the ground."

While Mrs. Burton was preparing a hurried dinner, Natachee told Hugh and Saint Jimmy the story of the tragedy, as he had read it from the tracks about the premises—signs which were as clear to the Indian as the words on a printed page.

"There were three of them," said Natachee. "They came from down the canyon. It was after everybody in the house was sleeping, because Sonora Jack would not start from where he was hiding in his camp until after dark. The third man was the Lizard. They left their horses and a pack mule at the gate. The marks of the Lizard's feet, where he dismounted, are very clear. Jack and the Mexican went to the corner of the house there at the back. They crouched close to the ground against the wall so they would not be seen easily in the dark, and waited, while the Lizard went to the barn and frightened the pinto so that the noise would waken the Pardners and cause one of them to come out to see what was the matter with the horse.

"Bob came out by the kitchen door and started for the barn. He did not see the men who were behind the corner of the house. When the old prospector was halfway to the barn, Jack and the Mexican ran upon him from behind. Bob fought them but he had no chance. Perhaps he called to Thad. I think not, however, from what happened in the house. Either Jack or the Mexican killed him with a knife, because the Lizard would not have had time to come from the barn.

"Then the Lizard went to stand guard at the front of the house to prevent Marta from escaping by that door, and to give warning in case anyone should come. His tracks are there by the porch. The two outlaws went into the house by the kitchen door. Thad probably had also been awakened by the noise at the barn, and while waiting for Bob to come back must have heard Jack and the Mexican. He was trying to prevent them from entering Marta's room when he shot the Mexican, and Sonora Jack struck him down.

"The Lizard, I think, is with Jack and the girl. He seems to have turned his own horse loose and taken the Mexican's. Marta is riding her pinto. They have taken the pack mule."

As Natachee finished, Mrs. Burton called them to dinner.

While they were eating, the Indian asked the Doctor about Thad's condition.

"I cannot say yet, as to his complete recovery," returned Saint Jimmy, "but I feel reasonably sure that he will pull through all right. I am quite certain that he will regain consciousness for a time at least. But the Mexican has no chance. He will live for several days, perhaps, but the end is certain."

"Good!" said Natachee. "You and Mrs. Burton will stay here until Edwards and I return, will you?"

"Indeed we will," returned Mother Burton quickly.

"Good!" said the Indian again. "We should be back the morning of the fourth day."

He looked at Doctor Burton inquiringly.

"We will save time getting started if we take your horses. The Pardners' horses are out on the range somewhere—and to go to Wheeler's for help would mean the sheriff."

"They are yours. Take them, of course," said Doctor Burton and his mother in a breath.

"We will take a little food for tonight and tomorrow," continued the Indian, "and a canteen of water. With a little grain for the horses and the Pardners' guns, that will be all, except"—he smiled grimly—"my bow and arrows."

CHAPTER XXVII
ON THE TRAIL

THE trail, left by Sonora Jack, led Edwards and Natachee down the creek and out of the canyon by the old road. But a mile or two beyond the crossing, the outlaw had left the road for a course more to the west through the foothills. And here, in the soft ground where there were no other tracks, the marks of the horse's iron-shod feet were very clear, even to the white man. But when Edwards would have urged his mount forward, the Indian checked him.

"There are many miles of desert ahead of us, my friend," said Natachee. "I must not permit your impatience to rob us of our horses before our journey is half finished."

Reluctantly Edwards restrained himself, and the Indian, riding a little in advance, set the pace.

They had not gone far when Natachee pulled up his horse, and springing from his saddle, held up his hand for his companion to stop.

"What is it?" asked Edwards. "What is the matter?"

The Indian, who was moving here and there as he studied the ground, did not answer until he was apparently satisfied with his examination of the tracks.

As he came back to his waiting horse, he said:

"They stopped here and the men dismounted to tighten the cinches. I was right about the Lizard. Those tracks there are his, and there are the tracks of his horse. Sonora Jack and his horse are over there. When the men had attended to their saddles, the Lizard went to look after the pack mule over there, while Jack went to the horse that stood there, which must have been the pinto. Now that we have identified the horses with their riders, we can follow the movements of each in case they should separate—unless, of course, they should change horses."

Again the Indian was in his saddle and they went on. At times they rode at a fast walk, again their sturdy mounts put mile after mile behind them with the easy swinging lope of the cow horse. Occasionally Natachee reined in his mount and, bending low from the saddle, studied the trail carefully, but he never hesitated for more than a moment or two.

At first, after leaving the old road, the trail led them straight west, but just before they crossed the Bankhead Highway they turned a little to the south, so as to pass the southern end of the Tortollita range. And here in the harder ground, and among the rocks, the trail became more difficult. Also, as Natachee had foreseen, the outlaw had separated his party; sending the Lizard with the pack mule one way while he with Marta went another. The Indian, explaining to Edwards what had happened, held to Nugget's tracks.

And now, as he proceeded, the outlaw had taken every precaution to throw any possible pursuer off his trail. Choosing the hardest ground, he had turned and twisted, doubled back and forth, riding over ledges of rock, avoiding soft spots of ground, and taking advantage of everything in his course that would be an obstacle in the way of anyone attempting to follow. At the same time, he had moved steadily toward the west and south.

Edwards, in dismay, felt that all hope of rescuing Marta was lost. To his eyes there was no mark to show which way they had gone. But Natachee smiled.

Dismounting, and giving his bridle rein to his companion, the Indian went ahead, stooping low at times and moving slowly, again running confidently at a dog trot. Three times he caused Edwards to wait while he drew a wide circle and picked up the trail at some point further on. Where Hugh could see not the slightest mark to show that a living thing had passed that way, the Indian moved forward with a certainty that was, to the white man, almost supernatural. A tiny scratch on a rock, a pebble brushed from its resting place, was enough to mark the way for the Indian as clearly as if it were a paved street. It was late in the afternoon when the trail finally drew away from the Tortollitas and again lay clearly marked in the softer ground of the desert. And here, presently, Natachee pointed out to Edwards that the tracks of the Lizard's horse and the pack mule had again merged with those of the animals ridden by Sonora Jack and his captive.

The sun had set when Natachee stopped his horse. There was still light to see the trail but it would last but a few minutes longer. For some time the Indian seemed lost in contemplation of the scene. Slowly his eyes swept the vast reaches of desert and the mountain ranges that lay before them. His companion waited.

At last Natachee said:

"Sonora Jack is going to Mexico. If he were not, he would have gone to the north of the Tortollitas back there. But Mexico lies there to the south and this trail is leading almost due west."

"What can we do?" cried Edwards. "It will be dark in twenty minutes, we cannot follow the trail in the night."

"Patience," returned the Indian, "and listen. The ways by which one may go through these deserts and mountains are more or less fixed." Pointing to the southwest where the ragged sky-line of the Tucson range was sharp against the glowing sky, he continued:

"The outlaw would not risk going straight south on this side of those hills because that is the thickly settled valley of the Santa Cruz with the city of Tucson to bar his way. Do you see, through that gap in the Tucson range, a domelike peak of another range beyond?"

"Yes."

"Well, that is Baboquivari. The Baboquivari, the Coyote, the Roskruge, and the Waterman Mountains are in a line north and south with the Pozo Verdes at the southern end of the line extending into Mexico. On this side of those ranges the country is rather well covered by cattle ranches and the main road to San Fernando, Sasabe and Mexico, and there is a custom house on the line. I do not think Sonora Jack would go that way.

"On the other side of that line of mountains lies the thinly settled Papago Indian Reservation. If this trail here continues its course to the west, it will pass north of those Waterman Mountains which are at the northern end of that line of ranges which mark the eastern boundary of the reservation. The Vaca Hills in the Papago country lie just beyond. They are surrounded by barren desert. There are no ranches—no roads. There is no place in all this country more lonely, and there is a little water there. Sonora Jack could have reached the Vaca Hills by daybreak this morning. If he spent this day there, he will turn south from that point and will be making his way tonight through the Papago Reservation to the Mexican line. I have heard that his old headquarters were in Mexico, south of the Nariz and Santa Rosa Mountains, which are on the border.

"But if I am wrong, and he went south on this side of the Baboquivaris, then he has gone through the Tucson range by the pass at Picture Rocks and we will find his trail there. Come!"

By midnight, they were at Picture Rocks—a narrow cut through the Tucson Mountains where the rock walls of the pass are covered with the strange picture writings of a prehistoric people. At places, the winding passageway is scarcely wider than the tracks of a wagon, so that it was not difficult for the Indian, by the light of an improvised torch, to assure himself that Sonora Jack had not gone that way.

With his customary exclamation, "Good!" the Indian swung into his saddle and, leaving the Tucson Mountains behind, pushed out into the desert with the sureness of a sailor steering toward a harbor light. And now, through the darkness of the night, he set a pace that taxed the endurance of the horses. The white man followed blindly.

Before they were out of the pass, Hugh had lost all sense of direction. In the desert, the darkness seemed to close in about them like a wall. The shadowy form of the Indian, the ghostly shapes of the desert vegetation, and the weird emptiness of those wide houseless spaces, gave him a feeling of unreality. Vainly he strained his eyes to glimpse a light. There was no light. Save for the soft thud of the horses' feet, the squeaking of the saddle leathers and the jingle of the bridle chains, there was no sound. He felt that it must all be a dream from which presently he would awake. And somewhere under those same cold stars that looked down with such indifference, Marta, too, was riding—riding. Where was the outlaw leading her and to what end? Where was she at that moment? What madness to think that Natachee could ever find them in that seemingly infinite space.

After a time, which to Hugh seemed an age, they were again riding among the lower hills of a small desert range. Another half hour and Natachee stopped. Slipping to the ground and giving his bridle rein to Edwards, he said:

"We are at the northern end of the Waterman range. If they went to the Vaca Hills, they came this way. We will pick up their trail at daylight. There is water not far from here. Wait until I return."

As noiseless as a shadow, the Indian disappeared.

Hugh Edwards, peering into the darkness, tried to guess which way the Indian had gone. He listened. On every side the mysteries of the desert night drew close. The shadowy bulk of the hills against the stars assumed the shapes of gigantic and awful creatures of some other world. The smell of the desert—the low sigh of a passing breath of air—the stillness—the feel of the wide empty spaces touched him with a strange dread. The wild, weird call of a coyote startled him. Faint and far away, the call was answered. The lonesome cry of an owl was followed by the soft swish of unseen wings. Suddenly, as if he had risen from the ground, Natachee again stood at his horse's shoulder.

"It is all right," said the Indian as he mounted, "there is no one at the water hole. We will camp there until daylight."

After watering their horses and giving them a feed of grain, the two men ate a cold lunch and lay down to rest until the morning. Natachee slept, but his white companion lay with wide-open eyes waiting for the light.

With the first touch of gray in the sky behind the distant Catalinas, the Indian awoke. By the time there was light enough to see, they were in the saddle.

They had not gone far when Natachee reined his horse toward the west and pointing to the ground said:

"They went here, see? And yonder are the Vaca Hills."

They were nearing the group of low hills that on every side is surrounded by unbroken desert when Natachee, with a low exclamation, suddenly stopped, and, standing in his stirrups, gazed intently ahead.

"What is it?" asked Hugh, trying in vain to see what it was that had attracted the red man's attention.

"A horse."

As he spoke, the Indian slipped from his saddle and motioned the white man to dismount.

Leading the animals behind a large greasewood bush, Natachee said to his companion:

"Stay here with the horses and watch."

Before Hugh could answer, the Indian had slipped away through the gray-green desert vegetation.

A half hour passed. Hugh Edwards watched until his eyes ached. From horizon to horizon there was no sign of life. The desert was as still as a tomb. Then he saw Natachee standing on one of the hills against the sky. The Indian was signaling Hugh to come.

When the white man joined his companion, the Indian did not reply to his eager questions, and Hugh wondered at the red man's grim and scowling face. Silently, Natachee mounted and started his horse forward.

Presently they rode into a low depression between the hills and Natachee called Hugh's attention to the water hole and the place where the outlaw had made camp. Pointing out that the trail from this camping place led south, the Indian said:

"They left here as soon as it was dark last night. They are now close to the border. Sonora Jack will not camp another day on this side of the line but will push on this morning into Mexico. We will make much better time today than they could have made last night."

"But that horse—what about that horse you saw?" demanded Hugh.

For a moment, although he stopped, Natachee did not answer. Then, as if against his will, he said curtly:

"Ride to the top of that ridge there and you will see."

Wonderingly, Hugh obeyed.

On the farther side of the ridge lay the body of the Lizard.

Not until the following day did Hugh Edwards understand why the red man's face was so grim, and why he would not speak of the Lizard's death.

Hour after hour the Indian and the white man followed the trail that led southward through the Papago country. Natachee set the pace, nor did he once stop or hesitate, for the tracks of the two horses and the pack mule were clear in the soft ground, and the outlaw had made no attempt to confuse possible pursuers.

Skirting the northern end of the Comobabi range, and leaving Indian Oasis well to the east, the trail avoided two small Indian villages that lie at the foot of the Quijotoas and then swung more to the west. Natachee, who for three hours had not spoken, pointed to a group of mountains miles ahead.

"The Santa Rosa and the Nariz Mountains on the Mexican line. Sonora Jack is making for the headquarters of his old outlaw band."

As mile after mile passed in steady, relentless succession, and the hours went by with no relief from the monotonous pound and swing of the horses' feet, Hugh Edwards found reason to be grateful for the past months of heavy labor that had toughened his muscles and hardened his body for this test of physical endurance. The sun rode in a sky that held no relieving cloud. In the wide basin, rimmed by desert mountains where no trees grew, there was not a shadow to rest his aching eyes. The smell of the sweating horses and the odor of warm, wet saddle leather was in every breath he drew. His lips were parched and cracked, his eyes smarted, his skin was grimy with dust, his clothing damp and sticky with perspiration. He felt that he had been riding for ages. He grimly set his will to ride on and on and on.

It was late in the afternoon when Natachee turned aside from the trail and rode toward a little desert hill near-by. When Edwards, following, asked the reason, Natachee answered:

"We are not far from the border. Sonora Jack must have friends in this neighborhood or he would not have come so far west before crossing into Mexico."

Dismounting, the two men climbed to the top of the hill, and from that elevation scanned the surrounding country. When Natachee was satisfied, they returned to their horses and rode on. But now the Indian held to the trail only at the intervals necessary to assure himself of the general bearing of the outlaw's course. At every opportunity he ascended some high point from which he could survey the country into which the trail was leading them. After two hours of this they were rewarded by the sight of a small adobe house and corral, a mile, perhaps, from where they stood.

As Natachee pointed to the place he said:

"That is not Indian. The Papago Reservation line, which follows the international boundary for so many miles, turns north at the foot of the Nariz Hills yonder and then after a few miles turns west again to the Santa Rosa Mountains over there. That little ranch is not on the Indian Reservation. It cannot be far from the border. It looks Mexican, and the outlaw's trail leads directly toward it."

At the possibility suggested by the Indian's words, Hugh Edwards cried:

"Do you think—are they—is Marta there?"

Natachee shook his head.

"No, I think the outlaw would take her into Mexico, but whoever lives there, they are Sonora Jack's friends or he would avoid the place."

Then with his eyes on his white companion's face, the Indian said slowly:

"Don't you remember the story you told me—how the old prospectors found the little girl?"

"Yes," said Edwards, not at first seeing the connection.

"Well," continued Natachee, "have you forgotten that Thad and Bob were coming in from the Santa Rosa Mountains, and that they found the child at a Mexican Ranch near the border?"

Hugh Edwards, fully aroused now, was trembling with emotion. He gazed at the little ranch house in the distance as if fascinated. Then, without a word, he went hurriedly down the hill to his horse.

Natachee was beside him, and, as they mounted, the Indian spoke.

"We must be careful, friend, it will not do to show ourselves here. If I am not mistaken, we will pick up the trail again beyond that ranch on the south."

Riding into the nearest opening between the hills of the Nariz range, the Indian again turned westward, thus leaving the ranch well to the north. At the western end of the range they found the outlaw's trail leading straight south into Mexico.

When the sun went down, Natachee and Edwards, lying in the grease-wood and mesquite on top of a low ridge a few miles south of the inter-national boundary line, looked down upon the buildings and corrals of a Mexican Ranch.

The nearest corral was not more than a quarter of a mile distant. The fence of a small pasture which lay between them and the corrals was less than a hundred yards away. In this pasture, within a stone's throw of where the white man and the Indian lay, the pinto horse Nugget was feeding quietly with another horse and a mule.

CHAPTER XXVIII
THE OUTLAWS

ALL through these lonely months following the disappearance of Hugh Edwards, Marta Hillgrove had lived in the firm conviction that the man she loved would come again. She had nothing to justify her belief. She could not understand why, if he loved her, he had left no message—no word of hope. But her woman instinct had persistently swept aside all the opposing facts and held her to the truth which her heart knew. She was so sure of Hugh Edwards' love that nothing could shake her faith in him or cause her to doubt that he would come again to claim her. With Saint Jimmy's help she had endured the long days when there had been no word from the man to whom she had given, without reserve, the wealth of her first woman love.

Marta never dreamed what it cost Saint Jimmy to help her. She would never know. Many, many times Saint Jimmy had told himself that the girl must never know how hard it was for him to help her through those weeks of her waiting for Hugh Edwards.

Then, at last, Natachee had come with the explanation of Hugh's silence, the story of the hunted man's innocence of the crime for which he had been imprisoned, together with the promises of the freedom and happiness that was now, through the gold her lover had found, so near at hand for them both.

Every moment of that day her heart had sung:

"Tomorrow Hugh is coming. Tomorrow he is coming." The hours were filled with rosy visions of the days, that were now so near, when she would be with him, with no fear of another separation. Again and again she assured herself that it was all true—that it was not another of her dreams. Hugh *had* found the gold that meant freedom for him, and happiness for them both. The Pardners, when they had talked with Saint Jimmy, were willing to do their part in carrying out the plan, as they would have been willing to submit to any hardship to insure the happiness of their daughter. Saint Jimmy was arranging everything. "Tomorrow, tomorrow, Hugh would come."

There had been a long talk with her two fathers that evening, and when at last they had said good-night, the girl had not found it easy to sleep. She was too excited, too thrilled with her happiness. Her mind was too active with thoughts of what the morning would bring. She heard the noise at the barn and wondered what mischief Nugget was in. At the same moment she heard the Pardners stirring in their room, and knew that they too had been disturbed by the noise that Nugget was making. The door of her room was open and she could hear Bob muttering about the pinto as he passed through the living room on his way out to the barn.

The noise at the barn ceased. She waited, listening for Bob's return.

There was the sound of steps in the kitchen and someone entered the living room. Thad moved in his room. She caught a whispered word outside her door. It was not Bob. What did it mean? Sitting up in her bed, she listened.

Suddenly all was confusion. Thad's voice rang out, challenging the intruders. There was a trampling rush of feet toward her door—a tangle of straining, writhing figures—a spurt of fire accompanied by the deafening report of a gun—a cry of pain—a dull, sickening blow—a moaning voice: "Hay mamacita de me vido"—a dreadful silence.

Then another voice spoke sharply in Mexican, followed by a groaning reply; and then a man stood beside her bed telling her that she must prepare to go with him and assuring her that no harm should come to her if she was obedient and made no effort to escape. Dumb with terror, the girl started to dress and Sonora Jack went back to the wounded Mexican. Marta heard him call to the Lizard to bring up the horses and the pack mule, and to saddle the pinto. But when the outlaw went again to the girl he found her kneeling beside Thad, overcome with grief.

Lifting her to her feet, Sonora Jack said sternly:

"Come, this is no good! The old man, he will be all right when he wake up. You do what I say an' make yourself ready to ride your own horse with me, or I finish him an' pack you on a mule."

He drew a knife and stooped over the old prospector.

With a cry, Marta sprang to do his bidding.

In those first hours of her enforced ride in the night with Sonora Jack and the Lizard, the girl was still too bewildered and frightened to think clearly. But when the outlaw ordered the Lizard to take the pack mule and go one way, while he with Marta went another, in order to confuse any possible pursuers, she caught, from her captors' words and actions, a gleam of hope. Hugh Edwards and Natachee would arrive at her home in the morning. They would not be long in setting out to find her. With this hope, and the assurance from the outlaws' manner toward her that she was in no immediate personal danger, the girl's courage returned and she was able to consider her situation with some degree of calmness. She did not know that Bob had been killed. But certainly he had not returned after being called from the house by that noise at the barn; nor had she heard his voice. This, together with the fact that neither Sonora Jack nor the Lizard had mentioned the old prospector or referred to him in any way, led her to believe that he was dead. She could not know how seriously Thad was hurt. Try as she might, she could find no hint of the outlaw's purpose in taking her away. When the Lizard would have talked to her, Sonora Jack ordered him, curtly, to keep his mouth shut and look after the pack mule.

Morning came and they were in the Vaca Hills. When Sonora Jack and the Lizard had made camp, and breakfast was over, the outlaw ordered the girl to rest and sleep because there was a long hard ride before her and she would need all her strength. Then, telling the Lizard that he would call him later to take his turn watching for anyone following on their trail, Sonora Jack went to the top of a hill, from which he could overlook the country to the east.

No sooner had his leader left the camp than the Lizard approached Marta. With a leering grin twisting his ratlike features, he said:

"You're a-ridin' with me after all, ain't ye?"

The girl, making no effort to hide her disgust, did not answer.

"Still a-feelin' high an' mighty, be ye? Wal, you'd best be a-gettin' over hit. You're a long way from th' Cañada del Oro right now an' you're a-goin' a heap further."

Marta forced herself to ask calmly:

"Do you know where we are going?"

The Lizard looked back at the hill toward which the outlaw had gone.

"I know whar Sonora Jack *says* we're a-goin'—whether we go er not depends on you."

"What do you mean?" faltered Marta.

"What do ye reckon I'm here a-mixin' up in this fer?" retorted the Lizard.

"I—I am sure I don't know."

"Oh, ye don't, don't ye? Can't even make a guess, heh? Wal, I'll tell ye, hit's like this: Sonora Jack, he's a-aimin' t' carry ye into Mexico. He 'lows he knows whar ther's a feller what'll be glad t' pay an almighty fancy price fer a likely lookin' gal like you an' he's goin' t' sell ye. Onct he's south of th' border, he kin work it easy enough. He's a-takin' good care of ye 'cause he's got t' deliver ye in first-class shape. Onct yer delivered an' th' other feller has paid Jack's price—wal, I reckon you'll be made t' earn yer livin' all right, an' pay right smart on yer owner's investment besides."

The explanation of the outlaw's purpose in abducting her was so plausible that Marta was stricken with horror.

After a moment the Lizard spoke again, emphasizing his words with significant care.

"That's what Jack *thinks* he's a-goin' t' do. Jist like he *thinks* I come along t' help him."

The girl caught the fellow's suggestion with desperate eagerness.

"But you won't help him—you—you couldn't do such a thing. You came to save me."

Then, as she saw the expression of the Lizard's face, her voice broke and she faltered:

"That is what you mean, isn't it?"

"What I mean depends on you. When Sonora Jack wanted me t' come along an' help him git you into Mexico, I seen th' chanct I been a long time waitin' fer. Hit'd be plumb easy t' git shet of that half-breed Mex anywhere this side of th' line. With th' outfit we got, you an' me could make hit on west t' Yuma an' California easy."

The girl was watching him as if she were under a spell. The look in his shifty eyes, the expression of his loose mouth fascinated her.

"But," he added deliberately, "you'll have t' go as my woman."

With a low cry, the girl hid her face:

"No! no!! no!!!"

"You kin take your choice. I'll help Sonora Jack sell ye t' that feller in Mexico er ye kin go with me."

Then the girl's overstrained nerves gave way. Springing to her feet, she broke into wild laughter.

The hysterical merriment with which she received his proposal maddened the Lizard beyond reason:

"Hit's funny, ain't hit?" he snarled. "I've allus been funny t' you—ye ain't never done nothin' but laugh at me. But I done made up my mind a long time ago that I'd have ye some day—an' now—whether ye want t' go with me er not—" He sprang forward and caught her in his arms.

The girl screamed.

A moment later the Lizard was caught by a heavy hand and whirled twenty feet away. As he recovered his balance and snatched at the gun on his hip, Sonora Jack said sharply:

"Drop it!"

The Lizard, with his eyes fixed on the outlaw's steady weapon, raised his empty hands.

When Sonora Jack, with the coolness of his long experience, had disarmed his companion, he turned to the girl.

"I'm sorry for this, Señorita. I have said that with me you would be all right. I don't want you should be scared like this. Tell me, please, what did this hombre say?"

"It is nothing," stammered the girl.

"You don't cry loud like that for nothin'," returned the outlaw. "You don't get scared so for nothin'."

For some time the girl, by refusing to answer or by giving evasive answers to his questions, tried to keep from telling him what the Lizard had proposed. But Sonora Jack, with persistent and cunning questions, with adroit suggestions and bold assertions, drew from her, little by little, the truth.

Then the outlaw faced the cringing Lizard.

"So you think you play a game with Sonora Jack, heh? Don't I tell you how the Señorita is worth so much gold to me that she must be guarded with great care? What am I goin' to do now? You're traitor to me. I no can trust you this much while I'm gone such a little way to watch the trail. 'Fore we get to the border there's goin' to be plenty chances for you to betray me. I ain't goin' to be safe with you, even in Mexico. Come—the Señorita must not again be scared. Come! You an' me we take a little walk over there behind that hill."

Grasping the Lizard's arm, he forced the frightened creature to accompany him.

The terrified girl, watching, saw them disappear over the low ridge.

Trembling, she listened.

There was no sound.

Presently she saw the outlaw coming back over the hill.

Sonora Jack was alone.

Leisurely he approached, and bowing low, said gently:

"I'm sorry, Señorita, you got so scared. It ain't goin' to be so no more."

All night they rode and in the gray light of the early morning came to that small adobe ranch house near the Mexican border.

Save for a half-starved dog that slunk from sight behind the house as they approached, there seemed to be no life about the place. But when Sonora Jack, riding to within a few feet of the door, shouted, "Buenos dias, madre," the door opened and an old Mexican appeared. He greeted the outlaw with a cordial welcome and came forward to take the horses. At the same moment an ancient crone hobbled from the house.

"Hijo mio! Gracias a Dios que volviste sin novedad," she cried. "My son! Thanks to God you have returned without mishap."

"Si, madre, sin novedad—Yes, mother, without mishap."

"You found the Mine with the Door of Iron?"

"No, Mother, but I found something else that will bring much gold to me."

He turned toward Marta and bade the girl dismount.

To the old man he said:

"We must eat and go on over the line quickly. Feed and water the animals but do not remove the saddles."

Then leading Marta into the house, he took her to a little room and told her to lie down and rest until their breakfast was ready, and left her.

When she was alone, the girl looked about with wondering interest. She had felt, even as they were approaching the house, that there was something strangely familiar about the place. She seemed to have been there before or else to have seen it all in some dream. That corral—the well—the water trough—the adobe building—the hard-beaten yard—the pile of mesquite wood—the heap of old tin cans and rubbish. Surely, she had seen it all before. The interior of the house, too, was familiar in every detail. The bed upon which she was lying—the old rawhide bottom chairs—the cracked mirror on the wall and that print of the Holy Family. How strange it all was! She was certain that once before she had been shut in that room, and, lying on that bed, had heard those voices talking in Mexican on the other side of that door.

In her wanderings with the old prospectors, Marta had picked up enough of the Mexican language to understand a little of the conversation. She learned that the old woman was Sonora Jack's mother. As she listened now, she gathered that they were discussing her. She caught the words prospectors, Cañada del Oro, and several times she heard, little girl, while the old woman and the man who had come in after caring for the animals exclaimed with astonishment. In a flash, the meaning of it all came to her. She was the little girl. This was the place from which the Pardners had taken her.

But try as she might, she could not bring back that childhood experience with any degree of clearness. It was a hazy fragment—a memory. She could not recall how she was first brought to that place, nor what her relationship to those people had been. If only Hugh and Natachee would come. If only they could be here now. Perhaps—perhaps, they could force these people to tell what they knew about her.

At breakfast, the old woman and the man treated Marta with great deference. Again and again, they assured her in Mexican and broken English that she must not be frightened, that she would come to no harm if she obeyed Sonora Jack. When, with Sonora Jack, she rode away to the south, they watched until she passed from sight.

They had ridden two or three hours when the outlaw said:

"Señorita, we goin' come now to the end of our ride, for a little time. This is Mexico. The line is ten mile back. Over them hills ahead is a rancho. We goin' stop there. It is not so good place as I like for you, but it is best I can do for now. Many men are goin' to be there—vaqueros—all kinds—bad hombres. All the time they come an' go. You no want to be scared, 'cause me— I'm goin' take good care of you. It is best if we make like you was my wife."

When the girl cried out with fear and he saw the horror in her eyes he hastened to explain:

"Señorita, you mistake—it is only that we make believe you are my wife. You sabe? If I take you to that place as Señorita Hillgrove, you goin' to be in much danger. I can fight them, yes—they know that I can fight, but—" He shrugged his shoulders, then: "Señora Richard would be safe, sure. Nobody is goin' make insult to the wife of Sonora Jack. They know for that Sonora Jack would sure kill."

When Marta would not, or more literally *could* not, agree, the outlaw impatiently spurred his horse forward.

"All right, Señorita, we goin' to see. I'm goin' to tell that you are my wife. I promise it is only a make-believe. If you goin' to tell it is not so—that you are not Señora Richards—then I can't help what comes next."

In a few minutes they were at the ranch. The house was a long, flat-topped, adobe building with several rooms opening on to a long ramada. In reality, the ranch was a general meeting place, or station, for cattle rustlers, smugglers and their kind from both sides of the border.

There were eight or ten men gathered in a group in front of the house as the outlaw and his prisoner arrived. All of them knew Sonora Jack, and, with two or three exceptions, greeted him cordially. When the outlaw told them that his wife was ill from the long ride and must at once retire, Marta made no protest. Frightened as she was at the villainous company, worn with the nervous strain and the physical hardship of her journey, the poor girl's appearance made Sonora Jack's statement that she was ill more plausible.

A room at the end of the building was soon made ready by a mozo who appeared in answer to a call from one of the men. The pack mule was relieved of his burden and the things taken inside. The room was rather large, with two doors—one opening on to the ramada in front and one connecting the apartment with another. Two windows supplied plenty of fresh air, and the place was fairly well furnished as a bedroom. Evidently it was the best apartment that the establishment afforded.

When the mozo was gone and the door was shut, Sonora Jack whispered:

"You done all right, Señorita. Now you goin' be safe for sure. Everything goin' be fine. You make like you too sick to get out of bed. Me, I bring what you want to eat, myself." He smiled. "I goin' tell them hombres a pretty story 'bout my poor Señora who is so sick. Then I'm goin' play cards with them. All night we play an' you will not be scared. *Adios*, Señorita, don't you be scared, rest an' sleep."

Marta threw herself on the bed and, in spite of her situation, fell into a deep sleep. When Sonora Jack brought her dinner, she awoke and, realizing that she must keep her strength for what might come, forced herself to eat. Then once more she slept.

When she was again awakened, it was dark. She could not guess the time. A strip of light shone under the door from that next room and she could hear the men who were drinking and gambling.

At times, their voices were raised in angry dispute or in boisterous laughter; again, there was only the slap-slap of cards as they were thrown on the table with the accompanying thud-thud of heavy hands, the click of bottle necks against glasses, the scuffling sound of a boot heel, the jingle of a spur, or the scrape of a chair on the rough floor. Then a drunken yell of exultation would ring out, accompanied by a heavy grumbling undertone.

The girl, trembling with fear, listened and waited. Would Sonora Jack keep his promise? Was the incentive, which led him to protect her from even himself, strong enough to endure when he had become inflamed by drink?

Slowly the terrible hours passed. It must be nearly midnight. The voices of the men in the next room were becoming louder, more quarrelsome and reckless. Suddenly the frightened girl felt, rather than heard, that front door opening. In the dim light she saw it swing slowly, inch by inch.

She held her breath. She wanted to scream but she dared not. The door swung a little farther and she could see the stars through the opening. Then a dark form slipped into the room as soundless as a shadow. Noiselessly the door was closed.

Cold with horror, unable to move a muscle, the girl cowered on the bed.

The shadowy form moved toward her. It stopped—then came a low whisper.

"Miss Hillgrove, do not be frightened, be very still. I, Natachee, have come for you."

CHAPTER XXIX
THE RESCUE

FOR a moment Marta could not speak. Then in spite of herself she gave a low cry of joy which brought another whispered warning from the Indian.

Moving closer, he said:

"Hugh Edwards is waiting with the horses. We have the pinto and your saddle but I fear you must leave everything else. Not all the men are in there gambling and drinking. There are three in front of the house at the farther end of the ramada. They are sitting with their backs toward your door so I was able to get in. I dared not wait longer because, from their talk, they are expecting someone to come any minute. Then the party in the next room will break up and it will be too late for us to move. We must hurry."

"I am ready," whispered the girl.

"You will be brave and do exactly what I say?"

"Yes."

"Good!—Come."

There was a burst of angry voices in the next room. The Indian waited until he was satisfied that the gamblers were continuing their play, then, leading Marta to the window in the end of the building toward the west, he slipped through, and from the outside helped the girl to follow.

At that moment they heard the sound of feet on the hard earth floor of the ramada. Some one was coming toward that end of the house. With his lips to the girl's ear, Natachee bade her lie down. She obeyed instantly, and the Indian, knife in hand, crept to the corner of the building, toward which the sound was approaching, where he stood, flattened against the wall.

The man who was coming along the front of the house walked leisurely to the end of the ramada and stood almost within reach of the Indian's hand, looking out toward the west and toward the corrals. Natachee was as motionless as the wall against which he stood. Had the fellow gone a step farther or turned his head to look past the corner of the building, he would have died that same instant. Presently he turned and started back toward his companions, calling to them in Mexican as he did so:

"It is strange that they are so late. They should have been here an hour ago."

In a flash Natachee was again at Marta's side. Lifting her to her feet, he whispered:

"Follow me and do as I do."

A hundred feet away, a hollow in the uneven ground made a deeper shadow. Lying prone, the Indian crawled to the little depression. The girl followed close behind. For a moment they lay side by side in the hollow, then the Indian rose and stooping low ran for the dark mass of a mesquite tree some fifty yards farther on.

Again Marta imitated his movements.

"Good!" whispered the Indian as she crouched, breathless, beside him. "But from here on there are too many dry sticks and things for you to stumble over and we must go swiftly."

Before she realized his purpose, he had caught her up in his arms, and keeping the tree between them and the house, was running swift and silent as a wolf through the brush. When they were at a safe distance, the Indian circled to the right and so gained the shelter of the corral fence, with the corral which was north of the house between them and the ramada where the three men were still sitting. Putting the girl down, he whispered:

"If you should make any noise now, they will think it is the horses, but be careful."

Following the back fence of the corral, they were soon some distance east of the house. Then, still keeping the fences between them and the three men on the ramada, Natachee led the way toward a mesquite thicket in a sandy wash between two low ridges where Hugh was waiting with the horses.

There was no time for greetings. Scarcely had they gained their saddles when a yell came from the house, and in the light that streamed from the open door of the room where the gamblers had been carousing, they could see the dark forms of the men gather in answer to the alarm. Clearly they heard the voice of Sonora Jack crying:

"Se fue la muchacha! Los caballos! A seguir la!—The girl is gone! The horses! To follow her!"

When the Indian made no move to go, but sat calmly watching the lights and listening to the voices of the outlaws as they called to one another while saddling their horses, Edwards said impatiently:

"Come, Natachee, we are losing valuable time here. If we go now, we will have a good start ahead of them."

"No," returned the Indian. "That is exactly what they expect us to do and their horses are much faster and fresher than ours. They think that we are making for the United States by the most direct route, which is there due north between those two mountain ranges—the Santa Rosas to the left and the Nariz to the east. They will not waste time trying to find our trail in the darkness but will try to outride us to the line and, by scattering, to cover the country so as to prevent us from crossing. Be patient and you will see."

Very soon the Indian's judgment was proved sound. The outlaws dashed away as fast as their horses could run toward that gap in the mountains through which Sonora Jack had brought Marta the day before. When the last rider was gone and the rolling thunder of the horses' feet had died away in the darkness, Natachee spoke again.

"Good; now we will go. When the day comes, we must be on the northern side of the Nariz Mountains and a little to the east of where Edwards and I struck the hills yesterday. As we start behind the outlaws, we need not fear pursuit, at least until daybreak."

For two or three miles the Indian followed the northern course taken by the outlaws, then, turning aside from the broad, well-traveled trail, he led the way at a leisurely but steady pace to the northeast. Another hour and they were well into the Nariz hills. By daylight they were on the northern side of the range—in the United States.

Leaving their horses, they climbed to a point from which they could look out over the wide plains of the Papago Reservation, with its scattered groups of hills and small mountain ranges bounded by the mighty bulwark of the Baboquivaris and the Coyotes on the east and by the Santa Rosa and Gunsight Mountains on the west. And Marta gave a low cry of delight when, far away to the northeast, they saw the blue heights of the Santa Catalinas lifting boldly into the morning sky.

For some time the Indian scanned the country at the foot of the hills where they stood. There was not a living creature moving within range of his vision. With a smile, Natachee turned to his companions and pointing to the west, said:

"Sonora Jack and his friends are very busy looking for us over there between these hills and the Santa Rosas yonder."

"Thanks to you, Natachee," the girl answered with deep feeling.

As if he had not heard, the Indian pointed more to the north and continued:

"That smoke which you see over there is from a little ranch—Mexican, I think—toward which we trailed you and Sonora Jack yesterday. Did you stop there?"

Marta told them briefly of her experience—of the old Mexican woman who was evidently Sonora Jack's mother, and of her conviction that it was from those people that the old prospectors had taken her when she was a little girl.

Hugh Edwards heard her story with many exclamations, comments and questions. The Indian, who continued to scan the country before them with ceaseless vigilance, listened without a word.

When Marta had finished her story, Natachee said:

"It is time we were moving, friends. Sonora Jack will be on our trail. When he has made sure that we did not take the course he thought we would take, he will ride east along the Mexico side of this range until he picks up our trail; for he will know that we would not go into the Santa Rosa Mountains. I think he will bring with him only one or two men, because he will not wish to share the profit of his venture with so many when one or two are all that he needs, now that it is no longer a question of heading us off before we cross the border. There would be a greater risk, too, with a large company—in the United States. He will know that there are only three of us and will plan to follow and pick us off at a safe distance when the opportunity offers or attack us tonight. When he has again taken his prisoner, he can easily rid himself of one or two helpers as he disposed of the Lizard."

A quarter of a mile from where they had left their horses, the low ridge, beyond which lay the open country, was broken by a narrow, sandy wash. One side of this natural gateway of these hills is an irregular cliff some twenty feet in height. The Indian, leading the way straight to this opening, passed close under the cliff and, leaving the hills behind, set their course straight toward the distant Santa Catalinas.

They had ridden but a short way when the Indian again halted. Pointing to a peak in the northern end of the Baboquivaris, he said to Hugh:

"That is Kits Peak. If you ride toward it, you will come to Indian Oasis. There is a store there where you can water and feed your horses and purchase something to eat for yourselves. I am going back to wait for Sonora Jack. I will overtake you later."

He was turning his horse to ride away, when Edwards cried:

"Wait a minute. Do you mean that you are going back to meet those outlaws?"

"Sonora Jack must be stopped," returned the Indian.

"All right," agreed Hugh, "but Sonora Jack is not alone. Do you think I am going to ride on and leave you to face those fellows single-handed?"

"You faced three of them single-handed for me. I, Natachee, do not forget."

"But that was different," argued Edwards. "There were several things in my favor. No—no, Natachee, it won't do. When you meet those fellows who are following our trail, I must be there to do my little bit with you."

"But Miss Hillgrove," said the Indian.

Marta spoke quickly. "Hugh is right, Natachee."

The Indian yielded.

"Come, then, we must not delay longer, or it will be too late."

Swinging in a wide circle to the right, Natachee led the way swiftly back to a point at the foot of the ridge, a short distance east of that rocky gateway. They dismounted at a spot that was well hidden and the Indian, directing Marta to stay with the horses and telling Edwards to follow, ran quickly along the ridge to the top of the cliff directly above the tracks they had made when first leaving the hills.

When he had assured himself that there was no one in sight following their trail, the Indian stood before his companion and Hugh knew that it was not the Natachee of the schools that was about to speak. Drawing himself up proudly, the red man said:

"Hugh Edwards, listen—seven days ago this stealer of women, Sonora Jack, and his companions, crawled like three snakes into Natachee's hut. Hiding, they struck, when Natachee alone crossed the threshold of his home. In the night, they bound the Indian to a rock, and but for you would have put live coals from their fire on his naked breast. One of the three who did that thing is dying in the Canyon of Gold—is even now, perhaps, dead, but I, Natachee, did not strike him. The body of another is over there in the Vaca Hills. He did not die by the hand of the Indian he had trapped. Sonora Jack alone is left. He is left for me. Do you understand?"

The white man, remembering the Indian's face and manner when he had found the Lizard's body, understood. Slowly—reluctantly, he said:

"This is your affair, Natachee, have it your own way."

They had not waited long when Natachee saw Sonora Jack and a Mexican riding down through the hills. The Indian, fitting an arrow to his bow, said to his companion:

"When I give the word, stand up and cover Sonora Jack with your rifle."

With their eyes on the tracks they were following, the outlaws rode swiftly toward the rocks where Natachee and Edwards were waiting. Sonora Jack was a little in advance. They were just past the cliff when the Mexican, with a cry, tumbled from his saddle. Sonora Jack pulled his horse up sharply and whirled about to see what had happened. At the moment he caught sight of the arrow in the body of his fallen companion, Natachee's voice rang out from the rock above with the familiar command: "Put up your hands."

And looking up, the outlaw saw the Indian with another arrow drawn to its head, and the white man with his menacing rifle.

While Edwards covered the trapped outlaw, the Indian relieved their captive of his guns and ordered him to dismount. Then Natachee motioned for Edwards to lower his rifle and stood face to face with Sonora Jack. From his position on the rocks, Hugh Edwards looked down upon them with intense interest.

At last the red man spoke.

"The snake that crawled into Natachee's hut to strike when the Indian was not looking is caught. One of his brother snakes he left to die in the home he robbed. Another, he killed with his own hand. It is not well that even one of the three snakes that hid in Natachee's hut should remain alive. When Sonora Jack, with the help of his two brother snakes, had bound Natachee to a rock, Sonora Jack was very brave. He was so brave that he dared even to strike the helpless Indian. Now, he shall strike the Indian again—if he can.

"When the snake, Sonora Jack, would have put his coals of fire on the naked breast of the Indian, he required the help of two others. If I, Natachee, could not alone kill a snake, I would die of shame. The one who frightened Sonora Jack and his brave friends so that they ran like rabbits into the brush is here. But Natachee is not bound to a rock now. Sonora Jack need not fear the one from whom he and his brothers ran in such haste. Hugh Edwards will not point his rifle toward the snake that I, Natachee, will kill.

"Sonora Jack boasted that with live coals of fire he would burn the heart out of Natachee's breast. There is no fire here, but here is a knife. Sonora Jack also has a knife. Let the snake, who was so brave with his two brother snakes when they hid in Natachee's hut and bound the Indian to a rock, keep his heart from the knife of the Indian now—if he can."

The two men were by no means unevenly matched in stature or in strength. Both were men whose muscles had been hardened by their active lives in the desert and the mountains. Both were skilled in the use of the knife as a weapon. Sonora Jack fought with the desperate fury of a cornered animal. The Indian, cool and calculating, seemed in no haste to finish that which in his savage pride he had set himself to accomplish. So swiftly did the duelists change positions, so closely were they locked together as they wheeled and twisted in their struggles, that the white man, who was trembling with tense excitement, could not have used his rifle if he would. At his repeated failures to touch the Indian with his knife, the outlaw lost, more and more, his self-control, until he was fighting with reckless and ungoverned madness. Natachee, wary and collected, smiled grimly as he saw the fear in the straining face of his enemy.

Then twice, in quick succession, the point of the Indian's knife reached the outlaw's breast but with no effect. Edwards gasped in dismay as he saw the baffled look which came into Natachee's face. Again the Indian, with all the strength of his arm, drove his weapon at the outlaw's heart and again Sonora Jack was unharmed. Suddenly the Indian changed his method of attack. To Edwards, the duel seemed to become a wrestling match. For a moment they struggled, locked in each other's arms, their limbs entwined, writhing and straining. Then they fell, and to Edwards' horror, the Indian was under the outlaw. But the next instant, while Sonora Jack was struggling to free his knife arm for a death blow, the Indian, hugging his antagonist close, forced his weapon between Sonora Jack's shoulders.

The muscles of the outlaw relaxed—his body became limp. Natachee rolled to one side and leaped to his feet. As if he had forgotten the solitary witness of the combat, the Indian calmly recovered his knife and stood looking down at the man who was already dead.

Sick with horror of the thing he had been forced to witness, Hugh Edwards called to the Indian:

"Come, Natachee, for God's sake let's get away from here."

"The snake that crawled into Natachee's hut is dead," returned the Indian. "The stealer of women will not again steal the woman Hugh Edwards loves."

Hugh was already starting back to the place where they had left Marta. When he noticed that the Indian was not following, he paused to call again:

"Aren't you coming?"

"Go on," returned Natachee, "I will join you in a moment."

And Hugh Edwards, from where he now stood, could not see that Natachee was examining the body of the outlaw to learn why the point of his knife had three times been kept from Sonora Jack's breast.

When Hugh reached Marta, the Indian was just behind him. To the girl, Natachee said simply:

"You can ride home in peace now. There is no one to follow our trail. Sonora Jack will never come for you again."

And Marta asked no questions.

On the homeward journey, Natachee did not follow the course they had come, but took a more direct route. Near Indian Oasis they stopped, while Natachee went to the store to purchase food. When they camped for the night, Marta would let them rest only an hour or two, insisting that she must push on.

In the excitement and dangers of that first night, there had been no opportunity for Hugh Edwards to speak to Marta of his love. And now, as the hours of their long, trying journey passed, he still did not speak. There really was no need for him to speak—they both knew so well. The girl was so distressed by her anxiety for Thad and by her grief over Bob's death and so worn by her terrible experience, that Hugh could not bring himself to talk of the plans that meant so much to him.

When they were safely back in the Canyon of Gold and Marta was rested—when she had found comfort and strength in Mother Burton's arms, then he would tell her his love and ask her to go with him to a place of freedom and happiness.

CHAPTER XXX
PARDNERS STILL

IN the Cañada del Oro, Doctor Burton and his mother watched beside the old prospector and the wounded Mexican.

The man who had been so heartlessly abandoned by his outlaw leader did not speak; but his eyes, like the eyes of a wounded animal, followed every movement of Saint Jimmy and Mother Burton. But as the days and nights of suffering passed, and he received nothing but the gentlest and most attentive care from the two good Samaritans into whose hands he had fallen, the expression of suspicion and fear which had at first marked his every glance gave way to a look of wondering and pathetic gratitude.

It was late in the afternoon of that first day following the tragedy, when Thad regained consciousness. Saint Jimmy, who was at the bedside when the sturdy old prospector looked up at him with a smile of recognition, said cheerfully:

"Good morning, neighbor. How are you? Had a good sleep?"

There was the suggestion of a twinkle in those faded blue eyes as Thad returned:

"There ain't no need for you to pretend none with me, Doc. I come to, quite a spell back. Got a peek at you, though, first thing when you weren't lookin' an' I jest naterally shut my eyes again quick. I been layin' here, figgerin' things out. Got 'em about figgered, I reckon." His leathery, wrinkled, old face twisted in a grimace of pain and his gray lips quivered as he added: "They got my gal, didn't they?"

Saint Jimmy returned gravely:

"You must be careful not to excite yourself, Thad. You have had a dangerous injury."

"Holy Cats! You don't need to think this is the first time I ever been knocked out. My old head is tougher than you know. You don't need to worry about me gettin' rattled neither. I tell you I know what happened up to the time that half Mex devil hit me with his gun. I know they must a-got her or she would a-been settin' right here, certain sure—tell me."

"Yes, they took her away, but Hugh Edwards and Natachee are on their trail."

"What time did the boys start after them?"

"About noon."

"Good enough. They won't throw the Injun off, an' him an' Hugh will be able to handle them if they ain't too many."

"There are only two with Marta—Sonora Jack and the Lizard."

"The Lizard, you say? Is he in on this deal too?"

"Yes."

"Huh, I always knowed he'd do some real meanness if he ever worked up nerve enough. That made three of them, then?"

"Yes."

"I got one of them, didn't I?"

"Yes, he is lying in the other room."

"Pretty sick, is he?"

"He is going to die, Thad."

"Uh-huh, that's what I expected him to do when I took a shot at him."

The old prospector looked at Doctor Burton appealingly, as if there was another question which he longed, yet dreaded to ask.

Saint Jimmy evaded the unspoken question by asking:

"Have you guessed who that fellow, John Holt, really is, Thad?"

"He certain sure ain't no decent prospector or he wouldn't be tryin' to carry away my gal like he's doin'—that's all I know."

"He is Sonora Jack the outlaw. Natachee found it out."

"Holy Cats! An' I wasted a shot on a measly Mex when I might jest as well a-picked the king himself first. But what do you figger he wants to carry off my gal that-a-way for?"

"I wish we knew," said Saint Jimmy.

"Wal, there ain't no good tryin' to guess. We'll know what we know when Natachee and Hugh comes back with her—But, say, Doc—"

The old prospector hesitated, and his gaze roamed about the room.

Saint Jimmy swallowed a lump in his throat.

"What, Thad?"

"Where—why—" The gnarled fingers plucked at the bedding nervously, and the faded blue eyes at last met the eyes of the younger man with such pathetic fear that Saint Jimmy's eyes filled.

"Why ain't my Pardner Bob here? Where is he? He didn't go with the Injun an' the boy?"

"No, Thad, Bob did not go with Hugh and Natachee."

The old prospector put out his trembling hand as if to cling to Saint Jimmy, and Doctor Burton caught it in both his own.

"They—they didn't get my pardner—Bob ain't cashed in?"

Saint Jimmy bowed his head.

Then his mother came to the door and the Doctor willingly made an excuse to leave his patient for a little. When he returned an hour later and Mother Burton had yielded her place to him and left the room, old Thad smiled up at him.

"That mother of yourn is a plumb wonder, sir. I always suspicioned it on account of what she's done for Marta, but I know now that I hadn't even begun to appreciate it. I reckon I'll be gettin' up now."

"And I reckon you won't," retorted the Doctor, putting out a firm hand and pushing him back on the pillow. "You'll stay right where you are until tomorrow morning. You have already talked too much. Here, let me fix the bandage. There, that will do. Now take this and turn your face to the wall—and keep quiet."

The old prospector obeyed.

But the next morning he was out of the house before either Saint Jimmy or his mother had left their beds. When Mrs. Burton went to call him for breakfast, she found him beside the grave under the mesquite trees.

"You see, ma'am," he explained with childish confusion, "I got to imagin' 'long in the night that my Pardner Bob must be feelin' all-fired lonesome an' left-out like, with me sleepin' in the house an' him out here all alone. Bob an' me ain't never been very far apart, you see, for a good many years now, an' so I felt like he'd kind of want me 'round somewheres. It's funny, ain't it, how an old desert rat like me could get fussed up that-a-way! I think mebby that Bob would feel some better too if only our gal was here. I'm plumb sure I would. But I know she'll be back all right. That Injun can hang to a trail like the smell follers a skunk, an' the boy will be here too, with both feet, when it comes to gettin' her away from them again. That half Mex an' the Lizard won't stand a show agin Natachee an' our Hugh. I wish they'd hurry back, though.

"Yes, ma'am, I'm comin'.

"So long, Pardner, I got to get my breakfast. I'll be back again directly."

Every day he spent the greater part of his time under the mesquite trees with Bob, and in the night they would hear him going out "to see," as he said, "if his pardner was all right."

It was there that Marta found him the morning of her return with Hugh and Natachee.

Later, when Mother Burton had put the tired girl to bed, old Thad roamed contentedly about the place, petting Nugget and going often to the door of

Marta's room to listen with a smile for any sound that would tell him the girl was awake. And that night he did not leave the house.

"You see, ma'am," he explained to Mother Burton in the morning, "Bob he's all right now that our gal is safe home again and there ain't nobody ever goin' to steal her no more. It's a good thing the Lizard is gone an' that the Injun done for that Sonora Jack, 'cause if they hadn't a-got what was comin' to 'em, I'd be obliged to take a try for them myself, old as I be. I couldn't never a-looked Bob in the face again nohow, if I'd a-let them hombres get away with such a job as that. But it's all right now—it's sure all right."

During the forenoon of the day following Marta's return, the Mexican at last spoke to Doctor Burton, who was dressing his patient's wound. As the man spoke in his native tongue, Saint Jimmy could not understand. Going to the door, he called Natachee. When the Mexican had repeated what he had said, the Indian interpreted his words for Saint Jimmy.

"He says he thinks he is going to die and wants to know if it is so."

"Shall I tell him the truth, Natachee?"

"Why not?" returned the Indian coldly. "He may have something that he wishes to say. Perhaps it is something the friends of Miss Hillgrove should know."

"Tell him, then, that there is no hope for his life. Death is certain. It may come any time now."

When Natachee had repeated the Doctor's words in the Mexican tongue and the dying man had replied, the Indian said:

"There is something that he wants to tell. He says that you and your mother have been so kind that he will not die without speaking of the girl you both love so much. I think you should call the others. It may be in the nature of a confession and it would be well to have them."

He spoke again to the Mexican and the man answered:

"Si, habla le a la muchacha y sus amigos."

Natachee interpreted:

"Yes, call the girl and her friends."

A few minutes later Mother Burton, Thad, Hugh Edwards and Marta were with Saint Jimmy and the Indian in the presence of the dying Mexican.

CHAPTER XXXI
THE MEXICAN'S CONFESSION

SLOWLY the eyes of the Mexican turned from face to face of the silent group. But it was upon Saint Jimmy's face that his gaze finally rested, and it was to Saint Jimmy that he addressed himself. The Indian, as coldly impersonal and impassive as a mechanical instrument, translated:

"He says that you, Doctor Burton, are a man who lives very close to God. When you are near him, he can feel God."

"God is never far from any man," returned Saint Jimmy.

Natachee translated the Doctor's words, and the Mexican replied in his mother tongue, which the Indian rendered in English.

"He says, yes, sir, that is true, but some men keep their backs toward God and refuse to see or listen to Him. He says he is one who has lived with his face away from God."

"Tell him, then, to turn around."

Again the Indian translated Saint Jimmy's words and received the Mexican's answer.

"He says he sees God when he looks at you—that if you will remain with him when he dies he can go with his face toward God."

"I will not leave him," returned Saint Jimmy. "Tell him not to fear."

When he received this message from the Indian, the man smiled and made the sign of the cross. Then he spoke again and Natachee translated:

"He says to thank you, and that now he will tell you all he knows about the girl you love."

It was well that no one in the room, save Natachee and the Mexican, could at that moment see Saint Jimmy's face.

"Tell him that we are listening."

With frequent pauses to gather strength or to shape the things he would say, the Mexican told his story. In those intervals Natachee's deep voice, without a trace of feeling, made the message clear to the little company.

"His name is Chico Alvarez. He was a member of Sonora Jack's band of outlaws in the years when they were active here in this part of Arizona.

"About twenty years ago they held up a man and woman who were driving in a covered wagon on the road from Tucson to Yuma and California. The man and woman were killed. There was a little girl hiding in the bottom of the wagon. They did not know the baby was there when they shot the man and woman.

"When Sonora Jack was searching the outfit for money and valuables, he found papers and letters that told him about the little girl. She was not the child of the people who were killed. They had stolen her, when she was a little baby, from her real parents who lived in the east.

"Sonora Jack saved all the papers and letters that told about the child, but burned everything else in the outfit so that no one would know there had been a child with the man and woman. He took the baby with him. He said her parents were very rich and would pay much money to have their little girl again.

"The officers were close after the outlaws who were escaping to their place across the border, and Sonora Jack left the little girl with his mother, who was Mexican and lived with her man, not Jack's father, on a little ranch near the border. When Sonora Jack went back to his mother for the child, after the sheriff and his men had given up trying to catch him that time, he found that two prospectors had taken the little girl away.

"Sonora Jack dared not come again into the United States because of the reward that was offered for him, so he could not follow the prospectors, and the little girl was lost to him. Sonora Jack went south in Mexico and stayed there where he was safe.

"Last year a man showed him an old Spanish map of the Cañada del Oro and the Mine with the Iron Door. Sonora Jack and this man, Chico, came to find the mine. They did not find the mine but they found again the little girl, whose people would pay so much money to have her back. Sonora Jack planned to steal the girl. He said they would take her into Mexico and keep her until her people paid much money. If it should be that her people were dead, then he and Chico would make from her enough money in another way to pay them for their trouble. That is all."

The Mexican closed his eyes wearily.

Saint Jimmy spoke quickly:

"Ask him what became of the things that told about the little girl's parents, and how she was stolen from them."

The Indian spoke to the man and received his reply.

"He says, 'I do not know. Sonora Jack he always keep those things for himself.'"

Hugh Edwards cried hoarsely:

"But the name, Natachee, ask him the name."

The dying Mexican opened his eyes as the Indian, bending over him, repeated the question. He answered:

"Eso nunca me dijo Sonora Jack," and with a look toward Saint Jimmy, sank into unconsciousness.

Natachee faced toward that little company of agitated listeners.

"He says, 'Sonora Jack never did tell me that.'"

Mother Burton led Marta from the room. Old Thad, muttering to himself, followed.

Doctor Burton turned from the bedside, saying quietly:

"It is all over. He is gone."

Natachee spoke:

"You, Doctor Burton—and you, Hugh Edwards, wait here for me. The others will not come again into this room for a little while. Wait, I will come back in a moment."

The Indian left the room.

Hugh Edwards and Saint Jimmy looked at each other in wondering silence.

When Natachee returned, he held in his hand a flat package, some six inches wide by eight inches long and about an inch in thickness. The envelope was of leather, laced securely, and there were straps attached. The straps had been cut.

The Indian addressed Hugh:

"As I fought with Sonora Jack, did you see that when I struck his breast my knife drew no blood?"

"Yes," returned Edwards, "I saw it and wondered about it at the time. But what happened immediately after made me forget. Now that you mention it, I remember distinctly."

"Good! When you had gone back to Miss Hillgrove, I looked to see why my knife had refused to touch the snake's heart until I found the way between his shoulders. This package was fastened to Sonora Jack's breast under his shirt. This strap was over his shoulder to support it. This other strap was around his chest to hold the packet in place. Look, there are the marks of my knife. Three times I struck—there and there and there."

The two white men exclaimed with amazement at the Indian's statement.

"I think," said Natachee slowly, "that you would do well to see what this thing is, that the stealer of little girls hid so carefully under his clothing and fastened so securely to his body."

Hugh Edwards drew back with an appealing look at Saint Jimmy, who took the packet from the Indian.

"Must this thing be opened?" said Edwards.

"Yes, Hugh, I think so," returned the Doctor gently. "Anything else would hardly be fair to Marta, would it?"

"No, I suppose not," answered Edwards with a groan. "All right, go ahead. You can tell me when you have finished."

He turned away and went to the window where he sat with his back toward Saint Jimmy, who seated himself at the table. Natachee stood near the door with his arms folded, as motionless as a statue.

Undoing the lacing of the leather envelope, Saint Jimmy found a number of newspaper clippings, so cut as to preserve the name and date line of the paper—several letters—and a diary, with various entries under different dates, rather poorly written but legible.

Swiftly he scanned the printed articles. The diary and the letters he read with more care.

Hugh Edwards was like a man condemned already in his own mind, awaiting the formality of the verdict.

When Marta's birth and the character of her parents had been under a cloud, the man who was branded before the world a criminal had felt that their love was right and that there was no obstacle to their marriage. He had reasoned, indeed, that their happiness would in a measure lighten the shadow that lay over the girl's life, and in a degree would atone for the injustice under which he himself had suffered. The unjust shame and humiliation that the girl had felt so keenly—the dishonor and shame that injustice had brought upon him, had been to them a common bond; while the knowledge of what each had innocently suffered and the sympathy of each for the other had deepened and strengthened their love.

But as he listened to the dying Mexican's story, he saw the barrier that was being raised to his happiness with the girl he loved. Marta's birth and parentage were not, after all, what the old prospectors, Saint Jimmy, and Marta herself had believed. What, then, was left to justify him in asking her to become the wife of a convict? If, indeed, her birth and name were without a shadow, how could he ask her to accept his name—dishonored as it was? And if it should be shown that her people were living—if they were people of importance and honor, how then could the convict who loved her ask her to share his life of dishonor?

When the Mexican had been unable to give the name, hope had again risen in Edwards' heart. But when Natachee brought the packet which Sonora Jack had treasured with such care, Hugh Edwards knew that it was only a matter of minutes until the identity of the woman he loved would be established, which meant that now he could never ask her to be his wife.

Saint Jimmy finished reading the papers and carefully placed them again in the leather envelope. To the watching Indian, he seemed undecided. He had the air of one not quite sure of his hand.

At last, looking up, he said slowly:

"You are right, Natachee, this envelope completes the Mexican's story and establishes the identity of the girl we have always known as Marta Hillgrove."

CHAPTER XXXII
REVELATION

HUGH EDWARDS rose to his feet.

"Well," he said desperately, "let's have it."

Saint Jimmy answered in an odd musing tone:

"Marta, or Martha, for that is her name, was born in a little city in southwestern Missouri—in the lead and zinc mining district. Her parents were both held in the highest esteem in the community where their families had lived for three generations.

"About the time Marta was born, her father, who was a real-estate speculator and trader on a rather small scale, purchased a tract of land from some people who could barely make a living on it. The land was hilly and stony and covered mostly with scrub oak, which made it almost worthless for farming and the man and his wife were glad to get the usual market price for such property.

"But shortly after, this same cheap farm land was developed as a very valuable mineral property—about the richest, in fact, in that district."

Hugh Edwards interrupted:

"Wait a minute—did you learn all this just now from the contents of that package?"

"No, Hugh, the fact is, I was born and grew up in that same Missouri town. It was the home of my people, and even after I went to St. Louis, I was in close touch with the old place. These papers here merely fill in some of the missing details of a story that I have known for years. I am trying to tell it to you so that you will understand everything clearly."

"Go on, please."

"When the property they had sold proved so valuable, the people who had been glad to receive the price they did for their supposedly worthless farm lands were very bitter. They considered themselves swindled and, being the sort they were, brooded over their fancied wrongs until they formed a plan of revenge. They stole the baby, Martha.

"The plan of the kidnappers, as it is shown here," Saint Jimmy touched the packet on the table, "was to hold the little girl until her father had made a fortune from the mineral lands he had purchased from them, and then to force him to pay a large part of that wealth back to them as a ransom for the child.

"The man and woman, with the baby, traveled west by wagon. They always camped. When supplies were needed, the man would go alone to purchase them. They rarely entered a town except to pass through, and then of course took every precaution to hide the child. Their plan to extort money from the father, led them to preserve carefully the evidence that would later prove the identity of the little girl. Their fears of arrest led them to conceal their own identity as carefully. It was more than a year later when they reached Tucson. The rest of the story we have heard.

"I should add that Marta's mother died six months after the baby was stolen. George Clinton, after his wife's death, sold his mining interests and moved to California."

Hugh Edwards started forward. His face was ghastly. His lips trembled so that he could scarcely form the words. "George Clinton, did you say?"

"Yes."

"George Willard Clinton?"

"Yes, do you know of him?"

Hugh Edwards, fighting for self-control, became very still. Turning his back on the others, he walked to the window and stood looking out.

"Yes," he said at last, and his voice was steady now, "yes, I know him. He lives in Los Angeles. I had heard that he was at one time interested in mines in Missouri. But of course I knew nothing of this story that you have told. He is a very wealthy man."

"What a splendid thing for Marta," exclaimed Saint Jimmy.

Hugh Edwards left the window and went to stand beside the body of the Mexican.

"Yes, it will be very fine for her."

And suddenly, as he stood looking down at the dead man, Hugh Edwards laughed.

Saint Jimmy sprang to his feet. Such laughter was not good to hear.

"Hugh!"

The man whirled on him. "You win, Saint Jimmy—congratulations." He rushed madly from the room.

Saint Jimmy gazed at Natachee, speechless with amazement.

"What on earth did he mean by that!" he said at last.

"Is it possible you do not know?"

The other shook his head.

Natachee said slowly:

"When everybody believed that the woman Hugh Edwards loved was one who had no real right to even the name she bore, then he could ask her to become his wife. Now that the woman is the daughter of honor and wealth, how can the convict expect her to go with him? Hugh Edwards is not blind. He sees it is now more fitting that the woman he loves become the wife of his friend, Saint Jimmy, upon whose name there is no shadow."

But Natachee, with the cunning of his Indian nature, had not given Saint Jimmy the whole truth in his explanation of Hugh Edwards' manner.

Natachee remembered that the man who had promoted that investment company, and who had used his power, as the president of the institution, to rob the people of their savings, and who, to shield himself, had sent Donald Payne, an innocent man, to prison, was George Willard Clinton.

CHAPTER XXXIII
GOLD

WHEN Hugh Edwards left Saint Jimmy and the Indian, he was beside himself with grief and rage. He had prepared himself, in a measure, to lose Marta. He had told himself that his love was strong enough to endure even that test, but to give her up because she proved to be the daughter of the man who, by making him a convict, had robbed him of the right to keep her, was more than he could endure.

As he rushed blindly from the house that had been to him a house of refuge, but was now become a house of torment, Marta called to him.

He did not stop. He must get away—away from them all. The old prospector, Saint Jimmy, Natachee, Marta, the dead Mexican—they had all conspired with God to sink him in a hell of conflicting love and hatred.

When he came to himself, he was at the cabin where he had made his home during those first months of his life in the Canyon of Gold. When he was seeking a place to hide, as a wild creature wounded by the hunters seeks to hide from the dogs, he had found that little cabin. He had learned to feel safe there. But he did not feel safe there now. The empty place was crowded with memories that would drive him to some deed of madness.

It was there his dream of freedom and love had been born. It was there that the dear comradeship of the girl had led him to believe there might still be something to hope for, to work for and to live for. He could not stay there now. The place was no longer a place where he could hide from his enemies; it was a trap, a snare. He must go, and go quickly.

Without consciously willing his movements, indeed, without realizing where he was going, he climbed out of the canyon and hurried away up the mountain slopes and along the ridges in the direction of Natachee's hut. With no clearly defined trail to follow, it is doubtful if in his normal mental state he could have found the place. He certainly would not have made the attempt, particularly at that time of day. But some subconscious memory must have guided him, for at sundown he found himself in the familiar gulch where he had toiled all through the winter for the gold that meant for him the realization of his dreams of freedom and happiness with Marta. When night came, he was seated on that spot from which he had so often, in the agony of those lonely months of hiding, watched the tiny point of light in the gloom of the canyon below.

With his eyes fixed on that red spot, which he knew was the window of Marta's room, Hugh Edwards brooded over the series of events that had ended in that hour of his dead hopes and broken dreams.

His thoughts went back even to those glad days when he was graduated from his university, and when, with a heart of honest courage and purpose, he had accepted a position of trust in the institution that seemed to afford such an opportunity for service. He recalled every proud step of his advancement from office to office, of increasing responsibility.

He lived again that appalling hour when he knew that he had been promoted only that he might be betrayed. Again he suffered the agony of his arrest—the trial, with his baffled attempts to prove his innocence—the hideous publicity—the hatred of the people—and again he heard the sentence that condemned him to years in prison, and to a life of dishonor and shame.

Once more he endured the horror of a convict's life—and the death of his mother.

Then came the terrible experiences of his escape—when he was hunted as a wild beast is hunted, with dogs and guns.

And then—the Canyon of Gold, with its promise of peace and safety—its blessed work and dreams and hopes—its miraculous gift of love.

One by one, the strange events of his life in the Canyon of Gold passed in review before him—the period when he lived in the cabin next door to the old prospectors and their partnership daughter—his comradeship with Marta and the sure development of their love—the story of the girl's questionable parentage that had made it possible for him to think of her as his wife—then the visit of the sheriff—his enforced life of torment with the Indian, and his fruitless toil for the gold that held him with its promise of freedom and Marta.

Again he lived over the coming of the outlaw, with the sudden turn of fortune that made Natachee his ally, and gave him the gold from the Mine with the Iron Door.

And then, with the gold in his possession and all its promises almost within his grasp, the tragedy and disaster that had followed. Until now, having gained the wealth for which, inspired by love, he had toiled and fought, he had lost the thing which gave the gold its value. The thing for which he had wanted the gold had become impossible to him.

The light in the Canyon of Gold went out. The hours passed, and still the man held his place on that wild spot high up in the mountains.

And now he saw and felt the mysteries of the night—saw the wide sea of darkness that engulfed the vast desert below, and felt the whispering breath of the desert air—saw the mighty peaks and shoulders of the mountains lifting out of the dark shadows below, up and up and up into the star-lit sky, and felt the fragrant coolness dropping from the pines that held the snows—saw the night sky filled with countless star worlds, and felt the brooding Presence that fixes the time of their every movement, and marks their paths of gleaming light—saw the black depths of the Canyon of Gold, and felt the ghostly multitude of the disappointed ones who had toiled there, as he had toiled, for the treasure they never found, or, finding, were cursed with its possession.

And then, as one who in a vision glimpses the underlying truth of things, this man, on the mountain heights above the Cañada del Oro, saw that life itself was but a Canyon of Gold.

As men through the ages had braved the dangers and endured the hardships of desert and mountains to gain the yellow wealth from the Cañada del Oro, so men braved dangers and endured hardships everywhere. Every dream of man was a dream of gold. Every effort was an effort for gold. Every hope was a hope for gold. For gold was life and honor and power and love and happiness. And gold was death and dishonor and murder and hatred and misery.

It was gold that had led Marta's father to purchase the rich mining property from the ignorant owners, for a price that was little more than nothing. The victims of George Clinton's shrewdness had stolen his child, in the hope that by her they might regain the gold they had lost. It was for gold that Clinton had robbed the people who, because of their need for gold, had trusted him with their savings. To insure himself in the possession of gold, Clinton had sent Donald Payne to prison and condemned him to a life of dishonor. Gold, to the escaped convict, had meant, at first, the bare necessities of life. It had come to mean everything for which a man desires to live. For gold, Sonora Jack had given himself to crime. Lured by the gold of the Mine with the Iron Door he had come to the Cañada del Oro and had been brought, finally, to his death. It was gold that had, at last, led to the revelations that brought the love of Hugh Edwards and Marta to naught.

The man saw that the story of his life in the Canyon of Gold, with its needs, its hopes, its labor, its fears, its victories and defeats, was the story of all life, everywhere.

He saw that the need of gold is a curse—that the craving for gold is a greater curse—that the possession of gold may be the greatest curse of all.

When Hugh Edwards went down to the cabin he found Natachee the Indian waiting for him.

CHAPTER XXXIV

MORNING

AND Hugh Edwards knew by the light that flashed in the Indian's somber eyes—by the expression of that dark countenance, and by the proud bearing of the red man, that Natachee had put aside the teaching of the white man's school. There was something, too, beneath the Indian's stoical composure which told Hugh that he was under the strain of some great excitement.

Gazing at Edwards with a curious intentness, the Indian said:

"My friend has been watching his star in the Canyon of Gold."

"Yes, Natachee, I have been up on the mountain."

Silently the Indian gave him a letter. It was from Marta.

Hugh handled the letter, turning it over and over, as if debating with himself what he should do with it.

"Open it and read," said the Indian, "then hear what I, Natachee, shall say."

Edwards opened the letter and read.

It was not a long letter, but it was filled with the strongest assurances of understanding and sympathy that a woman's loving heart could pen. Saint Jimmy had told her of the completion of the story that had been left unfinished by the Mexican, and had explained its effect on the man she loved. But it made no difference to her, that she was proved to be the daughter of George Clinton, except that she was glad for her future husband's sake that her birth was honorable—that she was not nameless, as she had believed herself to be. For the rest, everything must go on exactly as if she were still the old prospectors' partnership girl. Saint Jimmy had gone to complete the arrangements he had started to make when Sonora Jack carried her away. There must be no change in their plans. When they were safe out of the country, she could communicate with her father. Hugh must come for her at once. She would be waiting for him tomorrow morning.

With deliberate care, Hugh Edwards folded the letter and returned it to the envelope.

The Indian was watching him intently.

The man did not appear in any way surprised, elated or disturbed. One would have said that he had been expecting the letter—had foreseen its contents, and had already, in his mind, answered it. His manner was that of one who, having fought and lived through the crisis of a storm, methodically and wearily takes up again the routine duties of his existence.

Calmly, with a shadowy smile that would have caused Marta to think of Saint Jimmy, he spoke.

"What is it that you wish to say, Natachee?"

"I, Natachee the Indian, can now pay the debt I owe Hugh Edwards."

"You have more than paid that debt, Natachee."

The red man returned haughtily:

"Is the life of Natachee of such little value that it is paid for by the death of that snake, Sonora Jack, and his companion who stopped the arrow?"

"But for you, Marta would not have escaped from Sonora Jack and the other outlaws," returned Edwards.

"But for me, no one would know the woman Hugh Edwards loves, except as the Pardners' girl. Hugh Edwards, but for Natachee, would be free to make her his wife."

Indicating the letter in his hand, Hugh answered:

"She says here that it need make no difference. She says for me to come, as if the Mexican had died without speaking, as if you had taken nothing from Sonora Jack."

The Indian's eyes blazed with triumph.

"Good! That is as I, Natachee, wanted it to be. Now the way of my friend to the great desire of his heart is clear. Listen! When you left so hurriedly, after hearing the name of the girl's father, Doctor Burton wondered at your manner. I told him that now, when the girl was known to be the daughter of a man of wealth and honorable position, you felt you could not take her for your wife."

"That was true enough," returned Edwards, wondering at the excitement which the Indian, with all of his assumed composure, could not hide.

"Yes, but I did not tell anyone that it was the girl's father who sent you, my friend, to prison. No one but Hugh Edwards and Natachee knows that. No one shall know until you, Donald Payne, are revenged for all that this man

Clinton has made you suffer. When you have trapped this Clinton coyote—when you have made him pay for your shame—your imprisonment—your mother's death—when he has paid for everything your heart holds against him—then I, Natachee, will have paid my debt to you."

Hugh Edwards gazed at the Indian, bewildered, amazed, wondering.

"What on earth do you mean, Natachee?"

"Do you not understand? Listen."

"The girl, who does not know what her father did, will go with you. Good!—Take her. Let there be a pretense of marriage. Then, when her shame is accomplished, send her to her father. Let George Clinton, who made Donald Payne a convict, beg that convict to give his daughter a name for her children. The shame that he heaped upon your name—the dishonor that he compelled you to suffer—you will give back to him through his daughter."

The white man exclaimed with horror:

"In God's name stop!"

"Is not the heart of Donald Payne filled with hate for the man who has filled his life with suffering?"

"Yes, Natachee, I hate George Clinton."

"But you will not take the revenge that I, Natachee, have planned for you?"

"No—No—No!"

"The heart of a white man is a strange thing," returned the Indian. "I, Natachee, cannot understand."

The sun was not yet above the mountains, but the sky was glorious with the beauty of the new day, when Hugh Edwards stood in the doorway of the Indian's hut.

Against a sky of liquid gold, melting into the deeper blue above, wreaths of flaming crimson cloud mists were flung with the careless splendor of the Artist who paints with the brush of the wind and the colors of light on the canvas of the heavens. The man bared his head and, with face uplifted, watched.

He felt the soft breath of the spring on his cheek and caught the perfume of cedar and pine. He heard the birds singing among the blossoms on the mountain side. He saw the mighty peaks and crags towering high. He looked down upon the foothills and mesas and afar over the desert where gray-blue shadows drifted on a sea of color into the far purple distance. A squirrel, in a live oak near by, chattered a glad good morning. A buck stepped from the cover of a manzanita thicket and stood, for a moment, with antlered head lifted, as if he too sensed the beauty and the meaning of life. A timid doe came to stand beside her lordly mate. The man, motionless, held his breath. In a flash they were gone.

Natachee the Indian stood beside his white companion.

Hugh Edwards held out his hand to the red man.

"Good-by, Natachee."

"You go?" asked the puzzled Indian.

"Yes, you have paid your debt, Natachee."

The fire of savage exultation flamed in the red man's eyes.

"Hugh Edwards will take the revenge that I, Natachee, have offered?"

"No."

The Indian said doubtfully, as if striving for an answer to the thing which puzzled him so:

"There is something in the white man's heart that is more than hate?"

"Yes, Natachee. Yesterday I believed that there was nothing left for me in life but hate. Then you, last night, revealed to me what hate might do, and I knew the strength of love. I must go now—to the woman who is waiting for me, down there in the Canyon of Gold."

But Hugh Edwards, when he told Saint Jimmy that George Clinton was living, had been mistaken.

The very night that Natachee brought the girl from that place where Sonora Jack had taken her, Marta's father died in a Los Angeles hospital. In the same hour that the Indian and the girl were stealing from the Mexican house south of the border, the man for whose crime Donald Payne was sent to prison was dictating a confession. With the last of his strength, he signed the instrument.

Natachee, when he offered to Hugh Edwards his scheme of revenge, did not know that at that very moment every newspaper in the land was heralding the innocence of the escaped convict, Donald Payne. The man who went down the mountain slopes and ridges toward the Canyon of Gold that morning did not know that he was even then a free man. The girl who waited for her lover who had never spoken to her of his love did not know. But Doctor Burton, when he went to Oracle the evening before to complete his arrangements for that wedding journey, had received the news.

It was like Saint Jimmy to meet Hugh Edwards on the mountain side that morning, and to tell him what he had learned before Hugh had come within sight of the house in the canyon. It was like Saint Jimmy, too, to suggest that perhaps now Marta need never know, at least not until after they had returned from their trip abroad.

CHAPTER XXXV
FREEDOM

LATE in the afternoon of that appointed day, an automobile from Tucson turned off from the Bankhead Highway into the old road that leads to the Cañada del Oro.

At the point where the road enters the Canyon of Gold, which is as far as an automobile can go on that ancient trail, Hugh and Marta, with old Thad, were waiting.

The automobile would take them, without a stop, straight south through Tucson to Nogales, where they would cross the international boundary line into Nogales, Mexico. From there, immediately after the wedding ceremony, Donald Payne and his bride would travel by rail to Mexico City, from which point in due time they would go to the lands of the old world. Thad would return to the Cañada del Oro, and would, for a while at least, make his home with Saint Jimmy and Mother Burton.

It was the plan that had been arranged by Saint Jimmy when they all believed that it was unsafe for Hugh to make his real name known in the United States. For Marta's sake, the original plan was still to be carried out. When Marta and her husband were safely out of the country and on their way abroad, Doctor Burton would give the facts to the newspapers. In a few months the sensational story would cease to be of news interest to the press and would be forgotten by the public. Then Marta would be told that her husband's innocence had been established—that Donald Payne, no longer a fugitive from prison, was free to return again to his own country.

Saint Jimmy and his mother had said their goodbys at the little home of the old prospectors and their partnership girl.

From a rocky point on Samaniego Ridge, high above the Canyon of Gold, Natachee the Indian saw the black moving spot which was the automobile on the old trail that had been followed by so many peoples, in so many ages.

Motionless, as a figure of stone, with a face unmoved, the red man watched.

The automobile stopped.

The dark eyes of the Indian, trained to such distance, could see, as no white man could have seen, the three figures entering the machine.

The automobile moved away, winding down through the foothills, crawling cautiously over the ridges, laboring heavily across the sandy washes, growing smaller and smaller until even to the Indian's vision it was lost in the gray-brown plain of the desert. But still Natachee's gaze held toward the south where presently he saw a faint cloud of dust rising from the yellow threadlike line of highway. Then the cloud of dust melted into the desert air. A moment longer the Indian watched. Then slowly his gaze swept the many miles that lie between the foot of the Santa Catalinas and the far horizon.

A puff of air, fragrant with the scent of the desert, stirred the single feather that drooped from the loosely twisted folds of the Indian's headband. In the blue depth of the sky, a wheeling eagle screamed.

Lifting his dark face toward the mountain peaks that towered above his lonely hut, Natachee the Indian—mystic guardian of the Mine with the Iron Door—smiled.

MEADOWLARK BASIN,
by B.M. Bower

CHAPTER ONE
LARK RUSTLES A BOY

On the brow of the hill the horse Lark was riding stepped aside from the trail, walked to the very edge of the rim and stood there, gravely looking down into the valley. Where he stood the young grass was cut and crushed into the loose soil with shod hoofprints closely intermingled, proof that the slight detour was a matter of habit born of many pausings there at gaze. Except on pitch-black nights or when he rode in haste, Lark never failed to stop and drink his fill of the wide valley below—in his opinion the most beautiful spot on earth.

Straight down, a good four hundred feet below him, lay the bottomland known the country over as Meadowlark Basin, where old Bill Larkin had his stronghold in the old days. Across the wide meadows the Little Smoky River went whirling past like a millrace, the piled hills crowded close upon the farther bank. At the head of the Basin, nearly a mile away, other hills shouldered one another and the rumbling storm clouds just above; beyond all, the mountains with white peaks and purple canyons gashed the dark splotches of wooded slopes.

"Is down there—where we're goin'?" The small boy sitting within the circle of Lark's arms, his small legs spread across the saddle in front of Lark's long legs, pointed a soft, brown finger toward the valley below.

"You betchuh." One of Lark's arms snuggled the boy closer.

"Is all them horses—your horses?"

"Bet they are. Ain't they purty down there? Look at all them spraddly colts, son. Ain't they the purtiest sight you ever saw?"

"O-oh, one colt kicked its—its mamma!" The boy slapped his hands together and chuckled. "Can—can I have one colt—to ride?"

"Bet you can! Ain't it purty down there? Look at that green patch over next the river. That's lucerne. And up above there is the spuds, a different green yet. And that's timothy and clover on beyond. Listen, son. Hear 'em?

Meddalarks and frogs singin' a contest. Frogs is ahead, got all the best of it so far, 'cause they sing all night and the meddalarks lays off till daybreak."

"Can—can I have a frog—"

"Have to ask missis frog about that, son. Better shack along and get home ahead of the storm. See that lightnin' scootin' along up there among the hills; ain't it purty? Be blowin' rain in our faces if we don't hurry." Lark twitched the reins and the horse swung back to the trail that dipped down into a green fold of the encircling hills, shutting off their view of everything save the ink-black clouds with greenish-brown lights here and there that were swiftly blotting out the blue above their heads.

"Tired?" Lark bent his head to look into the flushed face of the youngster.

The boy shook his head, not wanting to confess. He wriggled one arm loose and wiped the dusty beads of perspiration from cheeks and brow, glancing up anxiously into Lark's eyes.

"They—can't find me here, can they?" He looked at the rock walls on either side with a certain satisfaction in their solid gray, as if they were put there for his especial protection.

"No," said Lark grimly. "They'll never git yuh away from here, son."

The boy heaved a great sigh and looked at the storm and the narrow pass and down at the twitching ears of the horse. The hard muscles of Lark's left arm pressed him close. He sighed again and drooped a bit in the embrace. It had been a long, hard ride that lasted through the night and half of the day, and, deny it as he would, he was tired to the middle of his bones.

At the foot of the steep, narrow pass the horse broke into a shambling trot, and once he whinnied eagerly. They brought up in a grassless, hard-packed space between two corrals, and Lark loosened his hold and swung stiffly from the saddle. His face was drawn and his eyes sunken as if he too were very tired.

"Well, here we are, son." He grinned and pulled the boy out of the saddle, setting him on his feet at a safe distance from the horse.

The boy's feet were like wooden clubs. He sat down with unexpected abruptness in the dirt. Over by the corral a man laughed.

"Still dragging in slick-ears; where did you find this one, Lark?"

Lark eyed the speaker across the saddle he was uncinching.

"In the wrong corral, Bud. Havin' the heart kicked outa him—game little cuss. Fit to wear our brand. Better take him up to the house and feed him and put him to bed. Been in the saddle since nine o'clock last night, Bud."

Bud lounged over to them—a slim, handsome youth with the peculiar, stilted walk of the cowboy—and bent smiling over the child, gathering the little body up in his arms.

"Shall I bed him with that broken-legged cougar, or nest him with the young eagle, or down in the calf corral, or where?" he bantered. "The Meddalark's about full up with orphan babies right now. How do you grade this one?"

"Ask maw. Bet she'll know his stall quick enough." He pulled off the saddle and, with a glance up at the approaching storm, walked to a near-by shed with the heavy, stamped saddle skirts flapping against his legs.

A sudden, blinding glare and rending crash of thunder sent the young fellow scurrying up the path to the one-story ranch house that sprawled against the hill as if it had backed there for shelter and still huddled in fear. Great drops of rain like cold molten bullets spatted into the dust. The young man laughed as he ran, the boy clinging to his neck with two thin arms. They reached the sagging porch just as another flash ripped through the clouds and let loose the full torrent of rain.

Turning to look back, he saw Lark almost at his heels, his broad hat brim flooded with the down-pour. The two halted on the porch and stood gazing out at the slanted wall of water, the thunder of it on the porch roof like the deep pounding of surf beating against rocks. Lark stared up at the high plateau beyond the Basin's rim, and his whimsical mouth widened in a satisfied smile.

"This'll wash out every track in the country," he yelled above the uproar. "Needn't have circled through the foothills if I'd known it was comin'."

Bud looked at him, glanced down at the boy now lying in the slackness of deep sleep on his shoulder. He shook his head in vague disapproval.

"Stole him, hunh?"

Lark hunched his wet shoulders, glancing sidelong at the flushed face of the boy.

"Damn' right," he growled. "So would you, Bud—or any man with a heart in him. Why—damn it, they had 'im out in the field, *workin'*. Followin' a big, heavy drag around. Made me so darn sore I just swiped him up into the saddle and rode for the hills." He took off his hat, tilting it so that the water ran out of the curled brim to the steps.

"You sure as hell annexed a bunch of trouble, Lark. Where was it you kidnaped him?"

"Got him off the Palmer ranch. Think he's a grandson of the old man. They'll hunt him, chances are. This rain's a godsend—they'll never track me home."

Bud grinned to himself and turned, carrying his burden inside and laying him on a roomy, cowhide-covered couch where the child sprawled slackly, without a movement of limbs to show he had been disturbed in his sleep. The two men stood looking down at him.

His light brown hair was curly, with damp rings clinging to his forehead. His lashes were long and curled up at the ends, his round face had the deep sun-tan of the prairies. Palmer was called a rich man, but the boy's overalls were faded and old, each knee a gaping, ragged-edged hole. His thin elbows stuck out through the ragged sleeves of a dirty, blue gingham shirt. Lark bent and twitched aside the loose collar, open for want of a button.

"Look at that," he gritted, exposing a long, greenish-blue mark on the shoulder. "Old man Palmer ain't paid for that yet, but he's goin' to some day. The kid won't forget it—I won't *let* 'im forget. You wait till he's full-growed."

"They'll come after him, Lark."

"Let 'em." Lark straightened and hitched up his belt. "Just let 'em try, that's all." His head swung toward a closed door. "Oh, Maw-w!"

Stodgy, flat-footed steps sounded in the next room. The door was pulled open from the farther side and a queer, goblin creature of the female sex looked in, smiling and showing just three lonely teeth in the full expanse of her mouth. Her head would reach to the Bull-Durham tag that dangled from Lark's breast pocket; a large head, much too large for so short a woman. The swelling goiter was not pretty to behold, and her graying hair was combed straight up and twisted into a hard little biscuit on top of her round head. But Lark's eyes softened wonderfully at sight of her, and Bud's lips twitched into a quick smile and his hand reached up automatically to take off his hat.

"What is it, boys? Lark, your coffee'll be ready in a jiffy. I've been kee-pin' the kettle on ever since breakfast. My, my, what a rain! If it don't wash the garden truck all into the river I'll be thankful. My peas are swimmin' for their lives already."

"Maw, come here." Lark crooked one finger, and the queer little old woman pattered forward, her face alive with curiosity.

"For the love of Moses!" Maw clasped her hands with a gesture of amazement. "Bill Larkin, what have you been a doing *now*? I'll bet you stole that little feller. I can tell by the gloat in your eyes. Who belongs to him? You never took him away from his mother, did you, Lark? If you did you must carry him right straight back."

Lark laid his hand on the biscuit of hair and gave it a gentle twist.

"Maw, you shut up and go get into your teeth. Want to scare 'im to death when he wakes up? What d'you suppose I went and got you fitted out with teeth for? Does he *look* like he had a mother? By Jonah, if he's got a mother she don't deserve him. Looks like an orphant to me, Maw."

"They'll be hunting him, Lark. You can't drag in boys like you would a calf; *did* you steal this child? You look me in the eye, young feller, and tell the truth."

Lark did not look her in the eye, but he told the truth without speaking one word. He bent, pulled aside the gingham shirt and pointed. Maw looked and turned away her head, sucking in her breath audibly as one does in pain.

"Shall I carry him back where I got him, Maw?"

"No!" Maw shuddered. "The dirty brutes! You fetch him right back into my room. Buddy, you go get that spring cot out of the lean-to, and bring in the top mattress off the spare bed in the wing. I'll rustle bedding myself." She bent and stared hard at the boy's face.

"This looks to me like the boy old Palmer brought home and said he was Dick's boy. If he is, there'll be a ruckus raised that'll make your old father's fingers itch in the grave to be up and shooting. Palmer hangs onto whatever he gets in his clutches, you want to remember that. And he's got a bad bunch around him."

"Well," Lark's lips tightened, "so've I got a bad bunch around me, Maw. I can't look back at a time when folks didn't hesitate some before they tackled the Meddalark outfit."

"The Meddalark never locked horns with old man Palmer yet. Lark, if you take my advice, you'll send a man up to the old lookout your dad fixed on the rim. That's the weak point of the whole Basin, Lark, and you know it. A man could stand up there with a rifle and pick off the whole bunch down here. There'll be trouble over this boy, sure as you live. If you got him away from Palmer there'll be shooting, and you better oil up your six-gun and get ready for it."

"Why, Maw, you danged old outlaw, you!" Lark laughed. "There wasn't any shootin' when I kidnaped *you*."

"Nobody cared about me, Lark. This is different."

"Yeah," Lark admitted thoughtfully, "mebbe it is."

CHAPTER TWO
SMALLPOX HAS ITS USES

Down through the pass came two riders, drenched with the storm that had lasted through the day, with intermittent gusts of booming wind and vicious lightning, then long, steady down-pours as if the whole heavens were awash and there would be no end to the falling water. From the window overlooking the Basin Bud saw them lope heavily into the meadow trail, small geysers of clean rain water thrown up into the sunset glow whenever the horses galloped into a hollow. Bud lounged across the room and put his head into the kitchen.

"Two riders coming, Maw. Better keep that kid out of sight."

Maw nodded, clicking the china white teeth she wore to please Lark. Bud closed the door, glanced toward another behind which Lark was sleeping heavily, and opened it.

"Oh, Lark! Riders coming. What time did you get in last night—if anybody wants to know?"

Lark landed in the middle of the floor, wide-awake as a startled mountain lion. One slim hand went up to pat his hair down into place, the other reached for his gun.

"Left Smoky Ford about three o'clock in the afternoon. Got here along about midnight, didn't I? Maw ought to know." Then he sat down on the edge of the bed and yawned widely. "You go on out, Bud. If it's the boy they're after, you holler to Maw and ask if supper's ready, soon as you hit the porch. Maw and I will look after the kid."

"Craziest thing a man could do," young Bud muttered, as he left the house and walked down the path to meet the riders. His hat was tilted a bit to one side, a cigarette was in his mouth and tilted to the same angle, his thumbs were hooked negligently inside his belt and his three-inch boot heels pegged little holes in the sodden path as he went. Mildly hospitable he looked, with no more interest in their coming than custom demanded of him. But he saw their eyes go slanting this way and that as they approached, and he saw the ganted flanks of their wet horses and the flare of nostrils that told of long, hard riding.

"Howdy, cowboys," he greeted, lounging closer. "Been out in the dew, haven't you?" He grinned as youth will always grin at the mischance of his fellows.

One lean, unshaven fellow slid out of the saddle and walked stiffly up to Bud, leaving the reins dragging in the wet, steamy muck of the yard. He did not answer the smile.

"We want you folks to get out and help hunt a lost kid," he stated flatly. "Palmer's grandson, it is. Or mebbe your Lark seen him yesterday. Some said he left town yesterday, comin' this way, and he musta passed by the Palmer place 'long about the time the kid disappeared. He might of saw him. He here?"

Bud jerked a thumb over his shoulder toward the house.

"Put up your horses, boys. Jake, over there forking hay, will feed them after you've pulled your saddles. Supper must be about ready. Oh, Jake!" he called, "take care of these horses, will you?" He turned back to the two who were jerking impatiently at wet latigo straps. "Lark didn't say anything about any lost kid, but you can talk to him about it. How about the town folks turning out? They're closer than we are. We'll go, of course."

"The town is out," the short man told him, grunting a little as he heaved his saddle to a dry spot under the shed. "Been out all night. Old man sent us over here because he seen Lark ride past right where the kid was workin' in the field. Looked like he stopped an' talked to the kid, he said, but it was so fur off he couldn't tell."

Bud turned and walked ahead of them up the path, and now he glanced over his shoulder at the speaker, a curious light in his eyes.

"A kid old enough to work in the field wouldn't get lost, would he?"

The thin man shook his head.

"That's what looked damn queer to me," he assented. "But it's about the only thing that could of happened—unless he was made away with," he added as an afterthought.

"How old a kid is he?" Bud's interest grew a bit keener.

"Eight—mebby nine. Too little to get anywhere on foot."

Bud considered this, shook his head as if the question was beyond him, and stepped upon the porch. "Oh, Maw! Supper ready? Two extra," he shouted, and turned squarely about to scrape his bootsoles across the edge of the porch.

"I'd run away," he said soberly, "if I wasn't more than eight or nine and had to do a man's work. Doesn't sound right to me." Having scraped all the mud from one boot, he began meticulously to scrape the other. The two from Palmer's followed his example and scraped and scraped, in evident fear of offending a careful housewife.

"Come right in, boys." Maw herself pulled open the door and stood there, smiling and showing the three yellow teeth like stripes dividing the glaring white ones. "Supper's about ready. What's these gentlemen's names, Buddy?"

"You'll have to ask them," Bud replied evenly. "They're in a hurry and upset, and didn't introduce themselves. Bat and Ed, the boys call them. Come on in, boys. They're out hunting a lost child, Maw. They think maybe Lark might have seen him last evening as he was riding out from town."

"Johnson's my name," the thin man introduced himself perfunctorily to maw. "This other man is named White. Is Mr. Larkin in?"

"Come right into the kitchen. Yes, Lark's here, going over his guns after the rain; leaky roof to the closet—Bud, you'd ought to patch that roof right away tomorrow. It was just an accident Lark went into the closet for something and found all the guns soaking wet. A child lost, did you say?"

"Don't seem to worry folks over this way very much," Johnson observed suspiciously. "How d' do, Lark; seen you in Smoky Ford, you remember."

"*Hel*-lo!" Lark, entrenched behind a table littered with guns, greasy rags, cleaning rods and odorous bottles, looked up and grinned a welcome. "Excuse me for not shakin' hands—coal-oil and bear's grease all over me. What was that, Maw, about a lost child?"

"They want to know if you saw anything of a boy back at Palmer's ranch. Old Palmer saw you ride past there about the time they missed the kid." Bud, pulling chairs to the supper table, spoke more rapidly than was his habit.

"I'll tell it," Johnson interrupted. "It's Palmer's grandson—Dick Palmer's boy. He was out in the field, and the horses come in without 'im. Palmer claims he seen you ride past, and he says you stopped an' talked to the boy. He wasn't seen after that, and the hull country's out lookin' through the hills for 'im. It seemed like you'd oughta know somethin' about 'im." Johnson's eyes clung tenaciously to the ivory-handled, silver-mounted six-shooter that lay close to Lark's hand on the table. The gun which Lark was working on at the moment was a shotgun, double-barreled and ominous.

"Yeah, I remember that kid." Lark spoke without haste, his eyes on the gunstock he was polishing. "Pore little devil, I rode along and found him hung up at the edge of the field, with the drag caught on a rock when he tried to turn around. He couldn't lift it off, and the team wouldn't pull it off, an' there he was, cryin' because he'd get a lickin' if he broke any teeth outa the harrer, an' if he didn't finish the draggin' along that end of the field, he'd get a lickin'—way he figured it, he was due for a whalin' any way the cat jumped." Lark inspected his work, broke open the gun and shoved in two pinkish cartridges.

"Too small a boy to be away out there, half a mile from the house, tryin' to do a man's work. I got off my horse and heaved the drag off the rock for him, and gave him a bag of gumdrops I was bringin' home to maw." He glanced at the old lady and smiled. "That's why you never got any candy this trip, Maw," he explained apologetically. "I gave the whole bag to the boy. It was worth it, too—way he began to put 'em away, two at a time. Mebbe he run off and hid from that lickin'," he added hopefully, picking up a rifle.

"The team come home," Johnson pointed out impatiently, "and the hull country for ten mile around has been combed. He never got off afoot." But he said it mildly and stared uneasily at the way Lark was handling the rifle; not pointing it at anyone, but holding it so that any man there could look down its muzzle if he but turned his wrist a bit.

"Set up to the table, folks," Maw invited briskly. "Larkie, can't you leave them smelly old guns long enough to eat?" Then she sighed, almost as an afterthought. "My, my, it's terrible to think of a child like that."

"Might as well finish this job, Maw. Hands all stunk up, now. You folks go ahead. Well, a kid like that can only be crowded just so far," he returned to the subject. "I know he was scared of somebody that would give him a lickin', and I know what a horse will do when it gets the notion it ain't being treated right. It'll quit the range, give it a chance. That boy was a mile from his lickin', just about, and he wasn't more than twenty rods from the hills. I expect a pound of gumdrops would look to him like supplies enough to carry him a hundred miles. Betcha a broke horse the kid beat it. And if he did I hope he makes it outa the country."

White and Johnson ate uncomfortably, more than half their attention given to the nonchalant handling of the guns across the room. Just behind Lark's chair was a closed door, and from behind that closed door came the sound of footsteps; rather, the creaking of boards beneath the weight of some person.

"Old man Palmer," Lark stated emphatically, "is the kinda man that would skin a louse for its hide and tallow. He'd likely keep every man in the country riding the hills and neglecting his work, huntin' down a little shaver of a boy that he can drive to a man's work and save, mebby, two dollars a day. Betcha a beef critter he won't say thank-yuh or go-ta-hell for the ridin'. No, sir, I don't feel called upon to put any Meddalark horses under the saddle for that kinda slave-chasin'. If the kid had the spunk to drift outa there, he's got my good wishes. And you can go tell him I said so."

"Ain't it struck yuh that might look kinda bad?" Johnson was stirring his coffee with his left hand, his right hand under the edge of the table.

"Think it does?" Lark very casually laid down the rifle—with his left hand—and picked up the six-shooter with his right. He seemed to be study-ing the W L filed on the metal behind the trigger, and while he was looking at that the muzzle pointed at the wall two feet behind Johnson.

"My Jonah, this gun of dad's is all specked with tarnish!" Lark ex-claimed, interrupting himself. "Four of the notches is plumb rusty, which they wouldn't be if my old dad was alive today. My Lord, how he could shoot! I've seen him wing a horsefly at forty yards and never ruffle the hair on the horse. Fact. Makes me think of what he used to say about how things *look*. He always told me to let my conscience and cartridges guide me, and tahell with the *looks*. Dad would likely ride over and beef the man that made that little kid stand and cry because he couldn't lift a heavy drag off a rock for fear a tooth might be broke and he'd get a beatin'. What I'd ought to of done is ride on up to the house and call old man Palmer out and shoot him. What do you think, Johnson?"

Johnson's hand came up and rested ostentatiously on the table. He shuf-fled his feet and nodded, his eyes on his plate. White cleared his throat and glanced sidewise toward the door that would let him out of the house by the shortest route.

"Have some goozeberry pie," Maw urged, and sucked her new teeth into place with a click of her tongue. "I hope they never catch that poor little feller. If they do, and I ever hear of old Palmer whippin' him again, I'll walk right over there with a black-snake and give him a good horsewhipping. I'll teach him!"

"I'll hold him for you, Maw." Bud Larkin reached out and patted her ap-provingly on the shoulder.

"Buddy, you go in and ask Mr. Smith if he could drink a cup of tea. You was vaccinated whilst you were off to school—"

"Somebody sick?" Johnson looked up, poising a knife loaded with mashed potatoes. "You ain't got smallpox here, have you?"

"No!" Lark spoke sharply. "Been a long time since I've saw a case, and I don't hardly believe this is smallpox. Sores break out on the forehead first, as I've heard it. These are on the back—back and shoulders, mostly. You take a close look, Bud, when you go in, and see if there's anything showin' on his face. And, my Jonah, be careful you don't pull down that sheet!"

Bud took the cup of tea that Maw had ready and walked to the door behind Lark. He opened it, letting out a whiff of carbolic acid from the soaked sheet hung straight across the doorway.

"Feller rode in here today in pretty bad shape," Lark observed soberly. "Couldn't turn him out, couldn't put him in the bunk house with the boys, couldn't do a darn thing but fix him up comfortable where we could watch him. But I don't hardly think it's smallpox. All the cases I ever seen, the sores—"

Johnson pushed back his chair with a loud scraping sound on the white boards of the floor. White duplicated the sound and the haste.

"I guess we better be goin'," said Mr. Johnson, stooping to retrieve his hat from the floor. "I—you folks better not ride over with us, seein' as you've got sickness. Might spread somethin'—with everybody millin' around."

"That's good sense," chirped Maw. "Lark don't think it's anything ketchin', but that poor feller caught it, didn't he? He don't make no bones of it. No use exposin' the whole country—and you may be mighty sure, Mr. Johnson, that we ain't going to take any chances."

"You let Bud Larkin set right at the table with us, and you been passin' us dishes—that's chances enough for *me*." Mr. Johnson, herding Mr. White before him, went out and slammed the door.

Maw stood with her head tilted grotesquely to one side, listening. A closed door, in her experience, did not always mean departure.

"Lark," she cried shrewishly, "what made you go and belittle that poor man's sickness to them fellers? They mighta stayed around here an' got exposed, an' you know as well as I do what ails that poor feller we took in. If they catch something, they needn't blame *me*, for I washed my hands good before I set the table. You'd oughta told them when they first come in—"

A board squeaked on the porch. Maw smiled, turned back to the stove and picked up the coffee-pot; hesitated, put up a furtive hand and pulled out the new teeth which she slid into her apron pocket.

"Come on and eat your supper, Lark, before it's stone cold," she said in a relaxed tone. "I guess the gun cleanin' can wait; they're gone."

Lark slid some more cartridges into the cylinder of the notched gun, slipped it inside his waistband and rose.

"You got a case of smallpox on the ranch now; what you goin' to do with it, Maw?" he demanded querulously. "A gun fight I can handle; I was raised on 'em. But how do you expect me to live up to smallpox? Answer me that!" Then he observed a certain vacancy in Maw's smile and frowned. "Where's your teeth? Swaller 'em?"

"No, I didn't!" Maw's leathery face showed a tinge of red. "You know as well as I do that I can't eat with them fillin' up my mouth. And as fer smallpox, how else you expect to keep folks from snoopin' around, lookin' fer that boy? Them men suspicioned you, Larkie, you know it as well as I do. It's a mercy I wrung out that sheet and hung it up—they heared the boy movin' around in there. Mebby you didn't see 'em wallin' their eyes that way, but I did. Lucky I could give 'em something for their pains of stretching their ears—you'd likely have two dead men on your hands to explain."

"Feller knows where he's at when it's straight shootin'," Lark contended in a tone of complaining. "This thing of lyin' out of a scrape—"

"I didn't lie, and neither did you. But I expect we'll all of us do some tall old falsifying before we're through. They ain't goin' to let the matter rest where it's at, Lark. You'd ought of thought about these things—Lark, do you s'pose them fellers will stop and quiz Jake about our Mr. Smith?"

"My Jonah!" Lark ejaculated under his breath, and went out bareheaded to see for himself.

He found Jake leaning against the shed wall with his hands in his pants pockets and his mouth wide open, laughing with a silent quaking of his whole body. He stopped when Lark walked up to him and pointed to where two horsemen were making one blurred shadow on the trail down past the meadow.

"Smoky Ford's goin' t' have a hell of a time supplyin' the demand fer carbolic acid and such," Jake declared maliciously. "And there goes two men that'll bile their shirts, I betcha." He gave Lark a facetious poke in the ribs. "Dunno what the idee is, but I rode right in your dust. They come down past the bunk house and wanted to know what we done with the outfit of the feller that rode in here with smallpox, and was he broke out bad. I played 'er strong, y' betcha. Told 'em I'd burnt saddle, bridle, blanket an' all the clothes the feller was wearin' at the time, an' shot an' cremated the hoss—by his consent durin' a loocid minute. An' as fer bein' broke out, I tells 'em you couldn't put a burnt match down anywhere on his face without bustin' a sore. Told 'em it was the worst case I ever seen. I kinda had t' play 'er with m' eyes shet, Lark, but if you'd saw fit t' have a man here that was down with smallpox, I knowed damn' well he'd oughta have it mighty bad an' be right down sick with it. Hunh?"

"You shore made 'im sick, all right," Lark grunted, and went off to the house without another word.

CHAPTER THREE
LARK DOES A LITTLE BRANDING

Lark stacked his cup and saucer in his breakfast plate, added knife, fork and spoon as range custom had taught him to do, and reached absently for his to-bacco sack and papers. Maw was going to spoil the kid, he thought. Already she was mystifying him with a fascinating game of "Two-little-birds-set-on-a-hill," with bits of the inner lining of an eggshell pasted on her fore-fingers to represent the two little birds, and sending the kid into hilarious squeals when Jack and Jill flew away and returned again with incomprehensible facility.

"Maw," said Lark, as he drew a match sharply along the underside of his chair, "looks like that smallpox is about cured, right now. I'm goin' to Smoky Ford, and I might be late gettin' back. Anybody you don't like the looks of rides into the Basin, why, there's the shotgun loaded with buckshot. She kicks, so hold her tight to your shoulder and pull one trigger at a time. You'll find extra shells in my room, in the cupboard behind the door. Don't stand fer no monkey work, Maw. The boys ain't likely to get in with that bunch of cattle before to-morra, so it'll be you and Jake to hold the fort; and Bud—" His eyes went to the glum face of his handsome young nephew.

"I'll ride with you, if you're damn' fool enough to go hunting trouble," Bud stated calmly, pushing back his chair.

"If Bat Johnson comes here again, I'll shoot him," said the boy abruptly, ignoring Maw's little white birds while he stared across at Lark. "He's a mean devil. Meaner 'n gran'pa. He—he goes an' tells gran'pa everything. He's a mean old tattle-tale."

"Now, Lark," Maw began worriedly, "there ain't a mite of use in you going to town. Them men was scared off last night. You couldn't hire 'em to come here and run the risk—"

"That's where you're fooled, Maw. They'll be back, don't you fret— leave 'em alone. My old dad brought me up to meet trouble halfway down the trail and shootin' as I ride. It's a good way—only way I know anything about. The Meddalark's never learnt how to lie and dodge, Maw, and now's a pore time to begin, looks like to me. Last night don't set well with me; when you come to think it over, I'm the feller that's got to live with me the closest and the longest, Maw. I'd hate to have to live with a feller all my life that I was ashamed of." He smiled suddenly with a boyish grin. "You see, Maw, I kinda put a spoke in the wheel of destiny, and she's liable to bust something if she ain't watched till she hits her stride again.

"Son, yore fightin' days are yet to come. How about some more gum-drops? You be a good boy today, and mind what Maw tells you, and mebbe there'll be a bag of candy in my pocket when I git back. You betcha."

Maw rose and stood goblinlike behind the boy's chair, her face turned grayish under the tan.

"Larkie, I know that town better than you do. There's a mean, low-lived bunch hanging around that I wouldn't put nothing past. If you must go, wait till the boys come with the cattle so you can have help. Six of you won't be any too many to face Palmer's bunch, and what saloon loafers he can drum up in town. Lark, I *know*. I was there when that trouble with the Willis boys come up, and I know just what that mob is capable of when they've got somebody to stir 'em up. You wait, Larkie. Don't go and do anything foolish, like riding to Smoky Ford today, right when——" Her voice broke and she turned her back on them, wiping her eyes surreptitiously on her apron.

"I like the way you count me," Bud cried with thin cheerfulness. "Never mind, Maw. I can rope and throw Lark any time he gets to horning in where he shouldn't, and I promise you that he isn't going to pull open any hornet's nest just to see how it's made. And Lark's right about one thing, anyway. The best thing to do, now it's pretty well known where we stand, is to ride in and show we aren't ashamed of ourselves. The Willis boys were afraid, Maw. They tried to run, and then when they were caught, they begged like whipped pups. And moreover, they were guilty as hell. Buck up, Maw." He went over and patted her on the shoulder. "Lark isn't going to do anything you'd be ashamed of."

"If you see gran'pa," said the boy fiercely, "you tell—tell him I'm goin' t' stay with—with you. Tell him I—I'm goin' t' kill him when I get big."

Lark looked down at him thoughtfully, smiled a bit at Maw's shocked expostulations, and turned to the door.

"I'll sure tell him that, son," he promised gravely. "And don't you worry a minute about me, Maw."

Maw did worry, however. She would have worried more if she could have seen and heard what was going on in Smoky Ford that morning. Old Palmer—who must have been old in sin, since he was not more than forty-five—had ridden in early with Johnson, White and two others of similar type. He did not go to the sheriff, as a man would have done whose cause was unassailable, but had talked in the saloons, his listeners for the most part those men who had joined in the search for the lost boy.

"Smallpox, my eye!" Palmer cried thickly. "There ain't a case in the country. It was my son's boy that they had hid away in that room—and us all huntin' the hills for him! It's like the Meddalark—an outlaw bunch if ever there was one. Look at old man Larkin! If ever a man deserved stringin' up, he did. And Lark and that kid nephew ain't any better. Stealin' calves from me right along—and now they take the boy and hide him away in a room—" There was a great deal of the same kind of talk, for Palmer was not the man to let anything slip away from him.

Smoky Ford men should have stopped to wonder why Palmer the tight-fisted was buying whisky for every man that joined the listening group around him. It never had happened before that anyone could remember, nor was it likely to happen again. But men do not as a rule stop to ask why, when the bartender is busy and makes no sign that he expects pay for every filled glass. Palmer's money was good that morning; he had a grievance and the men who had turned out to search for a lost child discovered that Palmer was a human kinda cuss, after all, and that it looked as if a crime had been committed boldly, in broad daylight. Then Bat Johnson artfully crystallized the growing sentiment born of whisky and Palmer's loud-mouthed denunciations.

"Hell, if it was a horse that was stole, that p'ticular Meddalark bunch would be busted up in short order. Being a kid that's made 'way with—" he stopped there to empty his glass "—why, mebby we oughta let 'em get away with it. Some places, though, folks count humans worth as much as horses, anyway."

"Damn' right," a Palmer man muttered. "I'm goin' t' ride up river, t'night, and ask how about it. Bat an' me figures we c'n clean out that nest by our lonely, an' git the kid back. Rest of you folks better pull the blankets over your heads t'night er you might hear shootin'."

"Rope beats that," suggested another, his tongue thickened by what had been poured over it.

Two or three grunted approval—a bit uncertainly, because in normal times they liked the Meadowlark outfit, Lark himself in particular, and they did *not* like Palmer.

"Better send the sheriff after the kid," one level-headed cowpuncher advised. "Lark just done it fer a josh, most likely."

"Yeah, better send the sheriff up there," someone agreed.

"Sheriff ain't here," said Palmer shortly. The crowd was colder on the scent than he liked. Had he known it, there had been hints among the searchers that the boy was better off in the hills than with his grandfather, and that he had probably run away. Which proves that they were human enough in their mental reactions if left alone.

He presently left that saloon and wandered into another, and there were plenty of half-drunken men by that time who would follow him for the free drinks that were in it. By noon the crowd was convinced that stealing a child is as serious a crime as stealing a horse and that the punishment should be as swift and sure. And it is a fact that when men dealt with the crime of horse-stealing they did not stop to inquire whether the owner had been kind to the beast. A horse was a horse, and stealing was stealing. So the Meadowlark outfit was declared outlaw, and at least fifty men prepared to stage a lynching that night in Meadowlark Basin.

They were making the last sinister plans and electing a captain of the mob—Palmer, of course—when Lark rode into town and down the road that was called a street, Bud's right stirrup swinging close to his left one. A man crossing the street to a saloon gave them a startled glance and dived inside bearing all the earmarks of one who is about to spill a mouthful of amazing news.

"Right there's the bee tree," Lark observed under his breath, and rode after him. The half door was still swinging when Lark's horse pushed in with a snort of distaste for the job, and Lark himself ducked his tall hat crown under the casing.

"Howdy, folks," he cried cheerful greeting. "Come on down to the Chester House, will you? I've got something to tell you—and I want Palmer there, particular. Fetch him along—I see he's here. Missed him at the ranch." He began backing out again. "If you please," he added carefully, as a polite afterthought.

Outside, he headed for the next saloon, looked in and found no one there but the bartender. Him he beckoned with a crooked finger, and rode on to the next, with Bud beside him and the mob hurrying curiously at his heels. Lark's restless eyes darted to Bud's right hand that fumbled the butt of his six-shooter thrust within his belt, and he grinned and shook his head.

"Don't think you'll need it, m' son," he said softly, as they reached the little hotel with the high platform in front, and he swung his horse to meet the crowd. There was no smile now on his lips, and his eyes were steady except for the light that flickered deep within.

"All right, folks. Just put Palmer up in front here, will you? I've got a message for him that I promised to deliver."

"Ransom, eh?" Palmer's teeth showed under his lifted lip. "You're crazy to come here and stick your neck in the noose—"

"You shut up, will you?" Lark's voice was so quiet that men in the rear crowded forward to hear what he was saying. "I'll do the talking for a minute. No, the boy you been hunting sent you a message. He said to tell you that he was going to stay with me, and that when he's big enough, he's going to kill you." Lark paused. "I think he'll do it, Palmer. There's good stuff in that kid and he won't forget." He lifted his eyes to the crowd behind Palmer.

"Folks, that little kid has got welts all over him, just about, where Palmer quirted him. He's between eight and nine years old, just the age when a boy plays the hardest and grows the fastest—and when I seen him he was out in the field following a heavy drag around (or trying to) and the team he had to handle was the kind you need a pitchfork to go in the stall with 'em. The black lammed out with his heels while I was there talkin' to the kid, and the gray was wallin' his eyes and watchin' for a chance. Palmer loves that boy, don't you think? He ought to have him back. Must save him a dollar a day, and don't cost as much to feed a kid as it does a man; not that kid, anyway. You can count his ribs as far as you can see him, when his shirt's off. Starved him, Palmer did. And beat him till—" Lark stopped and swallowed and blinked, and the crowd moved uneasily and sent sidelong glances at one another.

"So the kid will carry some of them marks till he grows up, and he ain't likely to forget. He'll kill Palmer as sure as God made little apples, if Palmer ain't killed already by the time the kid's growed up t' be a man. Palmer's got that to look forward to. But that's the kid's game, and I wouldn't for the world get in and spoil it for him. I hope Palmer lives with that in mind—that the kid he beat raw is growin' fast as he can and lookin' forward to the time when he can kill the devil that used him so.

"But, as I say, that's the kid's game. What I come after Palmer for is to put the Meddalark brand on him with my quirt. I never did try to draw that bird on a man's hide, but I'll never start younger, and I feel like I'm artist enough to mark this damn' long-ear, till the kid can get around to beef him. I been lookin' at the marks on the kid's back, so I've got them to go by. Palmer, don't make me kill you! I'd hate to cheat the kid like that."

Lark, easing himself to one side in the saddle, ready to dismount swiftly, halted Palmer's incipient flight as if he had caught him by the collar.

"All right, Lark. I've got him covered," snapped Bud, just behind him, "Go to it." He spurred forward. "Give me your bridle reins," he added matter-of-factly.

On the ground, quirt in hand, Lark advanced upon Palmer, who tried to shrink into the crowd and was shoved back into the open space as unhesitatingly as if these men had not been drinking his whisky and absorbing his viewpoint since morning. Palmer staggered under the impetus of the shove, and Lark caught him expertly by the collar, yanked his coat off, grabbed again and went to work, punctuating the swish and thud of the quirt by words that bit into the soul of the man like acid.

"Drop that gun!" This was Bud, cutting short Bat Johnson's half-formed determination to do murder. "This is no shooting match—unless some fool like you makes it so." Upon the close-packed, staring crowd Bud was calmly riding herd, Lark's horse dancing at the end of his reins and lashing out at any man who pressed forward. Strange as it might have seemed to those who had watched the slow forming of the mob idea, the strongest sentiment in that crowd was irritation against Bud, who blocked their view of the show. Men darted to the hotel platform and scrambled up to a vantage point, eager to miss no vicious cut of that flailing quirt.

Palmer, on his knees, begged for mercy. It was pitiable, nauseating, to hear how he wept and pleaded under the blows.

"Did you quit beating the kid when he cried?" Lark's voice was merciless, his eyes aglare with rage.

"He'll kill you for that," a man told Lark soberly when it was all over, and Palmer had slunk away with his shoulders bent and bloody, mouthing curses and threats. "You'll need a bullet-proof back from now on. Come have a drink."

"No—thank you just the same." Lark lifted a hand, stared dully at the way it was trembling, and wiped the beads of perspiration off his face. "I—the kid is waiting for some candy I promised him." He reached out a groping hand for the reins Bud was offering, and mounted like a man who is very, very tired. "I—guess we'd better be goin'. Maw'll be worried."

"And so," Bud remarked thoughtfully, when they had ridden a mile down the trail toward the Meadowlark, thirty-five miles away, "you've stopped a lynching party, marked the back of the richest and meanest man in the country for life, staked yourself to a feud that will keep you guessing from now on, and annexed another responsibility in the form of a boy you'll feel you've got to educate same as you did me. Lark, you damned fool, you're the kind of man King Arthur would have been proud of."

"Hunh?" Larked glanced up from tightening the scanty string on the lumpy bag of candy that was too big to go in his pocket and so must be carried for thirty-five miles in his hand. "Talk United States, darn you; I ain't ridin' the range fer no king!"

CHAPTER FOUR
BUD

Dust lay deep in the trail and spurted up in little clouds from under the tired feet of Bud Larkin's sweat-streaked sorrel. Smoky Ford squatted as always with her board shacks huddled about her one street and the rear windows staring stupidly at the hills beyond the swift-flowing river hidden behind the willows and the steep bank. The afternoon was half gone and the mid-July wind was hot and dry, and Bud had been in the saddle since early morning. He rode up to the hitch-rail in front of the Elkhorn saloon and dismounted, wondering a little at the crowd uproariously filling the place. Moving a bit stiffly, he went inside, the big rowels of his spurs making a pleasant *br-br-brr* on the boards, the chains clinking faintly under the arch of his high-heeled boots as he walked.

The whole of his high gray hat, the brim turned back and skewered to the crown with a cameo pin filched from the neck of a pretty girl whom he had kissed on the mouth for her laughing resistance, looked as if it were afloat on a troubled sea of felt as he pushed through the noisy crowd and up to the bar, his thoughts all of beer cold and foaming in the glass. The cameo pin and the pretty girl were forgotten, the smoldering eyes under his straight brown brows held no vision of gentle dalliance, though Bud was a good-looking young devil of twenty-two who gave blithe greeting to Romance when he met her on the lonely trails. His mouth, given easily to smiles that troubled the dreams of many a range girl, was grim now and dusty in the corners as he waited thirstily for the tall glass mug ribbed on the outside and spilling foam over the top; took one long swallow when the busy bartender pushed the glass toward him, and turned, elbowing his way to an empty table against the wall where he could sit down and rest himself and take his time over the refreshment.

Negligent greeting he gave to one or two whose eyes he met, but for the most of them he had no thought. It was not his kind of a crowd, being composed largely of the town drifters and a few from the neighboring ranches. The cause of their foregathering was not far to seek. Steve Godfrey was present and deeply engaged in letting his world know that he was having one of his sprees—during which he was wont to proclaim loudly that he was prying off the lid, taking the town apart, painting her red; whatever trite phrase came first to his loose lips. On such occasions he lacked neither friends nor an audience.

"*Ev*-rybody dance!" Steve was shouting drunkenly, his face turned toward the doorway where a man was entering whose back bore certain scars, they said, which Lark could best explain; Palmer, whose silent enmity was felt by the Meadowlark even though he had as yet made no open move against them, "Lock the door! 'S my saloon—bought 'er for the next two hours! Drink 'er dry, boys, and *ev*-rybody dance!"

Palmer laughed sourly and shut the inner door with a bang, pushing the bolt across. There was a general stampede for the bar, behind which Steve Godfrey was pulling down bottles with both hands and laughing widemouthed as they were snatched from him. Bud's lip curled.

A young fellow at the next table was sketching rapidly in a notebook, glancing up after each pencil stroke to catch fresh glimpses of some face in the crowd. Bud lifted his beer, took a sip and set down the mug, watching sidelong the careless, swift work of his neighbor. A stranger in the town, Bud tagged him. A tenderfoot, judging by the newness of his riding clothes, the softness of his hands, the town pallor of his face. He looked up and smiled faintly with that wistfulness of the lonely soul begging silently for friendship, and Bud's scornful young mouth relaxed into a grin.

"Great stuff—all new to me, though," the young man confided, nodding toward the massed backs before him.

"Crazy bunch of booze-fighters," Bud condemned the crowd tersely.

"Say, whyn't you up here drinkin' with the rest?" Steve Godfrey, standing on a keg behind the bar, bawled angrily at the artist. "You, I mean, over there by the wall. What's the matter with you? Sick at the stummick?"

"Why, no. Thank you just the same, but I don't drink liquor."

"Don't, ay?" Steve scowled and spat into a corner. "Well, if you don't drink, dammit, you'll dance!"

Bud moved his slim body sidewise so that his gun hung handily within reach of his fingers. The young man shrugged his shoulders, closed his notebook and put it away with the pencil. The crowd had swung round and was staring and waiting to see what would happen next.

"I don't mind dancing for you," smiled the artist, "but I can't dance without music, you know."

"Can't, ay?" Steve was happy now, bullying someone who would not fight back. "Say! you git up and dance to *this*!"

The stranger looked at the gun in Steve's hand, glanced into Steve's eyes and stifled a yawn.

"You know very well that's impossible," he said patiently. "I've always said that this dancing to the music of a six-shooter is a fake, invented by some Eastern author for melodramatic effect. I still believe you got the idea out of some book. I wouldn't mind dancing for you, but you couldn't possibly beat time with that gun. Six shots, and I'd have to stop and wait while you reloaded. The thing isn't practical. If anyone here could furnish some real music—"

"I have a mouth-harp, though you may not call that real music," Bud announced unexpectedly, and finished his beer with one long swallow. It amused young Bud to see the stupid indecision on the face of Steve Godfrey, who lacked the wit to handle an old range joke when it chanced to take a new turn.

"Good!" The young man smiled frankly. "Clear a space over there by the door, will you?" He looked inquiringly at Bud. "What can you play?"

"I can play anything you can dance," Bud grinned reply, well pleased with the small diversion. "How about a good old buck-and-wing?"

"All right, buck-and-wing it is." The stranger nodded, cast another glance toward that non-plused bully, Steve Godfrey, who stood on the keg with the gun sagging in his hand and his mouth half open, and took his place in the center of the makeshift stage.

Bud shot him a puzzled glance not unmixed with a certain tolerant contempt. The young fellow's manner gave no hint of fear, so why should he dance at the bidding of a drunken bully? Bud did not like to think that the tenderfoot had seized the first excuse for showing off before so sorry an audience.

However, the motive was no business of Bud's. He polished the harmonica on his sleeve, moistened his boyish lips that turned so easily to smiles, cupped his hands around the little instrument so dear to the heart of a cowboy and swung into a jig tune. Sitting on the edge of the table with his head tilted to one side, eyes half closed and watching the dancer while a well-made riding boot tapped the beat of the measures on the rough board floor, Bud never knew the picture he made.

The dancer's eyes studied the lines of his clean young face and throat, the tilt of his hat with the cameo brooch pinning back the broad brim, the slim, muscular body and straight legs; studied and recorded each curve and line in a photographic memory. And he could dance the while! Smoky Ford had never seen anything like it. Hornpipe and highland fling he did, never taking his eyes off Bud, but mechanically fitting the steps to each tune as it was played. Even the free whisky was forgotten as the crowd pressed close to watch him.

Then Bud awoke to the fact that his lips were getting sore from rubbing across the reeds, that time was passing and that he had urgent business in another part of town. Fifteen minutes or more had been spent when he had thought to drink a glass of beer and go on. He put away his mouth-harp and started for the door.

"Hey! Come back here with that music!" Steve Godfrey shouted arrogantly. "Where the hell you goin'?"

"Where did you get the crazy notion you could give orders to *me*?" Bud flung contemptuously over his shoulder as he slid back the bolt.

"You stay where you're at! That door stays shut till I give the word to open it!" Steve was off the keg and plowing toward him through the crowd.

"You'll stay shut a heap longer," flared Bud, and gave Steve an uppercut that sent his teeth into his tongue and jarred him cruelly. Behind Steve a lean face leered at Bud; the face of Palmer, who was edging forward as if he meant to take a hand. The key had been turned in the lock and removed—by Palmer, Bud would have sworn. The knowing look in his eyes betrayed that much.

Steve was coming at him again, gun in hand and mouthing threats; but the stranger who had danced managed to hook an agile foot between his legs and throw Steve so hard that he bounced. Then he swung a chair, and the crowd backed.

Bud opened the door by the simple expedient of shooting the lock off it, and went out with belled nostrils like a bull buffalo on the rampage. The strange youth followed close behind, the chair still held aloft and ready for a charge.

"Come on, Lightfoot," Bud snorted. "That bunch fights mostly with their mouths." A little farther down the street his temper cooled to the point where further speech came easily. "Darned chumps! I guess I quit rather suddenly, but it wasn't because I was tired of watching you dance. You're a dandy. But I have to get into the bank, and it's about closing-up time. I just happened to think of it."

"I'd danced quite long enough. I wanted to leave and meant to the first chance," the stranger dubbed Lightfoot confessed. "I guess they're a pretty tough lot in there; but I want to get acquainted, and I knew they'd probably enjoy my dancing and feel more friendly toward me. I'm anxious to shake down into the community and be considered just one of you."

"Are you classing me with that bunch back there?" Bud gave him a studying look.

"No-o—I meant the whole country, when I spoke. I'm a stranger here, and it seems pretty hard to get acquainted." He shook his head ruefully. "Now, I'm afraid I've only made matters worse, fighting like that."

"That wasn't a fight. They've gone back to lapping up free booze by now, and don't remember anything about it. Dirty sneaks, most of them are, and the less you shake down and be considered just one of them the better."

He went up the steps of the little, private bank at the end of the street, rattled the door knob, frowned at the green-shaded windows and looked at his watch.

"Three minutes to three, and I'm two minutes fast," he commented. "They've no business locking up ahead of time. I've just got to get in, that's all there is about it."

"There's a side door," the stranger suggested, and Bud gave a nod of assent and led the way around the corner of the building. A man with a pack-horse was riding out from the open lot behind the bank, going toward the river at a shacking trot. Bud gave him a casual glance, turned to the bank door and discovered that it was locked also, an unusual circumstance at that hour. He gave the door a kick or two by way of protest.

"This is one hell of a town!" he snorted. "Let's take a look at the back windows. The cashier surely must be inside, and I'll raise him—if I have to take the darn bank apart."

"I'm afraid I'm partly to blame," apologized the stranger. "I didn't know you were in a hurry."

"I quit in time. The bank doesn't close until three, and a fellow can always get in the side door any time within an hour after that. It's got no business to be locked up like a jail this time of day." They were inspecting the windows in the rear and saw that they were all closed in spite of the July heat. "Lightfoot, don't ever tell me you're living here because you like the place, or I'm liable to think you're crazy."

"Lightfoot" grinned.

"I'm here because my sister and I liked the name on the map. It seemed to be located right in the heart of the cattle country, where dramatic incident and local color should be at their best. Our name isn't Lightfoot, though. I don't understand how you got the idea it was. My name is Brunelle. I'm Lawrence Brunelle and my sister's name is Margaret; Marge and Lawrie we're always called. We've been here only a week."

"That's a week longer than I'd want to stay," Bud declared. "You picked about the meanest place in Montana when you chose Smoky Ford. I wish to thunder I knew where that cashier went. He doesn't drink, so it's of no use looking in the saloons. Say, if I stand on the door knob and get a squint over the curtain, could you hold my legs and steady me? The darn knob might bust." He stooped to unbuckle his spurs. "I tell you, Lightfoot, there's something wrong about this bank being closed up tight as a drum a good hour sooner than it should be."

With the ease of any other young broncho fighter he mounted the door knob, balanced there on the ball of one foot and bent to peer in through the three-inch space above the green shade that had been pulled down over the glass panel in the door. An awkward position, but he did not keep it long. When he dropped and faced Brunelle his eyes were wide and black with excitement.

"He's dead in there, Lightfoot! The whole top of his head is caved in, and the vault door's wide open!"

Spurs and crumpled gloves in one hand, Bud led the way across the street and down several doors to where James Delkin, the bank's president, ran a livery stable—he being a banker in name only, as is the way of village banks that cater to the local trade and find few customers, though these may carry rather large accounts. Delkin was swearing at his hostler when the two arrived, but he gave over that pastime long enough to hear the news. His face went tallow white.

"I told you first, Mr. Delkin. The rest of the town is boozing in the Elkhorn, and no one knows what has happened. I hate to push my private business into this, but it's a long ride to the Meadowlark, and Lark sent in a check to be cashed. Fifteen hundred dollars, it is. Will this murder make any difference?"

"*Difference?*" Delkin slowed his tottering run to stare at Bud. "If the vault's cleaned out, you can't get fifteen cents! My God, man, the bank will be broke!"

"Oh, say!" Brunelle's voice held panic. "My sister and I brought all our money with us and banked it here, just last week!"

Delkin was nervously trying to fit a key into the lock of the side door, and he did not seem to hear. They pushed in together, Bud thoughtfully closing the door behind them with the idea of staving off the excitement that would follow hard on the heels of the town's enlightenment.

Delkin lunged through the partition door, rushed to the open vault, gave one look and turned to the grewsome figure lying asprawl on the floor. He looked at the shelf behind the cashier's window, at the pulled-out, empty drawer beneath and slumped into a chair, his whole form seeming to have shrunk and aged perceptibly.

"Charlie dead," he wailed, "and the bank cleaned out—ruined! My God, what can I do?"

"Do?" Bud's eyes snapped. "Get after the gang that did it! You can get the money back if you pull yourself together. They can't eat it, and—the way Charlie looks, I'd say this happened not more than half an hour ago." He turned to Brunelle, the cameo brooch looking oddly out of place above his hard eyes and grim mouth. "You raise the town, Lightfoot, and I'll fork my horse and get after that pack outfit we saw leaving here as we came around the corner."

"You think he did this?" Brunelle looked startled. "One man couldn't, could he?"

"One man could have seen the gang leave here," Bud retorted impatiently. "Delkin, you stay here. Lightfoot will send someone." He whirled and was gone, running lightly down to where his horse was tied in front of the Elkhorn saloon, from which still rolled the uproar of boisterous celebration of nothing.

CHAPTER FIVE
THE SIGN OF THE GOLDEN ARROW

Still, clear moonlight lay upon the land, with the far hills like a painted back drop against the stars when Bud, having ridden far and fast, jogged wearily into town and dropped reins before the bank, where a light shone faintly through the curtained windows and figures were to be seen moving occasionally behind the green shades. He knocked, and after a hushed minute Delkin himself admitted him. Bud walked from force of habit to the grilled window and leaned his fore-arms heavily upon the shelf, his cameo-pinned hat pushed back on his head as he pressed his forehead against the bronze rods of the barrier.

"Well, I rode the high lines," he announced huskily because of the dryness in his throat. "I saw the bunch from town go fogging along the trail across the river, but I was back on the bench, following a mess of horse tracks that took off toward the hills.

"There's something darn funny about this deal, Mr. Delkin." Delkin had retreated again behind the partition as if that was what his office required of him. "Here's how she lies, but I don't pretend to understand it. I got my horse and rode back up here and out behind the bank, so as to pick up any trail they had left. The only horses that had stood for any length of time near the bank was a pack outfit that had been on the vacant lot back here all afternoon, by the sign. It was Bat Johnson had it—he works for Palmer. He rode away just as I came around the corner of the bank, thinking I could get in at the side door, and I overhauled him at the ford. He'd taken that stock trail through the willows, back here, and he told me he'd got a glimpse of three or four horses loping down through the draw to the ford ahead of him. He hadn't seen anyone leave the bank by the side door, he said, for he was over to the blacksmith shop for a while and came and got his horses just as I came in sight around the corner. He hadn't seen anyone that acted suspicious, but he hadn't been paying any attention, he said.

"I rode back up the draw and picked up the trail of four horses, shod all around. Your town posse crossed the river while I was in the draw, and I followed the four horses across. The riders ahead of me didn't pay any attention to the tracks. I suppose," he added scornfully, "they were looking for masked men with white sacks full of money in their arms! They just loped down the road, all in a bunch, as if they were headed for a dance." Bud cleared his throat; this painstaking report was dry work.

"Well, Mr. Delkin, those four horses—shod all around—took straight across the bench beyond the Smoky, heading for the hills. Here's the funny part, though: They didn't hunt the draws where they could keep out of sight, but sifted right along in a beeline, across ridges and into hollows and out again, until the tracks were lost where they joined a bunch of range stock that's running back there on the bench about eight miles. From there on I couldn't get a line on anything at all. I tried to ride up on the bunch, but my horse was tired and they're pretty wild, and they broke for the hills. There were shod horses among them, and I'm sure that no one had time to catch up fresh horses out of that band and leave the four—and, Mr. Delkin, those four horses didn't travel as if they had riders. I'd swear they were running loose, and beat it straight from town to join their own bunch of range horses."

"And that's all you found out?" Delkin's voice was flat and old and hopeless.

"That's the extent of it. It was a blind trail, I believe, and your holdups went some other way. Perhaps that posse will pick up some sign, though if they do it will be an accident."

The other men there asked a few questions, their manner as hopeless as Delkin's. They were the directors and other officers of the bank, and Bud sensed their feeling of helplessness before this calamity. The body of the cashier had been removed, and these were staying on the scene simply because they did not know what else to do.

"How's the bank? Cleaned out?" Bud was still conscious of his own personal responsibilities.

"Everything." Delkin waved an apathetic hand. "We're so far from other banks, and Charlie slept right here—so in spite of the fact that we sometimes didn't have more than a dozen customers in here all day, we kept more cash on hand than was safe. At least we had more on hand right now than usual. With the bookkeeper sick, Charlie was alone here part of the time. Near closing time especially. So few people came in, along in the afternoon. We did most of our business during the forenoons." He moistened his lips and looked away. "It looks as if Charlie had just set the time lock and was getting ready to close the vault when—it happened. Another half hour, perhaps, and they'd have had to blow open the vault, and someone would have heard. Maybe five minutes before you came—I can't see how they got away without being seen."

"Well, I can't do any more tonight, Mr. Delkin. My horse and I are both about all in. Of course you 'phoned for the sheriff."

"Right after it happened. He'll be here with a posse of his own before morning."

Outside Bud almost collided with young Brunelle, who caught him by the arm with an impulsive gesture.

"I recognized your horse. Come over to our cabin, won't you, Mr. Larkin? You see I've discovered what your name is. I've been watching for you to come back, for I knew you'd be hungry; and Marge—my sister Margaret—has supper all ready for you. We're pretty lonely," he added wistfully. "People here seem to be very clannish and cool toward strangers."

"That's because they're roughnecks and know it," said Bud, and picked up the reins of his horse. "If you'll wait until I put my horse in the stable I'll be right with you. Only I'm liable to clean you out of grub if I once start eating. There's over six feet of me, Lightfoot, and I'm all hollow."

"That'll be all right," smiled the other. "It's yours while it lasts—and that may not be long if the bank is really closed for good. We haven't any money to buy more."

Delkin's hostler took charge of the Meadowlark horse and the two men walked on to where a light shone through a cabin window, set back from the main street in an open space that gave a close view of the bluff. Bud very likely did not grasp the imminent poverty of his host, probably because he was not paying much attention to his last sentence; and that his ready acceptance of the invitation to supper was caused chiefly by a too intimate knowledge of the hotel cuisine.

"My sister," Brunelle explained on the way, "is an author of short stories. She has had one printed in the paper back home, and the editors of several Eastern magazines have given her quite a good many puffs on the stories she sent them. They were very sorry they couldn't use them and said it wasn't because there was anything wrong with the stories. I know all our friends at home are very anxious that she should make that her life work. But back in our home town there never seemed to be anything to write about, and Marge felt the need of going where there would be interesting subjects. So when mother died we decided to come right out West and write up some cowboy stories, and I could illustrate them with pictures drawn from life. Western stories are all the go now, and these ought to take pretty well with the editors, I should think—though of course one needs to have a pull to get right in. Still, these will be done right on the spot with pictures of the real characters, and that will make a hit with the editors, I should think.

"So that's the real reason why we came to Smoky Ford. We aren't telling everyone, because we don't want to make people self-conscious in our presence. We want to win the confidence of the people. That's why I danced in the saloon when they asked me to.

"We let it be known that my sister is out here for her health. That isn't so far off, either, because she was all worn out with taking care of mother, and the doctor advised her to go away somewhere for a while. So we sold the property—and every dollar we have we put in the bank here. We thought it would show our confidence in the town and help us get in with the right people."

"There aren't any right people to get in with; not to amount to anything," Bud told him bluntly. "Not in Smoky Ford. Delkin and—well, there are four or five pretty nice men, but I don't know what kind of wives they've got. Gossipy old hens, most of them, I suppose. I'd drift to some other range, I believe, if I wanted to feel confidence in my neighbors."

Budlike, he wondered if the sister was pretty and young. Tired as he was, interest picked up his feet and pulled the sag out of his shoulders when they neared the open doorway and he caught a glimpse of the girl called Marge. He took off his hat and held it so that the cameo brooch was hidden within the palm of his left hand, and gave his rumpled brown hair a hasty rub with the other as he entered—silent, positive proof that the young woman had already caught his roving young masculine attention.

He ought to be hurrying on to the ranch that night. He told them so, and then permitted himself to be persuaded into staying all night and sharing the bed of his host, whom he persisted in calling Lightfoot in spite of one or two corrections.

"Oh, I know why you call Lawrie that," cried Marge, who had been studying closely this young cowboy, the very first one she had met on friendly footing. "It's a custom of cowboys to give names to strangers, just as the Indians do. You know, Lawrie, Indians name their young and also strangers after the first thing that strikes their notice, the names for adults usually being suggested by some mark or trait in the individual that sets him apart from his fellows. Lawrie told me how he danced in the saloon while you played for him, and of course your custom demanded that you name him after his dancing. Don't you see, Lawrie? He has already given you your tribal, cowboy name—Lightfoot. I rather like it, I believe. So now you, at least, are initiated into the tribe—made a member of the tribe of cowboys!"

She had a pretty, eager way of speaking, and her eyes were the sparkly kind when she talked, yet Bud looked at her with a smoldering indignation in his eyes. Living next door to the Belknap reservation, he did not think much of Indians—less of their customs; he having known them long and too well. Nor did he approve of anyone calling cowboys a tribe. He had barked knuckles on a man's cheek for less cause before now, and he set his teeth into his lower lip to hold in a retort discourteous. But Marge was a pretty girl, as has been plainly intimated; her gray eyes sparkled like stars on a frosty night, her skin was soft and whiter than any range girl could ever hope to attain, and her mouth was red and provocative, daring male lips to kisses.

"Well, then, what are you going to call me?" she challenged fearlessly, as girls do who have been fed with flattery all their lives.

"I think perhaps I'll call you—Early," drawled Bud, a faint twitching at the corners of his mouth.

A range girl would have taken warning and let well enough alone after that. But Marge was not a range girl.

"But you aren't sure, so I can't accept that as final. And now, there's something I've been dying to ask you, Mr. Larkin. Just why do cowboys wear their sombreros pinned back like that? You know, I'm gathering local color of the cattle ranges, and I like to get right at the meaning of things." And with that, she pulled a notebook from her pocket and held pencil point to her lips. "Is it some special mark—an insignia of something? An insignia is a mark showing some certain rank," she explained kindly.

"Well, I guess it's an insignia, then," Bud confessed. "But it's a secret and I can't exactly explain. You won't see many wearing this particular badge—insignia." He rolled the word as if it were a new one and he liked the sound.

"Can't you even tell the name of the society or order?"

"Well—I can't go into details," said Bud gravely. "All I can say is it's the range sign of the golden arrow." (He thought she must surely see through that; she must certainly have read about that terrible young god, Cupid, who shot arrows of gold for love and arrows tipped with lead for hate. Surely she would remember that!)

But she didn't.

"The Golden Arrow? I don't—did you ever hear of that secret order, Lawrie?"

"No," said Lawrie indifferently, "not that I remember. But Mr. Larkin and I were going over to see if that posse has caught those bandits, Marge. If the bank doesn't get that money back, and has to close its doors, we're in a fix!"

"I know—but I want to find out about this secret society among the cowboys, Lawrie. It's important that I study cowboys when I get the chance, or how can I write about them realistically? And this Golden Arrow stuff is something no author of Western stories has ever mentioned. Can't you tell me a tiny bit more about it, Mr. Larkin?"

"Well, I know it's about the oldest society on earth," Bud elucidated gravely. "I believe the very first savage—"

"Why, of course! How stupid of me not to see at once that the Golden Arrow must be pure Indian!"

"Well, I dunno how pure it is, but I guess—"

"And you're a member! But what I can't understand, Mr. Larkin, is why that cameo pin should be an emblem of the Golden Arrow."

"Why," said Bud, looking at her with soft, dark eyes that simply couldn't lie, "the cameo pin is recognized everywhere as the paleface sign."

"Of course!" cried Marge, and wrote it down in her book.

Bud went out, holding his lips carefully rigid and unsmiling, though he made strange gulping sounds in his throat all the way down town.

CHAPTER SIX

BUD DOES A LITTLE BUSTLING

The volunteer man hunters had returned much soberer though no wiser than they had set out, and with them came Bat Johnson, who declared that his trip could be postponed until after the inquest, which would be held as soon as the sheriff and coroner arrived from the county seat. In the meantime Delkin had sent frantic word by telephone to the nearest points, and men were riding into town on sweaty horses, curious to see the corpse of the cashier and eager to join in the chase.

"For half a cent I'd borrow a horse and take the trail alone, with grub enough for a couple of days," Bud confided restlessly to his companion. "I'd do it, only Delkin says we'll be wanted at the inquest tomorrow; and after that the sheriff will be on the job and running things to suit himself. Seems mighty queer, the way those bandits plumb disappeared and never left a trace. Bat Johnson claimed to me that he was sure four riders went down the draw and crossed the river ahead of him, but now he admits that he only got a glimpse of the horses' rumps and can't swear to any riders. But what in thunder would range horses be doing right here in town almost? The whole thing's off color. I wish Lark was here—my uncle. He's pretty good at figuring out the other fellow's game."

"There must be some way to catch the murderers and get the money back," Brunelle worried. "Of course catching them won't help the cashier, but the money makes a big difference. This really does leave Marge and me in an awful fix, Mr. Larkin. All you people have homes and property, but here we are—perfect strangers; and a little over five dollars to face the world with! We didn't think it would be safe to keep any money in the house, out in this wild country, so every dollar we had was in the bank—where it would be safe!" He laughed a bit wildly. "Of course, I'll go to work at once. We both will. I wonder how much the robbers got?"

Bud shook his head.

"Delkin doesn't know, exactly; or if he does he isn't telling until he has to. He says Charlie Mulholland took care of everything while the other fellow has been sick, and all he or any of the others did was go in and act as teller while Charlie wrote letters and worked on the books forenoons. It's just a little whiddledig of a bank—plenty of money, but not many depositors. All the cattlemen and some horse raisers used it, and put in great wads when they sold off some stock, and checked it out in driblets. I could have run the whole works myself, almost. If the bank's busted, the robbers got a plenty. It's going to hit a lot of us, but it sure is too bad you folks got caught. What kind of work did you think of doing?"

"Well, Marge could teach school, of course. And once she gets a stand-in with the editors, she can sell all the pieces she writes, and I can sell the pictures to go with them. I can get a job as a cowboy for a while, I suppose, until we get on our feet again." His jaw squared. "We'll never go back, that's one thing sure; not even if we had the train fare. All the neighbors said we'd make a fizzle of things if we left there. I suppose there's a school somewhere that Marge can teach, isn't there?"

"I don't know of—wel-l—come to think of it, the Meadowlark sure needs a school teacher." Bud had caught another disturbing sight of Marge sitting with bowed head by the table, lamplight shining through loose locks of hair.

Tired as he was, bedtime came too soon for Bud that night.

* * * *

Marge would go to the inquest next morning, though Bud warned her that it would not be exciting and that she would only get herself talked about. These things could not daunt her. She must go, she said, because she was going to need murders and posses and sheriffs right along in her Western stories, and this was a wonderful opportunity to study the types at close range. She could not understand why Bud laughed.

So to the inquest she went, and thereby shocked the sober citizens of Smoky Ford, who liked their womenfolk shy and retiring. She mistook the big blacksmith for the sheriff, who was small and very quiet and kept his badge hidden under his vest. She was much disappointed in the coroner, who was pot-bellied and chewed tobacco frankly and untidily and spat where he pleased. Moreover, the corpse was in a back room out of sight, and Marge could not bring herself quite to the point of walking deliberately in to see how a man looks who has been murdered. She was the only woman present, and the room was crowded with men who stared at her; not even her notebook could furnish cause sufficient for her presence.

Then, after a few tedious preliminaries, they all trooped off to the bank to take a look around and left Marge all by herself in the empty storeroom. It did not help her temper any to have Bud ask her afterwards how she liked the wild, wild West as far as she had got.

"That man Palmer, who deposited five thousand dollars just before he came into the saloon, looked at you very queerly when you were giving an account of finding the cashier," Brunelle observed irrelevantly, thinking it best to change the subject before Marge said something sarcastic.

"He can't help that. He was born queer," Bud retorted. "Meanest old skinflint in the country. Took a quirting from my uncle before the whole town, and never has made a move to get back at Lark for it. Maybe that's why he looks queer when he sees someone from the Meadowlark."

"But he sneered as if he thought you were lying," Lawrie persisted.

"Well, so did I sneer as if I thought he were lying when he told about depositing five thousand dollars in the bank. I bet he keeps his money buried back of the barn or some other good place."

"I wish we'd buried ours," Marge sighed. "Or the editors would wake up and buy a story or something. We'll have to hunt some work to do, Lawrie—"

"Oh, I forgot to tell you, Marge. Mr. Larkin knows of a school you can teach. He says the Meadowlark school needs a teacher. And perhaps I can get a job somewhere close, as a cowboy. Do you think I could, Mr. Larkin?"

"How do we get there?" Marge began to untie her apron as if she meant to start within the next five minutes. Bud caught his breath and opened his mouth to explain, to temporize. But Marge was already beginning to pack her books, and her eyes were the brightest, dancingest gray eyes he had ever looked into. His own kindled while he gazed.

So that is how it happened that young Bud Larkin, leaving his own tall sorrel in Delkin's stable as hostage of a sort, drove blithely out to the Meadowlark with a hired team and a spring wagon and two passengers squeezed into the front seat with him and three trunks piled high and tied there with Bud's good grass rope.

CHAPTER SEVEN
WAYS AND MEANS

When the hired rig from Smoky Ford swung through the gate and on up to the very porch of the house, with Bud grinning impudently at his world from the driver's seat and a strange young woman wedged in between him and a young man who bore all the earmarks of a pilgrim, and three huge trunks lashed to the back of the vehicle to say that the visitors had come to stay, Lark stood in the doorway and stared dazedly, with never a word of welcome for the strangers.

But Maw did not hesitate or question. Instead, she hurried out—walking erect under Lark's braced arm in the doorway with plenty of room to spare—and waddled to the edge of the porch, smiling unabashed. Marge almost screamed at sight of her.

"Get right down and come on in," Maw cried. "Supper's about ready. As luck would have it, I killed that speckled hen that wanted to set and cooked her with dumplings. We're almost ready to sit down, and I'll bet you're hungry!"

Bud had swung his long legs out over the wheel and landed beside her, and Marge was shocked to see him lift the misshapen creature clear of the ground and kiss her on each leathery cheek before he set her down again and turned to help Marge out.

"Maw, this is Miss Brunelle. She's going to teach school here. And this is her brother, Lightfoot. He's going to be a cowboy. Hello, Lark. Say, I promised Lightfoot that you'd give him a job so he can be with his sister while she teaches school. Where's Skookum?"

"Oh, he went down to feed the cougar. I'm so glad we're going to have a school," cried Maw, without batting an eye or waiting for Lark to struggle through a sentence. "Larkie's real glad too. Of course he'll put Mr. Lightfoot right to work. Now, come right in, folks, and take off your things while I put on a couple more plates. Buddy, I'm afraid we haven't a room ready for Mr. Lightfoot—"

"He can bunk with me tonight," Bud interrupted, glancing up from unroping the trunks. "Say, Lark, the bank was robbed yesterday and the cashier killed. That's why I didn't get in quicker. I had to stay for the inquest this morning. No sign of the bunch that did it." The trunks thudded one by one to the porch. "It happened just before I went to cash that check. Say, Maw, Lightfoot's name is Brunelle, same as his sister, if you want to Mister him."

He stepped on the hub of the front wheel and went up, unwrapping the lines from around the whipstock as he did so. Lark came to life then and climbed in and stood behind the seat while Bud drove back to the stable.

Sprawled before the bunk house, the Meadowlark riders were taking in the smallest details of the amazing arrival and trying not to appear curious, or even interested. But Jake, permanently crippled in one leg from lying out all one night under his dead horse, got up and limped leisurely down to the stable to help take care of the team. Lark saw him coming and hastened his speech.

"Bud, where in the name of Jonah did you pick up them pilgrims? And what's this here joke about a school teacher fer the Meddalark? Where'd you git 'em—and their *trunks*?" The last three words sounded very much like a groan.

"Say, I didn't *steal* 'em," Bud flashed back meaningly.

"No—I'll bet you didn't git the chancet. I bet they grabbed you—"

Bud whirled on him, straight brows pulled together. If he began to see the foolishness of his impulsive hospitality, he never would admit it.

"Look here, Lark, these are nice folks, and they were up against it when the bank was robbed and they couldn't get a two-bit piece of their money out. Strangers, fresh from the East somewhere; came out here with the wild idea they can write and illustrate stories of the West and sell them to magazines. Maybe they can do it, but they sound too darned amateurish to me. And they were *broke*, I tell you!

"So she wanted to teach school or something—and you know darned well, Lark, that Skookum ought to be learning to read before he's sent off to school. All the kids would guy the life out of him if he landed without having some kind of a start in schooling at his age. And as for Lightfoot, he won't be the first tenderfoot that had to learn which end of a horse is the front." He stopped and glanced toward the house, where Maw was calling through the dusk that supper was all on the table. "And my thunder, Lark," he added as a clincher, "you never leave the Basin without bringing back something to take care of and feed; even if you have to steal him. You'd have done this yourself."

Lark lifted his hat, pawed absently at his hair and set the hat at a different angle as they started back to the house, waving their hands before their faces to keep off the mosquitoes whose droning hum was audible throughout the Basin after sundown when the dew began falling.

"Shore you'd 'a' done it, Bud, if the girl had been cross-eyed?" he thrust slyly at Bud's well-known liking for pretty faces.

"No, I don't know as I would," Bud admitted with shameless candor. "She isn't any prettier than Bonnie Prosser, though—and she hasn't the brains that Bonnie has, and no sense of humor whatever. I'll bet, if you pinned her right down to it, she'd admit that she thinks cowboys eat grass when they're on the range. You ought to hear the questions she asked about us, coming out.

"Lightfoot's all right, though. He'll break in and be human long before she will. You'll like Lightfoot, even if he is green; one good thing, he knows it. And Marge is a darn pretty girl, all right, even if she did get all her brains out of books. She can teach Skookum and get him ready for school—"

"Oh, all right, all right!" Lark yielded wearily to end the argument. "But if this habit of hauling in the helpless is going to run in the family, son, we'll have to start in ridin' with a long rope and a runnin' iron, to feed 'em all. And what'll Bonnie say, Bud, when she hears about it? And a dozen other girls that have kept their dads broke buyin' hair ribbons for you to decorate yore bridle with?"

"Say, there aren't a dozen girls in the country; not white ones, and I don't take to color," Bud retorted equably. "And as for Bonnie—I'm not halter-broke yet, if you want to know, Lark."

At the porch Marge stood looking out over the dusky Basin to where the moon was beginning to gild the clouds on the hilltops beyond the Little Smoky.

"You know, I never dreamed that you had frogs away out West in Montana!" she cried in her pretty, eager way when the two approached. "They sound exactly like the frogs back in Iowa, too."

"Well, they're Iowa frogs, that's why," Bud explained matter-of-factly. "Way it happened was this: When the first white woman came with her husband and settled in this country, she had to teach the kids herself and she was a real conscientious mother. Whenever she sung them that song about 'There was a frog lived in a well, humble-jumble-jerry-jum,' they kept asking her what frogs were. So the next time a trainload of beef went to Chicago she had the cowboys stop off in Iowa and catch a few jars of pollywogglers and bring back with them. There were twice as many as she needed, so she sent a jar over to the Meddalark. They've done real well," he added, stopping to listen to the steady singsong chorus down in the meadow. "One trouble is, they brought in mosquitoes same time. Said the farmers back in Iowa told them frogs wouldn't live where they couldn't get mosquitoes in season. The boys sure brought a plenty—or else our breed of frogs are light eaters. We've got more mosquitoes than we need right now."

"Well," said Marge, all unsuspecting, "of course I knew the frogs must have come from *somewhere*, and I noticed that they sounded exactly like our frogs back home."

That is why Lark kept eyeing the girl curiously all through supper.

But the unexpected addition to the Meadowlark family could not crowd from Lark's mind the startling news of the tragedy in Smoky Ford; nor from the uneasy thoughts of Bud, who felt keenly that he had failed Lark in a certain important matter.

The two gravitated together without a word or look that signified intention and strolled silently out away from the house to a bowlder fallen from the crown of the bluff and lying solitary and conveniently out of earshot yet within sight of everything. Even in Lark's tempestuous youth the bowlder had been called the Council Rock because of its frequent occupation when confidences were to be exchanged. A faint trail led toward it through the sparse grass at the base of the bluff, proof that it was still popular. Bud climbed up to the broad, flat top and sat down, dangling his legs over the edge of the gray rock while he produced tobacco and papers.

"That check—Lark, I feel that I owe you fifteen hundred dollars," he began abruptly. "I was so darned thirsty and hot when I came down off the reservation that I didn't go straight to the bank as I should have done. I stopped at the Elkhorn for a glass of beer. Lightfoot was in there and let himself be bullied into dancing for Steve Godfrey's bunch of souses, and I played the mouth-harp for him. I guess I wasted nearly half an hour altogether before I started to the bank. At that," he added, pausing to run the tip of his tongue along the edge of the filled paper, "I was in time—or I would have been if the bank had left alone. But if I had gone there at first I'd have been in time to prevent a murder and cash your check."

"Damn' expensive beer the Elkhorn's sellin'," Lark commented dryly. "What about the Fryin' Pan?"

"They've sure got a lot of dandy horses, Lark," Bud told him, relieved at the change of subject. "I had to do a lot of jewing on the price, but I got the promise of a hundred head for fifteen hundred dollars; forty young mares, and the rest geldings two and three years old. Just right to break, most of them are. You might be able to stand Kid off for the money, seeing the bank was robbed, but I don't know. I told him it would be cash down. Kid said he never bothered with checks at all—you had the right hunch there. He hinted strongly for gold too. Said he'd burned a thousand dollars of paper money by accident once, and he's nervous about having it around."

"Yeah, I wouldn't be su'prised if he is!" Lark laughed to himself. "My Jonah, I shore do want that bunch of horses! You say the bank's put out of business?"

"That's what Delkin said. They may get organized again after a while— or they may get the money back, of course. I'd have wondered if the Frying Pan didn't know something about that affair—" He stopped and emptied his lungs of smoke. "But I saw the whole outfit at the ranch. Butch Cassidy's working for them this summer. I wish we could get those horses some way. They promised to hold the bunch close in, because I told them you'd be right over. I expect they're watching the trail for us right now."

"Too bad." Lark absently reached for his own "makin's." "Forty young mares, you say. Bud, I expect my old man would just about peel the hide off me if he was alive, but I'll be darned if I can set still and let that bunch of horses git out from under the old Meddalark iron. I'm goin' to hit the trail fer Glasgow and borry a couple or three thousand dollars. That'll run us till shippin' time if Delkin don't open up agin. First time the Meddalark ever borried, but I plumb got to have them horses!"

"I'll give you a bill of sale of a thousand head of my cattle, Lark. I'll feel better about the whole business if you'll use my stock for security on a loan, and it will save the Meadowlark from having a mortgage plastered on it."

"You keep what cattle you got, son. I'll make out all right. Can't tell how soon you might wanta set up fer yourself. The marryin' notion hits kinda sudden when she strikes—"

"Say, I'll sell out the whole bunch if you don't shut up. I want you to borrow on my cattle if you must get a loan, and I suppose that's the only way out. Those Frying Pan horses are sure dandies. There's one favor I want to ask if you do get them, Lark. I'd like to have a couple of the geldings to break for my own string. There are two blacks, dead ringers for each other, that are beauts. I want them both. Half brothers, I'd say; going on four; clean-limbed and short-coupled, with forequarters like a lion, and their eyes are plumb human. They'd make a peach of a matched driving team, but I want them to ride. Butch says he got a saddle on one and started to ride him, and it bucked, high, wide and handsome, until it was a relief to get thrown clean over the fence. But I'll bet I can gentle the two of them so they'll be like pet dogs. Lark, I want them!"

"Yeah, I kinda thought mebbe you did," Lark chuckled. "All right, son. I'll take the bill of sale and use it for security on a loan (I know where I can get money in Glasgow without the hull darn country knowin' the Meddalark's borryin' money), and you can have your two black bronchs fer keeps. I'll give you the papers for 'em, and you can put the one-legged Meddalark on 'em to show they're yourn. That'll be for int'rust on the use of your stock for a few months. How's that strike yuh?"

"Fine and dandy, Lark. Maybe you'll want to back down on your bargain when you've seen them, but I'll hold you to it. Kind of low-down, but darn it, I fell in love with those blacks, and I'd have to fight the boys away from them if they got a sight of them before any promise passed. And I had a long, hot ride in the wind, going to the Frying Pan, and talked myself black in the face getting the hundred head at that price. Kid was asking two thousand even for the bunch, but I made him see where the cash in his hand was worth something, and I told him fifteen hundred was your limit. Any other outfit would probably stand him off for part of it, and that's what turned the trick. And by the way, Lark, you'd better go prepared to bring back the gold, because Kid might be persuaded to throw in a few yearlings extra. They've got some good-looking colts over there. Most of the mares have got sucking colts, by the way."

"I'll borry three thousand, and get it all in gold," Lark planned. "I'll take a valise along, and carry the weight easy enough without it being noticed. I'll likely stay over a day in Glasgow, anyway."

"Make it as quick a trip as you can, Lark. You must bear in mind that Kid expects us tonight, and I wouldn't want the deal to fall through because he got tired of waiting. He's touchy as the devil—and if I don't get those two black bronchs, I'll die!"

CHAPTER EIGHT
BUD HOLDS COUNCIL WITH HIMSELF

When he sauntered down from the Council Rock in the full flood of moonlight, left Lark to enter the house alone and continued to the bunk house, where the boys still lingered by the doorway, Bud did not look like a man whose life depends upon getting a pair of black bronchos into his possession. His walk and his softly whistled tune betokened care-free youth.

Cigarettes pricked little, red stars in the line of shadow before the long, low-roofed building where the riders of the Meadowlark were housed and fed to their complete content. The murmur of voices dwindled so that the frog chorus came sharp to the ears as Bud came up and squatted on his bootheels alongside a man whom he identified even in the shadow as his particular friend, Frank Gelle—called Jelly with a frank disregard for proper pronunciation.

"Have a good trip, Bud?" Not for a top horse would Gelle have betrayed his curiosity over the mysterious visitors.

"Pretty fair. Hot as blazes riding across the reservation yesterday. Oh, by the way, Rosy, I didn't get those socks you wanted if I rode back through town. I meant to, but when the bank was robbed—"

"Get out!" Gelle exclaimed, as an expression of surprise. "Some of these days, Bud, somebody's goin' to lose his patience all of a sudden. He'll just kill you and drag you off somewhere and leave you. I hate to do it, but you won't be human till somebody asks the question, so who's the girl you brought in?"

"The girl? Oh, she's Lightfoot's sister. She's going to teach our school, Jelly."

"School?" chorused six shaken voices.

"Now I *know* you're lying, Bud," Gelle mourned. "I've got to have a serious talk with you, I kin see that. This habit of lyin' where there ain't no cause or provocation—if you'll walk awn over to the Rock with me now, Bud, I'll tell you what I think about it."

"It's him that'll do the tellin', and that right now," a voice broke in ominously. "They's a certain Meddalark that won't have a damn' chirp left in 'im, time we git the pinfeathers plucked out. Us fellers have stood about all we're goin' to from Bud."

"Just another prophet in his own country," sighed Bud, reaching out a hand for Gelle's tobacco sack because he was too lazy to reach into his pocket for his own. "She *is* Lightfoot's sister. And the bank *was* robbed, and Charlie Mulholland was killed. I discovered him myself—"

Half an hour went to the telling of the story to the smallest detail, accurately as if he were talking before a jury. For when all the jokes were done, Bud appreciated the hunger these young men felt for news of their world after plugging hard on round-up. They were sick of their own stale company and they craved action, even the vicarious excitement of Bud's experiences. He gave them all he knew, and by the time he had exhausted his store of impressions each man there could visualize the whole affair so far as Bud knew it.

They discussed at length the mystery of its quiet perpetration on the edge of banking hours while forty or fifty men foregathered within gunshot of the place. Then Tony Scarpa, more American than his name implied, swung to the more immediate event.

"Who's Lightfoot and who's his sister, and what's the joke about teaching our school?"

"Straight goods." In the narrowing shadow as the moon swam higher they could see Bud's eyes gleam with mischief. "Lightfoot's a pilgrim; an artist, so he says. I know he's a darn good dancer, for I saw him dance. His sister's a pilgress. They went broke when the bank did, and had to rustle jobs—being perfect strangers in the country and having a bad habit of eating every day. She wanted a school to teach. That's the first and only thing a girl from the East ever thinks of when she comes West; that and marrying some cattle king and wearing diamonds. He wanted to be a cowboy—and I, being an accommodating cuss, gave them both jobs. I recalled the fact that there's a lot you fellows don't know yet, and while you're acquiring useful knowledge she can study your types. You see—"

"Study our *what*?" A man leaned forward so that the moon shone fully and clearly on his astonished face.

"Study your types. She's an amateur author and she means to write stories about cowboys. So she's looking for good types."

"Sa-ay!" Tony's irrepressible drawl cut musically through the amazed silence. "Loan me your type, will yuh, Bob? I lost mine back there where I bulldogged that roan steer."

"I will not! I'm goin' to need all the type I got. Is she purty, Bud?"

"She sure is." Bud glanced up at the moon and softly rhapsodized, "Big, devilish gray eyes—they'd drown a man's troubles so deep he'd swear he never had one. Her mouth—if her mouth has never been kissed it should be."

"It's goin' to be," Tony murmured, and made a motion of rising to his feet. Big Bob Leverett yanked him down.

"You ain't in this, Tony. Bud's givin' *me* the dope. You gwan to bed. You ain't got no type, and there ain't nothin' to set up for!"

"Law-zee, *boss*!" cried a tall young man with unbelievably small feet thrust straight out before him into the moonlight. "Here's one scholar that'll sure never be tardy!"

"I'm goin' to whisper an' stick out my tongue at you pelicans, and git to stay after school," Gelle declared.

"You—you fellers can go to her darned old school, but I won't," a young, rebellious voice cried from within the open door.

"Skookum?" Bud leaned and peered into the dark. "Come on out here, pardner. Why aren't you in bed?"

"How'd the kid git in?" Gelle swung his lean body sidewise, reached a long arm into the house and plucked the boy expertly by his middle. "Here he is, Bud. Clumb through the window, I reckon."

Skookum wriggled free and sat down in the dirt, crossing his legs and folding his arms in exact imitation of Bud's favorite pose when at ease among his fellows. He glanced up and down the row of cowpunchers leaning against the wall, and the moonlight gilded his hair like a halo and made of his eyes two deep, dark pools.

"I don't like her," he stated flatly. "She turned up her nose at—at Maw, and she asked her brother if he s'posed that hid-hid-e-ous creature was any relation to—to Bud. She said she couldn't bear to—to eat Maw's cookin' 'cause it was 'pulsive. And it was chicken dumpluns and—and pie!"

Dead silence for a space; then Gelle spoke diffidently, uncertain between apology and resentment.

"We get you, Skookum. But you see, Maw—well, she needs to be took kinda gradual, right at first. You know Maw's a kinda hard looker till you git used to her—"

"Maw's the purtiest woman in—in Montana!" Skookum declared hotly. "She's cute and—and sweet. When I get big, I'm agoin' to—to marry Maw. I asked her, and she said she—she would. You shut up about Maw. She's purtier than that darned old girl! Ain't she, Bud?"

"Handsome is as handsome does makes Maw the most beautiful woman in the world. You're right about that, pardner." Bud's voice had a queer note in it. "You stand up for Maw, Skookum, and I'm right with you. But I don't believe Maw would want you to pass up a chance to learn something. She thought it would be just fine to have a school here. It's that, or go to a boarding school where all the boys would laugh at you, and I don't believe Maw could stand that, pardner. It seems to me that your duty to Maw would make you want to learn just as fast as you can from Miss Brunelle."

"I don't care! She's a mean old—"

"Careful, Skookum. Never call a woman names—and besides, in this case it isn't fair. Miss Brunelle's an orphan, and she's among strangers, and she was all tired out—and you know yourself that even Lark can't stand it to see Maw with her teeth out and laid up on a shelf somewhere. I couldn't get her off to one side and speak to her about it before strangers, and neither could Lark. But Maw ought to have thought of it herself and put in her teeth when she saw company coming."

"Well, maybe she's purtier with—with her teeth on. But I bet if that old girl's teeth wabbled like—like Maw's teeth do, she wouldn't wear 'em, either. They tip up on the side and—and pinch. Maw showed me!"

"Well, then, we'll let Maw suit herself about it. Miss Brunelle will gentle down and get used to her, teeth or no teeth. It's like a horse getting accustomed to a yellow slicker," he went on. "He always stampedes at first. He'll pitch and strike and raise Cain generally—but there always comes a time when that same old yellow slicker feels mighty good spread over his back when he's humped up in a cold rain. We won't say a word, pardner. We'll just go along as if we didn't notice anything, and you'll see how soon Miss Brunelle will learn to love Maw."

"And—and Maw needn't wear her teeth if—if she don't want to," Skookum stipulated earnestly, "unless Lark ketches her w-without 'em."

"That's the idea, exactly," Bud assured him as man to man. "You see, Lark feels sensitive about Maw's teeth, because he took a beeswax impression himself and sent it to a dentist that advertised pretty extensively and wrote that teeth could be made by what Lark called absent treatment. He'd hate like thunder to admit he'd made a fizzle of the job, and Maw wouldn't for the world hurt his feelings by telling him straight out that they don't fit.

So there you are, and we'll just have to let them manage the affair themselves, and show Miss Brunelle what we think of Maw, teeth or no teeth."

Skookum nodded acquiescence, heaving a great sigh of relief.

"I was goin' to—to tell Maw what that girl said. But—but I'm glad I never."

"Real men don't repeat things that may cause hard feelings. You remember that, Skookum. If you'd gone tattling that, Maw would have felt badly and cried."

In the moonlight they could see how the boy's big eyes brimmed suddenly.

"Maw does—every time I change my shirt. It's where grandpa quirted me, and—and the marks is there."

"Grandpa—hunh! I'll grandpa that old devil if I ever run across him," Frank Gelle rapped out viciously.

"You leave grandpa alone! I'm waitin' till—till I get big as Bud, and then grandpa's—my meat!"

"There's Maw calling you to go to bed," Bud reminded him hastily—and unnecessarily, since Maw's voice was full size and not to be ignored. "Come on—I feel like rolling in, myself. Let's go pound our ears, as Shakespeare says."

But when Skookum had been safely delivered to Maw, Bud strolled back to the Council Rock, which was usually free from the humming hordes of mosquitoes, and where the acrid smoke of the smudges were but a pleasantly faint aroma. Thinking was not a popular pastime with young Bud Larkin as a rule, but nevertheless there were times when he felt the need of a quiet hour to meditate upon late impressions and events, especially when they came thick and fast, as the last two days had brought them.

For one thing, he was depressed over the murder of the bank cashier and he felt more responsibility in the matter than he had owned to Lark. There was no getting around the fact that he might have prevented the whole thing had he gone straight to the bank instead of stopping at the Elkhorn. When he thought how that one glass of beer had cost a man's life, Bud felt as if he never wanted another drink. He rolled and smoked a cigarette while he recalled each incident of yesterday afternoon.

Palmer's peculiar look when Bud had first tried to open the saloon door, for instance. Did that mean anything more than a natural enmity toward a Meadowlark man and a malicious satisfaction in knowing that the door was locked? According to his own voluntary statement at the inquest, Palmer had just come from the bank where he had made a deposit of five thousand dollars, the price of a herd of cattle which he had sold to the Government for the Indians; so he said, and two men present had borne out the statement regarding the sale. The pass book which he exhibited showed the amount, in Charlie's meticulous figures—perhaps the last he had written. Palmer, of course, couldn't have robbed the bank, for Bud felt sure that Charlie had not been dead so long when he discovered him.

The locking of the saloon door might have been a suspicious circumstance, but there also Bud felt baffled by the plausibility of the incident. Steve Godfrey frequently "bought" whatever place he chanced to celebrate in after a sale of stock that made him feel rich for a day or two. He too had sold cattle for use on the reservation. Buying a place in which to entertain all the loose men in town was merely a figurative purchase, meaning that all drinks were free for an hour or two, and that Steve would pay double for everything and waken next morning with a head the size of a barrel—according to his belief—and would forswear strong drink for a month or two thereafter.

No, Bud decided, the locking of the Elkhorn door had been merely a coincidence that facilitated the murder and robbery.

But there was the mysterious incident of the four shod horses which had no riders, galloping out across the river to mingle unrecognizably with the herd on the high plateau, mostly saddle horses and half-broken bronchos turned loose after the spring round-up to fatten on the sweet bunch grass of the higher ground until September brought shipping time and another strenuous season of work.

The Meadowlark horses had grazing grounds across the river, and so had several other outfits. Bud had not won close enough to read the brands on the herd which the four had joined, but he felt certain that they were not Meadowlark horses. Indeed, he could recognize their own herd as far as he could distinguish the individual animals.

But why had four riderless horses left the outskirts of town at that particular time and scurried out across the range to the west? To hide for a time the route taken by the robbers, Bud was certain; and admitted that it was a clever ruse, spoiled only by the quick action he himself had taken. Or had the robbers ridden the horses out of town and turned them loose to seek their own herd later on, hiding themselves and their saddles in some rocky gulch where the tracks would not show? Bud wished that he had thought of that sooner, though it seemed a far-fetched possibility.

Then there was Bat Johnson, a Palmer man and the only person Bud had seen in the vicinity of the bank. But Bat had made no attempt to escape, and he had volunteered the information about the horses that crossed the river. Bat had not taken the trail through the dry wash back of town where the four horses must have been concealed, because, as he explained at the inquest, his pack horse was barefooted, which Bud knew was the truth. The wash was gravel and loose rocks, and Bat had taken the longer trail through the sand grass and the willows. According to his statement to Bud and at the inquest, Bat had a glimpse of the horses moving out of sight among the willows near the ford, and had taken it for granted that riders bestrode them. But his pack horse, a little pinto, was hard to lead at the beginning of a trip, and Bat had been busy arguing the matter—Bat's side of the argument being the end of the lead rope or a quirt, Bud shrewdly guessed.

"I guess that lets him out," Bud muttered finally. "And I can't sleuth it out tonight. But there's another day coming. Marge will have to be blindfolded, I expect, to get her into what we'll have to call a schoolroom. Hm-m-m. Asked me where the town is, when we started down the pass. Wonder what time Lark wants to start in the morning? Have to explain to Lightfoot what a horse is, in the morning, and initiate him into the mysteries of a saddle. I like that geezer, somehow. He's the stuff, even if he is green. Wel-l—I guess I'll go to bed."

This, merely to show you that Bud could smile into a pretty girl's eyes and still keep his head clear for other things, and go about his business untroubled by dreams and fancies.

CHAPTER NINE
BUTCH CASSIDY GIVES ADVICE

Lark rode moodily up to the rim of the Basin and halted there, as was his habit, and gazed down upon meadow, field, small orchard and the chain of corrals, with the house and two or three cabins sitting back against the bold cliff that shut in the upper end of the river valley like a wall. Ages ago the river, then a glacial stream, no doubt, had gouged and dug at the hills until it had made a fair retreat just here along its bank; had shrunk as the climate changed and dried; left the valley a fertile place with seeds of trees and grasses and wild flowers imbedded in the soil. Birds had come there to nest, and in the spring the air was all vibrant with the sweet, rippling notes of the meadowlark and robin and the little wild canaries.

Old Bill Larkin had ridden into the valley by chance and had liked it well enough to appropriate it and build in it his home. Meadowlark Basin he called it—having come in the spring. Later he brought cattle and horses, when the pioneers were just awaking to the fact that Montana was an ideal grazing country. Some called old Bill a rustler—said his cattle and horses were mostly stolen. But they did not say it to his face, for old Bill was also called a killer. At any rate he owned a certain whimsical sentiment, for he fashioned the crude outline of a bird (though in the state brand book it was called the Half-moon-open-A) and stamped it deep in the hides of every hoof of stock he called his own. Moreover, he held his own against brand-blotters and prospered.

Now Lark stared glumly down into the Basin and wished his old dad was alive and able to take a hand in the fight he felt was coming. But old Bill lay deep in the grove of cottonwoods between the river and the house, and Lark glanced that way as he swung back into the road. Bud's horse—called the Walking Sorrel because of his gait—tilted his ears forward and picked up his feet with the springy, eager steps of a horse glad to be home after an absence. At the foot of the hill he broke into a gallop that Lark did not check until they reached the yard by the shed where the saddles were housed.

Lark slipped out of the saddle and was untying the valise from behind the cantle when Bud strolled down to greet him. He glanced over his shoulder, then handed the valise to Bud, who judged the weight of it and grinned.

"Got it, I see. You weren't held up then," he said. "I thought afterwards that you shouldn't have gone alone, but I see it was all right, after all."

Lark jerked off the saddle and led the horse to a gate and turned him through without speaking. The two started for the house, walking side by side up the roadway.

"Boys all here?" Lark spoke abruptly.

"Sure. They're eating supper. Butch Cassidy rode over from the Frying Pan yesterday to see why we hadn't come after the horses. I think Kid wants that fifteen hundred all right. Butch is waiting to ride back with us." Bud changed hands on the valise, for ten pounds added to the ordinary weight of a leather grip well filled is distinctly noticeable. "Have a good trip, and did you hear anything about the robbery?"

"Yeah, to both questions. Take that grip on into my room, son, and come over to the bunk house. I wanta talk to the boys."

"Oh—oh!" Bud exclaimed under his breath, and made off in a hurry. Lark in that mood promised action in plenty, and action meant joy in the heart of young Bud. He passed Marge without a word of teasing, which gave that young woman an uneasy half-hour, thinking she had somehow offended her perfect type of cowboy.

"Now's a good time to break the news to you pelicans," Lark began abruptly, when the preliminary greetings were over and Bud had arrived and sat down expectantly on the end of the long bench at the supper table. "Butch, it won't hurt nothin' for you to set in on this yoreself. Suspicions is like measles; once they start they spread through a hull neighborhood.

"To cut it short, they're tryin' their hell-darnedest, down Smoky Ford way, to pin that killin' and bank robbery on to the Meddalark. Soon as they find out where Bud come from that day they're liable to throw in the Fryin' Pan outfit fer luck. And my Jonah, I lost over fifteen thousand dollars to them thieves!"

"Pin it on us!" Bud voiced the incredulity of the group. "How do they make that out, Lark? I was in the Elkhorn—"

"Yeah—and Delkin told me they're sayin' that you was in there spottin' for the bunch that done the dirty work, son. You left the saloon and put straight fer the bank—to make sure it was all over and done without a hitch— and then you put out across the hills, mebbe for a blind, mebbe to help the get-away. Delkin don't believe nothin' like that, of course; but that's the story that's being circulated around town. He just give me the tip in a friendly way, so we'd know how to shape our plans."

"Pull in the corners, hunh?" Frank Gelle snorted.

"Pull in nothin'!" Lark's kindly hazel eyes hardened. "I'll tell you now, boys, I went on to Glasgow and borried some money to buy them Fryin' Pan horses and run the outfit on till the bank kinda pulls itself together again. Whilst the money lasts, I'm goin' to pay you rannies in gold. If yo're scared to show it, fer fear someone may think it's stole, you can go hide it under yore bunks. Delkin said he'd try and find out who's doin' all the gabbin' about us. He thinks it was started by somebody that's got a grudge agin the Meddalark—and, my Jonah! I can think of plenty that has! You dang pelicans go larry-whoopin' around the country, lickin' this one and that one, till the hull country's down on us, chances are!"

"Couldn't be somebody *you've* run a sandy on, of course," Gelle hinted mildly, and lowered an eyelid at the others.

"Palmer, you mean? He's got as good cause as anybody." Lark made no attempt to hedge. "Could be. Still, there's somethin' happened that Palmer didn't have no hand in, that I don't savvy. Up in Harlem I was waitin' to git my ticket, and my grip was settin' on a bench behind me in the waitin' room, and two different jaspers sneaked up and *hefted* it. Didn't know I seen 'em, but I caught 'em out the tail of my eye. *And that was goin' out!* At the time I thought they was lookin' fer easy stealin' and lost their nerve; or mebbe was curious to know if I had a gun or a bottle cached inside. Now, I know they was jest heftin' to see if I had the bank loot, er some of it. There was a lot of gold in the vault, Delkin told me. Detectives on my trail, mebbe. When I come back, I was packin' about ten pounds more weight, but I never let that grip outa my hands, you might say. I told Delkin about it, after he'd spilled his news, and showed him where I'd borried some money—just in case the talk gits too dang loud. He swore the bank never sicked no detectives on to us, nor anybody else in particular. Them bank officers don't dare give a guess at who done it, looks like to me. It *could* be what they call an inside job, and they know it don't look too good fer the bank officers."

"The thing to do," Butch Cassidy advised, "is lay low till somebody tips their hands. They'll do it—never knowed it to fail." He grinned and reached for the sirup can. "Way Bud was tellin' me, I'd say that hold-up job was a strictly home product. What do you think, Lark?"

"My Jonah!" Lark gave an exasperated snort. "I ain't any artist in that line, Butch. Looks to me like a daylight robbery with murder throwed in is something that takes nerve, and them town roosters don't qualify, if you want my opinion."

Butch chewed and swallowed a huge bite of hot biscuit dripping with sirup, his eyes staring vacantly before him as if he visioned things afar. Lark was calling for a clean plate and a cup of coffee, his long ride having given him a clamorous appetite which the supper table only aggravated.

"Bud was tellin' me about a few head of loose horses bein' hazed outa town and across the river right after the job at the bank." Butch came out of his trance and turned again to Lark. "Looks to me like that was meant fer a blind. Otherwise, the feller that drove 'em wouldn't make no bones of tellin' about it.

"And here's another point you don't want to overlook, none of you: Smoky Ford sets wrong fer a bank robbery to be pulled off durin' the day. Bank's away down at the wrong end of the street, and them cutbanks and washes where the bench breaks off down to the river bottom ain't rideable, except along the road. A bunch raidin' the bank would have to ride back through town and either cross the river or foller up the road to the bench, and take out across the reservation or come up this way. The trail across the river could be reached, uh course, by ridin' out back of town, the way Bat Johnson went with his pack outfit, but three or four riders foggin' along there would take big chances, seems to me. A job like that would need at least three men; two inside and one on guard outside the bank, jest in case anybody happened along. And even then it wouldn't be no picnic, right in daytime. With the town jammed into a pocket in the hills like that, and only two get-away trails, and them either leadin' around town or through it, they'd have to want money worse'n what I do." He laughed dryly.

"Them loose horses shod all around and takin' out across the river to the hills—that looks too much like a blind trail to me. Nobody was seen ridin' through town, so after a play like that, what I'd guess they done was git to the river bank and drop on down river in a boat." Butch Cassidy, vaguely rumored to be something of an outlaw himself, spoke as one who knew the tricks of the trade.

"River's too dang treacherous, down below the ford," Lark objected, with his mouth full. "It could be done, mebbe, but nobody in a hurry would ever think of doin' it. Moreover, what with rapids and bars and quicksands, there ain't a boat on the river anywhere; not that I know of."

"My—my grandpa was—was makin' a boat," the eager voice of Skookum broke in upon them. "In a shed where—where calves was weaned."

"Palmer, hunh?" Butch turned and stared reflectively at the boy, whom no one had noticed in the bunk house. A silence followed; a startled pause, as if each mind there took hold of the statement and turned it about and eyed it with surprised attention. Only Butch's light blue eyes, set close together, held a peculiar gleam.

"When was this, kid?"

"That was 'fore I come here with—with Lark. And—and—"

"Here! Quit that stutterin', kid, and take yore time." Lark spoke sharply, his eyes darting inquiring glances at Bud and the others. "Tell it slow, Skookum, and be dang sure you tell it straight. It's liable to mean a lot. You say yore grandpa was makin' a boat. Did he say what for?"

Skookum shook his head, his eyes big and round with the thrill of giving information to all these gods and heroes whose deeds and lightest words were things to dwell upon.

"Bat Johnson was makin' it, and Ed White. When they caught me—peekin' in, Bat s-shook me and swore. And—he took me where grandpa—was. He said I was—sneakin' around where I didn't have no—business. And—and grandpa—" Skookum shut his eyes tightly for a moment. "If you please, I—can't tell it—please. It's when grandpa made them cuts—"

"You can skip all that," Lark gritted, while the others shuffled their feet uncomfortably, their faces going glum with anger against Palmer for his brutal beating of the boy. "And you needn't to worry; yore grandpa's got more marks than what you've got."

"He oughta be strung up by the heels over a slow fire," Tony muttered, with the exaggerated malevolence of one who indulges in strong figures of speech.

"Go on, kid. Did you hear what they was goin' to do with it?"

"No—only Bat said sinkin' it was easy."

"There's the clue to the robbery!" Bud leaned forward, the light of revelation in his eyes. "It's the last thing anyone would think of, and about the easiest thing to do. Bat Johnson himself could have hazed those horses across the ford and come back after his pack horse. He could have done the murder and robbery too. If they had a boat hidden under the bank, he could have slipped out of the side door with all the plunder in a sack, packed it on his horse to the river, tossed it into the boat and gone on about his business—which was turning those horses loose and throwing them back across the river. I know where they were tied out of sight in the wash for an hour or two at least. It's so damned simple, Lark, it was practically safe!"

"It could be done," Lark agreed, "but they couldn't go on down river and stand a chance of getting anywhere."

"They wouldn't need to. Who would see a boat if it slipped down river from Palmer's place and went back the way it came? The farther bank is too rough to ride and too barren for stock to range close, and the current swings that way and cuts close to shore. This side it's boggy wherever you can get to the bank, so all the town stock waters at the ford, where there's a streak of gravel bottom. The willows are thick as the hair on a dog, most places—though of course a man could crowd through to the bank, close enough to throw a bag or two. Why, at three o'clock or a little before, even the kids were all in school down at the other end of town, and every footloose man was locked inside the Elkhorn!"

"Palmer was in town, you said." Butch Cassidy's eyes had squinted half shut as his mind focused upon the robbery and shuttled back and forth from scene to scene.

"You're darned right he was in town. It was Palmer who locked the saloon door, and it was Palmer who seemed to hate the idea of having it opened when I started to leave. Steve did all the bellowing, but Palmer's face gave him away; he wanted that door to stay shut. Of course, he had just deposited five thousand dollars in the bank, and he's been making quite a holler, I suppose—at least, he did at the inquest. But maybe he put that money in the bank for that very reason, to give him something to howl about. What do you think, Lark?"

"I'd bet on it," Lark answered sententiously, and with a three-tined fork turned over several pieces of beef fried so thoroughly that the meat was tender simply because it was too young to be tough under any mistreatment. He selected a particularly crisp piece, sawed off a corner with his knife and poised the morsel on the end of his fork.

"Oughta be some way to git the goods on that outfit. I've a dang good notion—"

"Better let it ride for a while," Butch counseled earnestly. "If it's them, they're bound to tip their hands; any mismove, and they'll be gone clean outa the country. Any of the bunch gone since it happened? What about Bat and his pack outfit? Did he leave with it?"

"Palmer sent him back home after the inquest. I overheard him telling Bat that some of them might have to join the manhunt and he'd better stay on the ranch in case he was needed," said Bud.

"None of 'em got out with the posse," Lark added. "Delkin told me the sheriff was handlin' it with his deppities, and said he didn't want the hull country messed up with tracks. Said it was time enough to make a general round-up when they picked up a trail of some kind. Good sense, too."

"How many men has Palmer got?" Butch wanted to know. "Not more'n three or four—he's too stingy to hire more'n he has to. Who works for yore gran'paw, kid?"

"Bat Johnson and Ed White, and—and Mex, and—and Blinker. But Blinker's no good. He—he's old and—and won't talk, and—and just whispers—to himself. He—he's afraid somebody's—comin' to—to kill him. And then there's the cook," Skookum added slightingly. "He's Sam, and—and he's a nigger."

"They're all to home," Gelle ended the discussion. "I and Bob met all three riders jest yeste'day drivin' a bunch of horses out towards the reservation."

"Got the stuff hid somewhere," Butch concluded. "That is, if they done the job. Thinkin' so ain't proof, we got to remember."

"Dang right it ain't," Lark agreed cynically. "They's folks in the country claims they think *we* done it, fur as that goes. That Maw callin' supper, Bud? You tell her I've et. By Jonah, I can't git no comfort out of a meal with them two pilgrims settin' there watchin' every mouthful and criticizin' my manners. I'll eat Jerry's cookin' fer a spell."

"I'm goin' to—to eat here," Skookum announced firmly. "I can't git no comfort, either. That old girl's learnin' me table etiquette! She makes me hold my fork like—like this!" To make his argument strong, Skookum grasped a fork as no human being would naturally hold one.

"Say," drawled Tony, "send her over here to eat with us, and you two gwan where you belong. Me, I never did know how to hold a fork in m' life. Why, I can't even hold a hayfork proper! You tell her, Skookum, that there ain't a one of us that's got the hang of makin' peas ride our knives without rollin' off. Jelly claims it's proper to mash 'em so they lay flat, but I say they was made to ride straight up. Gwan, kid. You tell 'er they's certain ones that needs to be learnt manners, and learnt 'em quick. Tell her we got a pelican here that whistles his soup 'stead of blowin' it gentle and then gulpin' 'er down. Gwan, kid."

"Yeah. Tell her I want t' know whether it's proper to say, 'Pass me those m'lasses,' or just 'Hand me them m'lasses.'" Bob Leverett winked at the others. "Tell 'er I'm liable to be invited out to a party, some time, an' I'm liable to make a bad break. Gwan, kid. You tell 'er that."

"Say, kid, you tell 'er I got another type she oughta study. Tell her this one is a sure-enough dinger, and that it's got the smile of a he-angel and the heart of a demon. It's this here sow-ayve kind, you tell 'er—"

"Soo-*ahve*, you darned knot-head," Gelle corrected disgustedly.

"Bud can tell her," Skookum stated calmly, and straddled the long bench to sit beside Lark. "I'm goin' to eat here."

"And hurt Maw's feelings?" Bud paused in the doorway and sent a glance of surprised disapproval at the boy. "She'll think you don't like her cooking any more."

"Aw, shucks!" Skookum threw down his knife and straddled back across the bench.

CHAPTER TEN
THE FRYING PAN

In that rare half-hour just before sunrise, when the cool breeze blowing across the meadows seemed saturated with sweetness and the vivifying essence of all life, as if here for a moment one might inhale the very breath which God breathed into his image made of clay and awakened it to the consciousness that it was a man, seven riders mounted at the Meadowlark corrals and went galloping down the trail, bound for the Frying Pan ranch, a long ride of forty miles through rough country.

Quivering drops of dew, scattered by eager hoofs, blinked at the first mellow sun rays and vanished from sight. Birds chirped and sang and flew here and there seeking breakfast for their hungry fledglings that would themselves soon be surprising the early worm. Every man's face was eager and alert, glad for no tangible reason save that it was good to be alive and on a horse, riding out in the cool of the morning once more after the leisurely two weeks just gone.

Lark was not among them, having made the excuse that he was tired from his trip to Glasgow; a thin excuse, for Lark could stay in the saddle as long as any man when the need arose. In reality Lark wanted to leave this horse-buying deal for Bud to handle alone. It was time, he thought, that the young man learned to assume some responsibility in a business way, and he was curious to see what sort of bargain Bud would make with the Frying Pan. So far Lark was secretly proud of his handsome young nephew whom he had cared for since he was a boy the size of Skookum, but for all that he was minded now to supplement Bud's schooling with a course of practical application of the lessons he had presumably learned from books.

The Meadowlark needed to build up its horse herd, and it was Bud himself who had suggested that they see what the Frying Pan had to offer. Lark did not think much of the Frying Pan, and Kid Kern, the owner, he did not trust at all; but he told Bud to go ahead and see what he could do over there with fifteen hundred dollars, intimating that he ought to be able to buy a hundred head of mixed stock for that amount.

Privately, Lark believed that the Frying Pan dealt mostly in "wet" stock—which is range parlance for stolen stock. A fresh brand is a "wet" brand. Stolen horses or cattle must be rebranded, the original brand hidden under another. That detail, combined with the fact that stolen stock is rushed by forced drives to distant localities, gave rise to the term, and that term was applied in undertones to Frying Pan horses. Lark wondered if Bud knew that. But wet stock is usually good stock, and cheap—for cash. So Lark did not say anything to Bud. If the kid wanted advice he'd probably ask for it.

So Bud rode proudly at the head of the little cavalcade with fifteen hundred dollars in gold coin wrapped in his slicker and tied behind the cantle, and the cameo brooch pinning back his hat brim while a blue satin bow stolen laughingly from Marge sat perkily between the twitching ears of his horse—braided into the short hairs of the mane for safe-keeping. And Bud, the young devil, was not thinking of girls at all, but dreaming of those two black bronchos he meant to tame, and trying to think of names worthy their magnificent beauty. Stirrup to stirrup with him rode Frank Gelle, who sent a glance over his shoulder to see how close were the others when they slowed for the climb up through the pass.

"What was Butch quizzing Skookum about last night, Bud, down by the little corral?" he broke ruthlessly into Bud's meditations.

"Butch? I don't know, Jelly. I heard him say something about teaching the kid some birdcall or other." Bud, brought back to the present, bethought him that now was a good time to roll a smoke. He slipped the reins daintily between his third and little fingers and reached for tobacco sack and papers.

"Didn't sound like no birdcall to me, Bud. He was pumpin' the kid about something. I couldn't ketch none of the words, but I could tell by the tonation of his voice that he was askin' one question right on top of another. Do you reckon, Bud, he was snoopin' around tryin' to pump the kid about our pilgress?"

"Marge? No reason he should pump the kid about her. That girl's an open book—printed in clear type. She and Butch were having a great old visit down by the corral yesterday when he was showing off his fancy roping. You saw them, Jelly. I bet she was giving him her life history. A girl that's lived the pure, simple life Marge has will tell all about herself without much coaxing. I don't believe Butch would be a darn bit backward about asking her anything he wanted to know. He must have been quizzing the kid about something else."

"She's a purty girl and a sweet girl, and no mother to guide her," Gelle eulogized solemnly. "No bonehead rustler like Butch Cassidy can run any rannigans whilst I'm on the job. If I was shore—"

"It wasn't that. Anyway, Marge can hold her own without any help. If you'd heard some of the roastings I've got, already—somebody told her I lied about our frogs. I never will be able to square myself, I guess. Say, Jelly, Butch may have been asking Skookum about that boat. He seemed pretty keen about it in the bunk house."

"Bud, I wouldn't put that bank job past the Fryin' Pan outfit, do you know it? From the way Butch talked, I'll bet they've been figuring on it, some time or other." Gelle sent another cautious glance over his shoulder.

"They didn't do it, Jelly. I left them all at the ranch, and rode straight across the reservation, the shortest way there is. I was expecting to make it home that night, you see. They couldn't have beaten me in. They were sitting around the house, whittling and telling it scarey, when I left, and their horses weren't caught up or anything. Butch may feel sore because someone beat them to it, and if he thought the boodle was cached somewhere within reach—

"Tell you what I'm going to do, Jelly. Soon as we get back with the horses I'm going to do a little scouting around. I've thought of several places I want to take a look at. That yarn about how I was spotting for the gang that killed Charlie Mulholland—well, the quickest way to stop that is to pin it on the guilty parties. If it's a home job, as it looks to be, we can do as much as the sheriff toward getting them with the goods. And, Jelly, I may need you before I'm through."

"Well, now, you'd have a heck of a time tryin' to keep me out of the muss!" Gelle laughed to himself. "Here comes Butch, so I'll drop back with the roughnecks. I wouldn't trust Butch if I was you, Bud. He's a nice feller and all that, but he's a horse thief and a killer and I wouldn't trust him fur as I could throw a bull by the tail."

Bud was grinning at that when Butch rode up on his high-stepping brown horse, but he did not pass along the joke.

The Frying Pan ranch, so called because of the brand most used by the owners, lay a good day's ride from the Meadowlark, over near the Missouri and close to that stretch of chaotic country called the Badlands. A small town might have stood on the level plateau against the hills, but as it was the Frying Pan ranch had a fine sweep of pasture land with a long lane running straight back to where the house, stable and corrals stood against the butte. Had the owners planned the place with an eye to the strategic possibilities, they could not have improved the smallest detail. First, the house, a two-story log building set well out in the open with a well and pump in one corner of the woodshed built against the kitchen. Beyond the house stood the barn, another log building with ample room for hay sufficient to winter eight or ten horses; and behind the barn the corrals, three of them in a string, with a branding chute between the two smaller ones and with a pair of funnel wings that never failed to ease the wildest broomtails into the enclosure left open to receive them. A somewhat elaborate arrangement, though the Frying Pan was a horse outfit that seemed to be making money faster than the cattlemen.

Range gossip is quite as malicious as a small-town club that is on the brink of disorganization. Range gossipers grinned at the Frying Pan brand, a blotched circle with the handle pointing downward; very convenient to cover any small brand and blot it forever from sight; handier still to have the choice of left hip or shoulder. One might guess that another brand was buried beneath that burned circle, but who could swear to the fact?

Whether Bud knew the gossip or not, he did know good horses when he saw them, and it was with a glow of pride that he climbed the fence of the largest corral and roosted on the top rail with the other Meadowlark riders, all staring down at the circling, kicking, squealing, nipping herd which the Frying Pan boys had just whooped down the wings and inside. A pretty sight they were—one that brought a shine into eyes other than Bud's.

"I trimmed the bunch down to about three hundred while we had them up waiting for you to come over after them," Kid Kern shouted, climbing up to straddle the rail and sit beside Bud. "I knew pretty well what you didn't want. Some good stuff there, hunh?"

"I've seen worse pelters than these," Bud grinned. "Got any fillies you want to throw in as an honorarium to me for having Lark dig up the full price in gold?"

"Say, Bud! If you bring any honorariums on to the ranch, by golly, you'll have to break 'em yourself!" Tony yelled, and winked at Jack Rosen. "They're tricky as hell, and you know it."

"Oh, I know you're not supposed to look a gift horse in the mouth," Bud retorted, "but I'll take a chance on five or six colts presented by Kid, here."

"If you put it that way, I might add half a dozen head; for you yourself, Bud. Gold is mighty useful to me, boy."

"You talk like good old greenbacks ain't money no more," Bob Leverett chided.

"There's a black gelding I'm going to build a loop for," Tony cried enthusiastically, and pointed to where a magnificent head and neck showed over the shoulder of a sorrel, the big brown eyes regarding curiously the strange row of figures on the fence.

"There's his twin, by golly! I speak fer him right now," Jack Rosen exclaimed.

"And they both belong to yours truly," Bud stated with outward calm. "Lark's giving them to me for making the deal, and my one-legged Meadowlark goes on tomorrow morning. You'll need darned fast loops, you fellows, to beat mine."

"My gosh, more honorariums!" wailed Tony. "Bud's bashful, I don't think!"

"Bud knows two good horses," Kid grinned, glancing sidelong toward Butch. "Them two blacks came"—he glanced again toward Butch and went on smoothly—"damn' near queering the deal. I didn't want to let them two go, but Bud, he couldn't see no bunch of horses that didn't include them, so I had to cave in or lose the sale. You'll have two dandy mounts, Bud, if you break 'em right."

"I don't intend to break them at all." Bud's eyes softened wonderfully as they rested on the nearest black horse. "All they need is to be taught. I'll have them both following me around like dogs, inside a month."

Butch lounged over and leaned against the fence near where Bud was perched. His hatcrown reached to Bud's knees, and he stared into the restless herd that crowded to the far side of the corral. His lip lifted a bit at one corner.

"Look out fer hydrophoby, then," he drawled. "One of 'em is a mankiller at heart; mebbe both. You'll have one fine time makin' pet dogs outa them two. I advise yuh to hogtie 'em and put a muzzle on 'em before you go caressin' around them birds."

Bud's cheeks darkened with the hot blood of anger, for Butch lied. Those big, intelligent eyes staring with shy wistfulness from the head of the nearest black betrayed the slander.

"Thanks for the advice, Butch. When I need more, I'll send word over," he said coldly.

The Meadowlark boys almost stopped breathing for a moment, and sent swift, sidelong glances at one another. But nothing came of the incident, save a tenseness in the atmosphere, a guarded note in conversations that had before been carelessly friendly. Not until after supper, however, did Bud speak his mind to anyone, and then it was to Gelle.

"I don't like the feel of this place, Jelly. We'll get out of here as soon as we can in the morning, and I wish you'd come with me while I turn over the money to Kid and get a bill of sale—and then I wish you'd slip the word to the boys that I'd like to have them keep out of the card games and turn in early.

"The Frying Pan thinks I'm young and green. I suppose they also think I'm a fool, and can't take the hints that have dropped around here. But it's like this, Jelly: We need this bunch of horses. I want that bill of sale signed tonight, and I want you to see me pay Kid the money. Butch doesn't want to see me get those two blacks, and the whole bunch may be slightly damp." He grinned, and Gelle laughed softly. "But if we lose any horses on that account, Kid will have to settle with the Meadowlark; don't think he won't!

"And when we've got them safe home," he added, after a reflective pause, "I'll have Lark let the boys off for a few days. They can go spend their good money in Smoky Ford while you and I take a little scouting trip around. How does that strike you, Jelly?"

"Fine and dandy; betcher life!"

"So come on, now, while all the boys are in sight and it's still daylight, and we'll dig up the gold and get the paper signed that will make these *our* horses. One hundred and six head of them, at least. Nothing like being young and innocent, is there, Jelly?"

"No, there ain't," Gelle agreed soberly. "I never did have much use fer the Fryin' Pan, and that's the truth. Now Butch is with 'em, they don't stack up near so good. Come awn, let's git that gold money paid over to Kid before they steal it. That's how *I* trust this bunch!"

CHAPTER ELEVEN
BUD TAKES A TRAIL OF HIS OWN

Have you ever watched a herd of horses come streaming down a hill at the end of a hard day's travel? There's a thrill in it such as comes when soldiers are marching by. First a drifting haze which is the dust kicked up by the traveling herd; then the faint, muffled sound of hoof beats; the heads of the point riders seen dimly through the cloud, and after them the upflung heads of the leaders.

As the freshly branded horses sighted the delectable green of the Basin, smelled the river rushing out of the encircling wall of rugged hills, they came streaming down through the pass in sudden forgetfulness of the weary miles behind them. At the foot of the hill riders spurred out from the veil of dust, swinging closed loops and shouting, forcing the eager band close to the bluff and away from the alluring green of the meadows. Tired muscles tensed again. Heads went up, dusty nostrils belled and quivered with the mingled scents of the valley. The leg-weary colts, dusty, lagging behind and then making sudden, shrill uproar when they missed their mothers, were sought with frantic whinnyings by the mares. Once found, they were torn from eager nuzzlings by the light thwacks of rope ends and the insistent, "*Hi! Hi-yee!*" from the hoarse throats of the tired riders; the cry that all day long without ceasing had dogged the laggards on the trail.

Even Maw left her endless pottering around the house and waddled down to the corral where Lark was already propping open the big gate, when Skookum came running with his body slanted perilously forward while he yelled that the horses were coming. Marge went back for her notebook and pencil, because you never know when cowboys are going to say something odd or picturesque, or a killing may take place—as she confided to her brother in passing.

(As a matter of fact, Marge was beginning to complain at the paucity of dramatic happenings on the ranch where she had confidently expected to find adventure galore. For however much the boys might boldly proclaim their gallant intentions, Marge saw them mostly at a distance and found them hopelessly shy when brought face to face with her. Young Bud talked with her gravely and misleadingly upon occasion, wherefore she called Bud bashful and slow—when in reality Bud was anything else, and was mostly preoccupied with other matters. So the coming of the new horses loomed before her as an event that promised something in the way of Western color and, possibly, drama.)

With a last flurry of hard riding and hoarse shouts, the leaders swung away from the tempting meadows and inside the wing fence that slanted down from the corrals to the road, the precipitous bluff forming the other barrier. The herd galloped in mass formation to the very gate before they realized that here they faced another one of those hated periods of captivity. They swerved toward the bluff, hurtled back along it and met the implacable Meadowlark riders; milled briefly and thundered again down the throat of the wings toward the corral. With a flick of heels, a last surge of upflung dust, they dodged inside. The big gate slammed shut behind them and the chain was pulled around the great post that looked as though rats had gnawed it just there—the hook rattled into a heavy link and that particular horse deal was completed. The horses were safe at home and milling inside the corral just as they had circled round and round within the Frying Pan enclosure that morning.

Six tired cowboys rode over to the open space beside the shed where saddles were kept, and with a backward swing of saddle-stiffened legs over the cantles they thankfully dismounted. A hot, windy ride—and the wind in their backs most of the way. Their throats were parched and raw from the dust and shouting.

"Me, I'm goin' to put sideboards on my chin, to-morra, and plug up my ears. That way I can hold more beer." This from Tony, who wished his world to know how dry he was.

"Yeah—if we git to go," Jack Rosen qualified pessimistically. "Lark may not let us off."

"Say, he'll let *me* off, if he has to fire me!" Bob Leverett threatened with a surface vehemence not meant to be taken too seriously.

"I'll see that you boys get a couple of days off, all right." Bud had ridden up and swung from the saddle, his face a gritty gray mask from riding point in the thick of the dust. "I'll fix it up with Lark this evening. Now's a good time to find out just what all this talk amounts to, and where it started. Of course, we think we know, but by the time you boys put a little gold into circulation, we ought to be dead sure we know. All I ask is that you boys keep your ears open and let me know what you pick up."

"Nice bunch of horses, Bud." Lark walked over from the corral and stood among them. "I s'pose you boys are framin' a trip in to the Ford, about to-morra. Better not say anything to Lightfoot about goin'. He's just fool enough to be game for anything that comes up, but he can't ride with you bunch of hellions yet. I'd hate to tell him he can't go, so if you'll leave without hollerin' it all over the ranch it'll suit me just as well. I'll be over to the bunk house after a while; you can draw what money you want then."

"Now, ain't that hell?" cried Tony after an eloquent pause. "Here we been gittin' ready to appoint a committee to approach the throne—aw, shucks. Lark, yo're a good boss, in some ways, but you'd keep men on the payroll longer if you was kind to 'em!"

Since no man ever left the Meadowlark of his own free will, even the weariest puncher laughed at that, Lark with the others; but his eyes held a shadow as he walked toward the house with Bud.

"What do you think of my two blacks? Aren't they peaches?" For the first time Bud's tone betrayed the fact that the black bronchos were not absorbing his full thought, but were being used to make conversation.

Lark grunted. They walked farther before he spoke.

"Horses are all right, I guess. Say, Bud, did you meet a feller ridin' a chunky little bay with the Acorn brand on its hip? He rode in here yesterday and stopped all night. Snoopy kinda cuss. Claimed to be a stock buyer, but he didn't show me no credentials, nor talk like he wanted to buy anything in p'ticular. Ast questions of everybody but me, seems like—mostly things that wasn't none of his business. He left right after dinner and said he was ridin' over Landusky way and would mebbe meet you boys somewheres on the trail. He didn't, hunh?"

"Never saw him at all, Lark. I don't see how we could have missed him, either, if he kept to the trail. How did you grade him, Lark? A detective?"

"Had the earmarks, son. Sicked onto us by some of them damn' granny-gossips in town, I take it. You goin' in with the boys to-morra?"

"No-o—well, I thought I'd take a ride around and see what sign I can pick up; on the quiet, Lark. I want to take Jelly with me, and I don't want the boys to know anything about it. They'll proceed to tarry with the wine cup, the first thing they do, and what they don't know they can't let slip when their tongues loosen a bit. I hope they stir things up and keep the town interested enough so Jelly and I won't be missed."

"Purty late to pick up anything on the range, Bud. Seven days now, it's been. That alleged stock buyer said they ain't got the first clue yet. He might of lied, though. Prob'ly did. You goin' to take a look around Palmer's place?"

"I thought we would, if we get the chance. I want to let the boys ride in ahead of us. I want to use them for a decoy. I believe Palmer and his men will follow them in if they see a bunch of Meadowlark boys go riding into town. They'll want to see what's taking place, and guilty or innocent, I believe their mental reactions will send them after the boys."

"Mebbe." Lark lifted his hat while he pawed at his hair. "I never went into fizzyology much, so I can't say what reactions will do to a feller. If you say they'll act that way, I ain't goin' to contradict. But what's the rule fer perventin' a killin' if our boys run into Palmer whilst they're lit up? I got a nice bunch of boys, now, and I don't want to see 'em killed off ner sent to the pen."

"Oh, you work that out by the rule of subtraction," Bud grinned. "Have the boys leave their guns with the bartender when they take their first drink."

"Hunh? No, sir, I won't ast the boys to do what I wouldn't do m'self. I'd ruther leave my pants with the bartender! You musta got that idee in school. What's the use of havin' a gun, if you got to hand it over to some slick-haired bar-wiper just when it looks like you may want it? I'd go in myself, but"—he paused to glance over his shoulder—"I'm goin' to fix up the Nest again. My old dad would raise up in his grave if he knowed how things has been let run down that way. The Lookout needs some work on it too.

"You go on and carry out what's in yore mind, son. I'll buy in later on, if it's necessary. But you kin make this yore fight, for the present, and if things look like they're comin' to a head, you kin send one of the boys back after me. I'll be workin' here, puttin' things in shape fer a show-down. Once these things start, they's no tellin' where they'll wind up. Callin' us a hard outfit to monkey with is one thing—that's somethin' to be proud of. But when it comes to sayin' we killed a man so as to rob the bank where we do our business—my Jonah, but that's damn' hard to swaller!"

"We aren't going to swallow it," Bud declared, promptly. "Where's Maw? I'm about half starved!"

Maw was coming, taking short, quick steps and waving the mosquitoes off with her apron. Behind her, Marge was walking with many short halts while she wrote something in her notebook, while whooping along in the rear came Skookum, driving Lightfoot and flailing him with a tall weed to keep him at a high gallop. Bud's eyes lingered on the bent head of Marge, and he loitered, waiting for her. Then, his glance going to the boy, his face hardened again with the purpose that filled his mind.

It was after he had eaten and Marge was waiting in the living room, hoping Bud would come in and talk to her after the deadly monotony of the past two days, that Bud artfully drew Skookum off by himself and turned the conversation very casually to Butch Cassidy. He wanted to know what it was that Butch had been talking about; but Skookum, unfortunately, had promised not to tell.

"Well, that's all right, pardner. If you promised, don't go back on your word; unless," he added, "it was something mean. In that case, of course, I ought to know."

"It wasn't mean," said Skookum, after a pause for reflection. "If you asked questions like Butch did, I'd tell you more'n I told Butch. I—I didn't tell him any more than—than I had to. I—wouldn't hold out on you that way, Bud. You're my—my pal."

Bud could have hugged the boy. There was a chance, then, that Butch had not learned much more than they all had heard in the bunk house. He did not see just what use Butch could make of the information gleaned in this manner, but he knew what he himself wanted to do. So Bud began to ask questions, and Skookum answered them as carefully and as completely as possible.

When he went to bed that night, Bud kept smiling in the dark until he fell asleep, and even then his lips were curved as if his dreams were pleasant. Skookum smiled also and dreamed of the pinto pony Bud had given him for his very own; a pony that was too small for a full-grown man; a pony with white eyelashes, one blue eye, a doglike devotion to anyone who would pet him, and the unusual name of Huckleberry.

The satisfaction of Bud and Skookum must have continued through the night, for both were up and out in the cool, dewy dawn when all the birds were ruffling feathers and puffing throats in rhapsodical melody.

Sooner than would seem humanly possible, Skookum went wading through dew-drenched meadows that straightway wet his feet, a frayed rope end dragging from the coil hung over his arm and in his two hands a battered basin holding oats enough to founder the pinto pony—or so Jake would have told him.

The pinto proved a willing partner to the new alliance, and let Skookum climb on his back and ride to the stable, obeying the guidance of a hand-slap on the neck, just as Bud had said he would. Picture any ranch-bred boy of eight or nine in full possession of a new and gentle pony, and you will have Skookum fully accounted for: riding reckless circles around and between Maw's flower beds to show her how Huckleberry neckreined; sending terror to the heart of a certain mother hen when he galloped full tilt and scattered her brood; roping gate posts, calves, old Jake, Lark—anything upon which a loop could settle. That was Skookum for the next few days.

As for young Bud, he was up and had a rope on one of the blacks before Skookum had so much as glimpsed the pinto pony. There was a certain shady corral with running water and a pole rack for hay, called the bronch corral, where he meant to leave them until his return, but already he was bent on making friends with them. He heard the boys making hectic preparations for the trip to town, and thought they must certainly be faring forth to carry out plans carefully laid in many conferences; whereas no man save Bud had any plan at all. They meant to ride to Smoky Ford and put a stop to the slander against the Meadowlark—how, they did not know.

"Funny Lark wouldn't do something about it," Jake Biddle grumbled, when the boys were saddling after breakfast. "Ain't like the old days—not a damn' bit. Old Bill would 'a' rode into town with a gun in each hand and a booie knife in his teeth, hollerin' his opinion of sech damn' liars. The fellers that started it—"

"I shore wisht he'd of lived to show us how to cuss and hold a knife in our teeth at one and the same time," fleered Tony. "You old broken-down riders makes me tired. Think us boys is kids?"

"Yeah. Where'd you git the idee we're goin' to run home bawlin' fer Lark to come show us what t' do to them bad men that's sayin' mean things about us?" Bob Leverett turned a shade redder. "Mebbe we ain't got the knack of carryin' a knife in our teeth whilst we cuss, but I betcha we can holler our opinions jest about as loud as old Bill ever done. And as fer wavin' a gun in both hands—why, me, I can look scarey enough with one gun to put Smoky Ford on the run. Come on, boys. We're keepin' Jake from settin' in the kitchen weepin' fer the days that is gone."

"Say, ain't Jelly goin' to town?" As they swung to the saddles Tony missed the tall rider. "Hey, Jelly!"

"You boys go awn," Gelle called from the far corral where he was killing time with Bud until the others were gone. "Bud and me'll be along after a while, mebbe. If we don't overtake you, you boys ride awn in and make yoreselves to home."

"Foolin' with them black bronchs," Rosen made indulgent comment. "Let 'em throw away good minutes if they ain't got better sense. Come on, let's be movin'.'"

They moved to such good purpose that presently a slow-settling dust cloud alone remained to tell of their haste.

CHAPTER TWELVE
THE MEADOWLARK BOYS HAVE A PLAN

Palmer's ranch, called so because the man himself came first to mind when one thought of his outfit—which bore the brand called the Roman Three—lay along the road from Meadowlark Basin to Smoky Ford. The fields lay farthest up river, but his house and stables stood in that narrower level where the river swung abruptly eastward toward the Indian Reservation and the hills. At that point the road drew in close to the house and not more than a long rifle-shot away from the river. Smoky Ford lay nearly seven miles farther down river; not a long ride for men accustomed to spend most of their waking hours in the saddle. Indeed, the Meadowlark boys thought of Palmer's ranch as being almost in the edge of town, and called their journey nearly done when they came loping up to the place.

"Let's wake the old devil up," Tony suggested recklessly, as they neared the gate and fired two shots into the Palmer roof-tree.

"Yeah! Let him know we ain't sneakin' past his door, scared he'll sick his dog on to us!" Jack Rosen lifted his gun and sent splinters flying from two shingles.

"Bet he don't keep no dog. Too darn stingy to feed one. Aye—Palmer! Yore roof's leaky!" Bob Leverett yelled, in a voice trained to carry across a restless herd, and splintered another shingle.

The front door opened abruptly and Palmer himself stood briefly revealed to the four riders halted in the roadway just outside the big, closed gate. Palmer waved a rifle and yelled obscene epithets until Tony stopped that with a leaden pellet planted neatly between his feet. Palmer jumped, banged the door shut and took a shot at them through a window. Evidently he had no intention of killing in broad daylight, for he shot high.

"His loyal henchmen must be gone somewheres. T' town, mebbe," Tony surmised shrewdly. "The old devil could hit someone if he wanted to, but he knows damn' well we'd git him if he did, so he's jest expressin' his sentiments in a general way, same as we are. What say, boys? Shall we take him along with us to town?"

"Hell, what'd we want *him* for?" Jack Rosen's voice was heavy with disgust. "He shore ain't good comp'ny."

"Oh, I jest thought mebbe we might take him along because he wouldn't want to go," Tony replied naïvely, slipping cartridges into his gun. "There goes that foolish jasper. Rest of 'em must be in town. Well, how about it?"

"Takin' him along would shore hurt my feelin's worse than it would his, fer I'd be in worse comp'ny than he would. What say we ride on in and see what's goin' on, and if the rest of these birds is there? If so, we can clean up on what's in town and come back out here later on. Mebbe Palmer'll foller us in. Be jest like him to have the law on us, don't you know it? I'm goin' to rip off another shingle and go about my business, I'm dry as a bleached bone."

They proceeded to rip off several shingles. But Palmer did not choose to retaliate, so they rode on, yelling derisively until they were out of hearing. Within a mile they had settled down and were tardily making plans calculated to stir Smoky Ford out of its lethargy and give it something to talk about. The idea was Tony's, and he was so proud of it that he could afford to give some credit to Bob as a true prophet when they topped a rise and had a glimpse of a horseman just riding out of Palmer's gate. Palmer, following them in, no doubt meant to stir up trouble for them before he was through. Well, let him. Trouble was what the Meadowlark boys were looking for today.

"I can see now how he come to take a quirtin' from Lark," Mark Hanley said contemptuously. "He's yeller as mustard, without the bite. Jest the kind that would cave in a man's head when he wasn't lookin'. 'Twouldn't a took much nerve to shoot up the bunch of us, him in the house like that and us in the open. We got to git that old coot in a corner, somehow. Now, Tony, that idee of yourn—"

"It's a darn good idee," Tony defended hastily. "They could guess everything else and lay plans to block it, but they couldn't guess we'd pull off anything like that. First off, we better ride to Delkin's stable and put him wise. Our horses is our excuse for going there."

Stirrups tangled, they rode so close together. Often a man would break into laughter and glance back at the trail to see if Palmer was still following them. They trotted up to the very door of Delkin's stable, ducked heads and rode inside, where they dismounted and unsaddled without help or interference from the stableman, who knew them of old. When their horses were turned into the corral behind the barn, where they speedily found hay and water and a place to roll, the quartet went trooping back down the long floor, spurs jingling pleasant accompaniment to their low-voiced laughter. Slightly bowed in the legs, they were—or it may have been the permanent kink in their chaps. Twitching hats and neckerchiefs into becoming angles, lest the eye of some young woman catch them in disarray, they made for the screened door of the office, where Tony peered in, saw Delkin sitting gloomily before his desk, and pushed open the door, entering with a slight swagger.

"Oh, hello!" Delkin's eyes went from one to the other in apathetic greeting. "You boys in for a good time, eh?"

"Yeah. We just stopped by to let you in on the joke. Seen anything of Bat Johnson and the rest of the bunch from Palmer's?"

"Why, yes. They rode in an hour or so ago, I believe. They don't put up their horses when they come to town, you know. Post hay is cheaper." Delkin did not know just how much resentment was in his voice, but his mood was bitter these days.

"Well, how's the scandal comin' along, Mr. Delkin?" Tony asked cheerfully. "Still shootin' off their mouths about the Meddalark?"

"Oh, about the same, I guess. But they'll never make me believe your outfit had anything to do with it." The mind of Delkin was so obsessed with the murder and robbery that it did not occur to him that scandal could focus on anything else.

"Well, we shore appreciate that, because we got a scheme for stirrin' up the bandits some. It's my idee," Tony informed him proudly. "I'd like to see what you think of it before we git to work on it. And mebbe it might be jest as well if you'd call in some of yore bank officers, so in case of a kick-back we won't git lynched without nobody to put in a word for us. That there," he added slightingly, "is Rosy's idee. He's scared to turn himself loose like he claims he kin, unless he's shore his imagination ain't goin' to be fatal. Rosy claims he's sech an eloquent cuss he's liable to git hung. Git the men that's handiest, will you? We're darn dry, and I can't hold these pelicans away from the flowin' bowl much longer."

Delkin glanced out through the open window, got up hurriedly and called to three men who were talking on a corner across the street. One threw up his hand to show that he heard, and they came over, tapering off their conversation on the way. Inside, they looked at the four Meadowlark riders and nodded, turning inquiringly to Delkin afterwards.

"I called you in to hear something or other that these boys have framed. Don't know what it is, but it ought to work. You know the Meadowlark has the name of putting through what it starts."

"So I hope they're starting in the right direction," grinned Bradley, vice president of the bank and proprietor of the town's principal store. "I've been wondering if the Meadowlark was going to tuck its head under its wing, with all the talk going round about it. I overheard one of Palmer's men saying in the store that the bank has put a detective on Bud Larkin's trail. I wonder where he got that idea?" Bradley sat down and thrust out his long legs before him in the attitude of one who has the habit of taking his ease whenever possible. He knew the boys well. He could have told you exactly how much each man there had paid for the shirt he had on—though what his own profit had been would have been carefully guarded as a dark secret. Every mouthful of food that went down the throat of a Meadowlark man when at home came from Bradley's store unless it had been produced on the ranch.

The other two men were also important business men of the town; one owned the hardware store and the other a small, fly-specked drugstore stocked mostly with patent nostrums. The boys could not have chosen four men more to their liking for this particular conference.

"Well, here's what we aim to do." Tony began rolling a cigarette as an aid to eloquence, and stated the plan.

The audience grunted and looked doubtful; then Delkin gave a short laugh.

"I admit it's original," he said dryly. "And it's lucky you told us before-hand, or you boys might find yourselves swinging from a limb somewhere before you could convince anyone you were only joking."

"Only danger," Bradley agreed, "is making too big a success of it. We've been watching Palmer and his men pretty close, and I must say we haven't a thing to go on, except that Palmer was the last man in the bank before Charlie was killed, and Bat Johnson was the first man seen near the bank afterwards. On the other hand, Bud and that young stranger—"

"Say, Bud's name don't sound purty to me, used that way; and that stranger's wearin' the Meddalark brand, Mr. Bradley," Tony interrupted meaningly. "Well, we're dry, and thank Gawd our duty calls us to git pickled or nearly so. And here," he added, glancing through the window, "comes the he-one of 'em all. Palmer's follered us in. Come awn, boys. Let's go git near-drunk. And, oh, say!" he added, reaching into his pocket, "here's the evidence agin us! Lark went and borried some money in Glasgow—I guess he told yuh himself—and us boys is plumb lousy with gold tens and twenties. So don't git nervous and think we're spendin' the bank's good money in righteous livin'. We worked fer this. Every dime was earnt in sweat and sorrow. Ain't that right, boys?"

"Damn' right that's right," they agreed solemnly.

"I'll tackle Bat," Tony announced, as they walked across the street to the Elkhorn, thumbs hooked inside their belts, hats atilt, eyes seeing everything. "Lordy, how this town's growed since I seen it last! There's a new dog, layin' right on Bradley's steps. Wouldn't that jar yuh some, hunh?"

"Who's goin' to tackle Palmer?" Bob Leverett wanted to know. "Me, I wouldn't come within ropin' distance of that old coyote. Rosy, you take 'im."

"Have to play the cards as they run," Tony warned them, pausing with one foot on the platform. "Make it look stagey, and my idee's plumb wrecked. Come awn in—like you hated to but had to. And we'll keep together right at first, hunh?"

"Shore. I wish't Jelly was here, and Bud." Bob cleared his throat, hitched up his belt and lounged in, the other three at his heels.

The four drank together, inviting the bartender to join them. Other occupants of the room may have noticed that they held their beer mugs in their left hands, and that they drank with their faces half turned to the room. Tony it was who paid in silver. They talked afterward among themselves in tones slightly lowered. Had they been men burdened with too much knowledge of evil, on guard against some overt move of an enemy, they would have worn that same air of aloofness, that faint challenge to the world hidden under the guise of careless ease. The dozen men lounging within knew without being told that the Meadowlark men were aware of the talk about them and felt themselves observed with suspicion. Indeed, everyone must have seen how these four watched the room in the mirror of the back bar, and how they studiously kept their right hands free and hovering near their belts.

It was the bad-man attitude, beautifully done. Had the Meadowlark boys murdered three men and robbed a dozen banks they could scarcely have been more careful. And they had the attention of every man there, thinly disguised, but all the keener for that. Bat Johnson, playing pool at the far end, lifted his lip in a sneer while he deliberately chalked his cue and raised a leg to rest it on the corner of the table for a difficult shot. But he did not make any audible remarks about the Meadowlark men, and he did pocket four balls in succession to show how steady were his nerves. In the back-bar mirror Tony saw that only two men were playing and that the game had just started. Bat would be occupied for the next half-hour, so there was plenty of time for certain necessary preliminaries.

Jack Rosen bought a bottle of whisky and paid for it with a ten-dollar gold piece. Bob Leverett watched the transaction and decided that he too wanted to drink out of a bottle and stop when he pleased. Bob fumbled in his pockets, looked uneasily over his shoulder and pushed a double eagle across the bar as if he were ashamed of having it. Indeed, Tony gave him a frown of disapproval and a shake of the head, and this was not lost upon the bartender nor upon others who were covertly watching the quartet.

"Well, gimme a bottle too. It's cheaper that way." Mark Hanley also paid with gold, explaining behind his hand to the others that he just had to have change, and he guessed it was all right. And thereupon Tony borrowed the price of a bottle from Mark, and they went clanking out and across to the stable, leaving tongues tickling to talk behind their backs, and a thoughtful look on the face of Bat Johnson.

In the far corner of the corral Tony was carefully spilling whisky on his undershirt and emptying the remainder of the quart on the ground.

"This is a hell of a way to get a jag on," he mourned, "but we got to stay sober and act drunk. Keep 'er on the outside, boys, till we put over this play. Actin's an art, and you can't be too clear-headed fer the parts you got."

"Ah, gwan!" Jack Rosen pulled the cork from his bottle and took a long, rapturous sniff. "Only way to act drunk is to *git* drunk. Me, I always git a glassy look in my eyes, and my face gits redder 'n hell. I can't git that way by pourin' three drops on my shirt front like it was perfumery. If I'm goin' to play drunken cowboy with no brains atall, I gotta put at least a pint under m' belt."

"Rosy, you *can't*! When you're drunk you wanta fight and beller out everything you know. We gotta play this thing fine." The anxious author of the idea snatched the bottle and broke it against the manger. "Say, you can git soused to the eyebrows when this play-actin's over. We'll *all* git drunker'n fools. Ain't that enough to make a man stay sober, if he's got to, in order to block their play? Come alive here, boys. We got a good chance t' make Palmer's gang show their hands. Do we go after 'em, or do we belly up to the bar and make hawgs of ourselves?"

"Oh, shut up! I'll bet yo're drunk before the rest is, Tony. No use addin' to our misery by chewin' the rag about it, is they?" Bob Leverett poured whisky into his palm and proceeded to wash his face with it. "Gawd, that's coolin'!" he exclaimed afterwards, licking his lips as far back as his tongue would reach. "Refreshin'est thing in the world! Betcha there ain't a feller in the outfit dast try it—wallop it all around your mouth without lettin' any go down. Betcha I'm the damnedest strong-minded cuss in the outfit!"

"Betcha five dollars," cried Mark Hanley, and swept off his hat to give his hair a whisky shampoo.

Jack Rosen washed face, neck, ears and hair, and saturated his handkerchief as a final flourish.

"By golly, that shore *is* refreshin'!" he testified earnestly, with his face lifted ecstatically to the hot wind. "Gimme some more. Tony went an' got fresh and busted mine. You owe me two bottles, don'tcha fergit that; one fer smashin' mine, and one fer misjudgin' yore betters."

They went swaggering through the barn and stopped at the office, where Delkin's three visitors still sat talking of the one big subject. The four leading citizens sniffed and leaned away.

"That's stage settin's," Tony informed them equably.

"Overdone," Bradley snorted, waving a hand before his face. "They'll think you fell into the barrel."

"Damned refreshin'," Bob told them soberly. "You fellers oughta try it in hot weather. You wouldn't never wash in nothin' else."

They backed out and went weaving across the street, arm in arm and stepping high. Apparently they were the drunkest punchers that ever spent money over a saloon bar, and their aloofness was all forgotten. They entered the Elkhorn singing raucously a sentimental ditty which must never see print, and Jack Rosen on the outside of the group stopped and attempted to embrace Palmer in almost tearful joy at seeing him. The others pulled him along to the bar and Tony swung round upon the crowd.

"Everybody drink!" he shouted thickly. "Drown yore sorrers whilst we drown ours. Money's made to spend—come on, boys, an' let's squander some."

There is only one answer to that, in a saloon. Not a man in the place but had a convincing whiff of the reason why the boys from the Meadowlark had suddenly changed their tone. The curtain was up on Tony's play.

CHAPTER THIRTEEN
BUD FINDS THE STOLEN MONEY

"There goes old Palmer himself," Bud exclaimed with some eagerness, as he and Gelle rode out from behind a low hill and started down the long, straight stretch beside Palmer's field of grain, fenced and rippling a green sea of wheat heads. "Now as the rest of the bunch is out of the way, it will be smooth riding. You know your part, Jelly. You just ride up to the house and do whatever you damn please, so long as you hold the cook and Blinker and any of the other men who happen to be home, right there at the house. I hope they've followed the boys to town, though. It's the logical thing for them to do unless they're bigger cowards than I take them to be."

"Say, if you're goin' to sneak up to the stables, you'd better be drifting right now," Gelle told him. "If there's anybody down around the corrals, I'll have 'em up to the house before you need their absence very bad. Don't you worry about that, Bud."

"All right. I did intend to ride past the house and come back the other way. It's just about as close. But this will do. Give me a few minutes' start, will you, Jelly?" Bud grinned, waved a hand in casual farewell and reined his sorrel out of the road and into the tangle of chokecherry bushes that grew in a shallow gully leading back toward the river.

Once away from Gelle, however, the grin left his face and a smoldering purpose glowed in his eyes. He was on enemy soil; if any of Palmer's men were at home and he were discovered he would probably find himself dodging leaden slugs before he got away. Midday was not the best hour for invading an unfriendly man's premises, but he had decided that it would be safer after all than midnight, when Palmer would be easily alarmed. Besides, the dogs were chained during the day and turned loose at dusk. Skookum had told him that: and for what he wanted to find he needed the broad sunlight.

Straight through the thicket he rode until he reached a barbed-wire fence extending up the river for a considerable distance. This, Skookum had told him, was the cow pasture which he would have to cross on foot, keeping one eye peeled for the big, black bull that had once killed a man and liked it so well he had been trying ever since to repeat the performance. Bud tied the sorrel well out of sight, unbuckled his spurs and hung them on the saddle horn, hitched up his belt and pulled his gun forward, and crawled through the fence. Skookum had advised him to pass the house, hide his horse in the bushes and come back up the river, keeping in the willows on the bank. In that way he would run no risk of the bull, of which Skookum seemed to be in terror almost as great as his fear of his grandfather. This was shorter, however, and Bud remembered how terrible a cross bull can look to a small boy; to a man it is not so formidable.

This end of the pasture was brushy, full of the twitterings of bird families, the scurrying of small furred creatures. Blue-bodied flies poised humming just before his face; great, long-legged mosquitoes sang a whining chorus around him. He made his way quickly toward the river, where the bank rose abruptly in a worn sandstone ledge. The pasture gate was built close against the ledge, and it was this point that held most of the danger. Some one at the stables might see him—Skookum had told him that the gate was in sight of the stable, but that the ledge was mostly hidden by the trees. Bud guessed that he would be obliged to walk in the open for a few rods, but with Gelle bullying the cook—or whatever it was he meant to do—even the dogs would have scant attention for anyone moving down by the pasture gate.

Once, when Skookum had ventured into the pasture after a rabbit that had been caught in a trap and lamed, the black bull had come grumbling ominously from the bushes. Skookum had scrambled up the ledge out of reach of the bull and had waited so long in the shade of a jutting rock that he had gone to sleep. When he awoke the bull was gone, but his grandfather was coming in at the gate, which was almost as bad, so he had cowered down out of sight and waited for that threatening presence to pass. His grandfather had stood for two or three minutes looking back at the house, while he pretended to be fastening the gate behind him, and then he had walked on past where Skookum was hiding and had begun to climb the ledge.

"And—and I didn't tell Butch what—what I done after he—he climbed up on the ledge," Skookum had declared earnestly to Bud at this point. "I mean, I never told Butch about me sneakin' along after—after grandpa went back to—to the house, and lookin' to see what—what grandpa was doin'. So I—I found all his money—but I never took any. I—I was scared!" Skookum was very careful to let Bud know what he had *not* told Butch, since he had promised Butch that he would not tell a soul the things he had revealed during the quizzing. Skookum believed in the letter of the law.

"I couldn't see grandpa after he climbed up on the ledge, because the—the rocks was in the way," he had explained further, and because he had told Bud so much more, Skookum was now in beatific possession of Huckleberry, the pinto pony.

"He's a smart kid. I suppose with the wrong training it would develop into foxiness like his grandfather. He sure described it perfectly," Bud made mental comment when, from a safe covert of wild currant bushes, he surveyed the ledge. He could even recognize the place where Skookum had scrambled up to get away from the bull, and the rock jutting out and away from the main outcropping where he had curled up and gone to sleep. From that point Skookum had drawn what he called a map, and crude though it was, Bud felt sure that he could find the place of which the boy had told him in a scared half-whisper.

He did one foolish thing. In crossing the open strip of trampled grass just inside the gate he nearly stepped on a huge rattlesnake lying asleep in the hot sunshine. To pass so venomous a thing without killing it went contrary to all Bud's instincts and training. Rangemen reason that every rattlesnake left to crawl away may sink its poison fangs into the next unwary passer-by, and that death may be the result of someone's carelessness. Bud picked up a rock and sent it straight at the ugly head, following with other rocks to make absolutely sure of the job. When the snake was dispatched, he took long steps into the fringe of concealing bushes and climbed to the rock which Skookum had described so accurately.

At the house Frank Gelle was holding in his horse, that backed and circled restively, fighting the tight rein. Gelle himself was insisting loudly that Palmer had better come out or he'd go drag him out. No use hiding under the bed, he argued contemptuously. He wanted to talk to him a minute, and he would stay until he did talk to him, if he had to sit there 'til his horse starved to death.

"Boss ain't heah nohow!" Black Sam protested, rolling his eyes so that the whites showed all around. "You Meddalahk boys done plowed up ouah roof a'ready wif youah bullets, an' Boss he gwine on in to talk to Mist' Shu'f man. He jes plumb *kain't* come out, 'cause he ain't heah. No, suh, ain't pawssible fo' him to come out, nohow."

"I think yo're lyin' to me, Snowball," Gelle declared firmly, and shook his head. "You gotta prove it."

"Lawsy, Boss, how Ah goin' to prove nothin' like dat air, 'cep'n' you git off'm dat hawse an' look fo' youahse'f? B-but 'twon't do no good nohow, Mist' Meddalahk, awnes, it won't! Dat ole house ain't got nobody into it *atall*. Ain't nobody undah no baid, Boss, Ah swah to goodness dey ain't. Blinkah, he's somewhah on de place, but he don' count no moah 'n Ah counts, an' Ah don' count nothin' *atall*." Sam backed warily toward the kitchen door as Gelle pressed closer. "Blinkah, he ain't got no sense nohow, Mist' Meddalahk, an' A'm jes' an old black cook what doan' 'mount to nothin'. Boss, he's in town—leastwise he's awn de way—yessuh, yo'all kin ride awn aftuh him, Mist' Meddalahk, suh, an' tawk all you'm a mine to. Yessuh."

Sam was so scared, so plainly and honestly helpless, so anxious to placate the man he believed a dangerous foe, that Gelle hadn't the heart to bully him further. At the same time he must give Bud time in which to make a thorough search. He looked around for Blinker, but that peculiar fellow was nowhere to be seen.

"Got any coffee?" Gelle demanded for want of something else to hold him there.

"Yessuh, Boss, Ah got whole pawt uh cawfee, yessuh, Mist' Meddalahk."

"All right, bring me a cup. No sugar, Snowball—"

"Lawsy, Boss, we doan' nevah have no sugah atall! Boss, he buy silk foah dishrags soon as evah he buy sugah foah cawfee an' sech." Sam grinned in spite of his terror, showing the strong, even teeth so characteristic of the negro race. "We got milk, 'cause milk doan' cos' nawthin'."

"How about buttermilk?" Gelle was better pleased with his task now. He thought he could keep this up for an hour if necessary.

"Yessuh, Boss, Ah jes' chuhned dis mawnin'. Buttah doan' cos' nawthin', neithah, an' it saves meat. An' aigs, we got aigs; hens, dey doan' deman' no wages, Mist' Meddalahk." Sam chuckled with a wry twist to his big mouth, as if the joke was barbed.

"What wages do you git, Snowball?" Gelle's tone indicated that he was prepared to be sympathetic.

"Me? What wages do Ah git? Ah doan' *git*. No, suh, Boss, time Ah wuhks out de cos' of pants an' shuht an' shoes an' hat, Ah doan' *git*!"

"You don't?" Genuine surprise was in Gelle's voice. "Git out! Say, Snowball, slavery days is over, don't yuh know it? You don't have to work fer *no* man that's too damn' stingy to buy sugar fer coffee, an' runs a sandy like that on yuh fer pay. Judgin' by them garments yo're draped in now, Snowball, I'd say you must spend as much as five, ten dollars mebbe, a year on clothes. What wages does ole Palmer claim he pays you, if it's a fair question?"

"What wages? Wa' now, Mist' Meddalahk, Ah doan' rightly know, suh. Boss, he claim lak Ah eats moah 'n what Ah kin earn nohow, cookin'. He talk lak he pay me ten dollah, mebbe. Mist' Meddalahk, suh, Ah wuhk an' wuhk, an' mos' Ah kin do is eat an' sleep, an' nevah much of dat. Doan' seem pawssible to git ahaid mo'n one shuht."

Sam wiped a ragged sleeve across his perspiring face, turned and went into the house, his terror of the Meadowlark man erased from his simple soul by the note of human understanding and sympathy. He returned presently with a big tin cup full of cold buttermilk over which Gelle promptly bent his eager lips.

"Say, Snowball," he remarked, when he came up for air, "our cook at the Meddalark gits sixty dollars a month. And he *gits* it—and buys his own pants and shirts. You're bein' robbed and you don't know it. And say! Lark buys sugar, five sacks at a lick, and nobody gits the bad eye for dumpin' three or four spoonsful into his coffee. 'Tain't none of my business, Snowball, but I hate to see even a coon git the worst of it like that. Say, here's a dollar. Don't let ole Palmer ketch you with it though."

Sam's eyes would not stand out farther if he were being choked. He was too stunned by this munificence to put out his hand for the money, so Gelle tossed the dollar in his general direction, finished the buttermilk in one long drink, set the cup down on an upturned barrel near by and rode back to the gate to meet Bud, who was coming at a swift gallop. Bud pulled up, his eyes snapping with excitement.

"Go back around the corner of the fence, Jelly, and down the gully about fifty yards," he directed crisply. "I left that old man Blinker tied up, and I want you to stand guard over him until I can ride into town and back. He came up on me before I could get away in the brush, and all I could do was glom him and bring him out with me. I won't be gone more than a couple of hours, but it's too hot a day to leave an old man tied up with ants and mosquitoes and flies raising merry hell with him. Will you do it, Jelly?"

"Sure, I'll do it. Thank Gawd fer that buttermilk! Say, you ain't leavin' me out of anything like a scrap, are yuh, Bud? If you are, I'll pack m' prisoner in under my arm but what I'll go to yore party."

"No—don't think there'll be a word of trouble. I'll be right back, Jelly, and then we'll both ride in and make merry. We'll have a right." He was galloping down the road before Gelle could answer him.

Even in his haste Bud took thought of the curiosity he would probably excite if he came pounding down the hill with his horse in a lather, and once on the subject of precautions it struck him forcibly that perhaps Smoky Ford would be just as well off if it failed to see him at all. At the foot of the hill, therefore, he turned sharply off the road on a dim trail that meandered up a wash and rounded an elbow of the bluffside, and so came out at the rear of Delkin's livery stable, where four Meadowlark horses took their ease in the corral, the sweat scarcely dried on their backs. The sight of them reminded Bud that after all he had not been so far behind the boys who were probably still feeling the thrill of their first cold drinks. Indeed, they had not been gone on their odorous adventure more than ten minutes when Bud led his lathered sorrel into a shadowy stall and went burring his spur rowels down the long stable so lately echoing to the footsteps of those other Meadowlark riders. With considerable abruptness he pulled open the screen door and stepped into the office, his eyes flashing quick glances at the four men who sat there talking about the one big subject.

"Howdy. Glad to see you all here, because you're the men I came after, and I don't know just how quiet you want to keep this business. I've found your money—or the bank's money, rather. If you folks will ride out with me, I'll show you where it's cached. I went on a still hunt around Palmer's on my way in; saw he was headed for town, so I took advantage of his absence. His grandson, the one he abused so that Lark took him away, told me some things that gave a clue to the whole business. Palmer's gang came down river in a boat, hid under the bank and then took the loot back up river, and probably sunk the boat after they were through with it. That's the way I've doped it out, at least. At any rate, I can show you the stuff, and you can bring it in; but you'll have to hurry. Unless you can get there, and the stuff is moved before Palmer goes home, he may discover us. And he'll be leaving probably—"

"No!" The front legs of Bradley's chair came to the floor with a thump. "My heavens, but you Meadowlark boys work fast when you get started! There's those young devils over in the Elkhorn, pulling off a bit of play-acting to make Palmer's gang give themselves away. And here *you* come, busting in here with the news—"

"No time for argument," snapped Delkin. "You men come along and bear witness to this. If we recover the bank's property, you have a right to be there, anyway. I think those boys over there will keep Palmer and his men interested for another hour or two, which will give us time. Bud, are you alone, or did your uncle come with you?"

"Lark's at home. I left Jelly on guard, back there; had to take that crazy old fellow at Palmer's and tie him up. He came and caught me at the cache, so there was nothing else to do. I wonder if I can borrow a fresh horse, Mr. Delkin?"

"By the lord Harry, you can have anything I've got, down to my last shirt!" As the news took hold of his imagination, Delkin was like another man. He led the way into the stable and on to the corral, choosing mounts for his companions and shouting orders to the scurrying hostler.

Stauffer and Kline, the two other bank directors, ejaculated futile comments but failed to contribute anything further than their presence to the venture. There are always men of that type in any gathering. They have little to say, they never take the initiative, but they do add the force of numbers—a useful incident at times.

"Better tie on some saddlebags, or take a grain sack or two. You know that stuff is a bit bulky," Bud reminded them. "There must be twenty-five or thirty pounds of gold, besides the other currency and papers. I was in too much of a hurry to go over it, after I'd fully identified it as belonging to the bank. And we'd better go out the back way by the trail I came in on. Mr. Delkin, I suppose you know whether your man here needs a gag, or whether he can be trusted to keep his mouth shut."

"Say, you don't need to worry about no gag fer *me*, young feller," the stableman retorted indignantly. "If it's the bank money you're goin' after, seven hundred and thirty dollars of it belongs t' *me*! I ain't liable to spill no beans off'n my own plate, I guess."

"You'd be a fool if you did," Bud laughed. "Well, we don't want a single solitary soul to know we've left town, or that I've been here. Mr. Delkin, are you ready?"

Five saddled horses, following five men who unconsciously held the reins in their left hands in preparation for any emergency, walked out of the doorway and into the hot sunlight that lay on the dim trail which joined the road at the foot of the grade.

The stableman stood with his back bowed in and his hands on his hips, teetering up and down on his toes, and watched them go, his jaws working in absent-minded industry on a tasteless quid of much-chewed tobacco.

"I golly, looks like I'll git m' money back, after all!" he cackled gloatingly, and followed the departing horsemen to the doorway, where he stood staring after them until not even their bobbing heads were longer visible as they trotted up the trail. When they were gone, he turned back grinning to his work.

* * *

CHAPTER FOURTEEN
"SOMETHING'S ABOUT DUE TO POP!"

"This seems a pretty tame proceeding," Bud observed whimsically, when they had dismounted in the hollow where Gelle was sitting cross-legged in the grass. "By rights there should be some shooting at the wind-up of a robbery the size of this one. I did take a prisoner, though, didn't I? But the old pelican doesn't seem to be very fierce—how'd you make out, Jelly?"

Gelle looked up sourly and pointed with his thumb. "I been keepin' the flies off your treasure trove, Bud, just as long as I'm agoin' to. If this is all they is to bandit-huntin', I'm goin' home and bug potatoes fer excitement. Where you goin' now? Snipe huntin'?"

"I'll watch this fellow," Kline the druggist offered promptly. "Give me a gun, somebody, in case he wakes up. Lord, that sun's hot!"

"Yeah, it's nice an' shady here—if shade's what you're after," Gelle told him dryly. "Bring any lunch baskets? Right nice, shady dell fer a buck picnic, and I could eat without bein' forced. And say, Bud, any time you feel like tellin' what you found or expect to find, I'll be willin' to listen."

"Come along and I'll show you," Bud grinned. "Palmer's whole outfit's in town, Delkin says—excepting the cook. We're going to investigate a rat's nest down here by the river."

"Yeah?" Gelle looked from one to the other, and then grinned in slowly awakening amusement that spread to his eyes and left a twinkle there. "Judgin' from that praise-God look on these plutocrats' faces—oh, well, come on!"

They filed down through the bushes after Bud, who led the way straight to the hedge and up over rocks that left no trace, to the place where Skookum had seen his grandfather at work like an old badger. A broken fragment of ledge lay piled there, and behind the rocks, hidden from sight until one climbed the pile and looked over, a dry, deep niche, narrow of mouth and roomy inside, lay revealed. Within it they saw a jumbled heap of sticks, dead leaves and twigs—a rat's nest, any chance observer would have sworn. But Bud picked up a larger branch and thrust away the litter. Delkin crowded past him eagerly and began clawing at the nearest of three ribbed, iron kegs with tight-fitting lids, such as are used for storing blasting powder.

"Gosh, is that money?" Gelle, peering over Delkin's shoulder, spoke in a hushed tone. "Gosh! Lemme heft one of them kegs, Mr. Delkin!"

His face red and sweaty with excitement, Delkin tilted the keg on its side, picked up a canvas sack as if it were very heavy and put it into Gelle's eager, outstretched hands. He laughed foolishly at the look of astonishment on the long cowpuncher's face and reached for another sack. He was like a boy clawing gifts out of his Christmas stocking and truly believing in Santa Claus. Bud, who had seen how despair could rack him, swallowed a lump that appeared mysteriously in his throat. It was worth a lot, he told himself, to see a man so overwhelmingly elated and happy.

"Brad, here are those bonds of Morgan's—why do thieves take stuff they never can use? Stauffer, here, you take charge of these—notes and mortgages, I guess they are. I wonder if Palmer was foxy enough to take out that note of his that the bank holds! God, if we could get Charlie's life back with the rest, I'd be the happiest man on earth! Well—that's all, I guess. No—but this isn't the bank's. This must belong to Palmer."

"Glom it!" Gelle advised grimly, but Delkin shook his head.

"No—all we want is our own. Well, no use putting back the rubbish, is there? If they come here at all, they're bound to find out the bank's property has disappeared. And if we have any luck at all, they'll never get back here. Jelly, do you want to carry the gold?"

"I should smile!" Gelle grinned widely to prove it as he held open the grain sack. "Any chances the gold might some of it rub off on m' shirt? How much is they, Mr. Delkin?"

"A little over twelve thousand dollars, according to the books. Brad's carrying three times as much; yes, Brad's got forty thousand dollars right there in his hands."

"Yeah?" Gelle cast a mildly disdainful glance at the package of bank notes which Bradley was stowing away in a bag. "Mebbe so, but it shore don't carry the same thrill as what this gold money packs. That why you left all that money in the keg?" He turned, shoulders slightly bent under his load, and stared at the emptied powder kegs, and at the one which was not empty. "It shore is a crime to leave all that good money there," he complained. "Chances are Palmer stole it, anyway. Me, I don't believe the old hellion ever did get an honest dollar in his life. It'd burn his fingers."

"But that doesn't give us any right to it," Delkin told him firmly. "Some one is liable to come on a long lope to see how about it. You fellows go ahead; I'll bring up the rear. And remember, that open stretch down there is in plain sight of the stables, so you'd better take it on the trot."

Gelle did better than that; he sprinted for the bushes ahead of the other three, got hung up in the wire fence because he tried to crawl through without slipping the sack of coin to the ground, and so caught a barb fast in the canvas and had to be helped by Bud, who overtook him while he was still wriggling like an impaled bug.

Delkin, Bradley and Stauffer went on and were jubilating in hushed voices with Kline when the Meadowlark contingent arrived. They stood apart from the old man, who still snored comfortably with his lips puffed out through his thin whiskers. Bud's capture was likely to prove embarrassing.

"What'll we do?" Bradley asked impatiently. "Can't turn him loose here—and Kline says he's been asleep all this while, so he doesn't know yet we've come on to the scene. Jelly, can't you stay right here and watch him for a while—till Bud comes back?"

Gelle stood with the sack of gold between his feet, as if he meant to protect it from all claimants, and stared glumly from one to the other.

"I can, yes. But I shore hate to like hell," he admitted sourly. "You'll go awn in an' have a scrap, chances are, an' I'll be settin' here like a knot on a log, watchin' this ole pelican's whiskers wave in and out. Excitin', ain't it? Damn fine way to spend an afternoon! When it comes to thinkin' up things fer me to do, you shore have got bright idees!"

"Seems to be about the only thing we can do about it, Jelly," Bud said soothingly. "We could tie him up, but even then it wouldn't be absolutely safe. You can't blame these bankers for not wanting to take a chance of losing all this money, now that they have it back. He might get loose and warn Palmer in some way. We'll go back by a roundabout way through the hills, just because they don't want a soul to know they've got the money. Once that's safe, we'll go after Palmer and his bunch, yes. But you must see, Jelly, that—"

"Oh, hell, go awn and leave me to m' thoughts!" Gelle pulled down the corners of his mouth, stepped over the gold, turned back and gave it a kick as if he would show his familiarity with it, and grinned at Bud. "I never did have no luck, nohow." He lounged over and sat down beside the sleeper, and spat disgustedly into the lush grass near by. He waved them toward town, made a derisive gesture and started to roll a smoke, giving them no further attention.

"Jelly's a fine boy, all right, and it's a damned shame he has to stand guard—but I'm darned if I'm sorry enough for him to stay in his place," Bud observed with futile sympathy, when they were riding townward by devious trails which kept to the hills and concealed them from any passer-by on the road. "Still—are you dead sure Palmer's bunch will stay in town?"

Bradley laughed.

"The way Tony and the boys had it framed, Palmer's gang will give no heed to the passing hours. You know, of course, what the boys meant to do?"

"I didn't know they meant to do anything," Bud confessed. "Darn 'em, they must have held out on me."

"Well, now, if they don't get hung before we hit town, they may stir up something interesting. The idea was to play off drunk, and when the crowd was pretty thoroughly worked up, seeing them spend money—gold money which they acted sneaking about—each one of the boys planned to get a Palmer man off in a corner, do the 'weeping-drunk' and confess that he went down river from Meadowlark Basin in a boat, killed Charlie and robbed the bank, and that he had the stuff cached and wanted a man he could trust to help him get the stuff safely out of the country. They had it planned out to the last detail: how long it ought to take them to get so drunk they'd confide in a man they never had chummed with, and just how they'd manage to lead up to the subject. Tony said he'd take Bat Johnson into his confidence, and Rosen was to tackle Palmer himself, I believe. Bob and Mark were going to buttonhole Ed White and the Mexican. It sure sounded like it might work—if they don't get lynched, as I said.

"They figure that one or all of Palmer's gang will get so uneasy there will be a general stampede to where the money's hidden to see if the Meadowlark boys have any of them found out where it's cached. Either that, or they'll give themselves away by wanting to fight or something. Of course," he added, glancing down with a grin at the bundle tied at the fork of his saddle, "they didn't know we'd have the stuff safely put away long before they could trail anyone to the spot where it was hid."

"And they expect to stay sober long enough to put that over?" Bud's lips tilted upwards with amusement.

"You bet they did! Just before you showed up, they'd poured whisky all over themselves, by the smell. On the outside," he added meaningly. "I don't see how they'd dare light a cigarette—they were sure saturated."

Bud touched his borrowed horse with the spurs.

"We'd better be riding," he called over his shoulder. "If I know anything about that bunch, something's about due to pop!"

CHAPTER FIFTEEN
"JELLY" GETS IN ACTION

Nothing is more disconcerting than to make elaborate plans which provide for every mishap save the one which afterwards looks absolutely inevitable. Tony had been deeply concerned over the integrity of his actors, and concentrated all his energies upon keeping himself and his fellow-actors sober, quite overlooking the obvious result of a meeting between Palmer's men and the Meadowlark boys. Tony should have remembered that a feud had existed since early spring; better still, he should have taken it for granted that the Palmer gang had circulated enough falsehoods just lately to render them self-conscious and a bit too ready to defend themselves if a Meadowlark man but looked their way.

Tony, absorbed in playing his part, was forced to take a drink or two at the bar—along with the three other members of his amateur comedy company—before he could plausibly detach himself from his fellows and wabble over to the pool table where he stood grinning a silly grin and applauding Bat Johnson's mediocre game. Tony did not know it, but his eyes held an unfriendly, calculating gleam and they clung rather tenaciously to Bat; which was not exactly reassuring to a man with as much on his conscience as made Bat's slumbers uneasy and troubled with bad dreams. A man with that silly grin stretching his lips, while above the grin his eyes stare with a malevolent intentness, need wear no other sign to warn a sober man. Bat Johnson was not drunk.

"Y're a good man, Bat," Tony burbled, when Bat had reached up his cue and slid the last set of buttons toward the center. "W' played out y'r string, Bat—played out y'r string, ain't yuh?"

"What's that?" Bat whirled upon him. "What do you mean by that, you drunken four-flush?"

"Y'r a good—what'd you say? Four-flush? Me a four-flush—me?" Tony remembered to shake his head in drunken grief. "Bat, I—I never thought you'd shpeak t' me like that, I—"

"It ain't me that's played out my string," Bat told him viciously. "You wait till a few Meadowlark necks git twisted! A string er two's been played out there, my fine buckaroo. Folks is gittin' damn' tired of them birds. You're one of 'em and you've about warbled yore last song. Git outa my way b'fore I kill yuh!"

Even the best actors may forget their parts when the proper cue is not given. Had Bat been friendly, or even neutral, Tony would have swallowed his feelings and gone ahead with his original lines. But you simply can't confide your guilt to a man like that, no matter what vital issue is at stake.

Still, Tony was vastly surprised at himself for knocking Bat head first over the pool table, because not even two unaccustomed drinks of whisky could convince him that this was a diplomatic opening to the confidential talk he had planned to have with Bat. He wondered dully whether he had spoiled the whole thing, or whether Bat would forgive the blow on account of Tony's irresponsible condition, and still consent to listen to the story which Tony had so carefully prepared to pour out at the urge of a drunken impulse.

But then Bat picked himself up and came at him with a billiard cue, and Tony decided quite suddenly that what he really wanted—and the only thing he wanted—was to show Bat exactly where to head in at (quoting Tony). He snatched up a ball and laughed when he saw how it bounced off Bat's head, leaving Bat dazed and waving the cue vaguely until his head stopped spinning.

"Yeah—you better go git into yore boat and drift on down the river!" Tony chortled recklessly. "I don't reckon yuh had a billiard cue handy at the bank, did yuh? Had t' kill Charlie with yore gun. Think nobody's wise to you an' yore bunch, ay? Well, you and—"

A big, firm hand slipped over Tony's mouth and stopped him at that point, and the arm belonging to the hand seemed in a fair way of throttling him.

"You damn drunken fool," Bob hissed in his ear. "Think us boys all stayed sober jest fer the fun of seein' you drunk an' shootin' off yore mouth thataway?"

Jack Rosen jumped a card table and kicked over two chairs, but he landed on Bat Johnson in time to spoil his aim, so the shot went wild. Big Mark Hanley grabbed Tex and Ed White, a hand on each collar, and butted their heads together while he whooped his glee at the way things were going. Other men scattered when they saw these two clawing for their guns.

"Hey! I ain't got nobody t' lick!" wailed Tony, seeing how the other boys were occupied, the whisky beginning to boil angrily in his blood. "Where's Palmer?"

No one seemed to know, or if they did they gave no sign. They made way for Tony's headlong rush for the door, where he saw that Palmer was already riding out of sight up the street. For a moment he was tempted to follow him; but time would be lost while he saddled his horse, and Palmer would have a start that would make it difficult to overtake him if he wanted to hurry. Moreover, sounds in the saloon behind him indicated that at least two fights were progressing with much vigor. Tony turned back to the fray and let Palmer go.

Had he ridden a bit faster Palmer would probably have seen Delkin and his party cross the road and turn into the hills on their way back to town with the bank's money. As it was, he rode at his usual racking trot and so arrived home not long after Gelle had taken his prisoner to the house and locked him in a room off the kitchen, where he promptly went to sleep again.

"Dass way Blinkah, he always do, Mist' Meddalahk, when Boss he go awn to town. Gittin' old, he is. Yass, suh, Blinkah he do need a pow'ful lot a slumbah. Wha' foh yo'all want wif dat ole cuss, skusin' de question?"

"Hell, I don't want him," Gelle denied pensively. "All I want is another drink of that buttermilk, and mebby a bite of somethin' to eat, Snowball. It's Bud that wants the old man. He come leadin' him along to where it was shady and cool, and then he told me I had to go and set with him fer company. I don't want him atall. I'm jest keepin' cases till I find out what Bud's idee was of havin' me day-herd the old coot. He ain't done a thing but sleep ever since I went on guard."

Sam grinned, showing an amazing lot of teeth.

"Yessuh, Mist' Meddalahk, he sho' kin sleep when chance comes along. Boss, he make a great ole niggah-drivah down Souf—yessuh, he sho' would do so! Ain' much sleepin' when Boss is home; nothin' but wuhk fo' ole Blinkah 'n' me.

"Ah sho' admire to git yo'all somethin' to eat, if Boss, he doan' come ketch me. Lawsy, Mist' Meddalahk, ef Boss, he come ridin' along home, Ah'd sho' 'preciate it ef yo'all lock up ole Sam jes' lak Blinkah. An' ef Boss, he s'picions Ah never made no desistunce, Ah'd lak lil small cut, mebby, on mah haid to show. Boss, he's pow'ful s'picious man, Mist' Meddalahk, yessuh."

"Say, the boys call me Jelly. Don't be so darn formal, Snowball, or I'll likely give you a lump about the size of a goose egg to show. You set out the grub, and I'll mebby lock you up jest fer a josh. I dunno but what I like the idee."

Thus it happened that Gelle was sitting with his mouth full and his jaws working comfortably when Palmer rode up to the gate, leaned and unlatched it, sidled his horse through and closed the gate afterwards. Perhaps he noticed fresh horse tracks that were strange, though Gelle's horse stood tied in the bushes at the edge of the gully. Perhaps Palmer saw the imprint of Gelle's boots. Whatever the cause, he eyed the house as if he knew some danger lurked within—or perhaps he was merely estimating the amount of damage done to his shingles.

Gelle had not expected him back. He took up his glass of buttermilk and washed down the mouthful of bread and butter with one huge swallow, drew his hand hastily across his mouth and did a rapid mental calculation.

"Yo're my prisoner, Snowball," he said over his shoulder. "I might give you another dollar if you do a good job of playin' dead till I holler when. Go awn and take a nap with the old man while I talk to yore Boss."

From the yard a harsh voice called Sam, and after a minute's hesitation Gelle motioned him forward.

"Act natural, Snowball, or I'll spill you all over the room," he muttered.

"Boss, he's pow'ful mean man. He kill dis ole niggah—" Sam held up his two shaking hands, the palms pinkish as if he had worn off the color.

"Gwan—answer him! He ain't goin' to have a chance at yuh. I want t' git him inside, Snowball. Gwan."

Palmer shouted again, and Sam caught up a chipped yellow bowl and stood forth bravely enough, though Gelle, standing just out of sight behind the door, could see how his legs were shaking.

"Yessuh, Boss, yessuh." Sam ducked his head propitiatingly.

"Sam, who's been here to the house? No lies, you damn' worthless whelp!"

"Heah? To dis house? Ah dunno zackly, Boss, Ah-h—" He took another breath and plunged. "Sho'ht time aftah yo'all rode off, Boss, man he comes lopin' along. Wants to speak wid yo'all, 'cawdin' to what he says. Ah says yo'all ain't heah an' 'tain't pawssible he kin speak wid yo'all. He hang eroun' awn his hawse, but he doan' shoot no gun, an' bimeby he ride awn off."

"Did, ay? Anybody you know?"

"No-suh, Boss, Ah doan' reckon Ah knows dat cowboy, nohow. But Ah notice, Boss, he's got Meddalahk brand on he's hawse—"

Palmer swore such fluent, heartfelt oaths that Gelle grinned and whispered to Sam that there was one thing old Palmer wasn't stingy with, and that was cuss words.

"Which way—here, come back here, you damn' lazy idiot, and tell me which way he went!"

"'Clah to goodness, Boss, Ah so plum tickled he's goin', Ah doan' rightly know! Awn up river som'ers, Boss." Sam rolled his eyes in terror, for Palmer was climbing down from his horse in the manner that promised blows delivered upon the first luckless object within reach.

"Scoot!" whispered Gelle, pointing toward the door of the small room beyond. Then remembering that the door was locked, he strode across on his toes, unlocked it and thrust Sam headfirst inside. He had just turned the key and faced the outside doorway when Palmer stepped in.

Surprise halted Palmer just an instant too long, for Gelle gave a long leap and landed a blow with his fist that rocked Palmer and brought both hands up and away from his gun, vaguely attempting to ward off another blow that landed full on the nose. Tears of pain started to Palmer's eyes, but he fought back viciously and shouted for Sam.

"The feller's locked up," Gelle told him between clenched teeth. "'Twouldn't help yuh none to have him here. Leggo that gun! Damn yuh, I could have shot yuh down like a dog if I'd wanted to!"

Before he had finished, Gelle was tempted to regret his fair dealing. They swayed the full length of the kitchen, locked in each other's arms. Palmer managed to get him by the throat and beat his head against the wall until points of light whirled before Gelle's eyes. He tore loose, filled his lungs with one great gasp and tripped Palmer, who pulled the table over on top of them as he went down, clawing like fighting cats. Gelle got the edge of a board in the ribs and felt a sickening crack and after that the flaming agony of a splintered rib prodding tender flesh, but he hung tenaciously with knees and fingers and managed to stay on top.

The fight ended when Gelle snatched up the heavy earthen pitcher that had held buttermilk and had come through the upheaval without a crack. He swung the pitcher aloft by the handle and brought it down on Palmer's head—breaking both. At least there was no doubt about the pitcher, and as for Palmer, he gave a convulsive shudder and went limp, and a cut on his head began to swell as the blood oozed out.

Gelle pulled himself up, grunting with the pain in his side, and looked down at the havoc he had wrought. He would have set the table back on its legs, but the effort was too painful, so he went staggering over to the bedroom door and unlocked Sam, bringing him out with an imperative, beckoning gesture, Palmer's gun in his hand. Sam came as if he were being kicked out, with his back bowed in and his fingers spread ready to ward off a blow.

"Get a rope or something to tie him up," Gelle ordered sharply. "I ain't goin' to hurt you, Snowball—not if you behave. That'll do. Pull his hands around behind him—no, he ain't dead. He'll come to after a while. Get a wiggle on."

"Yessuh, yessuh, Mist' Meddalahk."

"All right—fine. Now, jest drag him in there, will you, Snowball? And lock the door; or, no, jest drag him in there. The darn cuss might take a notion to die on my hands, and I want him alive; so you can keep an eye on him. When he comes to himself, I wanta talk to him."

"Yessuh, Mist' Meddalahk, yo'all sho' am a hahd man to git shet of bein' talked to!" Now that Palmer was safely tied, Sam could afford to take a full breath and to grin once more at his new friend. "When yo'all say you wanta talk wif a man, 'tain't no use to avoid de cawnvusashum—'tain't no mannah of use atall. Might as well make de bes' of it an' *talk*. Yessuh, Mist' Meddalahk, yo'all sho' am detumined!"

Gelle laughed, but that did not cause him to relax his watchfulness.

"What about the men that work here, Snowball? Purty good friends of yourn, ain't they?"

"Friends uh mine? Bat 'n' dat ah Mex, 'n' Ed friends uh *mine*? No, suh, Mist' Meddalahk, dey ain't no friends ob nobody but deyselfs. Dem fellahs, dey so plum mean an' awnery, dey jes' about hate deyselfs mos' awl de time. No, suh, Ah ain't got no friends—not on dis heah ranch, Ah ain'. Cusses an' kicks, dat 'bout awl Ah evah gits aroun' heah."

"Oh, all right. I just wondered, because if they come lopin' home, I'm liable to need more rope. Snowball—"

"Yessuh, yessuh, Ah gits moah rope direckly, Mist' Meddalahk. Lawsy, how dem fellahs do lie to dis heah ole niggah 'bout you gemman at de Meddalahk! Yessuh, dey sho' do lie!"

"Got anything to bandage a broken rib?"

Sam gave him a startled roll of eyeballs and hurried out. Gelle heard him clumping around overhead for a few minutes and wondered what he was up to. But when Sam came down he had a sheet, yellowed and smelling a bit musty; and over his arm was hung a coil of cotton clothes-line.

"Onlies' sheet in de house was up in de lof'. Big trunk awl wrop up wid dis heah rope. Mist' Meddalahk, suh, Ah mighty sorry yo'all done bruk a rib, kase mo' fightin' sho' is boun' t' come along when dem three gits heah, an' ole Sam, he ain' no good nohow."

"You can tie 'em up if I can get 'em into the house and pull down on 'em with my gun. Purty tame way to git 'em, but I guess it'll be best to play safe. How soon you reckon they're liable to come?"

But Sam, of course, did not know. All they could do was wait and hope for action before dark. There was, Gelle knew upon reflection, small chances that the three Palmer men would be left to ride unhindered out of Smoky Ford, once Delkin's party arrived. Palmer they had of course missed on the way, but unless his men left soon after he did, they would be captured and held in town until the sheriff could come and get them. It was just a bit of good luck that had sent Palmer into his hands.

And then, not more than half an hour after they had finished their preparations and time was beginning to drag, a scattered fusillade of shots came crackling thinly from the pasture, down near the ledge.

Gelle got up too carelessly and was obliged to sit down again, white and sweating. Sam was goggling at him as if in Gelle's face he could read the explanation of the sounds.

"Our boys chased 'em out, mebbe," Gelle muttered, speaking in that repressed tone which comes of not being able to take a deep breath. "Still—I dunno. Gee, I'd love to be down there! All I git outa this deal is sittin' around whilst the rest plays. Listen at 'em, Snowball! Darn the luck, anyway!"

CHAPTER SIXTEEN
"WHO SHOT BAT AND ED WHITE"

Life would sometimes be simpler if events were more evenly spaced and periods of inaction put to a better use by letting them hold the incidents that otherwise must pile on top of one another and crowd one day overfull of excitement. But so long as we remain unscientific enough to take things just as they come and let our emotions rule our hands and feet, life will continue to go steady by jerks.

Take this day in Smoky Ford and at the Palmer ranch, just seven miles out yet well within the trouble zone. If there is anything in thought vibrations, Tony and Bud must have owned powerful mental dynamos and set them working full speed that morning. The pity is that they did not work altogether in harmony, but instead set up different currents of violent thought action—and most of the mental activity gyrated around that money looted from the bank.

The money itself was safe enough, once it reached Delkin's stable. Delkin was a shrewd man when sudden misfortune did not upset him, and his method of safeguarding the bank's property was truly ingenious.

Among his horses was one with the significant name, The Butcher. His character lived up to his name, and with the exception of the stableman and Delkin himself, not a man in Smoky Ford would venture within reach of his teeth or his heels—and both had an amazing reach, by the way. Delkin studied long and deeply over the safest place—barring the bank—for the money and papers, and his cogitations brought him finally to The Butcher. The bank, he considered, was out of the question for the present. Some one would be sure to see them carrying the stuff inside, and the news would spread like scandal. Until Palmer's gang was safe behind the bars, it must be taken for granted that the money was still missing.

This naturally left Delkin thinking of The Butcher, and the more he thought of him the easier he felt in his mind. The Butcher had his own little corral for exercise, his own box stall. Moreover, the manger was built high and had a false bottom nearly two feet from the floor. Who in Smoky Ford would ever dream of finding anything in The Butcher's box stall, even if they dared look there?

Delkin did not say a word until they reached the stable and he had sent the stableman up into the office to watch for chance callers. The Butcher was out in the corral, and Delkin closed the stall door to make sure that the horse would stay outside for a while. Even then he took only Bradley into his confidence, after the others had gone to see what was doing in the saloons and whether the Palmer men were still in town, and what the Meadowlark boys had gained by confession. Not even Bud suspected Delkin of having a secret, but supposed that the money would be kept in the office until it could be transferred to the bank vault.

Instead, the two men carried it into the box stall, pried up a board in the manger and dropped everything underneath, replaced the board and the hay in the manger and heaved sighs of relief. Then Delkin waved Bradley out of the stall, opened the outer door and called The Butcher in. He came, nickering softly for a lump of sugar, got it and nibbled daintily while Delkin slipped out and shut the door. It was a bit early to shut up The Butcher, but the stableman would not bother with him unless he had to; Delkin knew that.

"There! We needn't worry about anybody stealing it tonight," grinned Delkin. "Unless the stable gets afire we're dead safe, Brad. We can leave it right here until we are ready to open up the bank again. Now, let's get after Palmer and his gang."

They met Bud coming with four much-ruffled Meadowlarks, a small, rat-eyed Mexican hustled along in their midst. Bud's eyes were once more snapping with excitement, the others inclined to glassy stares through red and swollen lids.

"Here's the one they call Mex. Took two knives off him, and the boys got a gun. Haven't located Palmer and Bat yet," Bud announced, as the two bankers hurried toward them.

"Aw, they crawled off t' die som'ers!" Tony pompously declared. "We licked 'em to a fare-ye-well. Didn't we lick 'em, boys?"

"Shore enough did," Mark Hanley boasted. "Put 'em both awn the run. One of 'em chawed m' ear off, purty near, but I got 'im."

"Sh'd say we licked 'em!" big Bob boasted. "Now I'm goin' to git drunk."

"Yes, y' betcha!" Jack Rosen approved gravely.

"Betcha they know now who the thieves is an' who the murderers is," Tony cried exultantly. "Told 'em m'self. Called the turn on that boat—made 'em swaller twice, that did! Told 'em I could put m' hands awn—"

"Good Lord!" Bud gave Delkin and Bradley a quick look that had in it a good deal of consternation. "They'll beat it out of the country now. Gone for the loot, and they won't stop short of the Badlands. Tony, you damn' chump, why didn't you keep your face closed?"

"Why? Had t' open it, didn't I, t' swaller a drink er two? Me, I don't drink only with m' eyes, I tell you those! Had t' open m' mouth, anyway—thought I might as well use it. Wha's matter with that? They *are* thieves an' murderers, ain't they? Told 'em so—licked 'em to a frazzle. Didn't we, boys?"

"Damn' right," three voices growled in chorus.

"Palmer, he run out on us, 'r we'd licked him too. This Mex, here, he's licked. Howled like a pup. Didn't you, Mex?" Tony turned gravely to the cringing captive, who nodded sullen surrender.

"Well, get your horses," Bud snapped. "You've got some riding to do now, you're so darn gay and festive. How long have they been gone? Do you know?"

They thought they knew exactly, but their answers were so conflicting that Bud and Delkin finally took the word of a boy who volunteered the information that Bat and Ed White had ridden out of town about ten minutes ago, headed toward home.

"We'll have to fan the breeze, boys, and we may wind up in the Badlands. Mr. Bradley, we'd better take a little grub—sardines and crackers, or something like that. Because if we don't overhaul them at the ranch, we'll just keep on going."

"I'll bring some stuff to the stable," said Bradley, and started on a trot to the store.

"Oh, hell, and we don't get drunk at all!" Big Bob Leverett complained disgustedly. "Wish I had the whisky I washed m' face in. A hull quart of Metropole gone t' granny!"

Bud whirled on the group and stared angrily from one to the other.

"You're drunk enough," he said contemptuously. "You fellows seem to think this is just a picnic. Do you want me to round up a posse here in Smoky Ford, and tell them that we've got the goods on the gang that killed Charlie and robbed the bank and that we're going after them, but our own men are too drunk to be of any use? I can take a town bunch, if you say so, and let you boys stay here and swill whisky. It would be a consistent finish to the damage you've done already—telling the gang that we're wise to them, roughhousing awhile like any other drunken chumps, and then letting them all get off except this greaser who may not know a thing about it." His lip curled in a sneer. "A hell of an outfit you are to round up outlaws!"

"Gwan an' git your Smoky Ford posse if you want to, Bud," Tony said stiffly, the whisky fumes swept clean from his brain by the hurt Bud had given. "While you're gittin' them, we'll hit the trail. Come awn, boys."

They took the remaining distance in a run, and they were saddled and ducking under the stable doorway and racing off up the road and out of town while Bud was still waiting for Bradley to come with supplies, and Delkin was telephoning the sheriff to come as quick as the Lord would let him. Smoky Ford itself saw only that the Meadowlark boys were in town raising Cain again, never dreaming that their one big tragedy of the summer was reaching a fortuitous climax, under the guise of a drunken fight in a saloon.

The Mexican, dropped unceremoniously when the boys ran for their horses, would have ducked out of sight completely if Bud had not seen his first furtive sidling and caught him by the collar. Him they turned over to the stableman for safe-keeping. He would be kept safe, because the stableman hated any man not of his own race, as is the way of certain cramped souls.

"Now, we'll have to fan it," Bud cried impatiently, "before those drunken punchers of ours do some other fool thing. How soon will the sheriff get here, Mr. Delkin?"

"Wel-l, it's about four-thirty now—little more. Oughta make it by ten or eleven. I was lucky to catch him in the office. Just got in off a wild goose chase down river, he said. I told him if we aren't here or at Palmer's, he better pick up our trail there. Didn't mention getting the money back—too darn many mule-ears on the line. Didn't say anything definite, only I needed him right away, and he'd find me out at Palmer's or somewhere beyond. He'll come on a long lope. And say, Bud, the way the boys shot out the door and took off up the road, I don't believe they were so darn drunk after all!"

"Why?" The harsh judgment of youth still held Bud's reason in thrall. "Think it takes brains to stay on a horse? I never saw our boys too drunk to ride, Mr. Delkin. It's all right—if they take it out in riding and don't attempt to *think*."

Unconsciously Bud maligned those four. They weren't so far from being sober, once they were out of the atmosphere of the saloon and pelting up the road in the cooling breeze of late afternoon. In spite of Bud's opinion of their mental condition, the four were beginning to think.

"Know what old Palmer done?" Bob Leverett, soberest of the four, half turned in the saddle to face the others as they raced along. "Went after the dough they took from the bank. I'd bet money on it. He heard them cracks you made to Bat about the boat, Tony. That's about when he beat it. Great friend, ain't he? Quit his men cold at the first word you let drop. Betcha he's got the money and gone with it."

"Betcha we ain't fur behind 'im," Tony flashed back. "Bud, he makes me sore! Tell you right now, I don't like the way he rares up an' gives us this high-schoolin' talk when things don't go jest to suit his idees. Hell, I punched cows before Bud was big enough t' keep his own nose clean! Drunk! Huh!"

"Bud, he's a good kid enough, but he's *just* a kid," Mark Hanley opined. "Swell-headed; knows it all; thinks a little schoolin' gives him a license t' ride herd on us boys like we was yearlin's turned out in the spring. C'm awn—mebbe we kin round up the bunch 'fore he gits there. Learn 'im a little somethin', mebbe."

"Well, I don't want to make any brash statements," said Rosen, "but I betcha Bud, he'll wish 't he'd trailed with our party, 'stead of his own, 'fore he's through. We got 'em runnin' for the boodle, and now we'll fog along behind and glom em jest about the time they git it."

Bob Leverett nodded and pricked his horse with the spurs, and the others lunged ahead to keep pace with him. They were yet some distance from the house when they heard the distant pop of gunshots—the unmistakable *pow-w* of a .45 fired several times in quick succession, or else one or two shots from several guns. And, riding hard to the gate, they were not too late to see the tell-tale blue haze down by the pasture gate to show where the shooting had taken place.

Bob, in the lead, opened the gate and let it swing wide to where the weight sagged it down so that it dropped against a rock and remained there. The three pounded through and took his dust to the stable and beyond, passing the house without a glance toward it.

"It's dem Meddalahks dat shot shingles off ouah roof, suh," Sam called excitedly to Gelle, who was standing in the kitchen door with his six-shooter in his hand and a longing look in his eyes. "Now moah shootin' takes place direckly, Mist' Meddalahk. Yessuh, dey shuah can shoot!"

"My luck—always settin' around in the shade watchin' the rest of the bunch have all the fun!" Gelle turned back, walked very circumspectly to the bedroom door, turned the knob and looked in. "Yore boss is showin' signs of life, Snowball. Guess I better camp here, seein' he's the old he-one of the bunch. Tell you what you do, Snowball. You go down there and tell the boys Jelly's here with a rib broke into a thousand pieces, an' old Palmer's hog-tied; so I can't leave, nohow. Will you do that?"

"Ah—Ah do anything awn uth fer yo'all, Mist' Meddalahk. Ah—ef dey all shoots ole Sam, Ah wish yo'all 'd kinely keep dis heah dollah fo' tokum ob ma gratefulness, Mist' Meddalahk, suh."

Gelle took the dollar, looked queerly at Sam and gave it back. He took what was left of the sheet, thrust it into the negro's shaking hands and grinned reassuringly.

"You wave that, Snowball, and they won't shoot. I'm kinda afraid they might go out the other way, up along the field to the road. You ketch 'em, Snowball, and I'll give you another dollar when you bring 'em back. Tell 'em what I said—I got Palmer hog-tied, but my rib is stickin' through my liver er somethin' like that, so I can't fan down there. Gwan."

Sam went, waving the torn sheet every step of the way; a brave thing to do, considering how scared he was. And Gelle, watching anxiously from the doorway, wondered why the shooting did not begin again, now that his fellows were at hand. For that matter, since it was not the Meadowlark boys who had started the gun-fighting in the pasture, down by the ledge, who was it? He had Palmer safe, and so far as he knew, Bat Johnson and the others had not returned from town. Certainly they had not passed the house, or Sam would have seen them. Yet they must have left town, or the Meadowlark boys would not be here.

"If I don't find out how about it right pronto, I'll bust!" Gelle complained to a lean cat that came walking up the path with a chipmunk in its mouth—earning its board, Gelle thought irrelevantly while he waited, sight and hearing strained to catch some indication of what was going on down there. It was too quiet. Gelle did not like it at all.

And then from the road to town came the pluckety-pluckety tattoo of galloping horses, and Bud, Delkin and Bradley swerved without checking their pace and came racing through the gateway; saw Gelle standing in the doorway and reined closer to the house. Bud's horse stopped in two stiff-legged jumps within ten feet of Gelle.

"It's down in the pasture, whatever's goin' on," Gelle called, without waiting to be asked. "I got Palmer tied up in here—the boys went foggin' past—there was some shootin', but it quit before they got there. For the Lord sake, go bring me some news!"

At that moment the boys came loping around the end of the stable, riding loose and in no great hurry.

"Show's over," Tony bellowed, with possibly a shade of mean triumph in his voice—for Bud's benefit. "Bat and Ed, they're down there in the pasture deader'n last year. That Mex and ole Palmer's about all there is left to hang, and we glommed the Mex and Jelly's got Palmer. Bud, you might as well gwan home. Us boys have wound things up for yuh."

"Yes? Did you get the money back?" Bud was young enough and human enough to take that fling at them.

"Oh, no-o—but that's a mere detail. We ain't come to that yet." Tony's manner was still charged with triumph.

"Say, who shot Bat an' Ed White?" Gelle's mind pounced upon the one puzzling point in the affair. "You fellers didn't. There wasn't a shot fired after you boys passed the house."

"Why—we figured they shot each other. Bat's gun was still smokin' when we got there, and Ed's gun was warm. Bat had fired three shots and Ed White two—"

"Yeah? Who fired them other four or five shots? I counted nine er ten, I wasn't shore which. How many 'd you hear, Snowball?"

Sam had just arrived, puffing from haste and excitement.

"Jes' what yo'all heah, Mist' Meddalahk, yessuh. Me, Ah doan' count good nohow, but Ah's shuah Ah huhd shootin' lak dey nevah would run outa bullits. Ah counts mighty slow, but Ah huhd jes' as many as what yo'all huhd."

"Sounded like more than five to me," Bob Leverett declared, now that the subject was opened. "More like about four guns in action than two; three, anyway. Reckon there's more in the gang that we don't know about?"

"That," said Delkin, "is what we must find out."

CHAPTER SEVENTEEN
"BUD AND JELLY; ONE OR BOTH"

With two of the boys—Mark Hanley and Bob Leverett—on guard over the bodies of Bat Johnson and Ed White, the remainder of the party returned to the house in a thoughtful mood. Certain small details puzzled them, and Bud appeared to be the most worried man among them, though he did not say much. What he did do was give Gelle a meaning glance and tilt of the head when no one was looking, and then stroll out to the well some distance away and down hill at that—too many ranchers seeming to believe that the cook needed exercise. In a couple of minutes Gelle came walking circumspectly down the slope, his face twisted with pain of moving.

"What's eatin' on yuh, Bud? Thought I told yuh I got about four inches of rib wound around my backbone," he complained, as he came up.

Bud's eyes were somber as on the day of the bank tragedy, and he gave no sign of sympathy—proof of how worried he was.

"Jelly, there's going to be a kick-back in this thing if we aren't mighty careful. Bradley and Delkin are wondering right now how polite they can be about Palmer's money being gone. Are you sure he came straight here to the house from town?"

"Yeah, I saw him ride up to the gate and open it and ride in. I wish now I'd throwed down on the ole coot before he got into the house. I'd 'a' saved me a busted rib. But I was scared maybe the rest was right behind him, Bud, an' I wanted to git 'em all. Gittin' Palmer inside the house, what I done to him wouldn't be publick. That's what comes of bein' a hawg," he added grimly. Then he came back to the meat of Bud's question. "Why, Bud, is Palmer's cash missin'?"

"Yes, and Bat Johnson and Ed White were dead before they reached the ledge. They didn't have any money to speak of; a little chicken feed in their pants pockets was all. Our boys don't know where the stuff was hidden, and I went with Delkin and the others to town and came back with them. So you see, Jelly—"

"Yeah, I see, all right." Gelle's eyes went cold as they bored into Bud's mind. "Well, what d' you think about it yourself, Bud?"

"I?" Bud looked at him straight. "Whatever you say, Jelly, goes with me."

Gelle stared longer, exhaled a long breath and relaxed to a mirthless grin.

"I oughta lick you, Bud, fer needin' my word. But friendship wabbles when there's money in sight, so—I never went near the damn' place after I packed that back-load of gold away from it. You was behind me—behind us all, fer that matter." Gelle's sudden grin turned a little sardonic. "Still, whatever you say goes with me! I kin be as good a friend as you kin, Bud."

Bud had to laugh, though he felt little enough like it.

"You win, Jelly. I'd have had to do some quick work, but I suppose it would have been humanly possibly for me to duck back up the ledge, grab Palmer's money and come along with it until I saw a place to ditch it where I could come back after it. Fast work—but I did stand in the fringe of the trees by the ledge and watch the stables here until you fellows were out of sight. I wanted to make darn sure you weren't seen."

"Well, I didn't go back either. But the fact remains that the cache is cleaned out—in a hurry, by the look of things around there. And these two dead men dropped in the open, just inside the gate and before they had been to the ledge. For one thing, Jelly, our boys weren't so very far behind them, so Bat and Ed wouldn't have had time to get the stuff, hide it somewhere else and then get into a fight over it and kill each other off before our boys came.

They'd have had to do faster work than I would to have raided the cave while you fellows crossed the open down there."

"And awn the other hand, you fellers rode off and left me in easy walkin' distance of the money, and the old man sound asleep and snorin'." Gelle reasoned it out soberly, stating the evidence against himself quite as impartially as Bud had done in his own case. "Yea, I'm the pelican, too, that told Delkin to grab the works. Looks like I'm bogged, right now, and sinkin' fast. Bud, on the face of it, you an' me both is guilty as hell. Ain't we?"

"On the face of it, yes." Bud studied the evidence while he finished rolling a cigarette. "Of course, we can't tell yet just how it will affect the case against Palmer. Not at all, maybe. That's something we have nothing to do with. I wanted you to know the money Delkin left in the cache was gone—how much, none of us know, of course. It's mighty mysterious, don't you think? Say, Jelly, what about those shots? Are you dead certain you heard more than five?"

"Shore I am. But I couldn't prove it, Bud—not in a thousand years. Snowball, his word ain't no good, so there y' are. I believe in my heart that somebody else was after that boodle and Bat and Ed White, they run into 'em, goin' after it theirselves. But that ain't proof. Say, Bud, d' you s'pose Butch Cassidy rode over on the quiet—"

"I've been thinking of Butch. He's that stripe, and so is the rest of the Frying Pan outfit in my opinion. But as you say, Jelly, opinions aren't proof. Besides, Skookum says he didn't tell Butch where his grandfather had his money hidden. I'll take the kid's word. He wouldn't lie—not to me, or anyone he likes. Butch tried to pump him, all right, but Skookum says he didn't tell Butch anything much that we didn't hear in the cook house."

"Did the kid say what ole Palmer's money was—gold or paper or whatever?"

"He said he saw a lot of gold money in a sack. You were looking over Delkin's shoulder, Jelly. What did it look like to you?"

"Gold. Jest about what the old thief would take and hide, Bud. Prob'ly most of it was stole, and bills has got numbers on. Then again, gold ain't spoilable. What you laughin' at, Bud?"

"At us, Jelly. Delkin certainly must know Palmer's money was in gold. And Lark's loaded up with gold coin—"

"So we got our alibi right there, Bud. Fur's that goes, the Fryin' Pan's got some honest gold money."

"And there is *their* alibi. And Delkin is sure to consider Lark's gold as an out for us, just as we can believe that Butch would account for any gold he flashed."

"Can't we ketch 'im? Why don't you take out after 'em an' see if you can't pick up their trail? Gosh, Bud, if the money's gone, you 'n' me *knows* Butch musta glommed it. I'd go, only fer this damn' rib."

"Better have one of the boys hitch up a rig and take you into town, Jelly. Old Doc Grimes isn't much force, but he ought to be able to fix you up all right. I'll take Bob and see if we can't pick up their trail. He'll keep his mouth shut."

"Yeah. Talk is what we want damn' little of, Bud. One word is all them pelicans would need to send them down into the breaks—and I ain't a doubt in the world but what they got hide-outs down in there where they kin live a year if they feel that way, and never show a head. You beat it now, Bud. I'll gwan down an' take Bob's place. I kin walk slow. An' I'll have some lie thunk up fer Delkin an' Bradley, time they git t' askin' questions about you. They're so tickled to git their claws on Palmer that they won't say much. We'll let on like you 'n' Bob had t' go home fer somethin'. I'll fix it."

At the house Delkin and Bradley were having quite enough to occupy their minds without watching the coming and going of the Meadowlark boys. Palmer was conscious, sitting up in a chair and getting somewhat the best of an amateurish third degree which Delkin and Bradley were attempting to give him. Palmer had a wet towel tied around his head, and the loose folds collected extra moisture and sent it trickling down his seamed, sallow face and his collar. Palmer's eyes were just as human as a snake's with an opaque, impersonal glitter that masked effectually the thoughts shuttling back and forth in his brain. Now and then he barked a question of his own which proved how well his brain was working in spite of the gash on his head.

"Killed two of my men, ay? Come on to my ranch and shot down two men in cold blood—that what you're tryin' to tell me I'm responsible fer?"

"We didn't shoot your men," Delkin explained, when he should not have replied to the charge. "They shot each other. They were after the loot from the bank, and they're lying down there inside your pasture fence, waiting for the sheriff to look them over when he gets here. Even you thieves and murderers can't hang together, it seems. They meant to get the plunder and leave you in the lurch."

"Plunder? What plunder is that?"

"The stuff you folks stole from the bank—"

"Looky here, Mr. Delkin. You be careful what you say! It ain't safe to make charges you ain't prepared to prove. I'm just remindin' you now that there's a law that takes care of malicious slander. I can't answer fer Bat an' Ed, but I want you to understand the bank owes me over seven thousand dollars that I had on deposit—and that was stole—so you claim. You been hand-in-glove with the Meddalark right along, and I'm the loser by it. Ef I was you folks, I wouldn't shoot off my mouth too much about that bank robbery."

Delkin and Bradley withdrew to talk it over, and it was then they discovered that Bud and Gelle were missing. With Tony and Jack Rosen on guard at the house, they hurried down to the pasture and found Gelle reclining in the grass with his hat over his eyes to shield them from the slanting rays of the sun, and Mark Hanley sitting cross-legged beside him, killing time by carefully whittling a stick to a sharp point and cutting the point off so that he could sharpen another; an endless occupation so long as the stick lasts.

"Bud? Him an' Bob, they went home quite a while ago. Us boys can't all of us be away more 'n a few hours at a stretch, an' Lark had give them first four a coupla days off. I jest come awn in with Bud fer the day, but now I'm kinda laid out so I can't ride, and Bob, he went home in my place." Gelle vouchsafed a glance apiece to Delkin and Bradley before he let the hat drop down again over his face. They could not know, of course, that beneath the hat his lips were twitching with ironic laughter.

"Yeah, they been gone half an hour, mebbe more," Mark contributed idly. "How long do we have to set here an' keep them unlovely dead from feelin' lonesome?"

Without answering, Delkin turned and walked back to the house, Bradley following close.

"What do you think about it, Jim?" Bradley asked, when two thirds of the distance had been covered.

"Brad, it doesn't matter what we think or don't think," Delkin told him irritably. "We'll do well to keep it to ourselves, no matter what it is. We won't mention Palmer's money to the sheriff, Brad. The Meadowlark boys have done a lot for the bank—we mustn't overlook that. I suppose they felt they had a right to collect their own damages from Palmer for starting all that talk about them."

"They?"

"Bud and Jelly; one or both. I wouldn't think Bud would have had time to do it, or the inclination. But you can't tell what's going on in a man's mind. Jelly, of course, had the chance and he's the one that suggested taking it. No, sir, we've got to keep our mouths shut for the present, anyway."

"Let it look like them two down there—Bat and Ed White—got away with it," Bradley suggested, all in favor of protecting customers as good as the Meadowlark outfit. "We've got Palmer dead to rights, anyway, and we've got the bank property back. I guess we can afford to let Palmer hunt his own money, eh?"

"They were both in on it," Delkin went on glumly. "I saw them holding a little private confab down by the well. Bud felt as if he'd better get the stuff into the Basin, I guess, before we asked him about it. But damn' it, Brad, I can't believe either of those boys would steal money!"

"You heard Jelly. They don't call it stealing, Jim, when they annex something that a thief has cached away. Buried treasure, maybe, is what they'd call it. Anyway, they'd have a name that made it sound all right. Well, we'll have to let it go for the present. But I wish they'd kept their hands off that money!"

CHAPTER EIGHTEEN
BUD GOES AFTER BUTCH

The two had ridden for a mile or more through the foothills bordering the western line of the Indian Reservation, boring into the wilderness to the east of the Little Smoky, following no trail, but taking the easiest course, Bud leading the way. Certain horse tracks had led off in this direction from a rocky hollow across the road from Palmer's fence corner, and Bud, having determined that point while Bob was sneaking their horses away from the corral where the others were tied before piles of Palmer's treasured new hay, was following a general course without attempting to trail the horsemen who had left their mounts in the hollow.

"Bud, if it's a fair question, I'd like to ask if we're the hunters, or are we the game?" Bob cocked an inquiring eye toward his grim-faced leader.

"Both," Bud made laconic reply.

Bob studied that for a while, reins held high, big body poised lightly in the saddle, while his horse negotiated a particularly complicated descent through rocks to a gully bottom.

"All right with me, Bud," he said pensively, when they could once more ride together. "What's on my mind right now is when do we feed this purty face of mine?"

"Didn't you eat in town?"

"Nh-nh. Tony, he went and got an idee in his head, and us boys was rung in on workin' it out. It was a hell of an idee, Bud. It started off with bathin' in whisky like they say the Queen of Sheeby done in asses' milk, without drinkin' none. Would you b'lieve that could be done? Well, it can't. But I done it, Bud. Tony, he got t' beefin' around about us fellers gittin' too dawg-gone drunk t' carry out this swell idee he had, so we done it. And then I'll be darned if Tony, he didn't git jagged and queer the hull entire play by tyin' into Bat Johnson! Made me so darn sore—and then after that, Bud, we was too busy whippin' them pups of Palmer's to go eat like white men. Gosh, I'm holler!"

"Well, so am I, if that will help you any."

"Don't feed a thing but my imagination, Bud. Whatfer party *is* this? Don't tell me a thing—but did you pick me to go off and starve to death with yuh? I'm a pore companion, Bud. Don't say nothing—I don't want t' hear a thing!"

"I know you don't, so I'll make it short. I found out from Skookum where Palmer cached his money, and I found all the stuff they'd stolen from the bank. Delkin and his outfit took that to town, and left Palmer's where it was. Now it's gone. They think Jelly or I got it—we could have, if we worked fast enough. I think I know where it went, Bob. I think Butch Cassidy got more out of Skookum than the kid realized, and went after the dough himself. We'd beaten him to it, and the bank money is safe. But Jelly and I are in wrong unless we can locate the stuff we left in that cache."

"So you and me is headed fer the Fryin' Pan by our lonelies, thinkin' we can make Butch let loose of Palmer's stuff?"

"That's one way to put it, Bob."

"Well," sighed Bob, after a long interval of deep meditation, "all right. Me, I'm a chancey cuss, anyway. I crawled into a wolf den once, and the old she come and crawled in with me by another hole I didn't know about, and caught me with about four pups in my arms." He heaved another reminiscent sigh. "D' you pick awn me, Bud, b'cause you knew I had the heart of an angry lion?"

Bud's brown-velvet eyes smiled briefly into his.

"I picked you primarily because I knew you'd keep your mouth shut afterwards."

"Primarily, it's a cinch I will," Bob agreed with melancholy assurance. "Dead men tells no tales outa school. That's why."

"Oh, I don't think it will be that bad. They can't be far ahead of us, Bob. We may not have to go clear to the Frying Pan."

"No, boy, we might not live that long. But that's all right—only I always did hate the thoughts of dyin' on an empty stomach."

"Why the sudden pessimism?" Having worries of his own, Bud leaned to sarcasm.

"Gosh, I'd *eat* that word if I could chew it!" Bob muttered longingly. "Say a softer one about that same length, won't you, p'fessor?"

"Go to the devil!" growled Bud angrily.

"I might, at that. I feel m'self slippin' that way," sighed Bob. "If it's a fair question, just what do you aim to do when we meet up with Butch? Ride up and say, 'H'lo, Butch, I'd thank yuh fer that money or whatever you swiped from Palmer,' and then fall back graceful outa yore saddle, or what? B'cause Butch is bound to shoot. Don't make no mistake about that."

"What I do," said Bud shortly, "will depend on circumstances. I'm not fool enough to draw a chart. If Butch has been over here, he got that money. If he got it, I'm going to get it away from him and turn it over to Delkin. Only a fool would plan the details at this stage of the game."

"Yeah, that's right," Bob admitted meekly.

For a time they rode in silence, Bud leaning over the saddle horn to study the loose soil of the canyon bottom. Bob, riding close behind him, studied each wrinkle and draw with eyes narrowed to keener vision in the soft half-lights of early evening when the shadows were sliding higher and higher on the western slopes and the peaks stood out all golden, clean cut against the tinted clouds.

"Three horses," Bud looked over his shoulder to announce. "All shod, but I've a hunch there's only one rider. Butch is so darned foxy I'm going to outguess him right here." He pulled up and swung round so that Bob, halting likewise, faced him. "Bob, you've done a good deal of riding over this way, so I'll let you take the lead from now on. Never mind the tracks. I believe Butch thought he'd try the loose-horse stunt, and brought a couple along with him. Farther on he'll turn them loose and haze them up different canyons—scatter the tracks. But I happen to know the shoe marks of that high-stepping brown he rides all the while. He's ahead of the other two, and back there where those rocks are lying helter-skelter Butch rode ahead and the other two followed him like led horses. Riders would have picked different trails among those rocks. You didn't follow my tracks, you remember. Each rider has his own notions of such things, and no man likes to trail right after another rider unless the path is so narrow he's got to. Ever notice that?"

"Ye-ah, now you speak of it. Gosh, you'll be a smart man, Bud, when yo're growed up."

"Well, right ahead here, I'll bet you a new hat the tracks will jumble a bit and then separate. And, Bob, I'm betting on another psychological twist. I bet you Butch will angle through these hills, and won't make straight for the Frying Pan. He'll be watching out behind—that's one reason why I'm holding back just here. We don't want to crowd him, come to think of it. What we want to do is hit straight for the Frying Pan by the shortest trail we know. Or the shortest you know. I lost a lot of trail lore in the years I had to spend in school."

"Yeah, I get you, Bud. I know a short cut through these hills, all right. But what if he don't show at the Fryin' Pan? Looks like a long gamble, t' me."

"He will. He's working there, and the Frying Pan is a bad bunch to break with. Butch is foxy. Also, he wants the big end, if I'm any judge. I'll bet you he hasn't said a word to Kid or any of the others about this deal. Didn't you see how Butch's eyes kind of glittered when I counted out that fifteen hundred to Kid? It was a pretty sight—gold twenties and tens stacked like poker chips on the table. Fifty twenty-dollar gold pieces—ten piles, five high, and fifty ten-dollar pieces, five piles ten high. It was enough to make anyone's mouth water for gold money, wasn't it, Bob? I saw Butch's face when Kid raked the gold back into the bags. I saw how his tongue went licking across his lips—"

"Made me lick m' chops too, Bud. And I ain't no thief," Bob put in fairly.

"Then think how you'd scheme if you *were* a thief!" Bud flashed back. "Put yourself in Butch's place. If you knew about where you could annex a fortune in gold and paper money—stolen goods that everyone knew you couldn't have taken from the bank—and all you had to do was to ride over on the quiet and swipe it away from thieves—would *you* tell anybody else and have to divvy? You know damned well you wouldn't, Bob. Neither would I. I'd want it all.

"And by thunder! Bob, that's why he brought along extra horses! I'll bet you he thought he might need one to pack away the bank loot. He wouldn't know exactly how bulky it was, you see. Well, maybe it was partly that, and partly to make enough tracks to confuse Palmer's bunch. If he got the stuff to the Frying Pan, and needed help to hang on to it, he could cache most of the gold and then take Kid in on the deal and split the rest. At least, that's what I'd do."

"And is this what you'd do too? Set here chinnin' all night an' let him git the money all spent b'fore we take in after him?" Bob's voice had lost its humorous patience. "Me, I'm ready to swaller m' saddle strings like they was egg noodles! You wanta git over to the Fryin' Pan by the shortest rowt. Nothin' like hunger to drive a man, Bud, so I'm goin' to lead yuh back to them rocks and take awn up over the ridge. It'll be nasty ridin' after dark, so I advise you to pry yore eyes loose from them tracks and come awn, if yo're goin' with me."

He reined his horse around and rode back the way they had come without another word or glance, and Bud followed him. Plainly, Butch had chosen to keep to the canyons where he could duck out of sight or even lay an ambush if necessary. That way must be longer, and in spite of the rough going Bud counted on making time.

The stars were out in a velvet sky when the two loped unhurriedly up the long lane which was the only feasible approach to the Frying Pan, and pulled up at the high, barbed-wire fence that warded off intruding animals from the dooryard. Kid himself came walking stiltedly down the beaten path to the gate, and behind the green-curtained windows the boisterous talk and laughter stilled. In the shadow of the house, away from the seeping light from the windows, darker shadows indicated the blurred outlines of Frying Pan men who were making unobtrusive investigation of these unheralded horsemen.

"Why, hello, Bud," Kid cried distinctly, for the comfort of his men. A note of genuine surprise was in his voice which Bud wished had been pitched in a lower key. "That you, Bob? Turn your bronchs in the big corral and come on in. Had yore supper?"

That word brought a groan from Bob so lugubrious that Kid laughed.

"Hey, Bill! Come take the boys' horses to the corral, will yuh? Bob's groanin' fer pie—I know that tone, Bob." Then he added carelessly, "Butch didn't come back with you, eh?"

"We've been scurruping around—looking for a couple of those horses," Bud lied. "Butch will be along, maybe. Was he coming back tonight?"

"Said he was when he started out this morning. But I dunno, Bud. That Eastern girl's a strong drawin' card, looks like. Guess you folks'll just about have to carry rocks in your pocket for Butch! Any time you ketch him ridin' into the Basin, you just rock him home, will yuh?"

"You know it!" Bob made emphatic declaration. "Say, our little pilgress ain't to be dazzled by no sech a hypnotizer as Butch. Say, d' yuh mind if I clean the Fryin' Pan plumb outa grub? I got an appetite, me."

Kid laughed and waved him toward the kitchen. He and Bud followed more slowly and Kid's mind still tarried with Butch.

"Butch kinda wanted to go back with you fellers, I guess," he remarked. "He never said a word about it, though, till you'd been gone an hour or so; then it was too late—I had to use him. B'sides that, I kinda got the idee you and him didn't hitch very well. Butch is kinda funny, that way. Takes streaks. You don't want to pay no attention to him, Bud."

"Why," said Bud, "I never had a word with Butch except that sneering remark he made about those black horses. I didn't mind that. They'll all be jealous before I'm through."

What Kid replied Bud could not have told five minutes after. His mind was keyed up to meet a crisis, and this desultory talk irritated him, distracting his thoughts at a time when he needed to be most alert. One thing he knew: Kid either was wholly ignorant of Butch's design, or he was playing his part so carefully that he would be dangerous later on when Butch came riding home.

Yet there was another point which Bud wanted to think upon. If Kid Kern knew of that bank money and bonds hidden away in Palmer's cow pasture, would he let Butch ride alone after it? Just one possible reason for that occurred to Bud, and that was Kid's wily caution that would think first of establishing an alibi that could not be broken. On the other hand, Palmer would never dare to accuse him openly; moreover, he would immediately suspect the Meadowlark. So far as Bud knew, the Frying Pan outfit had never been mentioned in connection with the tragedy at the bank, save as he and Gelle had spoken of the possibility of the Frying Pan's implication. In the face of Kid's untroubled manner and his evident indifference to Butch's movements, Bud decided that Butch was indeed playing a lone hand; snap judgment, he knew, because he was not left alone long enough to reason it out.

"Come on in and eat," Kid was urging hospitably. "I guess Bob ain't licked the Fryin' Pan clean, already." He laughed at his own joke, standing poised on the doorstep, perhaps wondering why Bud lagged behind.

"I don't feel like eating just now, Kid. Just let me sit out here in the dark for a while. One of those splitting headaches—I don't want the light in my eyes."

"Cup uh coffee'll do yuh good, Bud." Kid turned back with a solicitous air that was extremely well done if it was assumed to lull suspicion. "Tell you what. You go awn upstairs to bed, and I'll send up some coffee. You know where you slept last time; you go crawl in there."

"No." Bud's tone was sharp and decisive. "It's cooler out here, and—if you'll send out a cup of coffee, I'll drink it. And for the Lord sake, Kid, don't go and baby around about me! If you bawl it out to the bunch, I'll take a fall out of you, sure as you're born, when my head quits jumping. All I want is to be left strictly alone for a while."

"Well, I could lick you, but have it yore own way, Bud. Sick folks has got to be humored, they say."

Bud, lying on the ground with his head on his arms, wished with all his healthy young appetite that he dared go in and eat his fill. But that was a joy he must postpone—and then it struck him that Kid might dope the coffee!

The door opened and shut with a bang. Bud rolled over on his face, reached back cautiously and drew his gun from its holster and held it concealed under his folded arms. Lying so, he was as ready for instant action as is a cat that has drawn back its feet and tensed its muscles for a spring.

His nerves relaxed, his mind once more was at peace concerning the immediate future. Lying there on the ground, he could hear the faintest sound of far-off hoof beats when Butch came riding home. And unless Kid or some other began shooting bullets into his prone body without warning, he could take the initiative, could dominate any situation that might arise.

The cup of coffee he waved away when Kid brought it, though the delectable aroma maddened him after his long fast.

"Would yuh take a headache powder, Bud? I got some that shore would knock that pain." The voice of Kid Kern was full of friendly sympathy. He never dreamed that Bud's six-shooter was looking at him bleakly over Bud's left forearm.

"No—this is fine. I'm easy so long as I don't have to move." This was true enough, as Bud recognized with a fleeting grin. "Don't bother any more about me."

"Oh, I'll set with the sick any time." Kid squatted on his haunches, after the manner of outdoor men, and began rolling a cigarette. "Keep the boys from gittin' curious. They'll think we're talkin' private out here."

Silence fell, save for the creaking of crickets, the whisper of a cool breeze through the grass next the fence. Kid smoked, his big hat tilted back on his head, his eyes turned thoughtfully up toward the stars. Bud lay quietly with his face on his folded arms, his gun against his cheek, ready to come up shooting at the first breath of need. The cooling coffee sent faint whiffs of torturing fragrance to his nostrils. His eyes, half closed under the pinned-back brim of his hat, regarded Kid with unblinking attention. His ears, like faithful sentinels set on guard by his intrepid spirit, listened for hoof beats down the lane.

CHAPTER NINETEEN

"NEXT TIME, REMEMBER—BUTCH PACKS TWO GUNS!"

Bob came out fairly licking his chops over the enormous supper he had just gorged; took in the situation at a glance, hovered there help-lessly for a space and announced that he was going back in and have a game or two of high-five with the boys. He kicked Bud's foot in passing; a hint which Bud could interpret as he pleased, though what Bob meant to signal was his intention to guard against treachery from the house.

Kid asked Bud how he felt, received a mumbled assurance that he was all right, and rolled and lighted another cigarette. A tactful companion was Kid Kern upon occasion; one who knew the Indian art of absolute passivity. It shamed Bud a bit to know that if he had been really suffering as he pre-tended to be, Kid would have sat right there all night if necessary, with never a complaint.

Then it came—the far-off *clupet-clupety-clupet* of a shod horse loping up the lane. Bud moved his long body a bit, drawing up one knee for leverage when the moment came to spring erect, and shifting his forehead so that his left hand pressed palm downward on the ground.

"How's she comin', Bud?" Kid poised his cigarette between two stained fingers while he peered down at Bud through the bright starlight. "Worse? Better let me get yuh that powder."

"No use—it's easing up—by spells." In the pauses Bud was listening, gauging the swiftness of the approach. Kid, he could see, had not yet caught the sound that had come clearly to Bud's ear pressed against the sod. His heart began to thump heavily, high in his chest. He could feel his face grow hot with the uprush of blood, and knew it was not fear that rioted within his body, but battle fever instead; the excitement that sends hot young blood leaping when conflict is near.

"Somebody comin'. Butch, I guess." Kid ground his cigarette stub under his heel as he rose.

The action and the announcement together gave Bud the excuse to rise also to a half-crouching position, poised on the balls of his feet like a runner waiting for the signal to go; a posture that would pass in the starlight as the squatting of a man whose interest is not sufficient to bring him to his feet. A full minute they listened to the nearing hoof beats, then the dim outline of a horseman showed in the lane.

"Yeah, that's Butch. I'll go open the gate—er—no, that horse of his is broke to gates, come to think of it."

Bud said nothing. He was watching Butch Cassidy sidle up to the gate post, lean and push back the heavy wooden bolt, nip through as the gate swung open, catch it midway and sidle back, pushing it shut as he went. The horse stood quiet while the bar slid into place, then Butch came riding toward them.

"What's takin' place here? One of them garden parties yuh read about?" Butch laughed and swung a leg over the cantle to dismount.

"Yes. It's my party, Butch." Bud was up and standing so close behind him that Kid, ten feet away and in front of them, could not have shot without hitting both. "Keep your hands up—just like that." He reached forward, twitched Butch's gun from its holster and thrust it into his own.

"Why—what's wrong with Butch?" Kid's voice was surprised, but it had not lost its friendly note.

"Nothing much, only he shot a couple of men and stole a few thousand dollars out of Palmer's cow pasture, and the blame rests on Jelly and me until I take this pelican in and return the money."

"Aw, he's full of prunes, Kid. Don't you b'lieve a word of that." Butch stood with his hands raised—any man will who feels the muzzle of a gun in his ribs—and stared at Kid. "I ain't been near Palmer's place. Are you goin' t' stand fer this kind of a hold-up, Kid, right in yore dooryard?"

"I dunno, Butch, till I see how she lays." Kid's tone took on a silky smoothness. "Seems funny Bud would take the trouble to ride 'way over here just fer a josh to hold you up and accuse you of a thing like that. Must be a little something to it."

"He's crazy, that's all."

"I suppose you didn't leave a couple of horses tied in a draw just across the road from Palmer's fence corner! I suppose I didn't find your tracks, heading this way, when Bob and I struck out to overhaul you? I happen to know how you pumped Skookum to get all the information you could. He doesn't know how much he told you, but it was enough to make you feel sure you could put your hands right on the money the bank lost! Well, I took Delkin and some others out there, so they beat you to it, Butch. The trouble is, they left a lot that belonged to Palmer, and that's what you packed off with you after you'd shot Bat Johnson and Ed White. They were after it too, I suppose. Some of our boys in town scared them till they beat it out of town, and they caught you there at the ledge. You downed them both, and got away with the stuff.

"Kid, I don't think for a minute that you'd go in on a deal of this kind—but I'll bet a horse Butch never gave you a chance! That's playing real square with you, isn't it?"

"No, Bud, it ain't. I never dreamed Butch would pull a thing like this, and him workin' fer me. I hope you don't look on me as bein' capable of rusty work like that, Bud." He took a step forward, then halted. "How about this? Think you c'n trust me to help yuh go through Butch and see if he's got that money? How much was it? If he's got it with him, by Harry, he'll come clean. I hate t' turn in one of my own men, but I'll do it—I'll turn him over to the sheriff myself if there's a scrap of evidence t' hold him on. Can I come and look in his slicker, Bud?"

"I wish you would, Kid." Bud caught Butch by the slack of his coat and pulled him backwards, away from the horse. "I trust you, yes. Sure, I do! But I'll put a bullet through you, Kid, if you try a double-cross."

"That's all right. Can't blame you, Bud. Butch working for me, it does look kinda leery around here. But you can't do two things at once, very handy, and I'm damned if I'll stand for any man of mine pulling off a stunt like this and giving the Frying Pan a black eye with my neighbors."

"Go ahead and *look*, why don'tcha?" Butch challenged mockingly. "Sure, you'll try 'n' keep yore standin', Kid—you ain't got a man that don't know you'd quit him cold in a pinch, and save yore own bacon! Go ahead an' *look*!"

"You bet I'll look!" Kid picked up the reins, ran his hand reassuringly along the shoulder of the brown horse, grasped the horn and gave the saddle a little shake, and began untying Butch's slicker from behind the cantle, his fingers probing into the folds. "How much was it, Bud?"

"I don't know. It was gold, and there must have been several thousand dollars, at a rough guess. Nobody meddled with it—except the man that took it. Three or four regular coin bags, there ought to be."

Kid pulled off the slicker and slapped it on the ground, wide open and empty. Butch carried no saddle pockets, and there was no place on the saddle where a package of any size could be hidden.

Butch laughed unpleasantly.

"There ain't a darned thing, Bud." Kid turned and looked at the two. There was an awkward silence.

"Well, ain't somebody goin' to apologize?" Butch still had that mocking tone. "Bud's had a pipe dream, that's all. Now, I'll tell yuh where I been, and Bud c'n prove it easy enough. I been over to the Meddalark. I admit I went over there t' see Lark about gittin' a job. I stayed to dinner, and all the boys is gone but that pilgrim; yore black horses is in the bronch corral, Bud, and the kid's ridin' a pinto pony around he calls Huckleberry. Need any more proof, or does that convince yuh that I was *there*, all right?" Butch's tone was arrogant, though he was careful to make no offensive movement.

"Oh, you were there, no doubt. That doesn't let you out, Butch. Tell me where you were between four and five this afternoon!"

"Awn the road home," Butch drawled.

Bud twitched off Butch's hat and held it up in his left hand so that the edge of the brim was silhouetted against the stars.

"Look here, Kid. I suppose he'll say he bit that nick out of his hatbrim! Ever see a prettier bullet mark? Just about the size a .45 would make as nearly as I can tell in this light. Just for curiosity, Butch, how did you get that?" Bud's voice, that had been merely grim and unyielding, rang with triumph.

"None of yore damn' business. Is that plain enough, or shall I spell it?"

"No," said Bud softly, "you needn't spell it, Butch."

Followed another silence, which Kid broke placatingly.

"If Butch done what you think he done, Bud, I'm after him like a wolf. But if this is all the proof you got, why—you ain't got *any*, that's all." He stopped on the brink of saying more and looked from one to the other.

"Yeah. You ain't got *any*," Butch echoed, with that same faint mockery in his voice. "Goin' to hold me here all night? Me and my horse is hungry."

"Didn't anybody see him at Palmer's?" Kid asked doubtfully. And when Bud shook his head, Kid made a similar gesture. "Honest, Bud, I don't see what you're goin' to do about it," he said. "I'm with you if you've got any proof. But—"

"I'll get it," Bud declared harshly, and lowered his gun. "All right, Butch, this time you've got the best of it. But remember, I'll get that proof, and I'll get *you*. And I don't mean that I'll kill you, either."

"What the hell do I care what you mean?" Butch took down his arms, rubbing his muscles unthinkingly. "Only—if kids are bound to git underfoot, they're liable to git stepped on. Yuh goin' to give me my gun back? Or are yuh scared to?"

Bud gave him his gun haughtily, butt first according to the range code of good manners. Butch slid it into his holster and reached for the bridle reins.

"Kid, you spread my slicker so you c'n pick it up off the ground," he said, and pulled the reins up along his horse's neck. He mounted, sat looking down at Bud for a minute, gave a grunt eloquent of tolerant scorn and rode away to the stable at a careless lope.

The two stood looking after him until his figure blurred with the deeper shade of the barn.

"Bud, I'm sorry it turned out the way it did," Kid said under his breath. "I believe in my soul Butch done it—but what does that prove? I want to warn yuh, though. You've made an enemy there that ain't liable to forgit yuh. It's a darn good thing I happened to be out here with yuh, boy. Butch don't dare pull nothin' underhand when I'm around, but if you'd tackled him alone out here, it maybe wouldn't 'a' turned out so peaceful." He gave a little inarticulate exclamation. "Say, Bud, next time you bump into Butch, remember *he packs two guns*. He could of got you any time he wanted to t'night. Next time you pull a gun on Butch Cassidy I'd advise yuh as a friend to pull the trigger at the same time. May as well play safe, then it won't be you we'll have to bury."

"I suppose that's a friendly tip, and as such I thank you for it, Kid." Bitterness was all that was left to young Bud at that moment.

"Yes, and I wouldn't give it to everybody, either. Might as well come along in and have some supper, Bud—now yore headache's cured."

But Bud shook his head and said he couldn't swallow a mouthful, so Kid did not urge him. Perhaps he knew what it means when a young man must swallow his pride.

Bob came out to them, and all he learned was that they were going back home that night. Once again Kid did not urge Bud to modify his decision; instead, he approved it.

"Butch will shore be on the peck, now, and it'll be just as well to side-step. Here he comes—you boys can get your horses out, and I'll keep an eye on Butch. Too bad, but there ain't a thing more I can do, or you either."

"No," said Bud dully, "I guess not. I made a fool of myself, that's all."

They were riding down the lane before Bud came out of his black mood of depression, or Bob dared open his mouth to ask a question.

"It's a cinch he stopped and cached the money somewhere along the way," Bud cried hotly, when they had gone carefully over the whole thing together. "What we have to do now is try and find it."

"Yeah, and beat Butch to it," Bob reminded. "Now, I know all this end of the reservation like a book. Butch, he'd hide that money purty close in, I betcha, but not along the trail nowhere. Can't back trail him tonight, but by daylight—" He stopped there for a time. "Tell yuh, Bud, what we better do. Awn a piece here is that crick, and I betcha we could pick up Butch's tracks there where he cut across into the hills. It's about the only place where he could leave the trail without making signs a blind man could read; what's more, it's the only place where he could git into the hills without ridin' an hour er more extry.

"What we better do is you go awn home and git some chuck inside yuh, and take a sleep. I'll bed right down by that crick till daybreak, and pick up Butch's back track. I kin jest about read that jasper's mind, Bud. You put Kid wise, and Kid'll be watchin' Butch like a hawk. It'll be kinda funny if Butch gits a chance to ride back here fer a day er two. Right now is when he's got to take a big chance and leave the money where it's at. When you git ready, you come awn back with some grub. Foller the trail we took comin' over, and I'll meet yuh, Bud, right where that spring comes up under them sandstone cliffs. You know—where we watered our horses. They's feed, and we c'n make camp there if we have to. I know where we c'n crawl under a shelf if it storms, even.

"So you do that, Bud. It'll save time, and we'll find the dough—never you mind about that!"

"If it takes until snow flies, we've got to find it," Bud declared. "Well, I'll tell you when we reach the creek whether I'll do that or not."

CHAPTER TWENTY
"THINGS KINDA SLIPPED UP"

Two motley roosters and a black Minorca were craning necks to outcrow one another before the dawn. Out of the chill dark came Bud, the Walking Sorrel swinging automatically along in the long strides of the running walk that gave him his name and made him better than most horses on a long, hard trail. When he stopped, the sorrel's legs trembled with exhaustion. Bud's spurred boots dragged like an old man's on the path to the house, and his head buzzed until the roosters, the frogs and the humming of mosquitoes blended in one muffled, discordant chorus.

As he stepped upon the porch Maw sat up, rubbing her eyes, and got out of bed, dragging a faded, big-flowered kimono over her nightgown and thrusting tiny, bare feet into a shapeless pair of slippers much too large for her. Her muslin nightcap went up to a peak at the crown of her head. She looked like a female goblin fleeing from a midnight rendezvous as she came pattering into the kitchen with a lighted candle held aloft in her hand, her round eyes blinking with sleep.

"My, I bet you're about starved, Buddy! When a boy gets in this time of night, I *know* he's hungry. I set back a whole berry pie for you, and the cream for it is all whipped and ready. I thought I wouldn't spread it till you come, because if it stands too long the crust gets soggy. And there's plenty of cold fried chicken—I saved you the gizzards, Bud, and three wings. I know how you like them parts. Nev' mind washin' your face. You set right down and I'll have you eatin' in two seconds."

That was one of the reasons why the Meadowlark worshiped Maw.

"Drink this, Buddy. It's last night's milk—poured right off the top of the pan, cream and all."

Slumped into the nearest chair by the table, Bud put out a hand slowly and took up the glass, spilling milk on Maw's white tablecloth and down his shirt front because his hand shook so. But the rich milk refreshed him like a draught of wine, and when he had set down the glass—empty—he turned hollow eyes with some interest toward the plate heaped with chicken fried a golden brown as only Maw could do it. Maw was spreading fresh bread for him, two great slices, and she seemed blessedly unconscious of Bud's wolfish feeding, once he started to eat.

But finally, when Bud had finished the third wing and was biting into the bluish knob of a gizzard, Maw hooked her slipper heels over the top rung of her chair and nodded her head like a witch over her cauldron.

"Things kinda slipped up, I s'pose. They will do that no matter how careful we plan. I heard enough of what you and Skookum was talkin' about last night—"

"Last night?" Bud repeated, looking up in dull amazement. "Is that as long ago as it was, Maw?"

"Well, a course it's most mornin' now, so I s'pose I can say night b'fore last. When every minute is crammed and jammed with happenin's, it does seem to take an awful lot of 'em to make a day. The day has gone real quick for me, too. And there's Margy, sayin' Cranford would be real excitin' alongside this place. She got real put out t'day, because you boys went off first thing this forenoon, and then Butch Cassidy come over and spent most all the time foolin' around with Skookum and didn't talk to her much, and somethin' or other went wrong in her story—she was tellin' me all about it while we washed up the dishes.

"Margy's getting real friendly," Maw went on, after a pause spent in studying Bud's face and in deciding, no doubt, that he was not yet ready to talk of his own affairs. "This afternoon she come right up and put her arm around me and patted me on the shoulder! I didn't s'pose she'd ever get used to me so she could look at me without scringin', but she's got all over that, and it ain't much more'n a week since she come. She's just as sweet as she can be, and she tells me all about everything, real confiding."

"Cranford! Ye gods!" Bud exploded tardily, the full enormity of the outrageous comparison striking him in the middle of his demolishing the plate of chicken. He dropped a clean-picked thigh bone on the heap beside his plate and looked at Maw with a shadow of his old, impudent grin. "If Marge were a man I'd show her some excitement, maybe."

"She's writing a bank-robbery story, Bud, and—maybe I hadn't ought to tell you—she's got you for the hero of it. She—"

"Me for the hero? Good Lord!"

"Well," said Maw, blinking at him across the table, "looks to me as if you'd had about all the adventures she's put you through in her story, except I don't s'pose you've been arrested for the murder and throwed in jail and incarcerated, like Margy had 'em do to you. She says it's awful hard to make up excitin' things, when she come out here expectin' that things would happen right along that she could use fine. She says she's goin' to have the Indians break out and start massacreeing the whites, and she wanted all day to ask you about some secret order; Golden Arrer, she says it is. She wants to make it a religious outbreak of some kind, and either let 'em catch you and start in to torture you, or else have you save a girl from bein' tortured. She tried to get Lark to tell her, but Larkie's kinda queer about some things. She couldn't get a peep outa him. He told her there wasn't no such thing, but of course she knew he was just denyin' it for some reason of his own. She thinks maybe he's mixed up and implicated somehow—maybe a high priest of the order; but I told her I didn't hardly believe he was."

Bud gave a whoop and choked so that Maw climbed down from her chair and came around and thumped him between the shoulders until he could wave her off with weak gestures of refusal. He came to with his face red and blinking tears, but he had no sooner got his breath than he began to laugh.

"I s'pose I've said somethin' funny, but I don't see what." Maw spoke tartly when the first outburst had subsided. "I guess you oughta be in pretty good shape now after gorgin' the way you have. I'll go call Lark, and then I expect maybe you'll see fit to tell us what's happened, and what brings you home this time in the morning, lookin' like a string of suckers and eatin' like you'd starved for a week. And all I can say," she stopped to say pettishly, "is that small matters amuse small minds. If I used a word wrong, that's *my* business!" She scuttled off before Bud could explain.

Maw was further shocked to find Bud emptying the pantry of cooked food when she returned to the kitchen. Four loaves of fresh baked bread reposed neatly beside half a baked ham, and the cookie jar was in his arms.

"For the love of Moses!" snapped Maw. "Didn't you get enough to eat *yet*?"

Behind her, Lark glanced appraisingly at the devastated table and grinned. The pile of chicken bones beside Bud's plate was enough, to say nothing of the remnant of pie with the whipped cream scraped off in streaks.

"For the time being, maybe; but I may possibly want to eat again, Maw, before Marge has me put in jail and incarcerated!" Bud was still badly in need of sleep, and Maw's tone had not been conciliating.

"I ain't responsible for that word, Bud Larkin. Margy used it herself, and if it don't meet with your approval, it's none of *my* funeral. Here's Lark, wantin' to know what you've been up to, and why you come draggin' your feet into the house this time of night. Are you goin' to take all them cookies, Bud? I can't make any more till I get some sour cream. I churned every bit that I had."

"You did? Fine! Bob's out in the hills, and fresh butter will go dandy with this bread. You know, Maw, there's only one real bread-maker in the world, and she's just about four feet high and cross as a she bear with toothache."

"I ain't no such a thing! Do you s'pose you could carry a pie if I wrapped it up good?"

"Sure. I'll carry it inside, however. Then I *know* it will be well wrapped. Lark may want to carry one. How about it, Lark? Want to go hunting with me, after I've had an hour or so of sleep?"

Lark hitched up his belt, picked up Maw and set her on a corner of the table. Then, ignoring her indignant protests, he began his preparations significantly in the gun closet, choosing what weapons he would take. Bud eyed him from under straight brows while he wrapped the bread in one of Maw's choicest dish towels which she kept for "comp'ny", when some range woman would insist upon helping her with the dishes.

"You won't need a shotgun—and I'll just omit that hour of sleep. Maw's pie is a real rejuvenator."

"It ain't no such a thing! Bud, ain't you goin' to tell what you've been up to or where you've been? My land, I never saw such carryin's on!"

"Nothing exciting, Maw. Nothing that Marge could use in that story of hers. Come on, Lark."

CHAPTER TWENTY-ONE
LARK WOULD HAVE DONE THINGS DIFFERENTLY

"Well, so-long, Lark." Bud held his nervous buckskin to a prancy circling while he and Lark indulged in one of those last-minute dialogues without which two persons seem unable to part in complete satisfaction. "If you can get Jelly off to one side, you might tell him that Bob and I are going to stick to the trail like a burr to a dog. And of course you'll know what to say to Delkin. Use your own judgment about telling him the facts."

"You better bed down somewhere and take a snooze," Lark advised perfunctorily. "I'll go 'long and meet Bob. I know these hills better than anybody, I guess. You go awn into town and git into bed somewhere. Then you can attend the inquest if they hold one. Mebbe they might not, seein' it's a clear case, s' far as they know. You go awn, Bud, and let me handle this deal."

"No. This is my job, Lark. I'll take that rifle of yours, though. I was so afraid Maw would pump something out of me and tell it to Marge that I rushed off without anything much except the grub. I wanted it cooked, so we won't need to make a smoke. No, you go on in and say I came back home and you sent me out on the range. And, Lark, if I don't bring Butch in and turn him over to the sheriff, it won't do any good whatever to say anything to Delkin and the others. They'll believe what they please—and that won't be very favorable to Jelly and me. Just let it ride; and don't worry about Bob and me, will you? No telling how long we'll be out. One of us will ride in to the ranch if it's necessary—and I'd a good deal rather handle it without interference if it's all the same to you."

"Oh, all right, if you feel that way about it, Bud. You shore got me up early enough—jest to ride a piece down the road with yuh! Go ahead and handle it without interference then! Mebbe later on you'll be darn glad of a little plain old help! Needn't think Butch is goin' to be easy to take—he'll go down harder 'n cod-liver oil. But all right—have it yore way; you will anyhow." Whereupon, Lark put spurs to his horse and loped on down the trail towards Smoky Ford, talking to himself. He had been coolly pushed aside, robbed of a share in what promised to be a risky piece of business. Impudent, he called it, and forgot how he had deliberately pushed Bud to the front and encouraged him to use his own judgment.

No, Lark would have done it differently; followed old Bill's methods more closely. Old Bill would have taken his riders and gone boldly after Butch, and made what he would have called a clean-up over at the Frying Pan. Bud might believe that Kid was ignorant of Butch's plans, but Lark did not. It would surprise him to discover that Kid was in on the deal. Still, Bud might wake up to facts and realize that after all an older head might hold a few ideas worth considering.

Bud, however, was not awake to much of anything save the fact that he was beginning to lose interest in anything but sleep; and that the buckskin was a tricky brute in the hills and not to be compared with the Walking Sorrel. The buckskin had a way of climbing hills in leaps that gave no thought to secure footing, but left him winded at the top. His manner of descending a steep slope was quite as reckless and consisted of a series of slides interspersed with dancing sidewise and taking fright at various objects. Bud had saddled him because he happened to be in a corral where he was handy, but he was wishing now—when he roused sufficiently to wish for anything except sleep—that he had taken the time to catch a horse out of the pasture. It might have proved quicker in the long run.

So, slipping, sliding, fighting the buckskin and guarding as best he could his burden of food, Bud arrived in the course of time at the spring beneath the sandstone cliffs. By that time he was indifferent to everything. It would have taken Butch Cassidy himself to rouse Bud to the fighting point. He was glad, in a dull, apathetic way, that he had made the trip from the ranch so that Bob could eat before he got as hungry as Bud had been. He managed also to picket the buckskin in the middle of good grass, and to put the supplies up on a shelf of rock away from small prowlers. After that Bud dropped down in the shade of the cliff, pulled his hat over his eyes, gave one huge sigh and dropped like a plummet into the oblivion of dreamless slumber.

At the Palmer ranch black Sam was shuffling back and forth across the kitchen, clearing away the débris of a scanty breakfast well-cooked, where nine men had eaten silently and gone their ways; all except Gelle, who had volunteered to remain on guard over Palmer until the sheriff was ready to take him away to the county seat. The coroner had just arrived, and was down in the cow pasture looking over the scene of the double killing and arguing with the sheriff in the intervals of rolling a fresh chew of tobacco relishfully from cheek to cheek.

Sam turned scared eyes toward Lark before he remembered his manners and ducked his head in what passed for a bow. Gelle, on a bench before the door, grinned cheerful greeting.

"You musta heard the news and got up b'fore breakfast," Gelle bantered. "Bud git in last night?"

Lark swung down and sat on the bench beside his "top hand"—as Gelle loved to consider himself.

"Bud got in this morning before daylight. Hauled me outa bed and started me out thinkin' I was goin' to git some excitement, mebbe. Then he hazed me awn in whilst he took out across country to meet Bob."

"Which means, I guess, that they didn't have no luck last night." Gelle's voice betrayed his disappointment.

"Depends on what you call luck," Lark retorted. "That fool kid rode over to the Fryin' Pan, laid out in the yard with Kid Kern till Butch come ridin' in, then up and sticks a gun in Butch's ribs and tells him to come clean with that money he'd stole outa the pasture here. What's more, the darn chump got away with it, and come home without a bullet hole through him. I dunno how it strikes you, Jelly, but I'd call that *luck*."

"And didn't he git the money?"

"Naw." Lark stopped while he lighted a cigarette. "He got the laugh."

"How's that? I been awn the anxious seat all night, Lark, worryin' about Bud and that damn' gold of Palmer's. Aw, he can't hear. I've got him tied to the bed back in another room. And the coon's only about half there. Go awn, Lark. I'm achin' to know what happened."

"That's jest the trouble, Jelly. Nothin' atall happened. Kid, he sided in with Bud and said if Butch had come over here and robbed Palmer's cache he'd turn him over to the sheriff himself. Bud thinks he meant it, but I dunno. Butch didn't have nothin' on his saddle but his slicker, and he give Bud the laugh. That's about all there was to it, fur as I could make out. Bud, he come shackin' along home about three this morning, et everything in sight and packed off what's left to feed Bob with.

"Bob stayed out in the hills. They got the idee they can back-track Butch and find out where he cached the stuff. But I dunno—like lookin' fer a needle in a haystack, to my notion. My Jonah, what a mess! How'd you bust yore rib, Jelly? Bud said you'd done it, but he never said how. Gimme some facts, fer gosh sake!"

By the time Gelle had told all he knew, had heard or surmised, Delkin, Bradley, the sheriff and the coroner came walking up from the pasture, still arguing. They greeted Lark, then drifted back to the subject of the two dead men. The sheriff sensed the work of a third man there, but the others insisted that the killing had been an impromptu duel, the coroner holding that the position in which the men lay had no bearing upon that point, since death was not instantaneous in either case and both had evidently staggered a few feet before falling.

"Kinda funny they'd both be facin' the same way—toward that ledge where you folks got your money," the sheriff pointed out, with a stubborn tilt to his chin. "If they went down fightin' each other, wouldn't they be likely to fall *facin'* each other? They hadn't started to run, neither of 'em. Looks to me like they both went down shootin' at somebody up on that ledge. You can think what yuh please about it—that's what *I* think."

"There couldn't have been anybody on the ledge," Delkin stated positively. "Bud Larkin was with us; Jelly, here, was at the house with a broken rib; Palmer and the old man were tied up in the bedroom and the coon was here in the kitchen. The four Meadowlark boys had left town ten minutes behind the two Palmer men, and not more than five minutes ahead of us. They heard the shooting as they rode up. The four will swear that Jelly and the coon were here at the house—and as a matter of fact, the rest of us arrived so soon after the shooting that it would have been physically impossible for these two to get back up here."

"Well," retorted the sheriff, quickly, "are these all the men there is in the world, Mr. Delkin?"

"All that could possibly have known anything about what was on the ledge. Bud Larkin found the money and came straight in after us, leaving Jelly to guard the old man that works here. We came right back, got the money and took it on in to town, still leaving Jelly on guard out here. He brought his prisoner to the house—a very wise thing to do, I may say—and so was here when Palmer came, and while capturing him he broke a rib, as you know. You can ask the doctor here whether he would be able, with that broken rib, to run from the pasture up here in, say, one minute."

"Couldn't have done it without a broken rib," stated the coroner, expectorating a generous amount of tobacco juice. "They shot each other. No reason why they shouldn't, is there? They were both after the money, and each man wanted to get there first. Be funny if they *didn't* fight over it. Guess we better hold an inquest and thrash this thing out before a jury. How soon can you get a jury together, Stilson?" The coroner must have been out of humor with the sheriff, because usually he addressed him familiarly as Jim.

"Hour, maybe. That quick enough? You get your witnesses together, and a few *facts* to show, and I'll have the jury ready to listen to 'em quick enough to ketch 'em before they melt." He probably referred to the facts.

Lark, sitting quietly on the bench during the discussion, wondered why no one mentioned Palmer's money (or what was tacitly conceded to be Palmer's money) which had been left in the cache and was now missing. Delkin and Bradley seemed to avoid any unnecessary reference to money. Lark was on the point of mentioning the one great inducement to murder, the one thing that would call a man to the ledge. He was even tempted to tell what he knew of Butch Cassidy.

But while the others wrangled his caution came whispering and urging him to wait. If Delkin and Bradley failed to mention the mysterious disappearance of Palmer's gold, it was for one reason. They were grateful to Bud and to Gelle and meant to protect them. Lark appreciated that spirit even while he resented their suspicions. Both emotions held him silent after the first impulse to speak had passed. They knew all about that money being gone, he reflected. If they saw fit to cover up the loss before the sheriff, it would ill become him to drag the thing to the surface and tell the sheriff something that might throw suspicion—or worse—upon the Meadowlark. He joggled Gelle unthinkingly with his elbow, cautioning him to silence, and brought a yelp of pain from that tightly bandaged young man, and a stealthily vicious jab afterwards to show that Gelle had not missed Lark's meaning.

* * * *

There followed the usual commonplace running to and fro on horses sweating under the urge of their riders' haste to be somewhere else immediately. The coroner's inquest was called, and practically all of Smoky Ford bustled out to Palmer's ranch and squatted on run-over boot heels and drew diagrams in the dust with little sticks, explaining gravely to any who would listen that the robbery, the murder, and the killing of Bat Johnson and Ed White took place in this or that particular manner.

All I can say is, Marge should have been there with her notebook; two or three notebooks, rather.

Figuratively speaking, the various Sherlocks placed the noose on Palmer's neck a dozen times for a dozen different reasons. They openly mourned that Bat and Ed were past hanging, and there was not a man present who had not known all along that Palmer was at the bottom of the whole thing. So much for the loyalty of neighbors of that type when a man of Palmer's type is called to account for his sins.

The inquest might well be called an anticlimax, since the citizens of Smoky Ford had the thing all settled in their minds before the investigation was officially begun. Palmer puzzled and disappointed them and came near to a lynching, that day, merely because he refused to testify and would only say, with baleful self-possession, that since they were all set on laying the guilt on him, they could go ahead and think what they pleased; his lawyer would have something to say about it when the thing came to a trial. (It was at this time that Palmer edged close to death.)

The sheriff, being just a bit keyed up by opposition, made a clean sweep of it and took black Sam along with Palmer, and the old man Blinker as well. They might or might not be implicated in the crime, but at least they should prove useful as witnesses.

By mid-afternoon the inquest was over and the sheriff had left for the county seat with his three prisoners, leaving his two deputies ostensibly in charge of Palmer's ranch pending a more satisfactory arrangement. In reality, the sheriff had some hope of solving the mystery of the shooting of two men in broad daylight and within sound of the house, and he had left two men where one would have been sufficient, with secret instructions to make a careful search for some clue to an unknown member of the gang.

The last shovelful of moist, rocky soil had been carelessly tossed upon Bat Johnson's heaped grave, and the two rough mounds marked by stakes driven into the ground, each bearing a name and date burned hastily with a hot iron. The burial party, in haste to join their fellows, were riding through the gate on their way to town when Maw appeared.

Maw was mad. Never before since her arrival at the Meadowlark a few years before had she been treated as Bud and Lark had treated her that morning. Never before had they failed to tell her all that happened or was about to happen, and Maw did not propose to stand it much longer. She had waited until nine o'clock and then had ordered old Cap and Charlie hitched to the beloved "top buggy" which Lark had given her, and she had bundled Marge and a lunch basket in beside her and started for town. They needn't think, said Maw, that she was going to sit and fold her arms and act like a fool just because they treated her like one. Wherefore she challenged the nearest horseman, who was eyeing Marge with interest.

"How do? See anything of Bud Larkin around here?" Maw was pretty fair at reading signs, and the trampled yard just across the fence with jumbled tracks leading through the gate had told her a story of events.

"No, mom, Bud ain't been here t'day atall."

"Lark been here? Bill Larkin?"

"Yes, mom, Lark was here and he left right after the inquest." The horseman fiddled with his reins and kept his horse backing and sidling, showing off before Marge.

"Inquest! For the love of Moses, has old Palmer been killed at last?" Maw sucked so hard upon her new teeth that she almost swallowed them.

"No, mom, he's been took to jail. It's Bat Johnson an' Ed White the cor'ner has been settin' on. They was shot yeste'day."

Maw opened her mouth to speak further of her astonishment, then closed it abruptly, took the buggy whip from its socket and struck old Charlie smartly across the rump. Maw's face had gone the color of rancid tallow. There, conjured vividly before her by unreasoning fear, rode the vision of young Bud staggering into the kitchen hollow-eyed and ravenous; wolfing food sufficient for two ordinary appetites and going off with a sackful of supplies.

"I do hope I'll get some decently exciting material out of this," said Marge, all in a flutter. "Do you suppose something worth while has actually taken place, and I'll—"

"Put up that everlastin' notebook!" snapped Maw. "Things ain't picturesque when they're happenin' to your own!" She pulled the indignant horses from a lope as expertly as a man could have done, and sent them trotting their best down the road to town. "I've got to find Lark and see what's to be done—and it ain't a bit kind or p'lite to use the troubles of your own folks, Margy, to put in stories. If's Buddy's on the dodge for killin' a couple of men, you ain't goin' to put him into no story—you mark what I tell you. Buddy don't *want* to be no heero. And if he don't want to be, he sha'n't be. Time I put my foot down, I guess."

"I'd make Palmer the murderer, of course," Marge placated absently. "What's he been taken to jail for, do you suppose?"

"I dunno—and I don't care. Buddy's on the dodge. I knew it when he cleaned out the pantry without sayin' a word about where he was goin'!"

Maw sucked in her teeth, tapped both horses across their broad backs with the whip, and went lurching on down the road to town, leaving a cloud of dust behind her.

CHAPTER TWENTY-TWO
EAVESDROPPER

Five days may not seem long as a rule, but Bud's nerves were ragged with the strain of searching foot by foot the likely places along the trail Butch Cassidy had taken; with eating just enough to allay the sharpest hunger pangs, and with sleeping where dark overtook him, with no pillow save his saddle— which is mighty uncomfortable even though it may sound picturesque to those who have not tried it. Bob grew daily more lugubrious, but Bud began to talk rather wildly of riding again to the Frying Pan, getting Butch Cassidy by the throat and choking the truth out of him—a reckless notion which appealed to him more and more as the fruitless quest continued. He began to imagine how it would seem to go galloping up the lane, meet Butch and lash out at him with biting words until they fought. A vengeful dream that grew upon him.

On this fifth day Bob had ridden early to the Basin for more food; the baked ham being no more than a wistful memory, the cookies likewise and the four loaves of bread a dwindling, dried-out fragment. It was insufferably hot down in the canyon where he was dispiritedly searching the craggy walls for safe hiding places and thinking, among other things, that the country between Palmer's ranch and the Frying Pan held places of concealment for all the gold coin the world contains. Probably he was right. There surely was an ungodly amount of rough ledges and cliffs and heaped bowlders along the route indicated by the occasional hoofprints they identified as Butch's horse. In five days they had covered perhaps twice as many miles.

Off to the southwest a ragged blue-brown ridge of storm clouds crept slowly over the high peaks. A swashing rain would render their quest more hopeless still, for they would lose the tracks that now guided them sketchily from gully to bare ridge perhaps and into another canyon. The outlook was not cheerful, and the heat radiating from the rocks became unbearable.

It was then that Bud, climbing to a promising splinter of rock thrust upward like a crude needle from the broken ledge beneath it, sighted the cool, still pool sunk between banks of rock and gravel so that from the canyon floor it was invisible. Some sunken stream had risen there for a look at the sky, perhaps. Bud gave a hoarse whoop, forgetting caution in his sudden joy, and immediately began to climb down as eagerly as if he had sighted the gold.

The frivolous buckskin had long since lost all desire for prancing or taking the steep hills in jackrabbit leaps. He stood half asleep in the shade of a rock, with trickles of sweat running down thigh and shoulder; a tamed horse that had learned to conserve his energy and put aside his play. Bud mounted and rode to the pool though it was almost within pistol range.

Side by side he and the buckskin drank their fill before Bud stripped and went into it in a long, clean dive from a rock thrust up into the sunshine and so hot it curled his toes with pain during the few seconds he stood there poised for the jump. The water was cold, the shock to his fevered skin a gorgeous sensation of sheer physical thrill. Bud went deep, tilted and shot to the surface and spouted happily, the cobwebs washed from his brain, the gnawing rancor from his soul. For the moment at least he was his normal, care-free self; hungry, but enjoying to the full this glorious swimming pool set apart from the haunts of men, passed by a dozen times or a hundred, perhaps, without discovery.

And then, swimming and diving, floating and treading water and splashing in pure devilment, he heard someone laugh; a chuckling sort of subdued cackle which Bud knew quite well. By treading water and craning his neck he could see the spot where he had left his clothes, and Butch was there, sitting with his knees drawn up and his ungloved hands clasped around them, smoking and grinning between puffs, with his hat pushed back on his head and the knot of his neckerchief askew under his ear—where he would maybe wear a knot of another kind one day, Bud thought balefully. Butch looked a very good sort of fellow, a pal perhaps who had no whim for a bath that day. But he was not at all like that when he spoke.

"Divin' for it, Bud?" he fleered. "Better claw around there on the bottom, why don't yuh? Gold sinks, yuh know; or don't yuh? I savvy you've had lots of schoolin', but that don't mean you got good sense. What time yuh expect Bob back with the grub? Oughta be showin' up, now, most any time. I heard him say when he left he'd git here b'fore three o'clock. It's way past that now, by the sun." He squinted upward, then spat reflectively toward the pool.

"Of course you'll stay and eat with us," Bud invited urbanely. "Bob promised to bring some fresh eggs and a couple of chickens."

"Yeah, I know he did. I heard 'im." Butch's narrow, light blue eyes were studying Bud's black head, sleek as a wet muskrat, with some curiosity. He had expected a blasphemous series of epithets—and, fifteen minutes sooner, he probably would have heard them. He had not reckoned upon the steadying effect of that cold plunge.

"Then of course you'll stay." (Privately, Bud was certain that Butch was not to be shaken off before he had accomplished his purpose; and, frankly, Bud believed that murder was his purpose.)

"Might, seein' you insist. I'm purty well hooked up with grub, but my *kew*-seen don't include chicken. How yuh goin' to cook it, Bud?"

"Broil mine—and rub it with butter, salt and pepper now and then. How you want yours?"

"Sounds good t' me. I'll take the same."

To gain time for thought, Bud curved in his body and dived, expecting that he would come up to meet a .45 slug somewhere in his brain; between the eyes, he guessed—since Butch was called a good shot. As may be surmised, Bud did considerable thinking under water, but he could not think of anything better than he was already doing, since his manner was puzzling Butch and what puzzled Butch Cassidy also worried him. Still, he might shoot, and there was just one way to find out. Bud came up, shook the water from his eyes and saw that Butch was apparently much interested in the pinned-back hatbrim.

"Where'd yuh make the raise, Bud? I been kinda curious about that pin."

Bud hesitated. There is a fiction that two men must never let a good woman's name pass between them, but there was nothing secret about the pin—except before Marge. Every cowpuncher who went to dances in that country should have recognized it.

"Grandma Parker's," he lied shortly, and dived again as if he enjoyed diving.

When he came up, Butch had laid aside the hat and was looking speculatively at Bud.

"'Course, I could shoot yuh," he mused aloud. "Lots a things I could do. S'pose it'll be a bullet. Ain't yuh about ready to come out? Bob'll likely be startin' supper 'bout now. Come awn—git into yore clothes." Butch spoke as he would have admonished a small boy.

Because there was nothing else that he could do Bud came out of the pool, nipping over the hot gravel to where his clothes lay in a heap ten feet from where Butch sat smoking. Butch had moved while Bud was under water, and Bud's gun and belt had moved with him; also Bud's big clasp knife that was useful for so many things.

Bud dressed as unconcernedly as if the man sitting there in the shade had been Bob. Butch spun Bud's hat to him—without the cameo pin—and eyed Bud sharply when he picked it up and looked at the flopping brim with the two blackened pinholes. Bud looked up at him, his eyes black with anger.

"Pretty small, Butch! I knew you were a thief, but I did have some respect for you for taking a chance, anyway. A stunt like this is so low-down you'd have to climb a ladder to scratch a snake on the belly!" He stared a moment longer and put on his hat. To move toward Butch would have been one way of committing suicide, and even in anger Bud was no fool.

"Yeah—one more reason why I'll kill yuh, Bud. Some day." Butch got up, dusting off his trousers with downward sweeps of his palms—close to his gun, Bud saw with a curl of the lip.

"Yes? Well, you'll have to go some unless you play safe and do it now."

"I'll be willin' t' go when the time comes," Butch retorted. "Move awn— my mouth's waterin' fer chicken."

They moved on, Bud in the lead. Lark's rifle, he saw, was gone from the saddle. A foolish thing he had done, and a costly, to go swimming in that pool as carelessly as if he were down in the Basin pasture. He could find no excuse for it in his belief that he had the hills to himself that day. After so long a time he and Bob had both come to the conclusion that Kid Kern was watching Butch so closely that there would be no attempt made at present to retrieve the loot, and that they were therefore perfectly safe to search where they would.

At Butch's command, Bud dismounted some distance from the spring where they had made a makeshift camp. They approached the place on foot and so came upon Bob when he was least looking for callers, the supposition being that Bud would search until close to sundown before coming to camp. It was Butch's casual tones that brought Bob facing them in blank astonishment.

"I got a gun ag'inst Bud's backbone," Butch announced in a cheerful, conversational manner. "He'll git it, right plumb through the liver, first crooked move you make. Toss yore gun into the spring. It won't hurt the water none."

"Get him if you can, Bob," Bud countermanded. "Let the damned skunk shoot if he wants to; he will, anyway."

Bob looked at Bud, glanced over his shoulder into Butch's narrowed eyes, drew his gun and threw it into the spring with a muttered oath. Butch grinned.

"Got a knife? Throw that in too. All right, boys, let's go awn and have that chicken dinner. I an' Bud's been talkin' about it all the way over."

"'Better a dinner of herbs where love is, than a stalled ox and hatred thereby,'" Bud quoted under his breath with a grim humor not lost upon Butch, who overheard him.

"Nh-nh. This is goin' to be stalled chicken an' hatred thereby," he drawled. "An' I bet a dollar I'll hate harder 'n the both of yuh put t'gether. Wanta bet?"

The two ignored him and set about cooking their dinner, knowing that Butch would kill the man who made a hostile motion.

"Lessee. This is the first time you've had a fire sence you been down here," Butch observed pleasantly. "I'd a dropped in awn yuh b'fore, but it looked like purty slim pickin's. Then this mornin' I heard Bob say chicken, so I plumb knowed you was goin' to have comp'ny fer dinner."

"Say-ay," drawled Bob, after further small talk of the sort, "I'd ruther be shot than talked t' death, Butch."

"Yeah—but I'd ruther talk," Butch grinned. "Pass over the pepper 'nd salt, will yuh, Bud?"

"Certainly," said Bud politely, though his eyes were murderous.

They ate and were filled, but two of the trio did not enjoy the meal. Butch persisted in desultory talk, friendly on the surface but with a sting beneath. Now and then Bob grunted, while Bud relapsed into absolute silence.

"Can't figure out no way that'll work, Bud," Butch told him impudently, when the three were smoking afterwards—Butch performing nonchalantly the art of rolling and lighting a cigarette almost entirely with one hand. "Y' see, in the first place, I got yore guns. Y' won't jump me, so that lets you out. Anyway, I got t' be goin' in a minute. Main reason I give m'self an invite to supper was t' tell you fellers I'm shore tickled at the way yo're combin' these canyons. Y' see, I dunno but what yuh might run onto somethin' way yo're goin' about it, you shore ain't leavin' no stones unturned.

"When you've crawled all over these hills, mebbe you'll believe what I told yuh over to the Fryin' Pan, Bud; that I never got no money over to Palmer's place. Still, I dunno. Yo're so damn' pig-headed you won't believe nothin' you don't want to. Well, go ahead an' look. Look yore damn' eyes out, fer all me. You won't find nothin'. An' don't fergit I'll be right there, close hand by, all the time. So-long—shore enjoyed that chicken!"

While he talked, Butch had backed toward the bushes that grew near. At the last moment he drew something from his shirt pocket, looked at it, gave a snort of scornful amusement and tossed the object so that it fell between Bud's feet. Then he disappeared.

Bud stooped, picked up the cameo pin and turned it absent-mindedly in his fingers. His sign of the Golden Arrow. The red blood of youth crept upward and dyed his cheeks at the thought of the ignominy he would have suffered had he been obliged to go and confess to Bonnie Prosser that he had lost her pin; that Butch Cassidy had taken it away from him! In the pressure of events since that day when he had ridden blithely across the reservation with the cameo pin worn proudly above his forehead, he had not thought so much about it. He had fancied himself invulnerable to the young archer's barbed darts. Now—now he was suddenly aware of a great hunger, a longing that engulfed even his hatred for Butch.

"Hell!" said Bob, thinking of his gun lying at the bottom of the spring.

"Hunh?" said Bud, thinking that he had time in plenty to ride to Prosser's ranch before dark.

"Hell, you damn' fool!" Bob looked at him with his mouth drawn down at the corners like a child about to cry.

"Oh, sure," Bud agreed, without having the faintest idea of what had been said.

Bob's mouth opened, closed again very slowly. He was staring from Bud's face to the brooch in Bud's hand, and at the fingers softly caressing the carved face of the woman.

"Looks like her," said Bob with much sarcasm.

"A—a little." Bud's forefinger closed tenderly upon the profile.

"Say, come out of it!" growled Bob. "What about Butch?"

"Butch? Why, Butch will get killed if he crosses my trail again. Why?" Young Bud's eyes turned surprisedly toward Bob.

"Goin' to keep up the hunt, knowin' he's p'pared to jump us the minute we find it?"

"Why, sure! You don't think Butch cuts any figure with me, do you?" (Plenty of time—and he could get there before dark, if he hurried.)

"No—'course he don't!" cried a mocking voice somewhere among the rocks.

Bud started, closed his fingers upon the brooch and turned toward the voice. The softness had left his eyes, which snapped with their old fire.

"You know it, Butch! You heard what I said." Strange how the flinging of that cameo pin at his feet brought Bonnie so vividly before him that even his quarrel with Butch seemed irrelevant, a matter of secondary importance.

Now he knew that the illuminating truth had come upon him at the pool when he picked up his hat and saw that the brooch was gone. It was like losing Bonnie herself—and of course he had always known, deep in his heart, that he meant never to lose Bonnie Prosser out of his life; that some day—but the time of easy assurance was past, and it had taken the rough hand of Butch Cassidy to tear away the film from his eyes, just as he had torn the pin from Bud's hat.

"See you later, Butch!" he called defiantly, and started on a run for his horse.

"Yeah—yo're damn' right!" Butch's mocking laughter followed him, echoed and was flung back again and again from the farther wall of the canyon.

CHAPTER TWENTY-THREE
"DISARM THE PRISONER!"

"Got your notebook handy, Marge?" Young Bud, looking altogether different, though not so handsome, in a tailored suit left over from college, and a new straw hat that gave no excuse for wearing cameo pins in the brim, crossed the lobby of Fort Benton's best hotel to where Marge was sitting beside Maw staring out at the shifting crowds with puckered brows, her thoughts no doubt dwelling upon picturesque effects. "This is Miss Bonnie Prosser, and I thought you might like to make a note of the fact that she is the high priestess in the temple where I worship; the goddess of the Golden Arrow, and—"

"For the love of Moses, what kinda talk is that, Bud Larkin? Bonnie's too sweet and pretty a girl to be made fun of right in public, like this. I been waitin' for a chance to git you two girls acquainted," cried Maw, from the depths of a leather rocking chair.

"Why—why—she's *exactly* like my heroine!" cried Marge, her eyes dancing with excitement. "I wrote the sweetest love scene just before we left home—"

"Too late, too late," crowed Bud, his lips curving into the smile of a happy boy. "I beat you to it, Marge."

"Now, hush," drawled Bonnie, in a voice amazingly low and sweet and vibrant—just the voice one would want to hear from that smooth young throat and lips formed for laughter. "I'd love to be your heroine, Miss—may I call you Marge? I've so wanted a girl like you to come into the range country and give me a sympathetic ear now and then. Ever since I first heard about you I've been planning to come over and steal you. We live right next to the reservation, and there's the dearest old squaw I want you to write up. And I know so many places where I want to take you. When this trial is over, I want you to come home with me. We're going to be the best of friends. I always know, the moment I look at a person. Don't you?"

"Them girls don't need you, Buddy," Maw shrewdly observed. "Set down here where I can talk to you. Lean over here. Are you and Bonnie engaged?"

"Yes, ma'am," Bud confessed meekly. "Have been, Maw, for almost a month."

"Well, I ain't a mite su'prised, and I'm real glad. Set down, can't you? Let 'em alone till they get acquainted. I want to talk to you private. Now. What kinda luck did you have, Buddy? Are you goin' to be able to give that money back to Palmer—or the bank, or whoever it belongs to?"

All the joy went out of Bud's face. He shook his head, his lips pressed tight.

"Who told you, Maw?"

"Lark told me. Who else do you think? *You* wouldn't, I notice. I was so scared and worried when you stayed out in the hills like you did, Buddy, that I thought Lark oughta get you out of the country some way. I thought you was on the dodge for killin' them Palmer men, mebbe. So Lark told me what it was all about. Butch is in town, did you know it?"

Bud lifted his shoulders in a gesture of bitter defeat.

"I didn't know it, but I can't do anything, anyway. I saw Kid, and he told me he's been watching Butch and he hasn't got a thing on him. I'm certain Butch did it, but—Maw, there isn't a gopher hole between Palmer's and the Frying Pan that I haven't searched. Kid claims he combed the ranch too. If he turned up anything, he's keeping it mighty quiet—but I don't believe he has, I think Butch has simply outguessed us."

"Well, don't you have no trouble with Butch. You didn't bring no gun, did you, Buddy?"

"Butch took my gun away from me when he caught me in swimming." His eyes evaded hers. "You heard about that, I suppose."

"Yes, I did—and I heard too that Butch give your gun and Lark's rifle to Kid, and had him send 'em over home. Bob took 'em back down to you, so you needn't to think you can lie to me, Buddy. Don't you pack that gun around this town, or you'll get yourself into trouble, sure. You think what that would mean to Bonnie. I'm real glad she's got some say in the matter now, Bud. She'll hold you down—I'm sure I can't!"

"What do you expect me to do if Butch makes a crack at me? Stand and take it?" Bud's eyes grew stubborn.

"Butch won't make no crack at you. Kid told Lark he'd had a talk with Butch, and Butch promised him faithful he'd keep his own side the road. He ain't goin' to crowd you, Buddy, and you mustn't go glowerin' around edgin' him up to a fight. Them eyes of yourn git terrible stormy when you're all wrought up. You think about that nice girl and forget Butch."

"You dragged me away from two nice girls, Maw, and opened the disagreeable subject yourself."

"I know I did, but I was kinda lonesome for you, Bud. I ain't seen anything of you skurcely since that money was stole. Lark says Palmer's goin' to hold the bank responsible for it if it ain't returned. Palmer claims there was six thousand dollars, and he just as good as accused Delkin of takin' it himself. It'll likely come out at the trial. Lark says if the bank does have to stand good, he'll pay Delkin himself ruther than have 'em think—"

"And admit that Jelly and I took the money! I thought Lark had a little sense. Maw, if Lark does that, I'll choke the truth out of Butch Cassidy if I have to do it right under the judge's nose!"

"Now, now, Buddy, don't you go and git on your high horse again! You know as well as I do that Lark's soft-hearted as any old woman you ever saw. He can't bear to have Delkin feel—"

"Fine way to salve his feelings and sharpen his belief that Jelly and I are thieves! Where's Lark? I want to have a talk with him."

Maw stood up and looked around the lobby and sat down again with smug satisfaction.

"Lark ain't here. I dunno where he is, Bud. He was talkin' about ridin' out to some ranch or other to look at some cattle they wanted to sell. You wait and see how things works out at the trial. I heard someone sayin' the jury's most all chose, and the show'll commence in the mornin'. They say that Melrose feller that Palmer's got to keep him from gittin' hung is a wonder, Buddy. It's kinda s'spicioned around that he's got a pretty strong defense. I don't see how he can have. Can you?"

Bud brought his wandering glance from the two girls sitting in a corner with their heads together in confidential whisperings. He looked at Maw and cleared the impatience from his eyes. After all, who was more loyal than Maw?

"Palmer has an alibi, you know, and Bat Johnson and Ed White are conveniently gone where they can't turn State's evidence, even if they wanted to. A good lawyer can do wonders with a situation like that, Maw. Where's Lightfoot? He came with you, didn't he?"

Maw gave a sudden laugh, turned her new teeth sidewise in her mouth and necessitated some expert manipulations behind her handkerchief.

"Consarn them teeth! I've a good mind to throw 'em out the window. Lightfoot got right out of the hack as we was comin' from the depot and started in drawin' pitchers of that Injun camp up there on the hill. I wouldn't be a mite su'prised if the sheriff had to go up there after him when it comes his turn to testify in court. Buddy, you oughta take him over onto the rese'vation some time. He never seen any Injuns in Smoky Ford—and I never told him why the Injuns all hate that place so. Thought I'd leave that to you. There! See that big, fine-lookin' man comin' across the street, Buddy? That's Palmer's lawyer. They say the county attorney would give a good deal to know what he's goin' to spring on 'em tomorrow. Here comes the girls. Ain't they pretty and sweet? I bet they're up to somethin', the way their eyes is dancin'!"

Arms twined around each other, schoolgirl fashion, the two girls came up and perched on either arm of Maw's great upholstered chair. That buried Maw from sight of everything, so they laughed and accepted the chairs Bud was placing for them. Bonnie leaned forward, took one of Maw's tiny hands in her own and patted it.

"What shall be done to punish a young man who tells lies to an innocent young lady from the East?" she asked gravely. "I have just heard some awful whoppers which a certain person told Marge. And Marge," she said impressively, "is my best friend. I have heard about the Iowa frogs and—"

"I surrender." Bud interrupted her and threw both hands in the air.

Maw gave him a quick look, sucked in her teeth apprehensively as if she were afraid of losing them into her lap, and glanced at Bonnie's hand that had one finger extended and pointing like a gun at Bud.

"Yes, disarm the prisoner, Maw," said Bonnie. "I've got the drop."

Maw reached out and got the gun tucked inside Bud's waistband, where it had been hidden from sight; looked at it, blinking tears from her round eyes, and shoved it down beside her in the big chair.

"You may take down your arms and march ahead of us to that drug store on the corner. Two maidens in distress want lemon soda. Will you come, Maw?"

"No," said Maw in a voice that shook perceptibly, "I don't believe I will. You childern run along and—and have a good time!"

"Listen, Maw. We'll bring you some—some—" Bonnie leaned and whispered in Maw's ear.

"Yes—yes—all right—yes-s—" Maw's hand closed convulsively over the gun.

"And thank the good Lord for that!" Maw breathed fervently, while she watched the three cross the street. "My, my, what turrible liars men do make of us women—keepin' 'em outa trouble." She got up, looked shyly around to see if any there observed her deformity, and waddled away to her room, the gun hidden in a fold of her skirt.

CHAPTER TWENTY-FOUR
SNOWBALL TESTIFIES

"My, my, are you getting all this down in shorthand?" Maw leaned over and whispered to Marge—being of course obliged to look up, as a child must do.

"No," Marge whispered back, "it's too tiresome. I'm only making a few notes of funny people here. The trial itself is commonplace; hopelessly commonplace. I never saw such a tame crowd—and to think it's right in the West!"

"Tame, did you say?" Bonnie, on the other side, had caught the word. "I wonder what you're used to, Marge." She glanced across to where Butch Cassidy stood leaning against the wall with his hat dangling from his left hand, his arms folded—with his right hand hidden, Bonnie observed—and she smiled to herself.

Those tame persons most concerned did not consider the trial a commonplace affair. Palmer's lawyer was earning his money, and Palmer had reached the point where he could lean back in his chair and look the jurymen in the eye—though a close observer would have noticed that he avoided the judge's cold gaze. It had been proven beyond a doubt that Palmer had no visible connection with the murder and robbery. The facts so far as known were in his favor, and his testimony, given calmly under the adroit questioning of his counsel, brought to the attention of the jury many points which, though ruled out after sputters of argument between the lawyers, nevertheless carried their weight, just as was intended. Melrose was a clever man.

For instance, Palmer was not stopped before he had stated that he knew nothing whatever of the bank money being hidden on the ledge in his pasture. He had chosen to use a certain secluded niche in the rocks as a natural safe, he said. He had never placed much confidence in Delkin's bank and did not like to keep his last cent there. Something might happen. He had stored away six thousand dollars in powder kegs, just in case of need. He had not visited the place for a month. No, he did not go often to see if his money was safe. Nothing could bother it unless someone stole it, and he had felt sure that no one knew of the hiding place.

Yes, he understood that the bank's money and papers had been found there. He could not account for that, except that Bat Johnson and Ed White had discovered the place and had hidden the money there because it was the safest spot they could find. Well, although he had trusted them, he guessed if they knew he had six thousand dollars hidden away in there his life wouldn't be any too safe. He had no theory, except that if they were in a hurry they could have overlooked his money sacks. He admitted that was unlikely, and repeated that he believed he would have been killed if he had gone there before they removed the money.

Yes, he had been told that the money—his money—was gone. He thought that those who took away the bank money should be held responsible for his six thousand dollars. They may not have taken it, but they certainly knew it was there, whereas he had no idea that the bank's money had been secreted on his ranch in the very place where he had stored money of his own.

About the boat he was equally outspoken. The men had built a boat in which to cross the river, where there was a little feed and where stock occasionally drifted in to graze. Sometimes they mired in the mud while trying to drink; when the river was low that often happened. They had built the boat so that they could cross the river and haul out mired stock. He had never dreamed that it might be used for a more sinister purpose, but he could see how that would be possible without his knowledge or approval.

On cross-examination he named approximately the date of his last visit to the ledge. He had decided to store away six thousand dollars as a nest egg that could tide him over if hard times came upon him. The last time he had gone there was in the middle of June, when he had taken five hundred dollars in gold and put it away with the rest. That amount just rounded out his six thousand, he said. There had been no occasion to go there after that.

"Ain't that old pelican the damnedest liar you ever seen, Bud?" Gelle whispered behind his hand—they having given their testimony and been dismissed. "Gilt-edged, though. He'll git away with it."

Bud nodded gloomily. He had been watching Butch Cassidy and wishing hotly that he had a gun. It began to look as though Butch was going to get away with something—ride off scot-free and leave a smirch on the good name of the Meadowlark that, in the minds of the Smoky Ford bank's officers, would be harder to erase than Macbeth's haunting blood stain.

Butch glanced at the two, his light eyes narrowing under frowning brows. It was evident that Butch also had something on his mind. Beside him Kid Kern leaned against the wall, careless on the surface, but never missing a look or a movement anywhere, and paying especial attention to Butch and Bud.

"Gosh!" Gelle ejaculated under his breath. "Pore old Snowball's goin' to be pumped dry now—and he don't know a darned thing about nothin'."

"Character witness, maybe," Bud made ironical reply.

"It'll be a pippin," Gelle predicted. "Snowball don't know nothin' good about that old coot."

Sam rolled his eyes in mental anguish, probably imagining that he himself was being accused of something. He stuttered and didn't know anything he was expected to know. He was palpably terrified, and whenever he caught Palmer's eyes upon him he shrank pitiably in his chair. And then, mercifully, his wild eyes strayed to Gelle's face and clung there as to his savior. He blinked, swallowed twice, gripped the chair arms and began to talk—to his beloved "Mist' Meddalahk", who had given him human sympathy and a dollar. A question or two he answered intelligibly. Then, abruptly, his tongue-tied fear dropped from him.

"Yessuh, yessuh, Ah doan' know nuthin' 'bout no doin's mah boss he been up to. Boss, he want his dinnah awn time—dass all ole Sam consuhmed about.

"But one mawnin', 'long about noon, heah come dem Meddalahk boys ridin' and shootin'. Yessuh, Ah 'member what tooken place awn dat day. Considubble, suh, happens right 'long 'bout dat same time. Mist' Meddalahk, he come ridin' along, aftuh boss he go awn to town. Yessuh, boys dey calls 'im Jelly, but Ah doan' see nothin' respeckful 'bout names lak dat. Ah calls 'im Mist' Meddalahk, an' we talks along an' talks along, 'bout one thing an' anuthah—yessuh.

"Mist' Jedge, suh, Ah got somethin' awn mah min' don' consuhn yo'all. Ah been hearin' little sum'fin now an' ag'in 'bout some money what come up missin', and 'pears lak some gemmen, dey 'clined to think mah frien', Mist' Meddalahk ovah theah, he done mebby *took* dat money. Ah doan' rightly know jes' how dat come about, Mist' Jedge, suh, but Ah'd lak fo' to tell yo'all—"

"I object, your honor, on the ground that the witness is taking up valuable time to no purpose," cried Palmer's counsel, springing to his feet. "Your honor, this witness is incompetent—"

"This witness is trying to tell what he knows about some missing money," the judge rebuked. "Objection overruled. Go on, Sam. Tell us all about it. Plenty of time, so long as we get the truth."

"Yessuh, Mist' Jedge, dat what Ah'm comin' to right now. Mist' Jedge, it come about 'count of ole Blinkah. He go wand'in' off an' Ah hunts him up, 'cause sometime he jes' go to sleep 'mos' anywhere. Mist' Meddalahk, he bin gone fuh some time, an' Blinkah, he gone fuh some time, and Ah jes' starts off lookin' fuh Blinkah. Yessuh, Mist' Jedge, Ah'm lookin' for Blinkah.

"Time Ah gits down pas' de stable, Mist' Jedge, I seen fo', five men walkin' crost cow paschuh. Mist' Meddalahk, he's one, Mist' Delkin, he's one, Mist' Bud, he's one—looks lak mebby Blinkah he down thah an' mebby sick uh somepin'. So Ah goes awn down, Mist' Jedge, an'—an' awnes', Mist' Jedge, Ah doan' mean no hahm!

"Ah goes along in some bushes, lak, an' Ah watches t' see what all's takin' place, 'cause if it's Blinkah an' he's daid, ole Sam he ain't gwine be dah—no, suh! So, Jedge, 'clah to goodness, dem white folks dey diggin' aroun' an' talkin' 'bout *money*. Ah crope along, an' crope along, but Ah doan' see all dat money—no, suh. Ah waits, an' dey pack off all dey wants, an' Mist' Delkin, he say he leave wha's left.

"Mist' Jedge, Ah been luhned not to wast *nothin'*. Boss, he mighty p'tic'lah 'bout wastin' *nothin'*. Dey takes all dey wants, Jedge, and den Ah goes an' looks, and 'clah t' goodness, Ah seen *gol'* money lef' right dah! Mus' be fo' five dollahs. Ah—Ah tuk it, Mist' Jedge. Ah got it in mah baid, upstairs. Cawdin' t' what Ah huhd, Mist' Jedge, dat money consuhms mah friend, Mist' Meddalahk."

"Whoo-*eee*!" yipped Gelle, before he could stop himself, and caught the stern yet understanding eye of the judge and subsided, red to collar and hair line.

"That's the first dramatic moment I've seen since I came West," Marge confided to Bonnie, who was biting her under lip and staring straight before her, to where Bud's head had lifted and turned, his eyes seeking hers. Bonnie's eyes were bright and her lashes were wet, and she did not hear a word of what Marge was saying.

The sheriff was mumbling that there would be a recess of ten minutes. Bonnie stood up, helping Maw into the aisle. She was going to Bud. It was almost as if Bud had been cleared of some criminal charge—as if he had been the prisoner before the bar. But when she had taken a step or two down the aisle, Bonnie stopped, a queer little sound in her throat that may have been a laugh or a sob, or both. She turned and caught Maw by the arms and lifted.

"Stand on the seat, Maw, and look over there! He's going straight to Butch—to beg his pardon. Oh, isn't that the most splendid thing you ever saw?"

Maw, up on the seat, looked in the wrong direction and never knew it, because her eyes were so full of tears she could not have seen Bud anyway.

"Yes, it's grand," she quavered. "Larkie and Bud are good boys—"

"Say, Maw," Lark leaned over her shoulder to shout, "that coon's goin' to spend the rest of his days at the Meddalark and help you cook. Darn his black hide—and Butch too. He ast me fer a job and I turned him down cold.

Lemme past, will yuh, Bonnie? I want to ketch him b'fore he gits outside. My Jonah, about the worst thing can happen a feller is to be accused of somethin' he ain't guilty of. Hey, Butch! Butch! Bud! You 'n' Butch come awn over here! These wimmin has got me penned up here like a pet calf!"

"Moses, what a jam!" quaked Maw, when a dozen persons in her immediate vicinity began milling aimlessly in the aisle. "Larkie, I just hope Palmer gits let out. I don't believe any man on earth would lie like that under oath and all, and if he was tellin' the truth, he ain't no more guilty than I be."

"I don't think he is guilty at all," Marge complained. "I came clear up here to see a man sentenced to be hanged by the neck—oh, where? That handsome fellow over there? Lynched! Was he really? I wonder if someone can introduce him to me. Lark, will you—"

"Oh, Maw," cried Lark into the babel, "we got a new lark to set and chirp on our bough. Butch is goin' to start in quick as we git back."

"I'm real glad," said Maw, grinning vacantly with her teeth comfortably reposing in her pocket. "I wisht, Larkie, you could find somethin' for that poor old Blinker to do. Seems a shame—they say Palmer's bargainin' already t' sell out an' leave the country quick as they let him go—"

"Well," young Bud's voice rose cheerfully above the clamor, "Butch, you and I will have to go swimming first chance we get. How about it?"

"Gosh, let's *all* go," cried Gelle exuberantly.

"Me, I'll take mine in good ole Metropole," Bob pushed up and confided in Gelle's ear. "They say it's a cinch, now, that Palmer'll be cleared. Guess the old coot's got it comin'."

"Well, I'm real glad," Maw repeated. "It would be awful, wouldn't it, to think little Skookum's grandpa was a murderer? I guess they's good in all of us if it only gets a chance."

"Come on, girls—and that means you, too, Maw. It's all over now but the shouting, and I'm too dry to shout. Let's round up Lightfoot, and all go hunt that drug store. What do you say?"

"I say that means you want to get Bonnie out of here," Marge retorted. "I'd rather go with the other boys and Maw. I want to ask Butch a lot of questions, anyway."

"Ask me, little pilgress, why don't you? I could answer more questions a minute—if you asked 'em—than you could ask Butch in a year."

"Oh, all right. I don't think Butch heard me, anyway. Come on, Maw."

At the steps, Bud and Bonnie looked back and saw them coming; smiled and nodded, caught a warning scowl from Gelle and decided they would not wait.

TIMBER-WOLF,
by Jackson Gregory

CHAPTER 1

Big Pine, tiny human outpost set well within the rim of the great southwestern wilderness country, was, like other aloof mountain settlements of its type, a place of infinite and monotonous quiet during most days of most years. Infrequently, however, for one reason or another, and at times seemingly for no reason whatever, came days of excitement. And, as those who knew the place said, when the denizens of Big Pine bestirred themselves into excitement they were never content until they skyrocketed into the seventh heaven of turbulence. The old-timers recalled how, back in '82, a dog fight in front of the Gallup House started a riot; in spite of the dictum that it takes only two dogs to make a fight, the two owners present entered with fine esprit into the thing, and before nightfall men were carrying sawed-off shotguns and some of the oldest and wisest citizens had dug themselves in as for a state of siege.

This latest furore in and about Big Pine, however, had for cause an incident which since time was young has electrified both more and less sedate communities. True, it had begun with a fight; men, not dogs; yet it was what chance spilled from the torn coat pocket of one of them that transmuted slumbrous quiet into pandemonium. It was fitting that the Gallup House, centre of local activities, was the scene of the affair.

A mongrel sort of a man, one Joe Nuñez, known by everybody as Mexicali Joe, came in and demanded corn whiskey and paid for it on the spot. That in itself was interesting; Joe seldom had money. For twenty years he had been content to have his wife support him while he combed the ridges, always prospecting, always begging grub-stakes, always spending the winters telling what he would do, come spring. Tonight, looking tired and dirty, he was triumphant. He spent his silver dollars with a flourish, and an onlooker, laughing, announced that Joe must have stolen his wife's money. Joe resented the accusation with dignity; he knew what he knew; he wagged his head and stared insolently and tossed off his drink in solemn silence. Thereafter he dropped innuendoes while he had his second drink. The man, Barny McCuin, who had badgered him in the first place, carelessly called him a liar. Joe, who had accepted the familiar epithet a thousand times in his life, for once bridled up and spat back. From so small a matter grew the fight.

Onlookers laughed and were amused, taking no serious stock in the fracas because it appeared inevitable that in half a dozen minutes big Barny McCuin would have Mexicali Joe whimpering and apologetic. But it chanced that as Barny flung the smaller man about, the Mexican's coat pocket was torn and from it spilled a handful of raw gold. Men pounced upon the scattered bits of quartz, Barny among them; they caught it up and stared from one another to Joe, who became suddenly quiet and tense and alert. Then a great shout rumbled up:

"*Gold!*"

And that was the one word which set all Big Pine ablaze. Here, on the fringe of a gold-mining country, which the latter years had all but worn out, there had been made that fresh discovery which every man of them always kept somewhere in the bottom of his mind as a possibility for himself.

Gallup, called "Young Gallup," simply because he was the son of "Old Gallup," who had gone to his last rest twenty-five years ago, was a man eminently capable of dealing swiftly with unexpected situations; he did not know the meaning of tact, but he did understand force. This was his house and here his word was law; he broke into the room at the first outcry, took in everything with one flick of his black eyes, and issued his orders.

"Hand that stuff over," he commanded the men who still held bits of the Mexican's specimens. "It belongs to Joe, and no man's going to be robbed here under my nose, Mex or White."

The look which Mexicali Joe shot at his protector had in it far more of suspicion than of gratitude. But his grimy fingers were eager enough in snatching back the pieces of quartz from reluctant palms. Grown sullen, he returned to his corn whiskey, drinking slowly, and holding his tongue. When men asked him the inevitable quick questions he either shrugged impatiently or ignored them altogether. They looked at one another, and an understanding sprang up on the instant between big Barny McCuin and some of the others. Presently Barny went out, followed by the men who had caught his glance. Young Gallup, with eyes narrowing and growing darker, watched them go.

"They'll get you outside, Joe," he said bluntly. "And they'll make you open up for all you know."

Joe shifted uneasily; in his heart he knew himself for a poor fool caught up between the devil, which was Gallup, and the deep sea.

Besides the proprietor and the Mexican there were now but three men left in the room. One of them was Gallup's man, who cooked, did chores, and, when need was, helped with the still and served drinks. At a look from his employer he left the room. Of the others, one was old man Parker, an ancient to be despised because feebleness made of him a negligible quantity in any affair based upon the prowess of physical manhood; the second was a youngster who stood in awe of Gallup and who looked ill at ease as the hotel man stared at him.

"Better beat it, Tim," said Gallup. "And take old Parker along."

"But, look here, Gallup; you ain't got any right…."

"It's my house," said Gallup. "There's going to be no crooked work here and you know it. Joe goes clear. If he wants to talk later on, why, then he can come out and talk with you boys outside. You know you'll find Barny and his friends not so far away."

Tim's self-pride, unimportant as it was, perked up at the realization that Gallup was actually discussing a matter of import with him. He tried to play the man.

"You want to get him all alone!"

Gallup sighed.

"You make me sick," he grunted disgustedly. "Now shut up and clear out. You, too, Parker. It's closing time anyhow."

"I seen, didn't I?" clucked the old man, tapping nervously on the bare floor with his peeled willow staff. "It was gold! Joe's stuck his pick into the mother lode! Ain't I always told you young fools…."

Gallup, patient no longer, caught him by the thin old arm and jerked him to the door, thrusting him out and unheeding the querulous protests. Then he swung about upon the younger man.

"On your way, Tim," he commanded.

There was that in his voice which discouraged argument. For Gallup, in the full power of his strength, a big man and heavy and hard, was suddenly flaming with anger and the two great fists were lifting from his sides. Tim, muttering, hastened after old Parker; behind him the oak door was slammed and the bolt shot into its socket. He broke into a run, seeking Barny McCuin and the others.

Gallup strode straight back to Mexicali Joe, clamping a ponderous hand upon the shoulder which sought futilely to jerk free.

"Spit it out, Joe," he ordered. "Where'd that come from?"

"You let me go! I ain't workin' for you. You ain't my boss. What I got, she's mine! Now I goin' home."

Gallup, still holding him with one hand, probed at him with his eyes, seeking to fathom what powers of determination and stubbornness lay within a mongrel soul. Joe looked frightened; there were beads of sweat on his forehead, stealing downward from under his black matted hair. But there was in his look the glint of desperate defiance…. Gallup called softly:

"Hey, Ricky; come here."

His combination cook and chore man returned through the inner door with an alacrity which must have told his employer that he had never stirred a step from the threshold. He, like the others, was on fire with suddenly stimulated greed.

"Go get Taggart," said Gallup, his eye all the time on Joe. "Slip out the back way and go quiet. He's down at his cabin. I want him here in a hurry."

Ricky, though with obvious reluctance, withdrew. Once out of sight, however, he ran as fast as he could, anxious to be back with no loss of time.

"Taggart?" muttered Joe. "What for? For why you send for him?"

"Why does a man generally send for him?" countered Gallup dryly. "Know who he is, don't you, Joe?"

"Sure, I know! But I ain't done nothin'. I ain't no t'ief. This is mine."

"Thief?" Gallup having repeated the word thoughtfully, said it a second time: "Thief! I hadn't thought of that."

"Let me go," cried Joe. With a sudden fierce jerk he broke free and started to the door.

But Gallup, shaking his head, was at his side like a flash. He thrust the Mexican aside and stood with his heavy square shoulders against the oak panel. Joe, by now trembling with fury, slipped a hand into his shirt. But before the hastening fingers could close about the sheath-knife which Gallup knew well enough they sought, Gallup drew back a heavy fist and struck the Mexican full in the face. Joe went staggering across the room and fell, his battered lips writhing back from his teeth. Again his hand went into his shirt. Gallup ran across the room and stood over him, one heavy boot drawn back threateningly.

"Make one more move like that," he said coolly, "and I'll smash my boot heel in your dirty mouth."

* * * *

Outside, grouped expectantly in the middle of the road, Barny McCuin and his friends, joined by old man Parker and Tim, alternately speculated in quiet voices and watched for the door to open and Joe to come forth. Tim, in his anger and excitement, called them crazy fools; he warned them that Young Gallup, left alone with Joe, would be making some deal with the Mexican and that, if they were only half men they would come along of him and smash the door off and get in on whatever was happening. But Tim was only a boy and talked more than he acted; the others, knowing Young Gallup as they had cause to know him, hesitated to grow violent at his door. Gallup, defending his own property, would just as gladly pour a double-barrel shotgun load of buckshot into them as he would turn up a bottle of bootleg. They were not ready for murder and told Tim to shut up and keep his eye peeled.

But there was not a patient man among them, and tonight was no time for any man's patience. When they had waited as long as they could, perhaps half an hour, they turned back to Gallup's door, Barny leading the way and knocking loudly. In return came Gallup's voice, untroubled and cool.

"Locked up for the night," he said. And then, carelessly: "What do you want, boys?"

McCuin simulated laughter.

"That's a good one, Gal. All we want is a chat with Joe. And…."

"Joe's gone," returned Gallup. He came to the door and opened it, his lamp in hand. "Went about half an hour ago; just after you boys did. Out the back way and on the run!" He laughed. "Guess he's foxy enough to make a circle around you dubs. Oh, come in and look if you think I'm lying to you."

He stepped aside and let them come in. They knew that he was lying and they saw from his eyes that he understood that they were not fools enough to take him at his word. Yet Joe had gone. In that Gallup had told the truth; the lie lay in what he concealed.

"Where did he go?" demanded Tim earnestly.

Gallup jeered at him. "If I knew I'd tell you, wouldn't I, Timmy? Most likely where little boys like you ought to be by now. Meaning in bed, Timmy dear."

In time they went away; by now, drawn close together by a common burning desire, they were resolved into a committee with one objective. Late as it was they searched high and low for Mexicali Joe. They went first to his wretched cabin among the pines at the edge of the settlement; they got his wife out of bed and fired questions at her, receiving only blank looks of wonder; clearly she had not seen Joe and had no inkling of his sudden importance. They went away and in turn looked in at every likely place which Big Pine offered. But they found no sign of Joe. In a town of less than fifty houses he had vanished like one shadow engulfed and blotted out by another. They began to fear that he had fled, frightened, into the mountains.

A dozen men had seen Joe's gold. Before midnight no less than twenty tongues had discussed the one matter of moment. Men cautioned other men against letting too many people know; but such was the electric mood swaying them that early the next morning the news began trickling forth through the country surrounding Big Pine. By late afternoon word had penetrated far up into the mountains and, following the stage road, had gone fifty miles toward the distant railroad. And that same day it leaked out that Mexicali Joe, who had so strangely disappeared, had not fled at all but all the time had been in Big Pine. He had been arrested by Sheriff Taggart and thrown into the town jail, charged with disturbing the peace.

Taggart himself had nothing to say. He kept Joe shut up alone and let no one see him.

CHAPTER 2

A normal census gave Big Pine a population of about one hundred and twenty inhabitants, and the most normal thing which any census does is to exaggerate. But within forty-eight hours after the tearing of Mexicali Joe's coat pocket between nine and twelve hundred people, variously estimated, poured into the settlement. Wood-choppers and timber jacks and lone prospectors hurried down from the mountains; storekeepers and ranchmen came up from far below Rocky Bend and Red Oak; that strange medley of humanity which always rushes first in the wake of gold news filled Big Pine to overflowing, men and even women; all straining to one purpose back of which lay many motives. Spring was verging on summer; nights were cold, but the air was dry; they found rooms where they could, and when they could not they builded great camp-fires and found what comfort they might in the edges of the pine groves. Gallup doubled his prices and then doubled them again, and still his house was full. There were half a dozen empty houses, ancient disreputable shacks long in disuse; these found usurping tenants the first day. There were some few who had had forethought and took the time to bring tents. Almost in an hour a quiet, sleepy little mountain town was metamorphosed into a noisy, clamorous and sleepless mining camp.

Among the first to arrive was a young man named Deveril. Very tall and good-looking and gay and slender he was, making himself look taller by the boots he wore and the way he pinched his soft hat into a peak. Babe Deveril he was called by those who knew him, saving one only, who called him Baby Devil and jeered at him with a pair of mocking eyes.

Deveril had been in Big Pine before, though not for some years. Also he had seen his share of mining camps through Arizona and New Mexico and Nevada, and knew something of congested conditions and the hardships which accompanied the short-sighted. Before his arrival was ten minutes old, he had cast about him for a shelter. Already the Gallup House was full, but not yet had the disused, tumbled-down shacks been thought of. He found a dilapidated building which once, long ago, had been a log cabin; it stood in the pines set well back from the place of Mexicali Joe; it had a fireplace. Deveril preempted it coolly, neither knowing nor caring who the owner might be; he brought his slim bed-roll here, followed it up with frying-pan, bacon, and coffee-pot and considered himself established. Further, being just now in funds and always yielding to the more fastidious impulses at moments when fortune was kind, he secured a serving-maid. Maria, the dusky daughter of Mexicali Joe, consented gladly to come in and cook and make the bed and keep things tidy. He gave her a couple of silver dollars and made her a bow to bind the bargain, tossing in for fair measure a flashing smile which left the half-breed girl thrilling and sighing. Thereafter, bending his mind to the main issue, he sought to find out for himself how much of fact underlay the glittering rumors which had been pouring forth from Big Pine like rays from the sun.

This heterogeneous mass of humanity occupying Big Pine had broken up into numerous small groups, after the fashion of men who are so prone to break large units down into smaller ones. Cupidity, jealousy, and suspicion flaunted their banners on all hands; men watched one another like so many thieves. The old inhabitants went about bristling, resenting the presence of these outsiders who were rushing in to steal the golden secret. Among themselves they were divided into two antagonistic factions; there was the Gallup crowd, including Gallup and Sheriff Taggart and the men who did their bidding; and there were those who had heard Barny McCuin's tale and who were out to block the game of Gallup and Taggart, or know the reason why.

Babe Deveril, sauntering here and there, identified himself with no group; it was his preference always to hunt singly. But he went everywhere, his mind and ears and eyes co-ordinating in the work he set them. He listened to rumors and sifted them and went on to newer and always contradictory rumors. It was said that Mexicali Joe had been killed, his body found in a ravine three miles from town; that Gallup had spirited him off last night into the mountains; that Joe had made his strike in the old and long-deserted mining camp of Timkin's Bar; that his specimens had come from Lost Woman's Gulch; that Joe had never stirred a mile from Big Pine in his latter prospecting, and that, therefore, at any moment any one of the thousand gold seekers might stumble upon his prospect hole. It was said that Joe's pay-dirt would run twenty dollars to the ton, and while this was being advanced as though by one who knew all about it, another man was saying that it would run a thousand dollars. Deveril, when he had heard a score of empty though colorful tales, turned at last to the Gallup House; Gallup and Taggart knew all that was to be known, and, although they had the trick of the shut mouth and steady eye, there was always the chance of a sign to be read by the watchful.

He came upon Gallup himself standing in his doorway, looking out thoughtfully upon the road jammed tight with restless men.

"Hello, Gallup," he said.

Gallup regarded him briefly; again his gaze flicked away.

"Don't remember me, eh?" queried Deveril lightly.

"No," said Gallup, curt in his preoccupation. "I don't."

"Must have something disturbing on your mind," suggested Deveril as genially as though Gallup's attitude had been exactly opposite what it was. "Haven't looked in on you for half a dozen years, but you ought to remember." Gallup's eyes came back slowly, a frown in them, and the other concluded: "Known as Deveril…Babe Deveril, formerly of Cherokee…."

Gallup showed a quick, unmistakable sign of interest and Deveril laughed. But Gallup's frown darkened and there came a sudden compression to his lips.

"I got you, Kid," he said sharply. "You said it: There is a thing or two on my mind and I've got no time for gab. Just the same, take this from me: A certain Bruce Standing has been sent word the town can get along without him showing his face; and maybe, being his cousin, you'll trail your luck along with him."

"So you and Bruce Standing are still playing the nice little parlor game of slap-the-wrist, are you?" Deveril jeered at him. But, still highly good-humored, he went on: "He's no cousin of mine, Gallup. You've got the family tree all mussed up. What fault is it of mine if a thousand years ago Bruce Standing and I had the same murdering old pirate for ancestor? At that, Standing descended from him in the straight line and I am somewhat less directly related."

Gallup snorted.

"None of Standing's breed is wanted in my place," he said emphatically.

Deveril, though his eyes twinkled, appeared to be musing.

"So you sent him word to stay away? Didn't you know that he'd come, red-hot and raging, as soon as he got your message? Oh, well, you and my crazy kinsman fight it out to your liking; it would be a great thing for the community if you'd both do a clean job, cutting each other's throats.…. By the way, where does Taggart fit in? How does he work it to be hand in glove with both of you at the same time?"

"You heard what I said just now?"

"I did. Say, Gallup, where's Mexicali Joe? I've got some business with him."

Gallup, brooding, appeared not to have heard. Then, making no answer, he turned and went back into his house and into the big main room, where a crowd of men had foregathered. Deveril, his hat far back, his dark eyes keen and bright, followed him, almost at his heels. Gallup saw him out of the tail of his eye but for once gulped down his first hot impulse; his hands were full as things were and there were large stakes to play for, with nothing to be gained just now by a rough-and-tumble fist fight with a man who was obviously highly capable of taking care of himself. So he pretended to let Deveril's entrance go unnoted and thereafter ignored him.

For the first time in many days there were no drinks being served in Gallup's House. With so many strangers in town, one did not know how many federal agents might be snooping about. And, again, this was no time for the main issue to become befogged with side issues; Gallup did not want any unnecessary ruction on his hands. Nevertheless some of the men drank now and then, but from pocket flasks which they had brought in with them; flasks which for the most part came originally from Gallup's stock but which had been sold on the street by Gallup's man Ricky. The room was thick with heavy tobacco smoke; most of the men remained strangely quiet, watching Gallup or Barny McCuin, who glowered in a corner, or the sheriff who came and went among them. Deveril spent not more than ten minutes here; once more he returned to the street and to his passing from knot to knot of men.

"I'll bet a hat Gallup was lying about that warning to my mad kinsman," he told himself thoughtfully. "I don't believe he's man enough to get rough with Bruce Standing."

It was almost at the moment that Deveril came out of Gallup's place that the first shock of genuine news burst along the crowded road; Mexicali Joe had been located. He was in the stone jail, not five hundred yards from the thickest of his seekers, and had been there since last night, locked up by Taggart! The crowd split asunder as cleanly as though some gigantic axe had cloven its way between the two fragments; one group at full tilt ran to the jail, to prove to their own senses that here at last was a word of truth; the other streamed down to the Gallup House, seeking Taggart and an explanation. With the latter went Babe Deveril, who meant to keep his eye on Taggart and Gallup.

There were three steps leading up to Gallup's side door through which at last came Taggart, when the crowd clamored for him. He stood on the top step, looking stolidly at the faces confronting him. He was a big man, massive of physique, hard-eyed, strong-willed; he had been sheriff for a dozen years and after long office as the chief representative of the law bore in his look the stamp of that unquestioned authority which is the unmistakable brand of the mountain sheriff. He had looked straight into the eyes of many men in many moods and his own glance never wavered. Never a great talker, he stood now a moment in silence, tugging slowly at his heavy black mustache.

"Mexicali is my man right now," he said at last. "I got him in jail."

That was all. There was no belligerence in his tone; his look remained untroubled. Babe Deveril, beginning to understand something of what had happened and casting his own swift horoscope of the likely future, wondered to what extent it was in the cards that Jim Taggart should stand in his way. There was big game in the wind, or men like Gallup and Taggart, who were always big-game men, would not be taking things upon their shoulders thus. And today Jim Taggart was at his best; he stood as solid and unmoved as a rock, with never a flick of the eyelid, as he made his quiet announcement and awaited the breaking of any storm which his words might evoke.

There was a short lull while men murmured among themselves, and yet, digesting Taggart's statement, impressed by his manner, hesitated to speak the thought which was forming in dozens of brains simultaneously. Presently, however, a man at the far edge of the crowd shouted:

"What's he arrested for, Taggart? What did he do?"

Before the man had gotten his ten words out, the sheriff's keen eyes found him where his lesser form was half hidden by the bigger men in front of him.

"I hear you, Bill Cary," he said quietly. "And the only reason I'm answering a regular none-of-your-business question is that all of you other boys that have stampeded in here on a wild say-so will be worrying your heads off until you know what's what. I pulled Joe on two counts: First for disturbing the peace."

An uproar of laughter boomed out at that and even Jim Taggart smiled. But he went on evenly:

"Of course that was a blind until I got the goods on the second count. And I only got that a few minutes ago. This ain't any trial, exactly, and still I guess it will save trouble if you know all about it. So I'll let Cliff Shipton step up and testify."

Suddenly he stepped aside and a tall, hawk-faced man who had been holding his place at Gallup's side, just behind Taggart's massive bulk, stepped forward. Men craned their necks and crowded closer; nearly all of them knew Cliff Shipton. He was a Gallup man and always had been a Gallup man; for the last two years he had been in charge of a profitless "gold-mine" which Gallup pretended to operate at the head of the Lost Woman's Gulch; a property which, it was generally conceded in and about Big Pine, was merely the proverbial hole in the ground intended for sale to a fool.

"Last week, gents," said Shipton in his easy style, "we hit it rich out at the Gallup Bonanza. Pocket or ledge, we're not saying which right now. But we got the stuff. We been keeping it quiet until we got good and ready to spring something. I had the choice specimens in a box in my shack. That Mexican's been prowling around; I couldn't be sure until I'd glimpsed the specimens, but I just looked 'em over. That's the story; Mexicali, being half drunk and stupid generally, made his haul out of my specimen box."

As the first slow murmur, gathering volume, began, Jim Taggart threw up his hand and shouted:

"Now, men, go slow! I've seen a pack of gents before now get all het-up because they was sore and disappointed. And I can read the eye-signs! But pull off and think things over before you make a lot of howling fools out of yourselves. If you want me any time.... Well, I'll be right on hand!"

He stepped back swiftly, in through the open door, and it closed after him.

For a little while the men remained uncertain. Jim Taggart represented the law; further, he was no man at any time to trifle with. He had offered them an explanation and the worst of it was that it might be the truth. Discussions began on every hand; those who believed were in the minority and lost voice as the other voices, becoming heated, grew louder. Babe Deveril was turning away when a man caught at his sleeve.

"You know those men, Taggart and Gallup and the rest. What do you make of it? What had we ought to do?"

Deveril shook the man off.

"Go slow until you know what you're doing," he admonished curtly. "Then go like hell."

He skirted the crowd and went up to his cabin to be alone and do a bit of thinking on his own part.

CHAPTER 3

There was a crowd of men, tight-jammed, about the little square stone jail as Deveril made his way toward his cabin. Every man of them was striving for a glance through the barred slit of a window behind which Mexicali Joe glared out at them. In the throng Deveril marked a man who wore his deputy-sheriff's badge thrust prominently into notice and who carried a rifle across the hollow of his arm. Deveril shrugged and went on.

"In jail or out, the Mex is going to keep a shut mouth," he meditated. "He'll never spill a word now, unless Taggart gets a chance to give him a rough-and-ready third degree. And Taggart will get no such chance tonight."

Through the dim dusk gathering among the pines he came to the cabin. A light winked at him through the open door; Maria, Joe's daughter, was getting his supper. Well, he was ready for it; blow hot, blow cold, a man must eat.

"Hello, Señorita," he greeted her from the threshold. "How does it feel to be the one and only daughter of the most distinguished gentleman in town?"

Maria did not understand him, but her white teeth flashed and her large southern eyes were warm and friendly.

"They found your papa," he told her. "He's in jail."

"*Seguro*," responded Maria, unmoved. "That is nothing for him."

Deveril laughed and went to wash at the bucket of water which the girl had placed on a bench in the corner. Maria finished setting his table with the few articles at hand, putting a black pot of red beans in the place of honor before his plate. As he returned from washing and smoothing his hair down, he noted the plate itself; a plain, cracked affair of heavy crockery with a faded design in red roses. Plainly, Maria had raided her mother's home for that. She was looking at him for his approval and received it. At the moment she had both hands occupied and he stooped forward and kissed her. It was lightly and carelessly done; a gay salute to the girl's warm smouldering beauty. For beauty of its kind she did have, that of the young half-bred animal.

She gasped; her face, whether through indignation or pleasure, went a dark burning red. Deveril laughed softly and sat down upon the box which she had drawn up for his chair.

It was only then that he saw that he had a visitor. His eyebrows shot upward as he wondered. Another girl or young woman; in that light, as she stood just outside his door, nothing very definite could be made of her.

"Could I have a word with you, Mr. Deveril?"

He came to his feet almost at the first word, quick and lithe and graceful. Always was Babe Deveril at his best when it was a question of a lady. The voice accosting him was clear and cool and musically modulated. He tried to make out her face, but was baffled by the shadow cast by her wide hat. She was clad in a neat dark outing suit and wore serviceable walking boots; she was slim and trim and young and confident. Beyond that the dusk made a mystery of her.

"A thousand!" he returned in answer. "Won't you come in?"

"It is very pleasant outside. May I sit on your door-step?"

"Lord love you," he assured her, "you may do anything on earth that pleases you.... Maria, my dear, you may run home to your mama; I have affairs of state. And I'll be delighted to see you again at breakfast time."

Maria put down her things and fled. Again Deveril laughed softly.

"It was no tender scene that you interrupted," he told his visitor. "I was merely seeking expression in a bit of rudimentary human language of my gratitude for the loan of a cracked plate! Look at it!" He held it aloft.

"A gratitude which obviously springs from the heart," she returned as lightly as he had spoken.

She sat down on the door-step. He came toward her, meaning to have a better look at her.

"But you were just beginning your supper," she objected. "Please go on with it while it is hot. Otherwise I shall most certainly leave without talking with you as I had wished."

"But you? There is plenty for both of us."

She shook her head emphatically.

"No, thank you. It's very kind, but I have eaten."

"Then I eat, though it's putting a hungry man at an unfair advantage to watch him at such a disgusting pastime." He poured himself a cup of coffee, all the while trying to make out her features. He knew already that she was pretty; one sensed a thing like that. But just how pretty, that even Babe Deveril could not decide as long as the light was no better and she hid in the shadows of her provoking hat. "And now, how may I be of service?"

Thus of the two she was the first to be given the opportunity of clear observation. There were two candles stuck in their own grease on the rough table, and between them his face looking out toward her was unshadowed. A face gay and insouciant, dark and clean-cut, the face of devil-may-care youth. It struck her that there was an evidence of the man's character in the fact that, though she had caught him in the act of kissing his maid of all work, he was not in the least perturbed. She thought that it would be easy to like this man; she was not sure that she could ever trust him.

"I am Lynette Brooke," she said in a moment. "And I thought it possible that, if you cared to do so, you might answer a question for me."

"If I may be of assistance to you," he told her, cordially, watching her narrowly, "you have but to let me know."

"Thank you." He had inclined his head in acknowledgment of her introduction and now her head tipped slightly toward him. "My question has to do, naturally, with the one matter of general interest in Big Pine today. You see, I have heard of you; I know that you know some of the men here...Sheriff Taggart and Mr. Gallup, for example. And...I once had the pleasure of meeting you, Mr. Deveril. Small excuse for troubling you, I know, but when one is in earnest...."

"I'll tell you something!" said Deveril quickly.

"Yes?"

"I'd give a whole lot for a good square look at you! I am no hand for names; and I haven't been able to make out your face."

"A whole lot?" It was a fair guess that she was smiling. "Well, then, it's a bargain. You give me an answer to a question!"

"Done! Any question!"

With a sudden gesture her two hands went up to her hat. At the same moment she jumped to her feet and came three steps into his cabin. As she brought the hat down to her side and turned toward him, the candle-light streamed across her face and Babe Deveril sat back on his box and with a sudden lighting up of his eyes collected his share of the obligation by letting his admiring glance rove across her disclosed features. Pretty; yes, far and away more than pretty. He was startled by an unexpected, soft loveliness; an alluring, seductive charm of line and expression. Just now it was her mood to smile at him; and she was one of those rare girls whose smile is sheer tenderness. He marked the curl in her soft brown hair; the sparkle in her big gray eyes; the curve of the lips; in another moment the red mouth would be laughing at him. She held herself erect under his frank inspection; her chin was up; her eyes did not waver; she challenged him with her glance to look his fill and shape his judgment of her.

"I think you are mistaken on one point," he told her quickly. "I never saw you before, for I would not have forgotten."

"The obvious remark nicely made," she laughed at him.

He frowned.

"Through no fault of mine. You are welcome to know that I have a memory for pretty girls. And that you are absolutely the prettiest girl I ever saw."

"Thank you," she mocked him. She put her hat on again and went back to the door-step. "Nevertheless, it is true that we have met before. Of course," she amended hastily, "I am not going to claim any obligation on either side because of that. But it suggested that I should come to you now instead of taking my chances with utter strangers."

"If you care to do me a very great favor," said Deveril, "you will tell me when you think you and I met."

"Certainly. I have no desire to make a mystery of so common an occurrence. Last May you were in Carson?"

"Yes."

"There was a dance. You went with Mildred Darrel. When you called for her she was out on the porch. Another girl was with her and you were introduced."

"After all, I was right!" he cried triumphantly. "You were in the shadows that the vines threw all over the porch. I don't believe I even heard your name. Most positively I did not catch a glimpse of your face."

She dismissed the subject with indifference.

"At least I have made my explanation. And now may I ask my question?" And, when he nodded: "Are they telling the truth when they say that Mexicali Joe stole his gold from Mr. Gallup's mine?"

He had expected something like that; all along he had felt that this girl with the bright daring eyes and that eager confident carriage was in Big Pine because she, equally with himself, was concerned with the one occurrence which for the moment made the community a place of interest to such as found no lure in the humdrum.

"Of course, you know that anything I could say in answer would be but one man's opinion?"

"Yes. But knowing these men, your opinion would be of value to me."

"Well, then, I'd gamble my boots that they're lying. And I can advance no reasons whatever for my belief. But there's your question answered."

"As I thought that it would be. I was sure of it before I came here. You make me doubly sure."

He, for the moment, was more interested in her than in Mexicali Joe and his gold.

"You don't belong up here in the mountains? You're a long way from your stamping-ground, aren't you?"

"Of course. I happened to be down in Rocky Bend when the news came and I caught the first stage up."

He tried to make her out. She did not look the type of woman who followed in the wake of such news, adventuring. But then you could never tell what a woman was inside by the outer peach-and-cream softness of her, as Babe Deveril very well understood.

She appeared to be plunged deep into revery. Perhaps there was something of weariness in the droop of her shoulders; if she had come on the early stage, she might have had a hard day of it altogether....

"Were you able to get a room at the Gallup House?" he asked.

"Yes. I was one of the first, you know. As to how long I can keep my room, I can't tell. Mr. Gallup has doubled his prices and is likely to double them again."

"He's that sort," conceded Deveril. "He plays a big game and all the time has a shrewd eye for the little bets. By the way, do you feel entirely comfortable there?"

Her eyes drifted to a meeting with his.

"What do you mean?"

"There's as tough a crowd there and spread all over town as I ever saw. Are you alone?"

"Yes. Quite."

"You don't mean to say that you, a young girl and not overused to hardship, from the look of you, are up here to mix into such a scrimmage as may be pulled off? To match your wits and your grit and your endurance against the kind of men who go hell-raising into a new gold strike?"

She tilted back her head against the door-jamb and looked up, straight into his eyes. Thus he saw her chin brought forward prominently. It was delicately turned and joined, softly curving, a full feminine throat; and yet it was a chin which bespoke character and stubbornness.

"When men go rushing after gold," she said quietly, "more likely than not they go with empty pockets if not empty stomachs. There is always a chance, in a new mining-camp, for one who has a little money. A chance to stake a miner, going shares; and always, of course, the chance to stake one's own claim."

"But you…. What do you know of such things?"

"Not much, first-hand, perhaps. But it's in the blood!… You look a very young man, Mr. Deveril, but you and I know that looks are not everything; and it is quite possible that you are old enough to have heard of Olymphe Labelle?"

"Why," he exclaimed, "I have seen her. I was only a boy; it was twenty years ago. That was down at Horseshoe; why, bless your soul, I fell head over heels in love with her! I can tell you how she dressed and how she looked. Big blue eyes; golden hair; a pink dress; a great big picture-hat, with ribbons. I was only eight or nine years old, but forget? Never!"

"My father married her down in Horseshoe! That was the first time he ever saw her and he didn't let her get away! Dick Brooke; maybe you have heard of him, too? If so you won't ask why the daughter of Olymphe Labelle and Dick Brooke has it in her veins to mingle with the first of the crowd when there's word of a new strike!"

There was scarcely a community in all Arizona or New Mexico, certainly none within the broad scope of the great southwestern plateau country, which had not in its time, a generation ago, paid tribute to the gaiety and grace and beauty of Olymphe Labelle. She danced for them; she sang; she went triumphantly from one mining town or lumber-camp to another and men went mad over her. They packed the houses in which she appeared; they spent their money generously to see her, and night after night, captivated, they tossed to the stage under her pretty high-heeled feet both raw and minted gold. Olymphe was to this country what Lotta was to the camps of California in an earlier day. Then young Dick Brooke, a stalwart and hot-blooded young miner, saw her and that was the end of Olymphe's dancing career. They were married within ten days. And from this union was sprung the superb young creature now sitting upon an adventurer's door-step and looking straight up into his eyes.

"You see, it is only the thing to be expected, after all, that I should follow the gleam!"

She, like himself, was young and eager and unafraid and adventuresome; and within her pulsing arteries was that pioneer blood which, trickling down through the generations is ever prone to set recklessness seething.

* * * *

There was a man coming up through the pines on horseback. In the gloom all detail was wanting. But obviously he meant to come straight on to the cabin. Deveril, seeing this intent, stepped by the girl and a couple of paces forward. The man, sitting in a strange, sideways fashion in the saddle, drew rein and peered at him.

"Name of Deveril? Babe Deveril?"

"Right, friend. What's your trouble?"

"Offering to shake hands, to begin with. I'm Winch; Billy Winch. You and me know each other."

He leaned outward from the saddle, putting out his hand. But Deveril ignored it, saying coolly:

"Why should I shake hands with you? You and I are not friends that I know of!"

Billy Winch sighed, and used his hand to remove his hat and then rumple his bristly hair. Then he laughed softly. His horse, restless and fiery and well-fed, whirled, and for the first time Lynette Brooke made out the reason for that strange, lopsided attitude in the saddle; the man, a little, weazened fellow, had lost his right leg above the knee and managed a sure seat only by throwing his weight upon his left stirrup and thus maintaining his balance.

"Well," said Winch good-naturedly, "*he* said to start off by shaking hands. Just to show as I *was* friendly."

"*He?*" repeated Deveril. "You mean Bruce Standing?"

"Sure. Of course. When I just say *he* I mean *him*."

The girl sitting in the shadows smiled. Deveril, however, whose profile she could watch, appeared to have no good humor left to spend upon his caller. She marked how his voice hardened and how he bit off his words curtly.

"I have no business with either Bruce Standing or with you."

"Well," said Winch cheerfully, "here's the message: You're to meet him in half an hour or so at the Gallup House."

For a moment Deveril was silent; then the girl heard his barely audible muttering and knew that under his breath he was roundly cursing the man who sent him a message like that. In another instant he flared out hotly, forgetful of her or ignoring her:

"You go tell your Bruce Standing that I said that he is a land hog and a thief and a damn' fool, all rolled in one; and that I'll meet him nowhere this side of hell."

Billy Winch chuckled as at the rarest of all jests.

"I got a picture of *me* going to *him* with a mouthful like that! On the low-down level, Deveril, he means to be friendly, I think...."

"Do your infernal thinking somewhere else," snapped Deveril angrily. "Clear out or I'll throw you out!"

"I told him most likely you'd be sassy, so he won't be disappointed, I guess. Well, I'm travelling, so you don't have to mess your place all up throwing me off!" He was still chuckling good-naturedly as he swung his horse about with a light touch of the reins. Over his shoulder he called back: "He said it was important and he'd see you at Gallup's inside the hour!" The voice was taunting; Billy Winch threw his weight into his one stirrup, and even the attitude, though made necessary through his physical handicap, was vaguely irritating, so carelessly nonchalant did it appear. His horse bolted like a shot as he gave the signal and in a moment bore him out of sight among the shadows under the pines. Babe Deveril, hands on hips, stood staring after him. Then he swung about and came back to the cabin, and the girl on his door-step, seeing his face clearly in the candle-light streaming forth, caught her breath sharply at the outward sign she glimpsed of the rage burning high and hot in his breast.

"I'm of half a mind to meet him after all and break his confounded neck!" he cried out, a passionate tremor in his voice.

All along he had intrigued her, with his handsome face and devil-may-care air and light gracefulness; she estimated coolly that if, as he had said of himself, he had a memory for pretty girls it was something more than likely that more than one pretty girl had carried in her heart the memory of him. Now, suddenly, his good looks were sinister; his gaiety was so utterly gone that it was next door to impossible to imagine that he could ever be inconsequentially gay. The innate evil in the man stood up naked and ugly. And all because some man, a certain Bruce Standing, had sent a message commanding a meeting at the Gallup House.

It was not exactly the thing to do to put her question, but interest, mounting above mere curiosity, piqued her, and, certain of an answer in his present mood, she offered innocently:

"It seems to me I have heard the name Bruce Standing. Just who is he?"

Deveril glared at her and for a brief fragment of a second she was afraid of him; it was as though, by the mere mention of the name, she drew on herself something of the hatred he must have felt for this man Standing.

"You heard me read his title clear enough to his one-legged dog Winch," he told her harshly. "He is a man who came into this country with nothing a dozen years ago and who now rolls in the fat of his ill-gotten gains. He's a land hog who has robbed right and left and who has with him the devil's luck. He owns thousands of acres of land out yonder." A wide sweep of his arm indicated the endlessly rolling wilderness land, sombre ridges and ebony canyons, rising into stony barren crests here, thick timbered yonder where they slumbered under the first stars. "He operates mines; he gambles in gold and copper and lumber…and life, curse him! And in human souls, his own with the rest. He runs half a dozen lumber-camps and has a thousand of the toughest men in the world working for him at one place and another. Men hate him for what he is, a cold-blooded highwayman. They have sent him a warning not to show his face in Big Pine, and being of the devil's spawn he sends me word to meet him at Gallup's! That's his way and his nerve and his colossal conceit. May hell take him!"

"And," suggested the girl, watchful of him as she ventured to probe at his emotions, "on top of all of this…your cousin?"

"*No!*" He shouted the word at her angrily. "No cousin, thank God. Not so closely related as that. A kinsman of a sort, yes; but if you go back far enough to dig out the roots of things, we are all kinsmen since Adam. I claim no relationship with Bruce Standing."

"I should like to meet this wicked kinsman of yours," she said, as though thoughtful and in earnest.

"And," she added, "warned against coming into Big Pine, he will still come openly?"

"At least," he grunted back at her, "there is one thing I have never denied him; he's no coward. No Gallup was ever conceived who can tell him where to head in and get away with it. Of course he will come and in the wide open and on the run."

She rose to go.

"I wish you all success in your dealings with your bold, bad kinsman. And I do thank you for your frank answer to my question. And now…good night."

"I'll walk with you…if you will let me?"

"Thank you, but…."

They heard the clippety-clop of horses' hoofs, running. Not one horse this time, but three, bearing their riders like so many indistinguishable dark blurs through the night, sweeping on to the cabin. A man, one of the riders, was laughing, and Lynette Brooke knew that already here was Billy Winch returning. Babe Deveril, too, must have recognized the voice, for he jerked his head up and stiffened where he stood, oblivious of the fact that she had broken off with an objecting "but," conscious only of a hated man's impertinence.

Those three were expert riders, men who lived in the saddle. They and their horses seemed moulded centaurs for certainty and the grace of the habitual horseman. They came on at such a break-neck speed and so close that the girl whipped back, thinking that they would run her and her companion down. Then, with that quick light pluck at the reins, they brought their horses down from a mad run to a trembling standstill.

"He said you was to meet him…*about now!*"

That was Billy Winch, lopsided and cock-sure in the saddle, the chosen messenger of his impudent, reckless chief.

Winch flung out his arm. In the dark they could have made nothing of the gesture had it not been for the sudden sibilant hiss of the rope, swung by an iron wrist, cutting through the air. The noose fell with absolute exactness; Winch was not ten steps away and the rope thrown so unerringly settled about Babe Deveril's shoulders and with a quick jerk grew so tight that it cut into the flesh. On the instant the two men with Winch left their saddles and struck earth, both on the run forward. And, while Lynette Brooke thought with horror to see sudden death dealt, they threw themselves upon the man already fighting against the imprisonment of thirty feet of hemp.

She had never seen men battle as now these three battled while Billy Winch sitting back in his saddle with his rope drawn tight, watched and laughed and cried out in broken phrases expressing his satisfaction with the situation. Babe Deveril, roped as he was, gave her such proof of prowess as to make her admiration for the physical perfection of him leap high. She, too, cried out brokenly; she wanted to see him win against these unfair odds. But the men clung on and Billy Winch sat laughing and tautening his rope; blows and curses and throaty growls, the whole thing lasted not half a minute. Babe Deveril was down, mastered by three men.

"Well?" she heard him pant furiously. "What now? Murder or only robbery again?"

"Again? Robbery?" That was Winch's untroubled voice, always gay. "When was the other time, pardner?"

"He robbed me once of three thousand dollars. Now what?"

"Now," said Winch coolly, loosening his rope an inch or two but still on guard, "it's only what I said before: You are to meet him at the Gallup House, and I'm responsible for your coming. So we're taking you."

Deveril lay very still, two brawny men upon him. When he made no immediate reply Winch waited patiently and knew, as the girl knew, that a man must be given a moment in such circumstances to collect his wits. Deveril's panting gradually gave over to more quiet breathing; he lay flat on his back and saw the two heads bending over his own and, beyond them, the stars. He started once to speak, but clamped his lips tight. Still, in high tolerant patience, Billy Winch waited upon him while Lynette Brooke, trembling from head to foot with excitement, waited in burning impatience.

"You got me, boys."

She could scarcely recognize Deveril's voice; at first she thought that it was one of the other men speaking.

"That's sensible." That was Billy Winch. Again he loosened his rope.

"I guess," Deveril went on quietly, "that the three of you, jumping me like that, regular Standing sneak-style, can lead me down to Gallup's. Or, if you care to let me up, I'll save you the trouble, and will go without your help."

"That's your promise?" queried Winch.

"Yes...damn you."

"That's fair. Let him go, boys."

The two men holding him down, got to their feet and went back to their horses as if, their bit of work done, they had lost all interest, as perhaps they had. Deveril got to his feet and cast the rope off. Winch drew it in, coiled it, and tied it at his saddle strings.

"Most any time now," he said casually. "He's on his way and due in a dozen minutes. All you got to do is listen for him!"

Deveril stood, both arms stiffening at his sides, his head lifted high, looking straight at Winch.

"Some fine day," he said with low-toned quiet anger, "I'll get you or I'll get him. And it will be a great day!"

"It sure will, Kid," laughed Winch. "*Adios*, and all best wishes."

The three riders, all seated by now, sped away, their horses kicking up the fine dust fragrant with fallen pine-needles. Deveril remained, rigid and angry, looking after them.

"You don't know," he said heavily, as the pounding hoof beats dwindled and the scurrying blurs of figures faded, "you don't know and can't guess...."

And when he remained where he was, stiff, hands clinched at his sides and face lifted to the stars, she thought that for an instant it was given her to glimpse for the first time in her life something of the realities working in a man's very soul. Almost she could see the hot tears in his angry eyes.

She was very deeply moved. Clearly here was no concern of hers; these men, all of them including Deveril, were strangers to her and their loves and hates had nothing to do with Lynette Brooke. But none the less that current of men's lives ran so strong and swift that she felt as though she were being actually and physically drawn into it. Nor, though her eyes did not once leave the rigid figure of Deveril, did her thoughts concern themselves exclusively with him. She felt a sudden strange and burning interest in that other man whom she had never seen but of whose wild nature she had heard. She resented the work of Bruce Standing, done for him by his emissaries; she felt that she, no less than Babe Deveril, could hate a man like that. And yet already there had sprung up within her a strong desire to see him for herself.

"How can it be," she wondered, "that if he is the lawbreaker you call him, thief and worse, men allow him to go on his way?"

He looked at her curiously. Then he laughed his short angry laugh.

"He's a man for you to look into, girl with the daring eyes! A cruel, merciless devil if half the tales are true and, to top off his madness, a man who has not hate but an abiding contempt for all your gentle sex. But you wonder why men let him roam free? In the first place, haven't I told you that he rolls in wealth? That's one thing. Another is his cursed craft. You wonder why I say in one breath that he stole three thousand dollars from me and then merely growl that he remains outside jail?"

"I don't understand it, of course."

"Here you go, then: Half a dozen years ago I held that Bruce Standing and I were friends. He sent me word to come up here into his wilderness; I was to bring whatever money I could raise and there was the chance to double it. I came. When I met him, twenty miles off over yonder in a cabin where he lived like a solitary old bear, we talked things out. With all of his big ventures he was on the edge of bankruptcy. He was grabbing money in both hands from any source and every source. He wanted my three thousand to throw in with the rest, the damned selfish hog that he was and is. I laughed at him and you could have heard him growl a mile. We slept that night in his cabin. In the middle of the night in the pitch black dark, I felt a man on top of me in my bunk, his hands at my throat. I got a tap over the head with something; when I woke up my money belt was gone and it was morning and there was Bruce Standing, singing and grinning and getting breakfast and asking me if I had had bad dreams."

"But...."

"The law? When he wouldn't either admit or deny? When he just laughed and said, 'Where in this country, *my country*, will you get a jury to convict me?' And where, by the same token, was any money left in my pockets to do legal battle with a man intrenched as he is in his old mountains?"

"And he goes on prospering?"

"I tell you he was hanging on the rim of nowhere, broke. And he used my three thousand and God knows what other stolen funds, and now again he is the one power across a hundred miles up here!"

There was one other thing she meant to ask. Billy Winch had said just now that Standing was on his way; that all they had to do was *listen* for him. She supposed that he had meant the clatter of a running horse's hoofs; and yet something in Winch's tone implied something else. No doubt Deveril understood; she was parting her lips to ask when, across the fields of the silent night, Bruce Standing himself answered her. A sudden thrill shot through her blood.

As she was to learn later, there were many wonderful things about Bruce Standing. Among them were his reckless impudence and his glorious voice. Now, before ever she saw the man, she heard him singing, somewhere far out, under the stars, alone with his wilderness, sending far ahead of him into Big Pine the word of his coming. A coming which was in defiance of the order which had gone forth and which, with his superb assurance, he was ignoring. It was a voice as sweet and clear and true, for the high notes and the low notes alike, as a silver trumpet. She stopped breathing to listen. She felt her heart leap and quicken; a tingling quivered along her nerves. Never had she heard singing like that, wild, free, a voice to haunt and linger echoing in the memory.

And then, all of a sudden, she was set shivering. For the voice had done with the song and, at the end, with a great unexpected upgathering of sound was poured forth into a long-drawn-out call that was like nothing on earth save the howling of a wolf. The night call throbbed and billowed across the disturbed silences and all of a sudden was gone and the night was again hushed and still.

"There you have one of the two good reasons why men call him Timber-Wolf," said Deveril with a grunt.

* * * *

She scarcely heard. Somewhere, deep down within her, that golden out-pouring, that rush of fierceness at the end, echoed and lived on.

CHAPTER 4

Bruce Standing—Timber-Wolf, as he exulted in being called—was a man of few friends and many enemies. In and about Big Pine men disliked him wholeheartedly; many hated him so that they would have been glad to know that he was dead. And this was chiefly because he jeered at them and over-rode them; because at every opportunity, going out of his way to make opportunity more often than not, he thrust them aside and trod his unobstructed path through and over them, setting his heel upon many; because he spat upon their laws and made his own. And he, in his turn, held them in high contempt simply because always they stood aside for him. Those few who did not hate him were the handful of hard men whom, in the working out of his wide, overweening ambitions, he had drawn to him like so many feudal henchmen; they were, in their lesser degrees, of his stamp; they belonged in their hearts to an older day and a wider frontier; there were scores taking his pay whose blood ran hot and lawless.

So tonight he came riding down the winding trail from his mountains, singing. Thus he shot his spirit across the miles ahead of him, to invade Big Pine before his coming, to taunt before he brought his hard eyes to mock at them. He had received his word and his warning, and made his retort in the one way possible to him.

The road in front of the Gallup House, leading on to the pines and the aloof jail where Mexicali Joe glared out, was thronged. Half a dozen bonfires had been started, and in the ruddy light men stirred restlessly. Their talk was becoming purposeful; they gathered in knots about men who were showing impatient signs of initiative; they had murmured and were looking this way and that, over their shoulders, shifting their feet as they gave increasingly free expression to their determination. They were working themselves up to the pitch of defiance of the law, as represented by Sheriff Jim Taggart; as yet no man cared to be first and still they looked frequently at the deputy sheriff with the rifle across his arm, and meant to set Mexicali Joe free. A man broke away from one of these groups and ran back to the Gallup House, to carry warning to Taggart.

It was at this moment that Bruce Standing, Timber-Wolf, rode into town. He rode alone, on a powerful red-bay gelding, silent now, a great-bulked man sitting straight in the saddle. One saw nothing of his face under the wide black hat.

He had no word of greeting for any man of them; after his characteristic coldly insolent way, he appeared to ignore them utterly. On the instant he, rather than Mexicali Joe, became the central object of interest. Most knew who he was and what he stood for, and wherein his visit among them was to be regarded as worthy of interest; those who did not know, marked the hush which greeted him, and in lowered voices demanded the explanation which, in voices equally low, was briefly given. They looked for him to draw rein at Gallup's and swing down and go in. But, knowing that you could never be sure of him, they watched to see.

He disappointed them. That, in itself, was like him. No doubt he got his bit of glee out of knowing that, where they had looked to him for one thing, he had given them another. He rode on by Gallup's without turning his head. Where a tree grew at the road-crossing he dismounted, tying his horse. They saw that his rifle was in its scabbard, slung to the saddle; he left it where it was, and went forward on foot. Bigger than ever he loomed among them, appearing to walk leisurely, yet taking the long, measured strides which carried him along swiftly. They let him go on his way, their eyes following him with growing interest, some of the more curious of the crowd stringing along in his wake. And all this time no man had given him the time of day, and he had not opened his lips.

Meanwhile they saw him turn his head this way and that, as though he sought something. Before he had gone fifty paces he found what he wanted. A man was piling wood on his fire; the axe which he had used a moment ago lay on the ground, glinting in the firelight. Bruce Standing stooped and caught it up and went on—straight toward the jail. A sudden shout from many voices burst out; men came running to see, now that they understood what he meant to do. And those about the jail, when they saw, drew back to right and left hurriedly, leaving only the deputy with the rifle across his arm to block the way.

Now, the axe could mean only one thing in the world, and the deputy saw it, and saw who it was that carried it and called out a sharp, throaty warning. Standing came on, his stride quickened. He was not a dozen steps away, carrying his axe lightly in his right hand. The deputy jerked his rifle up, the butt to his shoulder, shouting:

"Stop, or...."

The man fired, but he was not quick enough. At that distance, had his finger touched the hair-trigger the tenth of a second sooner, he could not have failed to kill. But he was not the man, even though armed, to dictate to Timber-Wolf. For Standing made instant answer to that command, "Stop!" and hurled his only weapon, a heavy wood-cutter's axe, straight into the deputy's face. The bullet went wild; the man who had fired it, through the rarest chance left alive, went down in a heap, unconscious before he struck ground. For, though the axe blade had very narrowly missed his face, the hard hickory handle had taken him full across the eyebrows and came near being the death of him. His rifle clattered against the rock wall of the jail.

Bruce Standing, who had paused but the briefest moment, came on and stepped over the fallen man, and caught up his axe again. He stooped long enough to make out that the deputy's head was not split open; then he swung up his axe, high above his head, and brought it crashing down against the thick oak padlocked door. The sound of the stroke echoed and the echoes were lost in the striking of the second blow. And, when for the third time the axe rose and fell, flashing in the light of the fires, the door fell.

"Out you come, Joe."

Standing's deep, full voice rumbled in a sort of rich, placid content. And out like a rabbit, darted Mexicali Joe, looking pinched and starved and frightened.

"It is you, Señor!" he gasped.

"The crowd will be after you," said Standing. "And I'm not going to worry about what happens to you after this."

He was turning away when Joe caught his sleeve, and stood on his tiptoes and began a rapid, excited whispering. Standing hesitated, then laughed and shook the man off.

"You are a good little sport, Mexico," he chuckled. "Now, on your way."

Joe, with never another look behind him, turned and ran, disappearing about the corner of the jail, sending back an account of himself in the sound of his racing footfalls among the pines.

Once again came a great shouting from the crowd in the road; they had seen, and now that they had their hearts' desire in having Mexicali Joe free, they saw themselves losing all hope of coming at his secret because they were losing him. Their brief interest in Bruce Standing was dead for the present; Joe ran like a scared cat, and they, like so many yelping dogs, set after him. And Timber-Wolf, watching, standing where he was with his big hands on his hips, roared with laughter.

* * * *

Babe Deveril and the girl, Lynette Brooke, had seen much of all this. They were at the time on their way to the Gallup House, she to her room and he to his meeting with his lawless kinsman. Thus it happened that Deveril's first sight of Timber-Wolf in half a dozen years, and Lynette's first sight of him in all her life, was at a moment when he was engaged in an episode of the type which made him stand apart as the man he was.

"Taggart ought to kill him for that," grunted Deveril. "And he probably will before the night is over."

The girl shivered as she had done just now when she saw a rifle raised and an axe flung. And yet within her, being woman, there was the exultation which would not stay down, and the thought: "He is magnificent.... A brute, maybe, but surely magnificent!" And she knew that she would never be content until she had seen his face and looked into his eyes. Already, being woman, she was concerned with his eyes; whether they would be large or small, set wide apart or close together. She wanted him to be the lion, not the wild boar.

* * * *

The remainder of the night's happenings was to come, because of the simple arrangement of rooms at the Gallup House, within the experience of both Deveril and Lynette. They saw Bruce Standing go down the road and followed him. He did not once look back. When he came to his horse, he stopped only long enough to take down his rifle. Plainly now he meant to go direct to the Gallup House. All the while men were streaming by him, hurrying to join in the chase after the escaping Mexicali Joe. So, by the time he came to Gallup's door, there were not over a score of men remaining in the house.

The Gallup House was a long, squat building of two low stories, its three main rooms on the ground floor facing the road. These were the dining-room; a room given over to Gallup's office, and sufficient space for a dozen chairs and a big sheet-iron stove—a sort of living-room for Gallup's guests, when he had any; and, finally, a room which had in older times been the barroom, and which, despite changing conditions, remained in practice a barroom. At this hour both dining-room and sitting-room were deserted, and the score or so of men, Gallup and Taggart among them, were in the bar. Here were round tables, for it was a big room, for games of cards or dice.

Deveril and the girl parted at the centre door through which she entered direct into the general living-room. They saw Bruce Standing go to the last of the three doors and step in unhesitantly, still carrying his rifle lightly. Deveril followed him, and saw the looks on the faces of Taggart and Gallup and some of their following.

"I stepped in to buy the drinks for the crowd," Timber-Wolf said quietly, all the while his eyes flashing back and forth. "Gents, the treats are on me."

Jim Taggart, his hands on his hips, was eying him like a hawk, and in Taggart's face was a dull, hot flush. Gallup, however, standing close at Taggart's side, was the first to speak. He cried out angrily:

"No man drinks with you in my house! Not as long as I live. And...."

Bruce Standing drew a wallet from his pocket.

"About twenty men here," he said, in the same slow, steady voice. "As it's a night of celebration, we'll make it a dollar a drink. That's twenty bucks, easy money, Young Gallup," he wound up with a sneer in his voice. For all men knew Gallup's cupidity, which clutched at small as well as large amounts.

But Gallup, shaken with rage, only shouted back at him:

"To hell with your twenty dollars! And with you, Bruce Standing!"

"So? Well, twenty dollars isn't much, after all, is it? Gents, we drink tonight and damn the cost! Two bones for every glass of whiskey; that's forty of the iron men, Gallup. Call Ricky with the bottles."

A couple of men laughed at that. Gallup, however, seeing himself baited, roared out:

"I tell you, *no*! And out you go. You are not wanted here."

"Low bid loses, high bid wins," said Standing. Now he opened his wallet and disclosed a tight pad of bills. "Three dollars for each and every glass of imitation hootch! God, what a pirate you are, Gallup! Now, trot it out."

"Sixty dollars, clean-cut velvet, Gal," said a man at his elbow, willing to drink with the devil so the drink came paid for.

"And at last Young Gallup hesitates, his soul tempted by a row of dirty pennies," gibed Standing. "Look, men, and you'll see that pale-yellow soul of his snared clean out of his stingy hide. Look, Gallup! And if you can say no this time you have established a new record for yourself!"

Slowly, while they watched him, he counted off ten ten-dollar banknotes, and, with a careless gesture, tossed them to a table.

"That's for one round of your rotten bootleg liquor," he said contemptuously. "Now, step out, Gallup, and show them the sort of money-grabbing porker you are. You know you haven't got the guts to save your own besmirched pride at the price of a hundred dollars."

Gallup would have sold out for far less, but Timber-Wolf was not the man to haggle over what he termed dirty pennies. He shrugged his heavy shoulders and caught up the money, counting it carefully, stuffing it into his pocket and growling:

"You're not wanted here, Standing; but any time you're fool enough to pay a hundred dollars for the privilege, I'll take the rules down for a round of drinks! Hey, Ricky!"

Standing only grunted at that, though his eyes flashed.

"I come when I please and where I please, and you know it, Young Gallup! And if you think you are the man to throw *me* out, hop to it and don't let a little hundred dollars hold you back! Better than that; if you'll tie into me right now and chuck me out of doors, getting all your hangdogs that will take a chance with you to help you, you've got my word that I'll add a second hundred as your bonus! Or a thousand, by heaven! And right now you'll toe the scratch or back down and shut your mouth."

Gallup had never before in his life been faced down like that. And with so many men looking on! Yet in his heart, though no man had ever called him a coward, he was afraid of Timber-Wolf; mortally afraid. There was the look of death itself in the eyes flashing into his own. He sought to laugh the thing off, saying, with what semblance of fine scorn he could master:

"*Your* word!"

"I am no liar," said Standing wrathfully. "And no man in all Arizona and New Mexico ever called me liar. Do you, Young Gallup?"

"Bruce!" called Sheriff Taggart sharply, for the first time speaking a word. "What's the sense of trying to start a row? Drop all this foolery and let me have a word with you."

"That's fair enough," agreed Standing. "I've no desire to break Gallup's neck so long as he leaves me alone. But make it snappy, as I have another engagement."

"I want to talk with you privately, Bruce." Taggart obviously was angry, and yet it was equally clear that when it came to dealing with the Timber-Wolf, Jim Taggart meant to hold himself well in hand.

"I won't stand for corner-whisperings," Standing told him sternly. "If it happens you've got anything for my set of ears, they're listening. But it's right now or never."

Taggart's black and ominous scowl deepened, and he shuffled his feet back and forth, and in the end stamped them in his anger. But still he held the curb line upon himself.

"You always was a strong-headed man, Bruce, that would have things his way. So be it. And I guess, being a man myself that stands on his own two legs, I can say it all in one mouthful: You and me has always been friends. Are we that yet?"

* * * *

Now for the first time Lynette Brooke, looking in from the adjoining room through a door just ajar, saw Timber-Wolf clearly, his face under his big hat unhidden as he turned a little in order to look straight at Taggart. He did not see her, and she looked her fill at him; he gave her a start of surprise, and after that start came a surge of admiration. He was a young, blond giant of a man, eyes very blue and laughing and *innocent*! And wide-spaced! A man no older than Babe Deveril, one who bore himself like some old buccaneer or Norse Viking, before men who would have given much for the courage and the power to fly at his bared white throat and drag the life out of him; a man who overflowed with his superabundant vital energy, and who stamped his own character, through sheer force of unbroken will, upon others about him; a man who believed in himself and who was at once implacable and gay. Heartless he looked, and yet full of the dancing joy of life. She felt herself on the instant both strongly drawn to him and frightened; the mad vision presented itself to her of herself in his mighty arms. And the odd tremor which shook her body, as she whipped back with flaming face, was compounded of thrill and shiver. He confused her; at once she was amazed that he could be like this and convinced that the owner of that glorious voice which she had heard pulsing out across the fields of night could be no jot different.... While she drew back to a dim corner of the room, she managed not to lose sight of him.

His clear blue eyes kept on laughing; his was that silent laughter which arises from the soul, and which mocked and insulted and was like the cold mirth of Satan. And yet, in some vague way which she was all at loss to plumb, and which troubled her strangely, Lynette Brooke *knew* that this corsair of a man was laughing because there was cold anger in his heart and because, for some mysterious reason of his own, he was set on holding his anger hidden. It troubled her so that, within herself, she cried out passionately against *knowing* through leaping instinct anything of what might be going on within the dark caverns of the Timber-Wolf's mind and heart. She wanted him and herself to be as far apart as north and south; she meant them to be. And all the while that compelling interest which he awoke within her tugged mightily and she yielded to it in that, keeping out of his sight, she lost nothing of the play of expressions upon his face.

As yet she knew nothing of that one thing which Bruce Standing, forthright exponent of untrammelled manhood, held to be his greatest weakness; the one and only thing of which he was bitterly ashamed. A trifle, it amounted to; and a trifle he would have accounted it in any other strong man. Yet within his hard breast it awoke the intensest feeling of shame. And it was a thing which invariably sprang forth upon him and humiliated him whenever once he let his passions fly. A laughable thing, and yet one that put tears into his bright blue eyes. But, on guard against it, he strove to curb his anger.

Of all this and the thing itself she knew nothing. But she felt and she knew that the Timber-Wolf, laughing into Jim Taggart's gloomy face, was fighting down his own anger, as a man may fight wild beasts. She awaited, scarcely breathing, the answer he would make to that question from Taggart: "Are we still friends?"

"No!" shouted Standing, and laughed at him. "No, by God!"

That was man talk! Straight, simple words—words that left little enough to be said. But Taggart, though his face grew hotter and his eyes seemed burning in their sockets, demanded further:

"And why not, Bruce Standing? You and me have been pardners. You know and I know and a thousand men know what sort of a bond and an understanding has always, for more than a dozen years, been between us. And now, if that is busted and wiped out, I ask you, as man to man: '*Why?*'"

"And as man to man," cried Timber-Wolf, his eyes brightening, "I'll answer you, Jim Taggart. When I knew you for a man who played his game he-man style and stood up and fought hard and took his chances, I was for you! And I went out and shaped things up for you and made you sheriff. And, when men got to know you and wanted no more of you as master of law here in the mountains, I lifted you over their heads and made you sheriff again and again. And now that you are done for and are on your last legs, I would have done the same thing once more. But when you got panicky, thinking that this was your last term of office, and began to feather your dirty nest by running with the breed of this Young Gallup and his crowd, and when I found the sort of contemptible, hide-in-the-brush jobs you were pulling off, I got a bellyful of you and your new kind of ways. And you double-crossed me, thinking I wouldn't know! And on top of everything else, running neck and neck with Gallup, you threw Mexicali Joe into jail…knowing that Joe, puny blackbird as he is, had been a friend of mine. For that I've done two things, Jim Taggart: I've smashed your damned jail door off its hinges and I've thrown you over. And there, until I'm sick of talk about it, you've got your answer!"

Taggart, too, and with his own ulterior reasons, kept his head cool. He said ponderously:

"You broke the law, Bruce, when you let Joe go. For that I could run you in. But all Joe done was steal a pocketful of nuggets, and we got them back. And there's bigger things than that, anyway. You and me has been friends and so I'll go slow. But we got to have another talk. You've got me down wrong, old-timer."

Never had Lynette Brooke seen such utter contempt as that which now filled Bruce Standing's eyes. But he made no answer. At this moment the man Ricky came in with a gallon earthen jug and began to pour out the glasses set upon a table. Here was the Timber-Wolf's hundred-dollar treat. Standing himself waved it aside and:

"I drink no poison in this house," he said briefly. And as he spoke he saw for the first time Babe Deveril standing just inside the door, not two steps behind him.

"By the Lord, Babe, I'm glad to see you! Shake!" he shouted, thrusting out his big hand.

But now it was Deveril's turn to be cool and contemptuous.

"You and I, Bruce Standing," he said in that clear, insolent voice of his, "have gone a long way beyond the point of shaking hands."

Standing frowned as he muttered:

"Don't be a young ass, Babe."

But Deveril only shook his head, retorting:

"I have come, according to promise, for a word with you. Suppose we make it snappy."

"The same little Baby Devil!" Standing jeered at him, making Deveril stiffen with that look of his eyes. "I'll give you a new dance tune before I'm through with you. Come ahead!"—and with a suddenness which took Lynette Brooke by surprise he struck back the door leading to the room where she was and led the way in, Deveril at his heels.

But, though there were three or four coal-oil lamps burning in the room which he had just quitted, there was but one here where she was. And because its chimney was smoky and the flame burned crookedly and she was in a dim corner, he could make nothing of the look of her. Had she remained perfectly still he would scarcely have noted her presence. But now she was suddenly impatient to be gone, and went hurrying to a door which led into a hallway, the hallway in turn leading to her room at the back of the house.

"A woman," growled Timber-Wolf disgustedly, getting only a glimpse of a hastily departing figure. "It begins to look as though a man couldn't pick him a spot in the wilderness that the female didn't crowd in."

Lynette heard, and knew with a flash of resentment that he did not care whether she had heard or not, and that with the last word he would be turning to Deveril and forgetting that he had seen her. She went slowly down the hall, three or four paces only. There she paused and lingered; it was no such pale incentive as curiosity which held her now, but a peculiar fascination. Two men like those two, by far the strongest-willed and most dynamic men she had ever known, with the business which lay between them, made her ignore and give no thought to the convention of shut ears against the talk of others. So she stood here in the dim hallway, poised for instant flight if need be to her own door, a couple of yards farther on.

"Now," said Deveril impatiently, "what is it?"

Timber-Wolf's mood softened and the old bright laughter welled up in his dancing blue eyes.

"I pass it to you, Kid," he chuckled. "You've grown a man since last we met. We'll not forget, either one of us…will we?… that night in my cabin?"

"I'll not forget," returned Deveril coolly. "And some day I'll square the count."

"*You'll* square the count?" The keen eyes twinkled like bits of deep-blue glass on a frosty morning. "I was under the impression that always you have held that I was the man to square things. Accusing me, as you did, of so wicked a deed!"

"It was a treacherous thing at best," muttered Deveril, his own eyes bleak with that bitter hatred which never slept. "I didn't know then that you were, among other things, a damned thief."

Timber-Wolf's sudden laughter boomed out joyously, and he smote his thigh so that the sound was sharp and loud, like a gunshot.

"But you knew that always and always and once again always I take what I want! I asked you for the money, and I made you a fair proposition: I would guarantee that you doubled your dinky three thousand, and I'd see you had interest on top of it. And you hadn't the nerve to chip in…."

"Wasn't the fool, you mean!"

"And so…I went and took it! And I took from other quarters the same way. What I wanted I took. And when they all said I was busted in two, like a rotten stick, I fooled 'em, and laughed at the whole crowd. And now I'm whole again—and I've got what I want. That's me, Baby Devil! A man who goes his way and blazes his trail wide. A man you can't stop!"

"A cursed, insufferable, conceited ass, rather than wolf," snapped Deveril.

And still, in the rarest of high good humor, Timber-Wolf laughed, and his rich, deep voice went rumbling through the house.

"You're sore, Baby Devil. And you're envious."

"Not of you, Bruce Standing! You…."

"Let's chop out the Sunday-school stuff, Kid!" cried Standing impatiently. "I don't need your lecturings. Maybe I'm not what your puling moralists call a good man, and maybe I'm not 'clean-hearted and pure' and all that drivel. But, by God, I'm a man who's got his own code and who sticks to it, blow high, blow low! A code that, if more men followed it, would give us a world with more men in it and fewer mollycoddle pups!"

"It would appear," sneered Deveril, "that you remain well contented with yourself!"

"Like the rest of humanity—he, she, and it!" said Timber-Wolf equably. "And so much for friendly chatter. Now a word whispered in your pretty ear, since the Lord knoweth how many busybodies are straining their own ears to listen-in on us."

Lynette, in the hallway, stiffened and felt her face grow hot. But, with a strange new-born stubbornness, she remained where she was.

Timber-Wolf came a step closer to Deveril, and, lowering his voice so that Lynette lost the words, he muttered:

"I *am* under obligations to you, my dear kinsman, and since there is a tough crowd in town, any man of whom would whack you over the head for a handful of silver, I am keeping this between us." He took his wallet from his pocket the second time, and drew from it several bank-notes. These he proffered to Deveril, his eyes still bright with his cold mirth.

"Count it and stick it in your jeans," he said softly. "There's your three thousand. With it is another three thousand, the double of the bet which I promised you. And with that is another two thousand, which is a gain of ten percent for you for six years, all rough figuring. In all eight thousand in coin of the realm…and I'm much obliged," he ended mockingly, "for your generous loan!"

Babe Deveril, taken off his feet by the unexpectedness of this, stared at the bank-notes in the great hard palm, and from them to the grinning face. And slowly, from a conflicting tumult of emotions, in which, strangely enough, anger surged highest, Deveril's face went violently red.

"Damn you and your eternal posings!" Lynette caught those words, clear and high. But she missed the eloquence of the shrug into which Timber-Wolf's shoulders lifted.

"It's up to you, Kid," said Standing, and still he kept his voice low and quiet. The money lay in his outstretched palm. "The minute I make my offer I consider my obligation fulfilled. If you are too proud to take it…well, then, the devil take you for a fool, and I'll use the money elsewhere."

Deveril put out his hand, selecting from the several bills.

"My three thousand, I take," he said, "because it is mine. And the two thousand with it, judging that fair interest, considering the risks my money took. As for the rest—" he whipped back, and his voice, because of the emotions near choking him, was little more than a harsh whisper—"you can keep it and go to hell with it! I want none of your cursed charity!"

Timber-Wolf's thick eyebrows lifted, and a new look dawned in his eyes.

"By thunder, Baby Devil, you've the makings of a man in you!" he exclaimed. "You and I could be friends!"

"Don't fool yourself. We won't be!"

"I didn't say we would!" And Bruce Standing glared at him angrily. "I only said we *could*. There's a difference there, Kid. I could eat tripe, but I'm damned if I ever will!"

As the two men eyed each other, it was impossible to conceive of any earthly happening bringing them within the warm enclosure of man's friendship.

But there was money in sight, and money in the hands of Timber-Wolf was habitually offered to fate as free money. And always, in the heart of Babe Deveril, when there was money in his pocket and money in sight, there was the impulse to hazard, to win or lose, and know the wild moment of a gambler's pleasure. And so he said swiftly:

"Just the same, I have a claim on that three thousand of yours!"

"Yes?" And again the heavy eyebrows were lifted as Timber-Wolf's interest was snared.

"If it's mine, it comes to me. If it's yours, you keep it and take three thousand from me to boot. I'll flip a coin with you!"

"Baby Devil!" laughed Standing softly. "Oh, Baby Devil, if your mamma could only see you now!"

"Are you on?" demanded Deveril, in a suppressed voice.

"On? With bells, Baby Devil! Heads or tails, and let her flicker!"

Lynette Brooke could catch only enough of all this to set her wondering. The two men were agreeing upon something, and all the while jeering at each other, and, though they checked their words and subdued their voices, anger was directing whatever they did or meant to do.

Both men were eager and tense. For both made of life a game of hazard. With Babe Deveril three thousand dollars, to be won or lost in the flicker of an eyelid, was a large sum of money; to Bruce Standing, a man of millions, it was no great thing. Yet neither of them was more tense and eager than the other. The game was the thing.

Automatically, perhaps subconsciously intending to have a free hand, since his rifle was still held in his left, Bruce Standing stuffed his spurned bank-notes into his pocket. But it was Deveril who, having conceived the idea, was first to produce a coin; a silver dollar, and mate to those other silver dollars which he had presented to the girl, Maria.

"Heads or tails, Standing?" he demanded, holding the coin ready to toss ceilingward.

"Throw it," said Timber-Wolf, with his characteristic grin, "and I name it while it's in the air. For I don't know what sleight-of-hand you may have acquired these later years, and I don't trust you, my sweet kinsman! And shoot fast, as someone's coming."

For both had heard the rattle of hoofs in the road outside, as some horseman came racing up to the door.

"Name it, then," cried Deveril, and shot the coin, spinning, upward.

"Heads!" Timber-Wolf named it. "Always heads. My motto there, Kid!"

The silver dollar, with such zest had it been pitched upward, struck the ceiling and dropped to the floor, rolling. It rolled half across the room, both men springing after it, stooping to watch and know how fate decided matters between them. And in the end there was no decision at all. For the coin rolled half-way into a crack between the boards and stood thus, on edge, neither heads nor tails.

"Flip her again," growled Bruce Standing, deep in his throat. "And step lively!"

Already the horse's hoofs, as its rider plucked at the reins, were sliding outside. Deveril caught up the coin and tossed it again. And this time, true to his word, and not trusting the other, Bruce Standing called before the silver dollar struck the floor:

"Tails!"

And as the silver dollar struck and rolled and stopped, and at last lay flat, and the two stooped over it so close that almost the black hair of one and the reddish hair of the other brushed, they saw that it was heads. And that Timber-Wolf, repudiating his motto, "Always heads!" had lost three thousand dollars. And at the instant their intruder burst in upon them from the road.

Here, after his own strange fashion, came Billy Winch, Timber-Wolf's one-legged retainer. An able-bodied man and agile had been Billy Winch all of his hard life until, after a horse had fallen on him, the doctor had cut his leg off above the knee. "You'll go on crutches the rest of your life," they told him that day. And Billy Winch, weak and pale and sick and haggard-eyed, muttered at them: "You're a pack of damn liars! I'll cut my throat before I'll be a crutch-man." And he had kept his oath. Seldom did he stir save on the back of his horse. And when needs must that he go horseless some few steps, he went "like a man, one-leg style, hopping!" Now, hopping on his one foot so that, with his pinched, weazened face and small bright eyes, he resembled some uncouth bird, he bounced into the room.

"I got word for you, Bruce Standing!" he cried excitedly.

"Clear out, you fool...."

"I won't clear out! This is the real thing. Listen: A man, and it was a man paid by Young Gallup, has just went down the road with a double-barrel shotgun, and the dirty skunk has shot your horse, good old Sunlight...dead!" By now Billy Winch was whimpering; tears, whether of rage or grief, filled his bright eyes and streamed down his face. And all the while, to maintain his balance, he was hopping unsteadily about, his outflung hand groping for the wall.

And now at last Timber-Wolf's anger, a devastating, all-engulfing rage which mastered him utterly, was unleashed. And with its release came inevitably that one condition of which he was so terribly ashamed. He cried out aloud, in a great, roaring voice...and in the fierce grip of his wrath his utterance was so affected that his speech came enunciated in the most incongruous of fashions. For it was Timber-Wolf's burning mortification that he, the strongest man of these mountains, when in the clutch of his mightiest passions...*lisped* like an affected school-girl!

"Thunlight dead!" he stormed. "You thay that to me? Yeth? Then, by God, juth ath thure as I live, I'll...."

He cut himself short; his face, instantly red with rage, grew redder with shame. He snapped his great jaws shut, and across the room Deveril heard the grinding of his teeth. He swerved about, charging toward the door, which gave entrance to the room where Gallup was.

But a far more critical moment than Timber-Wolf knew was ticking in the clock of his life. In the hall stood the girl, Lynette. She had heard all of these words of Billy Winch, and she had heard Bruce Standing's bellowed rejoinder. And she, already taut-nerved and keyed up, what with fatigue and a strenuous night, was so struck by the absurdity of a strong man lisping his passionate utterance, that she broke out into uncontrollable laughter. And when Lynette Brooke's laughter caught her unawares, it rang out as clearly as the chiming of silver bells. Now, with nerves quivering, she was almost hysterical....

Timber-Wolf came to as dead a halt as though it had been a bullet instead of the mockery of a girl's laughter which cut into his heart. For only mockery he made of it, he who upon this one point, as upon no other, was so sensitive. And to have a human female laugh at him!

His rage threatened to choke him. But now, even as he had forgotten his lost bet with Babe Deveril, so did he forget a dead horse and Young Gallup. The entire violence of his anger was deflected, turned upon a woman who had eavesdropped upon his ignominy and then assailed him with the mockery of her mirth. He who held all womankind in such high scorn, to be now a woman's laughing-stock! He, Bruce Standing, Timber-Wolf! He snatched at the hall door, and under his attack one of the ancient hinges broke, and the door, flung back, leaned crazily against the wall. And all the while, though he kept his teeth so hard set that his jaws bulged with the strain, he was muttering curses in his throat. He burst into the dim hallway, his brain on fire.

She heard him coming. More than that, and before, it seemed to her that her instinct told her that he would come, bearing down upon her like a hurricane, in such violence as would stamp her into the earth. She had not meant to laugh at him; she did not want to laugh. And yet now all that she could do was clap her hands over her mouth and run before him as a blown leaf races before the storm. She sped down the hall, plunged into her room, slammed the door after her.

... And in the hallway she heard the pounding of his heavy boots. Already he was at her door. Before she could shoot the bolt, he had gripped the knob. When he flung his weight against the panel, it flew back, and under the impact she was thrown backward, and would have fallen had it not been that she brought up against her bed. Here she half fell, but was erect before he had stormed across the threshold.

"You...."

Why had she run from him? She was not afraid of him and she was not afraid of anything on earth. Or, at least, making a sort of religion out of it, that was the thing which she had always told herself. Just at hand, on the little table by the open window, was her revolver. And she could shoot and shoot true to the mark. She had told Babe Deveril that she could take care of herself. She stood, rigid and defiant, and in her heart unafraid.

On a bracketed shelf over her bed was a kerosene lamp which she had left burning when she had gone out. She could see the working of his lips. And he saw her.

* * * *

Now those who knew Timber-Wolf best knew this about him—that he had no use for womankind; that he held all of the female of the human race to be weaklings and worse, leeches upon the strength of man, mere outwardly glossed tricks of a scheming nature; things contemptible. And at this moment, surely, Timber-Wolf was in no mood to revise for the better his sweeping and deep-based opinion. But now, despite all trumped-up reasonings, no matter how sincere, his first clear view of this girl gave him pause.

She was superb. Physically, if not otherwise. For the first thing, her hair snared him. Strong men are always caught by films; a big brute of a man who may break his triumphant way through iron bands grows powerless under a frail wisp of a frail woman's hair. In the hall she had held her hat in her hands; her hair, loosely upgathered and insecurely and hastily confined, had tumbled all about her face as she bolted into her room. He saw that first of all. And then he saw her eyes. At the moment, already in her room with the door slammed shut behind him and his back against it, he looked, glowering, into her eyes. And he found them at once soft and still amazingly unafraid; those daring eyes of Lynette Brooke, daughter of a dancing-girl and of the dare-all miner, Brooke. Unafraid, though he who might have choked the life out of her between finger and thumb, turned his furious face upon her.

He paid her tribute with a flash of his shining blue eyes. That was for the physical beauty of her; that said, "Outwardly, girl, you are superb!" Yet it remained that, his one weakness shaming him, she had laughed at him. For the first time in his life a girl had laughed at him....

She saw the sudden changing fires in his eyes and stepped closer to the table on which lay that small, high-powered implement which puts the weak on a level with the strong....

"By God, girl...."

There came a sudden sharp rapping at the door against which his broad back leaned. There was Babe Deveril, who had lunged after him. Timber-Wolf, growling savagely, flung himself about, for the second ignoring the girl and facing the door. Deveril, just without, heard the bolt shot home. And then he heard the second, the sinister sound. A revolver shot, muffled by the four walls of a room. And he heard Timber-Wolf, whose back had been turned to Lynette Brooke and the gun upon the table, curse deep down in his throat, and heard almost simultaneously the scraping of the heavy boots and the crashing fall of the big body. Deveril shook fiercely at the door. Then he turned and ran back down the hall, meaning to go through the room he had just quitted and on through so as to come to Lynette's room by the rear.

But in the sitting-room Billy Winch, teetering on his one foot, grasped him by the arm, demanding to know what had happened. Deveril savagely shook him off, and Winch, raising the echoes with a shrilling voice, toppled over and fell. But little time had been wasted, and yet, before Deveril could free himself and run on, Lynette Brooke ran in upon him. Her eyes were wild and staring; in her hand was her revolver, so lately fired that the last wisp of smoke had not cleared from the barrel.

"Babe Deveril," she gasped. "They are after me!"

It was Sheriff Taggart who was after her. He was almost at her heels, shouting:

"Stop! In the name of the law! You are under arrest for killing Bruce Standing...."

Babe Deveril carried no weapon upon him. And he saw Taggart's pistols dragging at his belt, the heavy forty-fives which, as sheriff, he was entitled to carry openly. Taggart's hands were almost upon her.

Deveril did the one thing. He caught the gun in Lynette's hand and wrenched it free, and, having no time for accurate aim, did not fire, but hurled the revolver itself, with all of his might, full into Taggart's face. And Taggart, as though a thunderbolt had struck him, went down, with a steel barrel driven against his skull, near the temple, and lay a crumpled, still heap.

"The house is full of Taggart's friends!" Deveril cried sharply, warning her and, at the same time, thinking for himself.

But already she was running again. She ran out into the road; but there the brisk-burning bonfires made night into day. She dodged back into the shadow cast by the corner of the house, and ran about to the rear. Deveril hesitated only an instant; men were already rushing in from the room where they had been drinking. He followed her through the door, and here again he paused. Men were already stooping over the sheriff; he heard one cry out the single word, "Dead!" His brain caught fire. The girl had killed Timber Wolf; he had killed Jim Taggart. He and she were fugitives. He followed her again into the shadows, running to the back of the house.

And as he ran one thing angered him: He had won three thousand dollars from Bruce Standing, and that three thousand dollars was at this moment in Standing's pocket. And being Babe Deveril, who dared at least as far as most men dare, he meant to have what fortune allowed him.

And so, when he came to an open and lighted window, and looked in and saw the sprawling body of Timber-Wolf, Babe Deveril unhesitatingly threw his leg over the sill and went in. In his judgment Standing was as good as dead, shot in the back. Well, that was no affair of his, and certainly he was not the man to grieve. Let "Serve him right" be his epitaph. Deveril, in a feverish haste, began to feel in the fallen man's pockets.

He found the bank-notes and stuffed them into his own pocket. At the window, as he turned back to it, while he heard men hammering at the locked door, he saw Lynette Brooke's white face. She had been watching him. Yet even that, in the present need for haste, made no impression. He slipped through, hearing a discordant shouting of many voices.

"We are in for it now," he panted. "Run!"

He caught her hand, and, holding it tight, the two raced into the darkness under the pines.

CHAPTER 5

Billy Winch was the first to come to the bolted door. He hopped swiftly down the hall and beat at it with his fists. Snarling and snapping, growling and finally whimpering, for the world like a dog, he cried out through his fierce mutterings:

"I'm the only man here that can save him if he ain't dead already. And if he is dead...."

He hurled himself bodily at the door; he jumped up at it and kicked it with his one heavy boot and, falling, rolled over and crawled to his foot and struck again.

The Gallup House had become a vortex of violent excitement. It was shouted out that two men were dead, Bruce Standing shot by the new adventuress whom many had noted; Jim Taggart killed as he sought to put her under arrest. Voices clashed and so did thoughts and purposes. Men streamed out into the firelit road; they heard running feet marking the way the two fugitives had taken, and started headlong in pursuit, stumbling and falling in the dark, and for the first few moments making slight headway. Others, Gallup among them, were already with Taggart, lifting him up and bearing him off to a bed. Still others, hearkening to the strange word that a woman had killed Bruce Standing, were suddenly charged with the morbid curiosity to look upon this man dead. They found their way to the lighted window through which Lynette Brooke had escaped, and through it made their way into the room, until the small space was thick with their jostling bodies. All the while Billy Winch was beating at the door, yelling curses and, at last, when he heard them within, commanding and imploring to be let in. A man, stepping over Timber-Wolf's body, obeyed and Billy Winch hopped in. Immediately he was down at his chief's side, squatting, after his own awkward fashion, upon a knee and balanced by a stub of a leg.

"He *ain't* dead!" Billy Winch's breath was expelled in a long, grateful sigh, which, before his lungs flattened, was choked by a nervous giggle. "I'm here, Timber," he said softly. "You know me, old boy!"

"You damn little fool," was Bruce Standing's grunted answer. Yet his voice was gentle and his eyes for one rare and fleeting instant as soft as a lover's.

Billy Winch, a man of resource, was now himself again, cool and past all silly sentiment. He turned from the fallen man to the crowding onlookers, and his eyes darkened with fury. He snatched up the rifle which Standing had let fall, and, still kneeling, whipped it up over his head, brandishing it like a war club.

"Out of this, every one of you!" he shouted at them. "Give him air and give me room to work in, else I bash your brains out!"

Had he been less in earnest some man of them might have found occasion to mark the absurdity of a cripple, squatting on the floor, waving a gun over his head and ordering them about. But as things were, no man appeared to glimpse this angle of it. One by one, with his eyes and the eyes of Timber-Wolf glaring at them, they went hastily out through the window.

"Ought to get a doctor in a hurry," one of the retreating men was suggesting.

Billy Winch cursed him into silence. For Winch held himself as good a physician and surgeon as any, having served in the veterinary capacity for a score of years and having a natural aptitude for treating bad cuts and gun wounds. Further, he loved this Timber-Wolf; and beyond, with all his heart, Billy Winch distrusted and hated the breed of doctors. His stump of a leg he attributed to the profound ignorance drawn by the medical and surgical profession from their books of theories.

"You ain't even bad hurt, Timber," he growled, as though disappointed and angered that he had been tricked into a show of affection and fright. His look accused Standing of having wilfully deceived him. "Must have been just the shock, what we call the impack, that knocked you over…. Oh, lie still, can't you!"

But Bruce Standing gave him no heed, and continued in his attempt to draw himself up. While Billy Winch sat on the floor and looked up at him, the bigger man got slowly to his feet and stood leaning against the door.

"Anyway, get over on the bed and lay down and I'll look you over. You're bleeding like a stuck pig. And you're as white as a clean rag."

Bruce Standing's face was already haggard and drawn, his mouth hard with pain. Yet he ignored Winch's command, and walked slowly, forcing his steps to be steady, to the one chair in the room. He sat down upon it heavily, straddling it as though it were a horse, facing the chair-back, and thus leaving his own back clearly proffered for Winch's inspection. Winch got up and hopped to him, railing at him the while for not lying down and obeying orders.

"Help me get my coat off," commanded Timber-Wolf curtly. "Then you can dig around and find out what we're up against."

Men were still at the window, peering in.

"Scatter!" commanded Winch, waving the rifle at them. "And tell our boys to come here. Dick Ross and Charley Peters. They ain't far."

Reluctantly the onlookers withdrew, some two or three of them to pause in the shadows when once out of eye-shot, and look back. But from now on Winch disregarded them. He helped the wounded man off with his coat, yanked his shirts out from his belted waist, tore cloth freely when it was in his way, and thus uncovered the wound.

"*She* did that for you? That kid of a girl?"

"Yes, damn her," muttered Timber-Wolf angrily, as Billy Winch's fingers, already scarlet, touched the wound. "Turned my back a second…she ought to have shot me dead…either a rotten shot or in an awful hurry…."

"Or scared to death!" Winch's contempt was enormous. "That's the kind that does the most harm, the scared-stiffs that's always shooting the wrong time and the wrong man."

By now he had the shirts torn from top to bottom, and stood back, looking appraisingly at the broad, naked back and the small hole which a bullet had drilled. Against the great area of flesh, as white as a girl's and smooth and clean with vigorous health, the smear of blood, itself red with that same perfection of health, gave the wound an appearance of ten times its real gravity. But Winch was accustomed to blood, and knew that Bruce Standing could lose more of it than could most men and be little the worse for the loss. He diagnosed the case aloud, muttering thoughtfully:

"Thirty-two caliber, to begin with; a thirty-two ain't nothing, Timber. Now, if it had been a forty-five, at that close-up range…. Well, you see you was standing half-way slanting; it took you under that big shoulder muscle and drilled in and hit a rib, one of the high-up ones, and kept on going, sort of skirting round, skating on a rib, and popped out under your arm. Lift it a bit? That's it. A clean hole. I tell you, either you sort of slipped and fell, or it was the impack that knocked you over…. The boys will be here any minute, and will scare up a bar of castile soap for me and something to make a regular poultice, what we calls a comprest, you know; I can make one out of most anything; remember Sam True's thoroughbred stallion that got all cut to hell last fall, and I made him a comprest out of sawdust! You remind me," added Winch thoughtfully, drawing off one of his hopping paces, to take in with an admiring and practised eye the now virtually nude torso, a white, smooth-running engine of power and endurance, "of a wild stallion mostly as much as a man, anyhow. A good smear of mustang liniment on that shoulder, a application, you know; and a dose of physic and a couple days' rest and careful diet, and you'll be as good as new…."

"What happened in the other room?" demanded Standing, deaf to Winch's mutterings. "After she went through the window?"

"She came busting in where Deveril and I was, her eyes the size of two new dish pans. I put in *new* because they was shining like it too; I thought she'd seen the devil. She has a gun in her hand and she yells out, 'Save me!' or something like that. And after her, doubled-up running, comes Jim Taggart, yelling at her: 'I got you for killing Bruce Standing!' And then that cool-headed, hot-hearted young Baby Devil of yours grabs the gun out of her hand and whangs Taggart over the head with it so that he drops dead in his tracks. And I hear a man say he is dead, too; but I don't stop to see. Don't seem natural, and yet a man's close to mortal danger if he gets whanged with any hard object, such as steel gun-barrels, on the head, close up to the temple; we call it the parrytal bone, you know, and I've known men and even horses that was killed so quick...."

"Then what?" snapped Timber-Wolf.

"Then both him and her beats it like the mill-tails of hell! And that part's natural enough, him figuring he's killed the sheriff, and her figuring she's plumb killed you. They stampeded into the brush, ducking out toward the timber-lands where it was darkest, a bunch of hollering fools after them."

"And Jim Taggart?"

The "boys" whose presence Billy Winch had requested came hurrying in at the hall door, excitement and alarm shining in their eyes. One glance reassured them, and while Dick Ross gave expression to his relief in a windy sigh and sought hastily for materials to build him a cigarette to replace that which he had dropped as he raced here, Charley Peters stood and mopped at his forehead with an enormous dingy blue handkerchief and grinned. Billy Winch, who had the trick of pithy brevity when there was need of it, made his wants known sharply, and the two men, their spurs still dragging and clanking after them, hastened away for basin and soap and whatever else of Winch's first-aid materials might be had at hand. In the meantime, Winch was yanking a sheet off Lynette Brooke's bed, and ripping it into tatters for his bandages and rags and what he termed "mops and applications."

"It ain't necessary to probe for the bullet," he admitted, almost regretfully. "But I might poke around in there a mite, while the hole's good and wide open, to make sure that a piece of your shirt or something didn't get lodged inside...."

"I'll break your damned neck for trying it," threatened Standing.

"Well," sighed Winch, "all I'll do then is just take a pack-needle and put in a stitch or two. Remember when Dick Ross's horse...."

"You'll take some warm water and soap and wash me off," said Standing emphatically. "Then you'll make me one of your infernal compresses out of clean cloth; and after that you'll leave me alone.... Tell me about my horse, old Sunlight. So Gallup had him killed for me?"

"Somebody pretty near blowed his head off with buckshot," Billy Winch told him, and again twinkling fires of anger flickered in the little man's eyes. "If Gallup didn't have the job done, who did? I ask you!"

Timber-Wolf stared at the wall. Within him, too, rose scorching anger, that resurgent bitter flood which was not lessened now because in the first place it had leaped upon him unexpectedly, and had thus been the cause of his humiliation. But within him there was another emotion, one of deep grief; for he loved a good horse, no man more. And Sunlight was his pet and his trusted friend, and had been, for many a wilderness week, his only companion.

"You didn't leave him suffering any, Bill?" His voice sounded cold and impersonal and matter-of-fact. Yet Billy Winch understood and answered softly:

"I stopped long enough to make sure, Timber. But I didn't have to shoot him; he just rared his head up and looked at me straight in the eye, as man to man, so help me God, and fell back...dead. No; he didn't suffer much."

Bruce Standing was silent a long time, his eyes brooding, his brows drawn after a fashion which Billy Winch could make nothing certain of; anger and bitterness or a sign of his own bodily pain. They heard spurred boots in the hall, returning. Then a quick look passed between Timber-Wolf and Billy Winch, and Timber-Wolf said hastily, dropping his voice and speaking with a peculiar softness:

"When you get a chance, you take the boys and see that old Sunlight is moved out of this skunk town; he's too fine a little horse to take his last rest here. Out on a hilltop, somewhere; looking toward the east, Bill. And a good, deep hole and...leave the saddle and bridle on him, Bill."

"I get you," returned Winch gravely. And, by way of thoughtful acknowledgment of the justice of this thing, for Billy Winch, too, loved a horse, he muttered: "That's fair."

With the return of Ross and Peters, Winch gave them their orders, as a stern and dreaded head master might issue commands to a couple of his boys, securing unfailing and immediate obedience. For the one job of both Ross and Peters, and the one job which had been theirs for five or six years, was to do what they were told by Billy Winch and ask no questions, and look sharp that they did not seek to introduce any of their own and original ideas into the carrying out of his behests. For this they were paid by Timber-Wolf, who used them for many things, consigning matters of vital importance into their hands by way of Billy Winch's brains and tongue.

"Stand ready to hand me things when I ask for them, Dick," said Winch. He scrubbed his own hands with soap, and let Dick pitch the water from the basin out the window. Dick obeyed promptly, adding nothing of his own to the simple task beyond making sure that he pitched the whole basinful far out; far enough, in fact, to give a thorough wetting to one of the curious who had lingered outside, watching through the lighted window. "You, Charley," ran on Winch, "go down to where old Sunlight is, and stick there until me and Dick come out. His saddle and bridle ain't to be took off, and you'll have to keep your eye peeled some regular Big Pine citizen don't snake 'em, for their silver, under your eyes." Charley understood enough to do as he was told, and hurried out. "Now, Dick, stand by with them rags and warm water."

Winch went promptly to work, and, in his rough-and-ready fashion, did a good clean job of bandaging a simple wound. A raw wound like that must of necessity be intensely painful; yet Timber-Wolf's quiet and regular breathing never altered once, and not so much as the breadth of a hair did the muscular back flinch. They had just gotten the torn shirts lapped over into place and the coat thrown over Standing's shoulders, and his hat picked up from the floor for him, when a man walking heavily came down the hall and stopped at the door, knocking sharply.

"Who is it?" demanded Winch.

"It's me, Taggart. Is Standing all right?"

Bruce Standing himself, holding himself very erect, his head well up and his eyes cold and hard, opened the door.

"So the devil refused to take you, after all," he grumbled. "They had it reported that Deveril had killed you. At that, it looks as though he'd come close to doing a good job of it."

For Jim Taggart's face, too, was white, and there was a broad band about his head, stained in one spot near the left temple.

"The same kind thought rides double," rejoined Taggart, with a sudden flash of the eyes. "That wildcat of a girl came close to marking out your ticket to hell."

"Where is she now?" asked Standing eagerly. "Did they bring her back?"

"Gone clean, for the present," answered Taggart. "If that fool of a Babe Deveril hadn't butted in, just piling up trouble for himself, and knocked me out while I wasn't even looking at him, I'd of had her by the heels. And now the two of 'em, two of a kind, if you ask me, are off into the mountains together. And I'm starting after them in ten minutes, and will drag 'em back before tomorrow night, just as sure as you're a foot high."

"What have you come to sling all this at me for?" snapped Standing.

"I wanted to see if you was dead," returned Taggart coolly. "Now I just pinch both of 'em for assault with a deadly weapon with intent to kill. If you'd of died, it would of been murder for her."

"At least, I'm glad you blew in, Jim Taggart. There are two things it might be just as well to get straight. First: When you and I, a dozen years ago, were sidekicks, prospecting together, bunking together, grubstaking each other, taking chances a lot of the time on a quick, hard finish to the little old game of life, we had it understood that if I died all of my belongings went to you; and if you cashed in first, anything you had went to me."

Taggart nodded and said swiftly:

"My papers stand that way to this day! I never go back...."

"The more fool you, then," jeered Standing. "I'm done with you, and my papers are changed already...."

"Already?" Taggart started visibly. "Since when?"

"Since yesterday. Nothing I own, not so much as a wart on a log of mine, ever goes your way."

The bitterness in Taggart's soul overspilled into his voice as he cried out savagely:

"Sure, there you are! That's the way it goes. Now that your luck's been running high and you don't need me, now that my luck's been dragging bottom, why then you're ready to pitch me over...."

"Liar!" Timber-Wolf cut him short with the word which was like an explosion. But he did not pause to discuss a point of view, but continued immediately: "That's the first thing. Here's the second: You've decided to run neck and neck with Young Gallup. So you can take him a word from me. Tell him"—and Standing's voice, husky with his emotions, made even Jim Taggart wonder what was coming—"that I came into his skunk hole of a town tonight just because he had the nerve to tell me not to. Tell him that I know that was his work that my horse was killed just now. Tell it him that if I ever come into his skunk hole once more in my life, it will be to pull his damned town down about his ears."

Taggart chose to break into contemptuous laughter. But Bruce Standing, lost to all sense of his own pain, caught him angrily by the shoulder and shouted into his ears:

"And this, for the last word ever to be spoken between you and me, Jim Taggart. That rake-hell Jezebel that shot me, *shot me and not you*! Got that? I'm not asking you, sheriff or no sheriff, to chip in on my affairs; I'll attend to the little hell-cat, and you keep your hands off. And, as for Babe Deveril, since the cursed fool wants to show his hand by cutting in with her and trying to snatch her out of my reach, I'll attend to him at the same time. The likely thing is that they've headed into the wilderness, my wilderness, and I'm going after them. And you are to keep out of my way."

With a violent shove he thrust Taggart out of his way and strode by him, going swiftly down the hall, Dick Ross swinging along close behind him and keeping a watchful eye upon Taggart, little Billy Winch hopping along in the rear and spitting audacious venom at the sheriff with his baneful eyes. In this order the three came out under the shining stars.

CHAPTER 6

Bruce Standing, a man of that strong, dominant, and self-centred character which is prone to disregard the feelings of others, held both Lynette Brooke and Babe Deveril his prey. But Jim Taggart, whose professional business it appeared to be to bring in the girl, and whose sore and aching head would not for many a day lose record of the fact that it had been Babe Deveril who had forcibly put him out of the running, had his own human purposes to serve, and set his nose to the trail like a bloodhound. And yet, with these two bending every energy to run them to earth, the two fugitives plunging headlong into the friendly darkness were for the moment utterly lost to those who plunged into the same darkness and in the same headlong style after them.

Hand in hand, chance-caught, and running swiftly, Lynette and Deveril were in time to escape the first of their pursuers, a crowd of men who got in one another's way, and who were too lately from the lighted room of the house to see clearly outside. Behind Gallup's House was the little creek which supplied the town with its water; it wound here across a tiny flat, an open space save for its big cottonwoods. The two, knowing that in the first heat of the chase opening at their heels they were running from death, sped like two winged shadows merged into one. After a hundred yards they hurled themselves into breast-high bushes, a thick tangle—a growth which, in such a mad rush as theirs, was no less formidable than a rock wall. They cast quick glances backward; a score of men—appearing, in their widely spread formation and from their cries and the racket of scuffling boots, to be a hundred—shut off all retreat and made hopeless any thought to turn to right or left.

"Down!" whispered Deveril. "Crawl for it! And quiet!"

On hands and knees they crawled into the thicket. Already hands and faces were scratched, but they did not feel the scratches; already their clothes were torn in many places. In a wild scramble they went on, squeezing through narrow spaces, lying flat, wriggling, getting to hands and knees again. And all the while with nerves jumping at each breaking of a twig. It was only the shouting voices and the pounding boots behind them that drowned in their pursuers' ears the sounds they made.

"Still!" admonished Babe Deveril in a whisper.

And very still they lay, side by side, panting, in the heart of the thicket. A voice called out, not twenty paces behind them:

"They're in there!" And another voice, louder than the first and more insistent, they thanked their stars, boomed:

"No, no! They skirted the brush, off to the left, beating it for the open! After 'em, boys!" And still other voices shouted and, it would seem, every man of them had glimpsed his own tricking shadow and had his own wild opinion.

Thus, for a brief enough moment, the pursuit was baffled.

"Slow and quiet does it!" It was for the third time Babe Deveril's whisper, his lips close to her hair. "I see an opening. Follow close."

Lynette, still lying face down, lifted herself a little way upon her two hands and looked after him.

"String 'em up!" a voice was calling. It was like the voice of a devil down in hell, full of mob malice. She shivered. "They're murdering devils. String 'em up!"

"Catch 'em first, you fool," called another voice. Again pounding boots and…far more sinister sound…snapping brush where a man was breaking his way straight into the thicket.

Like some grotesque, curiously shaped snake, Babe Deveril was writhing along, ever deeper into the brush tangle, ahead of her. She began crawling after him. Voices everywhere. And now dogs barking. A hundred dogs, it seemed to her taut nerves. She knew dogs; she knew how they went into a frenzy of excited joy when it was a question of a quarry, any quarry; she knew the unfailing certainty of the dog's scent. She began hurrying, struggling to get to her knees again….

"Sh! Down!"

She dropped down again and lay flat, scarce breathing. But once more she saw the vague blot of Deveril's flat form wriggling on ahead of her, almost gone now. It was so dark! She threw herself forward; she threw her arm out and her hand brushed his boot. It was a wonderful thing, to feel that boot. She was not alone. She began again following him; dry, broken, and thorny twigs snared at her; they caught in her clothes and in the laces of her boots; they tore at her skin. Yet this time she was as silent a shadow as the shadow in front of her. On and on and on, on endlessly through an eternity of darkness shot through with dim star glimmerings, and pierced with horrible voices, she went. She came out into an opening; she stood up. She was alone! And those voices and the yelping of dogs and the scuffling of heavy, insensate, merciless boots….

A hard, sudden hand caught her by the wrist. She whipped back, a scream shaping her lips. But in time she clapped a hand over her mouth. She was not alone; this was Babe Deveril, standing upright…waiting for her! She brought her hand down and clasped it, tight, over his hand.

"Run for it again," he whispered. "Off that way…to the right. If we can once get among those trees…."

Side by side, their hearts leaping, they ran. Gradually, but steadily, the harsh noises grew fainter behind them. They gained the fringe of trees; they splashed through the creek; they skirted a second tangle of brush and rounded the crest of a hill. And steadily and swiftly now the sounds of pursuit lessened behind them.

"And now," muttered Deveril, for the first time forsaking his cautious whisper, "if we use what brains God gave us, we are free of that hell pack."

"If they caught up with us?" she questioned him sharply.

"Most likely we'd both be swinging from a cottonwood in ten minutes! There's no sanity in that crowd; it's all mob spirit. If it is true that both Bruce Standing and Jim Taggart are dead…. Well, then, Lynette Brooke, this is no place for you and me tonight! Come on!…"

"Babe Deveril," she returned, and now it was her fingers tightening about his, "I'll never forget that you stood by me tonight!"

Babe Deveril, being himself and no other, a man reckless and unafraid and eminently gay, and, so God made him, full of lilting appreciation of the fair daughters of Eve, felt even at this moment her touch, like so much warm quicksilver trickling through him from head to foot. He gave her, in answer, a hearty pressure of the hand and his low, guarded laughter, saying lightly:

"You interfere with the regular beating of a man's heart, Lynette Brooke! But now you'll never remember tonight for any great measure of hours, unless we step along. They'll hunt us all night. Come, beautiful lady!"

Even then she marvelled at him. He, like herself, was tense and on the *qui vive*; yet she sensed his utter fearlessness. She knew that if they caught him and put a rope about his neck and led him under a cottonwood branch, he would pay them back to the last with his light, ringing laughter.

In this first wild rush they had had no time to think over what had just happened; no time to cast ahead beyond each step deeper into the night. Where they were going, what they were going to do—these were issues to confront them later; now they were concerned with no consideration other than haste and silence and each other's company. Tonight's section of destiny made of them, without any reasoning and merely through an instinctive attraction, trail fellows. True, both carried blurred pictures of what had occurred back there at the Gallup House so few minutes ago, but these were but pictures, and as yet gave rise to no logical speculation. As in a vision, she saw Timber-Wolf sagging and falling as he strove to slew about; Deveril saw Taggart rushing in at her heels, and then going down in a heap as a revolver was flung in his face. Only dully at present were they concerned with the query whether these two men were really dead. When one runs for his life through the woods in a dark night, he has enough to do to avoid limbs and tree trunks and keep on going.

Big Pine occupied the heart of a little upland flat. In ten minutes Lynette and Deveril had traversed the entire stretch of partially level land, and felt the ground begin to pitch sharply under foot. Here was a sudden steep slope leading down into a rugged ravine; their sensation was that of plunging over the brink of some direful precipice, feeling at every instant that they were about to go tumbling into an abyss. They were forced to go more slowly, sliding on their heels, ploughing through patches of soil, stumbling across flinty areas.

"Down we go, as straight as we can," said Deveril. "And up on the other side as straight as we can. Then we'll be in a bit of forest land where the devil himself couldn't find us on a night like this…. How are you standing the rough-stuff?"

It was the first time that he had given any indication of realizing that her girl's body might not be equal to the work which they were taking upon them. Swiftly she made her answer, saying lightly, despite her labored breathing:

"Fine. This is nothing."

"If I hadn't forgotten my hat…among other things," he chuckled, "I'd take it off to you right now, Lynette Brooke!"

They paused and stood a moment in the gloom about the base of a big boulder, listening. Now and then a man shouted; dogs still barked. But the sounds were appreciably fainter, now that they had started down the steeply pitching slope into the ravine.

"We can get away from them tonight," she said. "But tomorrow, when it is light?"

"We'll see. For one thing, a chase like this always loses some of its fine enthusiasm after the first spurt. For another, even if they did pick us up to-morrow, they would have had time to cool off a bit; a mob can't stay hot overnight. But give us a full night's head-start, and I've a notion we've seen the last of them. Ready?"

"Always ready!"

Again they hurried on, straight down into the great cleft through the mountains, swerving into brief détours only for upheaved piles of boulders or for an occasional brushy tangle. In twenty minutes they were down in the bed of the ravine, and splashing through a little trickle of water; Lynette stooped and drank, while Deveril stood listening; again, climbing now, they went on. The farther side of the canyon was as steep as the one they had come down, and it was tedious labor in the dark to make their way; at times they zigzagged one way and another to lessen the sheerness of their path. And fre-quently now they stopped and drank deep draughts of the clear mountain air.

Silence shut down about them, ruffled only by the soft wind stirring across the mountain ridges. It was not that they were so soon out of ear-shot of Big Pine; rather, this sudden lull meant that their pursuers, done with the first moments of blind excitement, were now gathering their wits and think-ing coolly…and planning. They would be taking to horseback soon; scouting this way and that, organizing and throwing out their lines like a great net. By now some one man, perhaps Young Gallup, had taken charge and was directing them. The two fugitives, senses sharpened, understood, and again hastened on. They had not won to any degree of security, and felt with quick-ened nerves the full menace of this new, sinister silence.

Onward and upward they labored, until at last they gained a less steeply sloping timber belt, which stretched close under the peak of the ridge. They walked more swiftly now; breathing was easier; there were more and wider open spaces among the larger, more generously spaced tree trunks.

"We'll strike into the Buck Valley road in a minute now," said Deveril. "Then we'll have easy going...."

"And will leave tracks that they'll see in the morning!"

"Of course. Any fool ought to have thought of that," he muttered, ashamed that it had been she instead of himself who had foreseen the danger.

So they hearkened to the voice of caution and paralleled the road, keeping a dozen or a score of paces to its side, and often tempted, because of its comparative smoothness and the difficult brokenness of the mountainside over which they elected to travel, to yield utterly to its inviting voice. They turned back and glimpsed the twinkling lights of Big Pine; they lost the lights as they forged on; they found them again, grown fainter and fewer and farther away.

"Can you go on walking this way all night?" he asked her once.

"All night, if we have to," she told him simply.

They tramped along in silence, their boots rising and falling regularly. The first tenseness, since human nerves will remain taut only so long, had passed. They had time for thought now, both before and after. Mentally each was reviewing all that had occurred tonight and, building theoretically upon those happenings, was casting forward into the future. The present was a path of hazard, and surely the future lay shut in by black shadows. Yet both of them were young, and youth is the time of golden hopes, no matter how drearily embraced by stony facts. And youth, in both of them, despite the difference of sex, was of the same order: a time of wild blood; youth at its animal best, lusty, vigorous, dauntless, devil-may-care; theirs the spirits which leap, hearts glad and fearless. And when, after a while, now and then they spoke again, there was youth playing up to youth in its own inevitable fashion; confidence asserting itself and begetting more confidence; youth wearing its outer cloakings with its own inimitable swagger.

They had trudged along the narrow mountain road for a full hour or more when they heard the clattering noise of a horse's shod hoofs.

"I knew it," said Deveril sharply. "Damn them."

With one accord he and she withdrew hastily, slipping into the convenient shadows thrown by a clump of trees, and peered forth through a screen of high brush. The hurrying hoof beats came on, up-grade, hence from the general direction of Big Pine. Two men, and riding neck and neck, driving their horses hard. The riders drew on rapidly; were for a fleeting moment vaguely outlined against a field of stars...swept on.

They came with a rush, with a rush they were gone. But Deveril, who since he was taller, had seen more clearly than Lynette across the brush, turned back to her eagerly, wondering if she had seen what he had—if she had noted that one of the men loomed unusually large in the saddle, and how the smaller at his side rode lopsidedly. In all reason Bruce Standing should be dead by now or, at the very least, bedridden. But when did Timber-Wolf ever do what other men expected of him? If he were alive and not badly hurt; if Lynette knew this, then what? Deveril would tell her, or would not tell her, as circumstances should decide for him.

"Come on!" he cried sharply, certain that Lynette had not seen. "While the night and the dark last. Let's hurry."

On and on they went until the dragging hours seemed endless. They saw the wheeling progress of the stars; they saw the pools of gloom in the woods deepen and darken; they felt, like thick black padded velvet, the silence grow deeper, until it seemed scarcely ruffled by the thin passing of the night air. Thus they put many a weary, hard-won mile between them and Big Pine. Hours of that monotonous lifting of boot after boot, of stumbling and straightening and driving on; of pushing through brush copses, of winding wearily among the bigger boles of the forest, of sliding down steep places and climbing up others, with always the lure of the more easy way of the road tempting and mocking.

"We've got to find water again," said Deveril, out of a long silence. "And we've got to dig ourselves in for a day of it. The dawn's coming."

For already the eastern sky stood forth in contrast against west and south and north, a palely glimmering sweep of emptiness charged with the promise of another day. The girl, too tired for speech, agreed with a weary nod. She could think of nothing now, neither of past nor present nor future, save of water, a long, cool bathing of burning mouth and throat, and after that, rest and sleep. Her whole being was resolved into an aching desire for these two simple balms to jaded nature. Water and then sleep. And let the coming day bring what it chose.

Long ago the mountain air, rare and sweet and clean, had grown cold, but their bodies, warmed by exertion, were unaware of the chill. But now, with fatigue working its will upon every laboring muscle, they began to feel the cold. Lynette began shivering first; Deveril, when they stopped a little while for one of their brief rests, began to shiver with her.

Water was not to be found at every step in these mountains; they labored on another three or four miles before they found it. Then they came to a singing brook which shot under a little log bridge, and there they lay flat, side by side, and drank their fill.

"And now, fair lady, to bed," said Deveril, looking at her curiously and making nothing of her expression, since the starlight hid more than it disclosed, and giving her as little glimpse of his own look. "And when, I wonder, did you ever lay you down to sleep as you must tonight?"

But he did see that she shivered. And yet, bravely enough, she answered him, saying:

"Beggars must not be choosers, fair sir; and methinks we should go down on our knees and offer up our thanks to Our Lady that we live and breathe and have the option of choosing our sleeping places this night."

She had caught his cue, and her readiness threw him into a mood of light laughter; he had drunk deep, and his youthful resilience buoyed him up, and he found life, as always, a game far away and more than worth the candle.

"You say truly, my fair lady," he said in mock gravity. "'Tis better to sleep among the bushes than dangling at the end of a brief stretch of rope."

But with all of their lightness of speech, which, after all, was but the symbol of youth playing up to youth, the prospect was dreary enough, and in their hearts there was little laughter. And the cold bit at them with its icy teeth. A fire would have been more than welcome, a thing to cheer as well as to warm; but a fire here, on the mountainside, would have been a visible token of brainlessness; it would throw its warmth five feet and its betraying light as many miles.

So, in the cold and dark they chose their sleeping place. Into a tangle of fragrant bushes, not twenty paces from the Buck Valley road, they crawled on hands and knees, as they had crawled into that first thicket when pursuit yelped at their heels. Here they came by chance upon a spot where two big pine-trees, standing close together companionably, upreared from the very heart of the brushy tangle. Lynette could scarcely drag her tired body here, caught and retarded by every twig that clutched at her clothing. For the first time in her vigorous life she came to understand the meaning of that ancient expression, "tired to death." She felt herself drooping into unconsciousness almost before her body slumped down upon the earth, thinly covered in fall-en leaves.

"I am sleepy," she murmured. "Almost dead for sleep...."

"You wonderful girl...."

"Sh! I can't talk anymore. I can't think; I can't move; I can scarcely breathe. Whether they find us in the morning or not...it doesn't matter to me now.... You have been good to me; be good to me still. And...good-night, Babe Deveril... Gentleman!"

He saw her, dimly, nestle down, cuddling her cheek against her arm, drawing up her knees a little, snuggling into the very arms of mother earth, like a baby finding its warm place against its mother's breast. He sat down and slowly made himself a cigarette, and forgot for a long time to light it, lost in his thoughts as he stared at her and listened to her quiet breathing. He knew the moment that she went to sleep. And in his heart of hearts he marvelled at her and called her "a dead-game little sport." She, of a beauty which he in all of his light adventurings found incomparable, had ventured with him, a man unknown to her, into the depths of these solitudes and had never, for a second, evinced the least fear of him. True, danger drove; and yet danger always lay in the hands of a man, her sex's truest friend and greatest foe. In his hands reposed her security and her undoing. And yet, knowing all this, as she must, she lay down and sighed and went to sleep. And her last word, ingenuous and yet packed to the brim with human understanding, still rang in his ears.

"It's worth it," he decided, his eyes lingering with her gracefully abandoned figure. "The whole damn thing, and may the devil whistle through his fingers until his fires burn cold! And she's mine, and I'll make her mine and keep her mine until the world goes dead. And my friend, Wilfred Deveril, if you've ever said anything in your life, you've said it now!"

CHAPTER 7

Glancing sunlight, striking at him through a nest of tumbled boulders upon the ridge, woke Babe Deveril. He sat up sharply, stiff and cold and confused, wondering briefly at finding himself here upon the mountainside. Lynette was already sitting up, a huddling unit of discomfort, her arms about her upgathered knees, her hair tousled, her clothing torn, her eyes showing him that, though she had slept, she, too, had awaked shivering and unrested. And yet, as he gathered his wits, she was striving to smile.

"Good morning to you, my friend."

He got stiffly to his feet, stretching his arms up high above his head.

"At least, we're alive yet. That's something, Lynette."

"It's everything!" Emulating him she sprang up, scornfully disregarding cramped body, her triumphant youth ignoring those little pains which shot through her as pricking reminders of last night's endeavors. "To live, to breathe, to be alive…it's everything!"

"When one thinks back upon the possibilities of last night," he answered, "the reply is 'Yes.' Good morning, and here's hoping that you had no end of sweet dreams."

She looked at him curiously.

"I did dream," she said. "Did you?"

"No. When I slept, I slept hard. And your dreams?"

"Were all of two men. Of you and another man, Timber-Wolf, you call him—Bruce Standing. I heard him call you 'Baby Devil'! That got into my dreams. I thought that we three…."

She broke off, and still her eyes, fathomless, mysterious, regarded him strangely.

"Well?" he demanded. "We three?"

She shivered. And, knowing that he had seen, she exclaimed quickly:

"That's because I'm cold! I'm near frozen. Can't we have a fire?"

"But the dream?" he insisted.

"Dreams are nothing by the time they're told," she answered swiftly. "So why tell them? And the fire?"

"No," he told her, suddenly stubborn, and resentful that he could not have free entrance into her sleeping-life. "We went without it when we needed it most; now the sun's up and we don't need it; since, above everything, there's no breakfast to cook."

"So you woke up hungry, too?"

"Hungry? I was eating my supper when first you showed upon my horizon. And, what with looking at you or trying to look at you, I let half of my supper go by me! I'd give a hundred dollars right this minute for coffee and bacon and eggs!"

"You want a lot for a hundred dollars," she smiled back at him. Her hands were already busy with her tumbled hair, for always was Lynette purely feminine to her dainty fingertips. "I'd give all of that just for coffee alone."

"Come," said Deveril, "Let's go. Are you ready?"

"To move on? Somewhere, anywhere? And to search for breakfast? Yes; in a minute."

First, she worked her way back through the brush, down into the creek bed, and for a little while, as she bathed her face and neck and arms, and did the most that circumstances permitted at making her morning toilet, she was lost to his following eyes. Slowly he rolled himself a cigarette; that, with a man, may take the place of breakfast, serving to blunt the edge of a gnawing appetite. Long draughts of icy cold water served her similarly. She stamped her feet and swung her arms and twisted her body back and forth, striving to drive the cold out and get her blood to leaping warmly. Then, before coming back to him, she stood for a long time looking about her.

All the wilderness world was waking; she saw the scampering flash of a rabbit; the little fellow came to a dead halt in a grassy open space, and sat up with drooping forepaws and erect ears; she could fancy his twitching nose as he investigated the morning air to inform himself as to what scents, pleasurable, friendly, inimical, lay upon it.

"In case he is hungry, after nibbling about half the night," she mused, "he knows just where to go for his breakfast."

The rabbit flapped his long ears and went about his business, whatever it may have been, popping into the thicket. There grew in a pretty grove both willows and wild cherry; beyond them a tall scattering of cottonwoods; on the rising slope scrub-pines and juniper. And while she stood there, looking down, she heard some quail calling, and saw half a dozen sparrows busily beginning office hours, as it were, going about their day's affairs. And one and all of these little fellows knew just what he was about, and where to turn to a satisfying menu. When, returning to Deveril, she confided in him something of her findings, which would go to indicate that man was a pretty inefficient creature when stood alongside the creatures of the wild, Deveril retorted:

"Let them eat their fill now; before night we'll be eating them!"

"You haven't even a gun…."

"I could run a scared rabbit to death, I'm that starved! And now suppose we get out of this."

The sun was striking at the tops of the yellow pines on the distant ridge; the light was filtering downward; shadows were thinning about them and even in the ravine below. Walking stiffly, until their bodies gradually grew warm with the exertion, and always keeping to the thickest clump of trees or tallest patch of brush, they began to work their way down into the canyon. The sun ran them a race, but theirs was the victory; it was still half night in the great cleft among the mountains when they slid down the last few feet and found more level land underfoot, and the greensward of the wild-grass meadow fringing the lower stream. The canyon creek went slithering by them, cold and glassy-clear, whitening over the riffles, falling musically into the pools, dimpling and ever ready to break into widening circles, a smiling, happy stream. And in it, they knew, were trout. They stood for a moment, catching breath after the steep descent, looking into it.

"I wonder if you have a pin," said Deveril.

She pondered the matter, struck immediately by the aptness of the suggestion; he could see how she wrinkled her brows as she tried to remember if possibly she had made use of a pin in getting dressed the last time.

"I've a hairpin or two left. I wonder if we could make that do?"

"Just watch and see!" he exclaimed joyously.

In putting her tumbled hair straight just now she had discovered two pins, which, even when her hair had come down about her shoulders, had happened to catch in a little snarl in the thick tresses; these she had saved and used in making her morning toilet. Now she took her hair down again and presented him with the two pins, gathering her hair up in two thick, loose braids, while with curious eyes he watched her; and as curiously, the thing done, she watched him busy himself with the pins.

A few paces farther on, creeping forward under the willow branches, they came to a spot where the creek banks were clear of brush along a narrow grassy strip, which, however, was screened from the mountainside by a growth of taller trees. Here Deveril went to work on his improvised fish-hook. One hairpin he put carefully into his pocket; the other he bent rudely into the required shape, making an eye in one end by looping and twisting. The other end, that intended for the hungry mouth of a greedy trout, he regarded long and without enthusiasm.

"Too blunt, to begin with; next, no barb, too smooth; and, finally, the thing bends too easily. Hairpins should be made of steel!"

But at least two of the defects could be simply remedied up to a certain though not entirely satisfactory point. He squatted down and, employing two hard stones, hammered gently at the malleable wire until he flattened out the end of it into a thin blade with sharp, jagged edges. Then, using his pocket-knife, he managed to cut several little slots in this thin blade, so that there resulted a series of roughnesses which were not unlike barbs; whereas he could put no great faith in any one of them holding very securely, at least, taken all together, they would tend toward keeping his hook, if once taken, from slipping out so smoothly. He re-bent his pin and suddenly looked up at her with a flashing grin.

He robbed one of his boots of its string; he cut the first likely willow wand. Without stirring from his spot he dug in the moist earth and got his worm. And then, motioning her to be very still, he crept a few feet farther along the brook, found a pool which pleased him, hid behind a clump of bushes and gently lowered his baited hook toward the shadowy surface. And before the worm touched the water, a big trout saw and leaped and struck... and did a clean job of snatching the worm off without having appeared to so much as touch the bent hairpin!

Three quiet sounds came simultaneously: the splash of the falling fish, a grunt from Deveril, a gasp from Lynette. Deveril, thinking she was about to speak, glared at her in savage admonition for silence; she understood and remained motionless. Slowly he crept back to the spot where he had dug his worm, and scratched about until he had two more. One of them went promptly to his hook, while he held the other in reserve. Again he approached his pool, again he lowered his bait about the bush. This time the offering barely touched the water before the trout struck again. Now Deveril was ready for him, deftly manœuvring his pole; his string tautened, his wallow bent, the fat, glistening trout swung above the racing water.... Lynette was already wondering how they were going to cook it!... There was again a splash, and Deveril stood staring at a silly-looking hairpin, dangling at the end of an absurd boot-lace. For now the hairpin failed to present the vaguest resemblance to any kind of a hook; the trout's weight had been more than sufficient to straighten it out so that the fish slipped off.

Gradually, moving on noiseless feet, the girl withdrew; her last glimpse of Deveril, before she slipped out of sight among the willows, showed her his face, grim in its set purpose. He was trying the third time, and she believed that he would stand there without moving all day long, if necessary. In the meantime she was done with inactivity and watching; doing nothing when there was much to be done irked her.

Withdrawn far enough to make her certain that no chance sound made by her would disturb his trout, she went on through the grove and across little grassy open spaces flooring the canyon, making her way further up-stream. When a hundred yards above him, she turned about a tangled thicket and came upon the creek where it flashed through shallows. All of her life she had lived in the mountains; as a little girl, many a day had she followed a stream like this, bickering away down the most tempting of wild places; and more than once, lying by a tiny clear pool, had she caught in her hands one of the quick fishes, just to set him in a little lakelet of her own construction, where she played with him before letting him go again. Today…if she could catch her fish first! While Deveril, man-like, taking all such responsibilities upon his own shoulders, cursed silently and achieved nothing beyond loss of bait and loss of temper!

Up-stream, always keeping close to the merrily musical water, she made her slow way until she found a likely spot. At the base of a tiny waterfall was a big smooth rock; the water from above, glassily smooth in its well-worn channel, struck upon the rock and was divided briefly into two streams. One of them, the lesser, poured down into a small, rock-rimmed pool; the other, deflected sharply, sped down another course, to rejoin its fellow a few feet below the pool.

It was to the pool itself, half shut off from the main current, that Lynette gave her quickened attention. She crept closer, noiseless, peeping over. A sudden dark gleam, the quick, nervous steering of a trout rewarded her. She stood still, making a profound study of what lay before her; in what the rock-edged pool aided and wherein it would present difficulties. Scarcely more than a trickle of water poured out at the lower side; she could hastily pile up a few stones there, and so construct a wall insurmountable to the trout if minded to escape down-stream. Then she looked to the far side, where the water slipped in. She could lay a few broken limbs across the rock there and build up a rampart of stones and turf upon it, and so deflect nearly all of the incoming water. Both these things done, she could, if need be, bail the pool out, and so come with certainty upon whatever fish had blundered into it. She began to hope that she would find a dozen!

Twice, standing upon the glassy rocks, she slipped; once she got soaking wet to her knee; another time she saved herself from a thorough drenching in the ice-cold stream only at the cost of plunging one arm down into it, elbow-deep. She shivered but kept steadily on.

She heard a bird among the bushes and started, thinking that here came Deveril; she fancied him with a string of fish in his hand, laughing at her. Impulsively she called to him.

The close walls of the ravine shut in her voice; the thickets muffled it; the splash and gurgle of the tumbling water drowned it out. She stood very still, hushed; now suddenly the silence, the loneliness, the bigness of the wilderness closed in about her. She looked about fearfully, half expecting to see men spring out from behind every boulder or tree trunk. She longed suddenly to see Babe Deveril coming up along the creek to her. She was tempted to break into a run racing back to him.

She caught herself up short. All this was only a foolish flurry in her breast, conjured up by that sudden realization of loneliness when her quickened voice died away into the whispered hush of the still solitudes. For an instant that feeling of being alone had overpowered her, or threatened to do so; then her only thought had been of Babe Deveril; she could have rushed fairly into his arms, so did her emotions drive her. Now she found time to puzzle over herself; it struck her now, for the first time, how she had fled unquestioningly into this wilderness with a man. A man whom she did not even know. That hasty headlong act of hers would seem to indicate a trust of a sort. But did she actually trust Babe Deveril, with those keen, cutting eyes of his and the way he had of looking at a girl, and the whole of his reckless and dare-devil personality? Lynette Brooke had not lived in a cave all of her brief span of life; nor had she grown into slim girlhood and the full bud of her glorious youth without more than one look into a mirror. Vapidly vain she was not; but clear-visioned she was, and she knew and was glad for the vital, vivid beauty which was hers and thanked God for it. And she glimpsed, if somewhat vaguely, that to a man like Babe Deveril, taking life lightly, there was no lure beyond that of red lips and sparkling eyes. How far could she be sure of him? She went back with slow steps to her trout; she was glad that Babe Deveril had not heard and come running to her just then. But when Deveril did come, carrying two gleaming trout, she masked her misgivings and lifted a laughing face toward his triumphant one.

"We eat, Lynette!" he announced gaily.

Suddenly his eyes warmed to the picture she made, paying swift tribute to the tousled, flushed beauty of her. His glance left her face and ran swiftly down her form; she felt suddenly as though her wet clothing were plastered tight to her.

"You can finish this," she told him swiftly, "if you want to take anymore fish."

"But, look here! Where are you going? Breakfast...."

Her teeth were beginning to chatter.

"I'm going to try to get dry. You can start breakfast or...."

She fled, and called herself a fool for growing scarlet, as she knew that she did; as though two burning rays had been directed full upon her back, she could feel his look as she ran from him; she could not quickly enough vanish from his keen eyes, beyond the thicket. And how on earth she was going to get dry again until the sun stood high in the sky, she did not in the least know. She could wring out the free water; she could make flails of her arms and run up and down until she got warm.... If only she had a fire; but that would be foolhardy, the smoke arising to stand a signal for miles of their whereabouts....

And until this moment she had not thought of how they were to convert freshly caught fish into an edible breakfast! How, without fire? She began to shiver again, from head to foot now, and, confronted by her own problem, that of getting warm and dry, she was content to leave all other solutions to Deveril.

When half an hour later she returned to him, she found him smoking a cigarette and crouching over a bed of dying coals, whereon certain tempting morsels lay; Deveril was turning them this way and that; with the savory odor of the grilling fish there arose from the embers a whiff of the green sage-leaves which he had plucked at the slope of the canyon and laid first on his bed of coals. Crisp mountain-trout, garnished with sage! And plenty of clear, cold, sparkling water to drink thereafter! Truly a morning repast for king and queen.

"I hope they keep us on the run for a month!" Deveril greeted her. "I haven't had this much fun for a dozen years!"

"But your fire?" she asked anxiously. "Aren't you afraid? The smoke?"

"Where there's smoke, there's always fire," he told her lightly. "But when a man's on the dodge, as we are, he can have a fire that gives out almighty little smoke! It's all bone-dry wood, with only the handful of sage and a few crisscross willow sticks. Look up, and see how much smoke you can see!"

He had built his small blaze, ringed about by some rocks, in the heart of a small grove of trees which stood forty or fifty feet high; he had got his fire burning with strong, clean flames, from a handful of dry leaves and twigs; Lynette, looking up, could make out only the faintest bluish-gray wisp of smoke against the gray-green of the leaves. She understood; always it was inevitable that they must accept whatever chances the moment brought them, yet it was not at all likely that their faint plume of smoke, vanishing among the treetops, would ever draw the glance of any human eye other than their own.

"I'll tell you …" began Deveril, and broke short off there, as she and he, alert and tense once more, reminded that they were fugitives, listened to a sudden sound disturbing their silence. A sound unmistakable—a man at no great distance from them, but, fortunately, upon the farther side of the stream, and thus beyond the double screen of willows, was breaking his way through the brush. Both Deveril and Lynette crouched low, peering through the bushes. They could only make out that the man was coming up-stream. Once they caught a vague, blurred glimpse of his legs, faded overalls and ragged boots. Then they lost him entirely. They knew when he stopped and both waited breathlessly to know if he had come upon some sign of their own trail. But once more he went on, but now in such silence, as he crossed a little open spot, that they could scarcely make out a sound. Had it not been for the willows intervening, they could then have answered their own question, "Who is it?"—a question just now of supreme importance, of the importance of life and death. They lay lower; they strove as never before to catch some glimpse that would tell them what they wanted to know. The man stopped again; again went on. There was something guarded about his movements; they felt that he must have seen their tracks, that he was seeking in a round-about way to come unexpectedly upon them. And then, because there was a narrow natural avenue through the brush, they were given one clear, though fleeting glimpse, of him…of his face—a face as tense and watchful as their own had been…the face of Mexicali Joe.

CHAPTER 8

A glimpse, scarcely more it was, had been given them of Mexicali Joe's face. And at a considerable distance, at least for the reading of a man's look. But yet they marked how the face was haggard and drawn and furtive. Joe had no inkling of their presence. He had not seen their wisp of smoke; there was no wind setting toward him to carry him the smell of cooking trout. Plainly he had no desire for company other than his own. He, no less than they, fled from all pursuit. Again he was lost to them; he vanished, gone up-stream, beyond the thickets, no faintest sound of his footfalls coming back to them. From him they turned to each other, the same expression from the same flooding thought in their eyes.

"We're on the jump and we'll keep on the jump!" said Deveril softly. "And at the same time, Lynette Brooke, we'll stick as close as the Lord'll let us to Mexicali Joe's coat-tails! Don't you worry; he'll go back as sure as shooting to his gold-mine, if only to make certain that no one else has squatted on it. And where he drives a stake, we'll drive ours right alongside!"

"It's funny…that he hasn't gotten any further…that he should come this way, too…."

"No telling how long he had to lie still while the pack yelped about his hiding-place; that he came this way means only one thing. And that is that our luck is with us, and we're headed as straight as he is toward his prospect hole. Ready? Let's follow him!"

She jumped up. But before they started they gathered up, to the last small bit, what was left of their fish; Deveril made the small bundle, fish enwrapped in leaves, with a handkerchief about the whole.

"If he should hear us?" she whispered. "If he should lie in waiting and see us?"

He chuckled.

"In any case, we'll have it on him! He can't know that we're on the run, too; he got away too fast for that. And even if he should know, what would he do about it? He has no love for Taggart, anyway; and he has no wish to get himself into the hands of that mob that he has just ducked away from, like a rabbit dodging a pack of hounds. If he catches us…why, then, we catch him at the same time! Come on."

Thus began the second lap of their journey; thus they, fleeing, followed like shadows upon the traces of one who fled. For Mexicali Joe would obviously keep to the bed of the canyon; if he forsook it in order to climb up either slope to a ridge above, he must of necessity pass through the more sparsely timbered spaces, where he would run constantly into danger of being seen. The only danger to their plans lay with the possibility that he might overhear sounds of their following and might draw a little to one side and hide in some dense copse, and so let them go by. But they had the advantage from the beginning; they knew he was ahead, and he did not know that they followed; so long as they, listening always, did not hear him ahead, there was little danger of him hearing them coming after him. With all the noise of the water, tumbling over falls and splashing along over rocks, singing cheerily to itself at every step, there was small likelihood of any one of the three cautious footfalls being heard....

There were the times, so intent were they following the Mexican, when they forgot what was after all the main issue; forgot that they, too, were followed. For the newer phase of the game was more zestful just now than the other; they had neither glimpsed nor heard anything since the passing of the two riders last night to hint that any danger of discovery threatened them. They spoke seldom, only now and then, pausing briefly, in lowered voices, as the speculations which had been occupying both minds, demanded expression. Thus they were always confronted by some new problem; at first, and for a mile or more, they had full confidence that they had Joe straight ahead of them. But presently they approached a fork of the canyon; it became imperative to know if Joe had gone up the right or the left ravine. And here, where most they wanted a glimpse of him, they had scant hope of seeing him, so dense was the timber growth; he would keep close to the bed of the stream, at times walking in the water so that the network of branches from the brushy tangle on both banks would make for him a dim alleyway, like a tunnel. They could not hope to hear him; they could not count on finding his tracks, since none would be left upon the rocks and the rushing water held none.

But they were alert, ears critical of the slightest rustling, eyes never keener. And, their good fortune holding firm, when they came to the forking of the ways, that which they had not hoped for, a track upon a hard rock, set them right. For here Joe, but a few score yards ahead of them, had slipped, and had crawled up over a boulder, and there was still the wet trace of his passing, a sign to vanish, drying, while they looked on it. Joe had gone on into the deeper canyon, headed in the direction which last night they had elected for their own, driving on toward the heart of the wilderness country.

They were no less relieved at finding what was the man's likely general direction than at making sure that they were still almost at his heels. For they had come to realize that, to explain Joe's presence here, there were two directly opposing possibilities to consider: It was imaginable that Joe would be making straight for his gold; and it was just as reasonable that his craft might have suggested to him to head in an opposite direction. Now that they might follow him and still be going direct upon their own business, they were for the moment content upon all points.

Deveril, for the most part, went ahead; now and then he paused a moment for the girl to come up with him. But never did he have to wait long. He began to wonder at her; they had covered many hard miles last night; more hard miles this morning. How long, he asked himself, as his eyes sought to read hers, could such a slender, altogether feminine, blush-pink girl stand up under such relentless hardship as this flight promised to give them? And always he went on again, reassured and admiring; her eyes remained clear, her regard straight and cool. A girl unafraid; the true daughter of dauntless, hot-blooded parents.

And she, watching his tall, always graceful form leading the way, found ample time to wonder about him. She had seen him last night burst in through a window and take the time coolly, though already the hue and cry was breaking at his contemptuous heels, to rifle a man's pockets. There was an indelible picture: the debonair Babe Deveril, who had stepped unquestioningly into her fight, going down on his knees before his fallen kinsman…calmly bent upon robbery. For she had seen the bank-notes in his hand.

The sun rose high and crested all the ridges with glorious light, and poured its golden warmth down into the steep canyons. But, now that shadows began to shrink and the little open spaces lay revealed in detail, fresh labor was added in that they were steadily harder driven to keep to cover; all day long, at intervals, they were to have glimpses of the Buck Valley road, high above upon the mountain flank, and at each view of the road they understood that a man up there might have caught a glimpse of them. Ten o'clock came and found them doggedly following along the way which they held the viewless Mexicali Joe must have taken before them. They paused and stooped to the invitation of the creek, and thereafter ate what was left them of their grilled trout. Having eaten, they drank again; and having drunk, they again took up the trail.…

"If you can stand the pace?" queried Deveril over his shoulder. And she read in the gleam in his eyes that he was set on seeing this thing through; on sticking close to Mexicali Joe until he came, with Joe, upon his secret.

"Why, of course!" she told him lightly, though already her body ached.

It was not over an hour later when they set their feet in a trail which they were confident Mexicali Joe had followed; from the moment they stepped into the trail they watched for some trace of him, but the hard, rain-washed, rocky way which only a mountaineer could have recognized as a trail, was such as to hold scant sign, if the one who travelled it but exercised precaution. Babe Deveril, with his small knowledge of these mountains, held it the old short-cut trail from Timkin's Bar, long disused, since Timkin's Bar itself had a score of years ago died the death of short-lived mining towns. Brush grew over it, and again and again it vanished underfoot, and they were hard beset to grope forward to it again. Yet trail of a sort it was, and it set them to meditating: Timkin's Bar, in the late '80s, had created a gold furor, and then, after its short and hectic life, had been abandoned, as an orange, sucked dry by a child, is thrown aside. Was it possible that among the old diggings Mexicali Joe had stumbled upon a vein which the old-timers had overlooked?

At any rate, the trail lured them along, winding in their own general direction; and Mexicali Joe still fled ahead. Of this latter fact they had evidence when they came to the unmistakable sign…to watchful eyes…of his recent passing: here, on the steep, ill-defined trail he had slipped, and had caught at the branches of a wild cherry. They saw the furrow made by his boot-heel and the scattered leaves and broken twigs.

Gradually the trail led them up out of the canyon-bed, snaking along the flank of the mountain. And gradually they were entering the great forest land of yellow pines. If not already in Timber-Wolf's country, here was the border-line of his monster holdings: few men could draw the line exactly between the wide-reaching acres which were his and those contiguous acres which were a portion of the government reserve. Standing himself had quarrelled with the government upon the matter and what was more, after no end of litigation, had won a point or two.

Once they diverged from the trail to climb and slide to the bottom of the canyon for a long drink. But this and the sheer ascent took them in their hurry only a few minutes. Again they took up the trail. It was high noon and they were tired. But, alike disdainful of fatigue, driven and lured, they pressed on.

Suddenly she startled him by catching him by the arm and whispering warningly:

"Sh! Some one is following us!"

In another moment, drawing back from the trail, they were hidden among the wild cherries in a little side ravine.

"Where?" he demanded, his voice hushed like hers, as he peered back along the way they had come. "Who? How many of them?"

"I didn't see," she answered.

"What did you hear?"

"Nothing… I just know… I *felt* that someone was trailing us just as we are trailing Mexicali Joe! I feel it now; I know!"

"But you had something—something that you saw or heard—to tell you?"

She shook her head. And he saw, wondering at her, that she was very deeply in earnest as she admitted:

"No. Nothing! But I know. I tell you, I know. Can't you feel that there is someone back there, following us, spying on us, hiding and yet dogging every step we take? Can't you *feel* it?"

She saw him shaken with silent laughter. She understood that he, a man, was convulsed with laughter at the imaginings of her, a maid. And yet, also, since she was quick-minded, she noted how his laughter was *silent*! He meant her to see that he put no credence in her suspicions; and yet, for all that, he was impressed, and he did take care that no one, who *might* follow them, should overhear him!

"One doesn't feel things like that," he told her, as though positive. But in the telling he kept his voice low, so that it was scarcely louder than her own whisper.

"One does," she retorted. "And you know it, Babe Deveril!"

"But," he challenged her, "were you right, and were there a man or several men back there tracking us, why all this caution on their parts? What would they be waiting for, being armed themselves and knowing us unarmed? What better place than this to take us in? Why give us a minute's chance to slip away in the brush?"

"I don't know." She shrugged, and again he marvelled at her; she looked like one who had little vital concern in what any others, pursuing, might or might not do.

Despite his cool determination to adhere to calm reason and to discount feminine impressionism, which he held to be fostered by a nervous condition brought about by overexertion, Babe Deveril began to feel, as she felt, that there was something more than imagination in her contention. How does a man sense things which no one of his five senses can explain to him? He could not see any reason in this abrupt change in both their moods; and yet, none the less, it seemed to him, all of a sudden, as though eyes were spying on him from behind every pine trunk, and from the screen of every thicket.

"Joe won't escape us in a hurry," he muttered. "Not in this canyon. And we'll see this thing through. Let's sit tight and watch."

And so, with that inexplicable sense that here in the wilderness they were not yet free from pursuit, they crouched in the bushes and bent every force of every sense to detect their fancied pursuers. But the forest land, sun-smitten, a playland of light and shadow and tremulous breeze, lay steeped in quiet about them, and they saw nothing moving save the gently stirring leaves and occasional birds; half a dozen sparrows briefly stayed their flight upon a shrub in flower with pale-pink blossoms; a bevy of quail, forty strong, marched away through the narrow roadways under the low, drooping branches, with crested topknots bobbing; the forest land murmured and whispered and sang softly, and seemed empty of any other human presence than their own. And yet they waited, and at the end of their waiting, grown nervous despite themselves, though they had had no slightest evidence that pursuit was drawing close upon their heels, they were not able to shake from them that *feeling* that danger, the danger from which they fled, was become a near-drawn menace. And all the more to be feared in that it approached so silently, covertly, hidden and ready to strike when their guard was down.

"Just the same," said Deveril, deep in his own musings, "it can't be Jim Taggart, for that's not Taggart's way, having the goods on a man, and, besides, I fancy I put him out of the running." Then he looked at her curiously, and added: "And it can't be Bruce Standing, since you put him down and out and...."

It was the first time that such a reference to the past had been made. Now she startled him by the quick vehemence of her denial, saying:

"I didn't shoot Bruce Standing! I tell you...."

He looked at her steadily, and she broke off, as she saw dawning in his eyes a look which was to be read as readily as were white stones to be glimpsed in the bottom of a clear pool. She had made her statement, and, whether true or false, he held it to be a lie.

"In case they should somehow lay us by the heels," he said dryly, "you would come a lot closer to clearing yourself by saying that you shot him in self-defense than in denying everything. But they haven't got their ropes over our running horns yet!... Do you still feel that we are followed?"

His look angered her; his words angered her still further. So to his question she made no reply. He looked at her again curiously. She refused to meet his eyes, coolly ignoring him. A little smile twitched at his lips.

"It's a poor time for good friends to fall out," he said lightly. "I don't care the snap of my fingers who shot him, or why. He ought to have been shot a dozen years ago. And now I'll tell you what, I think, explains this business of someone being close behind us, if you are right in it. The big chance is that someone has been trailing Mexicali Joe all along; and dropped in behind us when we dropped in behind Joe. We've been doing a first-class job of sticking to cover; mind you, we haven't caught a second glimpse of Joe all this time, and therefore it is as likely as not that the gent whom you *feel* to be trailing us hasn't caught a glimpse of us. If this is right, we've got a bully chance right now to prove it. We lie close where we are for ten minutes, and see if your hombre doesn't slip on by us, nosing along after Joe."

In silence she acquiesced. That sense of the nearness of another unseen human being was insistent upon her. For a long time, as still as the deep-rooted trees about them, they crouched, listening, watching. She heard the watch ticking in Babe Deveril's pocket. She heard her own breathing and his. She heard the brownie birds threshing among dead leaves. Then there was the eternal whispering of the pines and the faint murmurings from the stream far down in the canyon. At last it would have been a relief to straining nerves if a man, or two or three men, had stepped into sight in the trail from which she and Deveril had withdrawn. For more certain than ever was Lynette Brooke, though she could give neither rhyme nor reason for that certainty, that her instincts had not tricked her. Therefore, instead of being reassured at seeing or hearing no one, she was depressed and made anxious; the silence became sinister, filled with vague threat; that she saw no one was explicable to her by but the one ominous condition: that person or those persons were watching even now, and knew where she and Babe Deveril hid, and did not mean to stir until first their quarry stirred. Why all this caution? She could not explain that to herself; if someone followed, why should that someone hide? Why not step out with gun levelled, and put an end to this grim game of hide-and-seek.

"You see," whispered Deveril, "there is no one behind us."

They had not moved for a full twenty minutes, and by now he began to convict her of nervous imaginings, fancies of an overwrought girl. But she answered him, saying with unshaken certainty:

"I tell you, I know! Some one has been following us, and now is hiding and waiting for us to go on."

"Well, you are right or wrong, and in either case I don't fancy this job of sitting so tight I feel as though I were growing roots. If you should happen to be right, we'll know in time, I suppose. Let's go!"

To her, in her present mood, anything was better than inaction. They left their hiding-place, found a silent and hidden way a bit farther down the slope, went forward a hundred yards and stepped back into the faint trail. Their concern, each said inwardly, was to forge on and to follow Joe; thus they pretended within themselves to ignore that nebulous warning that they, like Joe, were followed.

And so the day wore on, a day made up of uncertainty and vague threat. How full the silent forest lands were of little sounds! For therein lies the greatest of all forest-land mysteries; that silence in the solitudes may be made audible. Uncertainty struck the key-note of their long day. They sought to follow Mexicali Joe; they did not see him, they did not hear him, they did not know where he was. Was he still ahead of them, hastening on? How far ahead? A mile by now, not having paused while they lost time? A hundred yards? Or had he turned aside? Or had he thrown himself down flat somewhere, watching them go by? Was he following them, or had he struck out east or west, while they went on north? And was there someone following them? One man? Two? More? Or none at all? Uncertainty. And as they grew tired and hungry, the great silence oppressed them, and most of all this uncertainty of all things began to bite in upon their nerves as acid eats into glass, etching its own sign.

"I'm getting jumpy," muttered Deveril, glaring at her, his eyes looking savage and stern. "This nonsense of yours...."

"It's not nonsense!"

"Anyway, it's getting on my nerves! There's no sense in this sort of thing. We're scaring ourselves like two kids in the dark. What's more, we are allowing a pace-setter to get us to going too hard and steady a clip; we'll be done in, the first thing we know. And we've got to begin figuring on where the next meal comes from. What I mean is, that we've got enough to do without wasting any more nerve force on what may or may not follow after us."

"Joe is still ahead of us," she reminded him; "or, at any rate, we think that he is. He left last night in as big a hurry as we did; and he, too, came away without gun and fishing-tackle, and didn't stop to get Young Gallup to put him up a lunch. Then, on top of all that, Joe knows this country better than we do."

"I get you!" he told her quickly. "Joe's as ready for food and lodging as we are, and Joe, unless we're wrong all along, is hiking ahead of us. Who knows but we'll invite ourselves to dine with Señor Joe before the day's done!... Is that it?"

"I don't know how it may work out.... I hadn't gotten that far yet.... But if Joe is headed toward his secret, and if he does have a provision cache somewhere in the mountains...a few items in tinned goods and, maybe, even coffee and sugar and canned milk...."

"Let's go!" broke in Deveril, half in laughter and half in eagerness. "You make my mouth water with your surmisings."

Here in these steep-walled narrow gorges the shadows lengthened swiftly after the sun had passed the zenith, and already, when now and then they looked searchingly at what lay ahead, it was difficult to distinguish the shadows from the substance. They must come close to Joe if they meant to see him, and, by the same token, if a man followed them, he was confronted by the same difficulty. So they hurried on, walking more freely, keeping in the trail, climbing at times along the ridge flank, frequently dipping down into the lower canyon. Babe Deveril cut himself a green cudgel from a scrub-oak, trimming off the twigs as he walked on. If it came to argument with Mexicali Joe, a club like that might bring persuasion. And he fully meant that the Mexican should show himself generous, even to the division of a last crust. Always buoyed up by optimism, he was counting strongly on Joe's provision cache.

When they dropped down into the canyon again, they saw the first star. Lynette looked up at it; it trembled in its field of deep blue. She was faint, almost dizzy; her muscles ached; fatigue bore hard upon her spirit; she was footsore. But, most of all, like Deveril before her, she was concerned with imaginings of supper. She pictured bacon and a tin of tomatoes and shoestring potatoes sizzling in the bacon grease...and coffee. Whether with milk or sugar, or without both, no longer mattered. Then she sighed wearily, and had no other physical nor mental occupation than that which had to do with the putting of one foot before the other, plodding on and on and on. And all the while the shadows deepened and thickened in the canyons, and the stars multiplied, and the little evening breeze sharpened; she began to shiver.

She could mark no trail underfoot; always Deveril, before her, was breaking through a tangle, always at his heels, she kept his form in sight; but she began to think that he had lost the way, and a new fear gripped her. Instead of dining with Joe, they were losing him, and now, with the utter dark already on the way, they would see no sign of him. And in the dark they would not be able to snare a trout or anything else that might be eaten. She got into the habit of breaking off twigs and chewing at them….

And all the while Deveril was rushing on, faster and faster. It was hard work keeping up with him.

"We've got him! Stay with it, Lynette; we've got him!"

It was Deveril's whisper, sharp and eager; there was Deveril himself just ahead of her, pausing briefly.

"Come on. As fast and as quiet as you can."

Her heart leaped up; her life fires burned bright and warm again; the pain went out of her. She began to run….

"Sh! Look! Off to the left in that little clearing."

On the mountain slope just ahead of them she marked the clearing and, since there, too, the shadows were darkening, she saw nothing else. She wondered what he saw or thought that he saw. He pointed, and she, with straining eyes, made out a shadow which moved; Joe, going up a steep, open trail. And just ahead of Joe a dark, square-cornered blot….

"A house…a cabin…."

"A dirty dugout, most likely, and from the look of it. But, as sure as you're born, there's Mexicali Joe's mountain headquarters. A clump of bushes, willows, you can be sure, not ten feet from his door; that will be his spring. And inside his shack…a box of grub, Lady Lynette! And if Joe doesn't have company for dinner, I'll eat your hat."

"I haven't any," said Lynette. "But we'd probably have to eat our own shoes. Come on; let's hurry…. What are you waiting for?"

"I want to whet my appetite by loitering a while…. Listen, Lynette; after all, there's no great hurry any longer. First thing, a hot supper is what is needed, and Joe can make as good a fire as we can. You can gamble that he won't waste any time, and that he'll cook a panful!"

"He might have only one panful…and he might start in on it cold…."

"And if he has only that limited amount and it belongs to him and he wants it, you don't mean to say that you would seek to take it away from him? That's robbery…."

"We'll play square with him, Babe Deveril, and give him exactly one-third. And man may call it robbery, but God and nature won't. Come…."

"I'll come with you a few steps farther. And then we will possess our souls in patience and will sit down among the bushes and will wait until we smell coffee. And I'll tell you why."

She looked at him, wondering. And then suddenly she guessed somewhat of his thought, though not all of it. She had forgotten her own certainty
that someone followed them; it surged back upon her now.

"Yes," he said, when she had spoken, "you're on the right track. We are
going to wait a few minutes to make sure. If someone was following and
wanted you and me, he could have had no object in hanging back, spying
on us. But if that same gent were following Mexicali Joe, he would want to
hang back, trusting to Joe to lead him to something worth coming at. So, out
of your *feeling* I've built my theory: That this gent thinks all the time he's
trailing Joe, and doesn't know we are here at all; tracks in the rocky trail
wouldn't show him whether one or a dozen had gone over it. And I get to this
point: How did this gent pick up Joe's trail in the dark? And I answer it by
saying that he could have known that Joe had a dugout up here, and so lay in
wait for him. And, that being true, by now he would be sure that Joe was going straight to his camp, and so, at almost any moment, he would give up his
sneak-thief style of travelling and would come hurrying along. And, if that's
right, you and I can get a glimpse of this new hombre before he does of us.
It may come in handy, you know," he concluded dryly, "to get the first swing
at him if he's an ugly gent with a rifle. At short range, and in the dark, and
stepping lively, this club of mine is way up. And, if we can take his rifle from
him…why, then into the wilderness we go, without fear of starving. Which is
a long speech for the end of a perfect day, but I'm right!"

So insistent was he and so utterly weary she, they drew a few lagging
steps out of the trail, and sank down in the shadows. She lay flat; she saw
the stars swimming in the deepening purple; her eyes closed; she felt two big
tears of exhaustion slip out between the closed lids. There was a faint drumming in her ears; she no longer cared for food.

… "Get up!" Deveril was saying curtly. "I guess we're both wrong. And
I'm going to eat, if the devil drops in to join us."

She didn't think she had been asleep. Nor yet that she had fallen prey
to swift, all-engulfing unconsciousness. Only that she had been in a mood
of utter indifference to all earthly matters. She tried, when he commanded
the second time, to rise. He helped her. She sat up…. She saw a little sprin-
kling of sparks tossed upward from Joe's chimney; stars at first she thought
them—stars wavering and blurred and uncertain.

"We've waited long enough," said Deveril.

She rose wearily, making no answer. He went ahead, she followed. Her
whole body cried out for rest; this brief, altogether too brief, lingering had
stiffened her and made her sore from head to foot. She saw that Deveril was
going up the steep trail slowly; he still strove for caution, no doubt planning
to burst in unexpectedly upon Mexicali Joe. For Joe might have a gun there
in his dugout; and he might have no great stock of provisions and be of no

mind to share with others. So she, too, strove for silence…. A strangely familiar odor was afloat on the night air…coffee! Joe's coffee was boiling.

And then, at that moment of moments, jarring upon their nerves as a sudden pistol-shot might have done, there came up to them from the canyon they had just quitted the sharp sound made by a man breaking in the dark through brush. And, with that sound, another; a man's voice, a voice which both knew and yet on the instant were unable to place, crying sharply, unguardedly:

"Come ahead, boys. There's his dugout and we got him dead to rights!"

"Down!" whispered Deveril. "Down! There's three or four of them…."

She dropped in her tracks, he at her side. They were in the little clearing; if they went back it would be to run into the arms of the men down there; if they went ahead it was to go straight on to Joe's dugout. If they sought to turn to right or left, they must go through the longest arms of the clearing, and must certainly be seen. The only shadows into which they might slip were cast by the clump of willows grouped in a span of half a dozen yards, and not over as many steps, from Joe's door….

"Into the willows!" whispered Deveril. "Quick! It's our only show."

They crawled, wriggling forward, inching, but inching swiftly. Behind them they heard voices, and a sudden running of heavy boots; before them they heard a pot or pan dropped against Joe's stove, and then Joe's excited muttering and the scuffle of Joe's boots. They scrambled on; Deveril dragged himself, with a sudden heave, into the fringe of the willow thicket; at his side, so close that elbow brushed elbow, Lynette threw herself. They saw Joe come running out of his dugout; they saw him pause a second; he could have seen them, surely, had he looked down. But his eyes were for the canyon below, from which the sudden voices had boomed up to him. And now came a voice again, that first voice, shouting threateningly:

"I got you covered, Joe! With my rifle. And I'll drop you dead if you move! You know me, Joe…me, Jim Taggart!"

Still Joe hesitated…and was lost. Up the steep slope came Jim Taggart, and behind him Young Gallup; and after Gallup, Gallup's man, Cliff Shipton. And every man of them carried a rifle, held in readiness. Joe began to swear in Spanish, his voice shaken, quavering with the fear upon him.

Deveril put out his hand until it lay upon Lynette's arm; his fingers gave her a quick, warning squeeze. Taggart and the others were coming on swiftly; it was almost too much to hope that they could pass and not see the two figures outstretched in the willows. Still, there was the chance, slim chance as it was….

If only Joe, poor stupid fool, as Deveril savagely called him in his heart, would make a bolt for it! Then there'd surely be such a drawing of their eyes to him that they would not see a white elephant tethered at the door! But Joe stood as if his feet had grown into the ground. Save for his continued mutterings, as Joe poured forth his eloquent Spanish curses, he would have appeared a man bereft of all volition. And Taggart and Young Gallup and Shipton came on at a run. Deveril clutched his club; he turned an inch or two to be ready. Lynette, lying so close to him, felt his body stiffen and guessed his purpose, and this time it was her hand closing tight upon his forearm, warning him to hold to caution as long as there was hope.

The three came steadily on, hastening all that they could up the steep slope. A moment ago, when first Taggart called out, Joe might have eluded them had he been lightning-swift and ready to take chances. But now that he had hesitated, it was clear that his most shadowy hope of escape was gone. He stood motionless, cursing them and his luck.

Babe Deveril's fingers were tight, as tight as rage could weld them about his oak stick. At that moment he could have welcomed the excuse to leap out with the unexpectedness of a cataclysm and the rush of a catapult, to heave his club upward and bring it down, full force, upon Taggart's head. For now he had the added rancour in his heart that Jim Taggart, with his following, had chosen this one moment to come up with them, just as Babe Deveril was counting in full confidence upon the first square meal in twenty-four hours. Taggart, less than threatening his safety, was stealing the supper which he had counted on having from Mexicali Joe.

Jim Taggart began to laugh, more in malice than in mirth, and, most of all, in an evil, gloating triumph. He came on, hurrying; he almost trod on Lynette's boot. Instinctively she jerked away from him; yet only because Taggart was so gloatingly bent upon his quarry he did not note her movement, or must have supposed that he had set a stone rolling.

"Ho!" cried Taggart. "Joe's a good kid after all, boys! He's waited for us, and he's got us a piping-hot supper! Wonder how he guessed we were starved like wildcats?"

"Damn him!" Lynette heard Deveril, and her fingers gripped him with a new agony of warning and supplication for silence.

"What's that?" demanded Taggart, thinking that Gallup or Shipton had spoken.

"You robbers!" cried Joe nervously. "Already you tryin' rob me, las' night. Now you tryin' rob me! I tell you...."

"Shut up!" snapped Taggart. "Back into your dirty den and we'll have a nice little talk with you."

"I tell you...."

Taggart was close upon him now and caught him by the shoulder, flinging him about, shoving him through the squat door of his dugout. Slight enough was the diversion, but both Lynette and Deveril were thankful for it, for the two figures drew the eyes of both Gallup and Shipton and held them. Joe reeled across the threshold; Taggart, not knowing what weapon Joe might have lying on his bunk, sprang nimbly after him. And Gallup and

Shipton, to see everything, drew on close behind him. They passed the willows about the spring and, stooping, went in at Joe's door.

Lynette and Deveril lay very still, hesitating to move hand or foot. For both Gallup and Shipton stood on Joe's threshold, and that threshold was a few steps only from their hiding-place. The snapping of a twig, the crackling of a handful of dead leaves must certainly bring swift, searching eyes upon them.

CHAPTER 9

"The first half chance we get," whispered Deveril, guardedly, "we've got to sneak out of this! Lie still; I can see them without moving. That man with the hawk face is turned this way."

He could see neither Joe nor Taggart in the dugout. Gallup he could see, barely across the threshold now, watching Taggart and the Mexican. The man Shipton, evidently fagged from a hard day of it, had slumped down on the log that served as door-step, and faced outward, save when now and then he half turned to glance curiously at the sheriff and his captive.

"So we nabbed you, eh, Mexico?" gibed Taggart. "You damn little tricky shrimp! To think you could put one across on me!"

"Gatham you!" shrilled Joe. "You big t'ief, you try one time an' you see! I ain't do nothin' to you; I got the right...."

"Oh, shut up!" muttered Taggart impatiently. "Dry your palaver for once. I'll give you chance enough to spill over when I get good and ready." Outside Lynette and Deveril heard a sound which, in their hunger, they were quick to read aright; Taggart, also hungry, had stepped to the stove and had dragged a heavy iron frying-pan to him, investigating its content. "Phew!" growled Taggart. "You infernal garlic hound! Well, the jerked meat ought to go all right. And coffee, huh? Come on, boys; we'll feed up, and then we'll tell Joe what's in the wind."

"I ain't got much grub," Joe shouted back at him. "An' I need it mysel'. You go...."

There was the sound of a blow and of scuffling feet, the thudding of a body against the wall.

"Take that," Taggart told him viciously. And, his ugly voice thick with threat: "And thank your Dago saints I only used my fist! Next time, so help me, I'll bash you with a rifle barrel. Say, Cliff...."

"Say it," drawled Cliff.

"Scare up some dry wood; the fire's near out. And, Joe, you dig up a candle or lamp or something. I'd like a little light in this stinking hole."

Joe, though with infuriated mutterings, did as bid. Slowly the gaunt form of Cliff Shipton rose from the rough-hewn log.

"God, I'm tired," he said. And then, when no one thought to sympathize, he demanded querulously: "Say, Mex, where's your wood-pile?"

Gallup laughed at him.

"Imagine the lazy hound having a wood-pile! Skirmish around, Cliff, and pick up some dead sticks."

Joe had found a stub of candle, and now its pale light vaguely illuminated the dugout's interior. Since there was but the one opening, the squat door, Deveril still saw only Gallup. Gallup by now was sitting upon the narrow bunk at the back of the room, his rifle between his knees, the shadow of his hat hiding his face. Shipton set his own rifle down against the outside wall and began groping with his feet for bits of wood.

"It's getting awful dark for this kind of thing," he was telling himself in his eternally complaining voice. "Ain't he got a box or a chair or a table or something in there that'll burn?" he called.

No one paid any attention to him and Shipton, scuffling gropingly with his feet, widened his search. And now Lynette and Deveril scarcely breathed. For it seemed inevitable that he was coming straight toward the brushy-fringed spring where they lay. Deveril was now on his left elbow, his body raised slightly, his legs drawn up under him, so that he could readily fling himself to his feet, his oak club in his right hand. Lynette understood and was ready, too; if Shipton came dangerously near, she knew that it was Deveril's intent to drop him in his tracks. Then there would remain but the one thing to do; to leap up and run for it, run blindly, plunging into the nearest shadows, to run on and on while men shot after them.

Shipton came nearer. She felt Babe Deveril stir, ever so slightly. Her only concern now was: Would he strike just at the very second that he should? Would he strike a second too early, before it was necessary, and thus needlessly give himself away? Would he strike just a second too late, giving Shipton first the time to see and cry out?

"God, I'm stiff and sore," Shipton was muttering.

His foot struck something, and he reached down, thinking it was a bit of wood. But it was a stone, dirt-covered, and he kicked at it and came on. Now he was not two steps away. Again he stooped; as he stooped, Babe Deveril raised himself an inch or two higher. But now Shipton found a fragment of a pine log, half rotted and of little use as fuel. But in his present mood it served him; he picked it up and turned back to the dug-out. Lynette heard Deveril's slowly expelled breath.

Within there was a scraping of frying-pan on stove top. They saw a tin plate handed to Gallup on his bunk; Gallup began eating, noisy about it; eating like a dog. Shipton went in with his log. Taggart caught it from him, broke it up by striking it against the hard-packed dirt floor, and began stoking the stove. A fresh gush of sparks shot up from Joe's chimney. Shipton was demanding to be fed…and for God's sake give him a shot of coffee.

"Now's our chance," whispered Deveril. "None too good, but the best we're going to have! Ready?"

And her whisper came back to him, "Always ready!"

"Now," he whispered. "Off to the right; slow and quiet; if once we can snake across this open place and into the timber over there…."

"And now, Señor Joe," came Taggart's voice, and they knew from the sound that Taggart, mouth full, was eating ravenously, "we got you!"

"Sure you got me," Joe rasped out at him, and still there remained defiance in little Mexicali Joe. "Fine! But what you do with me? You can't eat me, an' nobody ever yet put any bounty on my hide, an' when you got me… you no got nothin'. An', *cabrone*, what I got I keep him!"

Taggart laughed at him in Taggart's ugly style.

"Talk big, little hombre, while you can! And now let me tell you something: Tonight, right now, inside ten minutes, you're going to tell me just exactly where you got that stuff you spilled out of your pocket last night. And in the morning, bright and early, you're going to take me there!"

"I die firs'!"

"You'll be a long time dying! Think I'm fool enough to kill you…now? Know what the third degree is, Joe?" Taggart's voice was terrible with its insinuation. "Me, when I give the third degree to any man, he spills his guts before I'm done with him! You'll cough up everything you know and be damn glad afterward to crawl off in the woods and die! That's me, Joe."

Gallup, who must have found amusement in watching Mexicali Joe's expression, laughed. After him Cliff Shipton laughed like an echo. Joe began cursing nervously.

"Ready?" whispered Lynette. Taggart's threats horrified her and set her trembling.

"No!… Don't you see? Taggart will make him tell everything he knows, if he has to knock his teeth out one by one and break every bone in his body! And I'm going to hear!… You crawl ahead while there's a chance; I can up and run for it after you if I have to."

She was silent. There was excitement in his utterance and another quality which sent a sudden chill to her heart. She stared at him through the dark as at a stranger; the gold fever was rampant in his veins, and she knew that he would lie here, never lifting hand or voice, while Taggart tortured his captive until Joe shrieked out his golden secret.

Before Lynette could speak or move, Taggart's voice once more cut harshly through the silence.

"You wouldn't know, Joe, unless you'd been sheriff as long as me, how many nice little ways there are of making a man hurry up about spitting up all he knows!" Taggart was steadily cramming into his mouth the half-cooked dried beef stew, appearing to have entirely forgotten his dislike for garlic. "Me, I'm a man of brains and what you call invention; I look around and see what I've got handy, and out of it I make what I need! Now, look here. You see us boys eating hearty, and, if I know what that look means in a man's eye, you got an appetite yourself? Well, you don't get a scrap to eat nor a drink to drink until you open up."

Joe sought to laugh at him. Taggart, still stuffing, went on steadily:

"Next, you see the stove with its hot lids? All right, pretty quick we hold you so the palms of your hands stick to the hot lids and the skin burns off. Oh, I know that don't hurt so much a man can't stand it; sure not. But it does sort to set him to thinking things over in a new fashion! And then, what next?"

"Make him eat salt," put in Shipton with a snicker. "And don't give him any water! Lots of salt does the trick, Jimmie."

Taggart, a man of no subtlety, snorted at him.

"Maybe you can tell gold when you see it, Cliff," he said briefly. "But that's all you do know.... Listen to me, Mexico. We got our rifles, ain't we? We stand you with your back to the wall and dare you to move! Then we practise shooting; just to see how close we can come! We don't hit you, us three being good shots. Anyway, we don't hit you often, and then it's only grazes! We make a game out of it; every man takes a shot and him that comes closest gets a dollar every time; him that draws blood puts up two dollars in the pot. And, pretty soon.... What are you looking so sick for, Joe? Nobody ain't hurt you yet!"

Joe's curses were suddenly faint, for Joe's mouth and throat were dry and he had grown limp and dizzy and sick.

"You see, I got you, Joe. Got you dead to rights!"

"The brute!" whispered Lynette, her own flesh set twitching. "The horrible brute!"

"Sh! Just listen!"

"I don't believe he'd actually do that! He is just frightening Joe—bluffing...."

"You the sheriff!" cried Joe, desperate. "You the one bigges' robber in all these mount'!"

"Call me robber, will you, you skunk!"

Again they heard the sound of the blow, struck fiercely by Jim Taggart, who, as he let all men understand, was the last man to brook an insult. And they heard Joe's slight body hurled back, so that he toppled and fell. And, thereafter, Taggart's brutish laughter. Tonight, Jim Taggart, no matter how disgruntled he had been during so many hours, was at last enjoying himself. For tonight he was secure in his expectations.

"You bleed awful easy, Joe," he jeered. "Ought to go get your teeth straightened up, too! Cup of coffee? No? Then I'll take one; *gracias, mi amigo!*"

"I hope you burn in hell!" screamed Joe.

"So?" And Taggart, swinging heavily, knocked him down again, and then reached out for the can that held sugar and sweetened his coffee. Shipton sniggered.

"You're a corker, Jim!" he declared.

"Me," acknowledged Taggart heavily, "I am what I am. But I never laid down for a Mex breed yet, and I ain't going to."

Joe lay where he had fallen. His body was pain-wracked, for when Jim Taggart struck in wrath he struck mightily, being a mighty man physically, and hard. Joe's swart skin had paled; his eyes started from his head; he feared, and not without reason, that a third blow like that would kill him. And he knew that Jim Taggart was no man to lie awake because he had killed another man.

"I got thirs'," said Joe thickly. He was sitting up, on the floor. "Give me cup water!"

"What did I tell you, Joe?" Taggart grinned at him. "I got you. Got you right."

"I burnin' up," said Joe weakly. "Maybe you killin' me. Give me drink water."

"I got you, Joe," said Taggart speculatively. No mockery now; just a vast, deep satisfaction. "I half believe one good kick in the belly would settle you and you'd tell all you know. I got a hunch...."

"Go slow, Jim." This from the avaricious Young Gallup. "No sense killing him, seeing you haven't found out a thing."

"You're right, Gal. Well, give him a drink, then; half a cup of water and let him think things over.... If he opens up then, O. K. If he don't we'll find the way to open him up."

"Let me go to the spring," said Joe. By now he was on his feet. "I was jus' goin' for water when you come. The spring, she's right there. You can see I don't run away...."

"Go scoop him up a can of water, Cliff," said Taggart. "You sit tight, Joe. You don't go out tonight unless we take you out to put you in a hole!"

"*Now!*" whispered Deveril sharply. "Now we've got to crawl for it!"

But Cliff Shipton demurred, saying surlily:

"I'm tired out, and I'm sore and stiff and stove-up. Let him go without his water."

"We were crazy for waiting so long!" complained Deveril. "Hurry!"

In the dugout Gallup was saying slowly, after his ponderous fashion:

"I'll go get him his water. After that, like you say, Jim, he'll open up— wide! Or, if he don't, I'll break his jaw-bone with my boot heel.... Where's a can?"

Already Babe Deveril had wormed his way out of the willows and began creeping about the edge of the tiny thicket that was farthest from Joe's cabin.

Lynette, feeling weak and sick, followed him like his own shadow. Thus they skirted the brushy fringe of the spring.

Then Gallup, carrying his can, came out. Deveril dropped flat and lay motionless, his body hidden, at least to careless eyes, by the spring willows. Lynette dropped flat just behind him. She knew that again Deveril was ready to leap and strike, mercilessly hard, if Gallup came too near. It was almost an even chance whether Gallup would come their way or not.... Lynette, cold and tired and hungry and at last afraid, shivered.

But, almost immediately, it became obvious to both of them that Gallup had been here before and knew his way about. He turned, as they had hoped that he would, to the right; they heard him reach the spring and dip his pan and fill it and turn back to the dugout, slopping water after him. They saw him step on the threshold; already Deveril was crawling cautiously again, and, after him, Lynette.

It was like life in a nightmare. So tortuously slow. So great a need for quiet, and, like jeering, mocking voices, there came so many little sounds, loud in their ears—twigs snapping, leaves rustling, tiny stones set rolling. At first, what with the dark and her sole thought to be gone, Lynette failed to understand just how Deveril was directing his course. When she did grasp, she wondered at him. Instead of hurrying straight across the clearing toward the haven of the timber-line, he was drawing nearer and nearer the west end of the dugout! Now she dared not whisper to him; she could not come up with him to catch warningly at his boot. So she followed, striving with all her caution to overtake him. And before she could do so, she glimpsed his purpose.

True to type, Joe's dugout had but the one door, and the rear of the building was a sort of timbered hole in the mountainside. Deveril planned that if he could gain the back of the dugout he could hear what was going on and run little danger of being detected; further, that in that direction, did he elect to up and run for cover, he and Lynette would have as good a chance as any to get away in the rim of the forest. If they moved with all possible silence, and especially if Taggart and the others within kept up their noise-making, snapping and snarling and knocking things about, it was more than an even break that neither Taggart nor any of his companions would come to suspect that they were being spied upon; and when did Babe Deveril ever ask more than the even break? Then...there remained one other consideration, one of exceedingly great importance in Deveril's estimation, of which as yet Lynette had no inkling: while in hiding down by the spring Deveril had made a discovery, or believed that he had, and no opportunity had been given him either to speak of it or yet to investigate.

Clearly now was the moment when Taggart and Gallup and the complaining Cliff Shipton concentrated every thought upon their captive; Joe showed signs of weakening, and every man of them held that if only Joe could be led to "open up" they would all be made rich at his expense.

Meanwhile Gallup had given Joe his water; Joe had drunk rapidly, gulping noisily. Taggart and Gallup and Shipton were eying him eagerly. Joe had taken a deep breath; again he started to drink. Taggart struck the can away from his mouth, commanding: "No more. You've got to talk first; fast and straight and no lies! Understand?"

"How you goin' tell if I lie?" muttered Joe, something of his stubbornness restored.

"Right now you tell us where the gold is. In the morning you take us to the place. And if you make a little mistake and don't take us straight, I'll make you sorry you were ever born!"

Deveril and Lynette passed within a few yards of the dugout's nearest front corner; they groped onward up the steep slope; they came in a brief détour to the rear, where the rude timbers supporting the shed roof were at this end embedded in the earth. Here they stopped and lay flat and listened. And they heard Joe mumbling: "If I tell, I tell true. But I don't think I tell. You kick me out; you steal everything; you get rich an' me—I die poor. Maybe better I die and fool you!"

"Listen, Joe." Gallup speaking—Gallup, who feared that Joe might be fool enough to die with locked lips rather than be robbed of his new fortune; Gallup, a man who could understand another man doing anything, standing any torture, rather than lose the one golden thing in life. "We'll make you a fair proposition, us three men. You found the gold; all right, you got a right to a share. You can't hog it anyhow; other men will come rushing in as soon as you drop a pick in it; they'll stake claims all around you; more'n likely they'll cop off the very cream of it, and you'll have just a pocket that will peter out on you. We brought Cliff along; he knows pockets and veins and all kind of gold signs, from stock to barrel. Now, you show sense; you take us along; we form a company, just us four. And you get one-fourth the rake-off. And we got the money to develop it; to make a big thing out of it. You ain't got the money and you ain't got the business brains, and you'd lose on it sooner or later, anyhow."

Silence. A long silence while three men watched him and while Deveril and Lynette listened. A long silence during which all that strangely blended craft which flowed into Mexicali Joe's veins from a mixture of Latin and Indian ancestry was hard at work…though this no one could guess now, so immobile was Joe's face, so guarded his tone when he spoke.

"That sound fine, Gallup! But how I know you don't cheat me? For why you don't hit me in the head with a pick when I tell? For why you don't take all…everything?"

"I'm telling you why!" cried Gallup. "Look here. Suppose we did that and croaked you and dug a hole and stuck you in. All right. Next thing we pop up with a new gold-mine! And there'll be men to say: 'That ore looks like the ore Mexicali Joe showed that night down to Gallup's house!' And they'll say: 'Where's Joe?' And they'll begin making trouble, all kinds; they'll want to run us out. They'll have us up for killing you. There'll be a lot of talk, and always the chance, as long's we live, they might pin something on us. And what would we make by that sort of work? *Only a one-quarter interest in your diggings!* Why, man, it ain't worth it! We got too much sense to kill any man for the sake of a little ante like that. Sure, Joe; dead on the level, if you play square with us, we play square with you."

Silence again. A longer silence than before. Then, while Joe must have appeared to hesitate, Taggart said abruptly:

"And if you don't take our proposition and talk fast and straight, I'm going to *make* you talk! And then you don't get no thanks but a kick and a get-the-hell-out! That's my way, you little greaser."

"Give him time, Jim," pleaded Gallup.

"All right!" cried Joe, seeming eager now. "I take the chance! You boys just tell me 'So help me God, I play square!' and I take the chance!"

"So help me God!" cried Young Gallup, first of all. "I play square with you, Joe!"

And after him, while Joe waited, both Taggart and Cliff Shipton said, with a semblance of deep gravity: "So help me God."

"We pardners now? Us four?" demanded Joe. And when he had had his three immediate, emphatic assurances—Deveril misjudged him a fool—Joe began, speaking rapidly: "*Bueno!* Now we talk. An' in the mornin' we start an' tomorrow I show you! I got the bigges' mine you can't beat in all New Mexico an' Arizona an' Nevada, too! For why I care take on three pardners? I tell you, we got the money to devil-him-up, we all rich like hell!..."

"Get going, Joe," growled Taggart. "Where? Down Light Ladies' Canyon, and not more'n three or four miles from Big Pine?"

Joe cackled his derision at Taggart's guess.

"Me, I fool ever'body!" he said gleefully. "Me, I'm damn smart man, Señor Taggart! Nowhere near Light Ladies'. The other way. We go all day tomorrow, way back up in the mountains. One long, hard day, walkin'. Maybe day an' a half. You know where Buck Valley? All right; you know, on other side, Big Bear Creek? An' then you know, little bit more far, two-t'ree mile, Grub Stake Canyon? You know...."

"By the living Lord," broke in Taggart. "That's right square in Bruce Standing's country!"

Again Joe cackled.

"You know whole lot; you don't know ever'thing! Timber-Wolf's lands run like this." (One could imagine a grimy forefinger set in a dirty palm.) "His line, here. My mine, she's just the other side. Nobody's land; gover'ment land." He chuckled. "An' ol' big Timber-Wolf, he goin' cry... *boo-hoo-hoo!*...when he find out we got gold not mile an' half from his line!"

Deveril was twitching at Lynette's sleeve. He began edging away. When she came up with him he was standing; she rose and, together they hurried across the clearing, and in a few moments were in the deep dark of the embracing forest land.

"I know that country like a map!" he told her excitedly. "We were already headed that way, and on we go! Why, it was right up by Big Bear Creek that I spent a night with Bruce Standing six years ago and he robbed me of my roll!… They start in the morning; we start tonight! We'll be there when they come; there are ten thousand places to hide out; we'll have a place on a ridge where we can watch them. And they'll never have the vaguest idea that anyone, you and I least of all, is ahead of them. Somehow, Lynette Brooke, our luck is with us and this whole game is going to play into our hands."

"If a little food would only play into them!… The smell of that coffee… the meat cooking…."

"Wait! Right here, by this tree. Don't move a step, no matter what happens. I'll be back with you in two shakes."

She was almost too tired and faint from hunger to wonder at him. She saw him go, and then she sank down, her back to the big yellow pine. He went as straight as a string toward the spring; she saw him walking swiftly, though with footfalls so guarded that she could not hear him when he had gone ten steps. She knew that he was recklessly counting upon a deal of quick chatter in the dugout, secure in his own bravado that no man of the four there would at this electrically charged moment have thought of anything but gold. He disappeared in the dark; he was gone so long that she jumped up and stood staring in all directions; but at last he was back at her side, chuckling, and then she knew he had not been away ten minutes.

"I struck it with my elbow, while we were hiding down there," he told her triumphantly. "Mexicali Joe's real cache!"

He had a square tin biscuit-box in his hands. She put her hand in quickly. The box, which had been half buried in the cool earth by the spring, was half full of tins and small packages.

Fatigue fled out of them. Hurriedly they went up over the ridge, deeper and deeper into the forest land. And when, in half an hour, they came down into the dark, tree-walled bed of another ravine, they made them their small fire and tumbled out into its light their newly acquired treasure-trove—sardines, beans, tinned milk…yes, coffee!

CHAPTER 10

"So the sheriff, Jim Taggart, is not dead, after all. And you…."

Deveril looked across their tiny fire at her, a strange expression in his eyes, and said quietly:

"No; he is not dead. All along I judged that unlikely. Though I slung your gun at him hard enough, if it hit a lucky spot. It's hard to kill a man, you know…. And, to finish your thought, I am not running wild with a hangman's noose hanging about my neck! And you…."

He took a certain devilish glee in concluding with an echo of her own words. And with the added insinuation poured into them from his own. He saw her jerk her head up defiantly.

"I told you…."

Again she broke off. He made no remark, but sat looking at her intently. They had eaten and drunk their fill; there remained to them a goodly stock of provisions; Deveril was smoking his cigarette.

"What now?" demanded Lynette, as one tired of a subject and impatient to look forward.

He shrugged.

"All troubles have slipped off my shoulders. The worst they could do to me, if they could lay me by the heels, would be to charge me with assault and battery! And we're in a neck of the woods where men laugh at a charge like that, and ask the assaulted one why the devil he didn't hit back! What now? For you I'd advise keeping right on travelling. For if Bruce Standing is dead it's up to you to keep on the move! As for me, I never met up with a sweeter travelling companion, nor yet with a nervier, nor yet, by God, with a lovelier! Say the word, Lynette Brooke, and we strike on together, over the ridge and deeper into the wilderness, headed for the land beyond Buck Valley, beyond Big Bear Creek. For the wild lands beyond the last holdings of the late Timber-Wolf, to be on the ground when Mexicali Joe leads Taggart and Gallup and Shipton to his gold!"

She understood how Babe Deveril, as any man should be, was relieved at knowing that the man he had stricken down was not dead; that he, himself, was not hunted as a murderer. And yet she was vaguely distressed and uneasy. She felt a change in him, and in his attitude toward her…. When he awaited her reply, she made none. Again fatigue swept over her, and with it a new stirring of uneasiness….

There was a drop of coffee left; she leaned forward and took it, thinking: "He had his tobacco, and it has bolstered up his nerves." She drank and then sat back, leaning against a tree, her face hidden from him, while she searched his face in the dim light, searched it with a stubborn desire to read the most hidden thought in his brain.

"I am tired," she said after a long while. He could make nothing of her voice, low and impersonal, and with no inflection to give it expression beyond the brief meanings of the words themselves. "Very tired. Yet necessity drives. And it is not safe here, so near them. I can go on for another hour, perhaps two or three hours. That will mean…how far? Four or five miles; maybe six, seven?"

Not only for one hour, not alone for just two or three hours did they push on. But for half of that silent, starry night. A score of times Babe Deveril said to her: "We've done our stunt; if any girl on earth ever earned rest, you've done it." But always there was that driving force and that allure, and another ridge just ahead, and her answer: "Another mile…. I can do it."

Deveril, with a lighted match cupped in his hand, looked at his watch.

"It's long after midnight; nearly one o'clock."

They found a sheltered spot among the tall pines; above them the keen edge of an up-thrust ridge; just below a thick-grown clump of underbrush; underfoot dry needles, fallen and drifted from the pines. Again he was all courtesy and kindliness toward her, seeing her hard pressed, judging her, despite her mask of hardihood, near collapse. So he cut pine boughs with his knife and broke them with his hands, and of them piled her a couch. She thanked him gently; impulsively she gave him her hand…though, as his caught it eagerly, she jerked it away quickly…. He watched her lie down, snuggling her cheek against the curve of her arm. Near by he lay down on his back, his two hands under his head, his eyes on the stars. A curious smile twitched at his lips.

And then, just as they were dropping off to sleep, they heard far off a long-drawn, howling cry piercing through the great hush. Lynette started up, her blood quickening; as she had heard Bruce Standing's warning call that first time, so now did she think to hear it again. Deveril leaped to his feet, no less startled. A moment later he called softly to her, and it seemed to Lynette that he forced a tone of lightness which did not ring true:

"A timber wolf…but one that runs on four legs! It won't come near." Then, as she made no answer and he could not see her face, he asked sharply: "What did you think it was?"

She shivered and lay back.

"I didn't know."

And to herself she whispered:

"And I don't know now!"

Here among the uplands it was a night of piercing cold. The nearer the dawn drew on, the icier grew the fingers of the wind which swept the ridges and probed into the canyons. For a little while both Lynette and Deveril slept the heavy sleep of exhaustion. But, after the first couple of hours, neither slept beyond brief, uncomfortable dozes. They shivered and woke and stirred; they found a growing torture in the rude couches they slept upon, in the hard ground and stones, which seemed always thrusting up in new places. Long before the night had begun to thin to the first of daybreak's hint, Lynette was sitting, her back to a tree, torn between the two impossibilities, that of remaining awake, that of remaining asleep. Deveril got up and began stamping about, trying to get warm and drive the cramp and soreness out of his muscles.

"A few more days and nights like this," he grumbled, "would be enough to kill a pair of Esquimos! We've got to find us some sort of half-way decent shelter for another night, and we've got to arrange to take a holiday and rest up."

It was all that she could do to keep her teeth from chattering by shutting them hard together; her only answer was a shivery sigh. She could scarcely make him out, where he trod back and forth, the darkness held so thick. She began to think so longingly of a fire that in comparison with its cheer and warmth she felt that possible discovery by Taggart would be a small misfortune. She could almost welcome being put under arrest; taken back to Big Pine and jail; given a bed and covers and one long sleep.

"Awake?" queried Deveril.

She nodded, as though he could see her nod through the dark. Then, with an effort, she said an uncertain: "Y-e-s."

"I'll tell you," he said presently, coming close to her and looking down upon the blot in the darkness which her huddled figure made at the base of the pine. "Taggart will be on his way soon; he'll hardly wait for day. He'll go the straightest, quickest way to the Big Bear country. That means he'll steer on straight into Buck Valley. If you and I went that way, we'd have him and his crowd at our heels all day, and never know how close they were; and I, for one, am damned sick of that *feeling* that somebody's creeping up on us all the time! So we swerve out from the direct way as soon as we start; we curve off to the north for a couple of miles; then we make a bend around toward the upper end of what I fancy must be the Grub Stake Canyon Joe is headed for. That way we'll always have two or three miles between our trail and theirs; at times we'll be five or six miles off to the side. That means, of course, that they're pretty sure to get to Joe's diggings ahead of us; not over half a day at that. For we're well ahead of them now. And, in any case, you can bet the last sardine we've got that they'll be a day or two just poking around, prospecting and trying to make sure of what they've grabbed off.... Agreed, pardner?"

"Yes. I could even start now, just to get those few miles between our trail and theirs. Then, when the sun was up and it was warm, we could have a rest and an hour's sleep."

So, walking slowly, painfully, carrying what was left of their small stock of provisions, they started on in the dark. Up a ridge they went and into the thinning edge of the coming dawn; they picked their way among trees and rocks; little by little they were able to see in more detail what lay about them. Along the ridge they tramped northward. They were warmer now that they walked; or, rather, they were some degrees less cold. Gradually their paces grew swifter, as some of the stiffness went out of their bodies; gradually the shadows thinned; the stars paled, the east asserted itself above the other points of the compass, softly tinted. The sleeping world began to awake all about them; birds stirred with the first drowsy twitterings. The pallid eastern tints grew brighter; as from a wine-cup, life was spilled again upon the mountain tops. A bird began a clear-noted, joyous singing; all of a sudden the morning breeze seemed sweeter and softer; there came a brilliant, flaming glory in the sky which drew their eyes; all life forces which had been at ebb began to flow strongly once more; the sun thrust a gleaming golden edge up into the upper world, rolling majestically from the under world. Deveril looked into her eyes and laughed softly; her eyes smiled back into his…. She felt as though she had had a bad dream, but was awake now; as though last night her nerves had tricked her into wrongly judging her companion. Doubtings always flock in the night; joy is never more joyous than when breaking forth with the new day.

"It isn't so bad, after all," said Deveril. "Now, if we only had a pack-mule and a roll of blankets and a bit of canvas…. What more would you ask, Lynette Brooke, for a lark and a holiday to remember pleasantly when we grew to be doddering old folks?"

"As long as you are wishing," returned Lynette lightly, "why not place an order with the King of Ifs for a gun and some fishing-tackle and a frying-pan and some more coffee? And a couple of hats; an outing suit for me." She looked down at her suit; it was torn in numerous places; it was gummed and sticky here and there with the resin from pines; it caught upon every bush. "Then, you know, a needle and some thread; a dozen fresh eggs, bread, and butter…."

"Too much soft living has spoiled you!" he laughed.

"If so, I am in ideal training to get unspoiled in short order!" she laughed back.

And for all of this was the rising sun and the new, bright day responsible; for the ancient way of youth playing up to youth.

What was happening within both of them was a great nervous relaxation. They knew where Taggart and Gallup were, or at least were confident that there was no immediate danger of Taggart and Gallup overhauling them; they knew where Mexicali Joe was and where he was going. For the moment they were freed from that crushing sense of uncertainty welded to menace which had borne down upon them ever since they fled from Big Pine. And consequently joy of life sprang up as a spring leaps the instant that the weight is plucked from it.

"It's our lucky day!" said Deveril.

For the sun was scarcely up when a plump young rabbit hopped square into their path, and Deveril, with a lucky throw, killed it with a rock. And just as they were speaking of thirst, they came to a tiny trickle of water among the rocks; and while Lynette was boiling coffee over a tiny blaze, Deveril was preparing grilled cottontail for breakfast. Savory odors floating out through the woodlands. Lynette was singing softly:

"Merry it is in the good Greenwood!"

They ate and rested and the sun warmed them. For a full two hours they scarcely stirred. Then they drank again; Lynette bathed her hands and face and arms; she set her hair in order, refashioning the two thick braids. She shut one eye and then the other, striving to make certain that there was not a black smudge somewhere upon her nose. They were starting on when Deveril said soberly:

"Shall I save the rabbit skin?"

"Why?" she asked innocently.

A twinkle came into his eyes.

"A few more days of this sort of life, and My Lady Linnet is going to require a new gown! Perhaps rabbit furs, if hunting is good, will do it!"

She laughed at him, and her eyes were daring as she sang, improvising as to melody:

> *"And for vest of pall, thy fingers small,*
> *That wont on harp to stray,*
> *A cloak must sheer from the slaughtered deer,*
> *To keep the cold away!"*

"Lynette!"

A flash from her gay mood had set his eyes on fire. He sprang up and came toward her, his two hands out. But as a black cloud can run over the face of the young moon, so did a sudden change of mood wipe the tempting look out of her eyes and darken them. Her spirit had peeped forth at him, merry-making; as quick as bird-flight it was gone, and she stepped back and looked at him steadily, cool now and aloof and dampening to a man's ardent nonsense.

"You have a way of saying something, Babe Deveril," she told him coolly, "which appeals to me. In your own upstanding words: 'Let's go!'"

He laughed back at her lightly, hiding under a light cloak his own chagrin. At that moment he had wanted her in his arms; had wanted that as he wanted neither Mexicali Joe's gold nor any other coldly glittering thing. Now he felt himself growing angry with her....

"Right. You've said it. Let's go."

He made short work of catching up the few articles they were to carry with them and of stamping into dead coals the few remaining glowing embers of their fire. Then, striding ahead, he led the way. And for a matter of a mile or more she was hard beset to keep up with him.

* * * *

The day was filled with happenings to divert their thoughts from any one channel. They startled, in a tiny meadow, three deer, which shot away through a tangle of brush, leaping, plunging, shooting forward and down a slope like great, gleaming, graceful arrows. "A man could live like a king here, with a rifle," said Deveril longingly. They saw a tall, thin wisp of smoke an hour before noon; it stood against the sky to the southwest of them, at a distance of perhaps two miles. "Taggart's noonday camp," they decided, deciding further that Taggart must have insisted on an early start, and therefore had found his stomach demanding lunch well before midday. Later, some two or three hours after twelve, they heard the long, reverberating crack and rumble and echo of a rifle-shot. "Taggart's crowd, killing a deer or bear or rabbit," they imagined. And all along they were contented, making what time they could through the open spaces, over the ridges, down through tiny green valleys and up long, dreary slopes, resting frequently, never hastening beyond their powers, secure in knowing that the Taggart trail and the Lynette-Deveril trail, though paralleling, would have no common point of contact before both trails ran into the country in the vicinity of the Big Bear Creek, the rim of the Timber-Wolf country.

"The whole thing," exulted Babe Deveril, "lies in the fact that we know where they are and they haven't the least idea where we are! We know where they are going, and they haven't a guess which way we are steering...."

"Do you know," said Lynette thoughtfully, "I don't believe that Mexicali Joe intends for a minute to lead them to his gold!"

Deveril looked at her in astonishment.

"You don't! Why, couldn't you see that Taggart put the fear of the Lord into him? That Gallup, slick as wet soap, tricked him? That...."

She broke in impatiently, saying:

"Yet Joe.... He seemed to me to give in to them in something too much of a hurry...as though he had his own wits about him, his own last card in the hole, as dad used to say. I wonder...."

He stared at her, puzzled.

"When you *feel* things," he muttered, none too pleasantly, "you get me guessing. I don't know yet how you came to know that the Taggart bunch was at our heels yesterday. But you did know; and you were right. As to this other hunch of yours...."

"You'll see," said Lynette serenely. "Joe isn't the biggest fool in that crowd of four. You wait and see."

"You'll give me the creeps yet," said Deveril.

They both laughed and went on—through brushy tangles; over rocky ridges; through spacious forests; across soft, springy meadows; up slope, down slope; on and on and endlessly on. Once they frightened a young bear that was tearing away as if its life depended upon it upon an old stump; the bear snorted and went lumbering away, as Deveril said, like a young freight-train gone mad; Lynette, as she admitted afterward, was twice as frightened, but did not run, herself, because the bear ran first and because she couldn't get the hang of her feet as quickly as he could! They came upon several bands of mountain-quail, which shot away, buzzing like overgrown bees; Deveril hurled stones and curses at many a scampering rabbit; once she and once he caught a glimpse of that dark gleam, come and gone in a flash, which might have been coyote or timber-wolf.... They did not speak of Bruce Standing. But they wondered, both of them....

Toward four o'clock in the afternoon they heard for the second time the crack of a rifle-shot. Farther to the south of them this time; a hint farther eastward; fainter than when first heard. Taggart, they held in full confidence, was following the trail which they had mapped for him; he was going on steadily; he was forging ahead of them. And yet they were content that this was so. They rested more often; they relaxed more and more.

And before the brief reverberations of a distant rifle-shot had done echoing through the gorges, they came to a full stop and determined to make camp. Not for a second, all day long, had Deveril swerved from his determination to "dig in in comfort for the night." They were, as both were willing to admit, "done in."

Deveril employed his pocket-knife, long ago dulled, and now whetted after a fashion upon a rough stone, to whack off small pine and willow and the more leafy of sage branches. He made of them a goodly heap. Then he gathered dead limbs, fallen from the parent trees, making his second pile. All the while Lynette kept a small dry-wood and pine-cone fire going hotly; little smoke, little swirl of sparks to rise above the grove in which they were encamping; plenty of heat for body warmth and for cooking. She was preoccupied, moving about listlessly. So this was Bruce Standing's country? She looked about her with an ever-deepening interest; this was a fitting land for such a man. Bigness and dominance and a certain vital freshness struck altogether the key-note here—and suggested Timber-Wolf. If he were not dead after all— Well, then, he would be somewhere near now for like a wounded animal, he would have returned to his solitudes.

Deveril found near by a level space under the pines. Here he sought out a scraggly tree which expressed an earth-loving soul in low-drooped branches. Against a low arm which ran out horizontally from the trunk he began placing his longer dead limbs, the butts in the ground, sloping, the effect soon that of a tent. Against these a high-piled wall of leafy branches. He stood back, judging from which direction the wind would come. He piled more branches. Into his nostrils, filled with the resinous incense of broken pine twigs, floated the tempting aromas which spread out in all directions from Lynette's cooking. He cocked his eye at the slanting sun; it was still early. He yielded to the insistent invitation, and came down into the little cup of a meadow to her, and she watched him coming: a picturesque figure in the forest land, his black hair rumpled, his slender figure swinging on, his sleeves rolled back, his eyes full of the flicker of his lively spirit.

When Deveril was hard pressed along the trail, worn out and on the alert for oncoming danger from any quarter, he was impersonal; a mere ally on whom she could depend. At moments like this one, when he was rested and relaxed, and grasped in his eager hands a bit of the swift life flowing by, he became different. A man now—a young man—one with quick lights in his eyes and a lilting eagerness in his voice.

"It would be great sport," he said, "all life long…to come home to you and find you waiting…with a smile and a wee cup o' tea! And…."

He was half serious, half laughing; she made a hasty light rejoinder, and invited him to a hot supper waiting him.

They made a merry, frivolously light meal of it. There was plenty to eat; water near by; there was coffee; above them the infinity of blue, darkening skies, about them the peace and silence of the solitudes. And within their souls security, if only for the swiftly passing moment. They chose to be gay; they laughed often; Deveril asked her where she had learned to quote Scott and she asked him, in obvious retort, if he thought that she had never been to school! He sang for her, low-voiced and musically, a Spanish love-song; she made high pretense at missing the significance of the impassioned southern words. He, having finished eating and having nearly finished his cigarette, lying back upon the thick-padded pine-needles, jerked himself up, of a mood for free translation; she, being quick of intuition, forestalled him, crying out: "While I clean up our can dishes, if you will finish making camp…."

He laughed at her, but got up and went back, whistling his love-song refrain to his house-building. She, busied over her own labors, found time more than once to glance at him through the trees…wondering about him, trying to probe her own instinctive distrust of one who had all along befriended her.

When she joined him a few minutes later, coming up the slope slowly, she looked tired, he thought, and listless. She sat down and watched him finishing his labors; all of her spontaneous gaiety had fled; she was silent and did not smile and appeared preoccupied. She sighed two or three times, unconsciously, but her sighs did not escape him. Always he had held her sex to be an utterly baffling, though none the less an equally fascinating one. Now he would have given more than a little for a clue to her thoughts…or dreamings…or vague preoccupation….

"My lady's bower!" he said lightly. "And what does my lady have to say of it?"

A truly bowery little shelter it was, on leaning poles in an inverted V, with leafy boughs making thick walls, through which only slender sun-rays slipped in a golden dust; within a high-heaped pile of fragrant boughs, with a heap of smaller green twigs and resinous pine-tips for her couch.

"You are so good to me, Babe Deveril," was her grave answer.

And not altogether did her answer please him, for a quick hint of frown touched his eyes, though he banished it almost before she was sure of it. Those words of hers, though they thanked him, most of all reminded him of his goodness and gentleness with her, and thus went farther and assured him that she still counted upon his goodness and gentleness.

"I am afraid, Babe Deveril," she added quickly, though still her eyes were grave and her lips unsmiling, "that I am pretty well tired out...all sort of let-down like, as an old miner I once knew used to say! It's going to be sundown in a few minutes; can't we treat ourselves to the luxury of a good blazing camp-fire, and sit by it, and get good and warm and rested?"

Had she spoken her true thought she would have cried out instead:

"What troubles me, Babe Deveril, is that I am half afraid of you. And, all of a sudden, of the wilderness. And of life and of all the mysteries of the unknown! I am as near screaming from sheer nervousness at this instant as I ever was in my life."

But Deveril, who could glean of her emotions only what she allowed to lie among her spoken words, cried heartily:

"You just bet your sweet life we'll have a crackling, roaring fire. Taggart and his crowd are half a dozen miles away right now and still going; our fire down in that hollow will never cast a gleam over the big ridge yonder and the other ridges which lie in between him and us. Come ahead, my dear; here's for a real bonfire."

That "my dear" escaped him; but she did not appear to have noted it. She rose and followed him back to their dying fire. He began piling on dead branches; they caught and crackled and shot showering sparks aloft. He brought more fuel, laying it close by. Already the blaze had driven her back; she sat down by a pine, her knees in her hands, her head tipped forward so that her face was shadowed, her two curly braids over her shoulders.

Deveril lay near her, his hand palming his chin.

"Tell me, pretty maiden," he said lightly, "how far to the nearest barber shop?"

"And tell me," she returned, looking at her fingers, "if in that same shop they have a manicurist?"

Having glanced at her hands, she sighed, and then began working with her hair; there was one thing which must not be utterly neglected. She knew that if once it became snarled, she had small hope of saving it; no comb, no brush, no scissors to snip off a troublesome lock; only the inevitable result of such an utter snarl that she, too, in a week of this sort of thing, must needs seek a barber who understood bobbing a maid's hair. And with hair such as

Lynette's, glorious, bronzy, with all the brighter glowing colors of the sunlight snared in it, any true girl should shudder at the barber's scissors.

All without warning a great booming voice crashed into their ears, shattering the silence, as Bruce Standing bore down upon them from the ridge, shouting:

"So, now I've got you! Got both of you! Got you where I want you, by the living God!"

CHAPTER 11

The one first thought, bursting into full form and expression in Lynette's brain, with the suddenness, and the shock of an explosion, was: "He is alive!" And in Babe Deveril's mind the thought: "Bruce Standing at last!… And drunk with rage!"

And Bruce Standing's one thought, as both understood somewhat as they leaped to their feet:

"Into my hands, of all my enemies are those two whom I hate most delivered!" For it had been almost like a religion with him, his certainty that he would come up with them—the girl who had laughed and shot him; the man who had stolen her away, cheating his vengeance.

Babe Deveril, on the alert in the first flash of comprehension, stooped, groping among the shadows for his club, his only weapon. He saw the sun glinting upon Bruce Standing's rifle barrel. That club of his…where was it? Dropped somewhere; perhaps while he was building a leafy bower for a pretty lady; forgotten in a gush of other thoughts…he couldn't find it. He stood straight again; his hands, clinched and lifted, imitated clubs. The first weapons of the first men….

Lynette heard them shouting at each other, two men who hated each other, two men seeing red as they looked through the spectacles which always heady hatred wears. Men, both of them; masculinity asserting itself triumphantly, belligerently; manhood rampant and, on the spur of the moment, as warlike as two young bulls contending for a herd…. She heard them cursing each other; heard such plain-spoken Anglo-Saxon epithets hurled back and forth as at any other time would have set her ears burning. Just now the epithets meant less than nothing to her; they were but windy words, and a word was less, far less, than a stout club in a man's hand or a stone to hurl. She was of a mind to run while yet she could; but that was only the first natural reaction, lost and forgotten instantly. She stood without moving, watching them. An odd thing, she thought afterward, wondering, that that which at the moment made the strongest, longest-lasting impression upon her was the picture which Timber-Wolf, himself, created as, with the low sun at his back, he came rushing down upon them. Just now the mountain slope had constituted but a quiet landscape in softening tones, like a painting in pastels, with only the sun dropping down into the pine fringe to constitute a brighter focal point; and now, all of a sudden, it was as though the master artist, with impulsive inspiration, had slung with sweeping brush this new element into the picture—that of a great blond giant of a man, young and vigorous, and at this critical hour consumed with hatred and anger and triumphant glee. He was always one to punish his own enemies, was Bruce Standing. And now one felt that he carried vengeance in both big, hard, relentless hands.

On he came, almost at a run, so eager was he. Came so close before he stopped that Lynette saw the flash of his blue eyes—eyes which, when she had seen them first in Big Pine had been laughing and *innocent*—which now were the eyes of a blue-eyed devil. He was laughing; it was a devil's laugh, she thought. For he jeered at her and her companion. His mockery made her blood tingle; his eyes said evil things of her. Her cheeks went hot-red under that one flashing look.

But he was not just now concerned with her! He meant to ignore her until he had given his mind to other matters! He was still shouting in that wonderful, golden voice of his; to every name in a calendar not of saints he laid his tongue as he read Babe Deveril's title clear for him. And, name to name, Babe Deveril checked off with him, hurling back anathema and epithet as good as came his way…. Lynette understood that both men had forgotten her. To them, passion-gripped as they were, it was as though she did not exist and had never existed. And yet it was largely because of her that they were gathering themselves to fly at each other! Man inconsistent and therefore man. Otherwise something either higher or lower; either of a devil-order or a god-order. But as it is…better as it is…something of god and devil and altogether—man.

And children of a sort, in their hearts. For, before a blow was struck, they called names! So fast did the words fly, so hot and furious were they, that she had the curious sense that their battle would end as it began, in insults and mutterings. But when Timber-Wolf had shouted: "Sneak and cur and coward…a man to rifle another man's pockets, after that other had played square and been generous with you…." And when Deveril, his hands still lifted, while in his heart he could have wept for a club lost, shouted back: "Cur and coward yourself…with a rifle against a man who has nothing …" then she saw that the last word had been spoken and that blows were inevitable. She drew back swiftly, as any onlooker must give room to two big wild-wood beasts.

"Coward? Bruce Standing a coward? Why, damn your dirty soul…."

Bruce Standing caught his rifle by the end of the barrel; at first Lynette, and Deveril also, thought that he meant to use it as a club. But instead he flourished it about his head but the once, and hurled it so far from him that it went, flashing in the sunlight, above a pine top and fell far away somewhere down the slope. Never in all his life had Bruce Standing had any man even think of naming him coward. As well name sunlight darkness. For all men who knew Bruce Standing, and all men who for the first and only time looked him square in the eyes, knew of him that he was fearless.

Thus with a gesture…he abandoned wordy outpourings of wrath and hurled himself into flesh-and-blood combat. He did not turn to right or left for the dwindling camp-fire; he came straight through it, his two long arms outstretched, seeking Deveril. And Babe Deveril, the moment he saw how the rifle sped through the air and understood his kinsman's challenge, leaped forward eagerly to the meeting with him. Their four boots began scattering firebrands….

Lynette, with all her fast-beating heart, wanted to come to Babe Deveril's aid. The one thing which mattered was that, at her hour of need, he had stood up for her; her soul was tumultuously crying out for the opportunity to demonstrate beyond lip-service the meaning of gratitude. She caught up a stone, and throughout the fight held it gripped so hard that before the end her fingers were bleeding. But never an opportunity did she have to hurl it as long as those two contended.

Once it entered her thought that she must have dreamed of Bruce Standing, shot and bleeding and senseless on the floor at the Gallup House. For now, so few hours after, he gave no slightest hint of being a man recently badly wounded. There was more of common sense in a man's dying of such a wound as his than in his striking such great, hammer-hard blows with both arms. He created within her from that moment an odd sensation which grew with her later; the man was not of the common mould. Something beyond and above mere flesh and blood and the routine of human qualifications inspired him. There was something *inevitable* about Bruce Standing….

Babe Deveril fought like a young, lissome tiger…. He fought with all of the might that lay within him, muscle and mind and controlling spirit. When he struck a blow he put into it, with a little coughing grunt, every last ounce of hostility which was at his command; with every blow he longed to kill. And, as though the two were blood-brothers, Bruce Standing fought as did Babe Deveril. Straight, hard, merciless blow to answer blow as straight and hard and merciless….

Timber-Wolf was a man to laugh at his own mine muckers when they could not thrust a boulder aside, and to stoop and set his hands and arms and back to the labor and pluck the thing up and hurl it above their bewildered heads. He smote as though he carried a war-club in each hand; he received a crashing blow full in the face, and, though the blood came, he did not feel it; he struck back, and his great iron fist beat through Deveril's guarding arms. No man, or at least no man whom Bruce Standing in his wild life had ever met, could have stood up against that blow. Babe Deveril, with the life almost jarred out of his body, went down. And Bruce Standing, growling like an angry bear, caught him up and lifted him high in air and flung him far away from him, as lightly as though he flung but a fifty-pound weight. And where Babe Deveril fell he lay still…. Lynette ran to him and knelt and put her hands at his shoulders, thinking him dead.

A short fight it had been, but already had the swift end come. So hard had that blow been, so tremendous had been the crash against rock and earth when the flung body struck, there appeared to be but a pale flame of life, flickering wanly, in Deveril's body. Timber-Wolf came and stood over him and over Lynette, gloating, mumbling; muttering while his great chest heaved: "Little rat that he is! A man to take advantage when he found me down; a man to cheat me of the she-cat that shot me. I could crush him into the dirt with my boot heel…."

"You great big brute!…"

It was then that she sprang to her feet and, almost inarticulate with her own warring emotions, grief and fear and anger and hatred, flung the jagged stone full into his face. He was unprepared; the stone struck him full upon the forehead; he staggered backward, stumbling, almost falling; his hands flew to his face. He was near-stunned; blinded. Deveril was on his elbow….

"Come!" she screamed wildly. "Quick! You and I…."

"Treacherous devil-cat!" There was his thunderous voice shouting so that she, so near him, was almost deafened.

Bruce Standing, wiping the blood from his eyes, his two arms out before him, came back to the attack. Deveril, on his knees, surged to his feet; Standing struck and Deveril went down like a poorly balanced timber falling. Lynette was groping for another stone. Suddenly she felt upon her wrist a grip like a circlet of cutting steel. She was whisked about; Timber-Wolf held her, drawn close, staring face into face. His other hand was lifted slowly; suddenly she felt it caught in her loose hair….

And then, inexplicable to her now and ever after, there was in her ear the sound of Bruce Standing's laughter. The hand at her hair fell away. It went up to his eyes, wiping them clear. And then she saw in the eyes what she had read in the voice…laughter.

"Well, Deveril, what now?"

Again Deveril was on his feet. He swayed; his face was dead-white; it was easy to see how fiercely he bent every energy at his command to remain upright. There was a strange look in the eyes he turned upon Timber-Wolf.

"I never saw a man…like you."

He spoke with effort; he was like a man far gone in some devastating lung trouble; his voice was windy and vibrant and weak.

"Baby Devil!" jeered Standing. "Oh, Baby Devil! And, when it comes to dealing with a real man…. Why, then, less devil than baby! Ho!…"

"I am going to kill you…."

"God aids the righteous!" Standing told him sternly. "You go. To hell with you and your kind."

God aids the righteous! This from the lips of Bruce Standing, Timber-Wolf!... Lynette, her nerves like wires smitten in an electric storm, could have burst into wild laughter.... She wrenched at her wrist; Standing's big hand neither tightened nor relaxed, giving her the feeling of despair which a thick steel chain would have given had she been locked and deserted in a dungeon.

Deveril was looking over his shoulder. In his glance...the sun was near setting among the pines, and they saw his face as his head jerked about... anyone might read his thought: down there, somewhere among the bushes, lay a rifle!

Standing laughed at him. And Standing, dragging Lynette along with him as easily as he might have drawn a child of six, went down the slope first. And first he came to the fallen rifle and caught it up and brought it back to the trampled camp-fire.

"You're sneak enough for that, Baby Devil!" he taunted. "For that or any other coward act. And so is this woman of yours. So I spike the artillery. God! If the earth were only populated by men!... Now I've got this word for your crafty ear: listen well." Instantly his voice became as hard as flint and carried assurance that every word he was going to say would be a word meant with all his heart and soul. And all the while he gripped Lynette by the wrist and seemed unconscious of that fact or that she struggled to be free. "I've given you a fair fight, you who don't fight fair. And I've knocked the daylights out of you. And now I'm sick of you. You can go. You can sneak off through the timber and be out of sight inside of two minutes. Yet I'll give you five. And at the end of that time, if you're in sight, I am going to shoot you dead!"

Deveril glared at him, his glance laid upon Standing's as one rapier may clash across another.

"Do your dirty killing and be damned to you!" said Deveril briefly.

Timber-Wolf looked at him in surprise; he began to cast about him for a fresh and clearer comprehension of a man whom he despised. He strove with all his power of clean vision to see to the bottom of Deveril's most hidden thought.

"Now," said Standing slowly, "I am almost sorry for what I said. It strikes into me, Kid, that you are not afraid!"

Deveril, breathless, panting, holding himself erect only through a great call upon his will, made no spoken answer, but again laid the blade of his glance shiningly across that of Timber-Wolf.

"You die just the same," said Standing coldly. "It's only because I gave my word; that you can take in man-to-man style from me, Kid; for once I am not ashamed to be related to you. Either you travel or, in five minutes, you are a dead man."

Slowly Deveril's haggard eyes roved to Lynette's face…Lynette chained to Bruce Standing in that crushing grip….

"I am going," he said. And both knew he said it in fearlessness but also in understanding of the power which lay in a rifle bullet and the weakness of the barricade offered to it by a human skull. And both understood, further, that it was to Lynette that he spoke. "I am coming back!"

"For God's sake!" she screamed. "Go! Hurry!"

"Hurry!" Bruce Standing, with his own word of honor in the balance against the weight of the life of a man whom he began to respect, was all anxiety to have his kinsman gone.

Deveril's last word, with his last look, was for Lynette.

"A man who doesn't know when he's beat is a fool…. But you can be sure of this: I'll be back!"

He went, walking crookedly at first among the knee-high bushes; then growing straighter as he passed into the demesne of the tall, straight pines. Not swiftly, since there was no possibility of any swift play of muscles left within him; but steadily.

"A man!" grunted Timber-Wolf. Whether in admiration or disgust, Lynette could not guess from his tone.

He had his watch in the palm of his hand; her gaze was riveted on it. It seemed so tiny a thing in that great valley of his hand; a bauble. Yet its even more insignificant minute-hand was assuming the office of arbiter of human life; she knew that the moment the fifth minute was ticked off Bruce Standing, true to his sworn word, would relinquish her wrist just long enough to whip his rifle to his shoulder and fire…in case the uncertain form of Babe Deveril, going up over the ridge, were still in sight. And she knew within her soul that just so sure as gun butt struck shoulder and finger found trigger, so sure would Babe Deveril toss his arms up and fall dead….

"Hurry, Kid…you damn' fool…*hurry*…."

All the while Timber-Wolf was muttering and glaring at his watch and clinching her wrist; all the while forgetting that he held her. And, this also she knew, regretting that he had the job set before him of shooting down another man.

Lynette, her whole body atingle, every sense keyed up to its highest stressing, knew as soon as did Bruce Standing when he was going to drop her wrist and jerk his gun up. The five minutes were passing; still, though at a distance far up on the ridge, seen only by glimpses now and then under the setting sun, Babe Deveril was driving on, a man half bereft of his sober senses, his brain reeling from savage blows and on fire with rage and mortification; they saw him among the pines; they lost him; they saw him again. Never once had he turned to look back. Yet it did not seem that he hastened....

Timber-Wolf, growling deep down in his throat, lifted his rifle. But Lynette, before the act, *knew*! She flung herself with sudden fury upon his uplifted arm; she caught it, and with the weight of her body dragged it down. He sought to fling her off; she wrapped both of her arms about his right arm; she jerked at it so that he could have no slightest hope of a steady aim....

He turned and looked down into her eyes; deep...deep. For what seemed to her a long, long time he stood looking down into her eyes.

Then, with sudden anger, he thrust her aside. Without looking to see if she had fallen or stumbled and run, he raised his rifle again.

But just in time Babe Deveril was gone, over the ridge....

CHAPTER 12

"And now that you're half scared to death, you'd like to make a man believe that you are not afraid of the devil himself!"

She flashed a burning look at him; chokingly she cried:

"At least, thank God, I am not afraid of you, Bruce Standing!... Big brute and bully and...Yes!... Coward!"

And yet, as never before in her life, her heart was beating wildly, leaping against her side like an imprisoned thing struggling to break through the walls which shut it in. His fingers were still locked about her wrist; his grip tightened; he drew her closer in order to look the more clearly into her eyes. Then his slow, mocking laughter smote across her nerves like a rude hand brushing across harp-strings, making clashing discords.

"You begin well!" he jeered at her. "We are going to see how you end."

"Let me go!" She jerked back; she twisted and dragged at her wrist, trying wildly to break free. His mockery stung her into desperation. With her one free hand she struck him across the face.

She struck hard, with all her might, with trebled strength through her fury. And, maddening her, he gave no sign that she had hurt him. Still jeering at her, all that he did was drop his rifle, so that with his other hand he could take captive the hand which had struck him. And then it was so easy a thing for him to take both her wrists into the grip of his one, right hand; held thus, no matter how she fought, hers was the sensation of utter powerlessness which is a child's when an elder person, teasing, catches its two hands in one and lets it cry and kick.... Suddenly she grew quiet....

"Well?" she demanded, panting, forcing her eyes to a steady meeting with his. "What do you intend to do with me, now you've got me? There doesn't appear to be anyone near to keep you from woman-beating!"

"What am I going to do with you? If I knew, I'd tell you! When I do know, I'll show you…. If I could catch you by the hair and drag you through hell after me…. I pay all of my debts, girl! I have followed you; I have found you; I have taken you, prying you loose from your running mate…. You thought it fun to laugh at me once, did you? Before I have done with you, you would give your soul for the power and the will to laugh…."

"It is because I laughed at you?" she asked wonderingly.

"For what else?" he said sternly.

"And not because of a pistol shot?"

"Less for that than for the other. I allow it any man's privilege to shoot at me if he doesn't like me; but no man's nor woman's privilege to laugh."

"How do you know it was I who shot you?… Did you see?"

"Had I seen, I should not have held it against you; for that would have meant that you struck in the open, any man's or woman's right! But to shoot a man in the back…. Here; help me!"

She was perplexed to know what he meant. He dragged her after him, a dozen paces from the fire; still holding her two hands caught in his one, he sat down upon a big stone. Suddenly it struck her that all this time, since he had dropped his rifle, his left arm had been hanging limply at his side.

"When I let go of you," he said, very stern, "if you try to run for it I'll catch you and drag you back. And I'm in no mood for gentleness!" At that he let her go. He put his right hand to his shirt collar and began unbuttoning it.

"My wound has broken open," he said, with a grunt of disgust. "That Baby Devil of yours didn't care where he hit a man!… Here; there's a bandage that has slipped. And I'm losing blood again. See what you can do."

"Why should I?" she demanded coolly. "What is it to me whether or not you bleed to death?"

Fury filled his eyes and he shouted at her:

"You, by God, drilled the cowardly hole; and you doctor it!"

"And if I won't?"

"Then, as I live, I'll make you! One way or another, girl, I'll make you. That's Bruce Standing's word for you. Now hurry!"

She cast a quick glance over her shoulder; she was on the verge of breaking into wild, headlong flight…. But certain knowledge restrained her; she knew that he would overtake her, that he would drag her back and…that he was in no mood for gentleness. Therefore, while her whole soul rebelled, she came closer, as he commanded.

… She had never dreamed that any man born could have a chest like that; nor such shoulders, massive and yet beautiful as the pure-lined expression of power; nor such skin, soft and smooth and white as a girl's, the outward sign of another beauty, that of clean health. Clean, hard, triumphant physical manhood…. It struck her at the time, so that she marvelled at herself and wondered dully if she were taking leave of her sober senses, that there was truer, finer beauty in the body of such a man than in any girl's; that here was a true artist's true triumph…. Physically he was splendid, superb…. In his own image did God make man….

With his right hand he was working with the bandage where it was taped about the bulge of his left breast; on the white cloth were fresh gouts of blood. Impatiently he tore at his shirt collar; on the bandage, where it passed about his left shoulder-blade, were red stains.

"Wait a minute," he commanded. "In my pocket I've got some sort of salve; some idiotic mess that Billy Winch cooked up; the Lord knows what it is or what he made it of; iodine and soap and flaxseed and cobwebs, most likely! But it will chink up the leak…and it feels good and hasn't poisoned me so far! Here, smear it on."

… She felt as though she were dreaming all this! That wild, uncontrollable laughter of hers which swept over her at times of taut nerves and absurd situations, threatened to master her. She fought it down. She touched his back. She, Lynette, administering to Timber-Wolf…it would be better for her, far better for her, if his wound were poisoned and he died!… Yet, as she touched his back, it was with wondrously gentle fingers. There was a wound there; the ugly wound made by a bullet, half healed, broken open anew under heavy blows. A little shiver, a strange, new sort of shiver, ran through her; here she was down to elementals, she, who with just cause and leaping instinct hated this man, ministering to him….

"Smear the stuff on, I tell you. Over the wound. Enough of it to shut out any infernal infection…. What in the devil's name is holding you? Waiting for the sun to go down and come up again?"

She bit her lips; he looked suddenly into her face, and could have no clue to her thought or emotion; he could not guess whether she bit her lip to keep from laughing or crying!… She spread over the gaping wound a thin film of Billy Winch's pungent salve. As she touched the wound she looked for a muscular contraction, for the flinching from pain. He did not move; there was not so much as the involuntary quiver of a muscle. She wondered if the man felt as other human beings did?

… "Now a fresh piece of tape. That idiot Winch packed me off with my pockets loaded like a drug-store shelf! That's all for this time; we'll make a new dressing and bathe the wound in the morning. Now…. Here! Let me look at you!"

He crimsoned her face with that way of his. She whipped back from him and her eyes brightened with defiance. He sat looking at her a long time, while with slow fingers he buttoned his collar; his face showed not so much as a flicker of expression; his eyes were keen, but gave no clue to his thought.

The sun was already down beyond the ridge; shadows here in the little hollow had gathered swiftly; dark was on the way. He rose and went to the fire, for an instant turning his back upon her as he piled on the dead-wood which Deveril had gathered. But over his shoulder he called to her coolly:

"I've warned you not to try to run for it!"

And from his tone she knew that he had easily guessed her thought; for the impulse to attempt flight had been strong upon her the moment that he turned. She remained where she stood; if only it were pitch-dark, if only he went on a few paces farther away from her, if only the fringe of trees offering refuge were a few paces nearer…. She was quick to see the folly of making a premature dash; the wisdom in allowing him to think that she could be looked to for obedience! Thus, later, when her chance came and his watchfulness nodded, she'd be up and away like a shot….

The fire caught the fresh fuel and crackled and blazed, sparks showering about her where she stood. Now Standing, his face looking ruddy in the glow, turned toward her, saying curtly:

"Come here. I want a good look at you…in the full light."

"Brute and bully!" she cried, struggling with herself for an outward semblance of calm. "You hold the high card. But the game isn't played out between you and me yet, Bruce Standing." While speaking she came closer, so that she too stood in the red fire glow. She held her head up; she returned his unswerving gaze unswervingly.

"You've got the vocabulary of a gambler's daughter," he said. "That's what you are, eh? A gambler's girl and, in your own penny-ante way, a gambler yourself!"

"I am the daughter of Dick Brooke!" she told him proudly. "Dick Brooke was a man and a miner and after that, if you like, a gambler."

"Dick Brooke? Dick Brooke's daughter? Why, then…the daughter also of a dancing-girl!"

Her face went white with anger.

"Oh…tI hate you! Oh, I hate you! You…yyou are contemptible!"

"Aha! So that hurts!" he jeered at her.

"It is a cruel lie. Olymphe Labelle was not a dancing-girl…. She was an artist! And a woman among ten thousand…."

The firelight cast its warm glow over her face. She lifted her chin defiantly. Her hair fell in loose, rippling strands of bronze and over her shoulders. She was very beautiful thus; no woman on whom Bruce Standing had ever looked was half so beautiful. And haughty, like a princess…llike a high-bred lady made captive, yet scorning to show sign of fear….

"You are Lynette Brooke," he muttered; "you are the girl who laughed at me, shaming me; you are the girl who shot me in the back! Those are the things to remember. A treacherous cat of a woman; a gun woman! One to go sneaking around with a revolver at hand to shoot a man in the back with…."

"Any woman, dealing with men like you, has need of a gun!"

"I'll tell you this," he muttered. "I'm a fair judge of men, if not of women. And when it's a case of a man…why just show me a man who carries a pocket-gun and I'll show you a cheap ragamuffin, a tin horn, or an overgrown kid…or a dirty coward. A man's weapon is a rifle carried in the open; give me a good pair of boots and I'll stamp the white livers out of a whole crowd of your little gunmen…. As for women, gun-toting women…." He broke off with a heavy shrug. "Now, girl, I'm hungry. The smell of your coffee has been in my nostrils a long time. See what you can give me to eat."

"So I am to wait on you…to be your servant…."

"To be my slave!" he shouted at her. "Proud, are you? So much the better. I swore to make you pay, and you begin paying now. Yes, as my slave as long as I like!"

"And you call yourself a man!"

"I call myself the best man that ever came into this wilderness country," he told her impudently. "If you are in doubt, bring on any other man of your choice and ask him, with your pretty smiles, if he cares to stand up against me! Yes, a man who goes rough-shod over everything and anything and anybody who stands in his way…."

"Boaster!" she named him scornfully.

He laughed loudly at that.

"I am no boaster and in your heart you know it!… There's another damn-fool convention for you, that business of great modesty! A man who is sure of himself doesn't have to walk easy and talk easy, but can tell other men what he is, and then, by glory, show 'em!"

Still she was scornful of him…though she could not keep out of her thought that picture which he had made when, axe in hand, he had laid an armed jailer in the dust, and single-handed had made a jail delivery which hundreds of other men wanted to make and held back from…through lack of that unrestricted confidence which was Bruce Standing's.

He was staring at her.

"You, too…for a woman…have courage," he muttered. And then, with a sudden arm flung out: "I'm hungry, I tell you."

"I'd rather die…."

"It's easy to die…for anyone who is not a coward. And I just told you that you had courage." He came suddenly close to her. "But there are other things that are not so easy! What if I put my two arms about you? If I hold you tight…and set my lips to yours…and…."

"You beast…."

"But my dinner?" he jeered at her.

She went hot and cold; she cast a quick glance toward the forest land where the night was thickening; she cast another glance at his rifle where it lay, a few feet from the fire. Then, her lower lip caught between her teeth, she went to the tin can in which she and Babe Deveril had made coffee.

"A funny thing," said Bruce Standing, watching her; "you skipped out, hot-foot, from Big Pine, thinking you had killed me! And your little friend, meaning Baby Devil, skipped along, thinking he had done Jim Taggart in! And, after all, nobody much hurt!… Glad to hear that Taggart did not die?"

"I knew it already," she said, just to cheat him of any satisfaction in telling her.

"Mexicali Joe skipped this way, too," he went on swiftly, so swiftly that he succeeded in tricking her into saying:

"I knew that, too!"

Then he laughed at her, informing her:

"Now there remains little for you to tell me. You knew Taggart was still on his feet and you knew Joe was travelling this way, and you've come up from the general direction of Joe's dugout! Which tells me one thing: where you and Baby Devil got the coffee and this tinned stuff. Now let's hear details!"

"Oh… I hate you!"

"You've told me that before. And…." He burst into booming laughter. And then, still laughter-choked, he cried: "Like a good old-time two-handled sword is the man Bruce Standing! And yet his wit, like a Spanish dagger, is good match for a girl's!"

She made no reply, though her blood tingled, and though her hand, with a will of its own, must be held back from striking him across the face again. She brought him his coffee and thereafter food which he called for from among the tins.

"What do you think has happened to your gentleman friend?" he mocked her. And when she refused to reply, he told her: "He's gone on…where? After Taggart? To get a rifle and come back? Planning to hide behind a tree and pop me off while I'm not looking? That would make a hit with you, wouldn't it? Like your own best game of shooting a man in the back! Or has he forgotten a pair of bright eyes and warm arms and red lips? And is he content to trail Mexicali, spying on him, trying to get in on the new gold diggings? Which, girl?"

"He hates you!… with cause. And he is no coward; he is as good a man, if less brute, as you, Bruce Standing!…"

When he spoke finally it was to say:

"We're going to be short on provisions for a day or so, girl. Hungry?"

Here was her first, altogether too vague clue to his intentions. Quickly she asked:

"Where are we going?"

"I to keep an engagement; you to accompany me."

He supposed that he had told her nothing. And yet she, quick-witted, having never let slip from her mind a certain suspicion when Mexicali Joe had too readily succumbed to Taggart, cried out:

"To a meeting with Mexicali Joe!"

"What makes you think that?" he asked sharply.

She pretended to laugh at him. He ate in silence; drank his coffee; thereafter, stuffing a pipe full of crude black tobacco, smoked thoughtfully. All the while the fire burned lower and the darkness, ringing them around, drew closer in. She had been on the alert, while looking to be hopelessly bowed where she sat. Suddenly he was at her side, his grip like a steel bracelet about her wrist.

"About ready to jump and run for it?" he taunted her. "Not tonight, my girl; and not tomorrow night nor yet for many a day to come. I've got my own plans for you."

"Are you going to take me back to Big Pine? To hand me over to the law, with a charge of attempted murder against me?"

"I am going to take you with me on into the wilderness. Into a country which is absolutely the kingdom of Bruce Standing. Haven't I told you that I have my own plans for you? I can hand you over to the cheap degradation of a trial and conviction and jail sentence whenever I am ready for it...."

"You can't keep me from killing myself...."

"But I can! I am master here, understand? And you.... By heaven, you are nothing but my slave so long as I tolerate you!... Look here, what I brought for you!... For I knew I'd find you!"

He began unwinding from his big body a thin steel chain, a chain which he had brought with him from his ranch headquarters, where it had served as leash for a wolf-hound. With a quick movement he snapped the end of it about her waist; there was a steel padlock scarcely bigger than a silver half-dollar; she heard the click as he locked it. Then he stood back from her, the other end of the slight chain in his hand...and laughed at her!

"The sign of your servitude!... Proud? One way to make you pay! Will you laugh again, girl? Will you, do you think, ever have the second chance to shoot me in the back?... Come; we must be on our way before daylight."

He caught up his rifle; that, together with the end of her chain, he held in his hand. He began putting out the fire, stamping on the living coals. Making her follow him, he went to the creek several times for water, which he carried in his big hat, which held so much more than any tin can in camp. When the fire was out, he turned with her toward the bowery shelter which Babe Deveril, working and singing, had made for her. With his shuffling boots he kicked the culled branches into two heaps. He wrapped the end of her chain about his wrist; she heard the snap as he fastened it. He thrust his rifle under him.

"I am going to sleep," he told her bluntly and cast himself down. "You with your payment just begun, may lie awake all night...wondering...."

... But it was a long, long while, a weary time of darkness sprinkled with stars before he went to sleep. She sat up on her couch of boughs, the chain about her waist galling her....

CHAPTER 13

It may appear a strange thing that Lynette Brooke slept at all that night. But a fatigued body, healthy and young, demanded its right, and she did sleep and sleep well. A far stranger thing was that, after she had sat in the dark a long time, there had at last come a little smile upon her lips and into her eyes, and she had gone to sleep smiling!

For in the deep black silence her quick mind had been busy, never so busy; out of tiny scraps it had constructed a mental patchwork. Nor were all dark-hued threads weaving in and out of it; here and there the sombre pattern had bright-hued spots. Her courage was high, her hopes always at surging high tide; her senses keen. And, after all, Bruce Standing was a blunt, forthright man, in no degree subtle....

He had given her the impression an hour ago of being entirely brute beast. That was true. Further, she told herself with growing conviction, that it had been his great intent to make her regard him as brute and beast; she had angered him, she had drawn upon herself his vengeful wrath; he meant to make her pay; and his first step had been to make her afraid of him.... She went on to other thoughts; Bruce Standing was the man to defy Gallup in his own lair; the man to defy the sheriff; to hurl an axe at an armed deputy...and yet the only man in Big Pine to lift an angry hand against the unfair play of shutting little Mexicali Joe up in jail! He, alone, had not sought to steal Joe's secret; he alone was ready, against all odds, to throw the door back and let Joe go. Not altogether that the part of the brute and beast!

Another thing: Bruce Standing did not lie. She *knew* that. And he was not a coward; he did not do petty, cowardly things.... He meant her to believe that there was nothing too cruel and merciless for him to inflict upon her. Yet she had struck him in the face with a stone; she had struck him with her hands, and he had not so much as bruised the skin of her wrists with his big hard hands!... Eager he had been to humiliate her, calling her his slave; eagerly, as soon as he had read her pride, he grasped at the first means of torturing it. Why that great eagerness...unless he, despite his threat, was casting about in rather blind fashion for means to make her pay?... He wanted her to be afraid of him...and it came to her in the dark, so that she smiled, that this was because there was little for her to fear!

"In his rage," she told herself, and, fettered as she was, a first gleam of triumph visited her, "he came roaring after me. And, now he has me, he doesn't know what to do with me! To make me his unwilling slave...*unwilling*!.... that is all that he can think of now."

And again there was comfort in the thought:

"If he meant to harm me, why should he have let me go tonight? An angry man, bent upon real brute vengeance, would have struck at the first opportunity. The opportunity was when he sent Babe Deveril away and had me to do what he pleased with. And he only played the perfectly silly game of making me his slave...*unwilling*...."

It was the thoughts which rose with the word that put the little smile into her eyes and brought the first softening of her troubled lips.... Several times she heard him stirring restlessly; once he awakened her with his muttering, and she knew that he was asleep, but that either his wound pained him or his sleep was disturbed by unwelcome dreams—perhaps both.

Bruce Standing woke and sat up in the early chill dawn. He looked swiftly to where Lynette lay. She appeared to be plunged in deep, restful sleep. She lay comfortably snuggled in among the boughs; the curve of one arm was up about her face, so that he could not see her eyes. Naturally he believed them shut; her breathing was low and quiet, exactly as it should have been were she really fast asleep.... She looked pretty and tiny and tired out, but resting. Suddenly he frowned savagely. But he sat for a long time without stirring.

Lynette put up her arms and stretched and yawned sleepily, and then, like a little girl of six, put her knuckles into her eyes. Then she, too, sat up quickly.

"Oh," she said brightly. "Are you awake already? And making not a bit of noise, so as to let me have my sleep out? Good morning, Mr. Timber-Wolf!"

She was smiling at him! Smiling with soft red lips and gay eyes!

He frowned and with a sudden lurch was on his feet.

"Come," he said harshly. "I want to make an early start."

She sprang to her feet as though all eagerness, exclaiming brightly:

"If you'll get the fire started, I'll have breakfast in a minute! There isn't much in the larder, but you'll see what a nice breakfast I can make of it. Then I'll dress your wound and we'll be on our way."

"Look here," muttered Standing, swinging about to stare at her, "what the devil are you up to?"

"What do you mean?" she asked innocently.

"I mean this cheap play-acting stuff...as though you were as happy as a bird!"

"Why, I always believe in making the best of a bad mess, don't you?" she retorted. "And, after all, how do you know that I'm not as happy as a bird? I nearly always am."

His eyes were blazing, his face flushed; she saw that she was lashing him into rage. She began to fear that she had gone too far; for the present she would go no farther. But meanwhile she gave him no hint of any trepidation, but kept the clear, unconcerned look in her eyes.

He strode away from her, toward the charred remains of last night's fire. He held her chain in his hand; she hurried along after him, so that not once could the links tighten; so that not once could he feel that he was dragging an unwilling captive behind him. Her heart was beating like mad; she was aquiver with excitement over the working out of her scheme, yet she gave him no inkling of any kind of nervousness.

"I don't know what you are up to and I don't care," he said abruptly. "You are to do what you are told, girl."

"Of course!" she said quickly. "I understand that. I am ready...."

"I am going to take the chain off you now, simply because I don't need it during daylight. But you're not to run away; if you try it I'll run you down and drag you back. Do you understand? And after that I'll keep you chained up."

"I understand," she nodded again. And, when he had removed the chain from her waist, all the time not looking at her while she, all the time, stood smiling, she said a quiet "Thank you."

"While I get some wood," he went on, "you can take some cans and go down to the creek for water. I'll trust you that far...and don't you trust too much to the screen of willows to give you a chance for a getaway! I tell you, I'd overhaul you as sure as there is a God in heaven!"

She caught up two cans and went down the slope toward the creek. To keep him from guessing how, all of a sudden, her heart was fluttering again, she sang a little song as she went. He stared after her, puzzled and wondering. Then with a short, savage grunt, he began gathering wood.

Was now her time? This her chance? She sang more loudly, clearly and cheerily. She wanted to look back to see if he was watching her every step; yet she beat down the temptation, knowing that if he did watch and did see her turn he would know that she was overeager for flight. She came to the creek; she passed carelessly about a little clump of willows. Now she looked back, peering through the branches. He was stooping, gathering wood; his back was to her!

"*Now!*" her impulses cried within her. "*Now!*"

She looked about her hurriedly, in all directions. There was so much open country here; big pines, wide-spaced. If she ran down the slope he must surely see her when she had gone fifty or a hundred yards. And then he'd be after her! If she turned to right or left, the case was almost the same. If it were only dark! But the sun was rising....

She began singing again, so that he might hear. A sudden anger blazed up within her. With all his blunt ways, the man was not without his own sort of shrewdness; he had known that she had no chance here to escape him; no chance for such a head start as to give her an even break in a race with him.

… After ten minutes she came back to him; she carried a dripping can in each hand; she had bathed hands and arms and face and throat; she had combed her hair out through her fingers, making new thick braids, with loosely curling ends. She had taken time to twist those soft ends about her fingers. He was standing over his newly built fire; his rifle, with the chain tossed across it, lay against a rock; he gave no sign of noting her approach…. Yet, while they ate a hurriedly warmed breakfast, she caught him several times looking at her curiously….

Her heart began again to beat happily; never was hope long departed from the breast of Lynette Brooke. She kept telling herself, over and over, that he was not going to be brute and beast to her. Soon or late she would find her chance for escape from him; she would let him think her that weakling which it was his way to regard women in general; there would come the time when, once more free, she could laugh at him…. And she, when he did not observe, looked curiously at him many a time.

When they had eaten and he had gathered up the few scraps of food and had very carefully extinguished the last ember of their fire, he wound the chain about his middle again, caught up the rifle and said briefly and still without looking at her:

"Come."

She followed him, neither hesitating nor questioning; thus she was glee-fully sure she angered him…. She wondered what the day held in store for her; she wondered what of good and bad lay ahead; and yet she was now less filled with terror than with the burning zest for life itself. Bruce Standing had told her that he was going to keep an appointment; he had been the man to re-lease Mexicali Joe; Mexicali Joe had whispered something and Standing had laughed; Mexicali Joe was now ahead of them, pretending to lead Taggart and Gallup and Cliff Shipton to his gold! Her thoughts were busy enough and she, like her silent companion, had small need for talk.

She wondered about Babe Deveril; how badly hurt he had been after Bruce Standing's mauling; what he was doing now; where he was? A hun-dred times that morning, hearing bird or squirrel and once a leaping buck, she looked to see Babe Deveril bursting back upon them…. Had he not gone far, last night? Had he remained near their camp and was he following them today?…

They passed over a ridge and turned into a little cup of a green valley; Standing, stalking ahead of her, went to a thicket and drew from it a saddle and bridle and saddle blankets and a small canvas pack. Then, standing with his hands on his hips, staring off in all directions, he whistled shrilly. Whis-tled, and waited listening, and whistled again. Lynette heard, from far off, the quick, glad *whicker* of a horse. And here came the horse galloping; kicking up its heels; shaking its head with flying mane; circling, snorting, with low-ered head; at standstill for a moment, a golden sorrel with snow-white mane and tail; a mount for even Timber-Wolf, lover of horses, to be proud to own and ride and whistle to through the forest land…. Lynette looked swiftly at Standing's face; he was smiling; his eyes were bright.

He went forward and stroked his horse's satiny nose and wreathed a hand in the mane and led the animal to the saddle, calling him softly, "Good old Daylight." The horse nosed him; Standing laughed out loud and smote the great shoulder with open palm…. Lynette saw with clear vision that there was a great love between man and animal; and she thought of another horse, Sunlight, slaughtered at Young Gallup's orders, and of Standing's lisping rage and of her own nervous, uncontrollable laughter….

There came a deep, ugly growling—a throaty, wolfish menace, almost at her heels. She whirled about and cried out in sudden startled fright.

"Lie down Thor!" Standing shouted sternly. "Down, sir!"

Lynette had never seen a dog like this one, big and lean and forbidding; as tall as a calf in her suddenly frightened eyes, wolfish looking, with stiff bristles rising along powerful neck and back, and eyes red-rimmed, and sharp-toothed mouth slavering. At Standing's command the great dog, which had come upon her on such noiseless pads, dropped to the ground as though a bullet instead of a commanding voice had drilled its heart. But still the steady eyes filled with suspicion and menace were fixed on her.

"He'd tear your throat out if I gave the word," said Standing. "Now you do what I tell you; go to him and set your hand on his head!"

"I won't!" she cried out sharply, drawing back. The deep, throaty growl came again; the dog's lips trembled and withdrew from the long, wolfish teeth; the whole gaunt form was aquiver….

"But you will! Otherwise…. He'll not hurt you when once I tell him not to. Go to him; put your hand on his head…. Afraid?" he jeered.

She was afraid. Sick-afraid. And yet she gave her taunter one withering glance and stepped swiftly, though her flesh quivered, to the dog.

"Steady, Thor!" cried Standing sternly. "You dog, steady, sir!"

The dog growled and the teeth were like evil, poisonous fangs. Yet Lynette came another step toward him; she stooped; she put forward her hand….

"*Thor!*" Standing's voice rang out, filled with warning. Thor began whining.

Lynette put her hand upon the big head. Thor trembled. Suddenly he lay flat, belly down; the head between the outstretched fore paws. He whined again. Standing laughed and began bridling and saddling his horse. Thor jumped up and frisked about his master; Standing fondled him, as he had fondled Daylight, by striking him resoundingly.

"To play safe," he flung over his shoulder at Lynette, "better come here."

When she had drawn close Standing stooped and patted the dog's head. Then, while Thor, snarling, looked on, he put out his hand and placed it for a fleeting instant upon Lynette's shoulder.

"Good dog," he said quietly.

Then he caught up her hand and placed it on Thor's head, cupped under his own.

"Good dog," he said again. And then he told Lynette to call the dog. She did so, saying in an uncertain voice:

"Here, Thor!… Come here, Thor!"

"Thor!" cried Standing commandingly. "Good dog!"

Thor trembled, but he went to her. He allowed her to pat him. Then, with a suddenness which startled her, he shot out a red tongue to lick her hand. Standing burst into sudden pleased laughter.

"Your friend…so long as I don't set him on you!" he cried out.

"You are a beast…who herd with beasts!" she said, shuddering.

He laughed again and finished drawing tight cinch and strapping latigo. He tied his small pack at the strings behind the saddle and said briefly:

"Since we're in a hurry, suppose you ride while I walk alongside? We'll make better time that way."

She was ashamed of herself—that she should have been afraid of a dog! Now she was Lynette again, quick and capable and confident. He was going to lend her a hand to mount; she forestalled him and went up into the saddle like a flash. It was in her thought to take him by surprise; to give Daylight his head and race away out of sight among the pines.…

But he was scarcely less quick; his hand shot out, catching Daylight's reins; he unwound the chain from about his middle and snapped the catch into the horse's bit.… And she began to analyze, thinking:

"He took time to explain why he let me ride while he walked! He is less beast and brute than he knows himself!… Less beast and brute than…simple humbug!" And, before they had gone ten steps, he heard her humming the air which she had sung at breakfast time.

"Damn it," he muttered under his breath, not for her to hear. "The little devil…she's taking advantage of me, every advantage. She…. Just the same…just the same.…"

And he, too, was wondering about Babe Deveril!

"We go this way," he said. "I'll lead; you follow."

"I know!" cried Lynette; she could not hold the words back. "Toward Buck Valley and Big Bear Creek…and Mexicali Joe. And…,"

"And what?" he demanded, snatching at her chain, sensing that something of import lay behind the abruptly checked words.

She only laughed at him.

CHAPTER 14

Another day of wilderness wandering. A cabin sighted, but so far away that it was merely a vague dot upon a distant ridge; miner's shack or sheepman's or wood-cutter's? Housing an occupant or deserted for years? No smoke from the rock chimney; no sign of any human being near it. And all view of it so soon lost!... And, afterward, no other human habitation of any kind; no road man-made; only trees and rocks, gorges and ridges and brush, and a winding way to be chosen between them. With, always, Bruce Standing driving on and on, relentlessly on, ever deeper into the wilderness.

A day of life like a leaf torn out of the book of hell for Lynette. He did not speak to her as they went on from dawn to noon and from noon until afternoon shadows gathered; he did not so much as turn his eyes full upon her own; for the most part he seemed altogether forgetful of the fact that, besides himself, there was another of his species in all the wide sweep of this land of mighty solitudes. For his dog, Thor, he had a kindly though rough-spoken word now and then; for his horse a word or a rude pat upon the shoulder or hip; for her nothing but his utter, unruffled silence.... At times she hummed little snatches of gay tunes, hoping to irritate him; at times she strove for an aloofness to match his own. Countless times she looked over her shoulder, looking for Babe Deveril. And so the day, a long day, went by until at last it was late afternoon.

"Here we stop," said Standing abruptly. "Get down."

He would seem to have all advantage over her; yet she understood that in one way, and in one way only, could she rob him of his advantage, and that was by giving him swift and cheerful obedience. So she slipped out of the saddle on the instant, giving him for answer only the light gay words:

"Oh, it is beautiful here!" ...

It was beautiful.... He glared at her and led his horse away to unsaddle; his big dog, Thor, had trotted along at Daylight's heels all day and now slumped down, ears erect and suspicious, while he watched his master and made certain of never losing sight for a second of his master's new companion, whom he tolerated but did not trust. Lynette, stiff from so many hours in the saddle, looked about her. They were in the upper, brief space of a valley; above reared the mountains steeply, rugged slopes with pines here and there, with more open spaces and tumbled boulders. The valley itself was a pretty, pleasant place, soft in short green grass, flower-dotted, smoothly curving down into the more open level lands below. Yet here was no proper place to pitch camp, especially at so early an hour when it was allowed to seek further; it was too open, it would be unsheltered and cold; there was no water....

"Come on!"

She started and turned again toward Standing. He had slung his small pack across his shoulders and was going on. She looked forward toward the ridge, which he faced; it rose sheer and forbidding. And she saw that his face was white and drawn; she wondered quickly how sorely his wound hurt him.

"Brute?" He could have been far more brutal to her…. He was dead-tired, white-faced; he had fought hard last night, scorning the advantage of an armed man against an unarmed; he had not harmed a hair of her head! Almost…almost it lay within her to whisper "Poor fellow!" And if only Bruce Standing could have known that!…

He led the way. She followed, since there was nothing else to think of doing.

They climbed steadily upward out of this narrow green valley, finding a steep but open way among the trees. Now and then they paused briefly to breathe, and Lynette, looking back, saw more and more of the long, winding valley, as it revealed itself to her from new vantage points. Far away she caught the glint of the sunlight upon a little wandering creek. They went on, and came to the crest of the ridge, in full sunshine now; Standing led an unhesitating way through a natural pass, and down on the other side, into shadows of a thick grove; through thickets; they splashed across a creek, a thin line of clear, cool water slipping through mountain willows, a tributary of the larger stream in the valley below. Down here it was almost dark. But twenty minutes later, climbing another slope where the larger timber stood widely spaced, they came again into the full sunshine…. Lynette began to wonder why he had left his horse so far back; how far did the silent, tireless man mean to walk? Also, she began to welcome the coming night with an eagerness which she was at all pains to conceal from him; he was always ten steps ahead of her; if he walked on another half-hour, she began to hope that they would come into a place of shadows and clumps of trees among which she might dare make the attempt for escape which had been denied her all day….

They came into a little upland flat, well watered, emerald-carpeted with tender grass, shot through with lingering flowers and studded with magnificent trees; it seemed the very heart of the great wilderness; here was such glorious forest land as Lynette had never seen and did not know existed in all the broad scope of the great Southwest mountain country. She looked upward. Dark branches towered into the sky, the tips still shot through with soft summer light. She heard the gush of water—the tumble and splash and fall of water. Somewhere above, at the upper end of the flat, where a dark ravine was an ebon-shadow-filled gash through the hills, was a waterfall. She could not see it, but its musical waters proclaimed it through the still air. She looked swiftly down the other way; there it was growing dark. She glanced hurriedly at Standing. And he, as though he had read her thought, stopped and turned and, before she could stir, was at her side.

After that, with never a word, they went on, deeper into this shadowy realm of big trees. He watched her at every step. Fury filled her heart, but with compressed lips she maintained a silence like his own. Thor trotted along with them, now in front of his master, as though this were a way he had travelled before and knew well, now questing far afield, now in the rear, eying his master's captive and setting his dog's brains to the riddle.

Before they had walked another ten minutes, Standing threw down his pack and said abruptly:

"This is as far as we go."

She sat down, her back to a tree, her face averted from him. She was very tired and now she could have put her face into her hands and cried from very weariness. But instead she caught her lip up between her teeth and hid her face from him and ignored him. But in her heart she was wondering; had he travelled all day long and then this far from the spot where he had released his horse, just to pitch camp in a clump of trees? Was this the spot toward which he had striven on so stubbornly since daylight? Where was he going? Why? Old queries and doubts rushed back upon her.... She was vaguely grateful that they were questions which he and not she had to answer; that responsibilities were his instead of hers. She was tired enough to lie down where she was and cease to care what happened.... It was not as yet pitch-dark; the sun was not down on the heights. But here, among the tall pines, in this hollow, the shadows were thick; nothing stood out in detail to her slowly closing eyes; here was a place of black blots, distorted glooms, the weird formless outriders of the night.... She had not the remotest suspicion that, where she had slumped down, she was almost at the door of a cabin.

Rather, it would have been surprising had she known. For surely there was never cabin like this hermit camp of Bruce Standing's! Two sky-scraping pines stood close together; between them was the door, framed by their own straight trunks. Smaller trees grew about the ancient parents; these hid the walls which to escape notice required little enough hiding at any time; a man might have passed here within a few yards at noonday and not noticed all this which Lynette failed to see in the dusk. For the walls of the tiny cabin were of rough logs from which the bark had never been stripped, walls which blended so perfectly with the greater note struck by the woodland that they failed to draw the eye; the chimney, of loose-piled rocks, was viewless at this time of day behind the tree trunks and inconspicuous at any time. And low, over the flat roof drooped the concealing branches of the trees. Of all this Lynette glimpsed nothing until Timber-Wolf said, looking down at her:

"When all the tavern is prepared within,
Why nods the drowsy worshipper outside?"

She had striven in one way and another since she had had her first view of him, axe in hand, for a clue to the real Bruce Standing. Now, again, he set her jaded faculties to work: Bruce Standing, Timber-Wolf, and man of violence, quoting poetry to her! And at such a moment and under such circumstances!... It is not merely the feminine soul which is indeterminable, mystifying, intriguing into the ultimate bournes of speculation; rather the human soul....

"I don't fancy guessing riddles this evening," she told him. "All that I can think of by way of repartee is: 'What meanest thou, Sir Tent-maker?'"

She thought that she heard him stifle a chuckle!

But, in this thickening gloom and through those heavy shadows which lay across her soul in an hour of doubtings and uncertainties, she could be certain of nothing.... He was saying merely:

"If you're not clean done in, I'd suggest you walk three steps into my cabin. On the other hand, if you can't make it, I'll pick you up and carry you in!"

At that she sprang to her feet; through the gathering dark he could feel the burning look in her eyes.

Then, groping mentally and physically, it was given to her to understand. For already he stood upon the rude threshold. She followed after him.

She gasped, astonished, when she realized that already, in so few steps, she had passed into the embrasure of four walls! Sturdy walls; walls rude and unbeautiful, but rising stalwart bulwarks against the cold of night mountain air. He, a blurred, gigantic form in the dusk, was before her; his wolfish dog was at her heels. She heard the scratch, she saw the blue and yellow spurt of a sulphur match. His form suddenly loomed larger, leaped into grotesque giganticness; the tiny room sprang waveringly out of darkness into the unreality of half-light; he found a candle; a steady golden flame sent the shadows racing into limbo; she looked about her wonderingly....

A room, bound in rough logs; a hastily, roughly hewn log set on other logs, offering its surly service as table; a stump which obviously made pretense at being a stool; a bunk against a wall, thick-padded with the tips from pines; a tin cup, a tin plate, an imitation of a box against a wall. And, hanging over a pole...her first certainty that Bruce Standing, though animal as she named him in her heart, was a clean animal...two or three blankets which, on last leaving this hut of his, he had stretched to air.... A primitive room, and yet clean. And, across from the narrow bunk, a deep, wide-mouthed fireplace made of big rocks.... He himself must have made that fireplace, for what other man could have lifted those rocks into place?

"I'm hungry," said Standing. "As hungry as a bear."

Already she was sitting on the edge of the bunk. She expected to hear for his next words: "Get me my dinner." But, instead, he said, his voice harsher than she had ever heard it before:

"And that's why I'm cooking for myself instead of making you do it! I don't want you to get it into your head it's because I'm getting sorry for you...."

She lay back, unanswering, and watched him. And presently, though not for him to see, a little smile touched her lips and for a short instant lighted her big gray eyes.... And in her heart she said: "He is so obvious, with all his thinking that he is a man whom a girl cannot see through! All day he has made me ride, while he walked! He said that that was to make better time! And, with every opportunity to harm me, he has not harmed a hair of my head! He has not even touched me with his big, blundering hands!... And he looks white and sick from his hurt...."

He rummaged in a corner; he made a fire in his fireplace; he ripped open a couple of cans and set coffee to boil in a battered black pot. Suddenly Lynette, who had been silent a long while, exclaimed:

"I know now! We are still on your land. This is the very cabin where, six years ago, you robbed Babe Deveril of three thousand dollars!"

"No!" he said. "You have guessed wrong!" And then: "So your little friend, Baby Devil, told you many a tale about my wickedness?"

"He told me that one."

"And did he tell you the sequel? How I squared with him?"

So he wanted her to think well of him! She made herself comfortable, leaning back against the wall.

"Have you the vaguest inkling of the difference between right and wrong, Bruce Standing?" she asked him impudently.

He laughed at her—become suddenly harsh.

"Come," he said, "it is time for food. And then, for a man who does not break his word, blow high, blow low, to keep an appointment."

With that conversation ceased. He drove Thor into a corner, and with a word and a glance made the dog lie down. He boiled his coffee and set a hurried meal; he caught up a tin plate and brought it to Lynette. She was about to thank him when she saw how he was planning to serve a tin platter like hers to his dog; then she could have screamed at him in nerve-pent-up anger.

The three—master, captive, and dog—ate their late dinners while the candle flame, pale yellow with its bluish centre, swayed gently in the mild draft of air through the open door. Windows there were none, saving the one square aperture over the bunk, boarded up now.

"What about Jim Taggart?" said Standing brusquely out of a long silence toward the end of which the weary girl was near dozing. "What do you know about him? Did he overhaul Mexicali Joe after all?"

She looked at him steadily; suddenly she was glad when a pine branch in the fireplace, full of pitch, flared up so that he must have seen her face more clearly than he could have done by mere pale candle-light; she wanted him to see it and read something of the defiance which she meant to offer him.

"So, after all, you have your engagement with Mexicali Joe? It was for that that you set him free? That you, instead of others, might steal his golden secret!"

"Then you won't answer, girl? You, whom I could crush between thumb and finger, refuse to answer me?"

"Yes!" she cried out at him. "Yes! I am not afraid of you, Bruce Standing!"

"Not afraid?" He glared at her, his flashing blue eyes full of threat. Then he laughed contemptuously, saying: "And yet, were I minded to, I could in a second have you on your knees, begging, pleading...."

"But you won't!" she dared fling at him. "And that is why I am not afraid!"

"I am not so sure!" he muttered. "Not so sure. Before morning, girl, you may come to know what fear is!"

She tried to toss back her fearless laughter, but at that look of his and at that stern tone of his voice her laughter caught in her throat.

"You've got nerve," he said grudgingly. "More nerve than I thought any girl could have...since it's far and away more than most men have. But just the same there's one thing you are afraid of! I've seen it a dozen times today, no matter how well you thought you hid it! You are afraid to death of old Thor, there!"

She shivered; she laid a quick command upon her muscles as upon her spirit, but they failed her; she tried to tell herself and to show him through her bearing, head up, eyes steady, that it was only fatigue and the growing chill of the coming night that put that tremor upon her. But he laughed at her and called his big dog to him and said heavily:

"Watch her, Thor! Watch her!"

Thor growled, a growl coming from deep down in the powerful throat; the red eyes grew hot; bristles stood up along neck and back; there came the gleam of the wolfish teeth. She shrank back against the wall.

"I have my appointment!... In an hour I must go. I give you your choice of coming along with me, in leash, or of staying here, with only Thor to guard, and taking your chances with him! Which is it?"

And she cried quickly:

"I'll go with you!" And then, lest he should think that he had triumphed, she added swiftly: "For I, too, am interested in Mexicali Joe!"

He caught down the blankets which had hung airing since last he came here and tossed two of them to the bunk where she half lay; the third he folded and placed on the floor, stretching out his own great bulk upon it, his shoulders against the wall. He found his pipe, filled and lighted it, and lay staring into the fire....

And she, drawing a blanket over her knees, crouched, looking into the same dancing flames, overwhelmed for the moment by a total sense-engulfing feeling of unreality. Could all of this which had happened, which was still happening, be an actual experience for her, Lynette Brooke? More did it resemble a long-drawn-out ugly dream than actuality! To be here tonight, so far from the world, her own world, in the heart of a gigantic wilderness, in a rude cabin; a giant of a man who, as he had said truly, might have crushed her between his powerful forefinger and thumb; a savage wolf of a dog watching her with unblinking eyes; another man, somewhere, with vengeance in his heart, following them; another man, clutching to his breast his golden secret, not far away;...nightmare ingredients! Did this man, Bruce Standing, Timber-Wolf as men called him, really know where to find Mexicali Joe? And, when he found him, would he come upon Taggart and Gallup and that hawk-faced man whom they called Cliff Shipton? And with them would there be Babe Deveril, who must have gone somewhere in his mad, hungering hope to have a rifle in his hands?... Above all else, was she the plaything of fate? Or the director of fate? Now it lay within the scope of her power to cry out to Bruce Standing: "When you find Mexicali Joe you will find others, no friends of yours, with him! With them, probably, Babe Deveril! And more than one rifle ready to stand between you and the Mexican!"... If she kept her silence, there might be bloodshed before morning; if she spoke her warning, she might be doubly arming Timber-Wolf. She grew restless; so restless that Thor, distrusting her, began growling.

And Bruce Standing, regarding her fixedly, demanded sharply:

"Well, what is it?"

Well...what should she say? Anything or nothing? If she kept her silence, would she in after-days know herself to blame for tonight's bloodshed in that, keeping shut lips, she allowed him to stumble upon all Taggart's crowd.

He was eying her sharply. She must make some answer, and so at last she prefaced her reply by asking him:

"You say that we are not on your land?"

"I did not say that. I said that this is not the cabin in which I had some years ago the pleasant experience of borrowing some money from Babe Deveril. He has never been here; has never heard of this place. No man other than myself, and until now no woman ever came here."

"That narrow end of a valley we crossed this afternoon...that was the upper end of Buck Valley? And the creek which came next was Big Bear Creek? And, right near us somewhere is Grub Stake Canyon?"

"You know the country like a map!" He spoke carelessly enough and yet was puzzled to understand how she knew; of course Deveril could have told her something of it and yet Deveril's knowledge was restricted to the slim gleanings of one short excursion of years ago, and he did not believe that even Deveril had ever heard of Grub Stake Canyon.

"And," she ran on swiftly, "you were to meet Mexicali Joe tonight at that other cabin of yours? Is that it?"

"Witch, are you? Picker of thoughts from men's brains?" He laughed shortly and got to his feet. "And so you elect to go along and see what happens? Rather than rest here with Thor to keep you company?"

She, too, rose swiftly.

"Yes!"

He took up his rifle, caught her hand and extinguished the candle.

"Down, Thor, old boy," he said as he might have spoken to a man, without raising his voice. "Wait for me. Good dog, Thor."

Thor whined, but Lynette heard the sound he made in lying down obediently; heard the thumping of his tail as he whined again. Standing began leading the way through the dark among the big trees, his fingers about her wrist.... She wondered how far they must go; suddenly as her great weariness bore down upon her spirit that was become the greatest of all considerations; greater, even, than what they should find at the end of their walk. Almost she regretted not having remained in the cabin...with Thor.

Standing, despite the dark and the uneven ground underfoot, seemed to have no difficulty in finding his way; he walked swiftly; she could sense his eager impatience. She began wondering listlessly if he were late to his appointment....

She had faint idea how far they had gone, a mile or two miles or but half a mile, a weary time of heavily dragging footsteps, when suddenly the silence was broken by men's voices. Far away, dimmed and all but utterly hidden by the interval of forest, was a vague glow of light. Standing came to a dead stop; she stumbled against him. There came, throbbing through the night, a man's scream. Standing stiffened; she felt a tremor run through his big body. A voice again, an evil voice in evil laughter; a deeper voice, too far away for the words to carry any meaning, not too far for the voice itself to be recognized by a man who hated it.

"Taggart and Young Gallup," Standing muttered. "They've got Joe! They'd cut his throat for ten cents!... Look here; what do you know about all this?"

She answered hurriedly; that thin scream still echoed in her ears; she remembered only too vividly Taggart's treatment of Joe at the dugout and Taggart's threats; she shivered, saying:

"All I know.... Jim Taggart and Gallup and another man caught up with Joe at his cabin; they made him bring them here...to show them his gold... Taggart threatened him with torture...."

"Come! Hurry! Why in hell's name didn't you tell me?"

Still with her hand caught in his own he turned and ran, making her run with him, back to his own cabin. Again they heard, fainter now since the distance was greater, that thin cry bursting from Joe's lips; she felt the hand on her own shut down, mercilessly hard.... Running, they returned to his hidden cabin.

He went in with her; hurriedly he lighted the candle; the fire was almost out. Wondering, she sank down upon the bunk.

"Down, Thor," he commanded; he made the dog lie again across the threshold. "Watch her, Thor!" Thor growled; the red eyes watched her.

"Don't you move from that bunk until I get back!" Standing told her sternly.

He ran out of the cabin. She heard him breaking through brush, going the shortest, straightest way down toward the spot from which voices had come up to them. Thor growled. She looked at the dog, fascinated with fear of him. The big head was down now, resting between the big fore paws; the unwinking eyes were on her.... She lay back on the bunk, staring up at the smoke-blackened rafters.

It was very quiet. No longer could she hear the sound of Timber-Wolf's running.... He, one man, pitting himself in blazing anger against at least three men,...perhaps four!... What if he were killed? Leaving her here, under the relentless guard of Thor? She was taken with a long fit of shivering. Thor growled.

CHAPTER 15

Every experience through which Lynette Brooke had gone until now seemed suddenly dwarfed into insignificance by the present. She was so utterly wearied out physically that muscles all over her body, demanding their hour of relaxation and having that relaxation denied them through the nervous stress laid upon her, quivered piteously. Hers was that frame of mind which distorts and magnifies, whipping out of its true semblance all actual conditions or building them up into monstrous, grotesque shapes. She was afraid of that great, staring dog on the threshold; more afraid of him than she had ever been of any man, Thor's master not excepted. For here was a fear which she could not throttle down. She would have sighed in content and have gone to sleep, her turbulent emotions quieted, if only it had been Bruce Standing's hard hand on the chain denying her her liberty instead of a great dog lying across the door-step.... Enough here to make her clinch her teeth to hold back a scream of panic-swept nerves; yet this was not all. For still that cry, heard through the woods, rang in her ears; still she built up in the picture which her quick fancy limned the vision of Mexicali Joe at the mercy of merciless men; Joe, who had lied to them, hoping to deliver them into the hands of one greater than they; Joe, who at the end, with them demanding to see what he had to show them, must be driven to the last extremity to fight for time.... And, blurring everything else at times, there swept over her another picture; that of Timber-Wolf, wounded and white-faced, stalking in that fearless way of his among them, confronting three armed men…or four?… and then man-killing…. They were all wolves! She shuddered. And Thor, watching her, filled the quiet cabin with the sound of his low suspicious growling.

"Thor!" she called him, hardly above a whisper. Her lips were dry. "Good old Thor!"

His throaty rumble of a growl, telling her of his distrust as eloquently as it could have done had Thor the words of man at his command, was her answer.

"Thor!" She called him again, her voice soft, pleading, coaxing. Then she lifted herself a few inches on her elbow; like a flash Thor was up on his haunches, his growl became a snarl, a quick glint of his teeth showing, a sharp-pointed gleam of menace.

Yet Lynette held her position, steady upon her elbow; she had never known a tenser moment. Her throat contracted with her fear; and yet she kept telling herself stubbornly that yonder was but a dog, a thing of only brute intelligence, while she had the human brain to oppose him with; that, some way, she could outwit him. So she did not lie back; to do so would, she felt, show Thor that she was afraid of him. She made no further forward movement but she held what she had been suffered to gain.

And then she set herself to dominate Thor, a wolf-like dog. She spoke to him; but first she waited until she could be sure of her voice. That brute instinct of Thor's would know the slightest quaver of fear when he heard it. She controlled herself and her voice; she made her tones low and soft and gentle; she kept them firm. She told herself: "Thor is but doing his master's bidding because he loves his master! I'll make him love me! He distrusts…. I'll make him trust instead!" And all the while she kept her own eyes steady upon Thor's.

"Thor!" she said quietly. And again: "Thor. Good old Thor. Good old dog!"

… Thor had set her down as an enemy; his master's enemy; his master had commanded him: "Watch her, Thor!" Thor's knowledge was not wide; yet what he knew he did know thoroughly. And yet Thor had had no evidence, beyond that offered by a chain, of any open enmity between his master and this captive; master and girl had travelled all day long together and neither had flown at the other's throat. More than that, it had been at the master's own command this very morning that Thor had felt her hand upon his head; a hand as light as a falling leaf. And now she spoke to him in his master's own words, but with such a different voice, calling him Thor, good old dog….

It was a soothing voice, a voice made for tender caresses. She spoke again and again and again. And she was not afraid; Thor could see no flickering sign of fear in her. A voice softer than had been the touch of her hand.

"Thor!" she called him. And his growl was scarcely more growl than whine. For Thor, before Bruce Standing had been gone twenty minutes, was growing uncertain. Lynette had had dogs of her own; she knew the ways of dogs, and in this she had the advantage, since Thor knew nothing of the ways of women nor of their guile. The dog was restless; his eyes, upon hers, were no longer so steady. Now and then Thor shook his head and his eyes wandered.

"Thor," said Lynette, and now, though her voice, as before, was low and gentle, there was the note of command in it, "lie down!"

There was an experiment…and it failed. Thor was on four feet in a flash; his growl was unmistakable now; the snarling note came back into it threateningly. She thought that he was going to fly at her throat….

Yet already was the lesser intelligence, though coupled with the greater physical power, confused.

Lynette moved slowly; she put her hands up above her head and stretched out her arms and yawned; Thor growled, but there was little threat in the growl; just suspicion. Again she moved slowly; close enough, in the restricted area embraced by the cabin walls, was the table; on it some morsels of food left from their dinner. Without rising from the bunk, she reached the tin plate; she took it up, all the while moving with unhastening slowness. Thor's eyes followed her straying hand; Thor had been fed, and yet the dog's capacity for food was enormous. He understood the meaning of her gesture; his eyes hungered.

She dropped the plate to the floor but, before it struck, not three feet in front of the dog, she cried out sharply, her voice ringing, her command at last emphatic:

"No, Thor! No! No, I tell you!"

Had she offered the dog the food she would have but awaked within him a new and violent distrust; he was not so easily to be tricked. But when she tossed before him something that he was slavering for, and then laid her command upon him to hold back, she achieved something over him; he would have held back in any case, but now he held back at her command.

"Watch it, Thor!" she cried out loudly. "Watch it, sir!"

The big dog stared at her; at the fallen morsels; back at her, plainly at loss. And then again, more sharply, she commanded him:

"Watch it, Thor!… Lie down, Thor!"

And Thor, though he growled, lay down…. And his wolfish eyes now were upon the plate and its spilled contents rather than upon her.

"If I can but have time!" Lynette was telling herself excitedly. "If only I can have time… I can make that dog do what I say to do!… God, give me time!"

* * * *

When Bruce Standing, rushing through the forest land, came upon them…Taggart and the others…they were grouped about a despairing, hopeless Mexicali Joe. For Mexicali Joe's *amigo*, the great Timber-Wolf, in whom next to God he put all trust, had failed him. And Joe had come to the end of his tether, the end of lies and excuses and empty explanations. And now Taggart, as brutal a man as ever wore the badge of the law, was impatient, and meant to make an end of all procrastinations. It was his intention to give Mexicali Joe such a "third degree" as never any man had lived to experience before tonight. Rage, chagrin, disappointment, and natural, innate brutality spurred him on. Even Young Gallup, who was no chicken-hearted man at best, demurred; but Taggart cursed him off and told him to hold his tongue, and planned matters to his own liking.

"Jim Taggart's got Injun blood in him, you know," muttered Gallup uneasily to Cliff Shipton…as though that might explain anything.

Even to such as Young Gallup, a man of whose humanity little was to be said, explanations were logical requirements. For Jim Taggart was at his evil worst. With cruelly hard fist he had knocked the little Mexican down; before Joe could get to his feet he booted him; when Joe stood, tottering, Taggart knocked him down again, jarring the quivering flame of life within him. And only at that did Jim Taggart, a man of no imagination but of colossal brutality, count that he was beginning. Then it was that Joe cried out; that his scream pierced through the night's stillness; that he pleaded with Taggart, saying:

"This time, I tell you the true! I tell you ever'thing…."

"You're damned right you will," shouted Taggart, beside himself with his long baffled rage. "When I get good and ready to listen. And I'm not listening now, you Mexico pup! First you go through hell, and then I'll know that you tell the truth! Fool with me, would you; with me, Jim Taggart? You—"

Then Taggart began his third degree, listening to neither Joe's pleadings nor yet to the voice of Young Gallup.

The four men were in Bruce Standing's old cabin; the door was wide open, since here, so far from the world, in the dense outer fringes of Timber-Wolf's isolated wilderness kingdom, no man of them…saving Joe alone, who had now given up hope…had a thought of another human eye to see; Shipton, at a curt word from Taggart, had piled the mouth of the fireplace full of dead-wood, for the sole sake of light, and it was hot in the small room. Taggart had bound the Mexican's hands behind him, drawing the thong so tight that it cut cruelly into the flesh…. Taggart had knocked Joe down and had booted him to his heart's content; the swarthy face had turned a sick white. Taggart's eyes were glowing like coals raked out from hell's own sulphurous fires; he was sure of the outcome, sure of swift success, and yet now, in pure fiendishness, more absorbed in his own unleashed deviltry than in the mere matter of raw gold, which he counted securely his as soon as he was ready for it. Whether or not Indian blood ran in his veins, elemental savagery did.

Mexicali Joe, unable to rise, or in fear for his life if he stirred, lay on the floor, his eyes dilated with terror, staring up into Taggart's convulsed face.

"I tell you the true!" he screamed. "This time, before God, I tell—"

"Shut up, you greaser-dog!" Taggart, a man of full measure, kicked him, and under the driving pain inflicted by that heavy boot, Joe's eyes flickered and closed, and Joe's brain staggered upon the dizzy black verge of unconsciousness. Taggart saw and understood and pitched a dipperful of water in his face. Joe gasped faintly. Taggart stepped to the fireplace, and snatched out a blazing pine branch.

"I've put my brand on more'n one treacherous dog!" he jeered. "You'll find my stock running across the wild places in seven States! Here's where I plant the sign of the cross on you, Mexico! Right square between the eyes!"

Suddenly he thrust the burning brand toward Joe's forehead. Joe cried out in terror:

"For the love of God!…" His two hands were behind him, but, galvanized, he fought the pine fagot with his whole body. He strove to thrust it aside; he fought against his weakness to roll over; Taggart's heavy foot was in his middle, holding him down; the burning branch in Taggart's heavy hands was as steady as a steel rod set in concrete; Joe's threshing panic disturbed it scarcely more than the wind would have done…. Another scream, shrilling through the night; the smell of burnt flesh; a red wound on Joe's forehead; Taggart's ugly laugh; and then suddenly, from just without the open doorway, a terrible shout from Bruce Standing, and then, in two seconds, Bruce Standing's great bulk among them.

"My God!" roared Standing. "*My God!*…you, Jim Taggart!…"

Shipton's rifle stood in a corner; Shipton, as lithe as a cat, leaped for it. Gallup's was in his hand; he whipped it to his shoulder. Taggart for one instant was stupefied; then he swept high above his head the smoke-emitting, redly glowing pine limb. Joe, weeping hysterically, writhing on the floor, was gasping: "*Jesus Maria!*"… God had heard his prayers; God and Bruce Standing.

But in tonight's game of hazard it was Timber-Wolf who chose to shuffle, cut, and deal the cards; his rifle was in his hands; it required but the gentlest touch of his finger to send any man of them to his last repose. His eyes, the roving eyes of rage, were everywhere at once.

"I'd kill you, Taggart, and be glad of the chanth! You, too, Gallup! Drop that gun!"

First of them all, it was Cliff Shipton who came to the motionless halt of shocked consternation; he lifted his hands, his face blanched; he tried to speak, and only succeeded in making the noise of air gushing through dry lips. Gallup stopped midway in his purpose of firing, for Timber Wolf's rifle barrel was trained square upon his chest; at the look in Standing's eye and the timbre of his voice, Gallup's gun fell clattering to the floor. Taggart mouthed and cursed, and slowly let his blazing fagot sink toward the floor.

For every man of them knew Timber-Wolf well; and they knew that incongruous *lisping* which surprised him and mastered his utterance only when his rage was of the greatest. When Timber-Wolf lisped it was because such a fiery storm raged through his breast as to make of him a man who would kill and kill and kill and glory in the killing.

"And I'd have given a million dollars to thee any man of you put up a fight!" he was saying harshly. "God, what a thet of cowardly curth! And you, Jim Taggart, I onth had for bunk-mate and onth thought a man!"

He reached out suddenly, and with his bare, open palm slapped Taggart's face; and Taggart staggered backward under the blow until his thick shoulders brought up against the wall with such a thud that the cabin shuddered under the impact.

"Get up, Joe!" growled Standing. "You're another yellow dog, but...get up and come here!"

Joe scrambled to his feet and came hurrying. Standing kept his rifle in his right hand. Using his left stiffly, he got out his knife and cut the Mexican's bonds.

"Go!" he cried savagely. "While you've got legth under you! And thith time keep clear, or hell take you! I'm through with you...you make me thick!..."

Mexicali Joe, with one last frightened look over his shoulder, fled; they heard his running feet outside. He was jabbering unintelligibly as he fled: "*Señor Caballero!... Dios!*...those devils!..."

Joe was gone. Bruce Standing's work was done. He looked grim and implacable, a man of iron heated in the red-hot furnace of rage. He yearned for Taggart to make a move; or for Gallup. Shipton, as a lesser cur, he ignored.

They saw how white, as white as a clean sheet of paper, his face was; they did not fully understand why, since a man's face, when he is in a terrible rage, may whiten, as an effect of the searing emotion; they did not know how he had driven his wounded body all day long nor how sore his wound was. They could not guess that even now he was holding himself upright and towering among them through the fierce bending of his indomitable will. That same will he bent terribly for clean-cut articulation.

"Taggart!" he said, and his voice rang as clear as the striking of an iron hammer upon a resounding anvil. "I'll tempt you to be a man such as you *once* were, before you went yellow clean through...and I'll show you, your *self*, how dirty a yellow you've gone! Pick up Young Gallup's rifle!"

Taggart glared at him and muttered and hesitated, tugged one way by hatred and the madness of wrath, tugged the other way by his fear of the certainty of death. Lights, bluish lights, flickered in Timber-Wolf's eyes. He said again:

"Pick up that rifle! Otherwise, in less than ten seconds you are a dead man!"

Taggart's face was red when Standing began to speak; ashen by the last word. Nervously and in great haste he stooped and caught up the gun.

"You've got your *chance*, Jim Taggart! Your last *chance*! To fight it out, or say, for *these* men to hear: 'I'm a dirty yellow dog!' If you're game we'll fight it out. I'll give you an even break; and we'll kill each other!"

Taggart held the rifle, not lifted quite to his waist; his hands were rigid upon it and did not tremble. He was not a coward; on many an occasion, when he had borne his sheriff's badge recklessly through violence, he had shown himself a brave man. He knew now that it lay within his power, if he were quick and sure, to kill Bruce Standing, whom he had come to hate, so that his hatred was like a running sore. And he knew, too, that killing, he would be killed. If it were any man on earth whom he confronted save Bruce Standing.…

So he hesitated, for brave man as Jim Taggart always was, he was a man who did not want to die. And Standing laughed at him and said:

"You've had your chance; you still have it. Now, fight it out or tuck your tail between your legs and do my bidding! And my bidding to you, so that I needn't expect a bullet in the back when I leave you, is to smash that rifle into flinders against the rock chimney. *And step lively!*"

The last words came sharp and sudden, and Taggart started. And then, hesitating no longer, he whirled the rifle up by the barrel and brought it with all his might crashing against the fireplace; the fragments fell from his tingling fingers. And again Standing laughed at him and again commanded him, saying:

"There are two more rifles; do the same for each one! And remember, Jim Taggart, every time you touch a gun you've got the even break to fight it out; and every time you smash a gun you are saying out loud: 'I'm a dirty yellow dog!' *Only make it snappy, Jim Taggart!*"

One after the other, and hastily, Jim Taggart smashed the butts off two rifles and jammed trigger and trigger-guard so that from firearms the weapons were resolved into the estate of so much scrap-iron and splintered wood.

"I'll take your two toy guns, Jim," said Standing. "And remember this; at short range the man with the revolver has the edge! When you drag a gun out you've got your chance to come up shooting! Don't overlook that! And remember along with it, that when you hand me a gun, butt-end first, you are saying aloud for the world to hear: 'I'm a dirty yellow dog!'"

"By God.…"

"Yes, Jim Taggart,…by God, you're a dirty dog!"

Lingeringly Taggart drew forth the heavy side-arms dragging at his holsters; all the while he was tempted almost beyond resistance to avail himself of his opportunity and of that quick sure skill of his; to shoot from the hip, as he could do with the swiftness of a flash of the wrist; he could shoot and kill. And within his heart, knowing Bruce Standing as he did, he knew, too, that though he shot true to a hair line, none the less, Bruce Standing would kill him…. He gave a gun into Standing's left hand and saw it thrust into his belt. Then was Taggart's time to snatch out his other weapon and drill that hole through the big body in front of him which would surely let the life run out; now was his chance, while for an instant one of Standing's hands was busy at his belt!… If it had been any other man in the world there confronting him! Any man but Bruce Standing! Jim Taggart was near weeping. But he drew out his second revolver and saw it bestowed as its fellow had been.

"Four times you've said it, plainer than words!" cried Standing ringingly. "Gallup will never forget; and he'll tell the tale! Shipton will remember and will blab! And, what's worse for the soul of a man, Jim Taggart, you'll remember to the last day you live!… And now you three can consider yourselves as so many mongrel curs whose back-biting teeth I've knocked down your throats for you! I'll leave you to your growlings and whinings!"

He swung about and went out. He knew both Gallup and Shipton, knew them and their habits well, and knew that neither man had the habit of carrying a pistol. Further, their coats were off, and he had seen that neither had a holster at his belt. So he turned his back on them to emphasize his contempt and did not turn his head as he plunged into the outside night and into the thick dark under the trees, going back to his hidden cabin and Lynette and Thor. He realized that he himself, despite a herculean physique, was near the tether's end of his endurance; he realized that Lynette was also heavily borne down by all that she, a girl, had gone through and that he had left her overlong with his wolfish dog.

What he could not know was that a revolver which had once already shot him in the back had followed him all these miles through the wilderness and was now lying on the bunk in the cabin he had just quitted; he could not know how, at the Gallup House after Babe Deveril had flung it in Taggart's face, Lynette's pistol had lain there on the floor until Taggart had been aroused to consciousness; nor how Gallup had picked it up, nor how Taggart had muttered: "Save it, Young. It may come in handy for evidence in court." Gallup had stuck it into his pocket; he had brought it with him; he had tossed it down among the blankets….

Taggart stared after him with terrible eyes; Taggart remembered and, when he dared, flung himself across the room, snatching for it among the covers. Standing, hastening, strode on. Taggart found the weapon; he ran out of the cabin with it in his hand; dodged to one side of the open door to be out of way of the firelight. Standing hurried on, he had not seen Taggart; Taggart could scarcely see him, could but make out vaguely a blur where he heard heavy footfalls…. It was all chance; but now no longer was Taggart himself running the desperate chances. He fired, one shot after another, until he emptied the little gun—four shots altogether; the hammer clicked down on the fifth, the empty shell.

Chance, pure chance; and yet chance is ironical and loves its own grim jest. The first bullet, the only one of them all to find its target, struck Timber-Wolf. And it was as though this questing bit of lead were seeking to tread the same path blazed by its angry brother down at the Gallup House in Big Pine. For it, like the other from the same muzzle, struck him from behind; and it, too, struck him upon the left side, in the outer shoulder, not half a dozen inches from the spot where he had been shot before....

Standing staggered and caught his breath with a grunt; he lurched into a tree and stood leaning against it. For a moment he was dizzied and could not see clearly. Then, turning, he made out the cabin behind him; the bright rectangle of the door; two dark running forms leaping through it, gone into the gulf of the black night. He jerked up his rifle, holding it in one hand, unsupported by the other, his shoulder, the right, against the tree. But they were gone before he could shoot. He waited. He heard a breaking through brush; men running. They were running away! They did not know that they had hit him; they could not tell, and they were afraid of his return! He lifted his voice and shouted at them in the sudden grip of a terrible anger. He listened to the noise they made and strove to judge their positions and began shooting after them. He fired until the rifle clip was empty. Then, while awkwardly, with one hand, he put in a fresh clip, he listened again. Silence only.

… He was strangely weak and uncertain; he had to draw his brows down with a steely effort to clear his thoughts. They were gone…they would not come back…it was too dark to look for them. And he had left that girl overlong…and he was shot full of pain. A surge of anger for every surge of weakness....

He started on toward his hidden cabin and Lynette. He blundered into a tree. He could feel the hot blood down his shoulder. He began using his rifle as a man may use a cane, leaning on it heavily.

CHAPTER 16

Bruce Standing came, weaving his way, like a drunken man, through the woods. He was sick; sick and weak. He muttered to himself constantly. Lynette was at the top of his thought and at the bottom; she dominated his whole mind. He was used through long years to such as Jim Taggart and their crooked ways; he was not used to such as Lynette Brooke, a girl like a flower and yet fearless. It had been his way to hold all women in scorn, since it had not been given unto him during the hard years of his life to know the finer women, the true women worth while, more than worth the while of a mere man. He had held his head high; he had mocked and jeered at them; he had been no man to doff his hat with the flattering elegance of a Babe Deveril for every fair face seen. So now the one thing which in his fiery and feverish mood galled him most was the thought of being seen by Lynette as a man borne down and crushed and made weak and sick. For most of all he hated weaklings.

"She laughed at me…damn her," he muttered. And, as an afterthought: "She shot me in the back, after the fashion of her treacherous sex!"

He had driven himself harder all day long than any sane man, wounded, should have thought of doing. Now the thought, working its way uppermost through the fomenting confusion of teeming thoughts, was: "I'll let her go. I'll be rid of her." For already, deep down in the depths of his heart, he knew that already a girl, a girl whom he despised and had meant to pay in full for her wickedness, had intrigued him; she had flung her defiant fearlessness into his face; she had kept a lifted head and straightforward eyes; and…those eyes of Lynette Brooke! Deep, fathomless, gray, tender, alluring, the eyes of the one woman for each man! Almost he could have forgotten, not merely forgiven, her greater fault of laughing at his infirmity; if only she had not been of the species, like Jim Taggart's, to shoot a man in the back.

He meant to let her go free and he had his own reasons for his change of front. Though she had laughed and galled him, though she had sunk to a cowardly act and shot him when he was not looking, at least she was not the coward which he had counted upon finding her; he gave credit where credit was due. He had humiliated her sufficiently, dragging her after him, humbling a spirit as proud as his own, making her his handmaiden, calling her his slave. That was one thing. And another, befogged as it was, was even clearer: In letting her go, in being rid for all time of her and the lure of her eyes, he was protecting himself, Bruce Standing, and none other!…fearless, he honored her for that. And yet a treacherous she-animal; so he wanted no more of her, no more of the look of her, the fragrance of her, the pressure of her upon his own spirit. He held himself a man; a man he meant to remain. And, for the first time in all his life he was a little afraid.…

And then, just at the moment when it would have been better for them both if he had not come…or when it was best that he should come…these are questions and the answers of all questions fate holds in her lap, hidden by the films of the future…he came staggering up to the door of the hidden cabin. And, at the sight of her, he pulled himself up, stiffening, as taut as a bowstring the instant that the arrow thrills to the command to speed.

There, in the doorway framed by the two big-boled pines she stood, vividly outlined by the firelight from within the cabin, superbly, gloriously feminine, her own slender soft loveliness thrown into tremendous contrast by the figure at her side, the figure of old Thor on whose head her hand rested as light as a fallen leaf! Her hand on Thor's head! She and Thor standing side by side, her hand on his head....

Sudden rage flared up in Timber-Wolf's heart; he gripped his rifle in both hands, contemptuously ignoring the pains which shot through his left shoulder; at that moment he could have thanked God for excuse enough to shoot her dead. She had seduced the loyalty and trustworthiness of Thor; she had done that! If a man like Standing could not trust his dog, when that dog was old Thor, then where on this green earth could he plant his trust?

"Back!" he stormed at her. "Back!"

She was poised for flight. He came at the instant of her victory over the brute intelligence of a dog, at the moment of her high hopes, when her heart hot in rebellion throbbed with triumph. She, too, at that moment, could she have commanded the lightnings, would have stricken him dead. Her hatred of him reached in a flash such heights as it had never aspired to before.

Back? He commanded her to turn back? Shouted his dictates at her in that first moment when she sensed escape and freedom and victory over him who had been victor long enough? Back? Not now; not though he flourished his rifle, threatening her with that while he shouted angrily at her. Briefly the sight of him had unnerved her, had created within her an utter powerlessness to move hand or foot. But before he could shout "Back!" the second time defiance, like a flood of fire, broke along her veins, warming her from head to foot; she sprang out from the area of light at the cabin door and, running more swiftly than Bruce Standing had deemed any girl could ever run, she sped away among the trees....

A moment ago he had but the one firm intention: To set her free and be rid of her for all time. Now, not ten seconds after holding that purpose, he was rushing after her, forgetful of everything, his wounds and sick weariness, except his one determination to drag her back! He was angry; in his anger, not admitting to himself the true explanation, he felt that he must blame her for a third crime...she had trifled with the integrity of his dog's loyalty... she had corrupted old Thor's sturdy honesty....

She ran like a deer. The moment that she broke into headlong flight that very act released within her a full tide of fright; it became a panic like that of soldiers once they have thrown down their arms and plunged into the delirium of disordered retreat. She ran as she had never done before, even when she and Babe Deveril had fled through the night. And Bruce Standing would never have come up with her that night had it not been that in the dark she fell, stumbling over the low mound left to mark the place where an ancient log had disintegrated. As she floundered to her feet she felt his hand on her shoulder. She screamed, she struck at him....

He caught her two hands as he had done once before; she could have no inkling of the tremendous call he put upon himself, body and will; she could hear his heavy, labored breathing, but she, too, was breathing in gasps.

She could see neither the whiteness of his face nor yet the blood soaking his shirt. He did not speak. He was not thinking clearly. He merely said within himself: "I got her!" That was everything. Until, as they came again into the outward-pouring firelight in front of the cabin door, he wondered somewhat uneasily: "What am I going to do with her?"

Lynette, panting and piteously shaken, dropped down on the edge of the bunk, overborne by disaster, hopeless, her face in her hands; she was fighting with herself against a burst of tears. Thus she did not see Bruce Standing as he stood at the threshold, looking at her. She heard his step; it shuffled and was uncertain, but she did not at the moment mark this. She heard a whine from old Thor, a Thor perplexed and ill at ease.

… Suddenly she thought: "He hasn't moved; he hasn't spoken!" She dropped her hands then and looked up swiftly. And, thus, she surprised a strange look in his eyes; his own thoughts were all chaotic and yet there was beginning to burn one steady thought among them like one bright flame in a whirl of smoke. He had closed the door when they came in; he had sat down upon the up-ended log which served here as a chair; Thor's head was on the master's knee and absently Standing's hand was stroking it. He had dropped his rifle outside when he started to run after her; he had not stopped to look for it as they came in. She saw that a revolver was half in and half out of his pocket…. Then she marked, with a start, the dead-white of his face and the way his left arm hung limp, and the red stain on his wrist and the back of his hand where the blood had run down his sleeve. Her first thought was of his old wound and how he was not the man to give a wound a chance to heal, but rather would break it open again and again through his violence. Then she recalled what, during these last few minutes she had forgotten—the shots which she had heard a little while ago. And she knew that, though he sat upright and stared at her with the old look again in his eyes, he had been shot the second time.

"I brought you back, girl," he said at last, and she knew that he was bending a vast resource of will to keep his tone clear and steady, "not because I mean to keep you any longer…but just to show you that with all the tricks of your sex you can take no step that I do not tell you to take! Now, I've the idea that I'd like best to be alone. You can go."

In a flash she jumped to her feet; she would scarcely credit her ears, and yet one look at the man told her reassuringly that he was in earnest.

"I don't know where you'll go," he said. "And I don't care. But I can tell you you'll find some good men and true, men of your own kind, since they shoot in the back, down below my other cabin; Taggart and Gallup and Shipton…. No, your friend Baby Devil isn't there! And Mexicali Joe has skipped out. If you like to take your chances with those birds…." He jerked out the revolver which recently had been Taggart's and tossed it to the bunk. "You can take that along, if you like."

She flushed up, her face as hot as fire, as he jeered at her, saying: "Men of your own kind, since they shoot in the back!"... She could come close to an accurate guess of what had happened; since Mexicali Joe was gone it must be that Standing had set him free; since Standing returned with a fresh wound, it must be that Taggart or one of his crowd had shot him in the back....

She had not meant to speak, but now she cried out hotly:

"I did not shoot you! You didn't see...if you had seen you would know. My pistol lay on the table...the window was open...someone reached in and picked it up and shot you... I was frightened, and when the pistol was dropped back to the table, I caught it up...."

His eyes grew brilliant with the intensity of the look he turned upon her.... But his brain was reeling, his weakness overpowered him...he was set with all the steel of his character against showing before her the first sign of weakness....

"Liar!" he flung at her. "To lie about it...that's worse than the shot...."

He leaned back against the wall. "You're free now," he said. "I would to God I had never seen you!"

For answer she flung her bright laughter back at him; defiant, angry, bitter laughter. She caught up the heavy revolver he had thrown to her.

"I could shoot you now...with no one to see...."

His own laughter, hard and ugly, answered while he found the strength to say sternly:

"But with me looking you straight in the eyes...you'd lose your nerve at that!"

She flung the weapon down to the floor, scorning any gift of his. Without another word, with never another glance toward him, she passed to the door, jerked it open and went out.

He sat staring into the fire. Thor began sniffing at the limp hand. Standing got to his feet; the fire was dying down and a sudden shiver of cold prompted him to pile on fresh fuel. He kicked Taggart's revolver viciously out of his way. He was going to the fireplace, but in doing so passed the bunk. He sat down a moment, wiping the sweat from his forehead...cold and sweating at the same time. He lay back, flat on his back, and shut his eyes. He wondered vaguely how much blood he had lost coming up through the woods from the lower cabin where he had been shot; how much blood he had lost while he ran like a madman after that girl.... His eyes were shut doggedly tight and yet it seemed to his dizzied senses as though he could feel the look of her eyes, bending over him.... Now, that was a strange thing.... Never once had she given him a look from those eyes of hers to show a single spasm of fear.... Fearless? She, a girl? Did fearlessness and cowardice blend, then, that the incomprehensible result might be known as woman? For it was the supreme stroke of cowardice to shoot a man in the back. And yet...she had said: "I did not shoot you!" While she spoke, he had believed!... He lay jeering at himself.... And all the while, as in a vision, he saw a pair of big gray eyes, soft and tender and alluring, bending over him....

"There's just one thing in the world," muttered Bruce Standing aloud, as a man may do when hard driven by perplexity and safe in solitary isolation from other ears than his own, "that I'd give everything to know! To know for sure!... Just one thing...."

CHAPTER 17

Lynette, running like one blind out into the dark silent forest land, her own soul storm-tossed, stopped with sudden abruptness, staring about her, striving to see what lay before her, about her. Free! As free as the wind, to roam where she listed. And alone! Alone with the wilderness for the first moment since she had fled the menace yelping at her heels in Big Pine. *Alone.*

And walled about by the wildest and most impenetrably blackly dark solitudes. She had but the one impulse; to flee from this man whose fellows termed him a wolf; but the one clear thought, that she *must* hasten in search of the very man from whom originally she had fled, Jim Taggart. For, since Bruce Standing had not been killed by that shot fired in her room at the Gallup House, she, like Babe Deveril, was no longer threatened with the most serious charge of murder. Let Taggart place her under arrest; let him take her back into the region of towns and stages and lamp-lit homes; let him accuse her. Suddenly it seemed to her, wearied with endless exertion and privation and nervous tension, that there could be no peace greater than that of being taken back and placed in custody in Big Pine!

Now she had to guide her but a general, a very vague, sense of direction. It was so absolutely dark! There were stars, but they seemed little sparks of cold distant light, blurred and almost lost beyond the tops of the pines. Standing had led her after him, on his way to his lower cabin, down the gentle slope. Yes; she knew the general direction. And the distance? She had little impression of the distance between these two aloof lairs of Timber-Wolf; half a mile or two miles, she did not know. She would go on and on, seeking a way among the trees; on and on and on, stumbling in the dark. Then, after a while, she would call; call and call again, praying that Taggart and the others were lurking somewhere within ear-shot; that they would hear and come to her...and place her under arrest! And she wondered, as she had done so many a time today, where was Babe Deveril? Was he near? Would he, by any chance, hear her? Would he, too, come to her? And, then, what?

She began hastening on; to be farther from him, though that meant to come at every step nearer Jim Taggart and Young Gallup and that other man with the hawk face. She could not be absolutely certain that the direction she set her course by would ever lead her to the lower cabin; but on one point she was assured: at every step she was getting farther from wolf-man and wolf-dog. What a brute, what a beast he was! *And yet…and yet….* There swept across her, like a clean, cold wind out of the north, a sudden appreciation of those finer qualities of manhood which his nature and his fate had allowed to dwell on in that anomaly, Bruce Standing. His absolute honesty, itself like a north wind, was not to be gainsaid even by his bitterest enemy; his courage, in any woman's eyes, was invested with sheer nobility. How he had befriended poor little Mexicali Joe; how, tonight for the second time, though handicapped by his wound, he had gone to Joe's relief; how he, one against three, had had his way, like a lion among curs. Wolf or lion?… And, finally, she abode wonderingly on that strange, distorted chivalry which resided in the heart of him, his brutally chivalrous way with her. For, no matter how harsh and bitter his tongue had been and no matter how hard his eye, he had not harmed her; when his hands had been like steel upon hers, commanding her while he jeered at her, they had not once so much as bruised her soft skin. In no way had he harmed her while it had been at his command, had he desired, to harm her in all ways…. She thought of being alone with any man like Taggart or Gallup or that hawk-faced hanger-on of theirs…and shuddered. Even Babe Deveril; he had looked at her last night, insinuating…. She remembered how Bruce Standing, rushing down upon them, had thrown his own rifle away to grapple with Deveril, man to man and no odds stolen; she would never forget the picture of him with his axe, attacking the jail and defying the law…. Her mind raced, her thoughts switched into a new groove: how he had set her free just now and tossed her the revolver….

And then came the most vivid picture of all, the latest one, that of Bruce Standing glaring at her just before she ran out of the cabin. A second time she came to a sudden stop. He had looked like a man dying! Too proud, with that vainglorious pride of his, to have her, a girl, watch him, a man, die. Too unyieldingly proud and defiant to have her, a weakling, look on while he, the strongest man she had ever glimpsed, yielded in anything, if even to death itself. What a man he was! A man wrong-minded, maybe; a man who overrode others and bore them down; a man who set up his own standards, such as they were, and battled for them wholeheartedly. Even in the matter of high-handed robbery…he had robbed Babe Deveril of three thousand dollars, and yet voluntarily, when he was ready to make restitution and not before, he had returned the full amount, estimating in his own way that he had merely borrowed it! There was the man disclosed; one who made his own laws, and yet who abode by them as loyally and as unswervingly as a true priest may abide by God's….

And he had looked like a man dying. She turned her head. The door of his cabin was still wide open, as she had left it; light, though failing, still gushed out. She told herself that it was only a natural curiosity, surely her sex's most irrefutable prerogative, that made her turn and look. She caught no sight of him; he was not striding up and down. And he had not come outside for his fallen rifle....

Her breast rose and fell to a deep sigh. Of relief, perhaps; perhaps for another emotion. Still she remained where she was, pondering. Which way lay the path to the other cabin, where Taggart and Gallup and the other man were? And what was Bruce Standing doing? He had named her "Liar!" He did not believe when she had cried out passionately: "I did not shoot you!" Darting considerations, flashing through her consciousness. The one question was: "Was Bruce Standing mortally wounded?" Shot in the back a second time; he had as much as told her that.

Babe Deveril was what the world names a ladies' man. Bruce Standing was a man's man. And the strange part of it is that the feminine soul is drawn to the man's man inevitably more urgently than to the ladies' man....

And all the while Lynette was saying to herself: "He is a brute and a beast and yet...he has not harmed me once and he has set me free and there is some good in him and...and he may be dying! Alone."

She had turned her head to look back; now, hesitatingly, her whole body turned. Slowly, silently, she retraced her steps. She came closer and closer to the hidden cabin; the light outlining the open door grew fainter, dimmer as the fire died down; she heard no sound; she caught no glimpse of a man within. She drew still closer; she heard the strange whining of his dog. Even Thor she could not see until, lingering at every step, she came close to the door. Then she saw both, the man on his back, his lax hand on the floor; the dog whining, distressed, licking the hand one instant and then looking wistfully into the master's face. A face bloodlessly white, save for one smear of blood, where a hand had sought to wipe his eyes clear of a gathering film.

Hesitating no longer, she stepped across the threshold. Thor looked at her and broke into a new whining, a note of sudden joyousness in it. Standing did not hear and did not know that she had returned; his eyes were shut and there was the pulse as of distant seas in his ears. She hurried to the fireplace and tossed into it the last of the wood he had gathered; then she came swiftly to where he lay. Her heart was beating wildly....

She saw that his jaw was set, hard and stubborn. She stood, uncertain, troubled, half regretful that she had come back, hence half of a mind to go hurriedly. But she did not stir for a long time, and then only to come the last step closer. His eyes flew open; he looked up at her. And, as the fire she had freshly piled blazed higher, she saw a sudden flash of his eyes...whether the reflection of the fire or the flash of the spirit within him, she could not tell.

"I thought you'd gone," he said. He sat up; it was a struggle for him to do so, yet here was a man who made of all his life a struggle and who thought nothing of a trifling victory over either nature itself or his fellow man.

"You have been cruel...."

He mocked her with his haggard eyes.

"That," she ran on swiftly, "is what you expected me to say to you, Bruce Standing, that you have been cruel! And, what I came back to say is: '*You have been good to me!*'"

She had not meant to say anything of the kind. But when she looked into his eyes, when she saw the clear-as-crystal soul of him, a soul as simple as a child's and…yes!… as clean; and when she remembered how she had ridden all day long while he had walked, and how he had steadfastly refused to so much as harm a hair of her head, the words gushed forth.

He eyed her, suspicion in his look and confusion. She could have laughed out aloud suddenly, since her whole emotional being was aquiver; for he, Timber-Wolf, like his own wolf-dog, Thor, distrusted her and regarded her with fierce eyes and yet…and yet….

"Your wound has not been dressed since morning," she said quietly. "And now you've got yourself another wound. I am going to help you with them."

His slave…. He had commanded her once to help him with his wound…. But his slave no longer, since he himself had set her free! Yet here she was, saying that she stood ready to help him care for his wounds. More, already she was getting warm water, and his old piece of castile soap…she was rolling up her sleeves….

He glared at her through a mist. He could be sure of nothing, since it *seemed* to him that she was half smiling! A tender, wistful sort of smile…as if she had it in her heart to forget injuries done, to forgive him who had done them, and to succor him now that there was little of man-strength left in his body…. Curse her! What right had she to forgive, to look at a man that way? He had asked nothing from her, save that she leave him….

He stirred uneasily. *Had* she smiled? In this uncertain light one could be certain of nothing; the flickering of the wood fire, casting quick-racing little shadows, breaking into their play with sudden warm, rosy gleamings, made it impossible for him to know if she had smiled, or if that semblance of a smile were but the effect of shifting lights. He held himself rigid, his back to the wall now, his right hand clinched on his knee.

"When I am in need of your help…you who shot me…."

She came to him unafraid; she set down the can of warm water on the floor; she began unbuttoning the neck of his shirt. He threw up his hand, the right, hard-clinched, as though he would strike her in the face; but he let the hand fall back to his side. She heard a great sigh.

"I told you once," she said quietly, "that I did not shoot you. And I am no more liar than you are, Bruce Standing."

He cursed himself for a fool; he was tired and weak and dizzy; his mind was the abode of confusions; he no longer knew what was fact and what was illusion. One thing alone he did know, a marvellous thing; there was in her low voice the ring of utter honesty when she said: "I did not shoot you!"…liars; all her sex, waging their weak wars from ambush, holding their place in the world through seduction and deceit, all were liars. And yet she troubled him, and with that voice and those eyes she bred uncertainty on top of uncertainty in his uncertain soul. Her steady fingers were unbuttoning his collar….

"Then why," he muttered, jeering and challenging, "did you run as you did after the shot? And how, since you and I were alone in the room…."

"The window was open! Under it was the table, my pistol where I had dropped it on the table. You turned your back; I was going to jump out the window and run because for the moment I was afraid! But someone, some man, was there; I saw his hand; it caught up the pistol. It was he who shot you in the back! And when he dropped the pistol back to the table…."

Again he demanded fiercely:

"But you ran…w*hy*? And with the gun in your hand! Why? *Why*, girl, if you are not lying to me?"

"Haven't I told you?" Suddenly she was aflame with passionate vehemence. "I was frightened; ready to run; keyed up to run! There came that shot, and you were hit; I thought you were killed! It flashed over me that I would be suspected and all evidence would point to me and I would be convicted of murder! Cowardly murder!… One does not think at such a time; there is only the rush of instinct and impulse. I was all ready to run; I had no time to think…."

"But you had the revolver in your hand as you went through the window!"

"Impulse and instinct, I tell you!" she cried. "Instinct to flee; and to snatch at the first weapon for protection, even though it was the weapon that had just shot you! I was a fool, maybe; and maybe by acting as I did I saved my own life!"

He was looking up into her face strangely; she saw the savage gathering of his brows; with all his might he strove for clear vision and clear thought. With a new, terrible keenness, he fixed his eyes upon her; then he said deliberately: "Liar!"

He saw the flash of her eyes, the angry set of her mouth; her hands were clinched now, and for a moment it was he who believed that he was to be struck full across the face. And thereupon his own eyes brightened; this girl did not speak like a liar; she did not carry herself like one; she had yet to show the first streak of yellow which is in the warp and woof of lying souls.

But Lynette curbed her quick temper and said only:

"You have no right to call me that; my word is as good as your word, Bruce Standing. Had I shot you I should not have waited for you to turn your back. One thing I did do for which I was sorry even while I did it, and ashamed; I laughed at you even while I sympathized with your anger against a man who, to be little and mean, could have your horse killed. And it was not at you that I laughed, after all…there come times when I can't help laughing, though there is nothing to laugh at…it was the shock, I think…the incongruousness, to hear you…."

She ended there, sparing him any further reference to his lisping of which he was so desperately ashamed; once more she began working at his collar…. And again there came into the blue eyes of Bruce Standing a flash as of blue fire, though he hid it from her; and a sudden great, utterly mysterious gladness blossomed magically. For, though he did not understand and though he would never rest until he did understand, yet already he began to believe that this girl with the fearless look spoke the truth! And this, because of the ring of her voice and the tip of her head, erect on its white throat, and the flash of her own eyes, as though the spirit of man and maid had struck fire, one from the other.

"If you'll help me…" said Lynette. "If you can sit a little bit forward?… Your shirt will have to be torn or cut; I can't get to your shoulder otherwise…."

He put up his right hand; as he jerked vigorously there was the sound of tearing and ripping; he thrust the cloth down from the left side and laid bare his great chest and the powerfully muscled left shoulder and upper arm. Lynette shuddered; he had lost so much blood! And against the smooth perfect whiteness of his healthy skin the blood was so emphasized. She found the new wound….

"Shot in the back…twice shot in the back," she said, and again she shivered. "And you don't know who shot you either time?"

"I have my own idea about both," he said curtly. And had nothing to add.

With the warm water and soap she cleansed the fresh wound and then the older one. Then, with gentle fingers, she did as he bade her with Billy Winch's salve, applying it generously.

When the thing was done they looked at each other strangely; man and maid in the wild-wood, with much lying between them, with each asking swift unanswerable questions, with the night in the solitudes advancing.

"It's a strange thing that you came back," said Standing.

"Where better had I to go?"

"I told you that Taggart and his friends were down there. You might have found them."

She turned from him abruptly and went back to the fireplace; he could see only the curve of her cheek and a curl and her shoulder.

"I have no greater liking for Sheriff Taggart than you have," she said.

He wanted to see her face, but she was stubborn in refusing to turn. He said curiously:

"Your friend, Baby Devil, ought to be overhauling them before long! If you think he decided to come this way?"

She did not answer. He began to grow angry with her for that; for refusing to reply when he spoke; for refusing to discuss Babe Deveril. But he kept a shut mouth, though with the effort his jaws bulged. He began feeling in his pocket for pipe and tobacco; he felt the need of it....

He would have sworn that she had not looked and could not have seen, but when he struggled over the difficulty of doing everything with one hand she whirled and came forward impulsively and finished the task for him, packing the tobacco into the black bowl of his pipe and handing him a lighted splinter from the fire.

He muttered something; she had gone back to her place at the fire and did not know whether his muttering was of thanks or curses; her attitude would have seemed to imply that either would find her indifferent. He smoked slowly; the strong tobacco, sharp and acrid, did him good; a man of steady nerve, he had come to a point where his nerves needed steadying; just now he wanted silence and his pipe and time to grope for certain readjustments. Sweeping in all his ways was Bruce Standing; in building up, tearing down, building up again; and always with him was the sheerest joy in building up.... And Lynette, for the first time in many hours, experienced a moment of bright happiness.

He knocked out the ashes of his pipe, rapping the black bowl sharply against his boot heel. Heavily he got to his feet. From the bunk he dragged a blanket tossing it on the floor in a corner by the fireplace. Obviously he was intending it for his bed....

"You must lie on the bunk," she cried impulsively. "You are worse hurt than you seem to know. In any case, I give you my word I'll not use it!"

"Why should I care what you do, girl?" he demanded, staring at her fiercely. "The bunk is there; take it or leave it."

Defiantly she snatched up a second blanket and folded it into the opposite corner, sitting down on it with her feet tucked under her, beginning swiftly to rebraid her loose hair. He turned from her to lie down. But since he had chosen the corner which he had, and since because of his wounds he was forced to lie on his right side, he faced toward her. She appeared not to notice him, having brooding eyes only for the fire; and yet she had had her clear view of his haggard face. Thor came to lie close to his master's feet.

There were three blankets. Lynette, only asking herself curiously what explosion of wrath she might bring upon herself, rose and went for the third, and, without saying anything, spread it over Standing. He looked at her amazed. But he did not speak. Instead, after the briefest of hesitations, he floundered to his feet, set one boot heel upon the edge of the blanket while in his good hand he gripped a corner; with one sudden effort he ripped the blanket fairly in two. He tramped across the small room and dropped half by her side; he went back to his own corner and lay down, dragging the other fragment up over his shoulders, like a shawl....

Lynette was tired almost to the end of endurance; further, this night had been no less a tax upon her than had the other nights. Now, suddenly, she burst into that inimitable laughter of hers, sounding as light and gay and mirthful as the laugh of a delighted child....

"Behold! The acme of politeness!" she cried merrily. "A perfectly good bunk and the two travellers going to sleep on the floor!"

He stared at her unsmilingly for a long time.

"I haven't thanked you, girl, for what you've done for me tonight. I am not without gratitude, but I'm no man for pretty speeches, I am afraid. At any rate here's this: I came hunting a cowardly sneak of a she-cat and I found a true sport. And I think I'm done with making war on you!... Unless...."

"Unless...what?" asked Lynette.

But he was lying back now, his eyes closed. He did not appear to have heard. She, too, lay down with a little weary sigh. Her last thoughts were three; they mingled and grew confused as all thoughts faded. But before they blurred they were these: Bruce Standing had dropped his rifle outside and had not gone out for it; Babe Deveril had not returned for her, but no doubt was still seeking her; and Bruce Standing was done making war on her, *unless*....

CHAPTER 18

Lynette awoke, shivering. It was pitch-dark; the fire had burned out; it must be very late, as she was stiff and cold. She had been dreaming and her shivering was half a shudder of fear. Her nightmare had been one of herself attacked and pursued hideously by wild animals; lions which in the fashion of dreams, changed into wolves, then into savages. She sat up, gathering her blanket about her. She heard Standing breathing heavily; she could hear, now and then, his mutterings of uneasy sleep. Perhaps it had been this which had awaked her? She began listening as one, startled out of slumber, inevitably does to another's incoherencies. It was hard to catch a word despite the cabin's hushed silence into which every slightest sound penetrated. The sounds were like those of a man babbling in fever. Once it seemed to her that he had hardly more than whispered "Girl!"

Always must the mind of one who listens thus be held under the spell of another spirit winging its way among dreams; the moment is uncanny if only because it brings in such close contact the commonplace of every day and the inexplicable of dreams. In the night, in the silence, under this strange spell, her own mind groping, she stirred uneasily.

It flashed across Lynette that it had not been Timber-Wolf's mumbling voice that had awakened her. That there had been something else, a new sound from without. She listened intently, straining her ears. *There was someone or something outside!* She started to her feet, though clinging to the security offered by her corner.

The door was open; it was a mere degree less dark outside than within. As she stared into the blackness she made out vaguely the mass of trees. A black wall in a black night. Some one out there? Then who? *Babe Deveril?*

All along she had held tenaciously to the thought that Babe Deveril would come for her. Perhaps he had come now; perhaps he lingered outside, not knowing positively that she was here, not knowing if Standing were awake or asleep, not knowing if Standing were sick of his wound or ready with rifle in hand.

Her thoughts began to fly like stabs of lightning; briefly they made everything clear only to plunge her whole world of thought back into even more profound darkness. Babe Deveril? It might be! Or it might be Mexicali Joe, lurking after his fashion. Or it might, equally well, be Taggart with Gallup and that other man at his heels. By now she was certain of only one thing: *There was someone out there.*

She stood rigid for ten or fifteen minutes; Standing had become quiet save for his heavy breathing; she strove with all senses upgathered tensely to read the riddle of the night. Once she was sure of a sound outside; but the mystery of a night sound is so baffling! A man's cautious tread? Or a limb stirring gently? Or a bird among leaves, or a rabbit? It was so easy a matter, with her senses so freshly aroused from a nightmare of wild animals and savage pursuers, to people the night with fantastic menaces.

Bruce Standing was unarmed; his rifle dropped somewhere outside when he had dashed after her. She, too, was without a weapon. He had given her the big revolver; she had refused it; she had flung it angrily to the floor, near the bunk. She remembered seeing it there, almost out of sight, under the bunk....

If it were Babe Deveril, she had nothing to fear. If Mexicali Joe, she had nothing to fear. If Taggart and Gallup and the other? What had she to fear from them? Merely arrest, at most, and not so long ago she had been eager for that! And if some prowling animal?

"There's nothing to hurt me," she told herself, fighting to throttle down that trepidation which had leaped upon her when she first awoke with the wildly beating heart of one threatened in sleep. "If I only had that revolver now…if it chanced to be wolf or bear or mountain-cat, one shot at it would send it scurrying. And, if a man, there is none for me to be afraid of."

She began, ever so slowly and guardedly, tiptoeing across the floor. She came to the bunk; she stooped and groped, and at last her fingers closed about the fallen revolver. She clinched it tightly and stood up, again rigid. This time she was sure of the sound which came again; a man's step, as guarded as her own had been, but betrayed by a little dry twig snapping.

Again she waited, without moving, a long time. And not another sound; only Standing's deep breathing. Once she thought that his breathing had changed; that he, too, was awake. But after a moment she persuaded herself that she had imagined that; that he was still sleeping heavily. But no further sound outside. What a cautious man, or what a cowardly, was he out there! What did he want?

Suddenly she thought of Thor. How was it that Thor, a dog, hence man's superior in as many matters as he was man's inferior, a thing of keenest senses, had given no sign? Why had not Thor stirred when she did; why had he not heard what she heard; why was he not already rushing out, growling, demanding to know what intruder lurked in such stealth at his master's door? Had there been a ray of light in the cabin she would have had her answer; for Bruce Standing was sitting up, his arms were about Thor, one big hand was at Thor's muzzle, commanding quiet. And when Standing commanded, Thor obeyed.

Some girls, some men…perhaps most girls and most men…would have remained in the protection of the four walls, resigned to uncertainty, until daybreak. Of their number was not Lynette Brooke, a girl little given to fear and greatly moved by a desire to *know*! She waited as long as she could bear to wait. Then, holding Taggart's revolver well before her and walking with one silent footfall distanced patiently from the other, she gained the door and stepped outside. She was trembling; that she could not help. But she was determined to go on. And on she did go, cautiously, until she had gone ten steps toward the sound which she had heard. She paused, turning in all directions, ready to fire and ready to run.…

"*Sh! Come here!*"

A whisper through the dark. And one man's whisper is much like another's. It could have been Deveril's or Taggart's or even Mexicali Joe's.

"Who are you?" her own whisper answered him.

"Is Standing in there?"

"Who are you?" she insisted.

There was a pause, a silence; a long silence. Then:

"Come with me…just a few feet. So we won't be overheard."

She found herself frowning. Was it Babe Deveril? She did not fancy a man's whispering; she could not imagine a man like Bruce Standing whispering at a moment like this! More like him, like any man who was a man, to roar out what he had to say rather than whisper in the dark. But that curiosity of hers, that inborn desire *to know*, lured her on. But under guard. She held her weapon so that it menaced the vague form so close to her and she whispered again, not realizing that she, too, whispered, but because she was under the spell of the moment.

"I'll go with you another ten steps…count them! And I have a revolver in my hand, aimed at the middle of your body!"

"You're a game kid! Dead game and I don't mind saying so!"

They had stopped; the whisper was dropped for a low-toned voice. It was not Babe Deveril! Not Mexicali Joe. Then Taggart?

"I want to talk to you. I take it he is in there. Asleep? So much the better. I'm Taggart."

"Well? What can I do for you, Mr. Taggart?"

"That gun of yours," he said. "I don't know how used you are to guns. Knowing who I am you can point it down!"

"Knowing who you are," she returned coolly, "I keep it just as it is! I have asked what I could do for you?"

"I've seen Babe Deveril. He's told me all about everything."

"Babe Deveril! When? Where is he?"

Jim Taggart, had time and opportunity afforded, would have laughed at her quickened exclamation, being an evil-thoughted individual with restricted mental horizons. She appeared interested. He had his own mind of her sex and it was not high, since those of her sex with whom such as Jim Taggart consorted were not such as to give a man a high idea of femininity. In the words which, had he spoken his thought aloud, would have been his, Taggart estimated that "he had this dame's number, street, and telephone."

"I'll tell you about Babe Deveril later; and what's more, kid, I'll give you your show to throw in with him again. Now I'm cutting things short; you know why. I was after him for hammering me over the head with a gun; I was on your trail for killing a man. Now, since the man you killed ain't dead at all and since I've had a good talk with Deveril, I'm ready to let you both go. And just to take in a man named Standing."

Through one of those odd tricks by which chance asserts itself at times, Lynette made a discovery while Taggart was talking. She had felt something underfoot—and that something turned out to be Bruce Standing's rifle.

… What had this lost rifle to do with matters as they stood? Why all Jim Taggart's caution, if he were armed? But then Standing had brought Taggart's revolver back to the cabin with him…. What part in tonight's game was this fallen rifle to play? Her thoughts had been withdrawn; so, standing so that for the present Taggart could not possibly touch with his own foot that which she had stumbled on in the dark, she made him repeat what he had said.

Thus she caught a free instant for thought; thus also she grasped all that he had to say and to insinuate. And at the end she answered him with a baffling, feminine:

"Well?"

"I've got to talk fast!" growled Taggart. "He's in there, I know. Is he hurt?"

"You know that he is…."

"I don't mean that shot at Gallup's…that you gave him…."

"I did not shoot him!" she cried out hotly, sick of accusation.

Taggart sneered at her, muttering threateningly:

"You did! For I saw you! I was right there, close by...."

* * * *

Within the cabin Bruce Standing, sitting very tense and straight, nearly choking his big dog into silence, grew tenser and harder. So, Taggart claimed to have seen her.... Taggart was *"right there, close by...."*

* * * *

"You say you saw me!" gasped Lynette. *"You!"*

"I tell you this is no time for palaver," said Taggart impatiently. "What do you care, so long as I agree to let you go free? And to let Deveril go free along with you! I guess that means something to you, don't it? If it don't mean enough, let me show you: I can grab you right now; me, I'm not afraid of any gun any woman ever waved! And I can put you across for a good little vacation in jail. But I'm letting that go by, wanting to get my hooks in one Bruce Standing, good and deep. And I got just that! Seeing as Deveril told me what happened; how Standing swooped down on you, how he beat Deveril up, how he put a chain on you and dragged you away after him! If you'll step into court and swear to that.... Why, kid, I got him! Got him right! Any jury in this country will land on him *hard* for doing to a woman like that. And you can tell the other things he's done to you by now, you and him all alone up here, him a brutal devil...."

Illogically enough it swept over her that it was she herself, Lynette, whom the man was insulting, and her finger trembled so upon the trigger that all unknowing Jim Taggart stood for the instant close upon the verge of the great final blackness. But, steadying herself, she managed to say:

"Babe Deveril told you that? That Bruce Standing had put a chain about me? How did he know? That was after he had gone!"

"But," muttered Taggart harshly, "he did not go so fast! He went up over a ridge and he stopped and rested, and in the dark he came back a bit and he hid and saw! Anyway, it's the truth, ain't it? And I know? So he must have come back to see!"

That thought became on the instant the only thought, one to rise up and obstruct all others. Deveril had seen; he had lingered, hidden in the forest land; he had watched her humiliation; he had known that Bruce Standing, though armed, was a man sorely wounded...and he had not come to her then!

"Where is he?" she demanded swiftly. "When did you see him? Where has he gone?"

"He came just as Standing, damn him, had jumped us tonight! All unawares Standing took us...when we were busy with other things. He had the drop on us and he made us let the Mexico breed go. Deveril was watching but he didn't have a gun and he couldn't step up and take a hand, knowing his cousin for a dead shot and a man who'd rather kill than not."

"But now," demanded Lynette. "*Now!* Where is he?"

"He's a wised-up kid and I'm with him, tooth and toenail! He came up then and he said his say…and I let him go! And he told me to look out for you and he hit the trail, dog-tired as he was, after Mexicali Joe! If there's gold to be had, why Babe Deveril means to be in on it. And me, so do I! And you, if you're on."

Underfoot, all this time, Lynette felt Bruce Standing's rifle….

There are times in life for methodical thought, other times for swift decisions, bred of impulse and instinctive urge….

She lived again through a certain pregnant crisis, saw in mind the whole scene as though some master artist with sweeping, bold brush had created the perfect vision anew for her, the struggle which had been hers and Babe Deveril's and Bruce Standing's, when Standing, with the sun glowing red over his head, had come rushing down on them by their camp-fire. She saw his rifle…the one she now felt underfoot!… go swirling over a pine top as he hurled from him any such advantage in fair fight as it spelled; again she watched the fight…she saw Babe Deveril go up over the ridge; she saw herself, striking in fury against Standing's arm, beating the rifle down….

"Well?" It was Taggart who spoke the brief word now. "Which is it? Jail for you…or a good long spell in the pen for him?"

… And Babe Deveril had come this close…she had proof of that in Taggart's knowledge of the chain!…and had gone on, following the golden lure of Mexicali Joe's trail!

"Well?" said Taggart.

"Suppose I were fool enough to refuse what you ask?"

"Then you'd go to jail as sure as hell! It's you or him! And I guess I know the answer."

Then Lynette said hurriedly:

"Step back…a little farther from the cabin. Let me make sure that he is asleep! There never was a man like him…. Back a few steps and wait…."

"There's no sense in that!"

"If you don't I'll scream out that you're here! Then you'll never take him; you know the man he is!"

Taggart mistrusted, and yet, hard-driven and urged by her voice, obeyed to the extent of drawing back a few steps. Not far, yet far enough for Lynette to stoop and grope and find the rifle. She caught it up and whirled and ran, ran as for her life, back to the cabin door. And she threw the rifle inside, crying out:

"Wake up, Bruce Standing! There's your rifle…and here's Jim Taggart outside, looking for you!"

She came bursting into the cabin and full into Bruce Standing's arms. For he was up on his feet, both arms, despite a sore side, lifted.

"By God!" he shouted.

He let her go and sought the rifle. She was first to find it and put it into his searching hand.

"He is a contemptible coward!" she cried. "As if...."

Standing had the rifle now, and thrust by her and rushed into the open doorway, Thor snarling at his side; and Standing's voice, lifted mightily, shouted:

"Come ahead, Taggart! I'm waiting and ready for you! Come ahead!"

Later he laughed at himself for that, and thereafter explained his laughter to Lynette, saying:

"He hasn't a gun on him! I cleaned him out, all but one pocket gun, and I fancy he emptied that at me...in the back. Come—we'll have a fire!"

Hastily she shut the door, lest Taggart might have one shot left. Standing set his rifle down against the wall; she heard the thud of the stock upon the floor. Clearly he had no fear of Taggart's return. He began gathering up bits of wood, kneeling to get a fire started. Presently under his hands the blaze leaped up and brought detail vividly blossoming from the dark of the room; his face, white, with the most eager, shining eyes she had ever seen; her own face scarcely less pale; the homely appointments of the place. He was still on his knees at the fireplace; he threw on the last bit of wood and watched the quick flames lick at it; he swerved about, and it seemed that his eyes, no less than the inflammable wood, had caught fire as he cried out in a voice which startled her and in words which set her wondering:

"I told you, girl, I'd let you go scot-free...*unless*! And here I bogged down like a broken-legged steer in the quicksands! But now...*Now*! I've got it all figured out. I don't let you go! Neither tonight ..." and he was on his feet, towering over her—"or ever!"

And, as quick as thought, he was at the door and had shot a bolt home and had clicked a padlock, and, swinging about again, stood looking down at her, his eyes filled with dancing lights.

CHAPTER 19

There was no more sleep through what was left of the night, and scarcely more of talk. Standing piled his fire high, and, unmindful of his discarded rifle, went out for more wood; Lynette dropped down on the blanket in her corner and named herself a silly fool. He came back, carefully relocking his door; kept his fire blazing, and made his coffee and smoked his pipe. And then, in that great golden voice of his, he began singing. And, through its wild rhythm, she knew the song for the same as that which she had heard for the first time when he had hurled himself both into Big Pine and into her life. His voice rose and swelled and filled the poor cabin to overflowing, and must have filtered through chinks and cracks and spilled out through the forest land, and for great distances through the quiet solitudes. And, at the end, in a sudden upgathering into all that tremendous resounding volume of sound of which his magnificent voice was capable, came that unforgettable wolf cry. If she required any reminding, here she had it, that she was housed in the same cabin with Timber-Wolf! A fierce outcry, to go resounding and echoing across miles and miles of forest lands, meant, as she was quick to realize, to carry both defiance and challenge to his enemies.

"You have had your choice, girl!" he shouted at her. "You could have gone free! I gave you your freedom. But you would not go. And that was because it was in the cards, in the fates, in the stars, if you like, that you and I are not to part yet! The door is locked; I stand between you and it. So, you stay here with me!"

For the first time she was truly and deeply afraid of him. But he went back to his place by the fire, and sat on the old stump seat, and filled his pipe again with hard, nervous fingers and glared at the fire. For a little he seemed to have forgotten that she was there. And then at last, when she saw that he was going to speak again, she forestalled him, saying swiftly:

"I am tired and sleepy. I am going to sleep."

He checked his speech, saving whatever he had to say to her. She lay back on her blankets, and, though she had had no such intention, soon drifted off to sleep. And he, with pipe grown cold, sat and glowered over his fire, and put to himself many a question, growing fierce over his inability to answer any one of them. But, at least, in his groping he forgot the pain of his wounds.

"You are not asleep," he said after a very long time. "I know that; I can tell. You are pretending. And you are thinking, thinking hard and fast! And so am I thinking! As I never did before now. You might as well save yourself the labor of struggling with your problems, since I am doing the planning for both of us right now; since everything is in my hands and I mean to keep it there."

She heard but gave no sign of hearing; she kept her face averted from him so that he could not see whether her eyes were open or shut. Open they were, and the man appeared to know it.

"Am I wise man or fool?" he cried. "He only is wise who knows what he knows and steers his craft by the one steady star in his sky!"

She would not answer him when he spoke; she could not just now. She lay still, as if asleep. He relapsed into a long silence, his eyes now on her, now on his fire.

"This neck o' the woods is getting all cluttered up with folks!" he muttered abruptly, with such suddenness that he startled her. "I've a notion to run the whole crowd in for trespassing!... Or better, girl, you and I move on. Where there's elbow room; room to talk in. We've got to quarry out our own blocks of stone and build up our own lives, and we want a bit of the world to ourselves. What's more, we're going to have it!"

She knew, as every girl knows when that mighty moment comes...and her girl-heart beat hard and fast...that after his own fashion Bruce Standing, Timber-Wolf, was making love to her.

"Dawn!" he said, and she understood that he spoke with himself as much as with her. "That's all we're waiting for, the first streak of dawn. Then we move on. Where? I know where, and no other man knows!"

He began impatiently stalking up and down; he seemed to have forgotten his wounds, and yet, stealing her swift glances at him, she could see that his face had lost little of its whiteness and that his whole left side was stiff. Again, bestowing mentally a strange epithet upon him, she regarded the man as "inevitable." Could anything stop him or divert his career into any channel but that of his own choosing? She *was* afraid of him.

"You told me that I might go! Where I pleased, when I pleased!"

He swung about and turned on her a face of whose expression in that dim, flickering light she could make nothing.

"You had your choice! You came back! Now I know something which I did not know before."

He began pacing up and down again, making the cabin's smallness further dwarfed by his great strides. He fascinated her; she watched him, and her fear, formless and nameless, grew until it seemed that it would choke her.

There was a boarded-up window. A thin slit of light showed.

"We breakfast and go," he told her.

"And if I refuse to go with you?"

"I have my chain and my good right arm!"

Then, as once before, tingling with anger born of foreseen humiliation, she cried out:

"I hate you, brute that you are!"

"Not brute, but man," he told her sternly. "And, ever since the world was young, men, when they were men, claimed their mates and took and held them!"

Again for a long time he was silent. And then, on his feet, his arms thrown out, he cried in a strange voice:

"I love you!"

He made strange mad music in her soul. She tried again to cry out: "I hate you!" She knew that still she was afraid of him, more afraid than ever. Yet he strode up and down and looked a young valiant god, and his golden voice found singing echoes within her soul and his wild extravagances awoke throbbing extravagances in her…. What can one know? What misdoubt? We are like babes in the dark. Of what can one be sure? Of the stars above?… Our hopes are like stars….

"I am no poet, though next to a strong fighting man I'd rather be a true poet than anything else God ever created! Were I a poet I'd build a song for you, girl! A song to ring through the eternal ages; going back to the roots of things when You and I were first You and I! It would be a song like one of the old troubadours', telling of great deeds and great loves only…for you and I have never been the ones for cowardly littlenesses! I'd make a song to hang about the world's memory of you like a golden chain. And I'd carry on, having the poet's soul and vision, into ten thousand lives to come; down to the end of time when eternity is only at its beginnings!… But I am only plain Bruce Standing, a simple fighting man, and no poet; one who at best can but mouth the voicings of the true poets. So I can only pour all my heart and soul, girl, into my brief poem: I love you. I have always loved you! Always and always I shall love you!… And I'll crack any man's skull that so much as looks at you!"

She was not sure of his sanity; not certain that a fever, bred of his wounds, was not burning into his marrow. *And yet—*

"It's dawn, I tell you! We boil our coffee, we pick up a mouthful of food. And then we move on! And why? Because we're sure to have callers here in another day or so, and just now I don't want other people; I want you, girl, and only you and the rest of the world can go to pot!… And now we go!"

CHAPTER 20

Lynette, in a mood to expect anything of fate, wondered vaguely where the steep trail of adventure now led. She would not have been surprised had Standing set his plans for some spot a hundred miles distant. But she was surprised to arrive so soon, after only two or three hours, at their destination. He looked at her, exulting.

"Here is Eden!" he cried out joyously. "Remember the name, girl; bestowed upon this spot no longer ago than this very minute! Eden! And as far from the world as that other distant Eden. Here we stop and here no man finds us!"

He had led the way, upward along a rocky slope. He had brought her into a spot which she would have named "The Land of Waterfalls!" A tiny valley with a sparkling mountain creek cleaving like flowing crystal through a grassy meadow; tall trees, noble patriarchs bounding it. Steep canyon walls shutting in the timber growth; a narrow ravine above with the water leaping, plunging, tumbling translucent green over jagged rocks, splashing into a series of pools, turned into rainbow spray here and there in its wild cascadings. The world all about was murmurous with living waters, with bees, with the eternal whisperings of the pines.

And here began an idyl; a strange idyl. A man asserting his power as captor; a maid made captive; two souls wide awake, questing, swung from certainty to uncertainty, gathered up in doubt. Life grown a thing of tremendous import.

All morning had Standing been wracked with pain. Yet none the less did he hold unswervingly to his purpose. Now he sat down, his back to a tree. Thor came and lay at his feet. Lynette stood looking down upon the two.

"Rest," he said. "Here is your home for a time. A day? Ten days? Who knows? Not I, girl! All that I know I have told you; here we rest and here we take life into our hands and mould it…as we have always moulded it! We are at the gates; we enter or we turn to one side! We go on or we go back. Which? When we know that, we know everything."

He had brought with him, slung across his back, a great roll from the hidden cabin. His rifle lay across his knees. He looked up into her face with eyes which, though haggard, shone wonderfully. She sat down, ten steps from him; her clasped hands were in her lap; her eyes were veiled mysteries.

"Taggart won't look for us here," he said. "He hasn't the brains of a little gray seed-tick! He'll be sure we've made a big jump, forward or back, ten times this distance. Besides, he has to go somewhere to get himself a new set of guns! Imagine him tackling anything with an ounce of risk in it unless he was heeled like an army corps! I begin to lose respect for that man."

Lynette was thinking but one thing: "She was not afraid of this man; not afraid to be alone with him in pathless solitudes. She might choose to be elsewhere…yet she was safe with him. For, above all, he was a man; and never need a true girl fear a true man." And, when she stole a swift glance at his face, it lay in her heart to be a bit sorry for him. Sympathy? It lies close to another eternal human emotion! He looked like one whom fate had crushed and yet whose spirit refused to be crushed. He looked a sick man who, scorning all the commands laid upon the flesh, carried on.

After a while he turned to look upon her, and for the first time she saw a new and strange look in his eyes, a look of pleading.

"Don't misjudge me, girl," he said heavily. "Rather than see your little finger bruised I'd have a man drive a knife in me! I'm just blundering along now…blundering…trying to see daylight. I won't hurt you. There's nothing on earth or in Heaven so sure as that. But don't ask me to let you go!"

She made him no answer. She began thinking of his wounds; he gave them such scant attention! He should be caring for them; what he should do was to hasten to a surgeon. She wondered if still he clung to his conviction, the natural one after all, that she had shot him? And she wondered, as she had done so many a time before: "Who had shot him?" Whose hand that which she had seen reach through her window and snatch up her revolver and fire the cowardly shot? Taggart, only a few hours ago, had said: "I saw! I was right there!" …

"Was it Jim Taggart who shot you in the back last night?" she demanded suddenly.

"Yes," he said. "At least, I think so."

"Is he that kind of man?"

Now his eyes were keen and hard upon hers.

"I begin to think that he is, girl," he said shortly. "Why?"

She shrugged and again turned away.

He lumbered to his feet. Thor, knowing where he was going, barked and leaped ahead.

"Come, I'll show you where we pitch camp."

She looked about her. Mere madness to attempt flight now; he would bear down upon her before she had run twenty steps. And did she want to run just now? She had her own measure of curiosity…. Was it only that?… and she had, locked away securely in her breast, her absolute positive knowledge that she had nothing to fear at his hands. She rose and followed him.

Suddenly he swerved about, confronting her, his eyes stern, his voice hard with the emotion riding him.

"Madman I may be," he said. "Fool, I am not, praise God! Last night I heard; you could have chucked that rifle into Taggart's hands and could have gone free yourself…and by now I'd be a dead man! But, glory be, there isn't a streak of yellow in your whole glorious being!"

The blood ran up into her face; it made her hot throughout her whole body. Praise, from him, to stir her like that! Her eyes flashed back angrily, for she was angry with herself.

"Come," he muttered. "Talk's cheap at any time. And I'm to show you where we make our first home."

With her teeth sharply catching up her underlip, she held her silence. He went on some two-score paces and stopped; with a sudden gesture he said:

"Here I've spent, God knows how many nights, when I had to be off by myself! No roof for us, girl, but who wants a roof with that sky above us?"

Here was a natural grotto which at another time would have made her exclaim in delight: a nook, set apart, thresholded in tender grass shot through with those tiny delicate blooms of mountain flowers. On one side a cliff, outjutting, thrusting forward a great overhanging shelf of rock which looked as though it must fall and yet which, obviously, had held securely through the centuries. Three big pine-trees, two of them leaning strangely toward the cliff, as though yearning to lean against the sturdy rock and rest there upon its iron breast. The whole ringed about by a dense copse of brush, thick as a wall and rearing high above her head. Almost a cave made of cliff and growing things, cosy and warm, with its opening fronting the stream which was never silent. Thor ran ahead into the dusky seclusion and barked his invitation to them to follow. A thick, dry mat, under Thor's feet, of fallen pine-needles.

Standing tossed his roll inside; he began, with one hand, to work with the knotted rope. Lynette came forward swiftly, saying:

"At least I have two hands…."

Their hands brushed over the labor. Again the hot blood raced through her, and again sudden anger, anger at herself, flashed through her being.

And a tingling, like that which shot through her, was in Bruce Standing's veins. He caught her hand.

"Girl!" he said huskily.

"Don't!" she cried in alarm.

He dropped her hand and rose swiftly to his feet.

"You are right," he muttered. "Not yet…."

How could this man at a touch make her heart beat like mad? She was afraid…she knew that she was not afraid of *him*…yet she was afraid.

"I'm sorry," he said roughly. Actually, marvelling, she saw that the big man looked embarrassed. "Look here, girl: I've come to know you a bit and, thinking what I think, I hold that I know you well! I'll take my chance that you are no petty crook, that you are no coward, that you are no liar! So…."

"Then," she cried, jumping to her feet, all eagerness, "do you believe me when I say that I did not shoot you?"

His eyes met hers steadily; he answered promptly:

"You have told me…and I believe. *I know!*"

A rush of gladness, an intoxication of gladness, swept over her. Her eyes were shining, soft and bright and happy like stars.

"But," she said, "if not I, then who?"

"Jim Taggart," he said as unhesitatingly as he had spoken before. "Jim told you that he saw, didn't he? That he was Johnny on the spot? Of course he was! And we'd had our plain talk. And he figured it out, that unless that very day I had changed my papers, I still named him in them my old bunk-mate and friend, and that I'd not forget him with a legacy! If I had died under that bullet, Jim Taggart would have had it doped out that he'd stand to win about a hundred thousand dollars! And for a tenth of that he'd crucify Christ!"

"But…."

"There are no buts about it! You did not do it; then Jim Taggart did. He shot me last night, a second time and the second time in the back! He was once a man; now he's a Gallup dog, a man gone to seed, a cur and one for such as you and me to forget about. I hope to high heaven I never see the man again; for the sake of what has been between Jim Taggart and me, when both of us were younger, I'd rather let the past bury its dead. For if he ever comes trailing his filth across my trail again, I'll smash him into the earth." He made a wide angry gesture, as though he would wipe an episode and a man out of his life. "But you interrupt me; I was going to say something. Just this: I'll leave you alone. For an hour, for a dozen hours! You want rest, you want solitude and a chance to think. So do I. I can chain you to a tree and be sure of you! Or I can ask you to give me your word that you'll wait here until I come back to you…and I already know you well enough to know *that* will hold you tighter than any chain that was ever forged!"

Lynette, without hesitating, answered:

"I do want rest and I do want to be alone. Is that to be wondered at? Until noon I'll wait for you to come back."

"Until high noon," he said. "And, girl, you pledge me your word on that?"

"Yes!"

"Come, Thor!" He turned and left her, his great dog at his heels, going up the narrowing canyon.

"I'll not spy on you!" he called back, when he had gone a hundred yards. "You'll hear me shouting to you well before I come within eye-shot."

And then she lost him, gone among the lesser, denser trees thick about the creek's margins.

She turned her back on the grotto of his choosing, and went out into the full sunlight. She found a spot in the open, ringed about by the majestic pines, a grassy sward with the cleaving silver line of the creek cutting across it. For the first time in hours…how many endless hours? how many days?… she was alone! No man at her side, either protecting or dominating. Her lungs filled with a deep sigh. Alone and secure in her aloneness for a matter of several hours.

There was a certain singing happiness, electric within her, and it sprang, bright-winged, from her own characteristic pride. Bruce Standing had left her to an absolute physical freedom, knowing her bound by that intangible and unbreakable bond of her promise. He, a man who did not break his own word knew her for a girl who did not break hers! And he knew, at last, that it had not been her hand that had fired that cowardly shot.

"It was cruel…to have laughed at him. I did not mean to laugh. Would to God…."

But if she had not laughed? Then what? Then how much of her adventure would have followed? How much of it did she, after all, regret?… She fell to wondering dreamily on Babe Deveril. Where was he? And would she see him again? And, if she should see him….

A thousand riddles and, as always, no answer to the riddles which spring from eternity. Only the merry voice of the purling creek to talk back to her, that and the rustling whisper ebbing and flowing through the pine tops. The stream, like a companionable human voice, called to her insistently. She rose and went down to it and stooped to drink; she bathed her hands and arms and face. How lonely it was here! She cast a quick glance up-stream; long ago Standing, with his big dog at his heels, had passed out of sight. And he had given her gage of promise for promise given…he would send his shouting voice ahead of him before he came back.…

So she bathed fearlessly, watched only by the solitudes, guarded by their sombre depths; she plunged, with a little shivery gasp, into the deep, cool pool below the slithering waterfall; the water slipped, gleaming like a bejewelled film over her pure-white body, making it rosy when she emerged, like rose petals…. She dressed in furious haste, all ablush and yet steeped in a confident knowledge that no eye, save the bright eye of a curious brown bird, had seen. She felt new-born; refreshed beyond belief. She ran back up the bank and sat down in the very spot where she had dropped first when Standing had left her. She began, always hurrying, to comb out her hair with her fingers. Sitting there in the open she let it sun.…

She rested. She drank deep, thankfully, of the hour. To be alone, to be secure in the moment, to have no danger pressing down upon her, above all to have no mind save her own dictating to her. It was glorious and life was good and glad and golden, infinitely worth the living. So passed an hour. It was so quiet here; so unutterably lonely. Only the voice of the creek and the million-tongued murmuring pines. Her swift thoughts raced ten thousand ways. They touched upon Big Pine; on Taggart; Mexicali Joe; a gold-mine still for men to find; Maria, the Indian girl whom Deveril had kissed; Deveril himself; that one-legged man who rode horseback and carried forth the word and the law of his master; Thor, a dog; Bruce Standing. Most of all, Bruce Standing. She wondered where he was, what doing? Caring for his own wounds? Lying on his back, his white face turned up, his eyes shut, tight shut? And he loved her?

Bruce Standing loved her, Lynette? Was that true? What was love? Whence came love? For what purpose? What did it do to the hearts and souls and bodies of men…and girls? Was love for her? She had never experienced it, not true, abiding love. Did Babe Deveril.…

Another hour. Shadows slowly shifting, moving like gigantic hands of eternal clocks. Time passing, time that answers all questions, man's and maid's, saint's and sinner's. She stirred uneasily and sat up. She looked at the pine tops and, beyond them, at the sun. It was almost noon!

Come noon.… What then? Come high noon before Bruce Standing, and she was free! Released from her promise, all bonds snapped! Free!

She jumped to her feet. Her eyes went questing, questing, everywhere. To be free again; to be her own self, Lynette, untrammelled…. And she felt awondering illogically: "Can it be that, after all, he was driving himself beyond any man's endurance? that he is more badly hurt than either he or I knew?"

But he returned a full half-hour before even the most eager could name it noon. True to his word, he sent his voice, like a glorious herald, ahead of him. She heard him call, not the wolf cry, but a rollicking shout. And ten minutes later he himself came, plainly in the highest of good humors. He was still pale and looked haggard, but his eyes were flashing and triumphant and untroubled.

He came to her, splashing across the creek, water flying about his boot-tops.

"I've had a bath," he announced from afar. "And I've plastered myself with the worst that Billy Winch can concoct, and Richard is himself again!" He came closer, towered above her and said: "You, too, have bathed! You look it, as fresh from the plunge as any Diana! It's good to be *clean*, isn't it?"

She flushed and was ashamed for it. She bit her lip and made no answer.

"Come," he said. "We'll lunch. And now, and from now on for some sixty years, my girl, it will be I who waits on you! The slave rôle reversed!" and he laughed.

"I promised to wait for you; I make no more promises!"

"That's fair enough! I watch you then!"

"Do you want to make me hate you?"

"Rather, I want you to come to love me."

"Could any girl come to love a man who treats her as you have done me?"

"Could any girl come to love a man," he demanded earnestly, "who thought so little of her as to let her escape him when once destiny had brought her and him together?"

CHAPTER 21

The most perfect of the summer months in this secluded mountain nook, not inaptly named "Eden" by Standing, was a period of time measuring itself in soft, fragrant loveliness. The days were balmy, perfect, halcyon; gentle hours of blue cloudlessness and golden sunshine and little breezes which scarcely ruffled the clear water in the bigger pools; night as clear as crystal, with flaring stars like distant torches above the yellow pine tops; nature in her gentlest mood here among the ruggedness of the wilderness, expressing herself in the most delightful of odors wafted through the woods, in the tenderest tiniest blossoms of wild flowers; a time of infinite hush and infinite solitude and peace.

To have chafed and been unhappy here, to a spirit like either Bruce Standing's or Lynette Brooke's, would have seemed next door to an impossibility. Even the girl, though restrained, a prisoner of a man's will when the bright star of her life had ever been one of splendid independence, found it easier to smile or laugh aloud at the sober-faced antics of Thor…when she and Thor were alone with none to see!… than to sigh. She knew her periods of restiveness and bitter rebellion; they were due not to her environment, but to the thought that another than herself was dictating to her. But for one reason or another these periods were rarer and briefer than her other hours of a strange sort of peacefulness.

"It's because I've been worn out and only now am resting," she tried to tell herself. "Recuperating from a condition of exhausted mind and body."

Thus four days and nights passed. There had been, during all that time, not the slightest opportunity to escape. The first day Standing had hurled the chain from him, as far as he could send it. But he had not lost sight of her for more than a few minutes at a time, saving such times that she gave him her promise that she would wait for him to come back. He accepted her word as he expected all the world to accept his. On other occasions, when he allowed her briefer freedoms, he had said merely: "No chance to run for it, girl! I'd overtake you, you know, in no time. Even if you hid, here'd be old Thor, nosing you out!" Then he laughed, adding: "For his own sake, the renegade, as well as for his master's! He's fallen in love with you, too." He made her bed in the rock-and-tree grotto; he labored, one-handed, over it for hours. With his heavy clasp knife he cut the tender tips of resinous branches; he heaped them high; he covered all with great handfuls of fragrant grass, thick with the tall red flowers that grew down by the creek, odorous with the tender white blossoms which shyly lifted their little heads to dot the grassy slopes.... He made her a bathing-pool: stiff and sore all up and down his left side, he worked with his right hand, dragging big boulders up out of their ancient beds, piling them in a ring about the pool, plastering them over the top with great handfuls of that carpet-like moss which thrived in these cool places.

"If you'd let me go!"

"No; not yet.... What man can read the mind of a girl? How do I know what you would do? Where you would go? My wounds are healing; until they heal I am only half a man. You might whisk away from me, I tell you; and I'd have to follow and seek you, if you led me through hell on the way to heaven; and I must be whole again. And I've got to get everything straight...."

Always when he left her he returned before the end of the time she had promised to wait for him. And always he sent, as herald of his approach, his golden voice forward to her. At times in an echoing shout. More than once in an outburst of singing which thrilled her strangely. What a voice the man had! And once, when he had elected to bathe in the starlight, he sent down to her that cry which she had heard the first time from the door of Babe Deveril's cabin in Big Pine...the wild, fierce call of the timber-wolf which, despite her naming herself "fool," sent a shiver into her blood.... Once this happened: He had left her in the forenoon, accepting her word that she would not stir until high noon. Usually he came well in advance; this time she watched the climbing sun and the creeping shade and suddenly her heart began its wild beating; it was almost noon and he was not here; no sound of his coming. When he shouted to her and then came rushing into camp, he found that she had been working frenziedly with a stick and a stone; driving the sliver of wood like a stake into the ground…. She started up, her face crimson.

"Well?" he said, his hands on his hips, staring down at her. "What's that?"

She blurted out the explanation and then was angry with herself for telling him. She had meant to stay until the tip end of the giant pine's shadow fell where it marked midday; she had meant there to drive in her stake; for him it would be a marker, an assurance from her that she had kept her word with him, that she had waited as she had promised to wait…that then, scorning him, she had snatched at her rights and had fled!

His first impulse was toward laughter. And then, strangely quiet, he stood looking at her and she saw a gathering mist in his eyes!

"Girl!" he muttered. "Oh, girl!… God, I love you!"

"I hate you.…"

… How many times had she cried out in those words! And how much of that did she mean? In her heart, in her soul…in the most hidden recesses of her most hidden being?

Thus she had hours to herself. And, therefore, had Bruce Standing hours to himself. For he wanted them. He wanted to be away from her, where he could not see her, could not hear that low music of her voice, could not catch that soft lure of her eyes, could not be tempted to have it happen that his rude hand brushed her hand…. Her hand, though she had been all these days and nights outdoors, roughing it, seemed to him a maddening realm of crumpled rose-leaves…pink-and-white rose-leaves. He left her, secure in her pledge that she would wait for him, and threw himself down on his back and stared up through slowly shifting branches and mused on her. He thought how like a flower she was, the queen of flowers…and he could have wept that he was so big and ungentle. He thought of Babe Deveril, and cursed him for being so slender and debonair; graceful and light of mood; gentle-voiced, with the knack of pretty words to pretty ladies. And Babe Deveril had befriended her; stood champion to her against him! He ground his teeth. He leaped up and paced back and forth, forgetful of all such insignificant nothings as trifling wounds of the flesh. He recalled how, man to man, he had broken Babe Deveril, and he laughed out loud…. Yet it remained that Babe Deveril had stood her friend and protector when he had pursued them both, linking them but the closer, with his wrath. She and Deveril had travelled together, side by side and hand in hand, miles and other miles of the open solitudes; they had been drawn close together, driven closer together. He, Bruce Standing, Timber-Wolf, and Fool, had done that! And what spark had been struck out of the flint of the adversity which he had hurled at them?… Had they loved… had they kissed…was *she* now longing with a sick heart for the return of Babe Deveril?

"Oh, Lord!" he cried out, his great iron fingers crooking as his arms were thrown out. "Deliver him into these hands!"

Lynette had no mirror. Standing began to grow a lusty young beard, as blond as his hair, shot through with red gleams. She knew the need of fresh clothing. When he was away she did her washing as best she could, pounding garments against the rocks in the creek; she dried them and hid them and donned them without his knowing...though of course he knew as she knew that he did his own rude washings. There was a spring at the side of the canyon, one of the many sources which fed the stream; a shadowed, tranquil place. Of this she made her pier-glass! She stooped and looked down into its glassily smooth surface. It gave back her own image; it reflected the dark green of the pines, the lighter green of the willows. Even the subdued colors of her worn suit. She washed her hair and groomed it; no comb, no brush, but agile fingers. Most of all, when secure through his promise in return for her own, did she enjoy her plunge in the pool he had made for her. The slender whiteness of her slipped hastily down under the translucent cover of the cool, flowing water; she was as swift in her movements as any slim-bodied trout that darted about her, scurrying into its retreat; the water shot a thrill through her; she emerged, dripping, charged with all the electric currents of well-being.

"If this were only a holiday...instead of imprisonment!"

She, too, thought of Babe Deveril, as was inevitable. And in many ways: One, always recurrent, was: "Could she have been as *sure* of Babe Deveril as she was of Bruce Standing? As secure in her utter conviction of safety?" And here was a question to which she found no ready answer. Babe Deveril, leaping full-breastedly into the stream which had swept her off her feet, had been a friend to her from the beginning; from the beginning Bruce Standing had been a menace.

... Best of all she loved the waterfall. It was her shower-bath. But, more than that, it was her friend and confidante, and, beyond aught else, a living, glimmering, varicolored thing of gossamer beauty. It talked with her, it was at once handmaiden and musician and troubadour; it plashed and sang and poured its cadences into quiet harmonies which sank into her soul. It had leapt and sparkled and poured itself onward unstintedly, unafraid, for a thousand years; for a thousand years would it keep up its merry dancings, uncaring if only the tall pines watched or if men and maids brought hither their loves and hates and hopes and fears. Unstable it was always, always falling; secure was it in its diaphanous veilings of its own merry immortality. She loved it for its abandon, for its recklessness, for its translucent myriad beauties. It lived; it sang and sparkled; it filled the moment with musical murmurings and recked not of all those vague threats and shadows of a vague future.... She sat here, quiet under the spell of its dashings and splashings and eerie flutings...musing, her soul drawn forth into all those vague and troublous musings which beset the heart of youth.

Youth? Young, too, was Bruce Standing! He hearkened to the cascading waters; he listened to the harp-tongued whisperings of the pines…. He had done everything wrong; he told himself that a thousand, thousand times. Yet he told himself savagely that throughout the insanities, the veritable madnesses of constricted human life there flowed always, onward and sweepingly upward, the great, triumphal, eternal forces of destiny. And, in the end…in the end…it all made for good. For eternal and triumphant good.

… After all, but the old, old story of man and maid, converging to the one gleaming, focal point though across distances oceans-wide removed.

He had his point of view; Lynette Brooke had her point of view. Yet it remains that from two widely separated peaks two eager hearts may see the same sun rise.

"Tell me," he said once. "What manner of man is this Babe Deveril? I know him as a man may know a man; you know him otherwise. Tell me; what have you found him to be?"

Never would she have been Lynette, had she not been ever quick of instinct…instinct leaping, never looking, yet so certain to strike true! She read the thought under a thought; there came a living, joyous gloating; she cried warmly, all the while watching him:

"A true friend and a gentleman! A man unafraid…one like a loyal knight of the olden time! Like one of the King Arthur's knights…."

"Like one," he growled, deep down in his throat, angrily, "who saw another Lynette across the four fords? That's not true, girl; else he would not have forsaken you so long! Nor would he have given up so easily when, in your view, I beat him down and sent him up over the ridge!"

"He'll come back!"

"You think so?"

"*I know!*"

Chance remarks of hers…this one above all others…rankled. She seemed so confident that Babe Deveril would come again, that he would carry in his breast the memory of sweet hours with her, that he would never rest until he, with her pleading eyes tender upon his, could rescue her from the bondage which Bruce Standing had set upon her! So it came about that nightly, and all night long, Bruce Standing dreamed of Babe Deveril and of battling with him and of beating him finally into such definite defeat as had not resulted from that other fierce struggle before her widening eyes.

Another day went by and another, with Bruce Standing obsessed, knowing himself for a man who yearned with all his soul for one thing and one thing only, a mere slip of a gray-eyed girl who made madness in his pulses. He had his moods of fierceness; on their heels came those other moods of tenderness. More than once he came toward her, striding through the woods, his mind made up to set her free, asking only her happiness. And then he saw her; and in his heated fancies he saw Babe Deveril; and he named Deveril a man of slight manhood and swore by his own manhood that never would he show so lax and flabby a hand as to let this priceless girl, drop into the graceful, careless hand of any Babe Deveril who ever lived.

"He'd never know how to love her as I do!" That ancient cry of all true lovers!

But all the while there bit into him doubtings, fears, those manifold darts flung from love's alter ego, jealousy. He stood ready to give this girl full-handedly everything; from her he craved with that direst of all cravings, everything…. And when he could no longer hold back the tumult within him and demanded: "What of this Baby Devil?" putting a sneer into his voice, always she cried out warmly: "A true friend and a gentleman!"

* * * *

All unexpected by both of them, the less by him than her, Billy Winch, Timber-Wolf's one-legged retainer, rode full tilt into camp. They were lunching; they sat under a tree in the noonday shadow like two at picnic. He had been saying: "We're running short of rations." Then it was that Billy Winch, anxiously spurring a big roan saddle-horse, rode down upon them and, seeing them, began waving his hat high over his head in sweeping, joyous circles and shouting:

"So you're still alive! That's something!"

"You fool! Who told you to come here!"

Standing leaped to his feet; he was hot with anger.

"I knew where to find you, Timber!" cried Billy Winch gleefully. "Unless, a fair bet, the devil had claimed you and taken you down under, I knew I'd find you here!… How's the sick wing? Been usin' my salve? Night and morning, keepin' it clean and…."

Billy Winch, headlong, stopping his horse with a sudden pluck of the reins when the gaunt roan had come near setting his four flickering hoofs in their midday fire, chose to ignore the fact that the Timber-Wolf was not alone.

But Standing, springing up, strode out to meet him, his mien anything but friendly.

"Damn you, Billy Winch," he muttered between his teeth, too low for the wondering Lynette to hear. She, too, had sprung up and stood leaning against the valiant pine-tree, wondering swiftly how this latest happening, the coming of Billy Winch into the wild-wood, was to affect her.

Billy Winch, as gay-hearted a rascal as ever stumped on one leg or rode a wild, half-broken horse in carelessly lopsided fashion, laughed gleefully.

"Ho, Timber!" he cried. "If I was a whole man, 'stead of half a one, I'd just jump down and naturally beat you to death! Bein' what I am, all carved to thunder, you're too much all gone to proud flesh to jerk me out of the saddle to stomp on me! So I got the age on you! And I asks you, Johnny Wolf, man-eater, how's tricks?"

"By God, Winch!" Standing in upstarting wrath had the roan horse by the bit, shoving it back with one savage hand so that it fell back on its haunches. "Just because I've stood a lot off you…."

"Slow does it, Timber!" cried Winch. "This is business. I've got a man back there, just out of sight, ready to go clean crazy unless he can have a word with you. To put a name to him…well, then, Mexicali Joe!"

Now Standing, deep down within him, knew why Billy Winch had come. Never did more faithful heart beat in human breast than that heart thrumming away beneath Billy Winch's faded blue shirt. Winch, having always a shrewd guess where to find his chief, when Standing took it upon himself to disappear from headquarters, had caught at the first excuse to come in person and make sure with his own keen eyes that all went well with a man whom many hated and whom he, above all men, loved.

"Hang Mexicali Joe to the first stout limb you come to!"

Lynette, of impulses ungovernable, could have broken into laughter. For the amazing thing was that what Bruce Standing, impatient almost to fury, said he meant. He had suffered enough inconvenience at Mexicali Joe's hands; he wanted nothing of the man nor of his dross of gold.

Winch did laugh aloud. And then, keen-eyed to see the play of his employer's expression, he grew sober and said earnestly:

"On the level, Mr. Standing, how's the hurt comin' along? Been usin' the salve I told you to?"

Lynette, though he had ignored her presence or because of this very attitude of his, could not hold back from exclaiming:

"He has two wounds now! Another shot in the back! And he gives them less attention than a sane man would give a cut finger!"

"The old fool! No more sense than a rabbit! Shot again? Twice in the back? Plugged a second time? The old fool!"

Like a flash in his quick movements he was down from the saddle; he left his horse with dragging reins to wait for him; over the uneven ground he came forward rapidly, hopping like an oddly oversized bird. He caught at Standing's shoulder, crying out:

"Let me see them hurts! I tell you, I got to see them hurts! Shot twice from behind? You bloody baby. Let me look at 'em. Blood poison most likely settin' in!"

"I could kill you…you interfering fool…."

But just then Billy Winch's one foot caught at a root and he came near falling, and Standing, instead of carrying out a threat, sprang toward him and steadied him; and Lynette saw a sincere rough affection in the way the big arms closed about Winch's body. Friends, these two.

"Who plugged you, Timber? And for the love of Mike, how come you to let it happen…*twice*? But tell me: Who plugged you the second time?"

"Taggart," said Standing; "at least that's my bet. And," he added hastily, "it was Taggart that shot me the first time, through the window at Gallup's!"

Billy Winch looked sharp incredulity; his eyes flickered away to Lynette as he gave sign of seeing her for the first time.

"But, man! I thought…."

"You thought wrong! She did not shoot me. You've got my word for that, Bill. *She did not shoot me!*"

Winch looked perplexed.

"Sure, Timber?" he demanded. "Dead sure?"

"Yes," said Standing. "Taggart didn't believe I had already changed my papers, ruling his name out. If he could have dropped me and made it seem clear that she had done it…. See it, Bill?"

"Well," said Winch slowly, "I guess you know or you wouldn't say so. And Jim Taggart was a real man once. But I've seen signs of late; he's mildewed inside, clean through. As comes of running with such as Young Gallup."

Suddenly he whipped off his battered hat and turned a pair of bright and smiling, and at last warmly admiring eyes upon Lynette.

"I beg your pardon, Miss," he said genially.

"Now," said Standing. "About this Mexicali Joe. You go back and tell him for me…."

Winch interrupted quickly, saying:

"No use, Timber. You got to see him. I tell you he's clean crazy to see you; he'll stick on your trail until he finds you. He wants only ten minutes; five would do it."

Lynette was mildly surprised to see Standing so easily persuaded; but she had no way of knowing the relationship of this man and his chief henchman nor how Billy Winch never took it upon himself to suggest unless he knew what he was about.

"All right," said Standing, though he frowned as he spoke. "Go get your man."

Winch jerked his head about and shouted; his long, halloing call pierced clear through the woodland silences.

"Hi, Joe! This way, on the run! *Pronto, hombre!*"

Joe came almost immediately, mounted on a scrawny mulish-looking horse, breaking an impatient way through the brush. His dark face still carried a frightened, furtive expression which had not been absent from it for a matter of days; not since a handful of raw gold had been spilled from his torn pocket.

"*Señor!*" he cried ringingly from a distance. "*Señor Caballero!* I tell you, they keel me! I got no chances! For sure, they keel me, robbers!"

Standing answered roughly: "And what do I care? Serve you right for the fool you are!"

"Now, he's here," said Winch. "Look here, Timber: you can take your time talking to him. Let me look you over. I want to see that second bullet hole."

"Winch, you idiot," Standing growled at him; "I got it close to a week ago. I've tended to it myself; it's all right. I don't look like a dying man, do I?"

"*Señor!*" Joe was crying, down on the ground now, tremendously excited.

"Are you usin' my salve?" demanded Winch. "Plenty of it, night and morning?"

"I have been using it...."

"And you're out of it *now*!" With a triumphant flourish Winch dipped into a pocket and extracted a small package. "Here you are, Timber! And this is extra special! I got all the ingredients this time; tried it out day before yesterday on that new pinto pony you bought from Ferguson; got cut in the wire fence down by the pasture. Say, it works like magic...."

Standing groaned. "Winch, some fine day I'll carve you all up with a hand-axe, just to give you a chance to use your own filthy mess...."

"I wouldn't have been shy a leg, would I, if that fool doctor had had a pint of this?"

"*Señor!*" Joe was crying. "You got to listen; you got to hear what I goin' tell you! My gold, my gold that I find, me, myself, all alone...."

"What do I care for you or your gold!" cried Standing. "I don't need it, do I? I don't ask you anything about it, do I? I don't want to know anything about it! Go wallow in your gold and leave me alone!"

But Joe explained, growing vehement to the point of wildness; as Winch had put it, "he was clean crazy over the thing." How could Joe wallow in it, much as he would like to, when always there were men like ugly hounds on his trail? What chance had he, poor devil that he styled himself, against such men as Jim Taggart and Young Gallup and Cliff Shipton and Babe Deveril and Barny McCuin.... He named a score. At the name of Babe Deveril Standing's eyes flashed and sped to a meeting with Lynette's; into hers, too, came a quick light. Joe had caught Standing's interest.

"What about these men?" he asked. "What about Deveril?"

"Him? The worst of them all!" wailed Joe. He went on, bursting with all the things he had to tell. That night when, for a second time, like God himself, the grand Señor Caballero had burst into the cabin and set him free, he had run! God, how he had run! But then he had thought of his savior alone against so many hard, merciless men; he had come to a sudden stop, saying to himself: "Joe, *mi amigo*, you must not desert him!" And then, of a sudden, had that young devil Deveril burst from the bushes upon him...and Joe had fled again and Deveril had sought after him. There was no shaking off this man; twice since then in the forest Joe had barely escaped him.... Lynette had come close, was listening breathlessly.

"I tell you where my gold is!" cried Joe. "You take what you like, I don't care! You give me what you like... I know you for one fair man. That way we save it. Any other way, they get me; they burn me with fire; they break my teeth and my fingers; they make me tell! And they get it all. Taggart and Gallup and Deveril and...."

He broke off, half whimpering, cursing them with all the eloquence of the Latin tongue.

Clearly Standing hesitated. Then, amazing them all, but with his own mind clear, he said bluntly:

"Clear out! It's your game. I don't want to know anything about it."

"*It's down in Light Ladies' Gulch!*" screamed Joe. "Not two mile from Big Pine! I lied to them...a big pine, with crooked roots sticking out...a washout.... Last year I make mistake; I think down under the Red Cliffs. But this time I find...four miles the other side...."

"Why, you shrivelled-souled...."

Then suddenly Standing caught himself up short; there came a new look into his eyes; he shouted, catching Joe by the shoulder:

"*Light Ladies'* Canyon! *Just* across from Big Pine? Only a mile or two!"

"As God hears me, Señor!"

Standing broke into sudden laughter. He clapped Joe upon the shoulder so that the little man staggered and paled under the jovial blow.

"With bells on! With bells, Mexico! By high Heaven.... Here, you, Winch! On the run, back to headquarters. Take Joe with you; mount guard over him night and day with a rifle. No man to have a word with him. And wait for me. And, all the while, Bill Winch, *keep your mouth shut*!"

Winch, with one arm out as a brace against a pine, stiffened.

"I guess I know how to take orders, Mr. Standing," he said, and his tone sounded angry. "You don't need...."

Him also Standing smote on the shoulder.

"Why, God bless you, Bill Winch, you're the only man on earth I'd trust! Those last words weren't necessary.... You're right and I apologize for them! But now, go! Go, I tell you; I'll do anything you say; I'll use your poison on me three times a day.... I'll eat it, if you say so! Only hit the high spots and keep Mexicali under cover until I come! No matter when or how long; there's your job...old friend!"

Billy Winch, galvanized, went hopping to his horse; he flipped after his own fashion up into the saddle; he loosened the rifle in its holster strapped conveniently; he called to Joe:

"Quick does it, Mexico! We're on our way!"

Bruce Standing watched them ride away among the trees and stood laughing! He had succeeded in puzzling two men; most of all had he set Lynette wondering....

CHAPTER 22

"I want a good long drink of fresh water," said Standing. "And you, after this lunch of ours, will be thirsty. Let's go down to the creek; down there, by the waterfall, after we've drunk, I want to talk with you."

He had turned to her, that flash still in his eyes, before Billy Winch and Mexicali Joe had ridden a dozen yards out of camp. She looked at him in silence, wondering what lay in his thoughts; what had been the sudden, compelling, and triumphant motive to actuate him when with his great shout of laughter he had dismissed the two men. He had Joe's secret now; she shared it herself: The gold was far from here and very near Big Pine; in Light Ladies' Canyon! The strange part of it was that Taggart's first surmise, when he and his companions had trapped Mexicali Joe at the dugout, was that it was in Light Ladies' Canyon that he had made his strike!... How many men and at least one girl had travelled how many wilderness miles from Big Pine, when the gold lay so snugly close to the starting-point! How Joe had tricked his captors, leading them so far afield!

"If I should escape from you now," Lynette could not help crying, "what is there to prevent me from staking the first claim? And bringing my *friends*... to stake claims!"

"If you should happen to escape me!" he laughed back at her.

Then he stepped to the tree where his rifle stood and called to Thor as he did always when he left the dog in camp: "Watch, Thor! Watch, sir."

It was not always that he carried his rifle. He explained, while he looked to her to come with him.

"We'll talk things over; but in any case it's clear that we're getting short of food. Maybe, while we talk, we can bring down something in the way of provisions with a lucky shot."

Willing enough was she today for talk; at least to listen to whatever he might say. She followed, stopping only to stoop and pat old Thor's head; already she counted the faithful brute a friend. Thor tried to lick her hand; for already Thor, like Thor's master, had bestowed an abiding love to the first true girl who had ever intimately entered the life of either. Thor wanted to follow; he whined and looked anxious, ears pricked forward, tail wagging.

"Down, Thor," commanded Standing, if only because already he had issued his command. "You watch camp for us; watch, Thor."

Thor dropped down at the entrance of Lynette's grotto; for one instant his great head lay between his forepaws; then he jerked it up again so that he might watch them as they went through the thickets to the creek.

Standing carried a cup with him. When they came to the waterfall leaping down a twenty-foot rocky spillway, glassily clear, making a pigmy thunder in the narrow-walled ravine, he rinsed and filled his cup and gave it to Lynette. She drank. Thereafter, and with no further rinsing, he drank. She sat upon a big rock, leaning back against a leaning tree trunk; he sat down close enough to her to allow of words carrying above the thunder of the falling waters and filled his after-lunch pipe.

"I know as much as you do of the place to find the gold!" she told him again. "And I, though a girl, have as much interest in a fortune to be made as any man can have. That's fair warning to you, Bruce Standing!"

He laughed carelessly. Then he said:

"It's neither your gold nor mine. By right of discovery, it belongs to a little shrimp named Mexicali Joe *Alguna-Cosa*. Our hands are off, so far as our own pockets are concerned."

"But…. You took quick interest when you learned where it was! You have some plan…you commanded your friend Billy Winch to keep Joe well guarded!"

His eyes were twinkling; and greed does not light twinkling lights!

"I've got gold of my own, girl! Gold enough to last me my life and you your life and both of us together our lives! And to leave a decent residuum after us…. But let's talk of Mexicali Joe's gold some other time. Today…. We have ourselves!"

"You have yourself!" cried Lynette with sudden bitterness. "I have not even my own personal liberty!"

"And what if I let you go, girl? As I have a mind to do today? What then? Where would you go? Where would I find you again? For find you I must and will though 'it were ten thousand mile.'"

"Am I to suffer your dictation during the days of actual imprisonment at your hands, and then, for all time afterward, render you an accounting of my actions!"

"Why do you try to hate me so, girl?"

"Why should I not hate you?"

"What have I done to you? Have I done anything more than put out a hand to stop time, to snatch time for you and me, for us to *know*!… Look you, girl, a man, at least a man of my sort, may go a third of his life or a fourth or a full half, and know much less than nothing of what a true girl is! *How can he know?* Already I have learned that you have instincts which leap; a man gropes like a blind mole and it takes him a long time to teach himself to see the stars…*the star!* Now it's a fair bet, and no odds given or taken, that one Bruce Standing happened to be an unruly devil, a blunt man, a man who has as a part and parcel of his religion to shoot square and to hit hard, so long as God lets him. I've done wrong and I've done right, and I'm doing as all the rest of the great mass, in a state of flux, is doing; growing up from the mud into something better. If not in this life or the next, well then, since the mills grind with exceeding patience, in some other life. At least I'm honest; at least, in plain English, I do my damnedest! Take it or leave it, there's the truth. If it happens that I'm a man of few friends.... Almost you can count 'em on Billy Winch's one leg!... if few men love me and many men hate...."

"Yes!" cried Lynette, and her own earnestness was caught and compelled by his own. "Most men, many, many men, hate you!... And yet you have it within you to make them love you!"

"Love and hate! What have I to do with the loves and hates of men as I know them? Shall I step to right or to left for all that? I play out my part in the eternal game. I live my life!"

"But you don't live your life! You miss...everything! If you would but be kind instead of cruel; open-hearted and generous always...you have in you the seeds of all that. Then men might come to know the real *you*; you could make them love instead of hate...."

But his eyes stabbed at her like quickened blue flames.

"So!" he said, and his tone was one of bitter mockery. "If I choose to pay them for the pretty, empty compliment, they will call me a good fellow and...love me! If I kick them they will call me villain and hate me. And there you have the epitome of that so-called love and hate of mankind which sickens me. I'll be eternally damned before I prostitute my immortal soul to pitch pennies out for a peck of treacherous hearts. For, I tell you, girl... Only Girl...the love that is to be bought is to be spat upon. I'll have none of it. Even your love, that I'd give my soul to have freely, I'd have none of if it were to be bought."

Lynette looked at him strangely, half pityingly. And she answered him softly:

"You twist things out of all reason to make, to yourself, your own acts appear something other than they are."

"A girl trying to turn logician?" he laughed at her, teasing.

Little effort on his part was required to set fire to her quick inflammable temper.

"It's magnanimous of you to jeer at me," she retorted hotly. "Because you have the physical strength of a beast and the beast's lack of understanding...."

Now his golden outburst of laughter stopped her. He shouted:

"See! There you go! As if to preach me the final word of love and hate! You'd hate me now, just because I tease you! If I said, with poets' roses twining through the saying, that you were most beautiful and no-end intellectual and beyond that of the heart of an angel, could you not better tolerate me?

And thus we come to the open pathway to most human loves and hates; two little doors standing side by side. For, I ask you, going back to your challenge to make men love rather than despise me, what in the devil's name is that sort of *love* but transplanted self-love? A damned-fool sort of selfishness masking like a hypocrite as something quite different.... If you loved a man who beat you there would be something worth while in that sort of loving; something divorced from plain selfishness and the eternal I-want-to-get-all-I-can-out-of-everything! Now, I love you! I love you so that my love for you comes near killing me! It gets me by the throat at night. That's love; and there's less of self in it, I swear to you, than there is of...y*ou!*"

"You! You talk of love. To me!"

She broke into her light, taunting laughter. And yet he had set her heart beating and the ancient fear...not fear of him...was upon her. "You, talking of love, are like a blind man lecturing on the colors of the rainbow! You...."

But he had started to his feet; his eyes went suddenly toward the camp, all sight of which they had lost on coming down into the creek bed.

"Listen!" he cried. "What was that?"

She had heard nothing; nothing above the splash and fall of water...and the beating of her own heart.

"Listen!" he said the second time.

"What is it?"

He caught up his rifle and leaped across the creek. He began running, back toward their camp.

"It's old Thor...there's someone...."

And now, Lynette realized clearly, had come her first opportunity to be free again! While Bruce Standing, because of something he had heard above the merry-mad music of the waterfall, or had thought he had heard, was running back to their encampment, she could run in the opposite direction. She stood balancing, of this mind and that. What had he heard in camp? What was happening there? As always, because of that volatile nature of hers which was *en rapport* with life's pulsings, she wanted to know! And then there was a certain assurance in her heart that after all these days the budding intention in Bruce Standing's heart was bursting into full flower to set her free again! She hesitated; she saw him running up the steep bank, charging back toward camp, vanishing among the trees higher up on the slope.

And, then, she followed him.

... Before Lynette came, through the trees, within sight of the grotto which Standing had given over to her, she heard a sound which brought her, wondering, from swift haste to lingering; she stood, her breathing stilled, listening, groping a moment blindly for an interpretation of that sound for its explanation. Harsh it was...terrible...never had she heard anything like it. At first she did not recognize it as a sound man-made. She paused; she came a step nearer, peering through the trees....

It was an inarticulate, stifled sound coming from the lips of Bruce Standing! He was kneeling on the ground, bending forward. He had dropped his rifle. There was something in his arms, upgathered into his embrace, something held as a baby is held in its mother's arms....

Thor....

And those sounds from Bruce Standing's lips! There were tears in them; his voice was shaken. He held Thor to him in a fierce agony of sorrow....

Lynette came closer, tiptoeing. She heard the sounds as they seemed to choke him, clutching like hands at his throat. And then suddenly, before she caught her first clear view, she knew when, into that first emotion there swept the second; when with the shock of deep grief there mingled white-hot rage. He began to mutter again...he was lisping...lisping as she had heard him do only once before...lisping because his one weakness had leaped out and caught him unaware. Lisping curses....

She ran closer. She saw old Thor, Thor who had learned to love her and whom she had learned to love, lying limp in Standing's arms. Thor dead? Some one had killed him, then, and Standing, above the booming of the waterfall, had heard? A sight, perhaps, to stir that wild, uncontrollable laughter of Lynette! The sight of a big, strong man half weeping over a dead dog in his arms.... Yet, when she came running to him and dropped down on her knees and put out her quick hand and Standing turned his face toward her...he saw that this time there was no laughter in her. Instead, her eyes were wet with a sudden dash of tears.

"He's not dead...we won't have it that he's dead! Thor!" she cried softly.

She did not realize that she had put her warm, sympathetic hand on Standing's arm before her other hand found the old dog's head.

"Thor!... Thor!"

Thor looked up at her; at Standing. The dog tried to stir; the faithful tongue strove to overmaster the terrible inertia laid upon it; to grant in last adulation the last farewell. For a stricken dog, like a stricken man, knows after the way of all creatures which have the spark of eternity within them, when the day's end is in doubt....

Standing tried to speak...and grew silent. How she hated herself then for that other time when he had slipped, through sorrowing rage, into his one unmanly failing...and she had laughed! Her tears began running down. He saw; he jerked his head about, focussing his eyes upon the eyes of a dog that he loved; a dog that had been faithful to him.

"Where is he hurt? He can't be shot," cried Lynette. "We would have heard a shot! If he is poisoned...."

Standing had mastered himself. He said coldly.

"Look!"

"Who did...*that*?"

"If I only knew! My God, if I only knew!"

Thor was not dead; his body jerked and quivered now and again, in spasms. Yet he seemed to be dying. And it grew clear to Lynette, as, at a glance, it had been clear to Standing, what had happened. Thor had been left in charge of camp; but the one word had rung in the faithful head: "Watch!" And then someone had come; Thor had been true to his trust; some man had struck him down with club or a rifle barrel; had struck and struck again. Thor's fore leg was broken; he had been battered over the head…bones were broken, the skull seemed crushed…the dog stiffened; fell back….

"Dying," said Standing, still on his knees. He placed old Thor very gently on the ground, striving after his own rough fashion to make a dog's last few minutes of breathing no more tormenting than was inevitable.

"Thor," said Standing gently. "Good old Thor!"

The dog tried to rouse. The old faithful head on Standing's knee stirred ever so little. The old steadfast eyes, red-rimmed but clear-sighted, were on Standing's. If ever a dog could have spoken….

Standing, with sudden thought, jumped to his feet.

"There's a chance for him yet! There is Billy Winch, the one man on earth to save a dying dog or horse…. Yes, or man!"

He cupped his hands at his mouth and sent forth, piercing through the leafy silences, that wild wolf-call which must bring Winch about in short order…if he was not already too far to hear it.

"He may be too far," cried Lynette. Already she was down upon her knees, taking his place and gathering Thor's head into her lap. "Hurry. If you can find your horse and ride after him, surely you can overtake him."

"God bless you!" He began running. But before a dozen swift steps were taken he stopped and came back to her, muttering: "But the man who did this for Thor? He'll not be far away; I can't leave you…."

"I am not afraid of a man like him," said Lynette. "A coward, or he would not have done this…. Leave me your rifle and hurry!"

"You'll wait for me, no matter what happens?"

"Of course I'll wait. Now, *hurry*!"

He placed his rifle at her side and with never a backward look was away again on a run, breaking through breast-high brush; splashing once again across the creek, calling to Winch as he ran…. He would be back with her almost immediately….

So he plowed through the thickets; plunged down a slope, sped up a slope, raced over a ridge. And, now with what breath was left in his lungs, he began to send out his whistled call. That summons, which his horse, if still lingering in these upland meadows, would welcome with quick response.

Lynette stooped and laid her cheek against the grizzled old face of Thor. And then, with a sudden access of emotion, she burst into fresh tears…. Thor tried to wag his tail…. Lynette, like Standing before her, felt that the dog was dying.

"Thor!" she whispered. "Can't you hold on? Can't you carry on? He will bring Billy Winch and Billy Winch will help us…."

Then there burst upon her a surprise which moved her immeasurably. There, almost at her side, stood Babe Deveril! A moment ago she was alone in the wilderness with a dying dog; now Babe Deveril stood close to her. With Thor's head still held in her lap she looked up into his face. She saw that it was tense, the muscles drawn, the eyes hard and bright.

"Lynette!" he cried softly. "Lynette! I've followed you half around the world! And now…. Come quick! We go free and the world is ours!"

She sat, staring up at him, still bewildered.

"You!" she whispered. "And…then it was you…who did this?"

He caught her meaning; he glanced down at the thick green club in his hands.

"I came to do what I could for you. That ugly brute stood up against me. I had no gun; I knew Standing was armed. I thought that maybe he had left his rifle in camp."

"What did Thor do to you that you should have done this to him?"

"Thor? That dog? He showed teeth and…look here, Lynette Brooke; now's your one chance. I've gone through hell to come to you…."

"Tell me," she cried. "When did you come?…"

Deveril was as tense as a finely drawn steel wire. Again she marked that hard glint in his dark eyes.

"It is up to you to do the telling!" he shot back at her. "I stood back there in the trees; I saw that damned henchman of his and Mexicali Joe come up to you! Joe, I've been following for days! I had no rifle; no weapon of any kind and both Standing and Winch were armed. But I could watch! Joe was terribly excited; I saw his waving arms. I heard him yelling…."

"Yes," said Lynette. "And then?"

"And then?" exclaimed Deveril. "What then? You know what we came for, don't you? You as well as I?"

"Yes! I know…."

He caught at her hand.

"Come! On the run. Before that madman gets back. We'll clean up on the whole crowd of them!"

But she jerked her hand away.

"There are certain things I don't understand…. Did you see the other night when he took Mexicali Joe out of their hands?"

"I saw; yes. It happened that I had just overhauled them at that minute! I could have cried for rage! He had a rifle, damn him, and was aching to use it! They laid down before him like pups…."

"*And you?*"

"What could I do, with a rotten stick in my hands!"

She looked up at him curiously.

"And, today?"

"Today?" His hands hardened in his grip upon his club. "Today, I tell you, I followed them into your camp and I saw. Mexicali Joe...."

"You are after Mexicali Joe's gold, Babe Deveril?"

"As you are! That brought us both into Big Pine in the beginning and then into the rest of it."

"And you were...afraid to come into camp while Bruce Standing was still here?"

He laughed at her, the old light laughter of debonair Babe Deveril.

"Afraid? Call it that if you like." He shrugged carelessly. "Yet, with an oak club against a man with a modern rifle...."

"Do you remember the last time? How he threw his rifle away?"

Deveril flushed hotly.

"Some day," he muttered, "when it's an even break...."

"What do you want with me, Babe Deveril?"

He stared at her.

"Want with you? I want you to come, to be free from this Timber-Wolf. Is he coming back soon?"

"I think so."

"Then hurry. Lynette...."

"Well?"

"Are you coming?"

She stooped over Thor.

"No," she said quietly.

"*What!* After all this.... You're not coming?"

"No!"

"But.... Then why?" he demanded with a sudden flare of anger.

"For one thing," she told him without looking up, "because I told him that I would wait for him. For another...."

"And that is?..."

She only shook her head, brown hair tumbling about her hidden face.

"I'll stay with old Thor," she said.

She had him cast away among the lost isles of bewilderment.

"But you'll tell me.... You and I have been friends; we've stood side by side...." He broke off to demand: "You'll tell me about Mexicali Joe's gold?"

"Gold?" she said. "Is gold the greatest thing in life?"

"But you know?"

"Yes! I know."

"Then listen: Taggart and Gallup and Shipton and a thousand other men are going crazy to find out! You and I can turn the whole trick if luck is good.... Why, we'll quit millionaires, Lynette!"

A shudder shot through the tortured body of old Thor. Lynette's long lashes lifted, wet with her tears.

"There are things…beyond millions…."

"I don't get you today!"

"Why did you kill this dog? What good did it do you? What harm had he ever done you?"

"He was in my way. I thought, I told you, that a rifle might have been left behind. And…it's Standing's dog, anyway! And, beyond that, no matter how you look at it, only a dog…."

"I think," said Lynette, and there was no music in her voice now and no warmth in the eyes which she lifted briefly to his, "that you had better go! Had you come, without rifle, upon Bruce Standing, at least he would have thrown his rifle away to fight with you! You know that. And…and I am not going to go with you, having given my promise. And I'll warn you of this: If he comes back and finds you here and knows you for the man who killed Thor…. He will kill you!"

Never in all his daredevil life had Babe Deveril made pretense at striking the angelic attitude. Now, in a rush of feeling, he grew black with anger and there came a look into his eyes which put the hottest flush of all her life into Lynette's cheeks, as he cried out:

"Tamed you, has he? So Timber-Wolf has taken a mate after the fashion of wolves! And I, fool that I was, let you slip through my fingers!"

She did not answer him. Had she answered she could have said: "You could have returned to fight with him; man to man and him wounded! Later, when he snatched Mexicali Joe from them, you could have fought with him. You could have followed him here, seeking me; and you followed Joe, seeking gold. You could have fought with him today; and instead you held back and spied and killed his dog and waited for him to go!…" So Lynette, stooping low over Thor's battered head, made no answer.

… She knew that Babe Deveril was no coward. She would always remember how he had hurled that gun into Taggart's face and himself into her adventures, reckless and unafraid. Yet Babe Deveril was no such man as Bruce Standing; rather was he like a Jim Taggart, and Taggart was no coward. But it remained that both these men, Deveril and Taggart, were afraid to come to grips with that other man, whose fellows named him Timber-Wolf. And he, the Timber-Wolf, was not afraid of life and all that it bore; and was not afraid of sombre death, in which he did not believe; was not afraid of God, in whom he trusted.

"You've thrown in with him!" Deveril cried it out angrily; his hands were hard upon his club. "Here, I've given days and days trying to see you through, and you've kicked in with him against me! He's had his will with you and he's made you his woman and…."

"You'd better go!"

She was trembling. A spasm shook her, not unlike that which convulsed Thor.

"You won't come with me then? You'll stick with him? After he put a chain on you!"

"At least he did not stand back and see another man put a chain on me!"

"Is that my answer?"

"Yes!" she cried in sudden fury. "And now...*go!*"

"I'll go, all right," said Deveril. And began to laugh. All that old light laughter of his, gay and untroubled, which so many a time had made dancing echoes in the souls of those who heard, bubbled up again. He looked, as he had done when first she saw him, a slender, darkly handsome and utterly care-free incarnation of debonair insolence. Still striking the right note, he shrugged his shoulders and tossed his club away as he said insolently:

"What need of all this heavy artillery...since the Queen of my Heart says Nay? I'll travel light after this!"

He turned away. But at the second step he stopped and swung about and told her:

"I have a guess where Billy Winch will be taking Mexicali Joe! And I'll be in on the final settlement. If you, with a rush of blood to the head, throw in with Standing, I'll play the game out! And what will you have left to trade to me for the pile I'm going to make out of this?... For I heard, too, when Mexicali yelled out! And I'm throwing in with Taggart and Gallup, headed straight for Light Ladies' Gulch!"

Lynette, unable to see anything in all the wide world clearly, could only stoop her head over the stricken dog. Her arms tightened about Thor.... If only Billy Winch would come in time, if only Billy Winch would save that flickering little fire of life...then, though she hated all the rest of the world she'd love Billy Winch....

CHAPTER 23

Bruce Standing running, breaking a straight path through the brush, came swiftly into the little upper valley. When in answer to his whistling his horse came trotting up to him, he did not tarry to saddle; he had picked up his bridle on his way and now mounted and struck off bareback through the woods with no second's delay.

"Get into it, Daylight!" he muttered. "We're riding for old Thor today!"

From a distance Billy Winch, hurrying homeward, heard that long call he knew so well. He pulled his horse down from a steady canter and turned, calling to Mexicali Joe to come back with him. Once within sight Standing waved and shouted again; Winch and Joe sensed urgency and dipped their spurs, riding back to a meeting with him. Winch stared and frowned while his employer made his curt explanation; Mexicali Joe gasped. But neither man had a word to say; Standing laid his brief command upon them and the three turned back, riding hard, into the mountains.

Again Standing called, when near enough to camp to hope that his voice would carry above the noise of the tumbling waterfalls; this time to Lynette, to tell her of their coming. He rode ahead; again and again he shouted to her; he leaned out to right and left from his horse's back, seeking a glimpse of her through the trees. And yet, when they were almost in the camp, there still came no answer to his shoutings and he caught no glimpse of her.... Suddenly, to his fancies, the woods seemed strangely hushed—and empty.

"She's gone," said Winch carelessly.

"No!" said Standing with such brusque emphasis that Winch looked at him wonderingly. "She said she'd wait for us, Bill."

But when they drew closer, so close that the various familiar camp objects were revealed, and still there was no response and no sight of her, Winch muttered:

"Just the same, gone or not gone, she ain't here, Timber."

"I tell you, man," snapped Standing, "she said she would wait. And what she says she will do, she will do!"

Now the three dismounted in the heart of the camp and still there was no sign of Lynette.

"Anyhow," said Winch, "it's a dog and not a girl we come looking for. Thor'll be here...if he's alive yet."

"He will be right where I left him." Standing led the way among the big trees, an arm about Billy Winch, hopping at his side the last few steps; they saw him looking in all directions and understood that while he led them toward Thor he was seeking the girl. But they found only the dog lying where he had been struck down; Thor barely able to lift his bloody head, his sight dim, but his dog's intelligence telling him that his master had come back to him; Thor whining weakly. Winch squatted down at the dog's side, become upon the instant an impressive diagnostician.

Standing stood a moment over the two, looking down upon them. Then he turned away, leaving Thor in the skilful hands of Winch and hurrying down to the creek, seeking Lynette. It was possible, he told himself, that she had gone down for a drink; that so near the waterfall she had not heard him calling. So he called again as he went on and looked everywhere for her.

But she was not down by the creek and she did not answer him from the woods. He came back, up into camp, perplexed. Winch was still bending over Thor; he was snapping out brusque orders to Joe for hot water and soap; Standing heard Mexicali Joe's mutterings:

"*Por Dios*, I no understan'. Somebody hurt one dog an' we wait, an' we look for one girl...an' all the time I got one meelion dollar gol'-mine down yonder...."

"Shut up," Winch grunted at him. And, seeing Standing coming back: "Say, Timber, we better take this dog home with us right away. We can make a sling of that canvas of yours, tying either end to our saddle horns, making a sort of stretcher; some blankets in it and old Thor on top of 'em. And I'll tell you this: if we get him home alive, and I think we will, I'll keep the life in him."

Thor was whining piteously; Winch shook his head; if only he had his instruments, his antiseptics, and a bottle of chloroform! For here he foresaw such an operation as did not come his way every day.

"Diagnosin' off-hand," Winch was telling the uninterested Joe, "I'd say here's the two important facts: first, old Thor has been beat unmerciful; his head's been whanged bad, but I don't believe the skull's fractured; his left fore leg is busted and he may have a cracked rib. Second and most important, after all that the old devil is alive."

Bruce Standing, still seeking Lynette, more than satisfied to have Thor in Billy Winch's capable hands, turned toward the grotto which he had set apart for Lynette. And thus upon his first discovery. There was a piece of paper tied with a bit of string so that it fluttered gently from a low limb where it was inevitable that it must be seen. He caught it down eagerly. On the scrap of paper were a few pencilled words, written in a girlish-looking hand. At one sweeping glance he read:

"I have gone back to Babe Deveril.

LYNETTE."

He stood staring incredulously at the thing in his hand. Here was a shock which for a moment confused him; here was something beyond credence. Lynette gone...to Deveril? For that first second his brain groped blindly rather than functioned normally. Lynette gone to Babe Deveril...that cursed Baby Devil! A handsome, graceful, and altogether irresistible young devil of a fellow to fill any girl's eye, to stir vague romantic longings in her heart. So she had gone to him? He had the proof of it in his hand; a word from her, signed with her name. A cruel, chill, heartless message of seven meagre words.... And she had broken her word; she had promised to wait for his return and she had not waited. She had left a dying dog to die alone and had gone to her lover...and she carried with her the key to Mexicali Joe's golden secret...to turn it over to Deveril!

"What's eating you, Timber?" shouted Winch. "Gone to sleep or what?"

Standing tossed the scrap of paper away. And then suddenly he laughed and both Winch and Joe were startled. Bill Winch had heard that laugh once before and knew vaguely the sort of emotion which prompted it: Standing's soul was suddenly steeped in rage...and anguish....

"We'll be on our way pretty quick, Timber," said Winch. "We'll ride slow and you can pick us up in no time. And…if you've got anything on your chest, any of your own private rat-killing to do, why, me and Mexicali will make out fine as far as headquarters, and once there I'll see old Thor through."

Standing only nodded at him curtly and went hurriedly to his horse.

CHAPTER 24

Timber-Wolf, his purposes crystallizing, did not attempt to rejoin Winch and Mexicali Joe. By the time he had ridden to the spot where his saddle was hidden and had thrown it upon Daylight's back, drawing his cinch savagely, he had begun to get his proper perspective. He knew that he could trust Billy Winch in all things; that Winch, with all of that persevering patience which the occasion demanded and that veterinary skill and love for animals which marked him, would do all that any man could to get Thor home and to care for him. And now, for Bruce Standing, beyond the stricken dog lay other considerations: There remained Lynette and Babe Deveril! He ground his teeth in savage rage and from Daylight's first leap under him rode hard.

Long before the early sun rose he was back at his own headquarters, a man grim and hard and purposeful. Rough garbed and still booted he strode through his study and into his larger office; and in this environment the man's magnificent virility was strikingly accentuated. Here was his wilderness home, a place of elegance and of palpitant centres of numerous large activities; not a dozen miles from Big Pine and yet, in all appearances, set apart from Young Gallup's crude town as far as the ends of earth. He stood in a great, hard-wooded room of orderly tables and desks and telephones and electric push-buttons. He set an impatient thumb upon a button; at the same moment his other hand caught up a telephone instrument. While the push-button still sent its urgent message he caught a response from his telephone. Into the receiver he called sharply:

"Bristow? In a hurry, Standing speaking: Give me the stables; get Billy Winch!"

All the while that insistent thumb of his upon the button! There came bursting into the big room, half dressed and clutching at his clothes, a young man whose eyes were still heavy with sleep.

"You, Graham," Standing commanded him. "Get busy on our long-distance wire. My lawyers…. Get Ben Brewster! It's the hurry of a lifetime!"

Young Graham, with suspenders dragging, flew to the switchboard. Meantime came a response from the inter-phone connecting him with the stables.

"Billy Winch?" he called.

"No, sir, Mr. Standing," said a voice. "This is Dick Ross. Bill, he got in late and was up all night nearly, working over a bad case that come in. Shall I...."

"That case," Standing told him abruptly, "was my dog, Thor. Find out who was left in charge when Bill went to sleep; call me right away and give me a report on Thor." With that he rang off.

All the while his secretary, Graham, had been plugging away at his switchboard. Standing, pacing up and down, heard his "Hello—hello—hello."

Within three minutes the stable telephone rang sharply. Standing caught it up. It was Dick Ross again, reporting:

"Bill didn't go off the case until three o'clock this morning. Had to operate again at about two; taking out a little piece of skull bone. He left Charley Peters in charge then; Charley's on the job now."

"Thor's alive then?"

"Yes, sir."

"Fine! I'll be out in a few minutes to see him. Bill's got him in the 'hospital'?"

"Sure, Mr. Standing. Thor couldn't be gettin' better care if he was King of England."

Standing rang off and came back to Graham from whose eyes now all heaviness of sleep had fled, leaving them keen and quick. Hardly more than a youngster, this Graham, and yet Timber-Wolf's confidential secretary, trained by Standing himself to Standing's ways.

"I've got Mr. Brewster's home on the wire," said Graham looking up. "He's not up yet but they're calling him...."

Standing took the instrument.

"I'll hold it for him. Now, Graham, order breakfast served here for you and me; plenty of extra coffee for the boys I'll be having in.... Get Al Blake on our wire to Red Creek Mine.... Arrange to have Bill Winch show up here as soon as he's awake; he's to bring Ross and Peters with him.... And Mexicali Joe; make sure that Joe didn't see anyone to talk with last night. I want Joe here with Winch.... Hello! Hello! Is this Ben Brewster?"

He heard his lawyer's voice over the wire; then, somewhere over the long line something went wrong; Brewster was gone again. An operator at the end of Standing's own private part of the line, seventy-five miles away, was saying:

"Just a minute, Mr. Standing... I'll get him for you...."

"Thanks, Henry," said Standing. And while he waited for the promised service which was to link him with a man nearly two hundred miles away, he was working hastily with pencil and pad. Graham was already carrying out his string of orders, getting dressed with one hand meantime.

"Brewster?" Standing spoke again into the telephone. "I've got something big and urgent on. Can you come up right away? Take a car to Placer Hill. I'll have a man meet you there with a saddle-horse, and you'll have to ride the last twenty miles in. We're forming a new mining company; I want to shoot it through one-two-three! Bring what papers we'll want; that will be all the baggage you need to stop for. Graham will have all particulars ready for you. Thanks, Ben. So long.

"Graham!"

Graham swung about expectantly.

"Get the stables. A couple of the best horses...."

"I've already got them," said Graham.... It was for such reasons that Graham, though a youngster, could hold so difficult position as private secretary to Bruce Standing, Timber-Wolf.

Al Blake was Standing's mining expert, general superintendent of all his mining interests and the one source to which he applied for advice on all mining matters. He was the highest salaried man on the extensive pay-roll and the shrewdest. In a few minutes Graham announced that he had the Red Creek Mine on the wire and that Blake was coming.

"I want you here on the jump, Al," said Standing. "And I need forty of our best men; scare up as many as you can at your diggings; I can fill the number down here. Just *good* men, understand? Men you know; men who at a pinch will fight like hell; every man with a rifle."

"Sounds like St. Ives!" grunted Blake, wide awake by now. "All right. I'm on my way in ten minutes."

Standing began pacing up and down again, his eyes frowning. He needed Billy Winch right now; needed him the worst way. For here was work to be done of the sort which invariably he placed in Winch's capable hands. But Winch had had a night of it and Standing was not the man to overlook that fact as long as he could put his hand on another man who would do....

"Have Dick Ross up, on the run," he told Graham.

Breakfast came, served on big massive trays by the Japanese servant. Almost at the same moment, and literally on the run, Dick Ross came in.

"Scare up ten good men for me, Ross. With rifles, all ready to ride. I'll have breakfast ready for them here." Graham caught the alert eye of the Japanese who set down his trays hurriedly and with a quick nod raced off to the kitchen. Standing looked sternly at Ross and said curtly: "I'm handing you a job that would usually go to Winch, Ross, but he's asleep...."

"He was just getting up again, Mr. Standing. Said he wanted to see for himself how Thor was pulling along...."

"Then," said Standing, "hop back and tell Winch what I said. He can tell you the men to pick...or, if he's busy working with Thor he can leave it to you. Of course I want you to be of the number; Peters also if Winch doesn't need him; Winch, too, if he says the word...."

Standing and Graham ate standing up. Men summoned began coming in. Each of them was given brief clean-cut orders and allowed brief time to gulp a hot breakfast. Billy Winch came first, bringing with him Mexicali Joe.

"He's going to be all right, *I think*," said Winch by way of greeting, and Standing understood that he was reporting on Thor. "I never saw man or animal worse shot-all-to-hell, either. I got him in bed now, strapped down; he's conscious this morning and had a fair night, all things considered. There's nothing more to be done right away, just be kept quiet...."

"I was coming out in a minute...."

"I can't have folks running in on him, Timber," said Winch, with a slow shake of the head, mumbling over a mouthful of ham and egg. "But if you'd just run in on him one second, to sort of let him know you was with him, you know, and then beat it, it might do him good."

"Can you leave for two or three hours? To go down with Al Blake and some of the boys to stake a string of mining claims down in Light Ladies' Gulch?"

"That's why the rifles?" said Winch. "Sure, I can go, leaving Charley Peters with full instructions. But I'll have to be back in, say, four hours at latest."

Standing turned to Mexicali Joe.

"Joe," he said, "how many friends have you got that we can put on the pay-roll for a few days at twenty-five dollars a day? To stake claims down in the Gulch?"

"*Jesus Maria!*" gasped Joe. "Twenty-five dollars a day? For each man? There would be one meelion men, Señor Caballero...."

"Take him in tow, Graham! Get a list of names from him, men to be reached in an hour's ride. As many as you can get, twenty or thirty or forty. And get them here...quick."

Al Blake arrived from the Red Creek Mine. Stringing along after him came a dozen men of his choosing; big, uncouth, unshaved, rough-looking customers to the last man of them and yet...as Standing and Blake agreed... *all good men!* Good to carry out orders; to put up a fight against odds; to hang on and fight to the last ditch. Graham saw to it that every man Jack of them was fed and had his cigar from the Chief's private stock. The men grouped outside and looked at one another, but for the greater part wasted little breath in speculations and questionings, each realizing that his fellows knew as little as himself.

It was a busy morning for Bruce Standing. Yet three times he found the time...rather he made it...to go out to the "hospital" to stand over old Thor and speak softly to him. Thor lay upon a white-enamelled bed; his bed was softened for him by many downy pillows; at the bedside sat Charley Peters, his face as grave, his eye as watchful, as could have been had it been Timber-Wolf himself who lay there. And when Standing came in Thor heard his step and tried to move; tried to lift his poor battered head. But at the master's low voice, "Down, Thor! Down, sir…good old dog!" Thor lay back and his tired sigh was like the sigh of a man. Standing's big hand rested gently upon the old fellow…then Standing went out, walking softly and Thor lay still a very long while, waiting for him to come again….

Al Blake left within fifteen minutes of his arrival, a little army of armed men at his back. With him, on the fastest horse in Standing's stables, rode a man whose sole responsibility was to race back with word of conditions. Fully Standing counted on hearing that already at least two claims had been staked. But he was not ready to see Lynette again so soon; he was not ready yet to see Babe Deveril. Never for a single instant since seeing that bit of paper hung to a tree with a girl's mockery upon it, had he doubted that this girl, whom he had thought that he loved, had cast in with the Baby Devil, the two racing side by side to steal Mexicali Joe's gold. He had said to Al Blake:

"Put them off…but don't hurt either of them. Leave them to me."

Attorney Ben Brewster, a man much shaken, arrived in record time. He could scarcely speak a word until Graham poured out for him a generous glass of whiskey. Then he glared at Standing as though he would highly enjoy killing him.

"You've got a fee to pay this trip," he groaned, "that will make you sit up and stretch your eyes! Good God, man…."

"Give him another drink, Graham," said Standing. "He's a lawyer and there's no danger of such getting drunk!… Curse your fees, Brewster. What do I care so you make an iron-clad job of it."

"And the job?"

Graham saw that he had a cigar.

"Something crooked!" muttered Brewster. "I'll bet a hat!"

"Otherwise," jeered Standing, "why send for you!… Now shut up, Ben, and get that infected brain of yours working. Here's the tale."

Ben Brewster, a man who knew his business…and his client…went into action. That day he took in businesslike shape all possible steps toward forming a new corporation, The Mexicali Joe Gold Mining Company.

"Lord, what a fool name!" he growled.

"Never mind the name," retorted Standing.

During the day many other men came in; among them no less than seventeen swarthy men of Mexicali Joe's breed. Brewster took signatures, and the men, showing their glistening white teeth, knew nothing of what was happening save that each man of them was to draw twenty-five dollars a day for driving a stake and sitting snug over it, rifle in hand and cigarette in mouth! Brewster got other signatures going down to Light Ladies' Gulch and among the men there. In all, he signed names of about sixty men. The Mexicali Joe Gold Mining Company was born. And the greater part of the stock, and the magnificently shining title of president was invested in…Mexicali Joe! Suddenly, though all day he had been a man as dark-browed as a thunder-storm, Standing burst out into that golden laughter of his. Not a single share in his name; all immediate expenses to be paid by him, and they were to be heavy; and yet he counted himself the man to draw a full ninety-nine percent of the dividends of sheer triumph! For it was to be a cold shut-out to Taggart and Gallup and Shipton and all Big Pine! And, most of all, for Babe Deveril and that girl! For early had come back the report from Al Blake: "Neither of them here; no claims staked!"

Standing could only estimate that the girl had misunderstood; that, hearing Joe's description of the place, she had not grasped the true sense of his words. He lingered over the picture of her and Deveril, hastening, driving their stakes somewhere else!

When Mexicali Joe came to understand, after much eloquence from Graham, how matters stood…how he swaggered! This, a day in a lifetime, was Mexicali Joe's day.

"Me, I'm President!"

President of a gold-mining company! Mexicali Joe! And of a real mine; for Al Blake had sent back the curt word: "He's got it; he's got a mine that I'd advise you to buy in for a hundred thousand while you can. It may run to anything. The best thing I've seen up here anywhere!"

Mexicali Joe on the high-road to become a millionaire…through the efforts of Bruce Standing.

To be sure, Joe, a man very profoundly bewildered, more dumfounded even than elated, took never a single step and said never a single word without going first to his friend "Señor Caballero." Before the end of that glorious day Joe was dead-drunk; didn't know "whether he was afoot or horseback." But in his crafty Latin way, he kept his mouth shut.

And then Bruce Standing, with an eye not to further wealth, but toward the confounding of all hopes of such as Young Gallup and Jim Taggart and Babe Deveril…*and a certain girl*…sprang his coup. With Ben Brewster guarding his rear in every advance, he "swallowed whole," as Brewster put it, every bit of available land above and below and on every side of Joe's claims. He recked neither of present difficulties and expenses nor of lawsuits to come. He wanted the land…and he got it! And he issued his proclamation:

"There's a *town* there, on Light Ladies' Gulch. You don't see it? It's there!… *Graham, get busy!* A contractor; lumber; building materials; carpenters! We build a town as big as Big Pine and we build it faster than ever a town grew before! A store, blacksmith shop, hotel. Shacks of all sorts. *Graham!*"

Graham, like a man with an electric current shot through him, jumped out of his chair.

"Send a man on the run to Big Pine with a message for Young Gallup! And the message is this: '*Bruce Standing promised to pull your damned town down about your ears…and the pulling has begun!*'"

"Yes, Mr. Standing," said Graham. And sent a man on a running horse.

And then took swift dictation. Standing made a budget of fifty thousand dollars, as a "starter." Even Graham wondered what impulses were rioting in his mad heart!

"We want scrapers and ploughs, a crew of road-makers! We build a new road…*on this side of Light Ladies' Gulch*! Got the idea, Graham? We cut Big Pine out. We go by them, giving a shorter road to the outside, a better road. We boycott Gallup's dinky town! Keep in mind we'll double that first fifty thousand any time we need to. Get this word around: 'Any man who buys a nickel's worth of tobacco in Big Pine can't buy anything, even if he has his pockets full of clinking gold, in our town! No man, once seen setting his foot down in Gallup's town, is going to be tolerated two minutes in our town.' Get the idea, Graham?"

"Yes, Mr. Standing!"

Standing smote him then so mightily upon the shoulder that Graham, a small man, went pale, shot through with pain.

"Raise your own salary, Graham. *And earn it now!*"

CHAPTER 25

What Bruce Standing could not know was that those few words signed *Lynette* and saying with such cruel curtness: "I have gone back to Babe Deveril," had been written not by Lynette, but by Deveril himself. Nor could he know that Lynette had not gone freely but under the harsh coercion of four men.

Deveril, when Lynette refused to go with him, had hurried away through the woods, his heart burning with jealous rage. Was the hated Timber-Wolf to win again, not only in the game for gold but in another game which was coming to be the one greatest consideration in Babe Deveril's life?

"Not while I live!" he muttered to himself over and over. And once out of sight of Lynette who still sat bowed over the dog he had struck down, he broke into a run. Jim Taggart and Gallup and Cliff Shipton were not so far away that he could not hope to reach them and to bring them back before Standing returned.

Thus, not over fifteen minutes before Bruce Standing came back, bringing Billy Winch and Mexicali Joe with him, Deveril had appeared before Lynette a second time. And now she leaped to her feet, seeing who his companions were and reading at one quick glance what lay unhidden in their faces. Greed was there and savage gloating and mercilessness; she knew that at least three of those men would stamp her into the ground under their heavy boots if thus they might walk over her body through the golden gates of Mexicali Joe's secret.

"You're arrested!" cried Taggart. "Come, get a move on. We clear out of this on the run!"

"It was you who shot him, not I! And I'll not go with you. In a minute he'll be back...."

Taggart was of no mind for delay and talk; he caught her roughly by the arm. Her eyes went swiftly to Deveril's; of his look she could make nothing. He shrugged and said only:

"Taggart's sheriff; he'll take you along, anyway. You might as well go without a fuss."

Gallup, his face ugly with the emotions swaying him, was at her other side. She looked to the hawk-faced man and then away with a shudder. Then, trying to jerk away, she screamed out:

"Help! Bruce...."

Taggart's big hairy hand was over her mouth.

"Come along," he commanded angrily. "Get a move on."

Half dragging her the first few steps they led her out of camp, down into the canyon and across among the trees. She gave over struggling; they watched her so that she could not call again; Taggart threatened to stuff his dirty bandana handkerchief into her mouth. Deveril alone held back for a little; she did not know what he was doing; did not see him as he wrote in a hand which he strove to give a girlish semblance those few words to which he signed her name. She scarcely marked his delay; she was trying now to think fast and logically.

These men were brutes, all of them; she had had ample evidence of that already and had that evidence been lacking the information was there emblazoned in their faces. Even Babe Deveril, in whom once she had trusted, began to show the brutal lining of his insolent character. And yet need she be afraid of any of them just now? If she openly thwarted them, yes. They would show no mercy to a girl. But at the moment their thoughts were set not upon her undoing, but upon Mexicali Joe's gold. And she knew where it was and they knew that she knew.... Taggart was speaking, growling into her ear:

"We followed Mexicali; we saw him come up here; Deveril followed him into camp. He told where his gold was. And you heard it all!"

"Well?" said Lynette, striving with herself for calmness. She was thinking: "If only I can have a little time. He will come for me.... If only I can have a little time."

"What do you mean by that?" demanded Taggart. "The whole earth ain't Joe's because he picked up a nugget or two. Anybody's got a right to stake a claim; I got a right and so has the boys...and so have you."

"Suppose," offered Lynette as coolly as she could, "that I refused to tell?"

There came a look into Taggart's hard eyes which answered her more eloquently than any words from the man could have done, which put certain knowledge and icy fear into her.

Always, when nervous or frightened, Lynette's laughter came easily to her and now without awaiting any other answer from this man she began laughing in such a fashion as to perplex him and bring a dragging frown across his brows.

"Are you going to tell us?" he asked.

"If I do," she temporized, "do I have the chance to drive the first stakes?"

"By God, yes! And say, little one, you're a peach into the bargain."

She did not appear to hear; she was thinking over and over: "Bruce Standing will come after us as soon as he finds I am gone. I must gain a little time, that is all."

If only she could make them think that the gold was somewhere near by so that Standing must readily find them. But now Deveril had rejoined them and she recalled how he had heard something, though not all, of Joe's triumphant announcement. For Joe had shouted out at the top of his voice, to catch and hold Timber-Wolf's attention: "Light Ladies' Gulch!" Deveril had heard that; and Light Ladies' Gulch was many miles away, down toward Big Pine....

Deveril was looking at her with eyes which were bright and hard and told no tales of the man's thoughts.

"This lovely and altogether too charming young woman," Deveril said lightly, his eyes still upon her, though his words were for the others, "has a mind of her own. It would be as well to hear what she has to say and learn what she intends to do."

"Will you try to lie to us?" demanded Taggart. "Or will you tell us the truth?"

She, too, strove for lightness, saying:

"Think that out for yourself, Mr. Taggart. Bruce Standing knows where the gold is now; both you and I know the sort of man he is and we can imagine that if he drives the first stake he will see to it that he takes the whole thing. Do you really think that after I came into this country for gold myself I am going to miss my one chance now?" She puzzled them again with her laughter and said: "Not that it would not be a simple matter to trick you, were I minded to let my own chances go for the sake of spoiling yours; Mexicali Joe fooled you so easily."

"Yet you yelled for Standing just now...."

"After you came rushing upon me as if you meant to tear me to pieces, frightening the wits out of me."

"Well, then, tell us."

"If I told you now, then what? You'd desert me in a minute; you would race on ahead; when I caught up with you there would be nothing left."

Deveril's eyes flashed and he said quickly:

"And give you the chance to send us to the wrong place, were you so minded, so that you could slip off alone and be first at the other spot! Very clever, Miss Lynette, but that won't work. You go with us."

And all the while she was trying so hard to think; and all the while listening so eagerly for a certain glorious, golden voice shouting after her. Deveril had heard part of Joe's exclamation....

"It is in Light Ladies' Gulch," she said quietly.

"Yes!" Here was Young Gallup speaking, his covetous soul aflame. "We know that; Deveril heard. But Light Ladies' Gulch is forty miles long. Where abouts in the gulch?"

She told herself that she would die before she led them aright. And yet she realized to the full the danger to herself if she tricked them as Joe had done and they discovered her trickery before Standing came. Yet most of all was she confident that he would come and swiftly.... Joe's words still rang in her memory; he had told first of the Red Cliffs, how he had found color there last year; how he had made prospect holes; how his real mine lay removed three or four miles. Still she temporized, saying:

"Bruce Standing and Billy Winch and Joe have horses. We are on foot. Tell me how we can hope to come to the spot first?"

"We'll have horses ourselves in a jiffy," said Taggart. "Stepping lively, we're not more than a couple of hours from a cattle outfit over the ridge. We'll get all the horses we want and we'll ride like hell!"

"You know where the Red Cliffs are? At the foot of the cliffs I'll show you Joe's prospect holes...."

The pale-eyed, hawk-faced Cliff Shipton spoke for the first time.

"Not half a dozen miles out of Big Pine! I told you last year, Gallup...."

Deveril, the keenest of them all, the one who knew her best, suspected her from the beginning. His eyes never once left her face.

"How do we know," he said quietly, "that there's any gold there? That Joe's gold is not somewhere else?"

"You will have to make your own decision," she told him as coolly as she could. "If you think that I am mistaken or that I am trying to play with you as Joe did, you are free to go where you please."

Taggart began cursing; his grip tightened on her arm so that he hurt her terribly as he shouted at her:

"I'll give you one word of warning, little one! If you put up a game on us now, you cut your own throat. In the first place I'll make it my business that if we get shut out, you get shut out along with us. And in the second place when I'm through with you no other man in the world will have any use for you. Got that?"

She knew what he had done to Mexicali Joe; she could guess what other unthinkable things he would have done. And she knew that if now she tricked Jim Taggart and he found her out…b*efore Bruce Standing came*…she could only pray to die.

And yet at this, the supreme test in her life, she held steady to a swiftly taken purpose. She would not put the game into these men's hands. And she held steadfastly to her certainty, knowing the man, that Bruce Standing would come. Therefore, though her face went a little pale, and her mouth was so dry that she did not dare speak, she shrugged her shoulders.

"Come, then," said Taggart. "Enough palaver. We're on our way."

And of them all, only Babe Deveril was still distrustful.

* * * *

And thus Lynette, accepting her own grave risk with clear-eyed comprehension and yet with unswerving determination, led these four men to a spot where she knew that they would not find that gold for which every man of them had striven so doggedly; thus it was she who made it possible for Bruce Standing to be before all others and to triumph and strike the death-blow to Big Pine and to begin that relentless campaign which was to end in humbling his ancient enemy, Young Gallup. Yet there was little exultation in Lynette's heart, but a growing fear, when, after hours of furious haste, she and the four men came at last into Light Ladies' Gulch and to the base of the towering red cliffs.

Cliff Shipton knew more of gold-mining than any of the others and Lynette watched him narrowly as he went up and down under the high cliffs. And she knew that she in turn was watched; in the first excitement of coming to the long-sought spot she had hoped that she might escape. But both Taggart and Deveril followed her at every step with their eyes.

Desperately she clung to her assurance that Bruce Standing would come for her. He had said that he would come "though it were ten thousand mile." He might have difficulties in finding her; she might have to wait a little while, an hour or two, or three hours. But it remained that he was a man to surmount obstacles insurmountable to other men; a man to pin faith upon. Yet time passed and he did not come.

They found indications of Mexicali Joe's labors, rock ledges at which he had chipped and hammered, prospect holes lower on the steep slope. And Cliff Shipton acknowledged that "the signs were all right." But they did not find the gold and they did not find anything to show that Joe or another had worked here recently.

"All this work," said Shipton, staring and frowning, "was done a year ago."

"He'd be crafty enough," muttered Gallup, "to hide his real signs. We got to look around every clump of brush and in every gully where maybe he's covered things up.... You're sure," and he whipped about upon Lynette, "that you got straight all he said?"

"I'm sure," said Lynette. And she was afraid that the men would hear the beating of her heart.

"I am going up to the top of the cliffs again and see what I can see," she said.

"If there's gold anywhere it's down here," said Shipton. "There's nothing on the top."

"Just the same I'm going!"

"Where the horses are?" jeered Taggart. "By God, if you have...."

"If you think I am trying to run away you can follow and watch me. I am going!"

She turned. Deveril was watching her with keen, shrewd eyes. Taggart took a quick stride toward her, his hand lifted to drag her back. Deveril stepped before him, saying coolly:

"I'll go up with her, Taggart. And I guess you know how I stand on this, don't you?"

"All right," conceded the sheriff. "Only keep your eye peeled. I'm getting leery."

It was a long climb to the cliff tops and neither Lynette nor Deveril at her heels spoke during the climb. They were silent when at last they stood side by side near the tethered horses. Deveril's eyes were upon her pale face; her own eyes ran swiftly, eagerly across the deep canyon to the wooded lands beyond. She prayed with the fervor of growing despair for the sight of a certain young blond giant of a man racing headlong to her relief.

"Well?" said Deveril presently in a tone so strange, so vibrant with suppressed emotion that he made her start and drew her wondering eyes swiftly. "What are you looking for now?"

"Why do you talk like that...what is the matter?"

His bitter laughter set her nerves quivering.

"Is the gold here, Lynette? Or is it some miles away, with Bruce Standing already sinking his claws into it, Standing style?"

Again her eyes left him, returning across the gorge to the farther wooded lands. Over there was a road, the road into which she and Babe Deveril had turned briefly that night, a thousand years ago, when they had fled from Big Pine in the dark; a road which led to Bruce Standing's headquarters. From the top of the cliffs she caught a glimpse of the road, winding among the trees; her eyes were fixedly upon it; her lips were moving softly, though the words were not for Babe Deveril's ears.

"Lynette," he said in that strangely tense and quiet voice, "if you have been fool enough to try to put something over on this crowd.... Can't you guess how you'd fare in Jim Taggart's hands?"

She was not looking at him; she did not appear to mark his words. He saw a sudden change in her expression; she started and the blood rushed back into her cheeks and her eyes brightened. He looked where she was looking. Far across the canyon, rising up among the trees, was a cloud of dust. Some one was riding there, riding furiously....

Together they watched, waiting for that *someone* to appear in the one spot where the winding road could be glimpsed through the trees. And in a moment they saw not one man only, but a dozen or a score of men, men stooping in their saddles and riding hard, veiled in the rising dust puffing up under their horses' flying feet. Now and then came a pale glint of the sun striking upon the rifles which, to the last man, they carried. They came into view with a rush, were gone with a rush. The great cloud of dust rose and thinned and disappeared.

"That road will bring them down into Light Ladies' Gulch where it makes the wide loop about three miles from here," said Deveril. "Have you an idea who they are, Lynette?"

"No," she said, her lips dry; "I don't understand."

"I think that I do understand," he told her, with a flash of anger. "Those are Standing's men and they are riding, armed, like the mill-tails of hell. Listen to me while you've got the chance! That's not the first bunch of men who have ridden over there like that today. Two hours ago, when you went down the cliffs with the others and I stopped up here, I saw the same sort of thing happening. If you're so innocent," he sneered at her, "I'll read you the riddle. I've told you those are Standing's men; then why the devil are they riding like that and in such numbers? They're going straight down into the Gulch where the gold is while you hold us back, up here. And Standing is paying off an old grudge and jamming more gold into his bulging pockets.... And you've got some men to reckon with in ten minutes who'll make you sorry that you were ever born a girl!"

"No!" she cried hoarsely. "No. I won't believe it...."

* * * *

He failed to catch just what she was thinking. She refused to believe that Bruce Standing, instead of coming to her had raced instead to Mexicali Joe's gold; that instead of scattering his men across fifty miles of country seeking her, he was massing them at a new gold-mine. Bruce Standing was not like that! She cried it passionately within her spirit. She had stood loyally by him; she had, at all costs, kept her word to him...she had come to believe in his love for her and to long for his return....

"If you saw men before...if you thought the thing that you think now... why didn't you rush on after them? It's not true!"

"I didn't rush after them," he returned curtly, "because I'd be a fool for my pains and would only give that wolf-devil another chance to laugh in my face. For if he's got this lead on us…why, then, the game is his."

"But I won't believe…."

"If you will watch you will see. I'll bet a thousand dollars he has a hundred men down there already and that they'll be riding by all day; they'll be staking claims which he will buy back from them at the price of a day's work; he'll work a clean shut-out for Gallup and Taggart. That's what he'd give his right hand to do. You watch a minute."

They watched. Once Taggart shouted up to them.

"Down in a minute, Taggart." Deveril called back.

Before long Lynette saw another cloud of dust; this time three or four men rode into sight and sped away after the others; before the dust had cleared another two or three men rode by. And at last Lynette felt despair in her heart, rising into her throat, choking her. For she understood that in her hour of direst need Bruce Standing had failed her.

"Taggart will be wanting you in a minute," said Deveril. He spoke casually; he appeared calm and untroubled; he took out tobacco and papers and began rolling a cigarette. But Lynette saw that the man was atremble with rage. "Before you go down to him, tell me: did you know what you were doing when you brought us to the wrong place?"

"*Yes!*" It was scarcely above a whisper, yet she strove with all her might to make it defiant. She was afraid and yet she fought with herself, seeking to hide her fear from him.

He shrugged elaborately, as though the matter were of no great interest and no longer concerned him.

"Then your blood be on your own head," he said carelessly. "I, for one, will not raise my hand against you; what Taggart does to you concerns only you and Taggart."

"Babe Deveril!"

She called to him with a new voice; she was afraid and no longer strove to hide her fear. Until now she had carried on, head high, in full confidence; confidence in a man. And that man, like Babe Deveril before him, had thought first of gold instead of her. Bruce Standing had spoken of love and had turned aside for gold; with both hands full of the yellow stuff he thought only of more to be had, and not of her.

"Babe Deveril! Listen to me! I have been a fool…oh, such a fool! I knew so little of the real world and of men, and I thought that I knew it all. My mother had me raised in a convent, thinking thus to protect me against all the hardships she had endured; but she did not take into consideration that her blood and Dick Brooke's blood was my blood! This was all a glorious adventure to me; I thought… I thought I could do anything; I was not afraid of men, not of you nor of Bruce Standing nor of any man. Now I am afraid…

of Jim Taggart! You helped me to run from him once; help me again. Now. Let me have one of the horses…let me go….”

All the while he stood looking at her curiously. Toward the end there was a look in his eyes which hinted at a sudden spiritual conflagration within.

“You’re not used to this sort of thing?” And when she shook her head vehemently, he added sternly: “And you are not Bruce Standing’s? And have never been?”

“No, no!” she cried wildly, drawing back from him. “You don’t think that….”

Now he came to her and caught her two hands fiercely.

“Lynette!” he said eagerly. “Lynette, I love you! Today you have stood between me and a fortune, and I tell you… I love you! Since first you came to the door of my cabin I have loved you, you girl with the daring eyes!”

“Don’t!” she pleaded. “Let me go. Can’t you see….”

“Tell me, Lynette,” he said sternly, still holding her hands tight in his, “is there any chance for me? I had never thought to marry; but now I’d rather have you mine than have all the gold that ever came out of the earth. Tell me and tell me the truth; we know each other rather well for so few days, Lynette. So tell me; tell me, Lynette.”

Again she shook her head.

“Let me go,” she pleaded. “Let me have a horse and go. Before they come up for me….”

“Then there’s no chance, ever, for me?”

“Neither for you nor for any other man…. I have had enough of all men…. Let me go, Babe Deveril!”

Still he held her, his hands hardening on her, as he demanded:

“And what of Bruce Standing?”

“I don’t know… I can’t understand men… I thought there never was another man like him, a hard man who could be tender, a man who … I don’t know; I want to go.”

“Go?” There came a sudden gleam into his eyes. “And where? Back to Bruce Standing maybe?”

“No! Anywhere on earth but back to him. To the stage which will be leaving Big Pine in a little while; back to a land where trains run, trains which can take me a thousand miles away. Oh, Babe Deveril….”

Taggart’s voice rose up to them, sounding savage.

“What in hell’s name are you doing up there?”

Then Deveril released her hands.

“Go to the horses,” he commanded. “Untie all four. I’ll ride with you to the stage…and we’ll take the other horses along!”

She had scarcely hoped for this; for an instant she stood staring at him, half afraid that he was jeering at her. Then she ran to the horses and began wildly untying their ropes. Deveril, smoking his cigarette, appeared on the edge of the cliff for Taggart to see, and called down carelessly:

"What's all the excitement, Taggart?"

"Keep your eye on that girl. Shipton thinks she's fooled us. I want her down here."

Deveril laughed at him and turned away. Once out of Taggart's sight he ran. Lynette already was in the saddle; he mounted and took from her the tie ropes of the other horses.

"On our way," he said crisply. "They'll be after us like bees out of a jostled hive."

* * * *

They did not ride into Big Pine, but into the road two or three miles below where the stage would pass. Deveril hailed the stage when it came and the driver took Lynette on as his solitary passenger. At the last minute she caught Babe Deveril's hand in both of hers.

"There is good and bad in you, Babe Deveril, as I suppose there is in all of us. But you have been good to me! I will never forget how you have stood my friend twice; I will always remember that you were *a man*; a man who never did little, mean things. And I shall always thank God for that memory. And now, good-bye, Babe Deveril and good luck go with you!"

"And Standing?" he demanded at the end. "You are done with him, too?"

Suddenly she looked wearier than he had ever seen her even during their days and nights together in the mountains. She looked a poor little broken-hearted girl; there was a quick gathering of tears in her eyes, which she strove to smile away. But despite the smile, the tears ran down. She waved her hand; the stage driver cracked his long whip.... Deveril stood in the dusty road, his hat in his hand, staring down a winding roadway. A clatter of hoofs, a rattle of wheels, a mist of dust...and Lynette was gone.

CHAPTER 26

Deveril went back to his horse, mounting listlessly like a very tired man. The spring had gone out of his step and something of the elasticity out of that ever-young spirit which had always been his no matter from what quarter blew the variable winds of chance. Lynette was gone and he could not hold back his thoughts from winging back along the trail he and she had trod together; there had been the time, and now he knew it, when all things were possible; the time before Bruce Standing came into her life, when Babe Deveril, had he then understood both himself and her, might have won a thing more golden than any man's mere gold. In his blindness he had judged her the light adventuress which she seemed; now that it was given him to understand that in Lynette Brooke he had found a pure-hearted girl whose inherited adventuresome blood had led her into tangled paths, he understood that in her there had come that one girl who comes once to all men…and that she had passed on and out of his life.

He caught up the reins of the horse she had left behind. His face grew grim; he still had Jim Taggart to deal with and, therefore, it was as well to take this horse and the others back to Big Pine and leave them there for Taggart. For the first thing which would suggest itself to the enraged sheriff would be to press a charge against him of horse stealing, and in this country horse thieves were treated with no gentle consideration.

"I'll leave the horses there…and go."

Where? It did not matter. There was nothing left for him in these mountains; Bruce Standing had the gold and the girl was on the stage.

But in his bleak broodings there remained one gleam of gloating satisfaction: he had tricked Standing out of the girl! That Lynette already loved his kinsman or at the least stood upon the very brink of giving her heart unreservedly into his keeping, Deveril's keen eyes, the eyes of jealous love, had been quick to read. It did not once suggest itself to him that Standing could by any possibility have failed to love Lynette. The two had been for days together, alone in the mountains; why should Standing have kept her and have been gentle with her, as he must have been, save for the one reason that he loved her? Further, what man could have lived so long with Lynette of the daring eyes and not love her? And he, Babe Deveril, had stolen her away from Bruce Standing, had tricked him with a pencil scrawl, had lost Lynette to him for all time. The stage carrying her away now was as inevitable an instrument in the hand of fate as death itself.

He turned back for the other horses which he had tethered by the roadside and led them on toward Big Pine.

"What the devil is love, anyway?" he muttered once.

It was not for a man such as Babe Deveril to know clearly; for love is winged with unselfishness and self-sacrifice. And yet, after his own fashion, he loved her and would love her always, though other pretty faces came and went and he laughed into other eyes. She was lost to him; there was the one great certainty like a rock wall across his path. And she had said at the parting…her last words to him were to ring in his memory for many a long day…that there was both good and bad in him; and she chose to remember the good! He tried to laugh at that; what did he care for good and bad? He, a man who went his way and made reckoning to none?

And she had said that she knew him for *a man*; one who, whatever else he might have done, had never stooped to a mean, contemptible act; she thought of him and would always think of him as a man who, though he struck unrighteous blows, dealt them in the open, man-style…. And yet…

the one deed of a significance so profound that it had directed the currents of three lives, that writing of seven words, that signing of her name under them....

"I am glad that I did that!" he triumphed. And gladdest of all, in his heart, was he that Lynette did not know…would never know.

Thus Babe Deveril, riding with drooping head, found certain living fires among the ashes of dead hopes: A row to come with Taggart? He could look forward to it with fierce eagerness. Standing and Lynette separated; vindictive satisfaction there. He'd got his knife in Standing's heart at last! He'd like to wait a year or a dozen until some time Lynette forgot and another man came despite her sweeping avowal and she married; he would like then to come back to Bruce Standing and tell him the fool he had been and how it had been none other than Baby Devil who had knifed him.

… And yet, all the while, Lynette's farewell words were in his mind. And he saw before him, wherever he looked, her face as he had seen it last, her eyes blurred with her tears. And he fought stubbornly with himself against the insistent admission: It was Babe Deveril and none other who, saying that he loved her, had put those tears there. Good and bad? What the devil had he to do with sticking those labelling tags upon what he or others did?

* * * *

Bruce Standing was still in his office. He was a man who had won another victory and yet one who had the taste of despair in his mouth. Gallup's town was doomed; it was one of those little mountain towns which had already outlived its period of usefulness and now with a man like Timber-Wolf waging merciless war against it, Big Pine had its back broken almost at the first savage blow struck. But Standing strode up and down restlessly like a man broken by defeat rather than one whose standards went flying on triumphantly; he knew that a new rival town, his own town, was springing into being in a few hours; he had the brief satisfaction of knowing that he was keeping an ancient promise and striking a body blow from which there would be no recovery, making Big Pine take the count and drop out of all men's consideration; he knew, from having seen it many times, that pitiful spectacle which a dead and deserted town presents; so, briefly, just as his kinsman was doing at the same moment, he extracted what satisfaction he could from the hour. He even had word sent to Gallup: "I am killing your town very much as a man may kill an ugly snake. I shall see to it that goods are sold cheaper here than at your store; there will be a better hotel here, with a better shorter road leading to it. And I will build cabins as fast as they are called for, to house deserters from your dying town. And I will see to it that men from my town never set foot in your town. This from me, Young Gallup: 'For the last time I have set foot upon your dung heap. I'm through with you and the world is through with you. You're dead and buried.'"

During the day, word came to him that several men and one girl had been seen hastily occupied at the foot of the Red Cliffs; the girl Lynette; one of the men, Deveril. And it seemed very clear to Standing that Lynette had led Deveril and the others in hot haste to the Red Cliffs only because she had misunderstood Mexicali Joe's directions, confused by his mention of these cliffs where he had prospected last year.

"I'll go get them." Standing told himself a score of times. "Just as soon as I know how to handle them. When I know how I can hurt him most and her...."

Mexicali Joe swelled about the landscape all day like a bursting balloon, a man swept up in a moment from a condition of less than mediocrity to one, as Mexicali regarded it, of monumental magnificence and the highest degree of earthly joy. Graham could not keep him out of Standing's office; the second time he came in Timber-Wolf lifted him upon his boot hurling him out through the door and promising him seven kinds of ugly death if he ever came back. Whereupon Mexicali Joe, shaking his head, went away without grumbling; for in the sky of his adoration stood just two: God and Bruce Standing.

Graham was still laughing, when another man rode up to the door, and Graham on the instant became alert and concerned. He hastened to Standing, saying quickly:

"Mr. Deveril to see you. He has ridden his horse nearly to death. And I don't like the look on his face."

"Show him in!" shouted Standing. "You fool...don't you know he's the one man in the world...."

Graham hurried out. Deveril, his face pale and hard, his eyes burning as though the man were fever-ridden, came into the room. The door closed after him.

"Well?" snapped Standing.

"Not so well, thanks," retorted Deveril with an attempt at his characteristic inconsequential insolence. "Here's hoping the same to you...damn you!"

"If you've got anything to say, get it done with," commanded Standing angrily.

"I'll say it," Deveril muttered. "But first I'll say this, though I fancy it goes without saying: there is no man on earth I hate as I hate you. As far as you and I are concerned I'd rather see you dead than any other sight I'll ever see. And now, in spite of all that, I've come to do you a good turn."

Standing scoffed at him, crying out: "I want none of your good turns; I am satisfied to have your hate."

Deveril, with eyes which puzzled Timber-Wolf, was staring at him curiously.

"Tell me, Bruce Standing," he demanded, "do you love her?"

"Love her?" cried Standing. "Rather I hate the ground she walks on! She is your kind, Baby Devil; not mine." And he laughed his scorn of her. But now there was no chiming of golden bells in that great volume of laughter but rather a sinister ring like the angry clash of iron. All the while Babe Deveril looked him straight in the eye…and understood!

"For once *you lie*! You love her and what is more…and worse!… she loves you! And that is why…."

"*Loves me?* Are you drunk, man, or crazy? Loves me and leaves me for you; leads you and your crowd to the Gulch, trying to stake on Joe's claim, trying to…."

"She did not leave you for me! I took Taggart and Gallup to her, and Taggart put her under arrest…for shooting you! And she did not lead us to the spot where she knew Joe's claim was; she made fools of us and led us to the Red Cliffs, miles away!"

Standing's face was suddenly as tense as Deveril's, almost as white.

"She left a note; saying that she was going back to you…."

Deveril strode by him to a table on which lay some letter paper and wrote slowly and with great care, laboring over each letter:

I am going back to Babe Deveril.

LYNETTE.

And then he threw the pencil down and stood looking at Standing. And he saw an expression of bewilderment, and then one of amazement wiping it out, and then a great light leaping into Standing's eyes.

"You made her go! You dragged her away! And you wrote that!"

Deveril turned toward the door.

"I have told you that she loves you. So it is for her happiness, much as I hate you, that I have told you…. She, thinking that you preferred gold to her, has just gone out on the down stage…."

"By the Lord, man," and now Standing's voice rang out joyously, clear and golden once more, "you've done a wonderful thing today! I wonder if I could have done what you are doing? By thunder, Babe Deveril, you should be killed for the thing you did…but you've wiped it out. After this…need there be hatred between us?"

He put out his hand. Deveril drew back and went out through the door. His horse, wet with sweat and flecked with foam, was waiting for him. As he set foot into the stirrup he called back in a voice which rang oddly in Standing's ears:

"She doesn't know I wrote that. Unless it's necessary…you see, I'd like her to think as well…." He didn't finish, but rode away. And as long as he was in sight he sat very erect in the saddle and sent back for any listening ears a light and lively whistled tune.

The stage, carrying its one passenger came rocking and clattering about the last bend in the grade where the road crosses that other road which comes down from the mountains farther to the east, from the region of Bruce Standing's holdings. The girl's figure drooped listlessly; her eyes were dry and tired and blank with utter hopelessness. Long ago the garrulous driver had given over trying to talk with her. Now she was stooping forward, so that she saw nothing in all the dreary world but the dusty dashboard before her... and in her fancy, moving across this like pictures on a screen, the images of faces... Bruce Standing's face when he had chained her; when he had cried out that he loved her....

The driver slammed on his brakes, muttering; the wheels dragged; the stage came to an abrupt halt. She looked up, without interest. And there in the road, so close to the wheel that she could have put out a hand and touched him, was Bruce Standing.

"Lynette!" he called to her.

She saw that he had a rifle in his hand; that a buckboard with a restive span of colts was at the side of the road. The driver was cursing; he understood that Standing, taking no chances, had meant to stop him in any case.

"What's this?" he demanded. "Hold up?"

Standing ignored him. His arms were out; there was the gladdest look in his eyes Lynette had ever seen in any man's; when he called to her he sent a thrill like a shiver through her. He had come for her; he wanted her....

"No!" she cried, remembering. "No! Drive on!"

"You bet your sweet life I'll drive on!" the driver burst out. And to Standing: "Stand aside."

Then Standing put his hands out suddenly, dropping his rifle in the road, and caught Lynette to him, lifting her out of her seat despite her efforts to cling to the stage, and took up his rifle again, saying sternly to the stage-driver:

"Now drive on!"

"No!" screamed Lynette, struggling against the one hand restraining her...and against herself! "He can't do this...don't let him...."

But in the end she knew how it would be. The stage-driver was no man to stand out against Bruce Standing...she wondered if anywhere on earth there lived a man to gainsay him when that light was in his eyes and that tone vibrated in his voice.

"He's got the drop on me...he'd drop me dead soon as not.... I'll go, Miss; but I'll send back word...." And Lynette and Bruce Standing, in the gathering dusk, were alone again in the quiet lands at the bases of the mountains.

"Girl... I did not know how I loved you until today!"

She whipped away from him, her eyes scornful.

"Love! You talk of love! And you leave me in the hands of those men while you go looking for gold!"

"No," he said, "it wasn't that. I thought that you had no further use for me; that you loved Deveril; that you had gone back to him; that you were trying to lead him and the rest to Joe's gold; that...."

There was now no sign of weariness in a pair of gray eyes which flashed in hot anger.

"What right had you to think that of me?" she challenged him. "That I was a liar, breaking a promise I had made; and worse than a liar, to betray a confidence? What right have you to think a thing like that, Bruce Standing... and talk to me of love!"

He could have told her; he could have quoted to her that message which had been left behind, signed with her name. But, after all, in the end he had Babe Deveril to think of, a man who had shown himself a man, who had done his part for love of her, whose one reward if Bruce Standing himself were a man, must lie in the meagre consolation that Lynette held him above so petty an act as that one which he had committed. So for a moment Standing was silent; and then he could only say earnestly:

"I am sorry, Lynette. I wronged you and I was a fool and worse. But there were reasons why I thought that.... And after all we have misunderstood each other; that is all. Joe's gold is still Joe's gold; I have made it safe for him and not one cent of it is mine or will ever be mine...."

"Nor do I believe that!" she cried. "Nor any other thing you may ever tell me!"

"That, at least, I can make you believe." He was very stern-faced now and began wondering if Deveril had been mad when he had told him that Lynette loved him. How could Deveril know that? There was little enough of the light of love in her eyes now. And yet....

"Are you willing to come back to headquarters with me?" he asked gently. "There, at least, you can learn that I have told you the truth about Mexicali Joe's gold. No matter how things go, girl, I don't want you to think of me that I did a trick like that...forgetting you to go money-grabbing...."

"You can make me come," she said bitterly. "You have put a chain on me before now. But you can never make me love you, Bruce Standing."

Now she saw in his face a look which stirred her to the depths; a look of profound sadness.

"No," he said, "I'll never put chain on you again, girl; I'll never lift my hand to make you do anything on earth; I would rather die than force you to anything. But I shall go on loving you always. And now," and for the first time she heard him pleading! "is it so great a thing that I ask? If you will not love me, at least I want you to think as well of me as you can. That is only justice, girl; and you are very just. If you will only come with me and learn from Mexicali Joe himself that I have touched and shall touch no single ounce of his gold."

She knew that he was speaking truth; and yet she could not admit it to him…since she would not admit it to herself! And she wanted to believe, and yet told herself that she would never believe. She was glad that he was not dragging her back with him as she had been so certain that he would…and she did not know that she was not sorry.

"Will you do that one thing? I shall not try to hold you…."

"Yes," she said stiffly. And then she laughed nervously, saying in a hard, suppressed voice: "What choice have I, after all? The stage has gone and I have to go somewhere and find a stage again or a horse…."

"No. That is not necessary. If you will not come with me freely, I will take you now where you wish; to overtake the stage."

And thus, when already it was hard enough for her, he unwittingly made it harder. She wanted to go…she did not want to go…most of all she did not want him to know what she wanted or did not want. She cried out quickly:

"Let us go then! I don't believe you! And, if you dare let me talk alone with Mexicali Joe, I shall know you for what you are!"

* * * *

Lynette was in Bruce Standing's study. He had gone for Mexicali Joe. She looked about her, seeing on all hands as she had seen during their racing drive, an expression of the man himself. Here was a vital centre of enormous activities; Standing was its very heart. The biggest man she had ever known or dreamed of knowing; one who did big things; one who was himself untrammelled by the dictates and conventions of others. And in her heart she did believe every word that he spoke; and thus she knew that he, this man among men, loved her!… And she loved him! She knew that; she had known it…how long? Perhaps with clear definiteness for the first time while she spoke of him with Deveril, yearning for his coming; certainly when she had started at the sight of him at the stage wheel. So she held at last that it was for no selfish mercenary gain that he had been so long coming to her, but rather because he had lost faith in her, thinking ill of her. That was what hurt; that was what held her back from his arms, since she would not admit that he could love her truly and misdoubt her at the same time. For certainly where one loved as she herself could love, one gave all, even unto the last dregs of loyal, confident faith. How confident all day she had been that he would come to her!

Lynette, restless, walked up and down, back and forth through the big rooms, waiting. Her wandering eyes were everywhere…upon only one of the shining table tops was a scrap of paper. In her abstraction she glanced at it. Her own name! Written as though signed to a note.

In a flash her quickened fancies pictured much of all that had happened: Deveril today had told Standing she was going out on the stage; Deveril had told Standing all that had happened…because Deveril, too, loved her and knew that she loved his kinsman. She recalled now how Deveril had stopped a little while in camp after Taggart had dragged her away. So Deveril had left this note behind? And Standing knew now; he had said there were reasons why he had been so sure she had gone to Deveril. She understood how now it would be with him; Deveril had told him everything and he, accepting a rich, free gift from the hand of a man he hated was not the man in turn to speak ill of one who had striven to make restitution, though by speaking the truth he might gain everything! These were men, these two; and to be loved by two such men was like having the tribute of kings…. She heard Standing at the door, bringing Mexicali Joe. There was a little fire in the fireplace; she ran to it and dropped the paper into the flames behind the big log. The door opened to Standing's hand. At his heels she saw Mexicali Joe.

"No!" she cried, and he saw and marvelled at the new, shining look in her eyes; a look which made him stop, his heart leaping as he cried out wonderingly:

"Girl! Oh, girl…at last?"

"Don't bring Joe in! I don't want to talk with him; I want your word, just yours alone, on everything!"

Now it was Mexicali Joe who was set wondering. For Standing, with a sudden vigorous sweep of his arm, slammed the door in Joe's perplexed face and came with swift eager strides to Lynette.

"It is I who have been of little faith and disloyal," she said softly. "I was ungrateful enough to forget how you were big enough to take my unproven word that it was not I who shot you, a thing I could never prove! And yet I asked proof of you! I should have known all the time that…'though it were ten thousand mile….'"

She was smiling now and yet her eyes were wet. She lifted them to his that he might look down into them, through them into her heart.

"Let me say this…first …" she ran on hastily. "Babe Deveril saved me the second time today from Taggart. And he told you where to find me. I think that he has made amends."

"He wiped his slate clean," said Standing heartily. "Henceforth I am no enemy of his. But it is not of Deveril now that we must talk. Girl, can't you see…."

"Am I blind?" laughed Lynette happily.

ATHABASCA BILL,
by Bessie Marchant

A TALE OF THE FAR WEST

CHAPTER I
OLD MAN ARLO'S DOGS

The three Crawford boys, on their way home from school, paused as usual at Deerfoot Corner to listen to the deep-throated baying of old man Arlo's bloodhounds, and to peer through the narrow openings in the high staked-fence with the hope of seeing the bent, wizened old fellow out with the dogs, practising their trade of man-hunting.

It was always a mystery to the boys, that old man Arlo should devote so much time and trouble to the training of his two bloodhounds, since no one in the district ever needed their services in tracking down thieves, or finding runaways, for he lived in a miserable fashion, and was always pleading poverty, yet spent enough on his dogs to have maintained himself in decent comfort.

The baying was coming nearer—plainly the hounds were on the trail, so in order to avoid accidents, they swarmed up into the lower boughs of some roadside trees to see the fun. As a rule, especially if Ella were with them, they took to their heels, racing at top speed down the slope through Golden Grove, and across Joe Armstrong's lot, to their own holding at the far end of the valley.

But Ella was not at school to-day, and being unencumbered with a non-climber, they quickly made their way up to a safe roosting-place in the spreading boughs, then waited for the fun to begin.

"Why, there are three dogs to-day, and they are not hunting, but held in a leash!" exclaimed Fred, who by reason of his seniority and superior strength had climbed higher than the other two, and so caught sight of the dogs first.

"So he has," cried Sam, peering through the yellowing leaves. "Then it must be true what Ross Johnson said about old man Arlo having bought a dog, that has come all the way from Montana, and can hunt a man through a crowded city street, yet never lose the trail. That is the one, that brown and white creature in the middle; easy to see which is the stranger, and, my word, but isn't it a beauty too!" and he gave vent to a long, low whistle of admiration, craning his neck so far out through the branches, that it was almost a miracle he did not overbalance himself and fall out of the tree, in front of the whimpering hounds that were straining so eagerly at the leash, as if anxious to be free and away across country tracking down something or someone from sheer love of hunting.

"Hullo, old man Arlo, where are you off to now?" piped out Johnny, the youngest of the three boys, in his shrill treble; he always wanted to know other people's business, and never scrupled to ask for information on the subject.

As a rule the old man was taciturn, and loth to gratify the curiosity of people, but today he was nearly as eager and excited as his dogs.

"I'm going to Millet—there has been a big robbery from the railway depôt, and the inspector has sent for me to bring my dogs to help 'em in tracking the thieves; so I'm reckoning that them wrong-doers are pretty nigh as good as convicted already," replied the old man, with a knowing wink, and a vicious pull at the leash, for the dogs were straining at it so hard that they nearly dragged him off his feet in their eagerness to go forward.

"When was the robbery?" called out Fred. "I was over at the depôt with our team yesterday, and I heard no talk of anything having been taken then, nor did there seem anything much to steal except a few empty freight cars, and nobody would want bloodhounds to track them with, I should think."

"Ah, it doesn't ever do to judge by appearances," retorted the old man, with a sly chuckle. "There was a little box standing in one corner of the office, that was worth double the value of every freight car on the depôt, and it is that box that was stolen last night, the thief getting clear away, and nobody none the wiser until this mornin'."

"What was in the box?" piped Johnny, whilst Sam whistled again, in wonder this time that anything so valuable should be left in the office, instead of being locked away in the safe.

"They say the box was chock full of dollars—five hundred of 'em, and they'd been labelled nails, so that no one should suspicion them for anything of more value. I reckon the thief that went for to steal that box o' nails made eyes as big as glass marbles when he saw what that box had in it really."

"Will your dogs be able to catch the thief?" called out Johnny, more shrilly than before, for the old man was moving on again, the straining of the hounds serving to tow him along.

But he turned to nod in token of assent, at the same time grimacing so hideously that the boys shivered in spite of themselves, because his face was so full of malevolence, and his reputation matched his appearance.

They watched until a bend in the road hid him from sight, then, with a little start of recollection, Fred began to scramble down from his perch among the branches. "Come along, boys, we must run for it now, for we've wasted quite ten minutes, and I promised mother I'd be home early to do the milking, because Dolty Simpson has to go to the mill this afternoon."

Away raced the three boys like the wind, Johnny's short legs twinkling along in the rear of the other two, as he made plucky efforts to keep up.

It was fairly easy going as they pelted down Golden Grove, but part of the way across Joe Armstrong's lot was very rough and heavy, so that Sam and Johnny speedily dropped behind, though Fred raced on, taking the short way across the potato-patch when their own land was reached, jumping the rows in a series of quick bobbing leaps like a kangaroo.

The Crawford homestead was only a small square house, standing in an enclosure, around which were built other houses and sheds, all of the same rough unpainted wood. A belt of spruce firs and hardy larches on the north broke the worst violence of the wind from that quarter, sheltering the young apple and pear trees planted there. It was a bare dreary-looking spot, but the Crawfords loved it because it was home, and a pang shot through Fred's heart as he neared it, knowing as he did that in all probability this time next year would see the old place in the hands of strangers, whilst they would be settled further away in the wilds, where land could be had for next to nothing.

Just as he reached the fence, over which he scramble preparing to take a flying leap to save time, instead of going round to the gate, a rosy-faced girl came rushing out of the house, and flung her hands up in joyful gesticulation about something or other, whilst she shouted something Fred could not hear.

"What is it?" he panted, thinking at first his sister was reproaching him for coming home late.

"Father has come home from Athabasca," she shouted again, her voice plainly audible this time.

"Hurrah!" cried Fred in a rather broken-winded fashion, owing to his want of breath, then without staying to shout the good news to Sam, who was ever so far behind, whilst Johnny was not even in sight, he rushed on towards the house.

"When did father come, Ella, and where is he now?" he panted, tugging at the strap of his bookbag, and nearly wrenching it asunder in his haste to get it off.

"He is out in the barn, I think; here, I will take your bag, and oh, Fred, he has found a place that he likes, so we shall have to go," she cried, catching her breath in a sharp little sob.

"Where?" he demanded quickly, pausing for her answer, whilst his heart gave a painful bound.

"He will tell you; I don't think the place has got a name yet, but it is somewhere by the Wabamun Lake, beyond Stony Plain and Spruce Grove," said Ella, in a tone which seemed to imply that the prospect was anything but inviting.

Fred whistled softly, but said nothing in answer, only rushed away to the barn to find his father, who had been away in the wilds prospecting for a fresh place of settlement ever since the close of harvest.

Maitland Crawford was a man with a passion for the wilderness pure and simple, and when a district became fairly settled, he felt crowded, and, longing for elbow room, yearned for a new location beyond the bounds of civilization.

It had not been an easy matter to take up new ground whilst the children were babies, but now that Fred was turned fifteen, and Johnny, the youngest, nearly nine, this obstacle seemed in a fair way of being removed, and so Mr. Crawford had set to work in good earnest on the task of finding a new home.

He was busy sharpening a saw when Fred entered the barn, but turned to greet his son with a bright smile, and a warm nod of greeting.

"I've got home again, you see, sonny; and, what is more, I've found what I have been looking for."

"Ella said you had dropped on a place you liked out by Wabamun Lake," Fred replied, with as much interest as he could muster on the spur of the moment, for he would not disappoint his father if he could help it, distasteful as he found the prospect of a change.

"Yes, that I have; it is rather rough at present, but when we've a house built, it will be a snug location, I can tell you; wood and water in plenty, and more game than you boys will manage to shoot in the next ten years. I saw a black bear the night I spent in a shack on the lake shore; but there, I mustn't begin talking of all I've seen and done, or I shall not be finished with this saw by supper-time," and Mr. Crawford turned back to his saw with a resolute air.

"I must stir round too, for I've got to milk, because Dolty has gone to the mill," Fred said, his face brighter now, and his voice eager, because of that mention of black bear.

There was over an hour of steady hard work got through before he had a chance to talk with his father again; by that time it was dark, and they were all washing their hands for supper, at the little sink out on the back porch, when Johnny, who was polishing his face very hard with a rough towel, asked shrilly—

"May I have that little wooden box that is out in the barn, father?—I mean the one you brought home with you today?"

"I don't know what box you mean, Johnny; but certainly I did not bring it home with me to-day," replied Mr. Crawford, turning to enter the kitchen where supper was spread.

"Then I wonder how it came there," went on Johnny, in a puzzled tone; "I asked Dolty Simpson if he had put it in the barn, but he did not know anything about it, and it wasn't there last night when I went to look for the eggs."

"What box are you speaking of, Johnny?" asked Celia, coming out just then from her bedroom, where she had been lying down most of the day with a bad headache. In age she came midway between Ella and Sam, but owing to her severe headaches and general weakness, was often compelled to stay away from school for weeks at the stretch.

"It is a nice little wooden box with a lid and a fastening, and it has 'copper nails' printed in big letters on the top; I found it hidden away behind the big board, where the two speckled hens mostly lay their eggs," explained Johnny, at some length.

"I know, I saw it there when I rushed out to the barn, after father came home, to look for eggs for supper," remarked Ella, who was hovering between the stove and the table busy with cooking. "I thought father had brought the box, because he went to the barn before he came indoors, but I forgot about it again until now."

"We will step out to the barn and have a look at it after supper, for certainly a box could not walk into the barn, having no legs," rejoined Mr. Crawford, with an easy laugh. "But supper is the first consideration."

"Yes, indeed it is," replied his wife; "for I expect you have not had very many comfortable meals during the last few weeks."

"I think I could reckon them up on the fingers of one hand," Mr. Crawford said, with a laugh, as he took his place at the table.

Then the children began to clamour for the story of his adventures, so that the supper-time seemed likely to be prolonged indefinitely. Dolty Simpson, the hired man, had gone home, and the father and mother were alone with their children, a re-united family once more; and no one was willing to break the spell of happiness by making a move to leave the table, until Mrs. Crawford said that it was high time Sam and Johnny went to bed. The latter began to clamour then for the little wooden box to be brought from the barn, and Mr. Crawford, reaching for his cap, said he would go and fetch it, when there came the sounds of dogs baying in the distance.

"Why, I believe it must be old man Arlo's bloodhounds on the trail!" exclaimed Fred, starting up in surprise.

CHAPTER II

A GREAT SHOCK

"Old man Arlo's dogs?" echoed Mr. Crawford, in great bewilderment. "What would he be doing with them out at this time of night? It is so dark that you can hardly see your hand, if you hold it up in front of your face, and it would be but little lighter out in the open."

"I suppose they want to work the trail while it is fresh," answered Fred. "Old man Arlo told us there had been a robbery from the railway depôt at Millet, and that he had been sent for to bring his dogs to track the thief. He would have had about time to go to Millet and come back again, if he stepped out briskly, that is, and the dogs were towing him along at a great pace when we saw him as we came home from school."

"I thought they only used bloodhounds when some big crime had been committed, like murder, for instance," said Ella, with a rather frightened face, coming to the door to peep out under her father's arm at the blackness of the night.

"I expect they are using the dogs now to save the expense of sending for a detective," said Mr. Crawford carelessly, putting his arm closer round her, and stooping to kiss her hair. "I came through Millet myself early this morning, but I heard nothing of the robbery. I ought to have been home a good bit sooner, but I was so dead tired, that when I sat down in that little wood bordering Pearson's lot, to eat my breakfast, I fell asleep, and didn't wake for nearly five hours."

"Poor, dear daddy! Didn't you go to bed at all last night?" asked Ella, in great concern, as she nestled closer in the arm that enfolded her.

"No, nor yet for a good many previous nights. It was cooler walking at night, and so I slept a bit in the day-time, when the sun saved the cost of blankets in keeping me warm; it will be a real treat to sleep in a bed tonight, and I don't mean to be late in getting there, but first we will go and get that box from the barn that Johnny is so excited about. Have you got the lantern, Fred?"

"Yes, father; here it is," answered the boy, coming forward with a lighted hurricane lantern, and the two went off together, Mr. Crawford coughing badly as he stepped out into the chill night air.

"Maitland, Maitland, put your comforter round your throat, or you will be getting bronchitis," called Mrs. Crawford, who had come to stand beside her daughter in the doorway.

"All right, mother," rang out the cheery response. "But I can't do it, by reason that I gave it away to a poor fellow who was sleeping rough last night, and I haven't screwed my courage up high enough to confess to my wrong-doing yet," he said to Fred, with a merry laugh, and little dreaming the misery that act of kindly charity was to bring to him and his.

"One of the girls can make you another, but you ought not to be out in the night air without something warm round your throat," Fred said, as he flashed the light of his lantern in at the doorway of the barn. His father had a delicate chest and throat, which made some little care necessary on winter or autumn nights.

Mr. Crawford did not reply at the moment; he was groping his way past a pile of hen-coops, to where the big board was leaning against the wall of the barn; then stooping down and feeling about with his hand, he presently drew forth the wooden box which had so excited Johnny's envy and admiration. It was well made and strong, but quite empty, and except the words "copper nails," had nothing about it to explain its use, or serve as a means of identification.

"Well, this is funny!" exclaimed Mr. Crawford, backing out from the neighbourhood of the coops, to where Fred stood with the lantern on the threshold of the barn. "I'm certain I never saw the box before—have you, sonny?"

"No, father," replied Fred with decision, and then there came flashing into his head what old man Arlo had said about the box of nails that was stolen from the railway depôt, and which had contained something so much more valuable than mere nails. It was on his tongue to speak of it, and to express a wonder whether the thief had brought the box to hide it in their barn, with the intention of diverting suspicion from the proper quarter.

But the words were never spoken, for as they stood there just outside the barn door, both absorbed in the mystery of the box, there came the sound of a panting breath close at hand, then a lithe brown and white body with gleaming eyes sprang out of the darkness, and with a roar like an enraged lion, sought to fix its fangs in Mr. Crawford's throat.

Taken by surprise as he was, however, he was yet too quick for the creature; thrusting his arm forward in a wild instinctive effort at self-preservation, he caught the animal's grip on the leather sleeve of his short jacket.

Before Fred, who seemed half paralyzed with fear, could spring forward to his father's rescue, two more dogs rushed out of the darkness to assist the first in dragging their quarry to the ground, but at the sound of Mr. Crawford's voice, as he shouted to his son, they suddenly commenced to fawn upon him with every appearance of love and affection, though the hound which had seized him first still clung to his arm with a fierce, unrelenting grip, growling horribly, as if daring the unfortunate victim to strike a blow in his own defence.

Mr. Crawford, however, stood quite still, talking in soothing, friendly fashion to the two dogs which crouched fawning at his feet, but not attempting to irritate the creature that had its fangs fixed in his sleeve.

"Father, what shall I do to help you?" cried Fred, in a voice quivering with horror, for this sudden attack out of the blackness of the night seemed to have robbed him of the resourceful courage which usually stood him in such good stead.

"Nothing. Stand quite still, and don't anger the beast, until its master comes up; I expect I happened to cross its trail, and so am the victim of an ugly mistake. Ah, here they come!" ejaculated Mr. Crawford, as the flickering lights of lanterns, and the sound of men's voices, came round the angle of the barn.

"Ah, the good dog has got him, sure enough!" cried an eager, rasping voice, then dim forms came plunging forward, and a man with a heavy hand gripped Maitland Crawford by the arm, saying gruffly—

"So the beast ran you, down, mister; well, it's no use crying over spilt milk, and seeing you've been found out, why, you'd best come along quietly; it will pay in the end, you know."

"No, I don't know; and I tell you plainly, officer, that I don't intend budging a foot from here until I know what it is I am accused of, and the nature of the evidence leading to this attempt at arrest; I am surely entitled to so much consideration in a free country like this. But I will thank you to call off this brute of a dog," said Maitland Crawford, in a steady tone.

"Why, surely it ain't never you, Mr. Crawford?" cried the thin, rasping voice of old man Arlo, in dismayed query, as he came up panting heavily, and holding his lantern high, in order that he might see clearly the face of the captive.

"It certainly is no one else. But are you going to call the dog off, or must I kill the beast in self-defence?" demanded Mr. Crawford impatiently.

"Down, Jenny; down, lass; good dog; leave it alone!" cried old man Arlo, seizing the hound by the collar, and slipping the leash through it, dragged the creature away by main force, though it whimpered and cried, struggling vainly to maintain the grip of its prey; but there was a quivering horror in the old man's tone, and when the dog was securely fastened, he exclaimed in consternation, "It surely wasn't never you what took them things from the depôt?"

"I may be able to deny the charge with more force, when I know to what it is you are referring," replied Mr. Crawford; and then he turned again to the man who was holding him in custody, demanding the explanation that was so tardy in coming.

That individual began at once to tell, in a jumbled and half-incoherent fashion, of the robbery at the depôt on the previous night, when a third man, who had been silent hitherto, chanced to flash the light of his lantern on the box which Mr. Crawford had been to the barn to fetch, but which the onslaught of the dog had flung from his grasp on to the ground.

"Why, here's the very identical box what had the dollars in it!" he cried out excitedly. "Why, we've caught him red-handed and in the act, as you may say."

"So it is; now, who would have thought it?" and the burly inspector, who had Mr. Crawford in his grip, let go his hold in sheer amazement for a moment, whilst he peered at the wooden box Johnny had wanted so badly. Then he said in a serious tone, "I'm afraid I must lock you up tonight, Mr. Crawford; for taken altogether, the case against you seems uncommon clear. That box labelled 'copper nails,' but containing in reality five hundred dollars, was stolen from the railway depôt at Millet some time during last night."

"But father didn't know the box was here until the children told him, and they only found it in the barn by accident. Father has been away for weeks, and only came home this afternoon," burst out Fred, with impetuous haste.

"Of course, if Mr. Crawford can prove an alibi, will let him go tomorrow with an apology, but we can't do without the pleasure of his company tonight nohow," replied the burly inspector.

"I should like to know how it was suspicion fastened itself on me to begin with, apart from that box, I mean," Mr. Crawford said, with a nod of his head in the direction of the box, which the third man had appropriated, and was holding with as jealous care as if it still contained the five hundred dollars.

"We found a scarf, a sort of long woollen comforter, lying in the office, as if the thief had dropped it by accident; there was a cap, too, but that was so soaking wet we thought it wouldn't hold scent, so trusted to the scarf. Then we sent a message to old man Arlo to bring his dogs along, and giving the scarf to the brutes for scent, they brought us straight here and pulled you down," explained the officer.

"Only one dog tried it on; look at the other two," said Mr. Crawford, pointing to the two hounds that lay resting at his feet, one of them licking his boot in an affectionate fashion.

"Ah, old Ruby would sooner pull me down, than stick a tooth in you, Mr. Crawford, and it's about the same with Smiler; they've long memories, them bloodhounds, and they don't forget in a hurry when a person has been good to them. But it is a mistake, Mr. Crawford; I am quite sure it was a mistake to arrest you," said old man Arlo, in tremulous agitation.

"That is my own opinion also, only, unfortunately, I don't seem able to prove it," replied Mr. Crawford, with a sigh of impatience, for he was very tired, and it was distinctly worrying to be met by a charge like this on the first day of his return, more especially as from the nature of his wanderings, he might find some difficulty in establishing an alibi; then he asked abruptly, "Have you the scarf here? I should like to see it."

"Here it is," said the officer, pulling from his pocket a knitted muffler of grey wool.

"I thought so," groaned Mr. Crawford, when he had inspected the scarf by the light of the lanterns; "that is, or was, my comforter, but I gave it away last night to a poor fellow that I thought was worse off than myself, and this is what has come of it."

"I'm sorry to hear it, Mr. Crawford, 'pon my word I am; it makes things so much more awkward for you. There don't seem no more to be said about it though, and so I suppose we'd better be moving. The moon will be up in less than another hour, so we shan't find it quite so dark going back to Millet," the officer said, with great concern in his tone, being honestly sorry for the farmer, who had borne such a good character before.

It was on Mr. Crawford's tongue to say that he must go indoors and make some sort of an explanation to his wife before letting the law take its course, when there came the sound of Ella's voice calling to him from the back porch, "Father, dear father, when are you coming indoors, or do you mean to stay out in the barn all night?"

He shivered then as if smitten with sudden ague, and said in a low, hurried tone to Fred, "I can't face telling them; you'll have to do it for me, sonny. The hardest bit of work you ever set your hand to, I guess, but you'll do it for my sake. Tell them, if you like, that I'm called away on sudden, unexpected business tonight, and you can leave the details to the morning."

"But, father, they will feel so bad about it, if you go without a word; and, besides, I'm coming too; they will lock us up together, then we can talk things over a bit," said Fred, tumbling his words out in a great hurry.

"Go in quietly, then, and ask your mother to come out here, but don't let the children come, for they would begin to cry, and I—I don't think I could bear it," Mr. Crawford replied, in a low, choked tone.

CHAPTER III

THE MYSTERY GROWS

Mrs. Crawford, although slight and frail in appearance, was endowed with more courage than most women; so when Fred called her out from the warm, lighted kitchen that night, into the chill darkness of the night, and told her of his father's arrest, she did not scream or faint, as a weaker woman might have done; but after a short gasp, as if the tidings of disaster had taken her breath away, said bravely—

"You must certainly go with your father tonight, Fred, and then if he is not released after examination tomorrow, you must come home to me, and we will see what is best to be done."

"Mother, you're a real brick!" cried Fred fervently, as he piloted her round the angle of the barn, to where the little group of men and boys awaited his coming.

She smiled faintly, and slipped a trembling hand through his arm to steady her steps.

"Most people have the capacity in them for rising to the occasion, whatever the occasion may be, and I would not add another straw to your father's burden of care just now," she whispered, just as they reached the group waiting for them in the shelter of the barn wall.

Mr. Crawford shook off the grip of the inspector's hand, and moving a step forward, took his wife in his arms.

"My poor Emily, if only I could have spared you this sorrow! But you don't believe I took those things, do you?" he asked, with a yearning pain in his voice.

"Of course I don't. What do you take me for, Maitland, if you think I would join the ranks of doubters at the first breath of suspicion?" she cried indignantly. "Why, I wouldn't believe you guilty though all the world declared you so, if only you told me yourself that you were innocent."

"As I am," he replied quickly; then went on in a slower, graver tone, "but it is easy to see that I shall have considerable trouble in proving it, for the evidence against me looks overwhelming. The finding of the stolen box in my barn, the fact that my woollen comforter was found on the floor of the room from whence the box was stolen, and then the bloodhounds running me down in this fashion, will all tell against me at the examination."

"Never mind," she said, in brave, encouraging tones. "And don't be depressed even if you are committed for trial, Maitland. Being innocent, it is next to impossible that you should be brought in guilty, since there is a God in Heaven to protect the weak and champion the cause of those who have no helper. The children and I can run the farm for a few weeks, as we have done since you have been away in Athabasca; and I will take care that Dolty Simpson has no chance to loaf round, wasting his time."

"I think we had best be moving soon, Mr. Crawford; it is a goodish step back to Millet, and there is nothing to be gained by delay," said the officer who had taken him into custody, feeling that it was really kinder to shorten the tribulation of the parting.

Mrs. Crawford let her husband go without another word; then bidding Fred hurry back in the morning, as soon as there was any tidings to bring her, she stood white-faced, but tearless, to watch the dreary little procession move off.

The man from the railway depôt, who had identified the box, walked first, and after him, the burly inspector, the prisoner and Fred, whilst old man Arlo and his three dogs brought up the rear, Montana Jenny still whimpering and straining at the leash, as if anxious to spring again on the quarry that she had run down so successfully. But the other two walked along with hanging heads, as if entirely ashamed of the business in hand, as indeed they would have been, poor beasts, if the full importance of that night's work could have been made clear to them.

Next to old man Arlo himself they loved Mr. Crawford, being sagacious enough to know that they owed their lives to his kindness; and as their master had said of them, they had long memories, and did not forget in a hurry.

One day in the previous winter there had been a fearful blizzard, and old man Arlo, who had gone to the town, was forced to stay there for three days, until it was possible for him to make his way back. But the dogs had been left at home, and must have been nearly starved, perhaps quite, had not

Mr. Crawford chanced to hear them howling, and guessing from the sound that something was wrong, gone to discover what ailed the creatures. Finding them shut up without food or water, he had stayed to relieve their wants, even lighting a fire to cook them a good warm meal, and thaw the water for them to drink. Being almost as sagacious as human beings, and endowed with a lively sense of gratitude, the dogs understood who it was had saved them from a lingering death of cold and hunger, and loved him accordingly. So that when the trail they had all three followed from Millet railway depôt ended in the man whose hand had fed them, the two lay down and licked his feet, leaving Montana Jenny to do her best, or worst, alone.

Although Mrs. Crawford had borne up so bravely under the terrible shock of her husband's arrest, she broke down completely when she had to go back to the house, and tell her other children what had happened.

Sam and Johnny were frolicking about like squirrels at nutting-time, whilst Ella and Celia, though pretending to clear the table, were in reality joining in the fun, when, white of face, and sick at heart, their mother entered the house, and told them of what had happened to their father.

They came about her then, the two boys crying noisily, the girls quiet but with quivering lips, and the sudden plunge from happy mirth to bitter sorrow broke her down utterly.

"Mother, don't cry so badly; why, you could not weep more if father were really guilty, instead of merely being accused of a thing," Ella said sharply, for to her such a demonstration of grief savoured of disloyalty to the father she loved so dearly.

"Hush, dear, it will make her feel better to cry," whispered Celia, who, although she was younger, had through suffering gained a keener insight into the hearts of others.

It was a night long to be remembered by the mother and her girls. Sam and Johnny went to bed and cried themselves to sleep in half-an-hour. But although Mrs. Crawford and her daughters put out the lamp, and lay down together on their bed, no sleep came to them, and they lay through the long hours waiting for the morning, longing for the cheerful light of the dawning, yet dreading with heavy, aching hearts what the day might bring.

The morning, however, did not end the sickening apprehension, and the hours lagged along more slowly than ever. Sam and Johnny were sent off to school, but Mrs. Crawford let the girls stay at home with her, knowing how impossible it would be for them to apply themselves to lessons, and glad to have the comfort of their presence in that silent house.

Dolty Simpson had taken holiday, and gone off to the inquiry before the magistrate, so that farm work was entirely at a standstill.

"It makes me think of Sunday somehow, though it is the most horrid Sunday I have ever known," said Ella, as she and Celia fed the poultry, then turned the horses and cows out to find their food in the pastures, where the pigs were already feeding.

"I think it is like that day two years ago, when mother was so ill, and father was not at home; do you remember how anxious we were, and afraid she would die, because she was in such fearful pain?"

"Yes, I remember," said Ella. "But Fred was at home that day, and things never seem quite so bad when he is on hand to help keep us cheerful. I suppose that is why today seems sadder than that other day."

"God heard our prayers then, and made mother well again, so maybe He will hear us now, and send our father back to us, cleared from this dreadful charge," Celia replied softly, with a rapt look on her pale little face.

Ella brushed her hand hastily across her face, to flick away the tears that would come, then the two went back to their mother, and to the weary waiting, which seemed as if it would never end.

The shadows were lengthening, and it was almost time for the children to be coming home from school, before Fred returned from Millet.

His face was white and weary, and his whole bearing so expressive of acute depression, that the questions which sprang to their lips were not uttered, and they waited in silence for him to speak.

"Father is committed for trial on the charge of having robbed the railway company," Fred said, in a dry, formal tone, as if he were repeating a lesson.

Mrs. Crawford moved her pale lips as if in reply, but no sound came, and there was a strained hush through the room, until Ella asked, in a puzzled fashion—

"Why did they send him for trial? I thought if a person stole a thing, or was supposed to have stolen it, they received punishment straight away."

"So they do sometimes; that is, if a man steals a pig, or a cow, or a load of fence-rails, and it can be proved against him, the magistrate sentences him to as big a penalty as the law will allow. But they can't prove anything against father, though the evidence is so strong; that is why they are sending the case for trial. Tom Saunders told me he believed a clever lawyer could have got father off today, by showing that there was no case against him, even though suspicion would have clung to him still," Fred said moodily, dropping on to a chair which stood just inside the door, as if he were too weary to stand on his feet any longer.

"How no case?" asked Mrs. Crawford, lifting her bowed head with a jerk, whilst a momentary gleam of relief and hope shone in her sad eyes.

"Tom says that to begin with, it was a fraud against the railway people to send five hundred dollars packed up as copper nails, and that the people to be prosecuted should be the consignees of the box. Then the evidence against father had so many thin places in it, that it must have broken down altogether, but for the finding of the box in our barn, and father's declaration that the comforter found in the station house belonged to him," Fred said vehemently, clenching his hands in sudden anger at the untowardness of things.

Mrs. Crawford sighed, shaking her head a little sadly, and remaining silent, for really things looked so black that for the moment she felt crushed.

Ella and Celia were also silent, but, after a moment's pause, Fred burst out passionately—

"There's more behind, only I get so choked with rage when I think about it that I don't know how to get the words out. You remember the cap, a fur cap it was, that was found just by the office window, only they couldn't use it as scent because it was so soaking wet?"

Mrs. Crawford nodded, and again the hopeful light came into her eyes, but she said nothing, for speech just then was impossible to her.

"Directly father saw the cap he knew it, and so did I, for it is pretty certain there can't be another cap in the Dominion like it."

"It was surely not that cap of Athabasca Bill's?" cried Ella with a jump.

"I am sure of it; you know what an extraordinary looking thing it was—the crown of silver fox skin, one lappet of squirrel, and one of white rabbit. Why, I should have known the thing if I had stumbled on it in Central Asia, or Peru," replied Fred stormily. "It is that which has put me in such a rage today, thinking what a wretch Athabasca Bill must be to try and throw the blame of his wickedness on father, by hiding the box in our barn!"

"Fred, I'm quite sure that Athabasca Bill would never do such a thing," interrupted Mrs. Crawford. "Think of the weeks we nursed and cared for him last winter, when he was so sick. Why, it isn't in human nature to be so ungrateful; there is some mistake somewhere, I am quite confident; he may even have given his cap away in charity, just in the same way that your father bestowed his comforter on the poor fellow with the cough."

"That is what father said, and he thinks if only Athabasca Bill could be found, we should most likely get some clue to who the thief really was," replied Fred.

"The trouble is where to find a wanderer like that," sighed his mother, pressing one hand to her throbbing brow.

"Father told me that he saw him only the day before yesterday; met him in the hilly country the other side of the railway," Fred answered excitedly.

"Then, my boy, you must go in search of him; if he is as near as that, it should not be a hard task to hunt him out. But, hard or easy, it must be done to save your father's good name," Mrs. Crawford exclaimed.

"I'll find him, mother, never fear," replied Fred blithely, little recking what the search would involve, or where it would lead him.

CHAPTER IV

WHERE WAS ATHABASCA BILL?

Fred awoke with a start, sat up, rubbed his eyes and shivered, wondering for a moment where he was, and what had happened to him.

Then in a flash recollection came back—he was on tramp in search of Athabasca Bill; this was his third night away from home, but the first time that it had been necessary for him to sleep out.

On the very first day of his journey, he had pounced on the trail of the man he sought, and gained so much information on the subject, that he confidently expected to overhaul him in the course of the next two or three days.

Fred's first night had been spent at Green Forks Creamery, twelve miles the other side of the railway from his home, and after earning his supper by two hours' work at wood-chopping, had turned in upon a lump of fragrant hay in the stable-loft to get his night's rest.

He was not alone, however; a genial Irishman, known in those parts as Creamery Pat, being his companion, and from him Fred learned that Athabasca Bill had called at the creamery on the previous day, and had taken orders for furs that were waiting for him there, telling Pat when he left that he meant to make his way by Strawberry Creek, and Rocky Raps, to Chip Lake, and Lobstick River, where there was a good winter hunting ground.

An hour's wood-chopping next morning had earned Fred as much breakfast as he could eat, with something over for dinner; and then he was away hot-foot on the trail again, heading now for Strawberry Creek.

The second night he spent in a lumber camp, where also Athabasca Bill had been heard of, one of the lumbermen having seen and spoken with him on the previous day. So Fred set forward again on the next morning in hopeful spirits, but so footsore as to be very much slower in getting over the ground.

Civilization was growing sparse and scanty now, and he had to chiefly rely for guidance on the section stumps, standing up here and there in the knee-high willow scrub, or the blazed and numbered tree-trunks in the heavy-timbered lands. A town boy must have been badly scared at the wide solitudes, but Fred's up-bringing had admirably fitted him for his task, and he was not nearly so frightened in the wilds as he would have been in a big city crowd.

A company of ragged Indians, journeying south-ward to the Ponoka Reservations, were the only human beings he had seen since mid-day, and when at dusk he came to a deserted lumber camp, he resolved to stay there until the next morning, through fear of going further and faring worse.

His supper that night was but a scanty one, whilst the prospect of breakfast was so remote as to be problematical; but being desperately tired with his long tramp, Fred ate what there was, then lay down to sleep, wisely leaving the question of the morrow's food to take care of itself until the next day should dawn.

But the day had come now, and something else with it, as he realized with a jump of amazement on opening his eyes and looking round. He had gone to sleep the previous night in the shelter of a half-ruined log hut, known in those parts as a shack, one side of which was open to the weather, whilst through the open spaces of the roof he could see plainly the opal-tinted morning sky. It was not the delicate tints of sunrise which so much surprised him, however, but the gambolling of some lively black animals in the open space before the shack.

At the first glance he had thought them to be goats, but a second look revealed them for what they were, the sprightly cubs of a huge black bear, which was quietly feeding a little distance away on some roots grubbed from behind a heap of fallen logs.

For a moment or two Fred lay quite still, watching the gambols of the sportive cubs, at the same time keeping a watchful, wary eye on Mrs. Bear, feeling uncommonly nervous all the while, black bears not being the kind of creature most desirable for companionship in the wilderness, to a person unprovided with the means of self-defence.

It would not have been so embarrassing if there had been a back door to the shack, since in that case he might have slipped out in an unobtrusive fashion, and so got clear off without disturbing the happy family. As it was, he had to think of some other way, and to make haste about it, for the cubs were rolling and tumbling nearer and nearer to where he lay, and who should say but what their mother might not take it in her head to stroll in that direction also?

The thought made him go cold all over; then summoning his courage up to one great effort, he sprang to his feet and rushed shouting and yelling from the shack, throwing up his arms, jumping and prancing as if he had gone suddenly crazy.

The effect of his noisy demonstration was magical; the two cubs went up trees like cats, jumping three or four feet up on to the trunks, whilst the portly dame, their mother, scuttled away into the willow scrub like a frightened rabbit.

It took Fred a minute to realize that the bears were quite as much afraid of him as he was of them, and then he burst into a loud laugh, which echoed and re-echoed through the lonely forest reaches.

When his mirth had subsided a little, he began to think of the scanty supper of last night, and to wonder where that morning's breakfast was to come from. He had some money in his pocket, it is true, but money was of little use in the wilderness, where there was nothing to buy; so drawing his belt a little tighter, he set forward again, steering his way as on the previous day, by means of the section posts.

It was terribly lonely work, however, and he was getting nervous and fidgety, as well as desperately hungry, when about two hours before noon, he stumbled on to a little encampment in the willow scrub on the banks of a tiny stream, where a young man and his sister were camping under a cart, until they had built themselves a hut to live in.

The latter, a brisk, bright girl of twenty or so, seized Fred by the shoulders, and gave him a kind of elder-sisterly shake.

"Have you run away from home, my lad?" she demanded, her comprehensive glance taking in Fred's carefully mended clothes, his good, stout boots, and his tired, hungry face.

"No; that I did not. My mother sent me, and I'm on the track of Athabasca Bill; but it is rather a long story, and if you, please, would sell me some breakfast, I would tell you more afterwards, for I am just dreadfully hungry," Fred said, with an eager sniff, for the odours coming from a pot simmering over a fire near by were quite tantalizingly savoury.

"Breakfast!" she exclaimed, with a merry laugh. "It is dinner you mean, I should think, Frederic John Crawford, unless, indeed, it is fashionable city hours that you keep."

"Oh, I got up early enough, the bears took care of that; they were as good as an alarum clock," Fred replied, with a laugh; then he sat down suddenly on a convenient log that lay near, feeling so sick and giddy that he could not think what was going to happen to him.

"Suppose we call it lunch, by way of splitting the difference," she said merrily, as, seizing an iron ladle and a tin basin, she proceeded to dip out a portion of the steaming, savoury stew, which she handed to Fred, giving him a wooden spoon to eat with. "I hope you don't object to tin basins and wooden spoons, Frederic John Crawford; it is a little difficult to get silver, porcelain, and cut glass in the backwoods. If you had happened along twenty years later, when Tom and I had made our fortunes, things would have been a bit grander perhaps."

"Twenty years is rather long to wait for breakfast, and, my word, isn't this just good!" exclaimed Fred, drawing a long breath of satisfaction, and then getting nearly choked by a lump of pepper.

"You look as if you needed something that was good; your face had such a yearning, hungry look when you came into camp, that I began to feel nervous lest you should want to make a dinner off me," said the girl, who had told Fred that her name was Saidie Marsh.

"There is no telling what I might not have been tempted to do, if you had not given me something to eat so quickly," he replied, as with great carefulness he scraped every fragment of the stew from the sides of the tin basin, in order that none of it might be lost.

Saidie leaned back against a tree trunk and laughed as if this were the very best joke that she had heard for weeks, until her brother, who was splitting logs at a little distance, called out to know where the fun came in, and whether there was enough left to make it worth his while to come and laugh too.

Then Fred, taking advantage of a momentary lull in her mirth, ventured to inquire whether she would prefer to take payment in money or labour, adding modestly that he could split rails, or cut firewood, or anything else that she preferred.

"Well, then, I prefer that you shall just sit there and tell me why your mother sent you roaming about the woods alone looking for—what was the man's name?"

"Athabasca Bill. But I can talk and work too, and, please, I'd rather, as I am in a hurry, and it will save time, for I'm getting hot on his trail, and I'm more than anxious to overhaul him as soon as I can," Fred said urgently, adding, rather shyly, "unless, indeed, you would rather have money."

"No, no, boy, I don't want the money, nor the work either; sit still and rest yourself whilst you tell me your story, and then I'll give you a lump of bread and cheese to take with you, to save you from having to wait as long for your supper as you did for your breakfast," Saidie answered good-naturedly. Then she sat listening with keen interest, whilst he told her about his father's arrest on charge of a robbery that he had never committed, the finding of a cap that was unmistakably the one worn by Athabasca Bill, and his mother's belief that the wanderer would be able to throw some light on the mystery of the robbery at the depôt, or at least give them some clue to the perpetrator.

"But, boy, can't you see that most likely it was this man—Athabasca Bill, as you call him—who stole the money, in which case it is not likely that he would be very anxious to assist in identifying the thief?" cried Saidie, in amazement at the innocent credulity which had sent Fred out alone on such a quest.

"Mother says she is quite sure he didn't steal the money, and father says so too. Besides, it is next to impossible that he could have been in Millet at the time when the box disappeared, because father met him about noon in the hilly country this side of Millet, but quite thirty miles away; he was then going west, and even supposing he'd turned round and tracked father back to the town, he would still have been too late to steal that box, which was missed very early in the morning," Fred replied, so earnestly that even Saidie was compelled to accept this view of the situation in part, though she still shook her head in a doubtful fashion.

"If this man, Athabasca Bill, could not possibly have committed the theft by reason of his distance from the depôt, then the same holds good of your father surely?"

"It would do if he could prove his alibi, but that is just what he can't do, for he did not see a single individual from the time he left Athabasca Bill, until the next morning, except a poor fellow tramping like himself, who had a terrible cough, and to whom father gave his comforter. We think that must have been the thief, because of the comforter being found afterwards in the depôt."

"Humph, I should think so too!" replied Saidie, with a dissatisfied frown wrinkling her face. "But what I fail to understand is what Athabasca Bill would be likely to know of this beggar, if he was so many miles away. Was the fellow wearing the cap when your father gave him the scarf?"

"It was dark, or nearly so, and father can't remember what the man had on his head, but he said that he had been surprised to see Athabasca Bill without a cap at all; and when he asked him if he was going to turn Indian, or if his funds didn't run to hats just then, Bill merely laughed, saying that he liked to be bareheaded."

Saidie drew a long breath at this explanation, then said, with an air of decision—

"I think your mother was quite right, when she started you off to find Athabasca Bill."

CHAPTER V
A STRANGE COINCIDENCE

Tom and Saidie Marsh were very good to Fred, trying hard to persuade him to stay until the next day, in order that he might get thoroughly rested.

But this Fred would not do, his burning anxiety to run down Athabasca Bill making him too restless to stay a minute longer on the way than necessity compelled him to do, so although he was footsore and tired, and the road to be traversed more lonely than ever, he was for setting forward again directly his hour of rest was at an end.

"Tom, how far is it across country to Errol's lumber camp?" demanded Saidie, with a puckering frown on her face, when she had exhausted all her eloquence in persuading Fred to stay longer, but to no purpose.

"A matter of fifteen miles, perhaps twenty; do you want to go over?" drawled Tom Marsh, in his slow, good-natured fashion, which was such a contrast to the brisk energy of Saidie's utterances.

"Yes, I do if you can spare me. I can sleep at Mrs. Errol's, and come back tomorrow. I shall take both horses, then the boy can ride one, and I can ride the other; you can manage single-handed for one day, then, when I come back tomorrow, I'll work double tides to make up for my little holiday," she said with a short laugh, and a little grimace which only Tom could see, and that was intended to inform him that she wished to go for the sake of helping their guest over a rough and tiresome piece of his road.

But Fred was quick to understand, and at once entered a protest.

"Oh, please don't trouble to come on my account; I can get through to Errol's by sundown, or if I don't I can sleep under a tree, a roof doesn't matter much anyway this weather."

"If that's your opinion it isn't mine, for I find the nights are getting uncommon cold, and that is why I'm in such a hurry to get on with my house-building, or I'd maybe take a run over as far as Errol's myself; so Saidie must go, for I want some nails—copper nails, if they have got them, and there are one or two other things we want in the housekeeping line," Tom replied. He had mastered the meaning in his sister's grimace by this time, and was acting up to it in a manful fashion.

"It will only take me five minutes or so to get ready, for the horses are hobbled, and I've nothing else to do but get into my riding skirt, so we will be starting right away," Saidie said, with a merry laugh at Fred's discomfited face, and then, whilst Tom went down to the little natural clearing by the stream to bring the two horses up, she dived into the shelter under the cart, to emerge two minutes later hatted and habited for her ride.

"You've a pretty location here," Fred said, looking round with an air of eager interest, when he had scrambled on to the back of the grey horse, whilst Saidie mounted the brown animal; he was thinking of their own projected move into the wilderness, and wondering if the shores of Wabamun Lake afforded possibilities equal to this bit of the wilderness.

"It will be all right when we get a house," replied Saidie, as she jerked the bridle as an intimation to her steed that she was ready to go on, then nodded in farewell to her brother. "But it is anything but comfortable, when it rains as it did last week, three days at the stretch, and we without a roof to cover us. Oh, but we were in a pickle, I can tell you," she said, with a shiver of recollection; then changing her tone, asked abruptly, "What is this Athabasca Bill like, and how is it that you know him so well?"

"We didn't know him very well until last fall, although we had often seen him at harvest times, for he most often happened along and helped us when we were at our busiest. But last year he took sick, got a chill or something, and was bad at our house until nearly Christmas; we had a doctor to him once or twice, but he begged mother not to do it again, because he couldn't pay the bills; so mother nursed him and did her best for him, till he was able to get about again."

"Humph! I think your mother must be a mighty good woman to do so much for a tramp," jerked out Saidie Marsh, with a funny little snort.

"He wasn't really a tramp, only low down through misfortune. He had been well educated, and should have been in a good position, only he got under a cloud, his family turned him adrift, and he'd just been drifting ever since. Most winters he goes trapping on the Athabasca Lakes, then comes south in the summer, and works on the farms," Fred explained, a little indignant that she should call his friend a tramp.

"What is his name?" she demanded sharply.

"I never heard anyone call him anything but Athabasca Bill, or Bill," answered Fred, saving himself from a tumble almost by a miracle, as the grey horse put its foot in a hole, then lurched heavily to one side.

"Rough going, isn't it? but we shall find it easier later on," said his companion, as the brown horse also floundered and slipped on the uneven ground; then returning with a strange persistency to the subject of his quest, she asked, "What is this nameless man like—is he dark and fierce-looking, a sort of Texas cow-puncher who has wandered north and got lost?"

"Not a bit of it; he is one of the meekest, mildest looking men that I think I ever saw. His hair is lighter than mine, his eyes are blue, and he doesn't look as if he could knock over a squirrel in an ordinary sort of way; but I saw him get roused once, and then he got as fierce as a Cherokee on the war path."

"What was it about?" demanded Saidie, with no lack of interest, and though he was always more than willing to talk about his friend, Fred was considerably surprised at the eagerness this stranger girl displayed on the subject.

"There had been a fire in a lot of dry bunch grass, and everyone had been hard at work putting it out, because it was near the schoolhouse, and they thought it would be fired too. Bill hadn't been among the workers, though he was in at the finish, when everyone was ready to dance with delight because the danger was over, and Micky Shute, the bar-tender, began chaffing him about happening along in time to fling up his hat and shout hurrah with the rest, but keeping out of the way till the work was done. Bill glared at the fellow for a minute or so, just as if he would scorch him out of existence with a glance, then he jumped straight for him, and knocked him clean into a tub of water that had been used for wetting fire mops in."

"Hurrah! I like that. What happened next?" demanded Saidie eagerly, clapping her hands.

"There was nothing to happen, except the laughter at the figure cut by Micky Shute when he was hauled out of the tub, for Athabasca Bill had walked away, and wasn't seen again that day. But the police told us afterwards, that Bill had been one of the first to turn out when the fire-guardian raised the alarm, and he had been working like a horse in the water-hole all the time, because the wheel didn't turn the water up fast enough, and the creek was nearly dry."

No response from Saidie at this, though Fred had expected quite an outburst of hurrahs; but when he turned to look at her, surprised by her silence, he saw to his amazement that her head was low down on the brown horse's neck, and she was weeping bitterly.

"Why, whatever is the matter with you?" he exclaimed, in extreme consternation. Tears always got upon his nerves, and, so far as he could see, this outburst was entirely uncalled for.

For a minute or so Saidie sobbed on, seemingly unable to explain the cause of her grief, whilst Fred grew hotter and hotter, feeling all the time as if he would very much like to kick his heels into the grey horse's sides, and make that worthy, though blundering animal carry him at the top of its speed from the sight of so much grief.

Presently recovering a little, she looked, with a wan smile.

"I am afraid you will think me rather silly," she said, in a choked tone, catching her breath in another sob.

"I couldn't think what I had said or done to make you take on like that," he replied reproachfully, looking as offended as he felt.

"It was stupid of me, and I know by experience how boys hate tears; besides, I almost never cry. But from what you have said, I can't help thinking that Athabasca Bill must be my eldest brother, who has been missing more years than I could count; indeed, ever since I was a little girl in short frocks."

"Oh!" Fred's eyes looked as if they would start out of his head with amazement, and he was plainly not capable of anything in the way of speech, saving the ejaculation which he fired off like a rocket.

"It must seem very funny to you, that I can be so sure of the identity of a man I have never seen; but that bit you told me about Bill knocking down Micky Shute convinced me that it must be the same," she said, gulping down a succession of sobs that threatened to choke her.

"But how—?" began Fred; then failing the ability to put what he wanted to say into words, stopped short in confusion.

"How did he come to be lost, do you mean? Ah, that is a long story, and a sad one," Saidie said, rubbing her eyes very hard with her handkerchief, which had the effect of making them even redder than before. "Bill, or Willie, as we used to call him, was the eldest of our family, and I am the youngest. There were ten of us altogether, but all are dead now but four; that is Willie, my eldest sister Mary, who is married and lives in Wyoming, Tom, and myself."

"Are your father and mother dead too?" inquired Fred, hastily scenting another breakdown, and anxious to divert her mind, even though his question had no cheerful tendency.

"All dead," she answered, with a sad little shake of her head. "Willie, as I said, was the eldest, then Mary, and then came Arthur, whom my father and mother always appeared to love better than any of their children. He and Willie had situations in the same store, and were very much attached to each other, seeming to care for no other companionship. But one day word came to my father that the boys had been gambling, and had taken money that did not belong to them; both stoutly denied it, but suspicion pointed to Willie, and in a fit of bitter anger my father cast him forth, declaring that he would never again look in the face of the son who had so dishonoured his name. Oh, they were sad years that followed; my mother drooped and drooped, my father grew into a morose, taciturn man, of whom his children were afraid, and a string of disasters followed on the heels of each other, until we seemed to be living over again the experience of the patriarch Job; and no sooner was the news of one tragedy told, than a messenger arrived in hot haste to inform us of another. Two of my brothers were drowned boating; then my sister Lucy, who had gone to stay with some friends at a distance, took fever and died; after which Arthur was run over in the street, and brought home mortally wounded."

"Look here, don't tell me any more if it hurts you so," interrupted Fred, seeing how white his companion had grown.

"It won't hurt me more to tell of it than it does to think of it all," she said, with a shiver. "When Arthur knew he was dying, he confessed that it was he and not Willie who had gambled, and then stolen money to make good his losses; when suspicion fell on Willie, he was too cowardly to own up to the truth, and so the good elder brother was cast out in anger to sink or swim as he could, whilst the guilty one stayed on in the comfort and love of the home. My father and mother never recovered the shock of Arthur's dying confession, and died within two years; they had advertised far and wide for news of Willie, but no word had come to them out of the silence. Tom, Mary and I lived on together until my sister married, then he and I decided to come north and try our fortunes in the wilderness. It was just about that time we chanced to hear from someone, who years before had come across Willie in Canada, and since then I have always felt that, sooner or later, we should come upon his trail."

"There is Errol's place, I believe," broke in Fred, pointing to some smoke rising from the valley below.

"Yes; that is it," replied Saidie, adding breathlessly, "and oh, suppose we find your Athabasca Bill there!"

CHAPTER VI
OLD MAN ARLO'S MONEY BAGS

The day after Mr. Crawford's committal for trial, old man Arlo rose early, and prepared for a journey.

As it was to be a journey by rail, his beloved dogs were, of necessity, left behind, carefully locked up with a good supply of food and water.

The old man lived alone in a little brown house, that stood back from the road in a weedy patch of clearing. Very few people ever came near the place, because of the unenviable reputation enjoyed by the dogs, so that he had little cause to fear that any of his neighbours would come prying about his premises during his absence.

A poor old object of pity he looked, as he set forth on his jaunt, his well-worn garments hanging in loose, flapping folds about his shrunken form; a battered old hat pressed down over his straggling grey hair, and a soiled, faded scarf tied in an untidy wisp about his throat.

He had a sideway motion in walking, that reminded one of a crab; and although he looked such a weak, frail old fellow, it was quite wonderful the pace he made, and the ease with which he seemed to get over the ground. When he reached the railway depôt, he boarded the cars on a trip to the town, haggling so fiercely with the official over some question of price, declaring that he had been charged a quarter of a dollar too much, that eventually a good-natured fellow-passenger paid the money for him, under the impression that the disputed coin formed a part of his bottom dollar.

Old man Arlo thanked the kindly stranger almost with tears in his eyes, and then subsided on to his seat, his wrinkled face screwed into a pucker of intense satisfaction, which never left it until the town was reached.

He made his way along the busy street from the depôt to the court-house, looking such a shaky, pitiable old man, that more than one passer-by turned to look at him, hoping that no harm would come to him in the bustling throng, where it was everyone for himself and no man for his neighbour.

When he appeared before the officials in the court-house, asking if he might be allowed to bail out Maitland Crawford, his request was looked upon as a sort of mild form of lunacy, and he was responded to in the half-bantering fashion supposed to best fit his case.

"All right; what is the figure?" demanded old man Arlo, with a rather dangerous gleam in the eyes, that were hidden away under their bushy, beetling brows.

"Five hundred dollars, money down," was the laconic reply, given in a brusque tone, for the official deemed he had wasted enough of his valuable time on this wandering lunatic, and was desirous of getting rid of him as soon as possible.

"Will you take it in notes or gold?" demanded old man Arlo, producing a bulky pocket-book, from which he proceeded to extract some very greasy notes. "Because, if you want it in gold, I'm afraid I'll have to trouble you to step along to the bank with me, or to send one of your young men to fetch it, for I'm not very good at carrying things now, and five hundred dollars would be something of a weight, eh?"

The energy with which the old fellow fired off the ejaculation made the official jump, whilst his amazement at finding the old tramp possessed of so much money was a sight to see.

"Notes will do, Mr. Arlo," he replied gravely, so soon as he had found his tongue again after the momentary shock. "But do you think you are wise to take such a risk? Think of the temptation to a man in Mr. Crawford's position to slope, when he finds himself free again; then where would you be?"

"Oh, I ain't afraid; Maitland Crawford is honester than most, and he wouldn't slope, to let a poor man in, as had tried to stand his friend," replied old man Arlo, in a quavering tone, shaking his head with an air of such pathetic helplessness, that the other was instantly more sorry for him than ever.

"Well, of course you know your own business best," he said tersely, then proceeded to sign the necessary documents that would ensure the prisoner's release.

"Rather hard lines on a man to be sent to prison on such flimsy evidence as was offered yesterday," commented old man Arlo, as he sorted over his bank notes.

"You think so? It seemed to me fairly circumstantial; and, really, we have so many of these robberies from railway depôts lately, that it was high time to make an example of someone, so there was nothing like commencing with the first offender caught red-handed."

Old man Arlo snorted in a fashion which savoured of disgust, then inquired in that feeble, cracked voice of his, if it was urgently necessary that his name should be made public in the matter of Mr. Crawford's bail.

"Not if you prefer to remain unknown," was the reply.

"Very well; you put it down as 'a friend,' same as they do on subscription lists, and I'll turn up all right to claim my five hundred dollars, when the time comes, don't you fret," and he laughed in a wheezy, cackling fashion, suggestive of machinery badly in want of oil. Then when the necessary forms had all been gone through, shuffled away as he had come, only for the present, at least, five hundred dollars the poorer, and looking as if he did not possess another dollar in the world.

When it was intimated to Mr. Crawford that he was a free man, until the date fixed for his trial, he was at first incredulous, for it had not seemed possible to him that anyone would come forward to bail him out. Then he asked to be told the name of his benefactor, but was informed that his surety wished to remain unknown, and was in consequence more puzzled than ever.

But he was free, and that in itself was a joy unspeakable. Without a moment's unnecessary delay, he hurried to the depôt, and because there was no passenger train for some hours, he boarded a train of freight cars, and travelled homeward on the rear platform of a horse car, dropping off when the cars stopped at Millet, and walking past the office he was supposed to have robbed, set out on the five-mile trudge to his home.

He was thinking how pleased they would be to see him—how the children would shout, and how his wife's face would shine with quiet joy; then came the thought of when he would have to leave them again, to be tried for a crime he had not committed, perhaps sentenced to a term of imprisonment, from whence he must return with a shamed and tarnished reputation, that nothing could restore to honour and uprightness.

"Oh, it was hard, cruelly hard to be made the victim of so foul a plot!" he muttered to himself, stopping short in the middle of the road, clenching his hands until the nails pressed into his horny palms, and his whole frame grew rigid with the intensity of his emotion, so that for a moment he was like a person in a cataleptic seizure.

It was growing dusk with the soft, enveloping gloom that marks the early autumn night, when suddenly a bird, perched among the yellowing leaves on a steeply wooded bank, burst into a sleepy trill of song, and then was silent again.

But it had done its work; the tension of the sorely tried man's limbs relaxed, the terrible rigour passed away, and he went forward with a free, springing step, because the tiny burst of bird-music had reminded him of the words in Holy Writ, that not one sparrow could fall to the ground without the Creator's knowledge, and so he was comforted, remembering that he was of more value than many sparrows.

His fancy had not over-painted the joy wrought by his unexpected return. Mrs. Crawford was sitting in a despondent attitude by the kitchen stove, and the children were getting their supper in melancholy silence, when he opened the door and walked in.

"Father!" cried Ella, with such a jubilant shout that her mother sprang up, knocking over a chair and a tin saucepan with a great noise and clatter.

"Maitland, is it really you?" she cried, with unbelieving joy, tumbling into his outstretched arms, whilst all the children crowded round, as uproarious now as they had been solemnly silent before.

"Really it is myself," he replied, laughing, yet with an odd quavering sound in his voice that betrayed the feeling lying behind; then with a quick change of tone he asked, "Where is Fred?"

"Gone in quest of Athabasca Bill; he set out at dawn this morning. I could not rest without doing something, and that seemed the only thing to be done. If Athabasca Bill can throw no other light on the mystery, he can at least help to prove an alibi for you," Mrs. Crawford said eagerly. She was still clinging to her husband, as if scarcely able to assure herself even now that he was not an apparition.

"I had thought of that myself—about the alibi, I mean, but not of sending Fred; he is such a boy to set out on a big journey like that," he answered.

"But he has a wise head on his shoulders, and I have no doubt of his doing his best. I gave him nearly all the money I had, and told him to earn his food where he could, so that he should not spend more than he could help."

"It was a good plan, and I hope the boy will find him; but Athabasca Bill would be precious hard to track down, I fancy, for he goes to such outlandish places for his winter trapping," Mr. Crawford said, as he sat down in his armchair by the stove, and began to realize how very tired he was.

"Ella, dear, hurry to get your father some supper, he must be so hungry; you might scramble some eggs, Celia will help you." Mrs. Crawford spoke to her daughter in an urgent whisper, then turned again to her husband with a question. "Maitland, you said someone had bailed you out; who was it, dear?"

"I haven't the ghost of a notion; when I asked, I was told that it was a friend, and that this unknown individual, whoever he or she may be, had considerately left enough money to pay my car fare home."

"It was very, very kind!" she murmured.

"Indeed it was. Amazingly kind! I did not know that I possessed such an influential friend anywhere."

"Father, I'm dreadfully sorry I asked to have that box; only it was such a nice, cunning little box, and I wanted it so very badly," Johnny said later on, when there was a lull in the talk, and he found a chance to say something on his own account.

"What box?" asked Mr. Crawford, in an abstracted fashion.

"The box that made the trouble. Dolty Simpson says that if you hadn't been found with the box in your arms, you would not have been taken to prison; and if I had not wanted it so badly, you would not have gone to the barn to fetch it just then."

"There is reason in that, certainly," said Mr. Crawford, with a look across at his wife; "though, I declare, I had not thought of it before. But don't worry yourself, Johnny, my lad; whoever put the box there meant it to be found on my premises, and it was not your wanting it merely that brought the trouble, though I don't say but what it may have hastened the catastrophe a little."

Johnny sniffed in a dolorous and uncomforted fashion; many and bitter were the tears he had shed since his father's arrest, because of his own innocent share in the business, and even now he could not feel himself free from blame.

But Mr. Crawford had more serious things to discuss that evening than even the sorrows of his youngest son, and sending him off to bed with a kindly word, began to talk to his wife concerning his plans for the future.

"I shall sell the farm and the stock at once, Emily, if I can get a customer for it, then matters will be easier for you if I am convicted and sent to prison for a term. Whilst if I should succeed in getting off, it will only hasten our going to the Wabamun country by a few months, and I shall be just as happy to be quit of this part of the world, after having to stand my trial for theft."

Mrs. Crawford nodded sympathetically, for she felt herself that the sooner they left the neighbourhood the better, after such a blow to their honour and respectability.

"But you couldn't go to the Wabamun country in the winter, and with no house built on your claim," she objected.

"You and the young ones could not. But Fred and I could manage very well with a shack under a sheltered hillock, well banked with snow. Then we could get a house built before the spring came and the land wanted us, don't you see; and meanwhile, you and the children could have lodgings in the town, till the weather got fit for you to join us in the new home.

"It sounds promising, if only we knew how the trial would go!" sighed Mrs. Crawford.

"Ah, if only we did!" he said, with an answering sigh.

CHAPTER VII
OLD MAN ARLO SHOWS A WAY OUT

For the next week Mr. Crawford worked as hard as it was possible for one pair of hands and feet to do. His long absence searching for a new location had left farm work very much in arrears. Dolty Simpson, though honest and faithful, not being endowed with an energetic temperament, was apt to run work to slow music, unless there was a leading spirit in command to push things forward.

But now that the boss was back again, Dolty was having to hustle in true Yankee fashion, very much to his own discomfort, but vastly to the good of the farm.

Mr. Crawford was coming home from the ten-acre lot with his team one afternoon, after a long day of ploughing, when he met old man Arlo and the three bloodhounds, which as usual were straining and tugging at the leash. Montana Jenny growled in a menacing fashion, recognizing the quarry she had so successfully run to earth nine or ten days before; but Smiler and Ruby were straining and whining in vain endeavours to lick their preserver's hands or feet, or indeed any part of himself or his clothes.

Mr. Crawford left his team a minute, to go and renew his acquaintance with the two friendly hounds, for he had that strong inborn love of a good dog, which is like an instinct in some people, but he kept a watchful eye on Montana Jenny, having no desire to find her leaping at his throat.

"So you're out of prison," said old man Arlo, in a disagreeable, croaking voice. "Who's your bail?"

"Ah, that is just what I should very much like to know myself," replied Mr. Crawford warmly; "just to say to him, 'Sir, I thank you warmly for your confidence in my honour, and I'll take care to do my utmost to show myself worthy of it.'"

"Which only shows that you are more of a lunatic than I had given you credit for being," growled the old man harshly, drawing his brows together in a frown of portentous blackness.

"What do you mean?" demanded Mr. Crawford in astonishment, going to his team, which were beginning to show signs of restlessness.

"What I say; that if you've got a grain of sense or sanity left, you'll slope, whilst you've got the chance," snapped the old man, with a vicious tug at the cord which held his dogs.

"So that the man who stood my friend, when there was no one else to help me, shall have to lose his five hundred dollars, I suppose? Well, you must think me a low down sort of scoundrel, to return a kindness in that fashion," Mr. Crawford retorted scornfully.

"No need to let your dander riz in that fashion, as I knows of," retorted old man Arlo, with another tweak at the cord which restrained the impatient dogs. "The fellow, whoever he was, knew the risks he was taking in standing bail; maybe did it on purpose to give you a chance to get away."

"Innocent folks shouldn't have to run away in dishonour," Mr. Crawford said, frowning almost as heavily as the old man who stood glowering opposite.

"Bah, that is all stuff and talk! Lawyers and police have got to live, same as other people; and if there ain't enough real thieves and villains to go round, why, they have to convict a few honest, respectable folk once in a way, just to keep their reputation going, so to speak. It ain't no business of mine, of course; but you've been a good neighbour. I don't forget that you saved my dogs for me, and if I could advise you for your good, why, it stands to reason I'd be glad to do it."

Old man Arlo's tone was so strangely earnest now, that the other looked at him in surprise, answering more gently than he would have done, but for the beseeching look in the eyes gleaming from under the bushy, beetling brows.

"It is very kind of you, old friend, to be so concerned on my account, and I'm just as grateful as if I could follow your advice. But I've more confidence in the laws of my country, than to think I shall be convicted, being innocent; or if such a thing should be that I am sent to prison, I shall still have the knowledge of my innocence to support me."

"Mighty poor comfort that, I should say!" scoffed old man Arlo, with a sudden change of manner. "Well, as I said before, it ain't no particklar business of mine; still, if I was in your place, I'd slope, and be quick about it."

"There wouldn't be much use in my running away, I'm afraid, seeing that those terrible hounds of yours would be safe to stick to my trail, even if I made tracks for Labrador," Mr. Crawford answered, with a laugh, reaching out his hand to fondle Smiler's ears.

"Now, you look here, neighbour," said old man Arlo, with an air of solemn earnestness, coming nearer and laying his wrinkled, dirty hand on the other's jacket sleeve; "if so be you've a mind to dodge the finger of the law, so to speak, I'll take good care that no beast of mine runs you down a second time. I'd sooner have choked the whole three of them, than that such a thing should have happened before. But there ain't no sense in crying over spilt milk, so I ain't going to waste time in whining about that; only once bitten, twice shy, and you give me a hint that you're thinking of sloping, I'll take jolly good care that there ain't no danger of the dogs following you up."

"You are very good; but it won't do, neighbour, for I've made up my mind to stay and face the music," rejoined Mr. Crawford, a little stiffly, for he was beginning to resent the old man's pertinacity.

"Well, well, do as you please; only perhaps you'll remember, if the worst comes to the worst, and you are convicted, that it is all your own fault," said old man Arlo, turning away in a huff, and dragging the unwilling dogs after him.

Mr. Crawford went his homeward way in a very brown study indeed. The way of escape pointed out by old man Arlo had been rankling in his own mind for days past, and it was only the exceeding ingratitude of leaving the man who had bailed him out to suffer, that had kept him from seriously meditating such a flight from the difficulties looming ahead.

He knew that, innocent though he was, nothing could save him from a conviction except the presence of Athabasca Bill, to swear to an alibi which even then might not hold good, or the detection of the real thief, a very unlikely prospect indeed, since the police would not stir further, or trouble themselves in looking for another victim, when they had one all ready and waiting close at hand.

If he chose to make a bid for safety in flight, the chances were greatly in favour of his getting off scot free; the country was so wide and so sparsely settled, that the mounted police would not be likely to trouble themselves over much in riding in pursuit of a fugitive, when there was so little to be gained by catching him.

But not to save himself from prison, or to save his wife and children from the poverty that must come upon them if he were convicted, would Mr. Crawford be false to his own idea of honour and uprightness. This unknown benefactor had believed in him, and trusted him to the extent of five hundred dollars, and he could not be the mean-souled ingrate to betray such a trust.

Strangely enough, his wife had been brooding over the same subject all the afternoon, and when supper was done, the two little boys gone to bed, and the two girls washing up the dishes on the back porch, she spoke of the trouble that had been so heavy on her mind.

"You will be ready to answer to your bail, Maitland?" she asked, half fearfully.

"Yes, I hope so," he answered, with a quick look at her, wondering if old man Arlo had paid her a visit before coming on to him.

"I am so thankful!" she exclaimed, with a deep breath of relief. "All day I have been haunted by the dread lest you should be tempted to keep your freedom, now you have it, by getting away before the trial comes on."

"Haven't you got a better opinion of me than that?" he asked, half banteringly, yet with an underlying reproach in his tone.

"I know how you love the children and me, and I feared lest your care for us should blind you to the duty you owe to yourself," she said softly.

He nodded, but did not speak for a minute; then he said, in a half query—

"So you are not very hopeful about the result of the trial?"

"How can I be, in the face of such circumstantial evidence? I am inclined to think it was a deeply laid plot to compass your ruin; yet even then it is amazing that it should have been planned with such consummate cleverness, since no one knew for certain that you were coming home that day, or that it would be so hard for you to prove your alibi; and then, again, no one could have known that you would take off that comforter of yours to give to that miserable tramp."

"Ah, but for that misguided act of charity, I should never have been in this plight," he answered bitterly.

"What do you mean?" she asked, in surprise.

"Why, but for that miserable comforter, they would have had no possible chance of fixing the guilt on to me; even the hiding of the box in my barn would have only served to throw suspicion on Dolty Simpson, or someone else, equally with myself. But the miscreant, whoever he was, to whom I gave the comforter, must have brought the box here, dragging the scarf after him, then have gone all the way back to the depôt, and stuffed the thing in at the office window."

"If only that tramp could be found!" sighed Mrs. Crawford, as she stooped a little lower over the garment she was mending, and hoped that her husband would not see the tears which blinded her eyes, and which she was furtively trying to wipe away.

"Aye, if only we could!" he echoed, staring moodily at the fire, yet seeing nothing in the blazing, crackling wood, but the bowed, suffering figure of the man to whom he had given his comforter, and whom he believed to be the enemy who had done him such cruel wrong. "But that, I am afraid, is by no means likely to come to pass, and the next best thing would be to get hold of Athabasca Bill."

"I wonder where Fred is tonight, and when we shall hear of him," said Mrs. Crawford, with motherly anxiety for the welfare of her first-born, whom she had sent out to the wilderness on his father's behalf.

"When we see him, I guess, and not before. Post-offices don't stand very thick on the ground in the districts where Athabasca Bill spends his winters," replied Mr. Crawford; then Ella and Celia, having finished with the dishes, came back to the fireside, and the talk veered round to other subjects.

The next day it rained and blew with tremendous force. Ploughing, or indeed any sort of out-door work, was out of the question. Dolty Simpson hitched a horse to the wagon to drive the children to school, covering them over with a bit of tarpaulin, as if they had been bags of meal from the mill. Then when that errand was done, he went to the barn to help Mr. Crawford, who was busy repairing farming implements, and other work, always left for such kind of weather.

Ella and Celia had both gone to school that day, and when the active part of her day's work was over, Mrs. Crawford sat down to her big work-basket, which was overflowing with garments in need of repair.

There was no bread to be baked that day, no washing, ironing, or churning, and the brooding hush of the house was almost like the quiet that comes with Sunday, whilst the storm raging without made all the pleasanter the peace and comfort of the tidy kitchen, with its cheerful, crackling fire, which glowed and sputtered through the half-open door of the stove.

A vague uneasiness had taken possession of Mrs. Crawford, despite the restful quiet of her surroundings. Every few minutes she rose and went to the window, peering anxiously through the murk of the falling rain drops, as if she expected something or someone.

"I can't think what is the matter with me, but I feel just as if something were going to happen. I suppose the anxiety and trouble of the last week or two has rather upset me," she said, as, laying down the garment she was repairing, she rose once more and, going to the window, peered out at the driving rain.

Some one was coming. A brown horse, with a huddled dripping figure on its back was approaching the house, and with her hospitable instincts fully on the alert, Mrs. Crawford hastened to fling wide the house door, to give her visitor a welcome.

"Are you Mrs. Crawford?" asked a brisk, girlish voice, as the dripping rider slid slowly from her horse to the ground.

"Yes, yes; do you bring me news of my boy?" she panted anxiously.

The girl put out both hands to grip Mrs. Crawford's, saying in a tremulous tone—

"I am Saidie Marsh, and I've ridden over fifty miles to bring you bad news; such bad news that I am afraid to tell it."

CHAPTER VIII
THROUGH DENAREE'S LEAP

Errol's lumber camp was also a store, and a recognized centre round which the units of civilization in that part of the world circled.

The man who gave the place its name, and was the mainspring of all its activities, was a stalwart backwoodsman, who had emigrated to the North West Territories from Ontario fifteen years before, winning himself a home and a living from the wilderness, becoming at length a highly prosperous individual, after a rough and ready fashion.

Mrs. Errol was a merry little woman, with a great longing for companionship, who found life at her husband's lumber camp so intolerably solitary, that it was only rendered endurable to her by entertaining and fussing over every wandering stranger, whose business or pleasure led him or her within reach of her eagerly proffered hospitality.

She welcomed Saidie Marsh with enthusiastic fervour, declaring that she would keep her a week, though she had seen her only once before.

"You are very kind, Mrs. Errol, and I shall be very thankful for one night's shelter, though I can't stay longer," Saidie replied gratefully; then drawing Fred forward, she said, "this is my friend, Frederic John Crawford, and the pair of us are out man-hunting."

"Dear, dear, only to think of it!" cried Mrs. Errol, with a gush of laughter. "I had no idea that the Dominion Government enrolled women in the mounted police corps; but we are always behind the times in the backwoods. Who is it you are hunting, pray—some terrible murderer?"

"No, indeed; our quarry has done nothing to be ashamed of, but he is badly wanted all the same. Is Athabasca Bill here, Mrs. Errol?" Saidie demanded eagerly.

"No; that he isn't. He went down to Denaree's Leap yesterday morning, on his way to the trapping grounds near Rocky Raps," replied Mrs. Errol.

"I am too late, then," groaned Saidie, blank disappointment settling down over her face.

"But I must go on after him," broke in Fred, finding his tongue now, though he had hung shyly in the background previously, feeling a little overawed by vivacious Mrs. Errol.

"You!" cried Mrs. Errol, with a sharp glance at him. "Why, you are much too young to go wandering about the world alone, man-hunting, and there are no hotels, or railway cars, where Athabasca Bill has gone."

"No, ma'am, I didn't suppose there were; but I have got to go after him, for all that, and to find him too," Fred replied, with a smile; he was finding Mrs. Errol easier to talk to now that he had once begun.

"Why is it you are wanting to find him so badly? Will you tell me, or is it a secret?" she asked kindly.

Fred told her at once, making his story as brief as was consistent with coherence. But he said nothing concerning the revelation made to him by Saidie Marsh, since that was her business, not his, and he had no right to make common property of it.

Saidie, meanwhile, had wandered indoors to renew her acquaintance with Mrs. Errol's three babies, who were pretending to help their old Indian nurse sort berries for pies, but were in reality rolling and tumbling over each other in a merry frolic, shouting and laughing in an abandonment of childish glee.

Sore as her heart was with the disappointment of finding Athabasca Bill had gone beyond her reach for the present, Saidie could not resist the temptation of joining the sport of the little ones, and in a few moments the shouting and laughing was redoubled, as she tossed them up in her arms, kissed the berry-stained faces, and rolled them over and over on the floor.

Fred coming upon the scene with Mrs. Errol a little later, was amazed at her mirth and high spirits; he was inclined to be a little resentful, too, because she seemed so happy and light-hearted, when she should have been, in his opinion, sad and melancholy at missing Athabasca Bill, whom she was so anxious to see and identify a short time ago.

But in reality he had more cause for gratitude than complaint, as he was speedily to find, for Saidie intervened so successfully on his behalf, with Mr. and Mrs. Errol, that he not merely did not have his supper, bed and breakfast to pay for, but his host offered to send him five miles down river in a canoe, to where Black Pine portage marked the limit of navigation in that direction.

"Will the canoe cost much?" Fred ventured to ask, for anxious as he was to overtake Athabasca Bill before that worthy plunged into the almost track-less wilderness beyond Rocky Raps, he feared to make inroads on his scanty stock of cash, knowing the stern necessity there would be for the money later on, when there would be two to provide with food instead of one, for he could not expect the man he sought to journey all the distance back to Millet at his own expense.

"Not a cent, my boy; I've got to send a man with some stores in a canoe down to Black Pine portage, and you may as well go too; it should give you a pull on Athabasca Bill, since he tramped the distance, and it is pretty rough going between here and Black Pine," George Errol replied.

"I'm very much obliged to you," Saidie broke in, before Fred had time to utter a thank you. "I have my own special reasons for wanting Athabasca Bill captured and brought back with as little delay as possible. Indeed, I was in two minds about pushing on myself with Fred, until we overtook him; only Tom will be so put to it to manage without me, especially as I have got the horses, and we were almost out of sugar and tea."

"It is just as well you can't go on, for I've no opinion of girls wandering about in such a fashion, especially one as pretty as yourself," George Errol replied, with a laugh and a bow, which was intended to emphasize the compliment, but only served to make Saidie cross.

"I am perfectly well able to take care of myself, thank you, Mr. Errol; but you need not trouble about me, as I intend setting out for our camp at dawn tomorrow morning," she said, with a toss of her head and a pout.

"No, indeed you will not. You promised to stay until tomorrow afternoon, and I just mean to make you keep your word," broke in Mrs. Errol, who was getting her own supper in the intervals of feeding her children.

"What is the river like beyond Black Pine portage?" asked Fred presently, when a discussion about hat trimmings between the two women gave him a chance of getting the ear of his host for a minute or so.

"Just as bad as it can be; twenty miles of whirlpools and rapids, with rocks sticking up in the middle; the Indians have a name for it, which means the Valley of Death, but it is mostly called Denaree's Leap," George Errol answered, pushing a great dish of corn-cakes and maple syrup nearer to Fred, and bidding him help himself.

"Why Denaree's Leap?" asked the boy, who was keenly anxious to know all there was to be known of the country through which he had to make his way.

"There was a French Canadian exploring this bit of country, a few years back, when the Indians were inclined to be troublesome; his guides deserted him, and he was in a fair way of being murdered in his tent on the cliff above the river bank, when just as he was hard-pressed and making a brave stand in his own defence, he espied a canoe that had somehow got adrift come bobbing and bowing down stream, and trusting to his luck, he turned and sprang right out into the current, by a wonderful chance grabbed the empty canoe, and scrambled in."

"What a plucky thing to do! Did he get safely away?" asked Fred eagerly.

"From the Indians, yes; from the Valley of Death, no. A few bits of the canoe were picked up a few days later, twenty miles further down river, but nothing was ever again seen of Jean Denaree, the ill-fated French Canadian explorer," George Errol replied, with a shake of his head.

"What a melancholy tale! And is it really true, Mr. Errol?" demanded Saidie, who had turned from the millinery discussion, to listen to the story her host was telling.

"I believe so. It was told to me by one of the Indians who saw Denaree jump," said George Errol. "My own opinion is that if he had only been a little braver, and shown a firmer front to the Indians, he need not have leaped to his death in that fashion; but you can never tell what a man will do when panic seizes him."

"All the Indians that I have come across have been the most arrant cowards; but perhaps they have become degenerate since the brave days of old," laughed Saidie, as she turned back to the question of millinery once more, with a shrug of relief in dismissing a topic so weird.

Fred could not get rid of it so easily, however, and in his dreams that night was taking Denaree's leap, and fighting for his life in the raging waters of the Valley of Death. So real was the vision, that he awoke himself struggling and choking, to find his head all entangled in his blanket, whilst the half-breed, named Potiphar, who was to take the stores down river, was tugging and shaking at his arm in order to rouse him for the start.

"Is it morning already?" asked Fred, sitting up with a shiver, for the air coming in at the open door of the hut was keen with the chill of coming winter.

"Boss do say, get away early down river wid dem stores, Potiphar, cos the boy he want to get along fast on the trail," said the half-breed, who rarely made a statement on his own account, but repeated the words of other people, as involving him in less responsibility.

"All right, I'm glad to be off early; but I declare I thought it was the middle of the night," Fred answered, with a yawn, promptly stuffing his head into a bucket of cold water, in order to banish his sleepiness.

But the fear and horror of his dream was on him still, and he shivered again, as he swallowed down half-a-pint of scalding hot coffee, and munched away at a great chunk of bread and bacon, by way of breakfast. He had no special concern about that day's dinner or supper, for the wallet strapped across his shoulders contained a supply of food that was more than sufficient for one day's needs, and beyond that there was no use in planning for, since at any time now he might find Athabasca Bill, and turn to retrace his journey homewards.

Saidie was up to look after his breakfast, to speed him onwards with her brisk, cheerful words of counsel, and to lay a special injunction upon him.

"Don't tell your Athabasca Bill anything of that little story I confided to you yesterday; only bring him to see Tom and me, as soon as your business will allow of the visit, and if he is the man I think he is, I shall just love to tell it to him myself. Meanwhile, it is a secret between you and me, Frederic John Crawford."

"I'll be careful to remember, and as a reward for my good behaviour, perhaps you will consent to call me Fred, instead of all that mouthful you seem so fond of, Miss Marsh," he said, with a laugh, as he took his place in the canoe, among the kegs of biscuits, flour, and sugar, the parcels of bacon, tea, and other stores with which the canoe was heavily laden.

Then Potiphar took his place in the bow as steersman, telling Fred to do the best he could with the stern paddle, and the little craft pushed slowly out to mid-stream, whilst Saidie stood on the bank in the dull grey light of the dawning, shouting farewells and waving her handkerchief, until they were out of sight round a bend in the river.

How the current raced along! Fred found little work in paddling, whilst Potiphar grunted and snorted in satisfaction at their progress, but spoke no articulate word until they were nearing a part of the river where a wall of black, funereal-looking pines loomed up to the sky line.

"Boss say stop at Black Pine portage; no through passengers for Denaree's Leap," he said, with a grating chuckle of laughter at his own small joke, which, however, in his peculiar fashion, he imputed to his master.

But the laughter proved his undoing, for in paddling inshore he failed to notice the low-hanging branches of a birch tree, which swept him from the canoe into the swiftly rushing current. Then before Fred could realize what had happened, or bend his strength towards paddling inshore, the canoe shot forward at a tremendous pace into the swirling waters of Denaree's Leap.

CHAPTER IX
THE TIDINGS FROM BLACK PINE PORTAGE

Saidie Marsh thoroughly enjoyed her morning with Mrs. Errol, whilst it was a satisfaction to be in a house for a few hours, after her experience of living for weeks in and under a cart. It is true the house was a very primitive one, being merely a log-cabin of rather larger dimensions than usual, well chinked, and fairly comfortable, but nothing more.

"Still, a roof is a roof, and you never know the comfort of having one over your head, until you have had to go without for a while," Saidie said, when Mrs. Errol reproved her in a laughing fashion for her enthusiastic praises of the backwoods abode.

"Yes, I know what the sensation is, for I have been through it myself, or something nearly akin to it; but you will be all right when you get your house built."

"I hope so; and now I must really see about getting those stores packed on to the grey horse's back. I shall miss my companion on the ride back to our camp; he is such a nice boy, that Frederic John Crawford! I declare I got quite fond of him," Saidie remarked, with a regretful sigh to think she had all the weary miles to ride, with no companionship saving that of the horses.

"Poor laddie! I wonder if he will succeed in overhauling Athabasca Bill; it is a big order for such a boy to undertake. And I wonder if his father is really innocent?" Mrs. Errol said, in a musing tone, as she led the way into the rough lean-to built at the side of the house, where the kegs of sugar and flour were kept, and which was called the store.

"Of course he is innocent; you can't imagine the father of a nice boy like Fred being a common low-down creature, capable of stealing a box of copper nails from a railway depôt," retorted Saidie, with some heat.

"I thought it was five hundred dollars?" objected Mrs. Errol, as she began to shovel sugar on to the scale in a businesslike fashion.

"It makes no difference; the box was labelled nails, even if it was stuffed with dollars," Saidie answered, indignant still that even a suspicion of possible guilt should cling to the reputation of Mr. Crawford in Mrs. Errol's mind.

"He might even have inherited his good qualities from his mother; it is often the case," Mrs. Errol went on, in an argumentative fashion, as she tipped a little more sugar on to the scale to make it go down nicely.

"This one did not—at least, not entirely," Saidie retorted, in a confident tone; then struck by a clamour of voices outside, moved hastily towards the door of the store, saying as she went, "I wonder what all the noise is about; it sounds as if something had happened."

Mrs. Errol followed her to the door, then cried out in surprise and alarm, for a canoe was being drawn up on the bank by two Indians, whilst out of it Potiphar was scrambling, dripping wet, his head bandaged with a dirty piece of cotton cloth, and one arm thrust into the bosom of his red flannel shirt, as if it had also been injured.

"What is the matter, Potiphar? You look as if you had been in the wars!" Mrs. Errol cried, with an involuntary smile, for the half-breed looked a ludicrous spectacle, with his dripping garments and dirty head-bandage.

"No, ma'am, but me have been in the water, which is a wusser," replied Potiphar, shaking himself as if he were a dog that had been for a swim.

"Have you had an upset with the canoe?" asked George Errol, who at this moment appeared on the scene, coming down from a lumber camp high up on the pine ridge.

Potiphar flung up his hand with a tragic gesture, rolling his eyes until only the whites were visible.

"There have bin a most disparate bad accident, an' the canoe, an' the passenger, an' the stores have all gone through Denaree's Leap together."

"Not that poor boy!" gasped Saidie, going white to her lips, and looking as she were about to faint.

"Whatever were you about to let such a thing happen?" cried George Errol stormily.

"Me?" ejaculated Potiphar, with another wave of his uninjured arm. "It wasn't me, Boss, for I was being drownded all the time."

"Yah!" broke in one of the Indians, who had paddled the half-breed back from Black Pine portage. "It have bin touch-an'-go with Potiphar, Boss."

"Touch-and-go," wailed that worthy; "Boss always say something bad sure to happen some day at Black Pine, cos de current am so strong dere, an' Boss always say true. Touch-an'-go, an' me so near drownded, that me ain't come to life again yet," he said, plunging into the story of how he was swept from the canoe, but telling it in such an incoherent fashion, that no one unused to his peculiar style could ever have made out his meaning.

He had been rescued himself by one of the lumbermen flinging a rope, and lassoing him as he was being swept down by the current past the landing place, in the wake of the canoe containing Fred and the stores.

"Still, the boy may not be drowned; there's just the chance of his getting through the rapids alive. I remember hearing of two men who did the journey in a birchbark, and living to tell the tale," said George Errol; not that there was much hope in his own mind, that Fred had survived the terrible journey through the rapids, but because he must say something that would soften the shock of the tidings to the two women, standing with shocked, white faces to hear the story of the accident.

"Yah!" snorted the Indian, who had spoken before. "Two men did get through once long time ago, but they had always bin up river, an' down river in a birchbark, an' knew all about it. Dis young boy, he sit an' stare while the canoe am sucked down by the whirlpool at Denaree's Leap, an' when the canoe come up again, it am empty an' floating like a bottle cork."

"Will they find his body, do you think?" asked Saidie in an awed voice, after a pause, during which no one had spoken.

But George Errol shook his head. He had seen too much of the river's vagaries, in the passage of the Valley of Death, to have any hope or expectation of Fred's remains being rescued from the long succession of whirlpools, in order that they might have Christian burial.

"Poor laddie, poor laddie, what a terrible fate!" murmured Mrs. Errol, standing with clasped hands, whilst the tears poured down her cheeks.

Saidie's face was white and pinched, but her eyes were tearless, as she held out her hand, saying, "I must be off as quick as I can, dear Mrs. Errol, for when I have delivered the stores at our camp, I must go over to Millet to break the news of this terrible affair to Fred's father and mother. Poor souls, how they will grieve!" and her voice choked and broke, as she turned her head hastily, to hide her working features from the gaze of the others.

"You had better write them a letter, and I will send Potiphar over to Knappsville with it tomorrow," suggested George Errol, feeling that for himself there was nothing he would not rather do than have to be the teller of such news.

"Oh, I could not treat them like that, poor things. I must go to them, if it were all the way to Newfoundland," exclaimed Saidie, with a quick, gasping breath.

"But the father is in prison, isn't he?" queried Mrs. Errol, whose tears were still falling.

"All the more reason why I should go to the poor mother. Why, a letter containing such news might kill her, coming like a knock-down blow in her loneliness. But if I am there to hold her in my arms and break it gently, she may not feel quite so bad," Saidie replied, with a thrill of deep feeling; then she hurried her preparations for departure with so much purpose, that in less than half-an-hour she was riding away up the long slope from Errol's, down which she had cantered in such buoyant eagerness and expectation on the previous evening.

But when once she was safely out of sight and sound of human companionship, and her horses were going forward at the steady pace which showed they knew themselves on their homeward way, her head drooped forward, and she commenced sobbing in a dreary, hopeless fashion, that lasted without stop or stay until she reached the little encampment by the river, where her brother Tom was triumphantly nailing the shingles on to the roof of his house.

"Hullo, Saidie! We shall sleep under a roof tonight, my girl; for Dan Shorter and his hired man came along just after you started yesterday, and put in a few hours' work on the roof. He wouldn't take money for it, either; but said he'd be glad of my help at a day's ploughing later on, when I was comfortably housed. Downright good of him, I thought it, especially as he knows a deal more about house-building than I do, and can get a power of work done in a very little while. But, I say, what is the matter with you, sis? You look as if you had been crying for so long, that you had forgotten to leave off."

"I believe that is just about the truth of the matter," replied Saidie, with a forlorn attempt at a smile, and then with quivering lips she told her brother of the tragic happening at Denaree's Leap.

"Why, whatever could that doddering old numskull, Potiphar, have been about, to get swept out of the canoe in such a fashion? He must have wanted to be upset," exclaimed Tom in surprise, for it seemed scarcely credible, that a man who knew the river so well as Potiphar did, should have been bowled over by such a blunder.

"It is just one of those bits of carelessness that do happen sometimes, I expect," Saidie replied, shaking her head in despairing fashion; "and through it that poor boy Fred has come to a terrible death."

"Pity Potiphar can't be sent the same journey, only the worst of it is that it wouldn't bring the poor boy to life again," Tom answered, picking up his hammer, and preparing to return to his work again, for time was precious in these shortening autumn days.

"Tom, I believe we are on Willie's trail at last," she said, with a catch in her voice, lowering her tone somewhat, although it is probable there were no listeners within five miles of that little backwoods camp.

"You don't say so!" he exclaimed, with a start, turning sharply round, his work forgotten in the absorbing interest of her words.

"Do you remember that poor boy, Fred, said he was trying to overhaul a trapper, whom he called Athabasca Bill?"

"Rather; to remember the boy was to remember his errand, he was so dead set on running his man to earth," Tom answered, with a nod.

"Well, unless I'm much mistaken, that man, Athabasca Bill, is our long lost brother Willie," Saidie said in a tone of conviction.

"Whew, what next, I wonder! Why, I've heard of this trapper myself, come to think about it; I may even have seen him, for aught I know, and yet it never entered my head that he might be Willie."

"Of course not, nor mine either, until Fred told me about the little affair with Micky Shute, and then I seemed to see Willie all at once; for if you remember, it was just the kind of thing he would be most likely to do," she said, smiling at the recollection despite her trouble.

"I suppose it is," and he nodded again, his face wearing a thoughtful look as his memory went back to the long ago, before Willie had been driven out of the home, because of the unconfessed sin of Arthur. Then he asked abruptly, "Do you want me to drop things as they are, and start out on the trail of this Athabasca Bill?"

"No, I don't," she cried hastily. "In any case, Athabasca Bill will return in the springtime with his skins, and we can look for him then. But if you were to follow him now, I should know no peace day or night, through fear lest harm should come to you, such as befell poor Fred. Besides, I must go off myself at dawn tomorrow, and I can't be back much under the week, by which time it would not be of much use to try and follow his trail, I guess."

"Where are you going?" he inquired, thinking only of her taking another jaunt over to Errol's to see if any further tidings had been received from Denaree's Leap.

"Over to Millet, of course, to tell that poor boy's mother; you won't mind being left, Tom dear; I'll work double tides when I come back to make up for going off like this. But it is a case, you know, of doing as you would be done by," she said wistfully.

"Oh, I'll get along, never fear," he replied good-naturedly. "And see here, Saidie, you might stay a day or two to help her out a bit if she's much driven, poor soul; it is hard on a woman to have a trouble like that, and her husband in prison, too. I guess you'll be worth your keep, anyhow."

"I guess I will; one must be lazy indeed not to be worth that—at least, with an ordinary sort of appetite," she rejoined, with a quavering laugh.

CHAPTER X

OUT OF THE WHIRLPOOLS

When the canoe shot forward into the hissing, seething waters of Denaree's Leap, Fred gave himself up for lost, sending one swift, agonized look around at earth and sky, whilst an awful regret chilled his heart, because he had been unable to find Athabasca Bill before death overtook him.

Then with a bump the canoe struck against something, knocking the paddle out of his hand, and almost upsetting him into the water. An instinct of self-preservation made him slide down to the bottom of the canoe, which righted itself as buoyantly as a cork, shooting forward again with the velocity of a railway train, whilst the roaring, angry waters foamed along by its side.

Stretched full length in the bottom of the canoe, clinging for dear life to the thwarts, Fred saw nothing of where he was going, heard nothing save the roaring of the rapids, and was conscious of nothing, saving a strained, painful waiting for the end.

Would it never end? He was just feeling that he could bear no more, and would prefer death to this terrible waiting for it to come, when suddenly the motion of the canoe changed, and instead of shooting forward as heretofore, the little craft commenced whirling round and round so swiftly, that he was giddy and sick with the motion.

Then he must have become unconscious, from the wriggling, squirming motion of the little craft, though his grip on the thwart did not relax, even when a rush of water levelled the seething maelstrom for a moment, sending the flimsy craft on its way again down the narrow channel, where rocks and fallen tree trunks bristled like death traps on either side, threatening a swift destruction had the canoe been driven against them; but it rushed scathless on to where the tall cliffs of the ravine receded, the channel grew wider, and the current more leisurely; and then, ceasing to dash along with the speed of a mail train, the canoe, with its living but unconscious freight, floated gently down river, until at length it attracted the attention of a solitary traveller, who was taking a noonday rest on the river bank.

Thinking that the canoe must have broken adrift from the last portage, but never dreaming that it had passed safely through the stormy turmoil of the Valley of Death, the traveller crawled out on the half-submerged trunk of a tree as far as he dared safely venture, then flinging a cord with a hook at its end, succeeded in catching the little craft and dragging it to the bank.

"Some one in it, asleep or dead!" he exclaimed, in surprise, talking to himself, after the manner of lonely people; then, with great care and tenderness, he proceeded to drag the stiff, drenched figure from the three or four inches of water which the canoe had shipped in its progress through the rapids.

"Now, where have I seen the laddie before?" he asked, in hoarse, yet kindly tones.

At that moment, with a long, sobbing breath, Fred opened his eyes and looked up.

For one moment he lay staring at the figure bending over him, as if unable to collect his scattered and bewildered senses. Then recollection returned with a rush, as he took in the details of the odd-looking headgear worn by his rescuer.

A cap of silver fox fur it was, of no particular shape, but distinguished by two big lappets, one of squirrel, and the other of white rabbit, which were tied down over the man's ears, giving him a peculiar sinister appearance, greatly belied by his kindly, gentle expression and humorous blue eyes.

"Why, you are Athabasca Bill!—but where did you get that cap from?" gasped Fred, his astonishment helping him to gain a temporary victory over his weakness.

"It ain't surely you, Fred Crawford?" exclaimed the man, in tremendous surprise, putting up a hand to rumple his shaggy hair into yet wilder disorder, but only knocking his outrageous cap further over one eye, until he looked the most comical object imaginable, and a veritable scarecrow as well.

"Yes, I'm Fred Crawford right enough, or at least I was before I came down river through Denaree's Leap," he said, trying to struggle to a sitting posture, but forced from sheer weakness to cling to the other for support.

"It isn't possible that you came down through the Valley of Death, and are alive to talk about it?" queried Athabasca Bill, in a tone of positive awe.

"I thought it was death I was going to, especially when the rotary current caught me, sending the canoe spinning round and round worse than a runaway whirligig at a fair. I don't remember anything since," Fred replied weakly, the reaction from the strain of his terrible voyage being almost more than he could bear, without breaking down and crying like a girl.

"For sure, it was a marvellous deliverance!" exclaimed Athabasca Bill, still with wondering awe in his tones; then his solicitude for the shivering boy awoke, and he said urgently, "But let me help you over yonder, laddie, where I've got a bit of fire; you'll catch your death, for certain, if you sit shivering here."

"I want to know where you got that cap from; did you lose it and find it again, or have you had it all the time?" persisted Fred, his gaze still fixed on the other's striking headgear, as if fascinated by its peculiarity.

"Why, I've had it ever since I've known you, and I've never lost or mislaid it that I can remember," Bill answered, with a laugh, as he half-led, half-carried Fred through the bushes to where he had a little fire burning in the lee of a great rock. "It isn't often I stop to camp at this time of the day, but I was walking from dawn to dark yesterday, and from dawn this morning, so when I got here I thought I'd take a little rest, on the off-chance of finding a canoe coming along to put me over on the other side of the river," he went on, half in apology, as if he felt rather ashamed of being caught taking his ease in broad daylight.

But Fred felt he must clear up the mystery of the cap—that strange and unmistakable headgear which his father had identified in the railway depôt at Millet, as being the property of Athabasca Bill, but which he was at this moment staring at on the head of its lawful owner.

"I must know about that cap," he said, almost irritably, for the thing was getting on his nerves. "It isn't possible that you've made yourself a new one, and given the old one away?"

"No, no, it's the same old tile I've always had; a most useful article for keeping the cold out, though not perhaps strikingly beautiful. I've never seen but one like it, though, and that—"

"One like it?" shouted Fred. "Oh, I say, where did you see it, and when?"

"Steady there, laddie, and take it easy a bit if you can; you must need a little rest after what you've come through, and it is quite a story about that other cap. You let me knock up a better fire, and get you in a fair way towards being a bit drier, then I'll tell you about it," Athabasca Bill answered, in a kindly but decided tone, against which Fred felt there was no appeal, and so was fain to submit with the best grace he could to a more or less patient waiting.

Making the best and biggest fire he could, Bill next proceeded to strip off as much of his own clothing as he could conveniently spare, which he then wrapped about Fred's shivering body, whose garments were then hung out on forked sticks about the fire to dry.

This done, and the steaming garments in a fair way to get fit for speedy wear again, Athabasca Bill next warmed up some stewed meat in an old tin pan over the fire, and standing over Fred, forced him to eat every bit of it, although the boy declared that even a mouthful would choke him.

"You must eat, laddie, or you'll be down with fever tomorrow, and this ain't no place for sick beds, I can tell you," Bill persisted, with so much decision in his manner, that Fred did his best to obey.

He fell asleep soon after his meal, being strangely drowsy and worn out from the strain of his terrible voyage, and when he awoke again it was dark, with the stars shining out of a frosty sky.

At first he wondered where he was, and what had happened to make him feel so weak and sore; then catching sight of the queer cap of Athabasca Bill, as that worthy sat bending forward over the fire, which was now a mass of glowing embers, he suddenly recalled the events of the day, and the unexplained mystery of the cap.

"Awake, are you, laddie?" said Athabasca Bill, turning his head as Fred roused from his long sleep.

"Yes; have I slept long?"

"A matter of four or five hours; long enough to take off the keenest edge of your scare, I guess. Stiff, are you?"

"Not very," replied Fred, as he rose slowly from his improvised couch, and crept nearer to the cheerful warmth of the fire.

"You will be tomorrow, if that's any consolation; but get into your clothes, boy; they are all dry, and you will be none the worse for as many garments as you can lay hands on tonight, for I can tell you it will be nippy by-and-by. Then I want you to tell me what brings you careering about this back country like a strayed yearling, and why you were so desperately anxious to know all about my old cap and its double."

"I'll tell you," said Fred, getting into his own clothes as quickly as he could, for, as Bill had said, the wind was nippy, and the frosty chill in the air made his teeth chatter; then he crouched down over the fire, telling over again the story of his father's arrest on suspicion of having stolen the five hundred dollars from the box, labelled copper nails, in the Millet railway depôt.

"Why, its monstrous, perfectly monstrous! to even think of suspecting your father; but there, it isn't the first time, by a good long way, that the innocent have had to suffer for the guilty," said Athabasca Bill, with great bitterness.

"I know that, but it mostly gets put right in the long run," retorted Fred, with the air of a philosopher. "But what I can't understand is that cap mystery; until I opened my eyes when you dragged me out of the boat, and I saw it on your head, I could have vowed and declared that your old cap was in the hands of the police at Millet. Father identified it as being yours, and the marvel to me is that the mounted police haven't ridden you down before this, to charge you with being concerned in the robbery; only perhaps they thought as they had got one prisoner, they need not trouble about hunting for another."

"I guess you've hit the right nail on the head there, boy, and it's not wonderful either, when you come to think what a big country it is to ride through on the off-chance of catching a thief. Still, I can but wish they had taken it in their heads to run me down, since then I could have put them on to the track of the real thief, and that pretty quickly too, or else I'm much mistaken," rejoined Athabasca Bill, in great excitement.

"What do you mean?" cried Fred eagerly.

"Why, I saw the fellow that owns, or did own that cap, so like my own that your father identified it as belonging to me; saw him only the day before yesterday, too, and asked him what he had done with his beautiful headgear, and he told me with a laugh, that he had left it in the hands of a bigger rogue than himself. I wish I'd known then what you've been telling me now; I guess we should not have parted so easily, that young chap and me," replied Athabasca Bill, with a suggestive reaching out of his thin, muscular arms, and a snap of his jaws which was like the click of handcuffs.

"But how—?" began Fred, then stopped, as the other held up a warning finger, as if impatient to proceed.

"It was like this, boy; the day I met your father, but an hour or two earlier, I fell in with a young man with a terrible cough, who was in a fine state of mind, declaring he'd lost not only all his money, which he declared had been filched from him at cards, or some other kind of gambling wickedness, but he had also lost his credentials and some other important papers, which he was tracking back to find. To my amazement, he was wearing a cap so like this old fur tile of mine, that I clapped my hand to my head to make sure I'd got it on, and in doing so gave a tug at the string, which broke it clean off. Not wanting to stop to mend it then, I stuffed the cap in my sack, and went bareheaded for the rest of the day; that is how it chanced that I'd nothing on my head when I met your father."

"I thought you said you had seen the young man since," said Fred.

"So I did, and I'm coming to that in a minute, if you'll only be a bit patient," rejoined the other.

CHAPTER XI
STARTING IN PURSUIT

"Oh, I'll be patient enough, if only you'll get on as fast as you can," Fred said, with a restless, excited wriggle of his body, which certainly did not look very patient.

"When I left your father," went on Athabasca Bill, after a pause spent in re-lighting his pipe at a brand taken from the fire, "I had to spend a deal of time tacking to and fro, doing bits of business as I went. There were orders waiting for me at the Creamery, and one or two other places, that kept me from getting on, and then the day before yesterday—that is, the day when I reached Errol's place at sundown—who should overhaul me, riding on a good horse, but my young bankrupt gambler of a few days before, whose headgear had been so like my own. He'd changed the fur cap for a felt wide-awake, but I knew him for all that, and asked him if he'd found his credentials again, and if the horse was one of 'em."

"Funny sort of credentials a horse would be; why, I thought they were letters, or something, to say you were honest and respectable," interposed Fred.

"There is more than one sort of credentials," replied Athabasca Bill, with an oracular air. "But this wandering tenderfoot, with his dissipated air, and desperate bad cough, declared that he'd found all he'd lost, and something more beside; when I asked him what it was, he said that was his own business, so I made up my mind he must have stolen the horse he was riding. However, I'd no evidence to prove it, so I parted from him as civilly as if he'd been proved honest by judge and jury. Then he asked me if Strawberry Creek didn't flow into the Saskatchewan River, and I told him yes; so he said he was glad to hear it, as he was going right away to Smoky Lake and Beaver River, and if he could get down the river, he'd travel so much faster than overland."

"Beaver River—but isn't that in Athabasca?" queried Fred, with a doleful lengthening of his face.

"Partly, and partly in Saskatchewan. Smoky Lake is just this side the boundary, and in Alberta; I know that country pretty well, for I used to go up there trapping regularly every winter—a regular no-man's-land it is, too; I've been for months and never set eyes on any human beings save Indians," Bill answered.

"Whatever would this fellow be going there for at this time of the year—was he a trapper?" Fred asked, in great surprise.

"I should say not. From the looks of him, I took him to be one of those Hudson Bay Company's people, who go from post to post taking orders, collecting accounts, and arranging the trade with the Indians; his talk about credentials made me the more certain about it, for, you see, he'd be sure to need something of the sort on such an errand," replied Athabasca Bill, tossing another armful of brushwood on the glowing embers, which smouldered for a few minutes, then burst into a roaring, crackling blaze.

"A pretty kind of creature to be put in a place of authority!" cried Fred, with a wrathful intonation, thinking of the trouble which had befallen his own home, in consequence of that mysterious robbery from the depôt.

"I've got a plan in my mind," the other said, after a long pause, filled only by the crackling of the brushwood on the fire.

"What is that?" demanded Fred eagerly.

"That chap—let me see, what did he say his name was? Oh, I remember; Guy Herrick—has got a clear days' start of us, to say nothing of his hitting the river at a point a good many miles lower down than this; but he hasn't had the experience, perhaps, with Indians at the portage that I have, and so we may overhaul him without much trouble."

"But you've got to come back with me to swear to father's alibi," broke in Fred, in quick protest.

"Now, boy, look here," said Athabasca Bill, in a judicial tone; "if I turn round tomorrow morning, and track back to Millet as fast as I can go, all that I can do when I get there, is to sit down and wait till the trial comes on, and then up and say that I met your father in a certain place on a certain day. But when I've said it, I shall know, and so will everyone else, that if your father had wanted to break into the depôt that night, he would have had plenty of time to do so."

"Then it was no good my coming all this way to find you?" cried Fred, in a bitterly disappointed tone, thinking of the weary miles he had tramped, and all that he had undergone in the passage of Denaree's Leap.

"Don't you make any mistake about that, and don't be downhearted, either," replied the other kindly. "If you hadn't come to tell me your father wanted help, I should not have known it until it was too late, maybe. Now, the very best I can do shall be done, for I don't forget what I owe your folks, and I'm going to pay as much of the debt as I can. If you and I go along after this Guy Herrick, and overhaul him, we can just take the law in our own hands, until we find a lawful person to help us, and take him back with us to the town in time to clear your father at his trial. If he should, after all, prove to be an innocent person, he will be able, at least, to identify his own cap, and free me from the suspicion of having been mixed up in the muddle."

"I see!" exclaimed Fred, with returning cheerfulness. "But how shall we manage the river, seeing that you haven't a canoe?"

"That's easy enough," began Bill, when Fred burst out excitedly—

"Why, of course there is that canoe I came in, with the stores; or was it too much damaged?"

Athabasca Bill shook his head.

"Now, if we took that without a word of explanation, we should deserve, and perhaps get the mounted police after us, for running away with George Errol's canoe, and appropriating his stores. No, boy, we must just get two of the Indians—and there should be plenty of them hereabouts—to carry the canoe and the stores back over the fifteen mile portage to Black Pine, with a letter or message to let the people know that you came safe through the racket of Denaree's Leap, then we'll get a birchbark of our own; I think I know where I can put my hand on one, and set off down river as fast as we can go."

"I've got a piece of paper and a pencil, so I can write a letter to Mr. Errol; then, perhaps, he will get a chance of letting our folks know that I am all right," Fred said, with a yawn, for though he had been so lately asleep, he was weary still, and badly in need of a good long rest.

"Tired, are you?" Bill asked, as he vigorously stoked the fire again. "Well, so am I; and the best thing we can do is to turn in and get what sleep we can, before it gets too cold for comfort. That blanket of yours was so sopping wet that I haven't got it dry yet, but it will do to hang up as a shelter to keep the wind away, and we can both lie down under mine."

Fred acquiesced cheerfully enough in this arrangement, and helped his friend hang up the wet blanket, as a sort of roofless tent to keep the wind away, though he was so stiff and sore that he could only move his limbs with difficulty.

Then the two lay down together as close to the fire as it was safe to get, and were quickly asleep. If danger menaced them in the long, dark hours, they knew it not, but slept on peacefully enough until the bitter cold awoke them, by which time it was nearly morning.

The fire had died down to a heap of dusty white ashes, and the blanket which covered them was stiff with frost, whilst the ground appeared covered with snow.

"Whew, it is like mid-winter!" exclaimed Fred, sitting up and trying to rub a little warmth into one half-frozen arm, whilst his teeth chattered with the cold.

"You wouldn't say so if you had ever slept in the open in mid-winter," remarked Athabasca Bill, who was busy restoring the fire.

"I wonder you don't freeze to death, in the long nights you have, with no comforts, no proper roof over your head even," Fred said, watching the other's handy way with the fire, and wondering what he should have done had he been left to his own resources.

"Don't you make a mistake; I mostly have a roof over my head, though it is usually made of snow. Capital stuff to keep the cold out, snow is. Whenever I've built myself a hut for trapping, I've always covered it in three or four feet deep with snow, and slept as warm and comfortable under it as if I'd had a Mansard roof, and the canopy of a four-post bed over my head," Bill replied, leaning over his fire with great satisfaction, as the cheerful flames leapt upward again.

"I think I should like to be a trapper; will you take me for an apprentice?" Fred asked, with a laugh; he had slept a good deal of his stiffness off, and was feeling fresh and fit again, except for the cold.

"Not if I can help it," answered Athabasca Bill, with sudden fervour. "Now, don't mistake me, and think it isn't that I wouldn't like your company; but, to my way of thinking, no one that has got a home, and people in it that love him, should ever take to a lonely life like a trapper's. If you've got anyone to love and trust you, then, I say, stop at home and enjoy it; time enough to take to trapping, when the home has slipped out of your grasp."

Athabasca Bill spoke with a stormy vehemence that would have surprised and startled Fred, had he not already been in possession of Saidie's story. As it was, he was strongly tempted to disobey her injunction, and drop a hint to the lonely, friendless man of the brother and sister who yearned so eagerly for his presence, and of the dispersion of the black cloud of suspicion and distrust which had hung over him so long.

But having given his word, Fred was in honour bound to respect Saidie's confidence, and was for turning the talk into other channels, in order to get as far as possible from temptation, when his companion started up, declaring that he heard someone coming.

"Which way?" asked Fred, whose untrained ears had caught no sound of approach.

"Over there, where your birchbark is lying. I think I'll step over that way and have a look round, or maybe some wandering red man may reckon the thing is his own because he found it, and then where would George Errol be?" So saying, Athabasca Bill strode away across the grass, that was crisp with frost, to where the canoe was lying which had made the perilous voyage of the Valley of Death with such little damage to itself or its contents.

He was away for some considerable time, during which Fred worked at the fire with such good effect, that he succeeded in getting some warmth into his chilled body, and was just beginning to wonder what Athabasca Bill had found to keep him away so long, when he caught the sound of voices and footsteps coming nearer at a quick rate.

"So Bill did hear someone over yonder," he muttered to himself, giving the fire a deft stir with a stick, which sent a shower of sparks flitting upward on the frosty air, followed by a crackling burst of flame, which illumined the darkness, and enabled him to see his companion returning, accompanied by two forms wrapped in blankets—Indians, he guessed them to be, although they both wore hats of the cowboy type, and wore store-shoes of a down-at-heel, squelchy description, which proclaimed them in the last stage of decrepitude to observant ears.

"Get your letter written with the first gleam of daylight, boy, for the chance of sending the canoe back to its rightful owner has come quicker than I expected," said Athabasca Bill, with quite a new ring of energy in his tone; and as day was already beginning to break, Fred was speedily able to comply with the injunction.

A brief scrawl it was, just explaining to Mr. Errol how he had come scathless through the seething whirlpools of Denaree's Leap, and was returning the birchbark and the stores to Black Pine portage, asking also that Mr. Errol would write to his mother, telling her that he had found Athabasca Bill, and was on the point of starting with him for the Beaver River country in pursuit of the real thief, whose tracks he had by good luck happened upon.

This communication being given to the two Indians, they prepared to carry the stores and the canoe over the fifteen miles rough ground to Black Pine portage. Being, however, overtaken by a fit of curiosity on the way, they stopped to examine into the nature of their load, and finding a package of tobacco among the stores, promptly annexed it for their own smoking. After that first yielding to temptation, the remaining fall was easy enough. Fred's letter was stuffed into the next supper fire, and the two trailed off into the wilderness with the stolen goods.

CHAPTER XII
ROUGH TRAVELLING

The Indians to whom Athabasca Bill entrusted the stores and canoe for Black Pine portage, possessed a birchbark of their own, which, to save time, he purchased of them, for the conveyance of himself and Fred down the North Saskatchewan River.

Perhaps if he had been a little less eager and absorbed by his project of thief-catching, he would have examined a little more closely into the condition of the canoe which he had purchased of the wily red men. As it was, when they had started on their journey, and he with Fred prepared to set out on their hastily arranged trip to the Beaver River country, he found to his dismay that the wretched little craft leaked at every pore.

"A pretty business, truly! The next time I buy a birchbark without seeing it in the water, I shall deserve to get sucked in and drowned off-hand!" exclaimed Athabasca Bill, rubbing his extraordinary cap to and fro on his head, as if he intended rubbing every bit of hair from the top of his head.

"They must have come up river in the thing. I wonder how they kept afloat; did they bale, do you expect?" Fred asked, as he stood staring at the frail thing, with the water pouring in at the cracks and seams, thinking that they must have baled with extraordinary vigour to keep the thing from becoming water-logged and swamped.

"They didn't come up river in it, the varmints! that canoe hasn't floated for a month or six weeks past," rejoined Bill, in a tone of exasperation, as he turned the thing over, then rubbed his head more violently than before.

"What will you do?" asked Fred.

"There's only one thing to do, and that is, caulk it," said Bill, in the short, sharp manner usual with him, when things were more contrary than usual. It was on the tip of Fred's tongue to ask how the caulking was to be done, seeing that no materials for stopping leaks lay handy, but second thoughts decided him to wait and see what his companion intended doing, instead of bothering him with questions.

"You make a better fire, as quick as you can; not a roaring, tearing blaze, but a quiet, glowing heat," commanded Bill, and Fred hastened to obey, though he rather wondered how the steady, glowing heat was to be arrived at in that region of brushwood and dried grass, where all the fuel flamed up, blazed furiously for five minutes or so, and then went out, leaving only a heap of hot dust and ashes.

However, where there's a will there's a way, most often, and having plied Bill's small hatchet to good purpose on the thickest of the brushwood, Fred laid the fuel in a conical heap on the fire, surrounding the whole with big stones and boulders dragged from the overhanging cliff where they had their camp. Half-an-hour of steady burning left a clear bed of red coals, the surrounding stones being also red hot.

Then Bill brought out his one cooking pot, which was neither more nor less than an old meat tin, with two bent skewers for a handle, and balancing it carefully on the hot stones, put into it some gum and balsam which had been stowed away in his pack, adding to it a little oil, and a cake of beeswax which he had made himself from a take of wild honey found on the previous day. When this precious mixture was boiling, he carefully daubed the outside of the canoe with it from stem to stern, going over and over the cracks and seams until they were well filled.

Fred watched the proceedings with great interest, lending a hand where he could, but carefully refraining from asking any questions, until the cooking-pot was empty, and Bill was cleaning it, by the simple, but effectual, method of rubbing it with handfuls of dirt.

"How soon will it be ready to use?" he asked then, with a nod of his head in the direction of the birchbark.

"Tomorrow morning; so we will stay where we are for today, cook what food we've got, and be ready to be off bright and early at dawn," answered the other, then started off to look at the traps he had set whilst Fred was asleep on the previous day, in the hope that they might yield something towards the replenishment of his larder.

Fred being left to look after the fire, set to work chopping brushwood into convenient piles, and heaping it near the camping-place; with the remembrance of last night's bitter cold fresh in his mind, he worked zealously towards gathering together a good supply of fuel for the ensuing night. He was making active play with the small but useful hatchet belonging to his companion, when he heard a shout, and looking round, saw Bill making his way through the scrub to the camp, laden down with game as the result of his forage.

Seizing the bundle of wood he had ready chopped, Fred hurried back to the fire with it, arriving in time to congratulate Bill on the good fortune which had attended his trapping.

"Now, don't you make any mistake about the traps, which were all empty except one, that had this hare in it," replied the trapper, holding up the only furred game he carried, though he was hung all over with birds which looked something like grouse.

"Then how did you catch them?" demanded Fred, in astonishment, for the shot gun, the trapper's only weapon, was lying in its place beside the pack.

Athabasca Bill laughed as he slung the birds from his back on to the ground.

"That was easy enough. They are what we call fool-birds, and the name fits 'em uncommon well, too, for they are about the most foolish creatures I ever came across. I happened upon a covey of six of them as I was coming back with my hare, and they flew into some branches about nine feet from the ground; so I got a long stick, tied a string with a running noose at the end of it, and bobbing it over the necks of the creatures one by one, brought down five of them, and only just missed the sixth, which flew away with a scream and a flutter, after sitting still to see me wring the necks of the other five."

"Well, I should think you are about right in saying their name suited them," remarked Fred, as he seized upon one of the birds and commenced stripping off its feathers, though he only succeeded in getting one bird done to the other's two.

Everything was put in readiness that night for an early start in the morning, and then, when darkness fell, the two curled down in the lee of the little hill to get as much sleep as the chill of the night would permit them to snatch.

They had two blankets instead of one now, whilst the cold was not so intense as on the previous night, or else their fire was bigger, for they slept in comfort, until the slow, reluctant dawn began to creep down the sides of the pine-clothed hills on the other side of the river.

"A night's rest that a millionaire swaddled in fine linen and eiderdown might have envied," commented Athabasca Bill, as he warmed some tea in a tin can over the embers of the fire, which they drank without sugar or milk. He carried tea in preference to coffee, as being lighter of portage, and sugar was a luxury entirely out of question, on account of its weight.

They were afloat before it was actually daylight, and to their joy and satisfaction discovered that the caulking was successful, for the present, at any rate, though how it would stand in rougher waters they had yet to discover.

Athabasca Bill appeared as much at home in a canoe as if he had been born an Indian, whilst Fred, by dint of keeping his eyes open and his wits about him, soon learned what to do, and what to leave undone in the matter of paddling. The journey was easy enough, and pleasant too, so far as the water part of it was concerned, but the numerous and difficult portages were exceedingly wearisome; for then, instead of paddling down the current in the light and buoyant birchbark, they had to tramp over rough trails, up steep hills and down precipitous descents, carrying the canoe and its contents on their shoulders.

It took four days of this sort of travel to get round to that part of the river into which Strawberry Creek flowed, and where they might hope to light upon traces of the man of whom they were in pursuit.

"There's an Indian village about five or six miles further down, and there we ought to get the news we want," Athabasca Bill said, as their light craft careered along on the swift current, caused by the confluence of the turbulent waters of Strawberry Creek with the steadier flow of the river.

"Is this reservation land?" asked Fred, glancing at the willow swamps on either side of the river.

"No; but the village is pretty permanent, for all that, and will be, I expect, until the land about here gets taken up and settled."

"Which won't be this year, or next, I should say," remarked Fred, looking at the willow-thickets on either side.

"Hullo, what's that?" exclaimed the trapper, becoming suddenly alert, ceasing to paddle, and leaning forward in an attitude of strained listening.

For a moment no sound broke on the dreary forest silence, saving the shiver of the crisping willow leaves, as the wind passed through them. Then followed a sound which almost made Fred's heart stand still—the deep-toned baying of a bloodhound.

"It is a tracker-dog," he whispered hoarsely. "Sounds just like one of old man Arlo's dogs, that he ran father down with," and he shivered again, thinking of the night when he had stood with his father in the darkness by the house door, listening to the baying of the hounds coming nearer and nearer, yet never dreaming of the disaster which loomed so close at hand.

Athabasca Bill thought he was nervous at the thought of a possible encounter with the creature, and spoke with intent to reassure him.

"No need to turn pale, laddie; by the sound there is only one beast singing to himself, and if he should chance our way, why he'll have to swim to reach us, don't you see."

"Oh, I'm not afraid of the dog; 'tisn't likely the creature would pull us down unless it was tracking us. I was only thinking that, unless all bloodhounds bay alike, that must certainly be an animal belonging to old man Arlo," Fred said, bending to his paddle with renewed vigour, as if anxious to reach the place from whence the baying came, and assure himself of the identity of the dog.

But though both were keeping a sharp look-out, neither he nor Athabasca Bill happened to notice the submerged trunk of a tree lying right in their track, but owing to the heavy shadow on the water at that point, invisible until they crashed into it, the sharp, scraggy branches ripping open one side of the canoe.

In a moment they were both floundering in the water, Athabasca Bill making frantic, but futile, grabs at their various bundles, which had so unexpectedly set out voyaging on their own account; whilst Fred's whole attention was absorbed in the task of keeping himself afloat by clinging to the birchbark, which, after upsetting them so treacherously, had righted itself, and was floating like a cork, the rent in the side being now about an inch above the water line.

Fortunately they were very close to the bank, and in a minute or so succeeded in scrambling on land by the aid of the overhanging willows. The ground was very soft and boggy, but in the first moment of deliverance they forbore to grumble at this, as they shook the worst of the water from their dripping garments, and took stock of the damage they had sustained.

Bill's shot gun was, as usual, slung in a waterproof case under his arm, and, in view of the constantly recurring portages, both had blankets and packs slung on their backs, but two other bundles of traps and stores had already made a rapid journey to the bottom of the river, whilst the damaged birchbark and the paddles were already floating down the current, voyaging on their own account.

"Well, folks say it's mostly the unexpected that happens, and I'm inclined to believe that there is a deal of truth in the statement!" exclaimed Athabasca Bill, with an air of gloomy philosophy, as, besmeared with mud and dripping from his ducking, he drew himself up among the willows for a moment's breathing time.

"There's a trail here," exclaimed Fred, who had worked himself further into the thicket. "And I can see boot-marks, as well as moccasins, so there is civilization somewhere not far away."

"Of a sort, perhaps," responded the other, with a doubtful shake of his head, as he dragged himself to his feet, and proceeded along the rough, but well-defined path in the direction from which the baying of the dog sounded nearer and nearer, whilst Fred pressed closely in the rear.

Ten minutes or so of walking, and they emerged on a little clearing with a log cabin, and a hound tied to a fence.

"It's Montana Jenny!" cried Fred breathlessly; "I'd know the creature anywhere."

CHAPTER XIII
A BID FOR THE FARM

The tidings brought by Saidie Marsh from Errol's place of the tragic fate which overtaken Fred, plunged his family into the deepest grief.

The children crept about with sad faces and red eyes, whilst Mr. Crawford looked as if he would never smile again; but it was on Mrs. Crawford that the heaviest weight of the trouble fell, because of the knowledge that it was she who had sent her son on the journey, which had ended in such black disaster.

"Better that you, though innocent, should have been convicted, and had to serve a term of years in prison, than that this should have come," she said, looking up at her husband with quivering lips, as they sat side by side in the darkest hour of their trouble.

"I may have to go still; and it will be all the harder to be compelled to leave you so unprotected," he rejoined, checking the complaint against this last bitter blow of fate that rose to his lips, as he remembered some words from the Book of Job, running after this wise: "In all this Job sinned not, nor charged God foolishly."

"You must not worry about us, dear, whatever happens; for I shall not be alone, you know, and Ella is very capable, whilst Celia has the brains and management of a woman," Mrs. Crawford answered bravely, rising above her own sorrow, from an unselfish desire to lessen her husband's heavy burden of care.

"Still, good as they are, they are only bits of girls, and so don't count much so far as earning a living goes. If only I can sell this farm, it may make matters easier for you. I will go over to Millet tomorrow, and see about having it advertised," Mr. Crawford said, rising from his chair, and beginning to pace up and down the narrow limits of the room.

Saidie, worn out with her long journey, had gone to bed at the same time as Ella and Celia, whilst the little boys had crept off before that even, to cry themselves to sleep over the loss of the big brother they loved so much. This left husband and wife alone, and they were looking forward into the black, dreary future, and planning to meet its emergencies as prudent people should.

But though they talked far into the night, then went to bed to toss there in wakeful restlessness until the morning came, they could see no light at all in the thick cloud of trouble overshadowing them.

Dawn found poor Mrs. Crawford too unwell to leave her bed, whereupon Saidie Marsh begged permission to stay until the next day, declaring that her horse would be quite worn out, if it could not have a little time in which to recover itself.

"Why, yes, of course we'll be only too glad for you to stay, for we are grateful indeed to you for all the trouble you have taken, in coming such a long way to break the sad news to us yourself, instead of leaving us to hear it haphazard," Mrs. Crawford said, in a low, faltering tone, when Saidie crept to her bedside with the request.

Mr. Crawford warmly seconded all this, and went off to Millet to take active steps in getting rid of his farm, feeling all the more comfortable about his wife, because he had left her in the vigorous, capable care of Saidie.

His errand did not appear very prosperous, however, for no one seemed in the least anxious to purchase a farm, or to know of anyone else who chanced to be buying land. It was the wrong time of the year, and he knew if a purchaser were to be found, it would doubtless make a hundred dollars difference on the wrong side, whether he sold his land now, or waited until the turn of the year.

But when fate holds the whip hand, a man must do the best he can, and not grumble; so having put matters in train for the speedy disposal of his property, Mr. Crawford turned his horse's head in the direction of home.

He was passing the last block of houses on the road out of Millet, when a man came striding towards him at a great pace, holding up his hand in token that he wished him to stop.

"Mornin', neighbour; I hope it isn't all true what I have been hearin' in the town?" he said, reaching up a hard, work-worn hand, and shaking Mr. Crawford's as if he meant to wrench it off.

"That chiefly depends on what you've heard; though, I fear, there isn't much chance of exaggeration in that direction just now," Mr. Crawford answered gloomily.

"I'm sorry, I really am, neighbour; I was downright cut up when I heard. You see, I hadn't bin this way for nigh a month, and it takes a goodish time for news of any sort to filter through to our place," the kindly stranger said, still working away at the other's hand as if it were a pump handle.

"Thank you, Sam Beresford; a friendly word goes a long way in these times, I can tell you; for there is more than one man in Millet today that forgets he used to know me before I saw the inside of a prison. It cuts in pretty deep, when they go by without turning their heads," Mr. Crawford said bitterly; he had been treated thus several times lately, yet might never have said a word about it, but for this touch of genuine good-heartedness from Sam Beresford.

"Let 'em be; they'll hang their heads and chaw the dust bime-by, when you're proved innocent, and come home with flags flying and a brass band blowing itself into fits for a hescort," said Mr. Beresford, with a deep, rumbling laugh, which seemed to begin somewhere in the region of his boots. Then checking this untimely mirth, so suddenly that it stuck in his throat and nearly choked him, he asked, in a lower tone, "I hope it ain't true what they're sayin' about your boy havin' come to grief over Black Pine way?"

"I'm afraid there is no room to doubt it," Mr. Crawford said, controlling his voice by a great effort. "Miss Marsh rode over to our place yesterday to bring us the news. She was at Errol's place when the—the accident happened, and was told of it by a man who saw the canoe tip over with the poor boy in it."

"Ah, now that is trouble, if you like; and, neighbour, my heart aches for you, that it do," said honest Sam, gulping down a sob, for his heart was as tender as a child's, and he thought it no shame to put up a hand and openly wipe his tears away.

"It is a terrible blow, especially to his mother; she sent him off on Athabasca Bill's trail, you see, in the hope of being able to establish an alibi for me. I was in prison then, but someone bailed me out next day," Mr. Crawford talked on, fearing he should break down if he stopped a moment, for the sympathizing face of his friend was strangely disconcerting.

Presently he made a move to resume his journey, and then the other suddenly bethought himself of something he wanted done.

"Going home, are you, neighbour?"

"Yes; is there anything I can do for you out our side?" Mr. Crawford asked, for Sam Beresford lived ten miles away on the other side of the railway, and the roads of the district were very much in their infancy.

"Just what I was going to speak about," ejaculated Sam, commencing to fumble at the breast pocket of his coat; "I owe a little bill to a man out your way—ten dollars it is, neither more nor less, but it's bin standin' a goodish while now—an' I'm blest if the old skin-a-flint hasn't sent me a letter sayin' he'd have the law on me if I didn't pay up sharp. So as I happened to have some cash drop in yesterday, I thought I couldn't do better than hurry up with the money. Old man Arlo is the party as it is owing to, and if you'd just look in and settle it for me as you go home, I'd be desperate obliged to you."

"I will do it with pleasure; shall I take the receipt and send to you, or ask him to forward it himself?" Mr. Crawford said, reaching down his hand for the money.

"Oh, there ain't no need to worrit about a receipt; I shan't pay the money over again, don't you be afraid; he can cross it off if he's got it writ down in black an' white against me, an' if he ain't, why there's no need to trouble. Good mornin', neighbour, and I hope you'll soon get righted, an' in smoother waters again." So saying, and with another hearty handshake, Sam Beresford went his way.

There was a smile on Mr. Crawford's face, as he told his horse he was ready to move on; and if it did not linger long, it at least served to show a temporary lifting of the clouds on his mental horizon.

The divergence of a mile on his homeward way brought him to old man Arlo's place, where a savage baying of dogs greeted him, until he shouted, as an intimation that he would have speech with the master of the house, when the angry barking changed instantly to an eager whining, the hounds having recognized their whilom rescuer by his voice, although they could not see his face, the outer door of their kennel being shut.

Thrice Mr. Crawford shouted, but receiving no answer, swung himself from his horse, and prepared to try the door. He had seen a thin, blue curl of smoke rising from the chimney as he approached the house, so imagined the owner could not be far away.

Nor was he. For just as his visitor's knuckles made active play on the door, old man Arlo came shuffling round the corner, as if he had but just become aware of someone seeking admittance.

"That door is barred to keep the draught out; you had best come in round this way," he croaked, in a hoarse voice, then began to cough as if he would choke.

"I don't need to come in. I met Sam Beresford in Millet this morning, and he asked me to look round this way, and pay you that ten dollars he has been owing you this good while back. Perhaps you will just let me have it in writing that I paid you," said Mr. Crawford, who meant to have a receipt himself, even though the man who paid the money was indifferent on the subject.

"Ha, ha, ha! are you afraid I shall go and say that you ha'n't paid me, eh?" queried the old man, then he was seized with another fit of coughing, which made him turn purple in the face.

"No, I'm not. But I'd rather have a receipt, for one never knows what is going to happen," replied the other.

"Then you will have to come indoors for it," old man Arlo said, gasping a little, and swaying in a weak, unsteady fashion, as he turned back round the corner of the house.

Throwing his horse's bridle over the hitching-post, Mr. Crawford followed him round to the back of the house, where the barn and piggeries were, and where also was the high-paled fence about the yard where the hounds took their exercise.

"Where is your other dog, the one that does not love me?" he asked, walking up to the palings and putting his fingers through for the dogs to lick.

"Montana Jenny? Oh, I got rid of the beast. I don't say she wasn't a good trailer, but she'd no discretion whatever, and was as obstinate as a pig," growled the old man, leading the way into the one miserable, squalid room, which served him as kitchen, parlour, and counting-house combined.

"The creature certainly did not love me. I hope you got a good price for her," Mr. Crawford said, glancing round the dirty, comfortless room, and wondering if old man Arlo was as poor as he looked.

"Oh, I did well enough. Glad enough to have her gone," he answered, coughing again; then with an abrupt change of tone he asked, "Well, are you thinking of taking my advice, and going off on the quiet one of these fine days soon?"

"No, I am not," the other replied. "But I've been to Millet this morning to have the farm advertised for immediate sale, for I must if possible get rid of that before the trial."

"It ain't the right time o' year to offer land; you'll only make a poor price."

"I know; but there is no help for it, as matters stand. I might have waited on the chance of getting off at the trial, but for my poor boy's death." Mr. Crawford stopped abruptly, and old man Arlo flung up his hands with an exclamation of horror and dismay.

"It's true, then, what Joe Armstrong was saying this morning, that your Fred had been killed, out yonder in Black Pine country?"

"Too true," said the bereaved father, in a dry, choked tone. "So I must get rid of the land somehow before the trial."

"How much are you asking for it?" queried the other.

"A thousand dollars as it stands, straw and hay included."

"Too much," rejoined the old man; "I know a man—leastways, he has sort o' commissioned me to buy him a farm in this district, and I don't mind bidding you nine hundred dollars on his account, cash down."

"It's a bargain, then," said Mr. Crawford.

CHAPTER XIV
OLD ACQUAINTANCES

At sight of the two dripping figures emerging from the willow thickets, the hound dashed forward as if to tear them down, at the same time raising such an uproar of barking, that the door of the hut speedily opened, and a man's rough, shaggy head was thrust forth, in order to discover what all the noise was about.

But he was a white man, and after a long, steady stare, Athabasca Bill claimed him as an old acquaintance.

"Why, if it ain't you, Blue Pete! And who'd have thought of coming across you in these parts? I heard you'd made your fortune a good while back, and gone to settle down at Calgary, or Toronto, I don't quite remember which."

"There ain't no call for you to go straining your recollection about it either, seeing that unfortunately it ain't true," rejoined the unkempt one, in an easy tone. "But come in, Bill, and make yourself at home, and the boy too; been having a bath in the river, have you, and with your clothes on? You look a bit damper than is ordinary on a fine day."

"And feel so, too," replied Athabasca Bill, with a shiver, as he followed his host into the log cabin, where a big fire was burning, and some kind of cooking in progress, whilst the place was strewn from end to end with garments, stores, and weapons, as if the owner had just come home from a journey, and had not yet had time to put things straight.

Blue Pete was hospitable, though shaggy; and if his cooking was primitive, and his methods of housekeeping somewhat lacking in the matter of cleanliness and tidiness, the warmth of his welcome left nothing to be desired.

He insisted upon clothing his guests in garments of his own, whilst their dripping raiment was dried at the fire; then dishing up a savoury mess of bacon, poultry and vegetables, all stewed together until they were indistinguishable one from the other, and the bones of the fowls stood out white and clean, he bade them fall to and feed.

With so much talk between the two men of past days, and the doings of long ago, there was no opportunity for some time for Fred to ask the question trembling on the tip of his tongue, as to the identity of the hound that was tied to the fence rails, and which every now and then voiced her complaints in a fresh burst of baying.

Presently Blue Pete, who, having finished eating, was smoking a short black pipe, and throwing out vast clouds of smoke, whilst he indulged in long-winded reminiscences of the days when he and Athabasca Bill had toiled in the same gang on the irrigation works at Lethbridge, stopped suddenly short in his talk, and asked Fred to take the remains of the stew to the clamorous dog outside.

"The beast is hungry, but she isn't likely to let any ventilation into you, boy, if you approach her down wind, so that she gets a whiff of something to eat first," he said, with a lazy stretch of his long limbs, as he threw another log on the fire.

Fred rose with alacrity; he had faced a savage dog before today, and armed with such a persuader as the remains of that dish of stew, he had no apprehension whatever as to the nature of his reception by the animal tied to the fence.

"I'll take it, and risk the ventilation. But I should like to know how long you have had that dog, and where it came from?" he said, pausing with the dish in his hand.

"That's easy answered; I've been away for a fortnight, sort of combining business and pleasure, down at Wetaskiwin, and having spent most of my available cash more or less wisely, I made out to tramp it most of the way back, specially as I had got some business to see to in Millet as I came through. But when I got to the town I found the man I wanted, Joe Armstrong by name, lived five or six miles east of Millet, so I had to tramp so far out of my way, and didn't feel very pleasant about it either. I did a stroke of business with him, though, that put me in a good temper again, and was tracking back to the railway, feeling that I could afford to ride after all, when I came across a poor, miserable old chap, a regular bag of bones; he was tied round with some old rags to keep him from collapsing, and he was leading that same animal as is chained to the fence outside."

"Old man Arlo, that was, I know," burst out Fred; then was suddenly silenced by a look from Athabasca Bill, warning him to be careful as to what admissions he made concerning himself.

"Well, the old chap wanted me to buy the brute; seemed reg'lar set on it, too; wouldn't take no for an answer, and all that sort o' thing, till at last I owned up I'd take it for a dollar and a quarter, not a long price as times go, but all I could afford, and he grabbed at the offer so eagerly, that I began to be sorry I hadn't said a dollar, without the quarter."

"Why, that dog cost I don't know how much money, and is a real trained tracker, that came all the way from Montana, and could hunt a man through a crowded city street without ever losing the trail; Montana Jenny, old man Arlo used to call her, and he set no end of store by her, because she was so clever," Fred burst out, in profound amazement that the dog should have been sold at such a price.

"Ah, I remember he said something about the creature being good at tracking; that's what made me think of buying her, for those thieving rascals of Indians come stealing my willows after I've got them peeled and ready for plaiting; but I guess they will be glad to keep away, when they find out what kind of an active partner I've taken into the concern," Blue Pete replied, laughing, and with a nod of his head, Fred took up the dish and went out.

At sight of him, Montana Jenny made a vicious spring, as if she would settle things up and make a meal of him in next to no time at all. Fred thought of the last time he had seen her, and how she had sprung straight for his father's throat, whilst he stood by, powerless to help or hinder. But the remembrance, instead of making a coward of him, put a startling new idea into his head, opening out a series of daring suggestions which fairly made him reel.

Picking out the skeleton of a fowl from the dish he was carrying, he approached the vicious Jenny with a word of good-fellowship, and making as if to tear a mouthful of flesh from the fowl, offered the bony fragments to the dog, as if sharing his meal with her.

Instantly the creature lost her ferocious aspect, and began greedily devouring the bones, whilst Fred, coming nearer, and bringing his dish, sat down, prepared to share the remains of the stew together.

His plan succeeded to perfection, and by the time the dish was empty and well licked out, the dog and the boy were the best of friends. Then slipping the chain from the post to which it was fastened, Fred first took Jenny to the water for a drink, then went back to the cabin with the dog trailing behind him.

The two men were still smoking and talking, while the reek from the drying clothes, and the fumes from the two pipes, made an atmosphere almost too thick to see through. But their conversation now was of the more immediate past of three or four days ago.

"If he'd just been satisfied to shelter for a night or even two, and taken just what food was necessary, I would not have been mean enough to grudge it him; but to make off with a couple of pounds of tea, after breaking the lock of the cupboard to get at it, and eating up most everything there was in the place, makes me feel I'd enjoy giving him a ducking in one of my peeling-pools," said Blue Pete, with a smoulder of indignation under his good-natured indolence.

"Serve him right, too; I wouldn't have minded lending a hand myself, if I had been here. Do you know who the fellow was, or what he was like at all?" asked Athabasca Bill, with an anxious inflection, which suddenly aroused the keenest interest in the breast of Fred.

"I didn't see him, and all I know of him is what Snaky-Shoes, one of my Indian willow-cutters, tells me; he found the rascal here sitting tight on my stuff, as if it belonged to him. Snaky-Shoes said he was a sickly, white-faced one, with a desperate bad cough."

"Bill, it's the man we want. I'm sure of it!" panted Fred, with so much haste and urgency in his tone, that Blue Peter turned to look at him in surprise, then saw, to his further wonderment, Montana Jenny curling herself down at the boy's feet, as if she had belonged to him for the last six months.

"Hallo, younker, are you out on the police lay? And oh, I say, you'd best keep a safe distance from that brute, for she may feel hungry again, and you'd feel sorry if she had a piece out of your leg."

"She'll not hurt me; we've eaten out of the same dish, and tracker dogs have long memories for friend or foe," Fred said, slipping an arm round Jenny's neck, and giving her an affectionate hug, an endearment she acknowledged by stuffing a cold, wet nose into his hand, and wagging her tail. Even as he spoke he had a vivid picture of her lithe brown and white body hurtling through the darkness to seize his father by the throat, but his sense of justice made him remember that the poor animal was only following its instincts and doing her duty; besides, with care and kindness she might be useful in tracking down the real transgressor, and so, conquering the momentary repulsion, he responded to the overture of the cold nose by patting her on the head.

"We are both on the police lay, for the matter o' that," said Athabasca Bill, in a slow, thoughtful tone, as he came to the conclusion that they could not do better than take Blue Pete into their confidence in the matter of their quest; then forthwith plunged into the story of the misfortune which had overtaken Fred's father, and their pursuit of the man, whom they believed to be the real culprit.

"Humph! A rather slender clue—a cap, a comforter and a bad cough; still, a man has been hanged on less than that before today," Blue Pete said, blowing out such a cloud of smoke that even Athabasca Bill had to cough, whilst Fred was nearly choked.

"I should like to see that red chap—what-do-you-call-him—Snaky Shoes," Athabasca Bill said, when he had recovered from all the tobacco smoke which he had swallowed.

"He's about," Blue Pete answered, with a vague wag of his head towards the back of the chimney, which seemed to imply that the Indian in question was being smoke-dried in the reek above the fire, but which really meant that Snaky-Shoes, ignoring the traditions of his ancestors, was working for wages in the osier beds behind the little hut.

Athabasca Bill rose slowly and stiffly to his feet, then taking a tobacco pouch from the pocket of his half-dried jacket, turned to leave the house.

Blue Pete also got up from his comfortable corner by the fire, as if the remembrance of neglected out-door work had just come into his mind.

"Holidays are desperately dissipating things; seems to me as if it was Sunday all the time now, and I'm always making mistakes and taking it easy now," he said, with a mighty stretch of his long, loose limbs.

"Can't I strike in somewhere and help?" demanded Fred, getting up, briskly alert. For although Canadian hospitality is so spontaneous and free, native etiquette demands a lively gratitude on the part of the benefited one, and he had been brought up to believe in paying his debts as he incurred them.

"Well, if you want something to amuse you, there's this place would be all the better for a little tidying up," Blue Pete answered, waving his hand in a deprecating fashion towards the litter encumbering floor, bed, table, and the big bench by the window. "I don't generally spend much time on that sort of thing myself, but that fellow who took lodgings here, free, gratis and for nothing, as they say down east, turned the place upside down, like pigs in a hay-meadow. I suppose he wanted to see if my things fitted him better than his own, for I found my best biled shirt gone, and a pair o' store shoes that didn't fit me quite enough were missing too."

"Oh, I'll clear up fine; it will be so tidy when you come back that you won't know it for the same," said Fred, setting to work with great zeal and energy, whilst Montana Jenny followed him round, sniffing suspiciously, as if she smelled a felon in every garment, and Blue Pete lounged away, well content to have someone else do his domestic tidying up for him.

Presently, in folding up a jacket which evidently came under the denomination of store clothes, though it was very old and ragged, he dropped a book from an inner pocket; stooping to pick it up, he caught sight of the name on the fly-leaf, "Guy Herrick, from a friend."

CHAPTER XV
MONTANA JENNY TAKES THE TRAIL

A thrill went through Fred as he read the name on the title page of the worn little book, which was a pocket edition of quotations from Shakespeare, very much be-thumbed, and a whirling sense of confusion and giddiness seized him, as he realized what a valuable clue had been put into his hands.

"Have a sniff, old lady," he said, holding out book and jacket to Jenny.

The dog came at his bidding, and smelled jacket and book in a distrustful fashion, wagged her tail, then whining in a plaintive manner, dropped her nose on the ground and commenced to hunt round the room.

"You'll do, good dog; maybe I shall live to be proud of you yet, only you mustn't make mistakes and run down the wrong quarry this time," he exclaimed, fussing over the dog in wild delight, then dancing round the room as if he had suddenly gone crazy, which encouragement so excited Jenny that she dashed round like a crazy creature, knocking down pots and pans, and upsetting furniture in her desire to find and pull down the owner of the ragged old jacket, that Fred was forced to tie her up to the leg of the bedstead, whilst he finished his task of clearing up the muddle in the place.

Then he went outside to see what he could find to do there, and espying a hatchet and a great pile of wood needing to be chopped, set to work upon it, only staying to bring out the dog, which he tied to the fence, where she could bask in the afternoon sun whilst he chopped.

But the tracker instinct had been awakened in Jenny by that invitation to smell the jacket and the book, and after restlessly pacing the length of her chain, with her nose on the ground, whining and crying, she flung up her great head in a melancholy and far-reaching howl.

Fred's heart beat faster as he listened. Suppose he had made a mistake, and that ragged old jacket belonged to Blue Pete, instead of the stranger who had taken such liberties with that worthy's house and wardrobe! The bare thought made him shiver, for he knew enough of the habits of tracker dogs to understand that it would not be wise to let Blue Pete come within reach of Jenny unwarned.

So he chopped on in feverish haste, keeping eyes and ears on the alert for some sign of his host's approach; then by-and-by, when he heard a cheerful whistle, and a rich, rolling tenor voice breaking out into a song, he dropped the hatchet in all haste and hurried to intercept Blue Pete, who was evidently coming up from the osier swamps at the back of the little clearing.

"Stay where you are, please; I want to talk to you," called out Fred, darting forward in the direction of the approaching forest, whilst Montana Jenny nearly choked herself with her chain in her efforts to get free and go also; then recovering a little from the strangulation, started howling worse than ever.

"What's up?" demanded Blue Pete, in mild astonishment, as Fred rushed towards him in a desperate hurry.

"I only want to be sure that I haven't made a mistake," panted the boy. "I found an old jacket, ragged and torn, amongst the muddle on the floor, and a book of poetry fell out of the pocket, with the name, Guy Herrick, on the fly-leaf; I thought it must have belonged to that man we are wanting, and I let Jenny smell it, telling her to go and find; then she got so eager she was ready to knock the house down, to get out and away, and I had to tie her up. But I am afraid lest I may have made a mistake, and given her one of your coats to smell, in which case it won't be safe for you to go too near her, until matters have been made plain to her again."

"Well, you are a pretty sort of a young varmint, to go setting my dollar-and-a-quarter dog against me in such a fashion!" exclaimed Blue Pete, throwing back his head in a guffaw of amusement. "But perhaps it wasn't my jacket after all, though 'ragged and torn' describes most of my clothes pretty accurately; but suppose we go and identify the thing, or will the dog tear me down *en route*, do you expect?" and again the great laugh burst out, as if the joke were too good to be dropped for some time to come.

"You'll be all right if you don't get near enough for her to get a smell at you," cried Fred, who was trembling in every limb, having taken the most serious view possible of the matter, because of his share in it; and then he hustled Blue Pete towards the door of the log-house, taking good care to keep himself between his host and the dog, which was still sniffing the ground, and making frantic dashes for freedom.

Once inside he shut the door, then brought forward the jacket from the corner, where he had laid it away for safety, then held it up for Blue Pete's inspection.

"It's a beauty, certainly; but it ain't mine, and, what is more, I couldn't get into it if I tried," said that worthy, taking the garment, and turning it round and round; then his eye was caught by something lying among a pile of personalties in the corner from where Fred had brought the jacket, and picking it up, he shook it triumphantly. "My best biled shirt, as I'm alive! So the fellow wasn't so much of a rogue as I thought him, though if he wore the shirt he might have washed and starched it—got it up, as the laundresses say—before he went away. Well, I'll forgive him the shoes he took, seeing that I never could wear them with any sort of comfort; but I did feel real mad about that biled shirt, for I've only got two, and this was out and out the best one."

Fred could not help laughing at the affectionate manner in which Blue Pete smoothed down the soiled cotton garment, which appeared so precious to him; then he picked up the ragged jacket with a relieved air.

"I'm very glad I didn't make a mistake, for I should have felt bad if Jenny had gone for you," he said.

"And so you'd oughter," responded Blue Pete, with another guffaw, as he rolled his much-prized shirt up into a tight ball, and stowed it upon a high shelf next to the coffee-pot, doubtless to await a good opportunity for washing and starching, he being something of a dandy with regard to his personal appearance, though rather lacking in the virtue of domestic tidiness.

But Fred was pulling and tugging at that part of his clothing in which his carefully hoarded money was hidden; he had not drawn upon the little store since leaving home, but now he felt the time had come to spend and not to spare, so he was prepared to do the thing handsomely, even though the doing left him all but penniless, with a journey of unknown length before him.

"What will you take for Montana Jenny? I want to buy her very badly, and I should like to have the jacket too, if you don't mind." His voice was fairly trembling with eagerness, and his breath came in short pants from the greatness of his excitement.

"What do you want a dog for?" demanded Blue Pete.

"I've got to follow up that man that was staying here; you heard what Athabasca Bill said about the fur cap that was like his own—so like that my father identified it as belonging to Bill. But in this wilderness we may overrun his trail no end of times if we don't have help; so I want Jenny and this jacket, and then I believe I can make her track him down."

"Not a bad idea that!" exclaimed Blue Pete. "How much money have you got, anyhow?"

"Five dollars. Mother gave me all she'd got in the house; but I haven't spent any yet, because I've mostly worked out my board, except since I've been with Bill, and he won't let me pay him for my keep, because of having been at our house so long last fall."

"I should think not. Good as a hospital, your house must have been for him. I only wish your folks lived out this way, so as I could drop in on 'em to be taken care of when I felt queer; only then, perhaps, the temptation to have a sickly fit would come so often, that I should develop into a confirmed invalid before I'd made my pile, which would be desperate inconvenient for everybody. But stow your money away, boy, and you shall have Jenny. Much good may she do you, too; though I don't mind owning that I am more than half afraid of the brute."

"It is very kind—" began Fred, with a flush and a stammer, being rather sensitive on the score of patronage, and feeling that he would have preferred to pay for the dog—at least, the dollar and a quarter which was the price his host had given old man Arlo.

"Not a bit of it, boy; you can take the dog as the first instalment of Bill's debt to your mother, and if you want to know why I'm taking his financial responsibilities on my shoulders, I can tell you that he kept my head above water once when we were working together down Lethbridge way, so I'm bound to do my bit in return, don't you see?"

"Saved your life, did he?" asked Fred, looking at Blue Pete's long length and powerful frame, and wondering a little how a small, weak-looking man like Athabasca Bill could have succeeded in towing such a big fish out of the water.

"Aye, that he did," replied Blue Pete, stooping to re-light his pipe at the fire, and then sitting down with a fatigued air, as if his short stroll through the osier beds had been quite too much for him. "We were patching up a dam that was risky near Magrath, when I happened to get caught by my foot through the sinking of one of the props against the barricade which kept the water back. Just at that moment, when Athabasca Bill was nearly smothering himself in mud, to try to get my foot free, with a crack like a gun going off, the barricade gave way and let the water down on us. It was every man for himself then, and everyone bolted, leaving me to drown, except Bill, who clung for dear life to the bit of the barricade that didn't give way, and held me above water till they were able to shut it off higher up, and set me free."

"My mother says that Athabasca Bill is as brave as they make 'em," responded Fred, with shining eyes.

"Aye, he's that, and more; for he is unselfish, and that is a very uncommon sort of virtue," Blue Pete said, with a windy sigh, as his pipe went out, and he had to stoop to re-light it.

When he was through with his wood-cutting, finding that he had still nearly an hour of daylight left, Fred slipped Jenny's chain from the fence, and winding it round his arm for security, brought her to the ragged jacket; then bidding her smell it well, told her to go and find.

Tugging at the chain, the dog went round and round the inner room, round and round the outside clearing, finally starting off by a narrow track leading to the higher ground away from the river.

Fred had gone as far as he deemed it wise, in view of the fading light, and was in the act of coaxing Jenny to relinquish the hunt that day, and return with him to Blue Pete's cabin for the night, when he heard a whistle, and saw Athabasca Bill coming quickly towards him through the deepening gloom.

"Did you think I had cleared on a new trail, without stopping to let you know?" asked the trapper, whilst Jenny gave one sniff at him, then turned away in disgust, because he was not the "find" for which she was seeking so ardently.

"No, I trusted to you to let me come too," replied Fred, and then, having at last induced Jenny to come back home peacefully, he turned and walked along the narrow path by the side of his friend.

"Blue Pete has given me Jenny to help in tracking down that Guy Herrick, and she is as hot on the trail as can be," he said eagerly; then bethinking himself of Bill's long absence, he inquired, "Did you find Snaky-Shoes, and did he know anything that might be likely to help you?"

"I found him, certainly, and I should say he's about as slippery as an eel; Snaky-Shoes isn't a bad name for him, all things considered. But if what he has told me is true, we've got some rather queer game to run down, Fred, my boy, and a precious long way to go to do it," Athabasca Bill replied, with a grave face.

"Oh?" the boy's tone and face were full of a questioning wonder, as he waited for the other to speak further.

"Snaky-Shoes says that this Guy Herrick, the young man with the desperately bad cough, is an official of the Hudson's Bay Company, and that he is to work right through Athabasca, visiting every outlying fort and trade depôt, in order to report on each."

"I don't care what he is; if he took that money, and threw the blame on my father, he has got to be found and made to answer for it," replied Fred stormily.

"So I think too," said Athabasca Bill, and the next morning, with their packs on their backs, they set off into the unknown, with Montana Jenny for a leader and guide.

CHAPTER XVI

'FOLLOW MY LEADER'

The travellers carried four days' provisions, which at a pinch might be made to serve one day longer; even Montana Jenny had a pack on her back, containing her own especial rations, and a pot and kettle for the use of the bipeds.

Carefully stowed away among his personal luggage, Fred carried the ragged jacket, which had to serve as a clue for the hound to work upon. By the advice of Blue Pete he had wrapped it in a bit of rubber sheeting, which not only served the purpose of keeping it dry, but also preserved the scent intact, by keeping it from mixing with other odours.

"This reminds me of the old game of 'Follow my Leader,' that we used to play when I was a boy at school," Athabasca Bill said, as he and his companion panted along in the rear of Jenny.

"We played it too, and jolly hard work it was sometimes, though I don't think we ever found it so tough as this," Fred replied, feeling as if his right arm was being pulled out by the roots, from Jenny tugging so hard at the leash, when the scent was good and the trail easy to follow.

"It was funny that old man Arlo was willing to sell a dog like that for a dollar and a quarter," Bill remarked, as they lay basking on the ground in the hot sunshine for a noontide rest. Though so late in the season, the weather was exceptionally bright and fine, the nights were certainly keenly cold, but the noonday sunshine was hot as summer.

"So I thought; why, the chain and collar must have cost all that," Fred said, passing his hand caressingly over the big brown head which rested on his knee; he had not felt much drawn to Jenny on their first acquaintance, but now that she belonged to him, and was doing her level best to run down the real thief, his affection for her, and admiration of her shrewd intelligence, grew with every hour.

"Perhaps the old man isn't quite so sane as he used to be, or too poor to pay for the creature's keep; a dog like that takes some filling up every day," Bill rejoined sleepily; the soothing warmth of the sun made him drowsy, and as this was the second day out on the trail, he was foot-weary, and glad of the noonday resting spell.

"What I can't understand is that Guy Herrick should have told you he was bound for Beaver River, when Jenny is keeping us due north; for Beaver River must lie a goodish bit to the north-east from here," Fred said presently, after a silence, which Bill had filled in by a gentle doze.

"I can," the trapper replied, with a stretch and a yawn. "It's one thing to talk about the Beaver River, and quite another to get there, for there ain't many trails like turnpike roads in North Alberta and Athabasca; so when that chap got across the Saskatchewan, if he knew the lay of the land at all he'd steer straight through here, as we are doing, to Morinville, and from there out to the main trail from Edmonton to Athabasca Landing. When he got there he could strike off into any one or the other of the hundred and odd trails that open from that one, and my opinion is, that if we don't catch him before he reaches the main trail, we've a precious poor chance of catching him at all, especially if it should come wet to wash out the scent."

"We had best be pushing on then," Fred said, all alert and eager to be off again.

Jenny was eager too; the scent was plainly strong at this point, though several days must have passed since the man they sought travelled that way, but there had been no rain, and nothing baffles the tracker dog like wet weather.

The trail they followed was one used largely by Indians, trading between the advancing tide of civilization and the Reservations, and it went for the most part through a country of rolling hills and gentle valleys, the rising ground clad in resinous pines, the lower levels abounding in osier beds, and willow swamps.

Here and there a solitary settler hailed their approach with a hearty welcome, and open-handed hospitality, asking nothing in return, saving news of the outside world, which in those wilderness solitudes was harder to obtain than gear, or gold.

There was a shed, partly filled with hay, designed doubtless as a shelter for horses and cattle later on in the season, that they reached about sundown, and into which Jenny led the way with a calm confidence due to a strong scent, and once she was under the shelter of the roof, she became wildly excited, plunging hither and thither, and leaping up at the stack of hay in frantic efforts to get free and swarm to the top, failing which, she threw up her great head, howling in a dismal and heart-breaking fashion.

Fred's heart began to beat so fast that it seemed almost as though his companion must hear its thumping, but he had not the courage to put his thoughts into words, looking instead for some means of getting to the top of that heap of dried grass, to investigate for himself the dog's reasons for being so excited about it.

Then he espied a handy piece of timber, with notches at the sides where the boughs had been lopped off short, and dragging it with some difficulty into position, dropped it against the side of the stack, and began to clamber up.

"Are you in such a hurry for bed that you have forgotten your supper?" Bill called out, looking up from his fire-building to wonder what had come to Fred, who was usually a steady help, not given to whims and fancies.

"I'll come and help you in a minute, after I have had a look up here," Fred called down, then just succeeded by a spring in launching himself on the top of the pile, though he narrowly escaped coming to the ground with a tremendous thump instead; still, as the old saying has it, "A miss is as good as a mile," and he was none the worse for so nearly falling.

Having with great care and skill got his fire laid to his liking, Bill was down on hands and knees, blowing and puffing to make the tiny flames spring higher, when he heard an eager shout of, "Bill, Bill, do come and look! I believe that fellow must have spent a night up here in the hay."

Athabasca Bill left his fire to its own devices, and proceeded to clamber up the rolling, slippery piece of timber, which swayed and shook in the most uncomfortable and disagreeable fashion; but he reached the top in safety, and crouched beside Fred, looking at a nest in the hay, that was like the form of a hare, only many sizes bigger, whilst tossed carelessly on one side was the fragment of a *Manitoba Free Press*, and an empty match-box.

"Some one has slept up here pretty recently, that's clear, and they weren't afraid of making a bonfire of themselves either," said the trapper grimly, as he picked up the box which had held matches, and dropped it again.

"He can't be far in front of us now; do you think we shall overhaul him tomorrow?" queried Fred, who was fairly panting with eagerness and impatience.

Athabasca Bill shook his head doubtfully.

"Can't say, I'm sure; but by the look of the sky, and the general feel of the weather, I should say there will be snow within twenty-four hours."

"Snow?" Fred's face was a pucker of wonder and dismay, for except in bad seasons they did not as a rule get snow for another fortnight or three weeks, by which time he had hoped to be safe at home again, with incontestable evidence of his father's innocence; but a snowstorm at this juncture might retard matters for weeks, might even bring their efforts to complete failure, and possibly cost them their lives, if they were out in the open when it began, for as a rule snowstorms in North Alberta were no joke.

"That's about it. You may think it early, but I've known a bad storm earlier than this; come outside and have a look at the weather," the other said, deftly swinging himself back on to the shaky timber, and sliding from thence to the ground.

Fred followed in silence; all the fine flow of his spirits had gone, dashed down by that one word, snow.

"See them white rags?" queried Athabasca Bill, with a lean forefinger upraised to the sky, where fleecy clouds, like billows of cotton wool, were piling themselves about the sun-setting.

Fred nodded, his heart too full for speech; then after a minute or two spent in battling with the big lump that had come into his throat, he said anxiously, "What do you think of doing?"

"Having supper, and a good warm; while that's in progress we can settle the next thing to be done," the trapper answered, going back to his fire, and working at it with great energy, until it was in a condition suitable for cooking him some tea.

Fred secured Jenny to one of the posts of the shed, then sat moodily down on the ground, staring at the leaping flames, and wondering for how many hours longer the trail would hold, which they had followed so successfully hitherto.

It was so cruelly hard to be faced with failure, just when he had imagined himself within reach of success. He would not have felt so bad about it, but for finding that nest in the hay, where, without doubt, his quarry had lain such a short time ago.

"Cheer up, boy; there's no sense in owning yourself beaten until you've been bowled out," Bill said, deftly lifting his kettle from the fire just as it began to boil.

"We shall be bowled out, and that pretty clean too, if the snow begins," Fred answered, feeling that he had no appetite for his supper even, with such a prospect in front of him.

"There's one thing we may do, if we have any sort of luck," said Athabasca Bill, casting one eye upwards to gauge the weather prospects; "we may beat the snow, unless you're tired out, that is."

"Oh, I'm not tired—not worth mentioning, that is," rejoined Fred briskly, though fifteen minutes before he had been feeling that it would be quite impossible to go any further without a long rest and sleep.

"And I feel pretty fit. So although that haystack looks uncommonly inviting, I propose that we take an hour to eat our supper, and then set out again as soon as the moon is up. A very good pace we shall be able to make, too, with the wind in our backs, and as we've been coming uphill steadily for the last two or three hours, the chances are that we may have downhill in front of us when we start again," Bill said, as the two started upon their supper, with Jenny crouching at Fred's elbow to share in the feast.

"I had forgotten the moon; but will it be up in an hour?" Fred asked, giving Jenny a push, as, forgetful of good manners, she thrust not merely her nose, but her whole head under his arm, and seized the fragment of food he was lifting to his mouth.

"Nearly, by then; it may be an hour and a half, but it won't make much difference, for we can rest until it comes up, take a taste of the haystack, don't you see, only it won't be wise to go to the top, as that friend of ours did, for fear we go off so sound that we forget to get up when the moon does."

"We ought to get a good distance on by that means," Fred said, looking up at the sky, where the drifting, billowy clouds hung, rose-tinted from the sunset, on the clear grey of the western sky.

"We ought, and so we'll hope that we shall," Bill replied, and Fred was too much absorbed in trying to drink some scalding tea to notice the dubious ring of his tone.

It did not take them long to finish supper, and then, when Bill had lighted his pipe, the two crept close under the haystack to rest until the rising of the moon.

They were both sleepy, and when Bill's pipe had dropped from his lips a second time, he rose to his feet, and going to a little distance, carefully knocked the ashes from the pipe, then stowed it away in his pocket.

"It always seems to me like tempting Providence to smoke under a haystack, especially when a man's drowsy," he remarked, coming back to settle down in his old position once more. "Now, boy, we've about three quarters of an hour, so let us make the best of it."

And make the best of it they did, huddled close together for warmth, with the dog curled up beside them, and adding not a little to their comfort. But when the three quarters of an hour were at an end, they still slept on, worn out with the long, weary tramp of the day before, while the moon came up, and after battling awhile to keep clear of the clouds, slid behind the billowy grey vapours, worsted in the struggle.

CHAPTER XVII
A BAD NIGHT

The hours went by, and Fred, who was cramped with his constrained position, and cold from keenness of the night air, began to dream that he had reached the courthouse, where his father's case was being tried, but though he had with him the clear and certain proofs of his father's innocence, old man Arlo barred his entrance to the court, even threatening to set the hounds on to him, if he persisted in trying to get in.

"Very well, set them at me, and see what will come of it," he was saying valorously; "for your Montana Jenny already loves me better than she does you, whilst Ruby and Smiler would never attack my father's son," when a burst of fierce and angry barking from Jenny brought him quickly out of dreamland, whilst the energy with which she tugged at the chain that was fastened on his arm, almost upset him.

"Hullo, what's wrong?" inquired Athabasca Bill, coming out of his heavy slumber with a groan and a sigh, for to a man as tired as he was, the process of waking could not fail to be painful.

"Have we slept too long?" cried Fred, with palpitating fear in his tone, for something seemed to have gone wrong with the quiet night, as sobbing bursts of wind swirled through the tree tops, and moaned away in the distance, while Jenny barked and raved, springing fiercely at her chain in the eager desire to pull down something or someone.

"Yes, we've slept too long, that's plain; past midnight I should say it is, by the look of the sky. There's not much moon either, and no stars. We shall have to be brisk to beat the snow now."

"Never mind if we do beat it," Fred said, as he fastened his pack on to his shoulders, and proceeded to harness Jenny into her burdens, a difficult task this, by reason of her dashing and straining.

"Quiet, old girl; quiet, I say; what is the use of making all that row?"

"I expect she has seen some ponies; they would be sure to gather on this higher ground if there is bad weather coming," Athabasca Bill answered, as he hung his burdens round his shoulders, slung his gun into place, then groped in the darkness for the stout staff, that was such a help in getting over soft places.

"Is there a horse ranch out this way?" Fred asked, in surprise at the other's mention of ponies.

Athabasca Bill laughed.

"They don't call them ranches, I guess; but for all that, the Indians raise scores of ponies every year for the southern markets, and for their own use; that is what the shack is for, and that stack of bunch grass. I expect a drove of the little beasts trotted up, thinking to be near shelter if the weather turned out bad, and then Jenny gave tongue; lucky she did, or we might have slept there like pigs until daylight."

"I expect we are all the better for what we have had, only I can't help feeling that I should like a little more," Fred said, as the procession moved on again in its old order: Jenny in front with her nose on the ground, himself next, and the trapper, with staff and gun, bringing up the rear.

Sometimes Fred would be towed along at a tremendous rate, Jenny pulling so hard as to nearly drag him off his feet; then she would stop dead so unexpectedly, that he all but tumbled over her.

Her course and her pace tonight were much more erratic than usual, and she overran the scent so many times, having to hark back to pick it up again, that Fred would have been seriously discouraged, but for his remembrance of Ross Johnson's words, that Montana Jenny could track a man through the crowded city street, yet never lose the trail.

The path they were following abounded with pitfalls, and as every hour the moon grew more obscure and the light fainter, they were presently compelled to pull up and spend the remainder of the time until daylight crouched close together under the shelter of an overhanging bank.

Jenny keenly resented this pause in her work, and it was as much as Fred could do to soothe her into quietness. Even when he persuaded her to sit down peacefully beside him, she would remain still for about two minutes and a half, then leap up with a tearing rush, and commence baying and struggling like a mad thing.

"What is the matter with the creature, do you expect?" said Fred, when for the fourth time he had dragged her back, compelling her to temporary obedience and quietness.

"Can't say. Them tracker dogs are altogether beyond me; it is possible we are pretty near what we want to find, or it may be she knows the weather is not what it should be. Hullo! what is that?" and Athabasca Bill craned his head forward in a listening attitude, whilst Fred strained his ears into listening also.

The wind swept through the trees with a moan and a shriek, branches creaked and groaned in every direction, but Fred could hear nothing else, and said so.

"I did; I heard a cock crow, and a dog bark. I don't think it will be long before the dawning, either; not by the look of the darkness, but I don't like the sound of that wind."

"And I don't like the feel of it. I could wish we had stayed in our snug quarters under the haystack, for there at least we had a roof over our heads," Fred said, as a swirl of wind swept round the corner of their bank, and nearly blew them out of it.

"You needn't wish it, for it is very likely that long before daylight comes, that shack, and the stack too, will be a heap of ruins. It takes a well-built place to stand a circular wind like this; don't you notice how every blast seems to twist and twirl almost like a humming top? I have been in an Indian village when a wind like this was blowing, and I have seen every wigwam in the place shorn of its topping; so I've come to the conclusion that I'd as soon be out of doors as anywhere, when such storms rise, until the downfall begins, that is, for then there is mostly such a smother, that it is as much as you can do to see your hand when you hold it up in front of your face," Bill answered, with the quiet philosophy which was a part of his nature.

"Ugh! I hope it won't begin to fall before daylight, then," the other said, with a shiver.

They sat in silence for awhile after that, as close together as they could press, and with nose and knees on a level, whilst Jenny sat just in front, with an air of fierce alertness bristling all over her brown and white coat.

Would the darkness never end, and morning dawn again? Cramped and shivering, chilled to the bone, Fred sat straining his eyes for some sign of the breaking of day, until from sheer exhaustion he slid into a doze, a kind of half-awake slumber, which left him keenly conscious of his physical discomfort, though it dulled his perceptions to what was happening around him.

"Here comes the light, such as it is; and now, boy, we'd best be moving," said the voice of Athabasca Bill, seeming to come from a very long way off.

Was that daylight? Fred scrambled to his feet, rubbing his eyes, because he thought the blame lay with his organs of vision.

"Is it a fog, or what?" he demanded, nearly toppling over, because one leg seemed to have no life or power in it, and gave way under him when he tried to put his weight on it.

"The clouds are hanging so low, that is what it is; come along, boy, we'd best get to shelter if we can, before the smother begins," the trapper said so urgently, that Fred made some sort of shift to get along, although at first every step was torture.

For a mile or two Jenny led them along at a fairly steady pace, then suddenly began to waver and grow uncertain, running this way and that, throwing up her head as if the scent lay above instead of below, then howling weirdly.

The trail, too, had become faint and confused, whilst with every mile the ground grew more broken and hilly, so that it was not merely the downhill that Bill had hoped for, and reckoned upon, but uphill also, and plenty of it.

"Here comes the snow," panted Bill, as a white cloud seemed to drop upon them, and all at once the air became too thick to breathe.

A groan from Fred was all the response he could make, for at this moment Jenny began pulling and tugging, uttering a low whimpering cry, which said more plainly than words, that she had found the trail again, and was for following it hard.

"Let her go, boy; I'll keep up. The scent won't last ten minutes longer, but maybe it will be enough," panted Bill, and Fred was fain to obey, even though it meant going at a run over very rough ground, then up a sharp, steep hill, where it was all he could do to keep from coming down on his hands and knees.

With every step the smother of whirling snowflakes grew thicker, and when presently Jenny slackened speed a little, giving him time to look round to throw a word to Athabasca Bill, who should have been toiling along in the rear, his words met no response, and to his horror he realized that he and his companion had become separated, in the gloom of the whirling snow-cloud.

"Bill, where are you, Bill?" he shouted, the quavering horror in his heart lending a penetrating insistence to his tones.

But no answering shout came back from the whirling smother, and Jenny was tugging so hard that he could scarcely hold her in.

Still he would have stayed where he was, or endeavoured to go back on his track in search of his friend, had it not been that he heard just then the bark of a dog, and what seemed to him the faint echo of a human voice.

Now dogs and voices meant, doubtless, help near at hand, and shouting wildly as he went, in the hope that some echo of his calling might reach his companion, he let Jenny pull him forward, which she did at a tremendous pace, though it was plain she was no longer following scent, since the snow already covered the ground, compelling her to depend on her instincts rather than her nose.

He was growing numbed and bewildered, being scarcely able to keep his eyes open because of the sting in the cold, when suddenly the path seemed to slip away from under his feet, and he shot forward with what seemed to be frightful velocity, getting mixed up with Jenny's chain as he went plunging downward.

Would he never reach the bottom? He thought of the bad dreams of falling that he had sometimes had after eating too many roast potatoes for supper, and of the relief it used to be when he bumped at the bottom to wake up and find himself safely in bed; but this fall seemed to have no bottom to bump upon, and he was just beginning to wonder if it was going on forever, when he came into violent collision with something or someone, there was a sharp, stinging pain in his shoulder, and then a chorus of grunts and ejaculations, shrill scolding in an unknown tongue, and then a blur of confusion that might have lasted two minutes or two hours, so little capable was he of measuring time, or understanding what had happened to him.

Then he came back to his senses again, to find Montana Jenny industriously licking his face, whilst a crowd of dusky faces were grouped in the background at a respectful distance, for Jenny, although chained, was not the kind of animal to be rashly intruded upon, or interfered with.

"Oh, I say, there's my chum Athabasca Bill away back on the trail; he can't be more than half a mile behind. We got parted; you see, the dog dragged me on so fast, and I didn't know he wasn't following," Fred said, with appealing eagerness, pushing away the dog's diligent tongue, and striving to sit erect.

"Smother too thick. Athabasca Bill all right. He know what to do when blizzard come," jerked out a particularly unlovely red man, who seemed to be in authority.

"I fell down somewhere—how was it?" asked Fred, trying to collect his wavering senses firmly enough together to make a still more imperious demand that his companion should immediately be searched for, even though the smother was so great that it had to be cut with a knife.

But at that moment Jenny sprang up with a roar, dragging so fiercely at the chain that his arm seemed to be wrenched out of joint.

CHAPTER XVIII
POTIPHAR'S FRAGMENT

There were several men lounging in the store at Errol's place, some of them with merchandise for barter, and others paying for goods with cash, or having them on credit, as the case might be.

Mrs. Errol was behind the counter, helping her husband to minister to the various needs of the buyers and sellers, putting a word into the conversation now and then, or letting her light-hearted laughter ripple out; for no cloud brooded long over her merry heart, and though she had wept copiously at Fred Crawford's terrible fate in the seething turmoil of Denaree's Leap, it was of no use to go on sorrowing, since no amount of grieving could undo the tragedy.

Naturally enough, the conversation turned on the accident, which, although over a week old, was still news to some of the customers thronging the store, and Mrs. Errol's smiles were waxing wan and tearful, when the half-breed Potiphar, whose misadventure in the water had been the cause of Fred's disaster, came into the store, his lank, black hair seeming to stick straight up with importance, whilst his face was screwed into a pucker of mystery.

"Back again, Potiphar; did you find any wreckage?" she asked, for the half-breed had been sent down to Black Pine, and over the fifteen miles portage, to the other side of the Valley of Death, in order to see if the river had flung up any wreckage, at the end of the twenty miles' succession of rapids and whirlpools; and he had taken his time in going and returning, not believing in over-much exertion of any sort.

"No wreckage whatsumever," he jerked out, in his own peculiar style; then seeing that all eyes were turned on him, and the running fire of talk had died down to an expectant hush, he went on, pulling something from under his arm and waving it in the faces of all present, "but I foun' dis here, half-a-mile off the portage trail atween Black Pine and the other end, and I say how come it there?"

"What is it?" demanded Mrs. Errol crisply, leaning forward to get a better view; then her husband reached his hand out over her shoulder, and caught the article which Potiphar was holding as if it were a banner.

"Why, it is one of our meal bags," he said, turning it and catching sight of his own name in letters two inches long on the other side.

"That is so," replied Potiphar, in a pompous voice. "It is that same one bag what went down in canoe to Black Pine portage, and tumble into Denaree's Leap."

"Nonsense, it could not be," retorted Mrs. Errol sharply, having little patience with the flights of fancy in which the half-breed was wont to indulge.

"It am," replied Potiphar obstinately. "See that hole in the corner; I tied it up wid the babby's hair-string, and cotched it arter for letting the papoose lose it."

"He is quite right, George; that is Mamie's hair ribbon, and I did grumble at him for letting her lose it," cried Mrs. Errol, examining the pink fragment with which the hole in the bag was tied, and instantly identifying it as having formerly belonged to baby Mamie.

"But how could it have got over to the trail?" queried Mr. Errol, in hopeless bewilderment, for river and trail were in some places as much as three miles apart, owing to the windings of the waterway, and the necessity which existed for making the portage as short as possible.

"Two legs and two hands kin carry a thing most anywhere," remarked Potiphar, fumbling in his clothing for something he had hidden there, yet failed to find on searching for it.

"You mean it may have been thrown up as wreckage, and found by someone, perhaps an Indian, who carried it to where you lighted upon it?" asked Mrs. Errol, knowing by experience that Potiphar's mind usually worked faster than his tongue.

"Whatsumever did it, the thing was there, the mark of a fire not many days old, and this," replied the half-breed stolidly, having at last found that which he was searching for, and which he handed to Mrs. Errol.

It was a half-burned fragment of paper with some writing on one side, and as Mrs. Errol bent forward to get a better light to read by, every head in the store was craned to, if possible, get a glimpse of the writing too.

"'But Bill and I are on his track, and we'll be sure to run him down in time to clear father, so don't worry about us. Your loving Fred,'" read Mrs. Errol, then cried out in amazement, "Whatever can it mean? If the boy really wrote this, he can't have been drowned in Denaree's Leap, that is certain."

"He was, for I saw him," announced a burly lumberman from Black Pine, who was stroking a rough-coated terrier, which tried hard, though unsuccessfully, to bite him.

"But 'Bill' must mean Athabasca Bill, and as Fred had not seen him before he got into Denaree's Leap, it is pretty plain this must have been written since," objected Mrs. Errol, who was going first red and then white with excitement.

"Perhaps it was a different person altogether who wrote that paper," suggested a man who lounged against a flour-barrel with the air of a person of leisure.

"Scarcely," replied Mrs. Errol quickly; "for in such a sparsely settled country, it is not likely that there could be two Freds wandering about in search of something to prove a father's innocence."

"So I should say," struck in George Errol, with an air of decision. Then chancing to turn his gaze in the direction of the open door of the store, he caught sight of an arrival on horseback, and hurried out to greet him.

This was Tom Marsh, who had ridden over directly Saidie returned from her journey to break the news of Fred's death to his people.

"Morning, neighbour, are we going to have some snow?" asked Tom, casting a weather-eye upwards, and not so much asking for information on the subject, as showing himself prepared to give it.

"I don't know; what do you think about it?" inquired George Errol, sending his gaze in the same direction, and looking as if nothing in the world interested him at that moment so much as the condition of the atmosphere.

"Well, I should say we are in for it, and that before very long, too, so I'll do my errands and start back as quick as I know, for I'm not keen on being caught in a smother, and Saidie will be more than a little worried if she is left alone in a snowstorm," said Tom, tying his horse up, then inquiring in a casual sort of way, as he turned to enter the store, "No news of that poor boy, I suppose?"

"We just got hold of something which may be news, or on the other hand it may not," replied George Errol; then walking up to his wife, who was still absorbed by the fragment of half-burned paper, he said, "Nancy, this is Tom Marsh, Saidie's brother; tell him about that piece of paper, will you?"

Tom Marsh proved readier of belief in Fred's continued existence than the other men had done, but that might have been owing to the fact that he had never seen Denaree's Leap, and so was no judge of the dangers to be reckoned with there.

"My word, won't Saidie be glad!" he exclaimed, rubbing his hands together with a gleeful air. "She has cried quarts since the accident, and if the youngster had been a matter of ten years older, I should have been as jealous as a yellow grasshopper, to think my sister liked another fellow best."

"But you ain't got no proof, only speculation, that he's still kicking," drawled the leisurely lounger by the flour-barrel, when the laugh raised by Tom's quaint tone had subsided.

"And I saw him drown, poor little chap," put in the lumberman. "Precious bad it made me feel, to hang like a great hulking coward on the bank, and never plunge in to try and pull him out; but in that race of water, he must have been washed half-a-mile by the time I could have jumped in."

"Just so," remarked Tom, with a nod. "But miracles do happen sometimes, even in these days, you know, and we shall see young Fred come marching this way again before long, or I shall be very much mistaken."

"Well, if it'll make you any happier, leave it at that for awhile," remarked the lumberman, with good-natured toleration, adding, however, with a lugubrious shake of his head, "But I saw him drown, poor little chap!"

Tom turned away, this kind of Job's comforter getting on his nerves to quite a serious extent. Moreover, he had his business to transact, and was more anxious even than before to get it done speedily, so that he could set out on his return journey.

He had brought both his horses, riding one for half the journey, and then changing to the other; but going back he would ride one animal all the way, whilst the stores were packed on the back of the other. His intention had been to stay at Errol's place for a couple of hours, to rest the animals; but the appearance of the sky, and the news he had heard, decided him on starting homeward with the least possible delay.

The stores were all laden, and he was tightening the girths of his saddle, when Mrs. Errol came tripping out of the door of the store to have a word in private with him before he went.

"Mr. Marsh, I don't think that you are half as nice as your sister, for she certainly would not have rushed away again in such an immense hurry, without telling me the news."

"It would not do for us all to be alike, ma'am; there'd be no variety in life. And as to the news, there is precious little of that stirring at our place, except that the speckled hen has laid four eggs since last Saturday; but I'm afraid she will leave off again, if we are going to have a cold snap."

"You are quite the most aggravating man of my acquaintance, Mr. Marsh," the little woman exclaimed, with an impatient stamp; "for you know quite well that the news I want to hear about so badly, is how that poor Mrs. Crawford bore the shock of hearing about her son's terrible end, and how the poor man is bearing his life in prison. I never felt so sorry in my life for anyone, even though I have not seen them, and had not heard of them even until your sister brought the boy along."

"Mr. Crawford has luckily been bailed out, so was at home to help his wife stand up under the most knockdown blow the poor soul had ever experienced, I reckon. But Saidie said she suffered cruel, because, you see, it was she who had sent the boy off into the wilderness like that," replied Tom, who felt very bad himself every time he thought of poor Mrs. Crawford, and the terrible remorse which she laboured under.

"I wonder if the boy did really write that scrap of paper, and whether he wasn't drowned after all!" Mrs. Errol cried, shivering a little, for the weather was growing colder, even though the sun had not left off shining. "You've got it safe, I hope, Mr. Marsh?"

"Yes, I've got it safe, and I will see that his people have it as soon as there is a chance to send over. I shan't get much clearing and ploughing done at this rate, with the horses away so constantly, but one must be neighbourly, you know."

"So I think, only it comes a little awkward when the particular neighbour you have got to befriend lives fifty or sixty miles away across country," Mrs. Errol said, with a laugh. "Well, good-bye, Mr. Marsh, and I hope next time you come our way, that you will have a little more leisure in which to cultivate my good opinion."

"I'm sure I hope so too, ma'am, if it will be any sort of gratification to you," Tom replied, and then he walked his horses up the long rise, giving them easy work at first, because he knew he should have to press them hard later on.

Anxiously he watched the sky as he rode, for although he was new to this part of the world, he was not new to that particular class of storm known as a smother, and he was very desirous not to be caught in it before he reached his own location, which already was beginning to wear the semblance of home.

In this he was successful, for although the heavens were black and lowering, while the wind moaned and shrieked through the tops of the pine trees, no snow had fallen before he reached the end of his journey.

Then Saidie ran out to welcome him, and to assist in caring for the weary horses, crying out as she came, "Tom, Tom, Mr. Crawford is here; he came about an hour ago, and was going straight on to Errol's, only I wouldn't let him, for he is clean done up; but he says that he must go and see for himself the place where his poor boy died."

CHAPTER XIX
MAKING THE BEST OF IT

When the smother began, and Athabasca Bill toiled along in the rear of Fred and the dog, he had the feeling that he could not possibly keep the pace up for long, only he said nothing about it, hoping that the distance to shelter might be short.

There was a tightness in his chest, a wavering in his legs, and a singing in his ears, which rendered his walking unsteady, and breathing a matter of difficulty. But he plodded on with painful perseverance, growing blinder and more stupid with every step, until chancing to catch his foot in the protruding root of a tree, he crashed forward on his face, falling the more heavily because of the load on his back.

He uttered no cry as he went down, however, and by the time he had picked himself up, re-settling the load on his shoulders, Fred and the dog were out of sight; out of hearing, also, for the roaring of the wind, and the creaking and snapping of the trees effectually deadened all other noises.

The very magnitude of his disaster served to rouse him, helping him to throw off the sensation of illness and lethargy which had been creeping over him. Hitherto his hope of reaching shelter and safety had depended on Fred and the dog; now he was flung upon his own resources, and it was marvellous what the knowledge did for him, in bringing back his courage, and whipping up his powers of endurance.

Toiling on with a fresh access of energy, it was soon plain to him, however, that it was a waste of strength to go forward, since he might after all be wearing himself out by walking round and round in a circle; so when in the gloom of the smother he butted against a tree, that was hollow on the lee side, he was grateful for his good fortune, and determined to stay there.

Luckily the tree was a big one, not only containing him and his baggage, but with a little room to spare as well, which enabled him to settle himself comfortably, mopping the encrusted snow from face and eyes, whilst he reviewed the situation.

Then in moving his foot it struck against a piece of dried wood, whilst another fragment hit him on the shoulder, the two blows serving to suggest a way of deliverance that might not have occurred to him until it was too late. He knew well that the danger of a smother like this lay chiefly in the keen frost accompanying the fall, which quenched the life out of man and beast unduly exposed to the fury of its piercing cold.

But with dry wood he could kindle a fire, the warmth of which might keep life in him until the storm was over, since the first smother of the season would not be likely to last many hours.

Going to work with the carefulness of long experience, he collected a little heap of dry chips, shredding them into fine shavings with his pocket knife, then lit one of his jealously-hoarded matches, his fingers trembling with eagerness and cold, so that it was a miracle that the tiny point of flame escaped extinction.

But escape it did, growing and increasing until it was a leaping, crackling fire, sending clouds of smoke into the cavity of the hollow tree, and nearly choking the man who crouched behind the cheery blaze.

Many times he wondered what had become of Fred, but it was of no use to worry about him, for the instinct of the dog would doubtless lead him straight to some habitation, where shelter and warmth could be obtained until the storm was over.

The warmth of the fire made him drowsy, so piling on more splintered fragments from the decaying trunk, he yielded to his desire for sleep, and slumbered on in blissful unconsciousness for hours.

When he awoke he was shivering with cold, and his fire was out, but the snow had ceased falling, and it was still daylight, or rather twilight, the clouds still hanging so low as to render the light obscure, with a promise of another fall later on.

Provisions were getting painfully low, and stopping only to munch a fragment of biscuit, and a small bit of bacon, Bill set out to find a more permanent sort of shelter before the next smother began.

There was no trail visible, of course, and having walked so far in the smother before taking refuge in the tree, he had no knowledge of the ground either before or behind, to guide him in the way he should take.

Then he espied a hill rising steeply in front of him, and as he had no remembrance of descending a hill when they were toiling through the smother, he decided on going that way, more especially as the higher ground would afford him a chance of seeing the lay of the land.

The fresh fallen snow was difficult to wade through, and the hill much steeper than it had looked in the distance; moreover, the cold was bringing back that sensation of illness which had troubled him so much before.

With all this to fight against, it was not wonderful that, instead of going straight up the steepest part of the incline, which was the way taken by Fred and the dog, he veered more and more to the left, where the slope was easier.

The top of the ridge was reached at last, and hardly had he gained the summit than a column of smoke, or rather a collection of smokes, arrested his attention away on the left.

"It's Morinville; I honestly believe it's Morinville. God send that the boy has reached there safe!" he ejaculated fervently, feeling that if one of them had to perish, it was better that it should be himself, who had, as he thought, no one to grieve over his going, than that Fred should lose his life in a vain attempt to track down the doer of the deed of which his father stood accused.

It was easier walking on the high ground, for the wind had blown the snow clear away, leaving the ground in places quite bare, and Bill was able to go forward at a good pace, increasing with every step, although he did not know it, the distance between himself and Fred.

The smoke was further away than it had looked, whilst the daylight was fading now in good earnest. No use for Bill to attempt an increase of pace; his walk, instead, grew slower and slower, as he descended from the high ground to the plain, with his boots sinking to the ankle in soft snow at every step.

The night came down black and impenetrable, when he plunged into a belt of pine trees intervening between him and his goal, and he had not fumbled and stumbled his way out to the open ground beyond, before the roar and rush of water caught his ear, pulling him up short with dismay at his heart, for water rushing along like that meant a stream to cross, and how was he to do it in the black darkness of the night?

Unable to answer the question with any sort of satisfaction to himself, he plunged forward again to investigate, so far as he could, the size of the watercourse, and the swiftness of its current, when he ran up against an unmistakable rail fence, whilst the dim outline of a log cabin showed faintly against the sky.

"A house, and here!" he exclaimed, in great amazement, for he had not looked to find houses until he reached the quarter from where he had seen the smoke rising, and which he calculated must be still quite a mile or more away.

But seeing there was a house, he was not minded to go any further in search of shelter, and scrambling over the rails, without troubling to search round to find an opening, he walked up to the house, and began to search for the door.

Finding this where he had expected to do, right in the centre of the log-wall, he rained a shower of resounding knocks on the panel, accompanying this exercise with shouts and cries, in order to arouse the occupants to a sense of his need. Then his heart sank lower, as it became evident to him that the house was empty, perhaps deserted.

Next he tried the door, for at least it would be a shelter, a place where he might lie down; and though he was hungry, food was secondary to rest, because of his failing strength, and the sensation of impending illness which had oppressed him so much all day.

But the door was locked, which for the moment nonplussed him; then taking that ever ready knife of his, he gently inserted it in the keyhole, withdrawing it with a smile of satisfaction, when he discovered there was no key in the lock.

Then he began to feel round the door, and between the interstices of the logs where the chinking was imperfect; he was searching for the key, and hoping against hope that it had not occurred to the owner to put it in his pocket when going from home.

Ah, there it was, hidden away in a nook under the shingles; and drawing it out, he fitted it in the lock, turned it, and lo! the door stood open.

He dragged himself across the threshold, then stopped, sniffing warily, after which he struck a match, looking about for lamp or candle.

A small kerosene lamp stood on a shelf near the stove, and lighting it, he paused to look round.

Some one lived there, plainly, since a heap of hay in an old sack, with a rug tumbled down upon it, plainly stood for a bed, whilst a home-made bench with a rickety leg represented a table, and a mighty block of wood reposing on the floor by the stove plainly served for a chair.

"Bachelor's diggings; might be worse," he said tersely, then turned to shut the door on the black night he had left outside.

If only Fred and the dog had been there, he would have been happy and content, despite the faint sinking of hunger, and the pain that already was beginning to tear at his frail body; as it was, a depressing loneliness was upon him, he who had been so solitary in his life, that often when away trapping in Athabasca he passed weeks, even months, without seeing a human being, saving an occasional Indian.

There was kindling wood lying ready by the stove, though it is doubtful whether, in his exhausted condition, he would have troubled to light a fire, had not a canister on the shelf beside the lamp suggested tea.

But when the fire was really crackling and roaring in the crazy, broken old stove, he was thankful indeed for the cheerful warmth, gaining strength and courage from it to prospect round a little in order to discover the chances, if any, that there were for supper.

There was no compunction in his mind about thus making free with another man's goods, for in that lone country, where shelter meant life, and exposure sometimes stood for death, every house was a hotel to a belated or hardly bestead traveller.

But there was a lack of cleanliness and order about this unknown individual's housekeeping arrangements which caused Athabasca Bill to shake his head in solemn disapproval several times, especially when he lighted upon a greasy, dirty old saucepan, the only cooking utensil the house afforded.

"I don't reckon he's much class, whoever and whatever he calls himself," the solitary man said to himself, as he carefully scraped the cookery accumulations from the inside of the saucepan, and scoured it with wood ashes from under the stove, before boiling the water for his tea.

A search round had revealed no water, but that was a small matter, for the supply outside was practically unlimited; so when the saucepan had reached the requisite condition of cleanliness, he opened the door to fill a bucket with snow.

The smother had begun again worse than ever, and nothing was visible from the door but a wall of whirling whiteness.

"I'm in luck today, that's certain," he muttered, as, filling his bucket with snow, he backed into the house again. A fierce spasm of pain shook him then, bringing the perspiration in great drops to his brow, and forcing him to sit and rest awhile before he could put the snow on the fire to melt for the tea.

"I'm in luck, that's certain, for I couldn't have walked much further, and I must have died sleeping out in such weather," he repeated later on, as he sat sipping his boiling hot tea, and soaking in it a bit of stale, mouldy bread that he had found pushed back on the shelf behind the tea canister.

But the pain was gripping him still, and he moaned with the anguish of it, as he muttered to himself over and over again—

"If only I could know that the boy was safe in shelter, I don't think I'd have a thing left to wish for."

CHAPTER XX
A FUTILE SEARCH

Fred uttered a sharp cry of apprehension and pain when Montana Jenny went on the warpath with such disconcerting suddenness, for there right in front of him was a huge deerhound, ready and eager for the fray, whilst the fierce wrench at his arm had appeared to almost dislocate the joint.

But it was not a moment for dwelling on personal pain, and though he could not use that arm to much purpose, he threw the other round Jenny's neck, dragging her down, and holding her so tightly that she was nearly choked, whilst the red men on their part dragged the ferocious-looking deer-hound out of sight and sound of the enraged newcomer.

Then Fred proceeded to examine into his hurts, which were quite numerous enough to make him feel very much of a cripple; the arm which Jenny had wrenched so violently being bruised and sprained, whilst his shoulder was very painful, having been cut by a jutting point of rock, which had sliced through jacket, underclothes, and flesh.

The red men among whom he had appeared so suddenly by crashing through the roof of the wigwam, were, as it turned out, old acquaintances of Athabasca Bill, and he could not have introduced himself more happily, than by mentioning the trapper's name, for the red man has a memory almost as long as a bloodhound, and Athabasca Bill had done this section of the tribe more than one good turn, so it was important, from the red man's point of view, to treat the young pale-face with kindness and consideration.

It was this reference to Athabasca Bill which made the red men willing to condone the damage to the roof of the wigwam, which had been built in that fashion under the hill, in order that it might have the shelter of the steep, cliff-like bluff, which, rising like a huge wall on the north-east, protected it from the worst of the tempests of the wild and stormy winter.

All this was made clear to Fred later, but his one absorbing thought and care at the first was to induce the red men to go in search of Bill, who might even at that moment be perishing in a snowdrift.

But the red men were wary, and weather-wise too. They knew that the storm would not be of many hours' duration, and they knew also the utter hopelessness of searching for anyone whilst the smother lasted, so they turned a deaf ear to Fred's entreaties, or answered only by grunts and ejaculations, until at last he was forced through sheer exhaustion to cease from his importunities, and await developments.

Meanwhile he lay on a couch of deer-skins piled on aromatic mountain hay, listening to the shrill scolding of the indignant squaws, as they set to work repairing the hole in the roof, whilst several dirty papooses rolled and tumbled about on the floor, to the imminent danger of themselves and everyone else, sending Fred into a tremor of fear every time they rolled his way, lest Montana Jenny should take it in her head to make a meal of one of them.

But the dog was quiet enough now that the deerhound was out of sight, and lay contentedly by Fred's couch, her great head resting on her paws, and with only the alert bearing of her ears or an occasional sigh to show that she was awake.

Except for the smoke from the smouldering fire, which had no outlet saving a tiny hole in the roof, the interior of the hut was comfortable enough, and Fred, despite his hurts, would have been happy and content had it not been for his wearing anxiety on Bill's behalf. So he was not a little relieved when the very ugly red man, who rejoiced in the name of Jumping Frog, on account of the agility of his movements, put his head into the smoky interior of the wigwam to announce that the smother was at an end for the present, and that they were ready to go in search of the missing one.

"I am going too," exclaimed Fred, rising with difficulty, for he was stiff and sore from his sudden descent through the roof of the wigwam.

"Pale-face not fit," objected Jumping Frog, with a grunt of disapproval.

"Oh, I am fit enough, and I just hate myself for having run away and left Bill in such a fashion!" retorted the boy, with stormy vehemence, entirely overlooking the fact that the running away had been entirely unconscious, so far as he was concerned.

"Ugh!" ejaculated Jumping Frog, in a tone which might have meant many things, but that was entirely untranslatable to Fred, who trailed painfully out from the smoky wigwam, to commence the search for his comrade, followed by Jenny, whose strong characteristic was her devotion to her master, whoever that master might be.

But Fred had entirely miscalculated his strength, and his attempt at a search was, after all, very much of a failure, for he fell down three times, and eventually had to be carried back to the wigwam on the shoulders of one of the stolid red men, where he lay fretting and fuming for the rest of the day.

Jumping Frog and his assistants returned just as darkness fell, declaring that they could find no trace at all of the missing man, although they had searched in every direction.

These tidings reduced Fred to a condition bordering on despair, in which the loss of the trail he had been following, and the fear of not being in time with the help his father needed, seemed as nothing in comparison to the loss of Athabasca Bill.

The night was one of the longest and most intolerable he had ever spent, the wigwam being crowded with well-greased but unwashed humanity, rolled in dirty blankets, and sleeping on the floor like pigs.

At another time he might have borne the discomfort with equanimity, for the glory of being able to say that he had really passed a night in an Indian wigwam; but the trouble of Bill's loss took the flavour out of everything.

He had learned from the red men that Morinville was only about five miles away, so when morning came he set about making arrangements to get there.

A difficult task it would be without snow-shoes, for snow had been falling all night, and although it was freezing, the surface was not yet hard enough to keep travellers from sinking in up to their knees at every step.

But he succeeded in getting the loan of these, and the services of a guide to Morinville for the sum of half-a-dollar, whilst another half-dollar went in satisfying the demands of Indian hospitality; the red man understanding to a nicety the art of getting money without the trouble, or, as they reckon it, the degradation of hard work.

Jumping Frog having elected to take the office of guide himself, because he chanced to have business in the town, took Fred by the shortest way, which led past that same hollow tree where Athabasca Bill had sheltered from the storm.

The sun was up and shining broadly, though its cheerful brightness had no power to warm, and Fred was skimming along in the wake of Jumping Frog, surveying the expanse of dazzling whiteness, and wishing it did not make his eyes ache so much, when the red man stopped so suddenly, that it was only with difficulty that he avoided a collision with him.

"What is up now?" Fred asked, though a much more correct rendering would have been to ask what was down, seeing that he himself was struggling on hands and knees in the snow unable to regain a perpendicular position, until Jumping Frog seized hold of him, and carefully set him on his feet again.

"There has been one fresh fire inside the tree," replied the red man, with imperturbable stolidity.

"A fire?" The puzzled wonder of Fred's tone was reflected in his face, as he turned it towards the tree, where Jumping Frog was carefully scooping away the drifted snow with his hands, and Jenny tugged hard at her chain in order to go to his assistance, just as if she knew all about it.

A sickening dread lest they might find Athabasca Bill lying stark and cold below crept into the heart of Fred, leaving him for a moment or two powerless to do anything; then, when it passed, he followed the example of Jumping Frog, by slipping his feet clear of the snow-shoes, and using one as a shovel to dig with.

A few minutes of strenuous toil served to clear a space down to the ground, revealing the brands and ashes of a burned-out fire, but nothing more.

"Then it might not have been Bill at all!" exclaimed Fred, in disappointed tones.

"Fire made yesterday," announced Jumping Frog, with an air of profound conviction; then putting his head into the hollow place in the tree, he uttered a further word of wisdom, "Some one shelter here from big smother outside. Ugh!"

"How do you know?" demanded Fred, with a sceptical air, as he too surveyed the cavity.

"Ugh!" snorted Jumping Frog, then fell to work again at digging away the snow with quite extraordinary vehemence for a red man.

Fred followed suit, and even Jenny scratched a great hole big enough to bury herself, barking every few seconds, as if she had come upon a find of great importance.

Presently, having excavated a great space all round the tree, Jumping Frog desisted from his labours.

"No use to dig; Athabasca Bill not here," he said, straightening his back, which ached with the vigour of his digging.

"Are you sure?" demanded Fred, still doubtfully, not having a very great opinion of the red man's wisdom and skill.

"Athabasca Bill dead, we find him here; alive, he walk away—Morinville pelaps," Jumping Frog replied, bringing out the last word with an air of triumph. He had learnt it from a Chinaman, and was tremendously proud of the acquirement.

"In that case we might as well be moving," Fred said, not a little relieved by this suggestion concerning Morinville, and trying hard to persuade himself that the red man must know best.

So they set out again, Jenny being with some difficulty dragged from her hole-digging, for she was of a rather obstinate turn of mind; and having once settled to a thing, hated to have her attention distracted from it.

Dropping down into the plain from a different angle taken by Bill when he left the tree, Jumping Frog led the way by a half-mile detour to the right, in order to gain a rough log bridge over the river, and by so doing the little hut in the pine belt was left far away in the other direction; and the ears that might have been gladdened by the sound of Jenny's deep-throated baying, heard nothing all through the long, weary day, save the sough of the wind through the pine trees, and the noisy babbling of the little brook, which would be a river, deep and wide, when the snow began to melt, but which now an active man might cross at a jump.

"What sort of a place is Morinville—a town?" inquired Fred, as the place which had been in sight for so long began to loom nearer and nearer.

"Ugh! white man live there," announced Jumping Frog, in a tone which seemed to imply that it could not be much good if a pale-face held sway.

Despite the rapidity of the pace they made on snow-shoes, it took some time to reach the row of straggling log houses which represented Morinville, and it was noon before they halted in front of the store, which was by far the most imposing building in the place.

The door was in the gable, and flanked by two windows crowded with various sorts of merchandise, whilst a goodly row of skins, hanging from pegs on the wooden walls, showed that the season of barter had begun, the long-distance Indian and white trappers bringing in their furs, and receiving provisions in return.

A crowd of men were gathered about the door of the store, shoring up the posts of the lean-to porch and peering in at the windows, from whence came the sound of angry voices, as if a pretty lively row was in progress within.

So absorbed were the loungers, that they had no time or attention to bestow on the new arrivals, although strangers—more particularly white ones—were not so common in Morinville as to pass unremarked.

"What is the matter—what is the quarrelling about?" asked Fred, pulling at the sleeve of a corpulent individual, who wore a coat made of white and grey hareskins.

"Hullo, younker, where did you spring from?" asked the man; then, not waiting for an answer, went on, "There's that H. B. C. man, Guy Herrick, inside, quarrelling with a half-breed, and they've come to blows."

CHAPTER XXI
WOULD HE DIE?

"Guy Herrick?" The name broke from Fred in an irrepressible shout of amazement, relief, and joy. He even forgot his anxiety about Athabasca Bill, in the excitement of knowing that he had run his quarry to earth.

"What, is he kin to you?" asked the corpulent one, bringing his attention now from the riot within the store to fix it upon Fred, who was chiefly of interest because he was a stranger, and life was apt to be monotonous up Morinville way.

"No, he isn't, I'm thankful to say, but I've been on his trail for days; tracked him right up from the Saskatchewan, and never lost scent until the smother came yesterday," replied Fred, tacitly calling attention to his companion by a caressing pat on Jenny's head, to which that intelligent animal responded by a whine of entreaty, for she had heard the riot inside, and earnestly desired to take an active part in the *mêlée*, according to her nature.

"That your dog?" The corpulent man surveyed Jenny with great admiration, for her beauty and the excellence of her points were undeniable, and he loved a good dog.

"While I want her, yes. She is Montana Jenny, one of the finest tracker dogs this side the boundary; will hunt a man through a crowded city street and never lose the trail," said Fred, repeating the well-worn formula, with all the more conviction because of the way in which he had himself proved the excellence of Jenny's nose; then he added, in a voice that had an odd, strained break in it, "I saw her run a man down once."

"Did you?" The corpulent man stared at Fred, as if he expected shortly to stand an examination as to the boy's looks and appearance, or to identify him from among a thousand or so of other similar youths. "What do you call yourself, now—mounted police?" this last with a wink to one or two other loungers, who were bringing their attention to bear upon the boy and his dog.

A laugh broke out at this sally; but Fred was equal to the occasion.

"No, I'm not in the mounted police, because I've nothing to mount on except Jenny, and she has quite enough to do on her own account, without carrying me. But I'm tracking this man down on my own account; my father has been arrested and imprisoned for a robbery he never committed, and which I'm certain this man knows something about; so Athabasca Bill and I have trailed right down the Saskatchewan, from Rocky Raps, to come up with him."

"Is Athabasca Bill here with you?" queried another lounger, craning his head round in eager search for the noted trapper.

"He was with me till yesterday, when we got parted in the smother; then I pitched head first down a bluff into an Indian wigwam, and though search was made, not a trace of Bill could be found when it left off snowing. This morning, when Jumping Frog guided me here, we came upon fresh traces of a fire in an old hollow tree, but nothing else; I was hoping you might have heard of him here in Morinville," and Fred's eyes scanned the face of the other with an anxious scrutiny.

"Not a sound. But don't you worrit, kiddy; Athabasca Bill is about as well fitted by nature and training to take care of himself as anyone I ever heard on, and you may reckon for him to turn up bright and smart sooner or later, most likely sooner."

"You think so?" Fred's relief at this was so great, that he forgot to be indignant at being styled a kiddy; and he was about to ply the man with eager questions as to whence he had come by his knowledge of Athabasca Bill, when his attention was distracted by Jenny, who for the last few minutes had been busy nosing among the trampled snow by the door of the store.

Now she began running hither and thither, pulling hard on her chain, and uttering the whimpering cry by which she made known the fact that she had found the trail again.

"Let me pass in, will you, please? it is pretty nearly a matter of life and death," urged Fred, his face drawn and white, as he realized how near he was to the end of his long quest.

"It'll be a matter o' your death if you poke your nose in yonder now," said the corpulent man, barring the way with his portly personality. "Rows like that between Guy Herrick and Sneaky Mose mostly have a way of ending in shooting; ah, they're beginning on it now," he exclaimed, as a noise from within made the crowd surge closer round the building. "No, they ain't; belike one of 'em knocked a pile of canisters over, and they ain't got no use for shooting irons yet, though I misdoubt but they'll be at it soon."

"I say, what makes you suspicion Herrick of robbery?" asked another bystander, who could not peer over the shoulders of the others thronging about the window by reason that he was, like Zacchæus, a man of short stature. "He is about the last man to do a thing o' that sort; indeed, the row going on in yonder is all because he caught Sneaky Mose cheating a greenhorn at cards.

The green 'un hadn't got any fight in him, and ran away d'rectly Sneaky Mose squared his fists; but Herrick 'lowed he'd punish him, and I reckon he's doing it, only it seems a pity they can't finish as they began, with their fists, instead o' taking to barkers, as they're morally certain to do if the half-breed gets the upper hand."

"I haven't anything but circumstantial evidence to go upon, but that is pretty strong," replied Fred, seeing instinctively that his best—indeed, his only—chance of forcing the man inside to a confession, or explanation of his share in the mystery of the robbery at the railway depôt, was to get this group of men on his side.

There was plainly no chance of getting inside yet, and so he used the time of waiting in telling the story of his father's arrest, the finding of the cap and comforter, and all the subsequent experiences and adventures which had befallen him since.

At first there were only two or three who paid any heed to him, but before his narration had gone very far, others joined in the circle of listeners, until, before he had done, the whole crowd had come pressing round him, finding his story of more interest even than the row inside the store, which had waxed momentarily tame, Herrick and Sneaky Mose being engaged in hurling hard words at each other, while they rested their bodies and recovered their wind.

"It sounds rather tall," was the comment of the short man, spitting thoughtfully; he had passed some years of his life in the States, and appeared to have spent the time in acquiring as many bad habits as possible.

"It's a mighty interestin' story, anyhow," applauded the corpulent person, admiringly. "Tell you what it is, kiddy, you'll miss your vocation if you don't go in for being a lawyer, or a parson, or one of them novel writer chaps; for it's plain you've got the gift o' the gab to an uncommon degree, and I've always maintained that it took a real born genius to make lies sound like truth."

The laugh that went round the circle at this was like a dash of cold water flung in Fred's face, and he searched in vain for that look of conviction on the countenances of any of the bystanders which should show that they believed what he had said.

"Why can't you believe I'm telling the truth? Do you think I'd have trailed all this way just to heap you up with an improbable tale at the end?"

His indignant questions provoked another burst of merriment, and there was not one among the loungers present but thought they were having a fine time of it that day, with such a red-hot row going on inside the store, and this stranger youngster weaving impossible yarns outside.

"If only Athabasca Bill were here to say I told the truth, would you believe me then?" he demanded, with such a tragic air that the crowd were once more convulsed with laughter.

"Aye, that we would, every word from beginning to finish," chorused the delighted circle, who by this time had decided that the boy's statement about Athabasca Bill was as much a piece of fiction as the rest of his story.

"Even that bit about your going through Denaree's Leap, and not getting sucked down in the whirlpools of 'the Valley of Death,'" put in another man who had not spoken previously, although he had joined heartily enough in the laughter. "I was lumbering down that way myself last winter, and tramped the fifteen mile portage more than once, so I know just how much to believe of that part of your adventures," and he threw back his head with a loud guffaw of amusement, in which the others joined.

It was lucky for Fred that he had learned some lessons in self-control, for a wave of over-mastering passion shook him now, and it was all he could do to hold in check a fierce desire to set Jenny on to the mocking mob, and bid her do her worst.

This, indeed, was what that intelligent creature most ardently desired to do, as she pulled and tugged at her chain, alternately growling savagely at the mirth-makers, and turning wistful, yearning glances at her master, as if asking in dumb, dog language why he let such insults go unavenged.

But white with anger though he was, Fred kept a steady grip of Jenny's chain, and faced his detractors with a steady, fearless air.

"Well, gentlemen, you must do as you like about believing what I say. But I do beg that you will let me have fair play, and if my dog pins that man Herrick down, that you will stand by me in insisting that he shall explain his part in that robbery business; or if he won't, that you will help me in handing him over to the police," he said, his quiet tones carrying more conviction with them than any amount of bluster or shouting could have done.

"That we will, kiddy," replied the corpulent man, in a jovial, hearty tone, speaking for the rest, some of whom nodded their approval. Then, because he was fond of fun, and loved a good laugh better than anything, which was perhaps one reason of his great bulk, he added slyly, "And we'll vote you into a berth in the mounted police corps too, as soon as you are big enough to ride a donkey without falling off."

The mouths of the crowd were agape for a fresh burst of laughter at this, when the sounds of revolver shots, followed by a hoarse, dreadful shriek, checked and choked the merriment back in their throats.

"I said there'd be damage done, if they wouldn't be content to settle it with fists," ejaculated the corpulent man, with a shake of his head, as he pressed forward with the others to gain the inside of the store.

A shiver of horror ran through Fred, whilst the sound of that death yell rang in his ears.

Suppose it should be Herrick that was shot! Then he would have lost his chance of being able to establish his father's innocence forever, and he ground his teeth in a sudden rage at his own helplessness.

But the suspense was unendurable. So, fastening Jenny's chain to a hook in the wooden wall of the store, he pushed and squeezed his way through the crowd, surging to and fro in the narrow doorway, until by sheer agility he had worked his way inside, where the crowd was even thicker than in the porch.

It was not a cheerful scene. The interior was in a state of wild confusion, as if the assailants had at first amused themselves by flinging bales and bundles at each other, before it came to a hand-to-hand fight.

But now one man lay on the floor limp and dreadful, whilst the other, supported in the arms of the storekeeper and his assistant, coughed in a terrible racking fashion, whilst a third man tried to stanch the red flow from a wound in his arm.

"Sneaky Mose is stone dead," said the storekeeper, in a tone of awed reproach, he holding that though wounding was justifiable in aggravated circumstances, murder was murder, and nothing could palliate it.

"It was his own fault; he fired first," said the wounded man faintly. "And I shan't be long in following him, for I'm deeper hit than you think."

"Sneaky Mose worn't no good anyhow—" began the assistant, when Fred, pushing himself forward, cried—

"Oh, you must not die until you have told me all about that robbery at the Millet railway depôt."

CHAPTER XXII
THE CREDITORS OF SNEAKY MOSE TAKE POSSESSION

Guy Herrick turned his head on hearing Fred's vehement speech, but the pure and undisguised amazement on his face was a sight to see.

"So you accuse me of that, do you, younker? Well, of all the absurdities I ever heard of, that is about the most absurd," and he laughed feebly, then coughed again.

"But you know something about it—oh, surely you must do?" burst out Fred, in tones of pleading, trembling agitation, for boy though he was, and inexperienced in the ways of the world, that look of amazement on Guy Herrick's face had told him more surely than speech that whoever was guilty of the robbery, this man was not.

"I know something about it, certainly; that is, I saw it done, but—"

"Look out, pard, he's fainting!" exclaimed the storekeeper, excitedly, as the wounded man ceased speaking suddenly, while his head drooped forward, and an ashen grey overspread his face.

"He's dyin'," cried the assistant, in a tone of horror. Being a young man and nervous, the tragic end of the fight had considerably upset him, and the prospect of there being two deaths instead of one filled him with horror.

"No, he ain't, he's only fainted from loss of blood and exhaustion; swab his face down with water, and pour a little brandy into him, he will soon come round again," replied the storekeeper, who, being a married man, had a wider experience of swoons than some of the others, for his wife was delicate and given to fainting.

But Guy Herrick's teeth were too tightly clenched for any spirit to be forced between them, while the water so liberally applied to his face had no effect, save to make him very damp.

"Looks to me more like a seizure than a faint," said the corpulent man. "Here, stand back, you fellows, and give the poor chap air, and for mercy's sake don't slop any more water over him, or he'll die of chill, without a chance to die of anything else."

Thus admonished, the crowd fell back a little, the hindermost ones being by this means forced nearer to that silent figure lying at the other side of the store than was pleasant, and from which they recoiled in horror.

"Ah, there'll have to be an inquest, I reckon," put in the storekeeper, who appeared to be master of the ceremonies. "Here, two of you fellows pick up Sneaky Mose and carry him round to that shed at the back, then go and tell the coroner he's wanted. It's as well to do things decent and in order when you can."

"Isn't there a doctor to be had here anywhere?" demanded Fred, who had grown sick with apprehension lest the man should die now with his explanation unspoken.

"There ain't one in the place," said the corpulent man. "We did have two, but one went south to get married, and ain't got back yet, and the other started for Klondyke this week. This place is so healthy, you see, that doctors ain't necessary as a rule—only in emergencies like this, which happily don't often happen."

At this moment a big, bony woman, weather-beaten, but kindly of face, entered the store, and approached Guy Herrick's unconscious form.

"Poor chap, he does look bad! and you've wetted him cruel," she said, stooping over him with a gentle, motherly expression on her face that instinctively inspired confidence and respect.

"Will he come round, Mrs. Sims?" asked the storekeeper, rather anxiously, for Guy Herrick's long swoon was beginning to frighten him.

"I hope so, but he won't stand much chance here; best bring him round to my house, and let me put him to bed; he's damp enough to get his death without anything else."

"Just what I said," put in the corpulent man, going to the assistance of Mrs. Sims, who was making energetic efforts towards the transportation of the sufferer to her own abode.

But he was so big and fat, so encumbered, too, with his voluminous fur coat, that he was glad to stand aside, and let the more nimble Fred take his place as burden bearer.

Slowly, and with difficulty, they carried the wounded man out of the store, and round the corner of the next block, to the small wooden hut Mrs. Sims called home; the very short man, who was also assisting in the work of transit, turned out to be the good woman's husband, a rather onerous post, if one might judge from the manner in which she ordered him about.

Jenny, who was still fastened to the hitching-post, whined and cried as Fred went past, making so much demonstration that Mrs. Sims found her attention momentarily called off from her patient.

"That's a handsome creetur; is that your dog?" she asked of Fred, who was toiling along at her side, bearing more than his share of the burden, whilst the short man opposite took especial pains not to work too hard.

Fred nodded; this was plainly no time for a long-winded explanation as to how he had come by the dog, or his own determination to regard it only as a loan to be returned to Blue Pete when he had done with it, despite the fact that it had come to him as a gift.

"Well, it is a handsome beast, and I do love a good dog," Mrs. Sims rejoined heartily; and then, before Fred understood what she was going to do, or could intervene a word to warn her, she walked straight up to Jenny, and putting her arms round the dog's neck, imprinted a sounding kiss on the great head.

Perhaps Jenny was taken unawares, or it might have been that she thoroughly appreciated the kindly notice, for she whined softly, put out her tongue to lick the woman's face, and wagged her tail in token of amity.

Deceived by this appearance of gentleness, one of the loungers following behind determined that he too would go and pat the dog's head; but with a resounding roar Jenny sprang straight for him, which so scared him that he rolled over backwards, whilst the dog raised such a clamour of barking, that the man who was being carried past in unconsciousness, stirred, opened his eyes, and looked about him.

"Not done for yet," he said, with a smile which was peculiarly sweet and pathetic.

"Feel bad, eh, dearie?" inquired Mrs. Sims tenderly, as she helped to lay her suffering guest on the bed in her tiny, but spotlessly clean abode.

"Rather," he responded with a sigh; then, as a fresh uproar of barking burst from Jenny, he said, "What a magnificent noise that dog can make! I haven't heard anything like it since that year I was in the state prison of Montana. Don't be scared, Mother Sims; I wasn't a prisoner, only a warder."

"I wasn't thinking that you were," she said warmly, adding, with a touch of beautiful womanliness, "Not that it would have mattered much, now that you are all bashed up and want nursing. Whatever made you go getting mixed up in a row with a low, dirty half-breed like Sneaky Mose; it was downright beneath you."

"He'd been cheating, Mother Sims; playing cards with that poor young Charlie Webster, till he'd swindled him out of his bottom dollar. I couldn't stand by and let that go unpunished; and Charlie, poor chap, hadn't the pluck to stand up to him."

"Well, he won't do any more cheating," said Mrs. Sims, with a strain of solemnity in her tone.

"I'm sorry I shot him. I truly am, Mother Sims; for it's awful to have murder on your soul," and the poor fellow groaned in anguish of spirit.

"There, there, it ain't no sort of use crying over spilt milk; he'd have killed you if he could, and not have groaned over it either," she said hastily, her eyes filling with tears at the sight of his misery; then turning from the wounded man, she ordered her husband to bring in more wood for the fire, then banged the door in the face of the crowd, yet took no notice of Fred, who stood in silent trouble at the foot of the bed, not liking to venture the question that trembled on his lips, and fearing lest the vigorous Mrs. Sims should order him from the place.

The wounded man appeared to have forgotten all about him, and lay in a half-doze, that was little removed from stupor, after his wounded arm had been bound up, and his wet garments removed.

Presently Sims, the short man, came hurrying back in a state of great agitation, but without the firewood.

"Betsey, Betsey! Bully Jim and Bob Jones are going off to the little house in the pine belt where Sneaky Mose lived, to lay hands on what he's left, because he owed them money; but he didn't owe them as much as he did us, anyway."

"What we've got to do, then, is to put our claim in first, and so I should recommend your setting off right away, dodging across lots; and when you get there, defy 'em to lay a hand on anything until we've got the worth of our lot; and as possession is nine points of the law, you oughtn't to come out so very badly. I'd go myself, if it wasn't for this poor chap."

"I'd be only one against two, and Bully Jim ain't an easy chap to stand up to," replied the small man, with a shiver.

His bigger, and more aggressive, better-half flounced round with an air of extreme exasperation, and in so doing caught sight of Fred, who stood well drawn back in a corner, and the sight appeared to give her a new idea.

"I tell you what," she said eagerly. "You get the boy to go with you and take his dog; I guess no one won't want to take liberties with you while that animal is in possession. You'll go with Sims, won't you, lad?" she asked, turning to Fred. "I'll pack the two of you up a bag of food, so that you shan't want for supper."

"But suppose—" Fred's eyes turned anxiously on the wounded man, as if fearing lest he should get up and run away, with the story untold.

"Oh, he won't die—not before tomorrow, anyhow; and equally he's too ill to get up and run away from you, which I don't for a moment believe; for whoever took that money, he did not. Wild, loose, and reckless he may be, but Guy Herrick ain't a thief. Now, will you go? I'll pay you two dollars, and find you in food, if you'll see Sims through this muddle, for he's neither very strong nor very plucky."

"I will go," replied Fred, swallowing down his reluctance by a great effort.

"Very well, then; you hurry along, and fetch the dog as quick as you can go, while I shovel some food into a bag for you. Spry is the word, now; for it is a case of first come, first served. And they do say that Sneaky Mose kept his money in a hole in the floor under the stove, so mind you keep your eyes open and stir well in the ashes."

Fred nodded, then shot out of the door to fetch Jenny; now that he had conquered his reluctance to leave Guy Herrick, the adventure rather appealed to him than otherwise, whilst the prospect of pay, and free food, was also eminently satisfactory.

He was unhitching Jenny's chain, and controlling her transports of delight, when he noticed the snow-shoes he had worn to Morinville standing outside the store, whilst Jumping Frog leaned against the wall, smoking stolidly.

Acting on impulse, Fred rushed up to him.

"I want the loan of those shoes for another day; how much?" he asked breathlessly.

Jumping Frog looked up at the clear cold of the blue sky, and round at the snowy waste for inspiration; then, because he thought Fred had only another dollar in his possession, and he coveted it, he said—

"No loan snow-shoe any more; sell outright one dollar."

"All right; there you are," said the boy, stuffing the dollar into the amazed red man's hand; he picked up the light framework shoes, and bounded away round the corner, while Jenny's joyful barking filled the air.

Fred was careful not to let the dog put her nose inside the house, fearing lest she should pick up scent of the trail she had followed so long, and fly at the helpless man on the bed; but strapping the generous bag of provisions supplied by Mrs. Sims on his back, and fairly routing out the timid and slothful Sims, started with him across lots, and down through some willow scrub to the pine belt that bounded the horizon.

"There go Bully Jim and Bob Jones," cried Sims, in a panic-stricken tone, pointing to two dark figures showing up against the snow away to the left.

"Hurry up, then; hurry, do, and we'll beat them yet," cried Fred, in tremendous excitement, shooting ahead, and setting a pace that was hard to follow.

CHAPTER XXIII
WHAT THEY FOUND

Bully Jim and Bob Jones, unconscious of rivals in the field, had taken the longest way round by the bridge, in order to avoid getting wet in crossing the river.

The two were proceeding leisurely enough, talking of the tragedy of the morning, and comparing notes as to the sayings and doings of the deceased Sneaky Mose, when their attention was attracted by the barking of a dog in the distance.

"Sounds like that younker's tracker dog; what's he doing out this way now, I wonder?" Bully Jim remarked, in a tone of query, sending a swift gaze over the snowy landscape, yet seeing nothing of his rivals in the field, because they chanced at that moment to be hidden by the sedges on the river brink.

"That dog is like an oil-painting—most appreciated at a distance," remarked Bob Jones, who had begun life as an artist, and could not quite forget all about it, now that he was a Morinville trapper, working two days in a week and lounging through the other five. It was he who had been obliged to tumble backwards, in order to get out of Jenny's way, and so he had no very pleasurable memories of their meeting.

"I'm puzzled to know what the creetur is out this way for now," Bully Jim said, sending another eagle glance in the direction from whence bursts of joyful barking still came; and then he caught sight of two figures emerging from the sedges and willows bordering the stream, and making their way into the pine belt, and then he began to dance and yell as if he had been stung.

"It is little Sims—I should know him anywhere, and the boy with that yelping brute of a tracker dog. They are going straight to the hut, and I know that Sneaky Mose owed Sims money—a goodish bit, too, without counting his debt to Mother Sims for nursing and medicine when he had cholera."

"I say, can't we run for it?" suggested Bob Jones, quickening his pace; he was lighter in weight than his companion, and fairly active when he chose.

"We may beat them, but I doubt it, especially if they see us coming; anyhow we can try," replied Bully Jim, gliding forward on his snow-shoes at a great pace, whilst Bob pressed after him, both absorbed in the task of getting over the ground as fast as possible.

Fred and his companion looked behind and saw the others coming, but they were well ahead, and knew themselves to be in no danger of being overhauled under ordinary circumstances. Then suddenly one of Sims's snow-shoes went snap, pitching him head first into a snowdrift, and the whole aspect of things was changed.

Luckily they were just inside the tree belt, and so their pursuers were for the present unaware of their disaster, but the situation was sufficiently serious.

"Take my shoes and go on; you'll get there in plenty of time," suggested Fred, stooping to free his feet for the sake of his companion.

"No, no," panted Sims, who was an arrant coward, and was turning all colours from fear and apprehension; "I can't go on alone, for the dog wouldn't come with me, and I should be scared of the beast if it would; besides, they do say the place is haunted by a white man, as groans awful when anything is going to happen."

"What are you going to do, then? We can't surely give up after coming so far; besides, what would Mrs. Sims say?" he demanded ruefully, thinking that failure to hold the fort would certainly mean the loss of the two dollars she had promised him.

"Oh, do you go on alone; you'll be in time, and the dog'll take care of you; then I'll just sneak round behind some of these trees, whiles I mend my shoe, and I can join you later. Go on, boy, for all you're worth; here they come." So saying, little Sims darted into the shadow of thick-growing pine trees, which completely hid him from view.

Then Fred flew forward again, giving Jenny a word of warning to be quiet, which the good dog chose to obey with commendable promptness, being pretty well winded with her long run.

Fred could see the little hut now, standing in the tiny clearing at the end of a long vista of pine trees, but he could also hear his pursuers behind him; while twice, when he had glanced round, he had seen them rapidly gaining on him.

His breath was failing him fast, and a wild despair was gripping him, at the thought of failure after so much effort, when there came a yell from behind, and a glance round showed him a great flurry of snow, and two prostrate figures struggling wildly to regain their footing.

The sight made him forget his fatigue, and he burst into a laugh of amusement over his fallen adversaries, as he reached the little hut, and paused a moment to slip his feet from his snow-shoes before entering the abode of the late Sneaky Mose.

To his relief the door yielded to his touch, and he crossed the threshold into the gloomy interior, his snow-shoes in his hand, and Jenny pressing close in the rear; when, to his exceeding horror and amazement, a deep groan sounded from the dark corner behind the stove.

All at once there flashed into his mind what Sims had told him concerning the ghost of a white man which haunted the hut, groaning its warnings of impending disaster.

For a moment he hesitated, with his foot on the threshold, whilst Jenny, who had also heard the sound, uttered a low growl of menace.

Then Fred heard the shouts of the men behind, who had regained their feet and were sprinting gaily down the glade.

That decided him. A ghost, whatever its nature, could scarcely prevent his earning two dollars, whilst those men behind could, and most certainly would, if once they set foot in the house. So he hastily stepped into the room, dragging Jenny with him, and banging the door, dropped a big wooden bar into the socket, and so secured the door against all comers.

But there was the window. And as he had no fancy for seeing Bully Jim's revolver stuffed through the glass, he slid the wooden shutter along, and then began to feel a little safer as to his chances of keeping the intruders out.

This arrangement, however, left him in almost total darkness, and whilst he was fumbling for a box of matches, another hollow groan sounded from the corner behind the stove, and then a voice said faintly—

"Who is there?"

"Bill?" he shouted in unbelieving joy. "Bill, is it really you, old fellow?" and in his hurry to get across the floor in the darkness he stumbled over Jenny and came crash down to the ground, whilst the good dog yelped with pain.

"Fred, lad, is it you—you and the dog? Then God be praised for His great mercy, and it don't matter at all what happens to me now," replied the weak voice, breaking down in a sob of utter thankfulness.

But Fred had by this time succeeded in finding his matches, and striking a light; then espying the lamp, lighted it, and stooped down by his friend.

"Bill, old fellow, what's the matter, are you ill again?" he asked tenderly, remembering how terribly Athabasca Bill had suffered a year ago.

"I've had a pretty bad time, what with pain and the worry of not being able to find you. Then I'm nearly clemmed, too, with hunger and cold, and I don't think I'd have been alive in the morning, if I had been forced to face another night of it. But where have you been, lad, and what is all the knocking about?" inquired Bill feebly, yet with a ring of hope in his tone, for no circumstances could be utterly disastrous all the time the boy was alive and well.

"Oh, my adventures will keep until I have got you something to eat, and the knocking don't matter either, unless it makes your head ache," replied Fred, as a loud knocking sounded at the door, which Jenny replied to with such a roar of barking, and such deep, menacing growls, that the besiegers thought it better to quit banging the door and attempt a parley.

But the boy in possession had no time to spare for them until his friend was warmed and fed, so he turned a deaf ear to the appeals from those outside, whilst he opened the package of food Mother Sims had given him.

He was hungry himself, not having tasted food since he left the wigwam of Jumping Frog that morning; but his appetite could be appeased later, and Jenny's also, for Mother Sims plainly understood the art of catering, and had provided very bountifully—a bird of some sort, a great slab of bacon, a wedge of cheese, a loaf, and some tea and sugar, promised a feast indeed.

"Can you sit up, old man, and get to work on this bird—I think it's a duck by the look of it—whilst I get the fire lighted?" he asked, hastily stripping off his jacket to make a pillow for the weak head to rest against; then slicing off a strip from the breast of the bird, bade Bill begin to feed.

There seemed to be no wood in the house for fuel, saving some odd sticks in the corner behind the door; but there was the table; and the bench, the latter of which he determined to break up and burn first, getting to work with great vigour.

Then the knocking began again.

"Hist, Jenny, at 'em, lass," he cried encouragingly, as he piled sticks in the stove, and the dog dashed at the door as if she would tear it down in order to make short work of the men outside.

"It ain't no go, Bob; we're plainly done, and by a bit of a boy that ought to be at school with his nose in a lesson book. If that shutter worn't shut, I'd try whether an ounce o' lead wouldn't act as a persuader in making him open that door," said Bully Jim savagely, as he fell back a pace or two, fingering his revolver with an eager touch.

"No, you wouldn't, Bully Jim; or if you did attempt it, I'd let a little daylight into that thick skin of yours. The boy is downright plucky, and he's got the laugh of us this time, no mistake," said Bob, in his slow, drawling tone, that yet had in it a resolute ring.

"But what are we to do? we can't hang round here all night, and it is beginning to get dusk already." Bully Jim looked fairly nonplussed, and the sight made his companion laugh.

"No, I guess we can't, or we shall be frozen stark in no time at all; our best plan is to go back to the town as fast as we can, then come out again in the morning; the boy will be hungry by that time, for I shouldn't think Sneaky Mose kept a very large stock of provisions on hand, so a hunch of bread and bacon for the boy, with a bone for the dog, may settle the business," Bob replied languidly, as if he had lost all interest in the affair.

"But there is Sims dodging round somewhere; perhaps he's got some grub with him, and so your bread and bacon won't be much good," sneered Bully Jim; who, though he was noted for the strength of his fists, and his skill in knocking people down, never shone at strategy, and, what is more, was well aware of it.

"Oh, Sims; I don't fancy there is much need to be afraid of him; I expect he is more than half-way back to Morinville by this time," replied the other. "Anyhow, he'd be scared nearly out of his life to spend a night in that place, for you know Sneaky Mose used to vow it was haunted by the ghost of that poor Pat Martin, that was found dead there with a bullet wound through his head a year ago."

"Folks did say that Sneaky Mose ought to know best who fired that shot," remarked Bully Jim, as the two, realizing the futility of waiting longer, turned to retrace their way homeward.

"Well, in that case Pat Martin has been avenged today; such things mostly meet their own punishment," Bob said thoughtfully. Then, as they emerged from the tree belt he burst out laughing, as he pointed to a black spot actively wriggling through the deepening dusk on its way back to the town. "There goes Sims; just see him sprinting along home, and won't his Betsey give him a welcome when he gets there!"

"All the more chance of the younker getting starved out the quicker," growled Bully Jim, with a ferocious growl.

"He's a plucky boy, though, and I admire that sort of thing—in other people," rejoined Bob slowly.

CHAPTER XXIV
UNDER THE ASHES

By the time Fred had made a roaring fire in the battered old stove, Athabasca Bill began to feel a little better, though he was terribly weak and exhausted from the fierceness of the pain he had endured, and his long fast.

"Now I'll make you a cup of tea, then you'll begin to feel quite fit again, and we can take the adventures at our leisure afterwards," Fred said, beginning to hunt round for water.

"I'm afraid it will have to be water without the tea, lad, for I took all there was in the canister last night; ah, what a night it was, and me not knowing what might have happened to you." Bill shivered as he spoke, at the remembrance of his long hours of bodily suffering and mental torture.

"Oh, I've got some tea. Mother Sims took care of that; she boards me while I'm on this job, don't you see, and she is a good generous sort where supplies are concerned, that is pretty evident."

"I'm more than a little curious to know what your job is, and why you have to blockade yourself in here," Bill said, in a stronger voice, as Fred displayed the tea and sugar among his other provisions.

"You shall know all in good time. But I say, I shall have to venture out for water, or at least for a pailful of snow, which is the same thing. I wonder if those two fellows are cooling their heels outside still, or whether they've decided not to wait. I think I'll take a look out. Any one about, Jenny?" he asked, for the dog was lying stretched out on the floor with her nose to the crack of the door.

But she only wagged her tail with resounding thumps on the floor, then got up slowly in order to let Fred open the door and peep outside.

His scouting happened at a fortunate moment, for he was just in time to see the figures of Bully Jim and Bob Jones turning out of the long vista between the pine trees on their way back to Morinville.

"Hurrah!" Fred cried, in a jubilant tone, coming back into the hut with his bucket of snow. "I thought they would take the hint, and not risk catching colds by hanging round here on the off-chance of finding me napping with the door open. I wonder though where Sims is, and how soon he will be along? I think it would be wise to take the keenest edge off my appetite before he comes, for he has got the look of a pretty good trencherman."

"It is just as well to be on the safe side," Bill replied, with a wan smile, as he leaned against the wall, basking in the warmth from the stove.

Before the light failed, Fred made several excursions to the wood pile, leaving Jenny on guard at the door. He was determined that there should be materials on hand for a good fire through the night, for it was freezing sharply now, and would be keener still later on.

When he had carried as much wood inside as he thought necessary, and replenished his water supply with another bucket of snow, he began to wonder not a little as to what had happened to Sims, for even supposing the snow-shoe to have been broken past repair, there was ample time for the little man to have waded through the soft snow and reached the hut long ago.

"Do you think I ought to go and look for him?" Fred asked his companion presently.

It was quite dark outside by this time, whilst the pleasant blaze of the wood fire shone through the open door of the stove, lighting up the grimy interior of the hut, the lamp having been extinguished with a view to husbanding the petroleum.

"No, I don't," said Athabasca Bill. He had been listening to the story of Fred's adventures with keen interest, and had already formed his own opinion regarding the character of little Sims.

"Well, I don't want to go, that's certain, for it is uncommonly comfortable here," replied the boy, yawning widely as he stretched his feet out to the fire.

"It wouldn't be any use if you did, for I expect he is on his way back to Morinville, or safely there, by this time, having left you and Jenny to tackle the ghost alone," Athabasca Bill said grimly.

Fred laughed.

"I own to feeling queer myself, when I came in at the door and heard you groaning, but as I had to choose between tackling the ghost with Jenny to help me, or being done out of my two dollar job, why, of course, I decided for the ghost. I'm jolly glad I did too, all things considered; and, by the way, that reminds me—"

"What about?" inquired Bill, as Fred went down on his knees, and commenced to stir over the heap of ashes under the stove with the aid of a piece of wood.

"Why, Mother Sims said that Sneaky Mose kept his money, when he had any, in the ashes under the stove, and so I'm going to have a look, for if he has left any cash behind him, my client might as well have the advantage of it," answered Fred, as he scooped the ashes out in a heap on the floor, leaving the cavity under the stove open and bare.

"It's a queer place to use for a savings bank, but I have heard of queerer," Bill said, as he leaned forward to peer into the little hollow. "It strikes me that stone is loose, try if you can lever it up; gently, mind, ease it a little, and worry it about a little; that's right, here it comes!"

Dropping the rusty iron bar which served as a poker, Fred seized the heavy stone in both hands and dragged it away.

"Nothing there but bare earth!" exclaimed Fred, in a disappointed tone.

"Scoop it about a little, gently—ah! that is right, I thought there would be something," said Bill, as, obeying directions, Fred stirred and dug in the soft earth with the poker, finally succeeding in bringing to light a small tin box, with the name "Patrick Martin" still discernible on the lid.

"Why it must have belonged to that poor Pat Martin, who was murdered here," said Fred, in an awed voice, when he had made out the name on the lid.

"Perhaps it was the very reason of his being murdered, if there was anything of value inside, that is; open it, lad, and let us see what it contains," urged Athabasca Bill.

But that was easier said than done, and it was some time before Fred, even with the help of Bill, succeeded in forcing open the lid of the box.

When it was done, a motley collection of articles were revealed, a pipe with an amber mouthpiece, the faded portrait of a sweet-faced woman, which bore on the back written in pencil, "My mother, died—" and a date which was ten years old. There was a tobacco pouch, filled with something that was not tobacco, and a canvas bag which was weighty after the same fashion.

"It is money by the feel of it," gasped Fred, in strong excitement, then he emptied the little bag on to the rough table, turning out a heap of dollars and half-dollars; but when the tobacco pouch was emptied there tumbled from it a bright rain of gold—ten English sovereigns, as bright as when they came from the mint.

"That is what that poor chap Pat Martin was murdered for," exclaimed Bill, when he saw the gold. "Then when the deed was done, Sneaky Mose, if it was he who did it, found that the money was of no use to him at all—not here, at any rate. So he set to work scraping and saving, witness the dollars and half-dollars, which were doubtless his own, in order to get the money to clear right out for Halifax, Montreal, or somewhere, that he might spend the gains come by in such an unholy fashion."

"Well, the money will come in useful for settling up with Mother Sims, for she is a great deal too good to be cheated out of her due," Fred said, as after counting the money he put it back again into the tin box with the other articles, then slipped it for safety into the big inner pocket of his leather jacket.

"If I were you I should put the stone back, and shovel the ashes into the hole to make it look natural and undisturbed; it isn't always wise to leave evidences of what you have been doing," Athabasca Bill suggested in that quiet way of his, and although Fred was so sleepy, that he could scarcely keep his eyes open any longer, he set to work restoring the place to the outward condition in which he had found it.

When this was done, he made up the fire again, then lay down by the side of Bill for the slumber he so greatly needed, whilst Jenny lay close by, and for a time deep silence reigned in the solitary hut, broken only by the soft crackling of the fire or an occasional growl from the dog, as if she was dreaming of foes to be encountered and overcome.

Bill was sleeping peacefully, with a smile on his face as of a little child, whilst Fred was dreaming that he was coming home from school with Sam and Johnny, when they met old man Arlo and the three dogs hunting a man, and were forced to take refuge in the trees from being hunted themselves.

The vociferous barking of dogs was in his ears, and he roused from his dream to find Jenny barking wildly, and dashing about the house as if she would batter the walls down to get at the foe outside.

There was someone knocking loudly at the door, and a voice shouting his name. What could it all mean? Trying to rouse himself more fully in order to understand the cause of the riot, Fred rubbed his eyes vigorously, calling on Jenny to desist from her noisy demonstration, so that he might hear what was being shouted from the outside.

"Have your friends come back from Morinville at this time of night, in order to catch you napping?" asked Athabasca Bill in a drowsy tone, for he too had been very fast asleep until awakened by Jenny's loud barking.

"Well, they succeeded pretty fair, for I was firm off and no mistake, but they did not get in, although they happened along so unexpectedly," laughed Fred, getting on to his feet and shaking himself in readiness for any emergency that might come.

At this moment the knocking was re-commenced, and a voice, rough but kindly, made itself heard calling—

"Laddie, laddie, don't be afraid, it is only Mother Sims, and she ain't likely to hurt you. Let me in, boy, I've come to keep you company."

"Do you hear, Bill, it's Mother Sims, and she's come all this way in the night, because she thought I was alone!" exclaimed Fred, whilst Jenny sniffed curiously at the door, and whined, because her instinct told her the intruder was a friend.

"Then let her in, lad, and be sharp about it. The night isn't warm enough to keep a lady standing out in the cold," replied Bill urgently, sitting up on the poor apology for a bed, and trying to give a day-time air to his appearance by putting his hat, which, by the way, was that peculiar article made of various kinds of fur, that looked so grotesque, yet was so comfortable.

Fred slid out the bar, and opened the door, keeping one hand on Jenny's collar to restrain her from leaping out upon the arrival.

A big woman, looking all the bigger for her heavy wrappings, was Mrs. Sims, and it seemed doubtful to Fred whether the doorway would be wide enough to admit her, but she sailed in comfortably, and then he saw that Sims was dodging along in the rear, looking meaner and more craven-spirited than ever.

"I was in such trouble about you, lad, that I could not rest, and I just had to come and see for myself that you weren't being frightened into lunacy by them tales about ghosteses that Sims has been stuffing into your ears; nor freezing to death for want of a fire," she said, turning a look on her husband that made the little man shake in his shoes, then catching sight of Athabasca Bill, exclaimed in wonder to see a stranger there.

"He's my chum that was lost in the snow. I found him sheltering here," Fred explained.

"I told you the boy would be all right till the morning, Betsey, without dragging me all this way at night," protested Mr. Sims, in a petulant tone.

"You might have stayed at home," she rejoined tartly.

"What! with that dead man—" he began, with a shudder.

"A dead man?" broke in Fred, in tones of dismay.

"It is poor Guy Herrick," said Mother Sims in a solemn tone. "He broke a blood vessel two hours after you started, and was gone in a few minutes."

CHAPTER XXV
THE EVE OF THE TRIAL

"There, mother dear, Celia and I have finished all that packing, and there is nothing more to do until supper-time, so couldn't you go and rest for awhile?" Ella asked, coming out from the bedroom, where she and her younger sister had been busy for the last hour or more.

Mrs. Crawford looked up from her sewing with a weary white face that was pitiful to see.

"I could not sleep if I went to lie down, Ella, and sewing is more bearable than sitting with my hands idle," she said, plying her needle the more swiftly, as if that were the only way in which distraction could be found.

Ella sighed a little impatiently, then stood staring out of the window, drumming her fingers on the wooden sill, as her gaze wandered over the stretch of snow-covered fields, yet saw nothing save the black cloud of trouble which had crushed all the joy and hope from the home-life.

Being so young, it was only natural that sometimes she should chafe and grow restless under the galling load of mortification which had been her lot during the past few weeks.

School was the worst part, and she evaded attending whenever possible, only as she had not told her mother the reason of her dislike to going, there were some days when she could not escape the ordeal, and had to bear as best she could the shrinking avoidance of her schoolfellows, and the taunting remarks about her father being a gaol-bird out on leave, a thief, and a person whom all respectable folk should shun.

When Sam and Johnny had things of this sort flung at them, they turned and fought, no matter how big the opponent, or how badly they were beaten; they had at least the satisfaction of incurring black eyes and bleeding noses in vindication of their father's honour, and that was consolation and satisfaction of a sort.

But girls don't fight as a rule, and their tongues are more cruel, their sarcasm more cutting than that of boys, so Ella had been compelled to bear a very heavy load indeed.

Yesterday had proved an especially trying time, and she had been thankful indeed this morning, when her mother had said there could be no school for her today, because of house-cleaning and packing that must be finished before evening.

"Can you see your father coming yet, Ella?" Mrs. Crawford asked, just as the light began to fade.

"No, mother, has he gone anywhere; I thought he was in the barn?"

"He said he was going over to old man Arlo's place this afternoon, to see when the new owner is coming into possession here, because he thinks it will be so awkward for me to be left in charge, with only that slow Dolty Simpson to look after things for me. Of course I shall be very thankful to be quit of the responsibility of taking care of a stranger's property, yet my heart does cling to the old home now that the time has so nearly come to leave it," Mrs. Crawford said, with a wistful look at the brown walls which had been her world for so long.

"Perhaps the new man won't want to live here yet, and then we might stay on for awhile, until—until we know what is before us," Ella said, with a hesitating break in her voice.

"I had thought of that, only old man Arlo told your father that the owner would be sure to live here," Mrs. Crawford replied.

"What a mysterious person old man Arlo is; if he were not so wretchedly poor, one would be disposed to think he had bought the farm himself out of pity for our troubles," Ella said, coming from the window to the fire, for her hands were blue with cold.

"Poor old fellow, I am afraid he will be pinched terribly in this bitter weather, and it has set in so early this season. I gave your father that little old flannel jacket of poor Fred's to take over for him. It is very old, but so thick and warm that it may help to keep a little of the cold out," Mrs. Crawford said, as she stooped the lower over her work too, because of the mist of tears which had gathered in her eyes at the mention of her missing son.

"Mother, don't you think it possible that Fred may be still alive?" Ella whispered, in an awed tone. It was another sharp sorrow at this time for them that hope should have been revived, only to die a lingering death again.

"Ella, I can't; I have tried so hard, hoping against hope, making allowance for delays, for bad travelling, for all sorts of contingencies, but it is all of no use, my own knowledge of the boy assures me that if he had been alive, he would have contrived somehow to let me know that he was all right, and doing his best," the mother said, dropping her work all of a heap now, because the tears would come.

Celia came stealing into the room at this juncture, more wan and white-faced than of old, whilst Ella, hearing a whistle outside which she knew to be her father's, caught a shawl down from a peg and hurried out to meet him.

He had to go to the barn before coming indoors, so she went with him, rejoicing to be out in the cold clear air and away, if only for a few minutes, from the brooding depression of the house.

Dolty Simpson was moving to and fro feeding the animals, his manner as slow and lethargic as ever, but he was honest and faithful in spite of it, and Mr. Crawford paused before leaving the barn, to settle the question of the future.

"Dolty, old man Arlo isn't sure even now when the new man will come in, so if I don't come back from the trial tomorrow, will you hold on here for a week or so, looking to old man Arlo for orders and wages?"

"I ain't going to work for old man Arlo if I knows it. Why, I'm skeered to death at the very sight of him, and the ugly faces he do make at me, sets the shivers a-running up and down my back most dreadful to feel," retorted Dolty, with a shudder, looking as if he were disposed to set off and run away at that very moment.

"It is quite true, father, for Sam and Johnny were in the cart with Dolty one day when old man Arlo met him, and he shook his fist at Dolty, saying that he would bring it all home to him some day—and serve him right too," chimed in Ella, with a thrill of indignation in her voice.

Mr. Crawford looked worried; there were so many things depending on him now, and he had only scanty time in which to make fresh arrangements, if such were necessary.

"Now look here, Dolty, do be reasonable, there's a good lad, and hold on here until the new owner comes to take things into his own hands, for my sake. You need not be afraid of seeing old man Arlo round here yet awhile, for he is too ill to leave his bed, and I have had to arrange with Dan Pearson's sister to go in and look after him, and you can go to her if you would rather, instead of facing the old man."

"Well, I'll catch hold for a few days longer then, for I do love the animals here, and the place is more home than anywhere, but I'm clean scared of old man Arlo, certain sure I am," replied Dolty, with another shudder.

"It is funny why that old man should display so much animosity against Dolty; I've seen it myself, and wondered at it," said Mr. Crawford to his wife later on, when they were sitting by the fire discussing the matter, whilst the children cleared away and washed the supper dishes.

"Perhaps he thinks that Dolty has injured him in some way," replied Mrs. Crawford. "But I am sorry the poor old fellow is ill; what is the matter with him, a chill?"

"It looked to me more like a regular break up of the system, and I should not be surprised if he does not live very long. He said some queer things to-day. I should have thought his mind was wandering, if it had not been that he is always more or less queer. What do you think he gave me as I was coming away?"

"It would be difficult to guess, for I never heard of old man Arlo giving anything away," Mrs. Crawford answered, with a smile.

"Well, this was not exactly a present, but a letter to the judge, which I am to give him before he pronounces sentence, if the verdict goes against me tomorrow; he said it may lighten the sentence," her husband said, half drawing a letter from his inner pocket.

"Maitland, what is it, I must see that letter?" and she stretched out an eager hand for it, but he drew back with a grave face.

"No, my dear, you can't do that. He made me take an oath, swear it on the Bible (I did not know that he had one until today), that I would not open that letter, unless the verdict was against me, or he himself was to die, and I can't go back from my word in any case."

"Of course you can't, but oh, suppose it should contain something which should lead to the conviction of the real culprit." Mrs. Crawford caught her breath in a half-strangled sob as she spoke.

"Not likely," replied Mr. Crawford. "I expect that it is merely a certificate of my good character from his point of view, and a recommendation to mercy on that account; for my own part I would rather not hand it in, since it may possibly make me look foolish, but I have promised and so I must do it."

"Yes," remarked his wife slowly and thoughtfully. "You must certainly do it if you promised."

"Here comes a horse, I wonder whose it is?" exclaimed Mr. Crawford, with a hasty step in the direction of the door as the hoofbeats of a horse sounded on the bit of road outside where the snow had been scraped away.

Mrs. Crawford turned a little whiter, and there was a sick flutter of hope and apprehension at her heart. It was always like that now, was since her husband had come back from Tom Marsh's place with that scrap of half-burned writing paper, which had been found by Potiphar on the fifteen mile portage. A quicker step, a raised voice, or an unexpected laugh was enough to enkindle the hope, which died so hard, of Fred's being still in life.

The children had rushed out in a body to identify the visitor, and now it was Celia who came scurrying back.

"Mother, mother, it is Miss Marsh, and she says that she has come all the way over here, on purpose to go with you to the trial tomorrow."

"Celia, Celia, did she say if she had heard any news of Fred?" cried the poor woman, standing erect now, but clinging to the table for support.

"No, mother, I'm sure she has not, for the first words she said to father, were to ask if we had heard of Fred," Celia said pitifully, creeping closer up to her mother and kissing her tenderly, as if the love of the living children should compensate the sore heart that grieved over the one supposed to be dead.

A momentary struggle for self-control, and then Mrs. Crawford moved forward to greet her visitor, who at this moment entered the house.

"I had to come, Mrs. Crawford, just to stand by you tomorrow. I'd been hoping I might have had good news to bring you to make up for the bad I brought before, but it does not seem as if I am to be favoured in that fashion," said Saidie Marsh, who looked as fresh and bright after her long journey as if she had only just had to ride over from Millet.

"It is very good of you to come so far, dear, on such a sorrowful errand," Mrs. Crawford replied, as she busied herself in removing her visitor's wraps and preparing a hasty meal.

"Perhaps it won't be a sad errand, it might even be a very joyful one, who knows!" cried Saidie, in a happy spirit of hopefulness which made them all feel better. "At least it is of no use anticipating the worst until the worst comes; it might even be an occasion for bonfires and crackers, so to be on the safe side I stopped in Millet as I came through, and bought that for the young ones," she went on with a laugh, producing a great package of nuts and candy from an inner pocket of her cloak and tossing it to Sam and Johnny.

But despite the cheery brightness of her manner, and her resolute attempt to inspire them with hope, they were sad hearts that lay down to rest in the little brown house that night, and the heavy cloud brooding over the home was unlightened by any instinctive foreknowledge of the relief the next day might bring.

CHAPTER XXVI
JUST IN TIME

So many people had come along in the cars from Millet to hear the trial that the court-house was crowded to the doors, and Mrs. Crawford, with Saidie Marsh, was squeezed away in a little odd corner near the dock, where she could see without being seen.

Mr. Crawford's case was the first on the list to be tried, and a very bad time he seemed to be having of it, every witness adding something to make the weight of evidence heavier against him, until even the good, faithful wife began to be assailed by doubts as to whether in a moment of temptation he might not have laid hands on what was not his own.

Not that she would have admitted the doubts, even to herself. But they were there, stinging and torturing her through the long time of examining the witnesses, and she was beginning to feel the strain so unbearable that she had turned to whisper to Saidie that she must get out of that crowded place, when there arose a commotion at the end of the room; a great pushing and struggling, then the bark of a dog, a deep, resonant roar, that made the crowd sway and break, then surge together again in a disturbed fashion.

"Silence!" said the judge, with a frown.

"Silence!" roared the ushers, making much more noise and commotion than the dog had done.

"Turn that dog out," shouted someone else, an order that no one appeared in the least hurry to obey; then the crowd surged to and fro again, like the restless waves of the sea, as a passage was forced through the thickest of the standing mass for two people and a dog.

A very battered, travel-worn pair the humans were, although the dog looked fresh and fit, and very much disposed to resent any undue familiarity from the crowd, who shrank respectfully backward on to their neighbours' toes, or anywhere else where standing room could be found, to give the great beast space in which to pass.

"Turn that dog out," shouted the official voice again, while a majestic wave of an official arm indicated that part of the building where a door might be found.

"If you please, sir, the dog is a witness; at least, it is evidence," replied a fresh young voice, which recalled Mrs. Crawford from a half-fainting condition into sudden life and vigour again, whilst Saidie sprang up, and stared around, crying out impulsively—

"That is Fred's voice; I am sure of it!"

"Silence!" roared the ushers again, turning such wrathful glances in Saidie's direction as made her sink down abashed, looking as if she wished the floor would open and swallow her out of sight.

Mr. Crawford, standing in the dock, turned sharply too, then cried out in amazement, as Athabasca Bill struggled through the crowd, and emerged into the open space before the judge's desk, wearing that selfsame cap which had been found in the despoiled station house, or, at least, one just like it.

Close behind Athabasca Bill, gaunt, pale, and desperately ragged, was Fred, but wearing a look of such beaming happiness as caused the father's heart to leap with a sudden tumultuous rush of hope, for surely the boy would not look like that if he had no good news to bring.

But Fred was alive, and well, and for the moment that was happiness enough, Mr. Crawford felt, as he clutched the narrow rail in front of him, and tried to gather his scattered wits together in order to understand what all the buzz of talk going on around him meant.

It was the lawyer whom someone had instructed to defend Mr. Crawford that made the next move, standing up with a paper in his hand, which he begged permission of the judge to read.

The buzz of talk and comment, which had seemed just like the noise of an angry swarm of bees, dropped into a silence so profound that the ticking of the clock over the press bench sounded quite unnaturally loud by contrast.

Jenny sniffed curiously at the counsel for the prosecution, greatly to that gentleman's discomfiture; then, when she had decided that he was not included in her list of suspected persons, laid quietly down and went to sleep, with one eye open, sighing profoundly, as was her custom when at rest.

Mr. Crawford had recognized the dog at once, but among so many causes for amazement had no time to spare for wondering how it fell out that she should be the companion of Fred and Athabasca Bill.

Before the judge would permit the paper to be read, he wanted to know what it was, and where it came from.

"It is the dying statement of a man named Guy Herrick, taken at Morinville, on the trail to Athabasca Landing," replied the lawyer. "And it throws new light on the robbery from the railway depôt at Millet, of which my client stands accused."

"Is it a confession?" demanded the judge, who was an irascible man, impatient of interruptions.

"No; this man, Guy Herrick, now deceased, was not the culprit," replied the lawyer, whose brows were creased in a thoughtful pucker.

"How was the paper brought here?" demanded the counsel for the prosecution, speaking in a nervous, jerky tone, for Jenny had roused from her one-eyed slumber, and lifted her head to look at him.

"That can be explained later; the paper should come first," said the other counsel, looking at the judge, who at once nodded his head as permission for him to proceed.

The lawyer cleared his throat, as if in warning to the keenly attentive crowd that he was about to begin; a very unnecessary thing, by the way, as everyone was already straining his or her ears for the first words.

"I, Guy Herrick, feeling that my end is drawing near, am making plain what I know of the robbery from the railway depôt at Millet, in order that the wrong person may not have to suffer for the crime; and that the brave boy who has followed so long and so perseveringly on my trail may not go home disappointed.

"On the night of the robbery, I was wandering about in a state of great misery and despair, for I had lost a pocket-book containing valuable papers, for which I was responsible, and money that was not my own, and as I had been loafing in bad company, I believed it to have been stolen from me.

"I had a bad, racking cough, and during an unusually severe paroxysm, a tall man with a kindly voice accosted me, expressing sympathy with my affliction, and asking if nothing could be done to alleviate it. I told him it was likely to get worse, rather than better, as, owing to my poverty, I should have to sleep rough; but that if it finished me off, I should not be sorry. He said a few kind words to me after that, then unwound the woollen scarf he was wearing on his neck, and gave it to me, and went on his way. I did not put the scarf on, but wandered aimlessly on, over the way I had come earlier in the day before discovering my loss, when suddenly my foot struck against something, which proved to be my pocket-book, with papers, money, and everything intact. I was so overjoyed at this that I could have shouted and danced with delight. As a matter of fact, I did nothing of the kind, but carefully putting my restored treasure in my inner pocket, and carelessly stuffing the scarf in an outer one, with a long end trailing out, I started for Millet as hard as I could pelt, because I knew I could procure a horse there with which to continue my journey.

"But I lost my way somehow, and, instead of following the road, came across lots clean into the yard of the depôt, which was all shut up and deserted for the night. I was pausing a minute to get my bearings, when I noticed a window open, and the figure of a man come stealing out of it, carrying a bag or box of something, which seemed uncommonly heavy, judging by the way he puffed and panted over it.

"Without a minute's thought or hesitation, I sprang forward then, intent on catching the thief, who, however, instead of running away, turned and fought; the two of us wrestling so fiercely, that I soon found I was getting the worst of it, and made a bolt for it as fast as I could go. When I got away, I found my hat, or rather fur cap, was missing, also the scarf given to me by the kindly stranger; and not being sure but that the robbery might be laid at my door, if the thief was as handy with his tongue as he was with his fists, I shook the dust of Millet off my feet with all speed, walking the best part of the night, and buying a horse next morning of a homesteader hard up for cash. The thief seemed to me to be a small man, with a harsh, croaking voice, and he panted considerably for breath, but he was so muffled about face and head that I could see nothing of him.

"This is all I know of the matter, and as I am a dying man, my word may be believed, for men do not pass into the presence of their Creator with falsehoods, written or spoken, on their tongues. Nor has this statement been wrung from me by force or fear, but I have made it of my own free will, so that, if possible, wrong may be made right.

"Guy Herrick.

"Witness, Betsey Sims, married woman."

The crowd, who had listened with bated breath, drew an almost spontaneous respiration of relief when the reading ceased; but the judge looked more gloomy and disgusted than ever, as well he might, poor man, considering what avenues of doubt and perplexity Guy Herrick's written statement had opened up.

Then the counsel for the prosecution had it out with Fred and Athabasca Bill, letting Fred off more lightly than he otherwise would have done, because of the glances the big dog, Jenny, bestowed upon him every time she lifted her great head.

Fred recounted his adventures modestly enough—as many of them as were required by the counsel, that is, and then gave place to Athabasca Bill, whose entry into the witness-box was made the occasion for a cheer from the crowd, who had been quiet for so long.

But Bill could only corroborate what the boy had said, producing a letter from the coroner in Morinville, as a sort of credential that they had come from that place; the letter also containing particulars of Guy Herrick's life and death, so far as the coroner knew of them.

Bill also attested to having met Mr. Crawford earlier in the day, and although, as he well knew, it was not sufficient to prove an alibi, it went a long way towards helping to a belief in the prisoner's innocency, since a man returning from an absence like that could have known nothing of a box labelled copper nails standing in the office of the depôt.

It was Guy Herrick's description of the thief, a small man, with harsh, croaking voice and panting breath, that was the strongest evidence in Mr. Crawford's favour, however, and secured him an acquittal in the end; for he was a big man, tall and burly, with a kindly voice; so, plainly, whoever the thief might be, they had not caught him yet.

There was quite a demonstration in the corner of the court-house when the trial was over, Fred and his mother standing with tightly-clasped hands, their hearts too full for speech, whilst Jenny sniffed at Mr. Crawford in a dubious fashion, as if remembering the time when she had tracked him down in the pursuance of her duty; then seeing that Fred treated him with every appearance of love and respect, whilst her own instinct told her that his nature was good and kindly, she decided to let bygones be bygones—and licked his hands.

Athabasca Bill, looking very wan, and old, and ill, feeling too that the future was not very rosy for him just then, seeing that he would probably get no trapping that winter, and was not strong enough to work at lumbering, was standing somewhat apart from the Crawfords, when to his amazement a pretty girl, bright and vigorous, walked up to him, and putting her arms round his neck, gave him a resounding kiss on his cheek.

"I should have known you anywhere, Willie, even if you hadn't given your name in the witness-box as William Marsh, for you've mother's eyes, and the worn, sad look that father had, when he tried so hard to find you, but could not. I'm your sister Saidie; Tom and I have come to Canada to find you, but I don't know that we should have ever managed it, if it had not been for that boy Fred."

She broke down in an odd, quavering laugh, which was much better than crying, although very near akin to it, whilst Athabasca Bill, standing with his arms clasped round her, and his head in a whirl forgot all his anxiety for the future, and remembered only that he was the happiest man of his acquaintance, let the next happiest be whom he might.

CHAPTER XXVII
A CURIOUS REVELATION

Athabasca Bill and Saidie went home with the Crawfords after the trial, and that night the little brown house was as full as it could hold of happiness and joy, the reaction from heavy trouble, and wearing apprehension, being almost more than some of them could bear.

Breakfasting next morning by lamplight, which is the western farmer's way of making the most of the short winter days, Mr. Crawford bethought him of old man Arlo, and determined to set off without delay to see how it fared with the invalid.

"May I come too, father, and bring Jenny along with me?" asked Fred; "I guess old man Arlo will be just considerably surprised to find that his grand Montana tracker dog belongs to me."

"Yes, my son, you can come; for I suppose you scarcely feel settled down enough after your travels to start on going to school again yet," the father replied, with a contented laugh.

"Not quite," said Fred, with a little grimace, he not being fond of books, and the kind of knowledge which comes from their study, although he was a keen student of everything that was to be learned out of doors. Then he turned to the trapper, asking—

"Are you coming too, Bill?"

"That is according to whether my sister says I may," Athabasca Bill rejoined, his eyes turning with wistful love and affection towards Saidie, as if it seemed to the lonely man an uncommonly beautiful thing to have a sister who would order him about, and extract from him a prompt and complete obedience to her commands.

"You will have plenty of time, for we won't start until noon; Tom does not expect me until tomorrow, anyway, and there is no sense in reaching the creamery until about sundown," she answered, with a smile.

The brother and sister had begged the loan of an old box sledge of Mr. Crawford, and as the snow was frozen hard enough for sleighing, the one horse which had brought Saidie over to the little brown house would take the two of them back with ease and comfort.

Athabasca Bill looked about ten years younger this morning, and as happiness is a very great beautifier, he looked almost handsome also, as he set out with Mr. Crawford and Fred across the snowy fields to old man Arlo's place.

They had not gone very far before a long-drawn and intensely mournful howl smote on their ears, followed by another which was almost weirder still. At the sound, Jenny, who had been walking thoughtfully along, with her nose nearly touching the snow, flung up her head and sent back an answering howl of a most dolorous description.

"Old man Arlo's dogs, poor beasts; it is pitiful how they miss the old man, now he is sick," said Mr. Crawford.

"Perhaps they are hungry," Fred suggested, remembering the time when his father had succoured the animals from death by starvation.

"I took care about that the day before yesterday, and left them enough to keep them from starving, in case of accidents, for some days to come; though Matty Pearson, who goes in to do for the old man, declares she is no more afraid of them than she is of her brother's calves," Mr. Crawford answered; then shading his eyes with his hands, to soften the glare from the snow, he peered at a figure stepping briskly along on the snowy path in front of them, and exclaimed, "Why, there goes Matty Pearson; she is late this morning, and we shall catch her up before she reaches the house."

So they did, and very full of congratulations the good woman was over the happy turn of yesterday's affairs for Mr. Crawford, whilst her delight at seeing Fred, alive and well, knew no bounds.

"La sakes, if that ain't Montana Jenny, or else I never saw a dog before!" exclaimed Miss Pearson, making a little dive forward as if she seriously intended embracing the great hound, but Jenny stopped short, uttering a low, warning growl, which caused the good woman to fall back in a fright. "La, what a great ugly beast, to be sure! I don't wonder old man Arlo was glad to get rid of her; and just hear how them other two dogs are a-howling; I declare it makes my flesh creep."

"How was the old fellow yesterday?" asked Mr. Crawford, laying his hand on the gate, to open it for her to pass through first.

"Just as bad as he could be all the first part of the day, and as restless as if he was possessed of an unquiet spirit; but when the telegram came as you'd got off, he turned as peaceful as a baby that has just had its supper, and went off to sleep beautiful. He was fast asleep when I left him, so I'm hoping to find him better this morning."

"Very good; go in and see how he is, and tell him I should like to have five minutes' talk with him if he is fit," said Mr. Crawford; and unlocking the outer door, Miss Pearson passed into the house, whilst they waited in the little yard before the door.

Then they heard a sharp cry, and the good woman came hurrying out with her face the colour of ashes.

"Mr. Crawford, the poor old man is gone. Dead and cold he is, and he must have passed away in his sleep, for the bed-clothes ain't rumpled, and everything is just as I left it—come and see."

They followed her into the house, with heads bared, and a look of awe on their faces, for death is solemn, let it come as softly as it may.

Very quiet and peaceful the old face looked, with half the wrinkles already smoothed away, and the wisps of his scanty white hair curling softly about the brows that would frown no more.

"What is this?" said Athabasca Bill, drawing a folded paper from under the dead man's face, as if he had slipped into his last long sleep with his head pillowed upon it.

"Instructions about his funeral perhaps; I see him with that paper yesterday, but he was mighty particular not to let me put a finger on it," Miss Pearson replied, and then Athabasca Bill handed it to Mr. Crawford, who spread it open and read—

"'I've left all my property to Maitland Crawford, because of the wrong I did him, and my will is at Lawyer Grimes's office at Edmonton.'"

"What does it mean?" said Mr. Crawford, in a bewildered tone. "He never did me any wrong that I know of."

"Fancy his talking about his property; he must have been a little gone in his head, poor man, for he's told me often enough that he was all but starving, and that this place was mortgaged for more than it was worth," Matty Pearson cried out, with uplifted hands and a face full of amazement.

"Grimes was the name of the man who bought my farm; it is possible it may be this same Lawyer Grimes; I think I must take train to Edmonton today to see him," Mr. Crawford said, as he left the house with Athabasca Bill, whilst Matty Pearson and a woman hastily summoned from the nearest house set about performing the last offices for the dead.

Fred had already gone to feed the dogs, Montana Jenny fraternizing with her former comrades in a rather patronising fashion, owing to her having travelled so far and seen so much, whilst they had merely vegetated at home.

"I think you had better bring Ruby and Smiler back with Jenny, Fred; they will only scare the women with their howling, and if, as the bit of paper states, the old man has left all he had to leave to me, why, I suppose the dogs are more mine than anyone else's," Mr. Crawford said, putting his head in at the door of the dog-pen, where he received quite an ovation of welcome from Ruby and Smiler.

"Father, what did the old man mean when he wrote about the wrong he had done you?" Fred asked, as they went back across the fields together.

"Ah, that is the very thing I am puzzling about myself," replied Mr. Crawford, and then he fell into a reverie so profound that neither Fred nor Athabasca Bill could rouse him from it.

When he reached the little brown house, he went straight to his bedroom, and feeling in the inner pocket of the jacket he had worn on the previous day, took out the sealed envelope old man Arlo had given him, with the injunction that it was only to be opened in the case of a conviction, or of the old man's death.

He was dead now, and Mr. Crawford felt that in view of that peculiar statement concerning the wrong done to himself, he must know what was contained in that sealed envelope.

It was blank on the outside, not being addressed to anyone, and he carried it out to the family room, and opened it there in presence of them all.

The enclosure was a folded sheet of letter paper, covered with writing in a very shaky hand, which was to the following effect—

"Maitland Crawford is not guilty of the robbery at the railway depôt, for I did it myself, and a fine lot of bother I've had over it, which of course serves me right, though not pleasant to bear. Happening to go into the office of the depôt on the day in question, I noticed a box of copper nails standing in a corner near the window, and as I happened to be rather badly in want of nails of that kind, I made up my mind to stay in town till after shutting-up time, and then help myself to that box. This I did, getting in at the window and walking off with the box as easy as possible. But no sooner had I set foot on the ground outside the window, than a man, who must have been watching, sprang upon me, collaring me by the throat and nearly choking me. I was mad then, and fought like a wild cat till the fellow was glad to take to his heels, and by his running and general appearance I judged him to be Dolty Simpson, Maitland Crawford's hired man, so I determined to pay him out in a way he wouldn't like. I therefore opened the box, shot the contents into a sack I had handy, then taking a scarf, or woollen comforter that I'd clawed off him when we fought, I carried the box and dragged the scarf all the way to Crawford's barn, where I hid the box, then tramped back to Millet and threw the scarf in at the office window together with a cap that the fellow had also left, but that was too wet to be of any use as trail; then I took the sack, and went off home, pretty well tired out. But when I had opened that sack and found five hundred dollars instead of the copper nails I'd reckoned on, I declare I felt as if I should go mad, and was more than ever keen on fastening the guilt upon Dolty. My dogs followed the made trail beautifully, for the comforter was very soiled with perspiration and carried the scent well, but when that beast Jenny pulled Maitland Crawford down, and he owned up to that wretched old comforter, I felt as if my heart would break, and I've known no peace nor happiness since. Everything has disappointed me in the way it has turned out. I bailed him out of prison with the five hundred dollars that I stole, but when I advised him to run away, he was too honest to go; so there is nothing left but for me to confess to my own wrong-doing, in order to save him from prison.

"Signed, Tobias Arlo."

"So the old man did it; I thought as much when you read that paper this morning," said Athabasca Bill.

"Poor old man, he must have suffered more than I did, for at least I had the comfort of a quiet conscience," replied Mr. Crawford. "But I think I had better take this paper with me for Lawyer Grimes to see, then he will let the proper authorities know, but the old man's memory will be spared the shame of a public exposure."

* * * *

The visit to the lawyer brought a great surprise, Mr. Crawford learning that old man Arlo had died a really wealthy man, his talk about mortgages and destitution being only fictions invented to keep people in ignorance of his possessions.

So the Crawfords gave up their idea of taking up ground in the Lake Wabamun country, and settled down to farm their broad acres in comfort and plenty, for it was old man Arlo's money that had purchased the stock and crops and land of Mr. Crawford before the trial, and thus it all reverted to him again.

Fred sent the price of Montana Jenny to Blue Pete, and that worthy animal lived to a good old age, maintaining her great reputation to the last, but Ruby and Smiler died the same winter as old man Arlo.

And so, as Athabasca Bill was wont to say, it all came right in the end.